THE SINNERS OF SAINT AMOS

A DARK BULLY ROMANCE (THE SINNERS OF SAINT AMOS FULL BOXSET COLLECTION)

LOGAN FOX

the sinners of
SAINT AMOS

THE FULL BOXSET COLLECTION

LOGAN FOX

DISCLAIMER

Kindly note that this book contains dark themes and violent situations that some readers may find triggering.

FREE NSFW AGE-GAP
ROMANCE

Want a copy of my deliciously dirty student-teacher book, Blackbird?
Click the link below to download your copy!
https://smarturl.it/ldfox-fm-cta

THEIR KINGDOM COME

Theme Song

The In-Between — IN THIS MOMENT

Playlist

Pet — A PERFECT CIRCLE

Never Enough — FETISH

Imagine — A PERFECT CIRCLE

Crawling — DREAM STATE

The Trauma Model — KING 810

Call Me Devil — FRIENDS IN TOKYO

Touched Your Skin — LANDON TEWERS

Soldier — FLEURIE

How Deep Is Your Love — THE BROS. LANDRETH

E xodus, Matthews, and Ephesians say you must honor your father and your mother. Guess it's only fair then—the day my parents and me have the worst fight in history is the last day I see them.

And what was the fight about?

Clothes.

New clothes. Since I'd literally worn holes in all of mine.

Mom promised we'd go buy some as soon as Dad came home. There was a sale on at the mall, so the timing was perfect. I knew exactly what I wanted too — we'd be back way before the night service at our church.

But Dad ran late, and because Dad didn't believe in things like cellphones, we had to wait for him. I mean, he knew they existed, obviously, but he saw them as materialistic trappings.

Clothes fell under that category too.

When he finally arrived, there wasn't enough time for us to go.

I guess the planets aligned or some shit because for the first time in my life, at the age of seventeen, I threw a tantrum.

I yelled. I screamed. I swore.

They said nothing. And then they left and went to church without me.

It's weird to think that if we hadn't had that fight, things would have been so much different.

For instance, I'd be dead.

But I hadn't been in the car when they'd hit the black ice on the road. I'd been in my robe and slippers, sulking into a cup of hot chocolate.

I never finished that chocolate.

I don't even know what happened to it.

Someone must have taken it to the kitchen, tossed it out, cleaned it.

But it wasn't me.

Because I was at a police station for most of the rest of the night, pretending to understand what they kept telling me.

My parents were dead.

Just like I should have been dead.

Something did die that night, something deep inside. Back then, I'd thought it was a precious, sacred thing like love.

Turns out I was wrong.

The only thing that perished that night were the invisible chains keeping me tethered to a life I silently hated with every breath.

I didn't die that night.

I was set free.

And it changed everything.

"For those who believe, no proof is necessary. For those who don't believe, no proof is possible."

STUART CHASE

CHAPTER ONE
TRINITY

There's a loud thump. My head bounces off the window of the cab, and my eyes fly open in surprise. I squint out at the blurring landscape as my mind scrambles to figure out where the hell I am while my heart tries to climb out of my throat.

"Sorry 'bout that. Road's not exactly in the best condition."

I glance over at the cab driver, and swipe the back of my hand over my mouth. Had I been drooling in my sleep? I'd been out cold—dreaming again. A happy dream this time. One where my parents were still alive.

"How long till we get there?" I mumble, trying to work out the kink in my neck. Outside, colossal birch and maple trees block out everything but a strip of gray sky. There's another thump, followed by a rattle, as the cab's wheels skate over another pothole.

"A few more minutes."

Hugging myself, I turn and stare out my window. Better than watching the cab driver's eyes in the rear-view mirror. We've spent over two hours together, and barely said a word.

We passed through the last town at least an hour ago and we've been heading deeper into West Virginia ever since. At least I know where I'm going. For the first time since that policeman knocked on our front door, there's some kind of order to my life.

"There it is," the driver says as we round a corner.

He didn't have to—my eyes latched onto the all-boys boarding school the second it appeared through the windshield.

Holy crap.

My mouth goes dry. "That's Saint Amos?"

I feel his eyes on me, and we make eye contact in the mirror. "Isn't it a little late in the year to be starting boarding school?"

Heat touches my cheeks. "I...don't have a choice."

The last hundred yards or so, the dilapidated tar road smooths into a hard-packed dirt road. The closer we get and the more the building looms, the deeper my stomach sinks.

This place looks more like Dracula's castle than a boarding school. There aren't statues of demons and things on the facade, but with its multitude of spires and fancy moldings, it's undeniably Gothic. Before Dracula could live here, someone would have to remove the enormous crucifix above the front entrance.

The trees thin. An immaculately trimmed lawn spreads like a pool of green algae around the base of the massive, sprawling structure.

The driver maneuvers the cab around a fountain where a concrete, pigeon-shit stained Virgin Mary is nursing baby Jesus.

Some of those streaks look like tears.

"Need help with your things?" the driver asks.

I huff as I shake my head. "I can manage, thanks."

He nods as he brakes and puts the car into park. "Good luck, and God bless."

My mouth tightens, but I give him another nod and drag my duffel bag out with me. That and my backpack are the only things I have with me. Our family wasn't big on material possessions like clothes, or jewelry, or furniture. In fact, the only thing they were big on was *that*.

I tip my head back and stare up at the crucifix.

I hope it stays up there. It could crush someone if it were to fall.

There's a rattle of gravel as the cab driver pulls away, and I turn to watch him until the shadow of the distant maples dapples the roof of his car.

The best way out is through, right?

I wince as I bang the big brass knocker on the door. Every person inside must have heard that racket.

But nothing happens.

I shuffle my feet and glance around as I wait, then try again.

The door shifts inward.

Guess there's no point in locking things around here. Who the hell's going to rob this place? It's miles away from anything.

I push open the door and step into cool, damp shadows that cling to me like a film. I'm in a vast entrance hall. Small, stained glass windows barely let enough light through to illuminate the double staircase. On a brighter day this place would look magnificent. Right now it's like I'm starring in my own horror movie.

"Hello?" My voice hurriedly warbles back to me as if it's terrified to venture deeper inside.

Lord, it's quiet in here.

Where is everyone?

Surely *someone* had to know I was coming.

"Are you Trinity?"

My heart leaps into my throat, strangling a gasp. I whirl around.

A kid a few years younger than me stands in the shadows beside the doorway. Dressed in brown slacks, a dress shirt with a brown tie, and a brown blazer, he looks like the adolescent version of Mr. Bean, especially with his dark, slicked-down hair. He squints at me like he's trying to figure out if I'm real or a ghost.

Where the hell did he come from?

"That's me." I try and sound jolly but I probably look more like a lunatic. "And you are?"

"Jasper. I'm your roommate." Judging from the faint scowl on his face, he's not thrilled with the fact. He strolls past me, heading for the left set of stairs winding up to a landing.

I tighten my grip on my duffel bag and readjust the strap of my backpack before following. Our footsteps echo hollowly until we reach the wooden stairs. "Roommate?" I call out after him. "So we don't get our own rooms?"

"Duh," he says dryly.

Holy crap, I'm just trying to make conversation. I didn't ask to be here any more than he did. And I know he's not here by choice, because no one would be here by choice. This is the place bad souls go to await sentencing.

Damp. Dark. *Dismal.*

Jasper turns into a hallway leading off the landing. Almost immediately, he takes another turn. Then another. A minute later, I stop trying to keep track of where we're headed.

Flickering sodium lights cast an ugly yellow glare over the doorways and somber portraits we pass.

Holy crap, it's cold. Two weeks until summer break, and it could be the middle of winter.

I'm wearing a black cardigan, a vest, and jeans with the hems turned up so I don't step on them. The thin wool covering my arms could have been tissue paper for all the protection it's offering me. I'm tempted to let down my mass of black curls, if only for some extra warmth around my neck.

What I know about Saint Amos could barely fill a serviette. It's an all-boys, faith-orientated prep school specializing in training new priests. But I didn't come here for their theological program—I'm here because it's the only place where even a remnant of my previous life still exists.

His name is Father Gabriel. Technically, he's all the family I have left. If it weren't for him, I'd still be a ward of the state. Enrolling at Saint Amos wasn't my first choice, but I'm starting to realize orphans don't get a say in how their lives are run.

Luckily I'm used to having all my major life decisions made for me.

"So how long have you been here?"

"Too long," Jasper replies stiffly.

What did I do to piss him off? Is this because he has to share a room with me? I glance at the multitude of doorways we've passed in this stretch of hallway alone. It's impossible that every room in this place is occupied. So why do I have to share with a boy?

I should make an effort to be friends, especially if I'm going to be living with this kid. "I'm sorry if I kept you waiting," I say.

He lets out a sigh and gives a half-hearted shrug without looking back at me.

On this level, we pass several stained glass windows, none of which look as if they can be opened. Most are random arrangements of colored glass, but the larger ones form crude images.

Doves flying toward rays of heavenly light.

Various saints and angels.

People tilling the soil under a watchful eye. Literally, an eye in the sky—lead strips for lashes and everything.

"Place used to be a Catholic orphanage," the kid says.

"It's..." I want to say beautiful, but that would be an outright lie. "Impressive."

We take another set of stairs, putting us on the fourth floor. Wooden doors crowd the walls of the passage. Small cards slipped behind tiny brass frames centered below each doorway's arch bear the room's number.

Jasper leads me to room 113.

He opens it and steps inside.

"You don't lock doors around here?"

He turns and gives me a dead-eyed stare. "You got something to hide?"

I laugh as I enter the room, but I cut it off a second later.

It looks more like a prison cell than a bedroom. Even the small window is meshed with a steel frame as if to stop anyone from climbing out and jumping. Two cots—one against each wall—fill most of the space. What's left is crowded out by a double-door closet and a desk with a set of drawers on each side of the gap where the chair fits in.

Jasper points at one of the beds. "That's mine."

"You sure?" I mumble to myself. The beds look identical. In fact, I wouldn't have been surprised if he'd told me no one lived in this room.

"That's yours," he says, pointing at the left-hand closet door. "Stay out of my side."

"Why, you got something to hide?"

He turns angry eyes on me, and I bite down on my lip.

It's been a long day. Hell, it's been a long month.

My duffel bag and backpack thump to the floor. This place reeks of mothballs and stale air but if I can open the window that might help.

The window is sealed shut.

Jasper grabs something out of his drawer. "I got class," he says before walking out.

I rush over to the door and poke my head out in the hall. "Hey!"

My voice booms back at me. Jasper swings around, but he doesn't stop walking.

"Where do I go?"

Jasper shrugs. "Only told me to show you the room!" he yells back before disappearing around the corner.

"Mother of God," I mutter to myself as I step back into the room. I stare out the doorway, and shiver when a damp breeze slips inside. "Surprised no one gets pneumonia." I push the door closed and let out another sigh as I sink onto the corner of my bed.

It groans theatrically under my weight, and I roll my eyes.

This is what happens when the only thing going through your head for days at a time is the mantra, *what else could possibly go wrong?*

I challenged the Universe, and it came at me swinging.

CHAPTER TWO
TRINITY

I'm glad everything I own fits into two bags. There's barely enough space on my side of the closet to hang the few dresses and jeans I have. Even the four cubbyholes on my side of the cabinet are barely large enough to fit a pair of shoes.

I take my fat, leather-bound bible and perch reluctantly on the creaky bed with it my lap. I trace my fingers over the gold title embossed on the cover. Then I flip it open and take out the photo nestled between the first few pages.

My father's stern eyes stare out at me from a decade past. He looks dashing in his full clerical vestments, despite his no-nonsense expression. I wish I had a photo of mom too—even better, the three of us together—but my parents considered photos a form of vanity, much like having more than three sets of clothes to rotate out during any given week.

Or makeup.

Or jewelry.

If they knew they would die months before my eighteen birthday, would things have been different? Would we have spent less time in church and more time in the park, or going to the beach, or playing ball in the backyard?

Nope.

I open the first drawer and put the bible inside, shoving it as far back as I can.

I have no intention of reading it. I only brought it along because Mother treasured it so. I didn't even know about the photo until I accidentally dropped the book on its spine while I was collecting my things from home a week ago.

Twenty-seven days.

Not even a month since they've been gone, and it already feels like a lifetime ago. I only remember bits and pieces since then, and most of those I try to forget.

Fuck you.

I kick the drawer closed with my ballerina pump.

"First day and you're already destroying school property?"

I'm on my feet in a second and whirl around to face the door. There's a guy in the doorway, leaning with his shoulder against the jamb.

He's tall and lean-muscled with a sharp nose, angular jaw, and hooded blue eyes. I wouldn't be in the least surprised if he turned out to be a fashion model despite his military-style haircut that leaves little more than a layer of fuzz on his perfectly shaped head. We didn't have magazines around the house, but I saw them once or twice in the library. He's wearing Saint Amos's school uniform, but his collar is loose, and his tie crooked.

A smug smile carves a dimple into his cheek. "You miss the turn off for Sisters of Mercy or something?" He runs his gaze down my body before snapping them back to my eyes. "Or did you somehow miss the fact that this in all-boys school when you enrolled?"

What the hell is he talking about? I shake my head, and stagger back when he slips inside the room.

"Can you talk?" He glances about the room as if the answer doesn't concern him. "Or are you an orphan and a mute?"

I'm starting to wonder the same thing, because I seem incapable of forming words. It doesn't help that he keeps moving closer, and the only way to keep my distance in this tiny room would be to climb over the bed.

"'Cos I'm pretty sure they'd tell the hallway monitor to expect a mute orphan." His eyes flicker to me. "Especially one as adorably fuckable as you."

Hallway monitor? My cheeks flare with heat. "Excuse me?" I bark out before I can stop myself.

"Aw," the guy says, pouting lush lips. "You just became slightly less tragic."

"Who the hell are you?"

Air whistles through his teeth. He rushes forward. The closet door bangs as he pushes me up against it so hard, the air knocks out of my lungs.

"Blasphemous little slut," he hisses. I open my mouth to scream.

His fingers wrap around my throat, and suddenly yelling for help isn't an option anymore. He leans close enough for his breath to caress my lips. "I don't like surprises." His voice is dangerously low.

"Please," I manage, grabbing his wrists and digging my fingernails into his skin.

He doesn't even seem to notice. "Maybe you're not even a girl," he whispers, his mouth so close to my ear that his lips brush my skin. "Is that why they sent you here?" His free hand skims across my stomach and latches onto the top of my jeans. With a twist of his wrist, the button pops open.

"Only one way to find out, isn't there?" he murmurs. His fingertips slide behind the elastic band of my underwear.

My body goes stiff. Nothing exists but his creeping fingers.

A gong sounds out.

It's not exceptionally loud, but it's so unexpected I jerk in surprise. His fingertips slip out from behind my underwear.

He steps back. Cool air rushes down my throat. I cough, sagging against the closet as he studies me.

"Saved by the bell," he says through a laugh. His face transforms into a hard, unfriendly mask. "See you around, slut."

Then he's gone.

I count ten thundering heartbeats before I dare go over to the door and check if he truly has left. The hallway outside is empty. Slamming closed the door, I back up into the room until the bed knocks into the back of my knees. I sit on automatic, staring at the door through wide eyes.

How the hell am I supposed to process what just happened?

Who was that guy?

Why on earth did he—

I flinch at a knock on the door. Swallow.

He's back.

But of course it's not him. He's not the kind of guy to knock.

So what fresh hell is this then?

"Trinity?"

Another knock.

I jump to my feet and race to throw open the door.

A man in his late thirties regards me from across the threshold. His mouth is set in a gentle curve.

"Good to see you again, Trinity," he says, his warm chestnut brown eyes wrinkling in the corners as his smile inches up.

"Father Gabriel! It's—"

A wave crashes down on me, choking the words. His is the first familiar face I've seen in weeks.

I'd never known what loneliness was. The longest I'd been apart from my parents had been a few hours. But from that moment the bell rang, and I opened the door, and I saw a police officer standing where I'd been expecting my parents—perhaps Mom juggling a bag of groceries while she hunted for her keys, or Dad looking sheepish because he'd left his pair inside the house—I'd had no one.

No one.

A week later I realized the policeman hadn't come to tell me my parents had died in a car accident. He'd come to say nothing would ever be the same again. I was destined for a dark, lonely future where flowers didn't bloom, the sun no longer shone, and food had lost its taste.

For weeks, I've been handed from person to person like a goddamn parcel with no return address, the receiver simply marked as 'To Whom it May Concern'.

Strong arms wrap around me, squeeze me, warm me. Cigarette smoke and candle wax waft up to me in a familiar and oh so comforting smell.

A sob wracks me. I cling to Father Gabriel like I'd fall if I were to let go.

My knees weaken when he strokes my head and murmurs, "Hush, child. You're safe now."

CHAPTER THREE
TRINITY

Pulling away from Father Gabriel is one of the most difficult things I've had to do in weeks, and that includes identifying my parents at the morgue. But I'm behaving like a kid, and he's the last person I want to disappoint. So I suck up my sorrow, and wriggle out of his arms. My smile isn't as steady as I want it to be, but at least it's there.

I know I should tell him about the guy who was just here. What he'd been about to do. But the thought of relaying those sordid details makes my stomach shrivel up with humiliation. What'll it change, anyway? It might make him even angrier.

"Are you all settled?" Gabriel asks, using a knuckle to swipe a tear from my cheek.

"Yeah."

"Then I'll show you around." He holds out an arm, his smile inching up when I take it.

He looks odd in his pale, cable-knit sweater and dark slacks. His loafers barely make a sound as he leads me out of the room. I guess he only wears his official clerical garb when he's visiting a member of his congregation.

I pause, and then lean back to pull the door closed. He pats my arm, his smile growing a little sad around the edges.

"You're safe now, child. This is the Lord's house. He will watch over you while you're under His roof."

I think back to the stained glass window, the one with that big eye in the sky with the people toiling beneath it. And then the guy who slipped into my room.

If God was watching me, then it seems He was more interested in seeing how far he'd get than putting a stop to it.

But then a bell rang, and he stopped. I'd call that divine intervention, wouldn't you?

"Thank you," I murmur, dropping my gaze. My cheeks grow hot again. "I don't know what I would have done if you hadn't become my guardian."

"A foster home is no place for a child of God," he says. "Especially one as bright and talented as you. I'm more than happy to help."

I manage a smile. Seeing Gabriel has brought back too many memories. They fill my mind as he leads me down the hall, and my mood dips ever lower.

Father Gabriel had been the bishop of our parish for close to five years before he left the country for missionary work a few months ago. My father, the priest of our local congregation, had known him since the start of his seminary training, where Father Gabriel had been one of his tutors.

Gabriel was at our house at least three times a week, and often ate dinner with us. He was my parents' closest friend, and from what I could gather, their confidant when their marriage became a little rocky. That was way back before I was even born.

"I must apologize for not meeting you when you arrived. This close to summer, I have a hundred and one tasks." Gabriel laughs. "I'm sure the staff is looking forward to this break as much as the students."

I laugh with him and it sounds strange out here in the dimly lit hallways. "This place is enormous. How many students are here?"

"Just shy of five hundred."

My mouth sets. I shouldn't be ungrateful, but it begs the question. Before I can bring myself to ask it, though, Gabriel says, "You're wondering why you don't have your own room." His mouth forms that all too familiar neutral line. "As much as I'd like to give you one, doing so would set a bad precedent. Students at Saint Amos must earn their privileges."

"And a private room is a privilege," I say, nodding along. I guess it would be unfair for me to be elevated above students who've been here for years already. And the last thing I want to do is stand out.

"So...does that mean Jasper lost his privileges?"

"God rewards our faith in many ways, Trinity. But he also demands penance for our sins."

"What did Jasper do?" I ask, voice hushed. I'm guessing a private room is one of the best privileges around here. I could be wrong, but it would make sense why Jasper is acting so damn sulky.

"That's between him and God."

Gabriel pauses by a window. It's the first one with clear glass I've noticed, and the first with a latch. I glance down both sides of the hall. I have no idea where I am. How long is it going to take me to figure out this place?

He pushes open the window and breathes in the air rushing in from outside, then beckons me over with a flip of his hand.

I go to stand beside him. My breath catches.

"Oh my Lo—" I cut off, biting down on my lip just in time.

Blasphemous little slut.

"If you think it's beautiful now, wait till the leaves turn." There's a reverential hush to his voice.

"I can't wait."

Even though we're on the third level of this majestic building, trees soar up and around us. It's as if the school was dropped into the middle of the forest and left to its own defenses.

"Can you see where the grounds end?" Gabriel points, and I follow his finger.

"Yeah?"

"Anything past that fence is out of bounds," he says firmly. "Understand?"

I look at him and nod. "I understand."

"It may look innocent, but the forest is a dangerous place," he adds, his brown eyes searching mine. "We've lost more students than I care to admit out there. I wouldn't want that to happen to you, child."

Lost them?

My neck moves like a rusty joint when I turn to look out the window again.

The forest doesn't look like a place I'd want to go anyway. Why on earth would anyone have to be warned to stay away?

"Come on. Lots to see before lunch."

This time, Father Gabriel doesn't hold out his arm. I wish he had—the dark and the cold of this place is pressing in again. I suppress a shiver as I follow him down the hall, and glance back at the window. From this angle, only a sliver of gray sky is visible.

What happened to those kids? Did they lose their way and starve?

Or did something else find them first?

"I'M sorry I wasn't there for you when your parents passed," Father Gabriel says out of nowhere. We've been walking for about ten minutes, and passed another two windows—both with dramatically different views than the first.

Saint Amos is more like a small town than a school. This building contains the staff quarters, the student's rooms, the administration office, the kitchens, the washrooms, and the dining hall.

Outside, there's a chapel, a building that houses the classrooms, and even a crypt. From the window we viewed it at, the rectangular shapes of concrete slabs placed on the handful of graves beside the crucifix shaped building were visible.

Yet another place I have absolutely no interest in visiting, although Father Gabriel hadn't warned me to stay away this time.

Further back on the property are the stables and some sports grounds—even a gymnasium with an indoor pool.

"Trinity?"

I snap out of my thoughts. "The social worker said you were away on missionary work?"

He smiles at this. "South America. It's so rewarding to share God's message to impoverished nations."

Father Gabriel did a lot of missionary work. My father's even been overseas with him more than once. They would stay away for up to months at a time. Dad always seemed different when he came back, but I could never figure out why.

I guess spreading the gospel changes you.

"Judging from your grades, your parents did an excellent job home-schooling you." Gabriel chuckles. "Our classes are slightly larger, but trust me, your academics won't suffer. We have excellent teachers. Some of them past students, in fact."

Dad taught me scripture. *Mom* taught me everything else. But I don't say anything—I've never been one to pick a fight.

We descend a stairwell and arrive in a vast hallway. Several yards away, it ends in a set of double doors. Through the small windows set in them, I can make out a bustle of activity beyond.

The dining hall? My stomach grumbles. When was the last time I ate something? It might have been yesterday, but I can't remember if it was breakfast or lunch. They'd served supper on the train last night, but I'd been too nervous to eat anything.

I start forward, expecting Father Gabriel to move ahead. I come up short when he grasps my elbow and gently turns me around to face him.

My chest grows tight at the look on his face. "What?" I ask quietly.

He releases me and grasps his hands in front of him.

I know Father Gabriel well. He looks older today. He's still far from an old man, but his face has lost some of its youthful glow.

"Anyone can lose their faith, Trinity." Tiny creases form at the corners of his eyes. "It happens so quickly. So, so easily. But that's exactly what the devil wants."

My chest closes. I can't speak, or think, or breathe. Pressure builds behind my eyes as Father Gabriel presses his mouth into a thin line.

"We can never comprehend the full extent of God's plan. Especially if we turn our back on Him during difficult times."

Difficult times?

Sadness turns to anger. The pressure is still there, scalding my eyeballs. Moisture builds, but these aren't tears of mourning.

These are tears of rage.

Not the first I've shed. I'm sure not the last.

There are so many things I want to say to Father Gabriel right now. Bad things. Blasphemous things.

Hussy.

But I don't.

If he senses my anger, he doesn't acknowledge it.

"One last stop before lunch," he says as he sweeps out an arm. "In case you ever need to get something off your chest."

There's a small alcove a few feet away. The arched door set within has a brass crucifix hanging at eye level.

Father Gabriel opens the door, revealing darkness beyond.

He steps inside.

I can either follow or stay out here, stranded and alone. As much as I want to fade into the shadows, I'm done with being alone.

I trust Gabriel.

I know he wouldn't allow harm to come to me.

I follow him inside despite my tight chest and my pounding heart and my dry mouth.

I follow him into the darkness, and it swallows me whole.

CHAPTER FOUR
TRINITY

Candles emerge from the gloom once my eyes have adjusted to the low light. They don't do a good job of illuminating this place—but there isn't much for them to light up anyway.

This is the tiniest chapel I've ever seen. The nave consists of six short pews, three a side, with a narrow aisle leading to the chancel.

The person on his knees in front of the altar seems too big and brawny for this intimate space.

Candle flames flicker as we move deeper inside.

As if sensing us, the figure in front bows his head a little deeper and slowly gets to his feet.

"My apologies for interrupting, Reuben."

The figure turns.

I thought it had been a man, perhaps another priest, but as the flames light the stranger's face, I realize he's a kid like me.

Okay, *kid* isn't the right word. Young man works better. He couldn't be more than a year or two older than me, but he's tall and broad and the darkness in his eyes doesn't come solely from this shadowy room.

He's dressed like Jasper was, but without the blazer. On him, his dress shirt skims defined muscles and his collar hugs a thick neck. The top button of his shirt is undone, and his tie slightly loosened, as if he was getting hot.

Unlike Jasper, he's handsome as hell.

I suddenly feel much too small for my age.

"Trinity, this is Reuben. He's in the same grade as you."

"Hi," I manage, although I doubt he can hear my whisper all of a yard away.

His dark eyes take me in, not changing one bit, and then fix on Father Gabriel. "She's a girl." His voice is deep, like I expected, but so melodious. The sound tugs loose a contraption that releases a million butterflies into my belly.

"Acute observation," Father Gabriel says through a laugh. "Trinity is my—"

Gabriel's cell cuts him off. He lifts a finger, sending an apologetic smile first my way, then Reuben's, before he slips out of the room to take the call.

When I turn back, Reuben's standing less than two feet away.

My heart jumps out of my chest as I stumble back.

"What are you doing here?" Reuben demands.

"Um…Going to school?"

His dark eyes scour mine. "You don't sound so sure."

I open my mouth to protest, but then I hear fabric rustling behind me.

"Reuben, child, show Trinity to the lunchroom."

I turn pleading eyes to Father Gabriel, willing him to understand the psychic message I'm yelling at him.

Don't leave me alone with this guy! He's a fucking psychopath!

But Father Gabriel just gives me a warm smile and a pat on my shoulder before saying, "Jasper should be in the lunchroom. He can show you to your first class this afternoon."

My skin itches, and I'm sure it's because Reuben's staring at me.

"Father—!"

"I'm sorry, I must go."

Reuben watches Gabriel leave then his eyes flicker back to me. He ducks his head and slips a rosary around his neck with reverential care. The wooden beads rattle as he tucks it under his shirt.

When he looks back up at me, my spine turns to ice.

Eyes like pools of frozen tar pin me where I stand. If I could have turned tail and run, I would have been scampering out of here like a mouse who's spotted a cat. And the cat was ready to pounce.

Reuben steps past me. I catch a whiff of something sweet and musky in the air he disturbs as he reaches back and grabs my wrist. I have no choice but to trot after him. It's that or have him rip off my arm. He doesn't walk fast, but big as he is, he covers a lot of ground even at his slow pace.

Reuben says nothing as he leads me from the prayer room and down the hall to the lunchroom. I catch a glimpse of Father Gabriel before he disappears around a corner. If I'd had a shred of common sense, I'd have called out to him. All he'd have to do was glance back. When he saw how Reuben was manhandling me he'd realize something was wrong.

But he doesn't look back.

Guess he's forgotten all about his newest charity case.

I watch Reuben's back the rest of the way, both mesmerized and horrified by the way his muscles move under his shirt.

How easily he could have snapped my neck back there.

No one would have seen.

No one would have known.

My skin crawls at the thought.

He pushes open the door. A wave of chaotic noise and intoxicating smells wash over me. Reuben releases me and steps through. The door almost crashes into my face as it swings back on a hydraulic hinge. I catch it just in time. When I push it open, Reuben's disappeared into the bustle of boys moving around as they go to find their seats.

Thankfully, no one seems to notice me standing here.

The crowd thins at just the right time, creating an open channel to the far side of the room. Call it a miracle, but through some disturbance in the fabric of the universe, I spot Jasper. He's sitting at the end of one of the long benches chatting with the boy sitting opposite him.

Just another boy in a room filled with boys. But at least I know his name. At least he didn't just murder me with his eyes.

I push back my shoulders and head for the edges of the room, trying to find the most inconspicuous way to reach him.

Definitely not the welcome I was expecting.

JASPER DOES a double-take when he sees me standing beside him. It took every bit of courage I had to walk through the bustling hall and make my way over here. Even more to detour and grab a plate of food. I was expecting some kind of buffet line, where staff in hair nets dished up whatever you wanted onto your plate. Instead, I had to grab the second-last food tray covered in plastic wrap from a nearby counter.

Today's lunch is thin stew and bread.

This place is really starting to remind me of a prison.

Jasper sits back, the hand holding his fork sagging. "What are you doing here?" he whispers furtively.

"Eating?" I grip my tray a little harder. The closest boys turn to stare at me. Those next to them look, then the next, then the next.

Everyone is watching me.

The entire dining hall is silent.

Dear Lord.

"Can you move up a little?" I ask quietly as my cheeks heat up.

"Fuck off," Jasper says under his breath, glancing askance at the kid next to him like he's embarrassed by my presence.

I grit my teeth. "Please?"

He shakes his head, keeping his eyes on his plate. I glance around in panic and spot a gap at the table next to us.

Before I get there, the gap disappears.

Now my cheeks are on fire.

It feels like every boy in this room is staring at me but when I look around no one meets my eye.

Screw this.

My nose can't go any higher into the air, so I push back my shoulders and strut down the middle of the room like I belong here.

Technically, I do. I'm a student here as much as any of these pricks. They have no right to treat me like a turd.

Despite my flaming cheeks, or the way my skin is intent on crawling right the fuck off me, I make it all the way to the other side of the room without wetting myself. I push open the door, my heart thundering in my chest as the door hisses closed behind me.

Relief is brief, but delicious. The plastic wrap has crept up at one edge of my tray, and I catch a whiff of the food beneath. It doesn't look like much, but it sure smells good enough to eat.

You can do this, Trinity Malone.

One day at a time, same as before. One day at a time, one after the other, thy kingdom come, thy will be done.

A-fucking-men.

MY INTENTION HAD BEEN to eat my lunch in my room—if I could find my way back there. But I'd barely gone a yard before someone emerges from the nearest stairwell. A stocky woman at least two decades older than Father Gabriel latches eyes with me.

I smile weakly.

She frowns—*hard*.

My smile wilts. I stop dead in my tracks. She picks up her pace, the skirt of her habit snapping around her thick-set ankles.

"Just what do you think you're doing?" she demands as she storms up to me.

"Lunch?" is all I get out before the woman grabs my elbow, spins me around, and shoves me back the way I came.

I stumble into the dining hall amid a cacophony of sniggers and giggles and chuckles.

A second later, everyone's mouth snaps shut.

"Move," the woman snaps.

I start forward on instinct, but she catches me above my elbow. "Not you."

She surges ahead, stabs out a finger at the boy seated closest to the door, and drags a line to the side. "Move it, Nelson!"

The boy shoots to his feet, grabs his tray, and almost trips over his own feet in his hurry to get out of the woman's way as she drags me across the floor.

"Sit."

My ass hits the bench so hard, my teeth click.

"Eat."

The woman steps back and claps her hands. "Children, this is Trinity Malone. She is a new student here. Each and every one of you will make sure that she understands and obeys the rules of our school, or I shall punish each and every one of you. Do I make myself clear?"

"Yes, Sister Miriam," the school choruses.

I'm staring so hard at my food I'm surprised it's not setting alight.

Sister Miriam lets out a huff, turns, and starts pacing the length of the hall. For a few minutes, there's only the sound of her shoes hitting the tiles. Then, with another slap, she barks, "Eat!"

Plastic knives and forks scrape plastic plates.

No one says another word.

No one looks up from their plate except me. And I only risk peeking through my lashes.

My heart slows from a gallop to a trot, but I couldn't eat if I'd crawled out of the desert having wandered forty days and forty damn nights.

One day at a time? I'm wondering if I could even get through the day at this rate.

Seriously, what else could possibly go wrong?

CHAPTER FIVE
ZAC

*C*ASSIUS: *We have a problem.*

I tap my finger against the side of my phone, stroking my bottom lip with the other hand.

"Afternoon, Brother Zachary."

I glance up and give Simon a curt nod. Students file neatly into my class, seating themselves like a beautifully choreographed dance. My AP Psychology class is one of the smallest in Saint Amos—I only teach up to a dozen students in each grade.

I return the smattering of 'hellos' and 'good afternoons' before facing the chalkboard. "Today we'll be discussing epigenetics. Can anyone tell me—?"

My classroom door rattles. I glance back at my class.

All my students are present. It's highly unusual for a staff member to interrupt me once my lesson has begun. Word has long since gotten around how much that annoys me.

"Who is it?"

The door immediately stops rattling. Then a hesitant, high-pitched voice says, "Trinity."

She cuts off when I open the door and snatches away her hands. Looks like she'd been pulling at the handle instead of pushing.

I tilt my head. "May I help you?"

The girl steps back, and huffs a dark curl away from her face. She's wearing street clothes and a thoroughly confused expression. "Yeah... uh...is this Psychology?"

T. Malone.

My new student.

I'd barely glanced at the memo slipped under my door this morning. My mind had been on other things. More *important* things. So much so, I'd even forgotten to assign her a seat.

I step back and wave her inside, my mind moving a mile a minute.

I'll be the first to admit I'm set in my ways. Which is saying something for someone who's turning twenty-one in a few months. A strange girl showing up at my door shouldn't have rattled me, but it did.

She stands at the front of the class, notepad clutched to her chest like a shield. A moment later, her amber eyes come back to mine, now even more confused than before.

I snap my fingers at a student in the front row and point to the chair behind my desk.

He hurries over, picks it up, and sets it by the wall.

"You're late," I say, when the girl keeps staring at me like she's had a stroke. "Don't let it happen again."

Still, she doesn't move.

"*You're* my teacher?"

I straighten as my hand drops to my side. "Were you expecting someone different, *Miss* Malone?"

As if she realized what she said, she shakes her head and hurries to her seat. There's a soft hiss as she plops down on my chair and the air leaves its pillow. Her fair skin looks even paler as her cheeks turn rosy with embarrassment.

It takes me a moment to gather my thoughts. As I turn back to the board, the text message on my phones comes back to me.

Could this be the 'problem' Cassius mentioned?

She's not wearing a uniform which indicates her presence took others—such as Sister Ruth, who runs the laundry—by surprise. Else she'd have been decked out in Saint Amos colors.

Her slim body, her poorly fitted clothes, the nervous energy vibrating through her—I put her at sixteen. But her eyes tell a different story. They're underlined with shadows, as if she hasn't had much sleep, and don't hold my eyes longer than a moment before she looks away.

Could be she's shy, but I suspect it's more a matter of her not wanting to give away more than she already has.

"Have you submitted your transcript to the administration office?" I ask, turning my back on her as I scratch out a note on the chalkboard.

"I...I don't have one."

I turn back to her, subtly aware the other students in my class are following our exchange like a particularly slow—if fascinating—tennis match. "Which school did you attend? I'll have it sent over."

"I was...homeschooled."

"Ah." I click my fingers at the student closest to her and turn back to the board. "Sit with Alex. He can share his textbook with you."

She drags her chair over to the closest table, and the boy reluctantly slides his textbook to the side so she can lean across and read with him.

Homeschooled? That's a first for Saint Amos. At least, since I became a teacher here. Most of our students are children from across the state who couldn't afford private tuition and whose parents—for whatever reason—had decided they didn't want them in a public school.

Those who still had their parents, of course.

Many students at Saint Amos are orphans.

Is that the case with Trinity Malone? If so, why isn't she at the all-girls school up in Devon? Sisters of Mercy never turns anyone away.

I glance over my shoulder. Trinity immediately drops her gaze back to the textbook, and her cheeks turn rosy again. I take in the rest of the class. Most of the boys are surreptitiously peeking over at her, some hiding the fact behind hands or raised up textbooks.

I'm fully aware of her presence through the rest of my lesson, and find myself watching her more often than my students. Perhaps it's because she's a new and shiny thing in a place usually full of shadows and cobwebs.

I need to find out what she's doing here.

If this is in fact a coincidence, then so be it. But if there's any chance she'll disrupt our plan, then we'll have to get rid of her.

THE NEW GIRL doesn't have anything to pack up except her notebook. She clutches it against her chest as she makes a beeline for the classroom door. The bell is still sounding its last gong when she disappears out the door without so much as a glance in my direction.

My regular students stream out of the room, each pausing to thank me or bid me a good afternoon before they leave.

Many of them used to have abysmal grades before they joined my class last year. The devotion and passion I pour into each class are beginning to show. With my help, these boys will get a head start on their degrees.

Moments after the last student leaves my class the door opens again.

I glance up. My body tenses soon when a student slips into my class. He peeks outside before silently closing the door and turning the lock.

"What's so important it couldn't wait?" I ask dryly, straightening the things on my desk as Cassius Santos slinks closer. "And fix your fucking tie, Santos."

"You can drop the act," Cassius rests his thigh on the corner of my desk as he crosses his arms over his chest and leers at me. "It's just us."

"Hallway monitors don't mock the dress code. Or did you forget that you're supposed to be a star pupil?"

The eighteen-year-old student is tall and well put together. Stark blue eyes contrast a dark buzz cut that accentuates his features even more than a mop of hair would have. He pretends to adjust his clothes, but when he drops his hands his tie is still crooked and his top button still undone.

"Whatever," Cass mutters. "And it's not a what, by the way. It's a *who*." He stabs a thumb over his shoulder. "She just left your class."

I close my drawer and sink into my seat, leaning back and crossing an ankle over my knee. We shouldn't be meeting like this, but the other classrooms should already be empty by now—the chances of someone seeing us are slim to none.

"It's not the first time we've had a female student, or an enrollment so late in the term."

"That's what I thought." Cassius narrows his eyes to blue slits. "But then Rube came to talk to me. Told me Old Scratch was showing her around like a tour guide. He seems to think they're pretty tight."

I shrug. "I'll take a look at her file this afternoon." I grab my ankle, pressing my thumb into one of the tendons. It's an old injury, one that usually doesn't pester me this much in warm weather. Its twin on the other ankle starts aching too, but I leave it be. "If there's cause for concern, you'll be the first to know."

"What if she fucks this up, Zac?" Cass's arms tighten as he ducks down a little. "It's taken us *years* to get to this point. If she's going to be one of those closet nuns who hang around Lucifer the whole time, how are we supposed to..." he lowers his voice, leans close "...get rid of him? You told us it would only work if no one misses him for like a week. If this chick's his niece or something, don't you think she'll notice if he suddenly disappears?"

I recognize the storm brewing in Cassius's eyes. "Tell Apollo to keep an eye on her, if you're so damn worried," I say.

"Will as soon as he gets back. He's been out in the woods most of the day. Somehow managed to convince the old hag to let him leave the grounds."

My eyes shift to the window panes. They're high up on the wall, and less than a foot across each. They don't show anything of the world outside except a few pieces of the sky—classrooms are for learning, not for daydreaming. But I know this place well enough to know how far away those trees are. It's one of the things the staff of Saint Amos drill into every student who attends—no one goes past the fence. If they're caught, they're expelled.

Too many students have gotten lost in those woods, most of their bodies never recovered. Those that were? Hardly recognizable once the wild animals out there had finished with them.

Trust Apollo to charm his way into being allowed to spend the day out there. He hasn't even been here the longest. This is my second year at Saint Amos. Apollo graduated last year, and Reuben and Cassius will be graduating this year.

We made sure not to arrive at Saint Amos in the same year. We couldn't risk anyone piecing together the fact we knew each other. That's why we've always kept our relationship on a need to know basis.

A dry chuckle escapes my lips. "Fuck my life."

"I'd rather fuck her."

My eyes snap back to Cassius. "Not a chance. You don't go near her until we know who she is."

Something flickers over Cass's face, but it's gone before I know what it means.

"Don't fuck her." I narrow my eyes at him. "In fact, don't even *look* at her."

"Aye, aye, Boss." He gives me a mock salute before leaving my classroom as surreptitiously as he entered.

My muscles loosen, but not as much as they should. If my brothers are all as restless and uneasy as Cassius, then we could be facing disaster.

But he's right—we're running out of time. And this girl could be no one...or the person who causes this web to unravel. A web we've been building for years.

My ankle throbs, but I ignore it this time.

I'm stronger now. My body doesn't have full control over me anymore.

But I don't have full control over my mind.

It was a tradeoff I was happy to make. One we've all made at some point in our journey.

That's why we stuck together. That's why we formed our brotherhood of revenge.

Alone, we were nothing but prey.

Together, we've become the ultimate predator.

SISTER STELLA GIVES me a warm smile when I step through the door to the administration office that afternoon. While Saint Amos only has two female teachers, all of the administration staff are women. Students' grades, school supplies, and everything else the school needs to run are handled from the cluster of offices on the east wing of the school's main building.

Framed by her black-and-white habit, only the center of Sister Stella's face is visible.

"Good afternoon, brother. Something I can help with?" she asks, rising from her desk.

Saint Amos has telephone lines and electricity, but everything looks like it's from the 1960s. No computers. No internet. And since the telephone lines are down more often than they work, everyone relies on their cellphones to maintain contact with the outside world.

When there's service, of course.

Certain places on campus don't get any service, like the libraries nestled deep in the disused catacombs.

Originally a church, all of the original buildings remain intact. When this place became an orphanage, the catacombs were used as an infirmary. These days, it houses the library. Unconventional, since the classrooms are a good fifteen-minute walk away, but more cost-effective than building a new structure. In fact, the low, squat building housing the classes is the newest structure on the property.

"I'd like to take a look at Trinity Malone's transcripts, if she has any. May I see her file?"

Sister Stella widens her eyes at me, and gives her head a tiny shake. "I'm sorry, brother, I only requested it this morning. We didn't even know she was coming until the provost mentioned it after prayers."

"That's strange," I say, resting my elbows on the reception desk and leaning in a little. "Why was no one notified?"

Stella shrugs. "Perhaps it slipped the provost's mind. He's under a lot of stress at the moment, what with—"

"Yes, I understand." I shouldn't have interrupted her—I'm supposed to be the kind of person who cares deeply about Father Gabriel's state of mind.

In a way, that's *all* I care about these days.

I was hoping her file had arrived already. Why did her arrival at Saint Amos take so many people by surprise? I doubt it slipped Gabriel's mind. He's the most intelligent and cunning man I've ever had the displeasure of meeting.

Her file would have told me all I needed to know. Where she came from, what her connection to Gabriel and the school is. No one just *enrolls* at Saint Amos—students have to be referred by the bishop of their diocese.

If I know who her emergency contact is, I could contact them and find out even more.

But not without her file.

And maybe that's exactly what Gabriel wanted. Maybe he didn't want anyone knowing who she is, or how she's connected with him.

Why?

"When is he leaving?" I ask, keeping my voice casual.

"Let me confirm." She lifts a finger, giving me another honey-sweet smile. Then she turns her head a little and calls out, "Sister? When does Father Gabriel leave?"

"Thursday afternoon," a voice replies from one of the rooms branching off this reception area.

"And her file?" I ask. "When are you expecting it?"

Stella turns back to me. Her shrug is nearly invisible beneath her habit. "I'll let you know as soon as it comes in. But I doubt there'll be a transcript. Probably a few report cards and her family history. She was homeschooled, you know?"

"I'm aware," I murmur. "Thank you, Sister."

How long will I have to keep Cassius in check? I refuse to make a move until I know how she fits into all of this. From the sounds of things, she was brought here by the provost himself.

I'm not okay with an innocent being caught up in the fray. We planned this so there would be no collateral damage.

Our window of opportunity is closing. Fast.

And there will never be another chance like this.

"Hey, wake up!"

I scramble to a sit, blinking hard as I try to focus.

Jasper's leaning over my cot. He's dressed in his school clothes. The last time I saw him he'd been wearing athletic shorts and a vest.

That had been yesterday afternoon.

"What time is it?"

"Didn't you hear the bell? It's breakfast," he snaps. "We all say prayers before. They won't let you lie in unless you're sick. Are you sick?"

I wish I could have convinced him I was. But the only thing wrong with me is the sudden conviction I've lost my freaking mind. I slept right through dinner? No wonder my stomach feels like a black hole.

I'd been planning to take a quick nap. After all, no one had told me what I was supposed to do after I finished Calculus, my last class of the day. Jasper must have come to bed at some stage, but I don't remember that at all.

What I *do* remember is how tongue-tied I'd been at meeting my Psychology teacher. I guess he's not too young to be a teacher, but he's definitely too good looking. How is anyone supposed to concentrate?

Maybe that's why he chose to teach at an all-boys school.

Jasper scans my rumpled cardigan and jeans. "You can't wear that."

"Yeah, God, I know."

"You can't say that."

"You know what?" I hop off the cot, so close to him I could knee him in the groin if I wanted. And dear Lord, how I want to.

"You can't tell me what to do." I poke his chest.

"If you don't obey the rules, *I* get punished," Jasper says, tilting his head. "Think I like getting lashes? *No one* likes getting lashes." He spins around, yanks open his closet, and tears a set of clothes from one of his hangers.

I don't have time—or space—to move out of the way. He shoves the bundle of fabric against my chest so hard I stumble back and end up sitting on my bed.

It creaks.

I scowl up at Jasper.

He glares back.

"Put that on and haul butt to the chapel outside." He points at me. "And don't you dare try to sit next to me."

With that, he's gone.

I THROW on Jasper's clothes and hurry into the hall but he's nowhere in sight. This hallway only has two exits, both with staircases. I pick the east side, and sprint down the hall before thumping down the stairs two at a time.

I breathe a sigh of relief when I spot Jasper turning the corner.

Jogging after him, I try and neaten my clothes on the way.

His shirt is too tight around my breasts, but not if I keep the top three buttons open and use his tie to cover my cleavage. His pants are tight around my ass. I'm hoping I can sit down without splitting them.

The outfit looks ridiculous with my ballerina pumps—there'd been no time to change those—but at least I only have to turn up the hems once so I don't step on them.

My hair is a train wreck. It's super curly on a good day, and I must have been rolling around in my sleep last night because now it's a tangled mess. Even trying to get the elastic band out of it brings tears to my eyes, so I decide to leave it in.

At least I'm wearing a uniform. Now Jasper can stop fantasizing about being whipped because I'm in jeans.

I arrive at the downstairs hallway alone with no roommate in sight.

The dining room doors are standing open.

It's empty.

Where the hell is everyone?

We all say prayers before

Shit.

In my hurry to chase down Jasper, I'd forgotten about prayers.

I'm in the wrong building.

My boobs jostle each other as I turn and sprint for one of the side doors leading out of the dormitory. I followed a group of students from the lunchroom yesterday—that's how I found my way to class. If it hadn't been for them, Jasper wouldn't be able to sit down for the lashes he'd have gotten.

What a prick.

I head for the chapel. The crucifix poking out from atop its little tower makes it easy enough to spot.

Far ahead, a handful of students hurry toward the chapel. I'm almost there when movement catches my eye. I glance over my shoulder, and stub my toe the same instant I catch sight of someone breaking away from the shadow of a nearby maple tree.

I lose sight of the figure as I hop on one foot and grit my teeth against the pain. When I look back, he's gone.

The fine hairs on the back of my neck lift up.

Someone *was* standing there. Shoulder length hair, sandy or blond, and a video camera in his hand. Not a cellphone or anything—a proper video camera with a lens.

Maybe I am hallucinating.

It wouldn't be the strangest thing to happen since I've set foot in this place. My toe aches in time with my hammering heart as I step inside the chapel.

Awe washes away the pain.

THIS IS nothing like our church in Redmond. That place always reminded me of a converted barn. It could seat two hundred and store a bunch of hay bales at the same time.

This place?

Oh my fucking Lord.

Whoever built this place must have been blessed with visions of heaven. Maybe he'd been dying of syphilis or something. You'd have to be on the spectrum to create something this...

"Gorgeous, isn't it, Little Hussy?"

I instantly recognize the voice. It's the guy who threw me up against my closet yesterday morning.

I try to swing around. He clasps my shoulders, keeping me facing forward.

The thought of this guy touching me makes my insides clench. I should be horrified, *terrified*...but for some reason my body isn't on the same page as my mind.

His touch sets everything inside me squirming.

"You'd think it was some crazy-talented architect who built this place, wouldn't you?" His breath tickles the hairs alongside my face. "Turns out, it was just some religious nut who knew how to use a hammer."

Still rooted to the spot, I don't have a choice but to take in—I mean *really* take in—this place. Everything from the vaulted ceiling to the immaculately designed stained glass windows. The floor is a ceramic artwork of mesmerizing patterns so glossy it reflects the rows of pews like a mirror.

It must have taken years to construct.

"Better take your seat, New Girl. Old Scratch hates it when we're late to prayers."

Then he slaps my ass.

Hard.

My gasp travels through the chapel like a whip crack. Everyone turns around to look at me, some grabbing hold of the backrest of their pew to twist in their seats.

I can't imagine what I look like, standing in the doorway with my hands clutched at my chest, hair disarrayed and cheeks glowing like hot coals.

I'm not in the least surprised when most of the boys start snickering into their hands.

Moving on wooden legs, I force myself to the closest pew.

I don't bother looking behind me. I already know the guy who'd been standing there whispering into my ear like Satan himself is gone.

But he must still be watching me from somewhere, because someone's staring at the back of my head.

I take a deep breath, and let it out slowly.

At least my pants haven't split. Today might even turn out to be a good day.

IT SEEMS the first two rows are reserved for the teachers and staff. I glance at them all and try to figure out who they are.

Dressed in full clerical vestments, Gabriel strides onto the chancel. I'm so relieved to see a familiar face I'm blinking away tears.

I hope I can talk to him before school starts. I know I'm the only female student here, but for heaven's sake, this can't be normal. Maybe if he makes an announcement or something, like that other woman— Sister Miriam?—did. He can tell the boys to leave me the hell alone.

I push back my shoulders and sit up a little straighter.

But then I remember what he told me yesterday. That the boys around here earn *privileges*. I guess there's no way he'd consider showing me any kind of special treatment.

After a short sermon, Father Gabriel leads us in the Father's Prayer.

Our father, who art in heaven.

Hallowed be thy name.

I barely murmur the words loud enough to move my lips. I wouldn't be praying along at all, but I guess it won't hurt.

What else is there to do but keep playing along like I have been all my life? What's a few more weeks, months, years?

Maybe by becoming the perfect student, I'll earn myself a private room. Perhaps even some kind of protection against the boys.

It's a lot to hope for, but I have Mom's stubbornness on my side.

I duck my head and squeeze closed my eyes. My lips tremble as I fight with myself. But this time, I lose the battle.

Thoughts pour into my mind like rancid oil.

How could you abandon me like this?

You weren't even supposed to be in that car with him.

You were supposed to be at home, with me.

You're my mother.

You told me you loved me, and then you chose him over me.

You always did.

I bite the inside of my lip until I taste copper.

I hate you.

I hate you!

I fucking hate—!

A hand lands on my shoulder. "Trinity?"

I jerk away from the touch, and turn brimming eyes up to Gabriel. "Father," I manage in a wobbly voice.

"May I join you in prayer?"

I'm vaguely aware of boys streaming past him in the aisle watching us intently.

If I spoke, I'd start sobbing like a kid so I scoot silently aside. Father Gabriel takes a seat beside me, his thigh warm and hard where it presses against mine. With a quick smile at me, he sits forward and rests his elbows on the backrest in front of our pew. Then he clasps his hands and bows his head.

Guilt eats through me like a heap of maggots.

He thought I was praying when he walked past, when in truth I was cursing my dead mother.

I fold down, pressing the tips of my steepled fingers to the skin between my brows hard enough to bruise. It helps with the shaking, and at least now I'm hidden behind Gabriel's figure. If the boys walking past want to gape at me, they won't be able to see much.

But even now, like this—shielded by the provost—someone's watching me.

Are they waiting for me to fuck up and expose myself as the heretic I am?

Or are they intrigued by this stranger in their midst?

Well fuck them.

Whoever they are, they can go straight to hell.

CHAPTER SEVEN
TRINITY

I don't bother trying to find anyone to sit with at breakfast. I hadn't even planned on going to the dining hall after the terrible time I'd had at the chapel. But on my way back to the main building, Sister Miriam makes a beeline for me and falls in step beside me.

"I trust you are keeping well, Miss Malone?"

Miss Malone.

A faint tingle works its way deep inside me. I don't know why, but my entire body came alive when Brother Zachary had spoken my name yesterday. In fact, that had happened every time he'd looked at me too.

"Yes, thank you." My voice is still thick with emotion. I don't know how long Father Gabriel and I sat praying in the chapel. It felt like hours had gone by before he shifted in his seat and let out a soft, "Amen," before excusing himself.

"What are you wearing?" Miriam asks, in exactly the same tone she'd used to greet me with.

"A uniform?" I look down at myself. My tie has shifted, exposing my cleavage.

I turn bright red. It must have been the run over here that did it. So was it like this the entire time Gabriel sat beside me in prayer?

Despite what I'd always thought, dying from shame is not only a possibility, but it seems destined to be *Miss* Malone's fate.

"Come see me after breakfast." She breaks away and heads for the classrooms.

Someone's watching me again. I scan all around me.

There's no one sight.

I stare at the distant trees. It's so dark under that dense canopy, they could easily move around on the edges of the grounds without being seen.

Goosebumps break out on my skin.

I ALMOST GET ALL the way through breakfast without incident.

En route to the table to put down on my empty tray, I feel eyes on me again. This time I don't hesitate—I immediately scan the entire dining hall to see who's looking in my direction.

Quite a few of the boys still seated at the benches are looking my way, but they duck their heads when I make eye contact.

Except the pair at the far back of the room. There beside the table with hot water urns for tea and coffee is the same sandy-haired guy I'd seen outside the chapel.

This time there's no mistaking the video camera in his hand.

Or the fact it's trained on me. He's not looking through it. He's watching the little fold-out screen.

I hastily put my tray on top of the others. Time to get the hell out of here. My tray upsets the entire pile. I wince as the trays clatter to the floor by my feet.

Not all of them were empty.

My pants—*Jasper's* pants—are now splattered with oatmeal and runny eggs. Some of it even got in my fucking hair. On instinct, those same disastrous words start playing through my head.

It can't possibly get any worse than this.

It can't *possibly* get *any* fucking worse than this.

But it does.

Everyone starts laughing.

"Gees," someone says behind me. "Were you born under a ladder or something?"

I half-turn to Jasper, scared the ceiling might collapse on me if I make any sudden moves. "I'm sorry about your clothes."

"Yeah, me too." Jasper shakes his head. "But it's kinda impossible to stay pissed off at you."

I shake a glob of oatmeal from my hand with a sigh. "At least I got that going for me."

"You gotta take a shower." He makes to grab my elbow, but I've had about all the manhandling I can, well, handle.

I move away from him, lifting my hands. "Just tell me where it is."

He stares at me for a second, and then laughs and shakes his head. "Bet I'll hear about a busted water main in an hour or so." He shrugs. "But hey, it's your funeral."

AFTER USING the restroom on the third floor, I'd assumed the bathroom would be one of many. A private room with a tub and a shower— possibly even a combo, for efficiency—and a basin for the boys to shave in. Maybe even some stalls.

How very naive of me.

Saint Amos was *definitely* a prison in one of its earlier incarnations. Church, prison, orphanage, boarding school. Isn't that the natural progression of places like this?

Situated on the second floor, the bathroom looks more like a locker room. On the left, a row of basins and mirrors. To the right, a wall of showers. *No* shower curtains. A low wall separates every pair of showerheads from the next.

A long bench splits the room down the middle.

Because showering with your roomie adds to the fun.

I shudder at the thought.

Where the hell am I supposed to put in my tampon? Or do I go and squat next to the bench when no one's looking?

I'm dimly aware I need to get a move on—Sister Miriam said to meet her after breakfast, and I think I have class with Brother Zachary first thing, but I'm so busy trying not to lose my shit all that stuff fades into the background.

I strip and hurry to the closest showerhead. I fully expect only cold water to come out, but after a few seconds I'm delightfully surprised by a lukewarm stream.

I slather no-name brand soap and shampoo—no conditioner, duh—over myself while I try not to think about athlete's foot. The fact this feels so good is a dire testament to how shitty the past few days have been.

As much as I'd love to stand here for a few minutes and let the warmish water batter out some of my stress, I'm pretty sure I'm tempting fate. The longer I stay here, the higher the chance someone will decide they need to shower or shave or sit down on a bench for no reason.

I dry off and put on the dress I brought with me. It's far from flattering—nothing in my sparse wardrobe can *possibly* be considered seductive—but I still feel overly exposed as cool air washes over my bare legs and arms. Even slipping on my cardigan doesn't help.

I hesitate, and then toss Jasper's dirty clothes into what I assume is the laundry basket in the corner of the room.

I wring out my hair and pat it dry with a towel as I hurry back to my room. Since I have no idea how long this thing with Sister Miriam will take, I'd rather fetch my notebook so I have it on me before Zachary's class.

I don't dare show up late to his class again.

There's an envelope on my bed.

I tear it open and pull out a class schedule typed out on a typewriter.

TUESDAY

7:00am - Prayer

7:30am - Breakfast

9:00am - English

10:00am - AP Psychology

11:00am - Free

12:00pm - Lunch

On and on it goes, spelling out every minute of my day till the last bell—lights out. I'd literally been lights out when that one rang last night.

I haven't had much time to consider how different things would be. I loved being homeschooled, but I'd never known anything else. Mother was an excellent teacher, but she'd also get into a mood sometimes and give me the day off to do what I wanted. Days like that I'd usually end up at the local library, reading whatever I could get my hands on.

Maybe structure is exactly what I need. I can just follow my schedule day after day until it becomes my new norm. No need to think.

Hopefully, by then, I'd have fooled myself into believing there could be such a thing as normal again.

I toss the towel on the foot of my bed, snatch up my notebook, and head down the hall.

I'm halfway down when the school bell tolls.

Shit! It's already nine?

I glance through one of the windows I pass, but it's impossible to make out where the sun is through the stained glass.

Who would I rather *not* piss off: Zachary, or Sister Miriam?

Since I have no idea where Sister Miriam is—does she have an office or something?—I choose Zachary.

With my dress flapping around my knees and my hair dripping water down my neck, I sprint over the grounds and hurtle into the classroom hallway.

I remember to push the door and not pull on it this time.

One point for Miss Malone, nine-hundred ninety-seven for the universe.

Brother Zachary glances at me from the blackboard. Forest green eyes narrow. His dark hair is long but carefully brushed back from his diamond-shaped face and dimpled chin.

Oh Lord, he's just as intense as I remember. And, like yesterday, my body reacts in the strangest way. Everything inside me goes tight and then, when I think I'm going to pass out from lack of oxygen, my lungs fill with air.

That breath calms me a little, despite how Zachary's face hardens when he sees me.

But it does nothing for the tingle dancing between my legs.

"Late again, Miss Malone."

My heart thumps in time with his words, as if he's controlling my organs.

If he is, then he's one cruel bastard.

Because as I force myself to walk across his classroom, it's as if he slides inside me and starts toying with my guts.

I should hate him for having such an effect on me.

Instead, all I can think about is him touching me. Not with his eyes, but with his hands.

I know I've missed out on a lot in my sheltered life.

Playdates, sleepovers, movies at the mall.

Kissing.

Sex.

I've always been intrigued by the concept. What would it feel like? Who would be the one to finally deflower me?

Against all logic, I'd resisted the thought it would be with the scrawny, pimple-faced kid from our church Mom kept trying to set me up with.

My dreams had centered around someone a lot more like Zachary. Tall and handsome and charismatic in his own way.

Maybe that's why I'm reacting like this. Since I'd started here, I've been bombarded with good looking boys.

Well, four, anyway.

I doubt I'd have felt the same way about anyone in this class. But it's not just the way they look. There's something else. At least with Brother Zachary, it's a little more obvious. He exudes a dark aura. His steely eyes, and the way he walks like he owns the room and every stick of furniture inside it.

Even the students.

Especially me.

Every time I step into this class, it's blatant I'm entering his domain, and I'm only here because he allows it.

CHAPTER EIGHT
TRINITY

Yesterday I spent my entire Psych lesson trying to ignore the fact I was apparently head over heels in love with my teacher. Today isn't going much better but at least I'm taking some notes.

Every time he happens to glance at me, I blush.

"...next stage, which is postnatal. Those can include neglect and *what?*"

It's the quiet that drags me from my thoughts. I've resorted to staring at my notebook and doodling circles in the margins so I won't catch on fire.

I look up.

Yup—everyone's staring at me.

What now?

Reluctantly, I look over Zachary.

He's holding a piece of chalk against the board, poised to write.

"Neglect and *what?*" He taps the chalk, dipping his head a little.

Dear Lord—he wants me to answer? My mouth opens as my eyes take in the diagram he's drawn. This stuff all sounds very familiar. I'm sure Mom already went through this part of the curriculum, but for the life of me I can't remember anything.

"I don't know."

My heart turns to lead when disappointment darkens his eyes.

He turns and points to one of the boys. "Eric?"

"Abuse?"

Zachary says nothing, but the tap-squeak of his chalk speaks volumes as he writes down the answer.

"Thank you, Eric. Abuse and *neglect* can affect genetic change during the postnatal stage of an individual's life."

I keep my head down for the rest of the lesson, not even daring to look up when I hear silence. Unless he calls on me directly, I'm not fuck risking it.

Thankfully, he ignores me for the rest of the lesson. By the time the bell sounds, I'm such a bundle of nerves I drop my pencil twice before I can shove it into my dress pocket. It sticks out halfway, but at least it's got a better chance of staying in there than in my hand.

I try and merge with the boys leaving class, ridiculously assuming they'd provide camouflage.

Instead, I cause chaos.

Some of them step back to let me through the door first. Others, as if sensing Armageddon is seconds away, speed up so they can exit first. I end up getting bounced around like a pinball.

Zachary watches impassively, not even bothering to catch me when I stagger. For my own safety, I wait to the side until everyone's left.

"A moment, Miss Malone," Zachary says, like I knew he would.

I try and keep the door open—it's set on a hydraulic hinge like the lunchroom—but Zachary puts his head to the side and that's somehow a command for me to approach.

The door hisses closed.

I creep closer and try to disappear behind my notebook.

"I'm not like the others," Zachary says.

A downright hysterical laugh escapes me before I can press my lips closed.

Zachary's eyes darken to the green of tree shadows as he perches on the edge of his desk. "Which part of this amuses you, Miss Malone?"

I bite the inside of my lip and hope it will be enough to stop me from losing my shit. But he waits me out, so I shake my head and try to look meek.

"Is it the part where you receive penance for continuously showing up late to my class?"

Continuously? Dude, it's the second day of my miserable stay at Saint Amos. Have a little—

"Or is it the part where you fail this class because you can't be bothered to apply yourself?"

My face heats up. I wish I could say something, but I don't trust myself to speak, especially since I still feel like laughing.

Who does he think he is? He's treating me like a ten-year-old. I can't believe I liked this guy. He's horrible.

"I only got my schedule this morning." The words are out before I can stop them.

Zachary tilts his head. My guts worm around in my belly at the intensity of his stare. "And your voice? Did that also just arrive?"

I just shake my head.

His eyes flicker away, as if he's suddenly lost his patience. He stands, steps closer. "I'll tell you again. I'm not like the others." He bends and reaches down.

He's going to touch my bare leg. Is that why he kept me back? He's so close I can make out the patterns in his irises.

His perfect skin, his expressive mouth, the tendons in his neck that tense as he stretches out his hand.

Oh, Lord, how badly I want him to touch me.

But not on my leg.

I squeeze my thighs together.

There.

That's where I want him to touch me.

Right between my—

Zachary holds up my pencil. "I don't give second chances," he says before tucking it back into my pocket. It must have fallen out when that guy bumped me. "I'm writing you up for this, and I suggest you do whatever it takes to be on time for my next class."

His words mean nothing to me. I'm hypnotized by the way his mouth moves.

"Do I make myself clear, Miss Malone?"

He's still a foot away, but I want him closer. I want to know if his touch will be gentle or firm. I imagine his large hands will demand from my body what he demands from my mind.

"Miss Malone." It's not a shout, but the snap in his voice goes right through me like he yelled.

"I'm sorry, Sir," I babble. "I promise I won't be late again."

The door whooshes open. Sister Miriam steps inside, ruddy face framed by her habit. "There you are!" Her mouth turns into a cruel curve. "Wait in the hall for me." She stabs out her finger, and my body moves without a single thought from my brain.

It's blessedly cool in the hall, blessedly quiet.

I can hear them speaking, but I can't understand a word through the closed door. I press my back against the wall and close my eyes, gathering myself with effort.

If the tingling between my legs is anything to go by, I'm going to have a hell of a time getting Brother Zachary out of my head today.

What the hell is wrong with me? Why am I suddenly acting like a teenager with raging hormones?

Yes, technically I am still a teenager, but I've never been—

A hussy?

When Sister Miriam comes out, she looks a touch calmer than she did going in. Zachary seems to have that effect on everyone except me.

"Follow me," she says in a snippy voice.

"Uh...I have English—"

"Not today. I've already spoken with your teacher."

Miriam leads me to the main building, then through the dining hall and into the big kitchen. A few people move around the large space—I guess if you're feeding so many students, meals take hours to prepare.

There's a guy kneading bread nearby. His arms are dusted in flour up to his elbows, and his long blond hair swept under a hairnet. He looks up when we enter the kitchen, and his eyes stay on me the entire time as Miriam leads me across the floor.

There's something familiar about him, and I only catch on right before Miriam opens another door and leads me through.

He was the one with the video camera.

I turn, glancing back over my shoulder.

He's standing up straight, a smudge of flour on the tip of his nose. He'd be handsome if his features weren't so gaunt.

I hesitate, and then wave.

He gives me a smirk.

THE LAUNDRY ROOM'S air smacks into me like a warm, damp towel. There are a handful of women and two younger boys in here, all drenched with sweat. Massive washers rumble along one wall. Clean linens drape a row of tables in the center of the long, narrow room.

Further down, racks of pressed uniforms stand waiting to be delivered to the boys's rooms.

"Strip," Sister Miriam commands.

I stop walking and cough like I've swallowed a fly. "Excuse me?"

She turns, clasping thick arms over her stomach. "I need to take your measurements. Ruth!"

An older woman looks up from folding a bedsheet, and hurries over.

"Did you find any?"

"Yes, Sister." Ruth detours and heads over to one of the emptier racks. Hangers clatter as she drags it closer to us on squeaky wheels. With a glance in my direction, she starts going through the clothes hanging on the rack.

"Are you deaf?" Miriam asks. "I said strip!"

I glance at the other people in the washroom. All of them have their back to me, but the two boys are staring so hard at their soapy buckets I know for a fact they'll peek over their shoulders as soon as no one's looking.

I grit my teeth and force down a swell of irritation. Fighting this won't do me any favors.

I slip off my dress and hand it to Ruth. I move my hands around to take off my bra.

"Leave it."

My skin crawls, but a quick glance at the boys shows they're still engrossed in their task.

"Turn."

I pivot on my heel, and then hold up my arms so Miriam can measure me. It's the weirdest thing—standing still while a complete stranger takes stock of how big and small you are in all the important places.

My parents raised me not to be vain, but there's no way you can sprout a pair of breasts and not stare at yourself a little longer in the mirror. I know I'm far from perfect—my hips and thighs are too large and my breasts too small in comparison. I kinda hoped they'd grow a little to balance things out but that never happened.

Invisible eyes drag over my skin again.

Not the boys. Not the other washerwomen.

I scan the laundry room.

"Got it?" Miriam says.

"Yes, Sister. But I don't think any of these will work."

"They'll have to. I can't stand seeing her walking around like this."

Their voices become white noise.

The laundry doors, like the ones on either end of the dining hall, have little windows set at eye level. I barely noticed them on the way in.

The baker is on the other side of the door. With his hair net gone, his long, sandy hair hangs in his face. He drags it away with thumb and forefinger, but it just falls forward again.

He's the one watching me.

What the hell is his fascination with me? First the video camera, now this?

I get an overwhelming urge to cross my arms over my bra, but I'm not sure if the sisters are done measuring me yet. Ignoring my reddening cheeks, I lift my chin and glare at him.

So what if he wants to look? There's not much for him to see. Just a girl in her underwear.

His lips quirk up in a smile that immediately spreads into a wide grin. He takes the first two fingers of his hand and presses them to his lips. Then he touches them to the glass.

I stiffen. In a blink, he's gone.

"Turn around," Miriam says in a long-suffering voice. "Arms up all the way."

They slide a shift over my head. It's at least two sizes too big for me, and comes to mid-calf. The armholes expose the side of my bra, and the belt is two inches lower than I'm assuming it should be.

"Good gracious, this is the closest you have?" Miriam asks Ruth.

"She's a tiny little thing," the sister replies.

"Well, she can't walk around in those whorish clothes of hers anymore."

Whorish...?

I turn stunned eyes on Sister Miriam, but she's glaring so hard at the shift, she doesn't seem to notice.

Then again, they're all wearing habits.

Wait...

"Do I have to wear a habit?" I whisper.

I hope they don't hear the horror in my voice. Ruth shakes her head, lifting a finger to tut me. "No, no. There's a school dress. We just haven't made many of them."

Thank. *Heavens.*

"Bring the dress."

Lo and behold, there *is* a girl's uniform for this place.

It's brown.

It's hideous.

And it looks like they made it out of felt. I can already tell it's going to be scratchy as all hell. I take a step back before I can force myself to hold still and let them slide it over my head.

Yup. I look like a turd.

I peek over my shoulder, but there's no one by the window.

Is it weird I'd rather let that guy see me in my underwear than in this monstrosity?

"You come back here this afternoon," Miriam says, slipping a pale belt over my waist and yanking it tight.

"Oh, I won't have it ready by then, Sister," Ruth protests.

"Not for the dress." Miriam turns me around adjusts my dress as if she can somehow make it two sizes smaller by tugging it here and there. Her eyes fix on me. "This is where you'll spend your afternoons."

I open my mouth, but from the look on Miriam's face, I know there's no reasoning with her.

"Yes, Sister," I manage.

Lord, I've *got* to start earning some brownie points with Father Gabriel. I don't know how else I'm going to survive this place.

CHAPTER NINE
TRINITY

My other teachers are mostly middle-aged men and women, none of whom are even remotely as interesting as Zachary. My mind drifts in each of their classes, and it's increasingly difficult to bring it back to the subject at hand.

The dress has given me a rash along my collarbones. I scratch the rest of my body as surreptitiously as I can, but I'm sure everyone in my class thinks I have leprosy.

For the first time since I arrived at Saint Amos, I'm relieved when the bell gongs for lunch.

I don't bother trying to find Jasper—he made it clear he'd rather stick a fork in his eye than spend any more time with me than he has to. I head for the first open seat I see.

As luck would have it, I recognize the boy sitting opposite me a few minutes into my meal of sausages, gravy, peas, and mashed potato. He doesn't look like he's going anywhere, so I might as well get some answers.

"You're Jasper's friend," I say, pointing at the kid with my fork.

He leans back from me as if he's worried I'll reach over and stick him with my cutlery. "Yeah, so?"

"So what's his problem? I mean, is he genuinely just a prick, or did I do something shitty to him a previous life?"

Jasper's friend watches me with owlish eyes. "He...he doesn't like girls."

"No one in this place does." I stab a stray pea and shove it in my mouth, bursting it between my teeth. "Tell me something I don't know."

His friend shakes his head, and then ducks down.

I'm all hot and cold inside. I so badly want to thump my fist into the table and make his friend look me in the eyes. I've got a bad temper sometimes, but I never let it show back home. I'd rather suppress it until I'm alone.

Things are always easier to handle when you're alone.

"What's your name?" I ask, switching to a softer voice.

Jasper's friend glances up at me, and then shifts in his seat as if even that question makes him uncomfortable. "Perry."

"Perry...I'm going to level with you." I put down my fork and place my palms on the table, spreading out my fingers. It helps me keep calm, and Perry can see I'm not palming a switchblade or something. "I've had a horrible few weeks. I..."

Why is this so difficult?

Come on, Trinity. Just open your mouth and—

"My parents died. Recently."

Perry's eyes go even wider.

"This place is all I've got left. I'm not picking a fight with anyone. Why would I? That would just make my life miserable."

Perry nods a little.

"So why is Jasper treating me like his enemy?"

Perry picks up a pea and presses it against his lips, but he doesn't eat it yet. "Because you're a girl."

"Bullshit."

Perry shrugs.

"So he just straight-up hates all girls?"

I sit back. Perry looks relieved as he pushes the pea into his mouth and swallows.

"How can I show him I'm not a bad person?"

Perry shakes his head. Eats another pea. I pick up my fork, toying with it. "Nothing, huh?"

"I guess..."

I sit forward. "Tell me."

"I mean...he's getting really bad grades for English Lit. And you're like two grades up. Maybe you can teach him? I tried, but I'm not good at explaining stuff."

I have no idea if I *can* teach anyone anything. Then again, I've never tried. It can't be all that difficult, right? And since I don't have a clue what I'm going to do with myself after I graduate, I guess staying here for a year or two to teach would give me time to figure things out.

If I can convince Jasper to let me help him.

That's going to be the hardest part of all.

CHAPTER TEN

ZAC

Gravel crunches under my shoes. With no moon out tonight, this path is as dark as those heading toward the stables and sports ground. This time of night, the students and staff should all be snug inside their beds.

There's a light fixture outside the crypt, but the bulb's been busted for months. The tomb isn't exactly a place students care to go, and even the staff avoid it. Superstition, of course. The only corpses nearby are those in the handful of graves outside in the cemetery.

Warm light spills out when I open the door. Should someone happen to glance out of a window, they could see me enter, but hopefully I wouldn't be recognizable.

It's one of many reasons I chose this place for our meetings.

The crypt's interior is cool and, despite the size of the room, stale.

A double row of columns cut the room in half, forming a square in the center where they meet the second row of columns intersecting diagonally.

I don't know who would ever hold a class or an impromptu sermon in this place, but if they did, it appears the maximum seats allowed would be no more than the dozen inside that sunken square.

Twelve seats

Twelve apostles.

Only three of those seats are taken.

Apollo chuckles as he leans forward, turning his video camera so Cassius can see the playback screen. Reuben's watching the entrance. He sits up even straighter when I enter the square.

The smell of weed hits my nose.

"Christ, I almost feel sorry for her," Cass says, and then glances up at me. "You took your time, Boss. Everything okay?"

"Never better," I say as I sink down in the seat closest to Cassius.

"Apollo taped her," Reuben says, his voice steeped in disapproval.

"That was the plan." I hold out a hand for the camera.

"I didn't know why she went in there," Apollo drawls through a grin as he passes the camera to me. "Would've tried for a better shot if I had."

Him and Cassius laugh at this. I turn the camera.

Trinity's a blip on the small screen until Apollo moves closer with his camera.

I flip the screen closed without bothering to watch more.

Apollo throws up his hands. "You missed the best part."

I hold up the closed camera. "This is not what I meant."

"You said t' watch her. This is me watching her."

"Showering?"

Any normal guy might have dropped his eyes at this point. Apollo's grin grows wider. "She did a good job. I'm sure there wasn't a single spot she—"

As soon as I move my gaze from Apollo's eyes, he cuts off. With a huff, he slumps in his chair and runs his hands through his hair, unsuccessfully tucking the bulk of it behind his ears. He's almost twenty-two, but you'd think he's the youngest of the Brotherhood.

I stare at each of my brothers in turn.

"She's not a threat."

"You saw her file?" Cass sits forward, a blunt dangling from his fingertips. "What does it say?"

Sister Stella had sent a message for me this afternoon. Trinity's file had been faxed through.

From her social worker.

Trinity Malone was an orphan, like I'd suspected. Homeschooled by her parents since she was a kid, her file only had a few report cards and some very basic details. Addresses, contact numbers, that kind of thing. All useless, since both her emergency contacts were now deceased.

No referral. No indication why she'd ended up here at Saint Amos.

"Someone wants us to think she's a nobody."

Cass and Apollo groan. Reuben says quietly. It takes a lot for him to involve himself in a conversation.

"If there's some kind of relationship between her and Gabriel, the file doesn't mention it."

"We're doin' this?" Apollo asks, his voice warbling with nerves. Putting his camera down by his feet, he shoves his hands under his armpits and narrows his eyes at me.

I flick my fingers at Cass, and he passes me the blunt. I glance at each of them in turn as I hit it, diagnosing their mental states best I can.

I'm a year into my psychology major. The human psyche has fascinated me ever since I realized how fucked up a person could be.

Or, become.

Nature versus nurture.

We need to have our shit together before we act. Asking my brothers straight out if they're of sound frame of mind will earn me anything from the unvarnished truth to a flat out lie. But I've known them for fifteen years. We're brothers through and through. I can read them like I read scripture—cutting through all the bullshit metaphors and anecdotes, straight to the bone.

"You're wrong. She *is* somebody," Reuben says, as soon as my gaze settles on him.

He could put any of us on the ground in a heartbeat. But he's always been cautious. Sometimes too cautious for his own good, just like Apollo does shit without thinking things through.

Cass and I, we're somewhere in the middle. Sometimes cautious, sometimes rash.

"Why?" I say.

"He's known her a long time."

I don't even try and second guess him. Honest to God, I wish Reuben would join my psych class. What he understands on an intuitive level about most people, it would take me years to learn. Maybe it's because he listens before he speaks. He's the one that put us onto

Father Gabriel in the first place, through a happenstance meeting at one of the provost's parishes.

For close to a decade, we'd been chasing a ghost. After Reuben met Gabriel in person. Then our ghost suddenly had a name and a face.

"Don't mean she's—" Apollo begins.

Reuben doesn't even pause. When he speaks, he doesn't allow himself to get interrupted. "He treats her like family."

Everyone tenses up at that.

Everyone.

Gabriel doesn't have any family. DNA like his isn't meant to be passed on. God only knows what evil his offspring would bring to this world. If he ever knocked up some chick, she'd give birth to a two-headed goat.

There's a pause while everyone makes sure Reuben is done. Then Apollo sits forward in his seat and clicks his fingers at me. I pass him the blunt without taking my eyes from Rube. "Nothing in her file indicates that he even knows her."

But, like Rube, I'm convinced that's intentional.

"If you saw what I did, you wouldn't think she was so fucking special," Apollo says in a tight voice as he passes the blunt to Cass. When he continues, smoke leaks from his lips. "That hag stripped her down like she's one of those window dolls." Apollo gestures with long hands and spindly fingers. "Wasn't being polite about it, neither."

"Get that on tape?" Cass passes the blunt to Rube, but the guy ignores him.

"Nah, man. I was working." Apollo scratches his arm. "Guys don't like it when I film them in the kitchen."

"'Cos then we'd all know who spits in our food," Cass says through a smirk.

Apollo barks out a laugh.

I'm still watching Rube. And he's watching me.

"Even if she's his fucking daughter," I say, "how could she fuck this up for us?"

Reuben shrugs—an impressive gesture on a guy with his shoulders. "We can't risk it. This is the last chance we get."

"Exactly!" Apollo's foot starts tapping. "It's our fuckin' last chance. We don't do this, we've got shit. Nothing. Fucking *nada*."

"Relax," Cassius murmurs, handing the blunt back to Apollo. "We'll figure this out."

Apollo's right. For once, time isn't on our side.

I make eye contact with Cass. He's watching me with such intensity I already know what he's going to say.

"We have to try." Cass stands. "Even if it's a fuck up. Even if we get outed, this ends with him, one way or the other."

"Sit down," I murmur.

"You knew this day was coming."

"Sit. Down."

He does, but with ill grace and the type of sulky mouth I'd expect on Apollo.

Rube's staring a hole through my head. I prop my elbows on my knees and lace my fingers together. My ankles are starting to throb, but I don't want to draw attention to the fact by rubbing them.

"Then I vote yes." I glance aside at Reuben when he remains silent. "Got to be unanimous, brother."

Reuben's chair creaks when he shifts his weight. Apollo and Cass finish the blunt between them in the time it takes him to speak. When he finally looks up at me, determination gleams in his eyes.

"No," he says.

I only realize I was holding my breath when it streams out of me in a hiss.

No.

Of course not.

Reuben doesn't take chances. If there's the smallest chance something could go wrong, he backs off.

Apollo springs up. "Jesus *fucking* Christ." He stalks out of the crypt.

Cass lets out a sigh, picks up Apollo's camera, and shrugs at us before trotting out after him.

Silence filters down between Rube and me for long minutes before I let out a sigh and rub my eyelids. "Sure about this?" I ask quietly.

"Of course," Reuben says. "She's..."

"What, Rube?" My next sigh is exasperated. "What is she?"

He taps his thumbs against the side of his knees and then slowly looks up at me. "She's one of us."

CHAPTER ELEVEN
TRINITY

I make sure I'm awake before the first bell rings. While I was slaving away in the laundry yesterday afternoon, I had a lot of time to think.

I meant what I said to Perry.

This place *is* all I have.

So I've got to make this work. Fuck knows how, but if I'm going to spend a good three or four years here, I need to make peace with the natives.

Starting today.

I run a hand through my curls as I sit up in bed. It was too cold to sleep in my usual pajamas—cotton boxers and a vest—so I put on a sweater before crawling under the covers.

Jasper shoves away his blanket with a groan and then swings his legs over the side of the bed and yawns. When he sees me staring at him, he freezes.

"What?" he snaps, going to get his clothes from his closet.

"Did I tell you I'm thinking about becoming a teacher?"

Jasper scratches his hip without answering. He yanks out a pair of clothes and tosses them to the bed. I guess he's not going to shower this morning. Though, from the smell of sweat rolling off him, he really should.

I'd still love to know what he did to get himself stuck with me as a roommate. But that'll come in time. Right after I turn him into my BFF.

"Thing is, I was homeschooled," I go on as I start untangling my curls with my fingers. "I've never really had anyone to practice on."

Jasper's shoes thump to the floor, and he slips them on without bothering to put on socks first.

"Boo for you," he mutters, and exits the room in his trunks and vest.

I guess he's used to the cold.

"Fuck," I mutter to myself.

Guess he's not a morning person. Well, at least I planted the seed. I'll try again at breakfast.

Should I shower before school starts?

Jasper left the door open. Half-dressed boys of all ages stream this way and that across the hall, some with towels slung over their shoulders.

I sniff at my pits and shrug. At least I don't smell as bad as Jasper.

Father Gabriel leads us in prayer at the chapel. Since I got here early, I had my choice of seats. I didn't want anyone creeping up on me again, so I'm sitting near the front. This way Gabriel can watch over me.

But as soon as the provost is done addressing the school and reading today's scripture, he walks off stage. Not even a glance in my direction. It's like he's forgotten all about me.

I hesitate for a second, and then hurry after him before I can second guess myself. I hope this isn't a restricted area, because I need to know what I can do to earn my own room. And a proper school uniform. One that doesn't come pre-installed with lice.

I push open the door Gabriel disappeared behind and walked right into him.

"Trinity?" He frowns at me, and for just a second there's something very unfriendly in his eyes.

"Father. I'm—I'm sorry to just—"

His eyes soften from wood to velvety chocolate. "Gracious, I've been so caught up, I haven't had a chance to check in with you." He grabs my arm and leads me to a nearby table with a set of chairs. "How are you, child?"

I sink down, but he remains standing, forcing me to crane my neck to look up at him.

"It's been an adjustment," I admit. I was going to honey coat it—no use complaining when I'm trying to show him how well I can adapt—but he's always had a way of drawing the truth out of me.

Did he have that same effect on Mom and Dad? Did they tell him things without wanting to?

Bad things?

Sinful things?

I push away the thought. This place is making me jump at shadows. How can anyone stand it?

"I would imagine so. Tell me, how are you finding the classes? Have your teachers been accommodating?"

Teachers.

Of course! That's my way in.

"That's actually why I'm here." I twist my hands in my lap and force out the words before I can lose my nerve. "Is there a chance, I mean, do you think I could try and...?"

"You may speak freely, child," Gabriel says. He shifts his weight, looking for all the world as if he could stand there all day while I fought my tongue.

"I want to be a teacher."

He nods, waits.

"I'd like to teach here when I've finished high school. Is that...would that be...?"

Gabriel cups my face in a hand. I start at the intimate gesture, but I don't pull away. The last thing I want is to offend him. His usually vacant smile deepens. It's not the first time I've seen his dimples, but I can't remember when last he looked so happy.

"You truly are a remarkable girl."

Pressure wells behind my eyes. I drop my eyes, but he keeps me looking up with that gentle pressure on my jaw. His hands are warm, slightly calloused—which is strange for a man of the cloth. "Is that a yes?"

"I would love nothing more," he says.

He turns to leave, and then pauses and turns back. "I'll send someone to collect you tonight."

I was in the process of standing. My knees lock, leaving me in a weird half-crouch. "Uh...why?"

"We shall have dinner. God bless, Trinity."

I almost manage to reply.

Almost, but not quite.

CHAPTER TWELVE
TRINITY

Morning prayers ran shorter than yesterday. Despite my meeting with Father Gabriel, I get to the dining hall way ahead of everyone else. Since I don't know when Jasper's arriving, I decide to lurk in the corner close to the urns and have a cup of coffee. Which means I'm alone with the blond-haired film student when he wheels out a trolley full of breakfast trays.

At first, he doesn't see me.

The coffee must give me a spark of courage, because by the time he's done unpacking the food trolley, I march across the hall and come up behind him.

I open my mouth, but he beats me to it.

"Nice dress," he drawls. "Really brings out your eyes."

I freeze to the spot. Nice *dress*? This fabric is so stiff I could prop it up in my closet—no need for a hanger.

"Why do you keep filming me?"

"Filming you?" He turns, watching me for a second from the corner of his eye. I take back what I said before—he *is* handsome, perhaps because of his sharp nose and blade-like cheekbones. It makes him look like a fox, especially when he narrows his honey-brown eyes. "Now why'd I do that?"

"That's what I'd like to know."

"D'you really think you're that pretty?" He sets down the tray he was holding and turns to face me. When he steps forward, I step back on automatic. "Or are you just that vain?"

Now I'm regretting walking over here. I thought I'd have the upper hand, but—

Without warning, the guy tucks a stray curl behind my ear. When his fingertips brush my cheek, they leave behind a static charge that's both terrifying and exhilarating.

"Stop filming me or I'll report you."

The guy narrows his eyes again. "Who you gonna tell?"

My mind scrambles to the scariest person in this place. "Sister Miriam," I say, jutting my chin into the air. "She won't stand for it."

"What if she's the one who told me to film you in the first place?" He reaches for me again, and this time I take two steps back.

By now, boys are starting to file into the dining hall. Thankfully, one of them is Perry. The blond guy glances toward the doorway and then back at me. "I got work to do, pretty thing," he drawls through a wicked smile. "I'll catch hell if you distract me much longer."

He hurriedly offloads the rest of the trays and pushes the trolley away without looking back. I start after him, but then stop. I don't have the guts to demand his name. I mean, I barely stood my ground.

I grab a tray and hover around the table until Perry comes up to get one too. He spotted me from the doorway already. When he gets close, he moves around like a skittish deer, as if he's convinced I'm going to go for his throat.

"Morning!"

He flinches. "Hey."

"Sleep well?"

"What do you want?" he asks, frowning at me as he grabs a tray and steps back. Did I look like that when I was dodging the blond-haired guy? Like a nervous rabbit facing off with a wolf?

I'm such a wuss.

Here I am, minutes after the provost tells me how remarkable I am, and I can barely hold a conversation?

Screw that.

I've been in the passenger seat for way too long while some anonymous driver takes me from point A to point B. Time to take the wheel.

"I wanted to thank you," I tell him.

He glances back warily when I trail him to his seat. I sit beside him before he has a chance to object, and a moment later another kid boxes him in on the other side.

"What for?"

"I really think I can help Jasper." I lay my hand on top of Perry's. "I want to help him. And if I can, and he passes, then he's got you to thank for it."

Perry stares at me for a second as if I've totally caught him off guard.

"What the hell are you doing here?"

Perry snatches away his hand and ducks his head. I turn and beam up at Jasper. "Waiting for you, silly." I point at the empty space opposite us. "I want to talk to you about something."

Jasper growls out something that could have been a curse—was definitely a curse—but he sits anyway, wincing the last inch of the way as if he can't bear the thought of spending breakfast with me.

"So talk," he says, taking a noisy sip from his cup without making eye contact.

"I need a student to tutor. Do you know anyone that needs help?"

Jasper frowns at me, and then moves that look to Perry. "No," he says. "Ask the teachers."

"Oh, right!" I snap my fingers and point at him. "Of course. Why didn't I think of that?"

Because I don't want to try and teach just any kid. Jasper doesn't like me, but he seems bright enough. I want to show Father Gabriel I can do this so I'll aim for some low hanging fruit first. Plus, if I can get him to stop treating me like shit while I'm still his roommate, it would make my life that much easier.

Two birds, one stone.

Jasper scrapes his spoon through his oatmeal for a few seconds. I slurp at my coffee and take a bite of my toast, happy to shut up and wait.

I don't think he's going to go for it, when he suddenly asks, "Will it get me out of swimming practice?"

"Will what?" I ask through a mouthful of toast. I know I'm pushing it, but I need him to think this is his idea.

"Extra classes."

"What, for you? You need extra classes?"

"You said you need practice."

"I do." I drop my toast and dust my hands. "Yeah, I guess I could do a few with you. Just while I figure things out. What do you need help with? Is it math? I could def—"

"English," Jasper cuts in.

I nod, frowning a little. "Okay. Let's do it." I hold out my fist.

He stares at it until I put it back in my lap. "See you at three," he says.

I salute him with my mug of coffee.

And that, ladies and gentlemen, is how it's done.

I DON'T RISK PISSING off Jasper by joining him at lunch. Instead, I sit off to one side and munch on a slightly soggy cheese and tomato sandwich while I steal glimpses at the rows of boys. Sister Miriam pops in on our meals as randomly as if she's doing a spot check. The boys seem to have developed a sixth sense around it. Seconds before the dining room doors or kitchen doors swing open, the entire hall hushes.

As soon as Miriam's walked up and down a few times, she leaves. Seconds later, noise levels return to normal.

Maybe I *can* get the hang of this place. It can't be that hard—not if all these boys manage to coexist.

I don't have Psych today, and that suits me fine. If I did, I'd probably sprain my ankle on the way to Zachary's class and arrive late...again. Heaven knows what penance he'll assign me.

Is he the kind of teacher that would go old school and draw me over his knee? I don't think that shit's allowed anymore, but Jasper didn't look like he was kidding about getting lashes.

I head to my room just before three. I don't want Jasper to wait for me in case he loses his nerve and bails on our first lesson. Honestly, I'm a bit nervous. I paid close attention today in each of my classes, trying to figure out if there was anything specific I needed to do if I was going to start teaching. But nothing really jumped out at me, so I'm going into this blind.

"Not here," Jasper says as soon as he steps into the room.

"Oh, okay." I stand up, my notebook and math textbook pressed to my chest. "Then where—?"

"Library." He flicks his fingers, and I follow him.

He leads me out the building and across the grounds. I slow down when I realize where he's headed.

"That's where the library is?"

"Relax. It's not haunted or anything."

"But…"

Who in their right mind puts a library in a cemetery? Thankfully, our path doesn't lead us too close to the gravesides, but it's still eerie having to walk within sight of the gravestones.

The inside of the crypt is emptier than I thought. There are some chairs in the center, as if this place is used for bible study groups or AA meetings. Most of the space is filled with columns.

He leads me to the back of the enormous room and then down a circular stairwell. When I clear the stairs, I pause for a second to gape.

This chamber is huge. It's not in a cross shape like the crypt, so I'm pretty sure it extends beyond the upper building's walls.

I guess they didn't have enough dead bodies to put in here, so they decided to use it as a library instead.

Row upon row of books line the walls and form narrow aisles. Closer to the stairwell are two sections with overstuffed chairs and sofas for people to read or study. A few feet away is a podium with a large, leather-bound bible on it. A spotlight set in the ceiling illuminates it. Dust motes disturbed by our presence catch fire in that beam of light.

It's so quiet down here.

As if the books are all waiting for something…or someone.

I guess the only thing a book ever wants is to be read. It's sad to think no one ever comes down here—that's obvious by the film of dust on everything and the staleness in the air. If I ran a place like this, I'd make sure it was clean and filled with curious minds.

"We've only got an hour," Jasper says.

"Sorry." I run my hands down my thighs, grimacing at the touch of the coarse fabric. "Just…taking it all in."

He takes a seat on one of the couches and leans back, watching me expectantly. "Do that on your own time."

I roll my eyes as I take a seat on the chair closest to him.

Lord, I hope this isn't a big waste of time.

CHAPTER THIRTEEN
TRINITY

I'm in the laundry room, suds up to my elbows, when a boy comes inside and walks straight up to me. He's young, perhaps no older than thirteen.

"Father Gabriel is looking for you," he says.

"Now? I thought he said I'm having dinner with him."

The boy frowns at me. "It *is* dinner."

I must have lost track of time. There's no bell until six again, and the last one signaled the end of my lesson with Jasper. I snort quietly to myself as I flick suds off my arm and start rolling down the sleeves of my dress.

Lesson?

What a joke.

Teaching Jasper had been like trying to talk to a tree. He moved about like he had ants in his pants, but from his jaw-cracking yawns, it was obvious nothing was sinking in.

I called it quits after forty-five minutes.

"I need to change," I tell the kid as he leads me out of the laundry.

"He said to bring you straight up."

Lord, is everyone in this place missing a screw? I guess after following orders for so long you forget the meaning of independence.

Whatever. It's not like Father Gabriel would actually care what I look like. And after two hours in the laundry, I smell more of suds than sweat. I wipe my hands on my dress, hoping enough of the scent will soak into the fibers to last through dinner.

As the kid leads me up flight after flight of stairs, I take down my hair and try to get it to conform. I can only hope it doesn't look like a rat's nest.

The kid takes me to the fourth level of the building where the doorways are spaced several yards apart. The lighting is better, the floors are carpeted, and it doesn't smell like a bunch of boys crammed into a shoe closet. While my room is on the east wing of Saint Amos, Father Gabriel's is on the west.

The kid leaves me in front of a wide, arched doorway with a brass plaque:

PROVOST

No name? Guess the position suffers from high turnover.

"So do I knock, or—?"

But the kid's already gone. I push back my shoulders, paste on a smile, and knock.

No one answers.

I knock again.

No answer.

Maybe I'm too late. He could have decided to go and have dinner with the rest of the staff.

Where *do* Zachary and the rest of the faculty have dinner? Do they take their plates to their rooms, or is there a separate dining room for the staff?

On my third knock, a muffled voice calls from inside. "Come."

I turn the handle and step into a small antechamber. There's an umbrella stand, a table with a set of keys in a bowl, and a small stool beside two pairs of shoes. A second door opens into a living area.

A multitude of candles flickers as I push the door closed behind me. Polished mahogany gleams, and thick carpets eat the sound of my footfalls.

Father Gabriel is sitting in front of a fireplace on the far side of the room. There's a footstool in front of him, and he has his socked feet propped on it.

Cigarettes, wood smoke, and candle wax cloy the air, making my eyes water.

He's wearing a white t-shirt and dark jeans. Nothing like the cable-knit sweater and slacks he greeted me in on Monday morning.

He glances at me over his shoulder, and beckons. "You came straight from the laundry?" he asks as I approach.

There's a cigarette in one hand, and he flicks it against the edge of a glass ashtray without looking. He's been a smoker as long as I can imagine. Mother would never let him smoke inside our house, though. Even Dad had to smoke outside on the porch.

"Bit late to be working down there, isn't it?" he adds before taking a drag from his cigarette.

Of course I could tell him I lost track of time. But I'd rather he think I'm an overachiever than a daydreamer.

"I thought I'd stay a bit longer. They really appreciate the extra pair of hands down there."

Gabriel nods, his smile fading a little as he turns his attention back to the fire. There's a wine glass on the side table beside his ashtray—ruby liquid swirls as he brings it to his lips.

"Care for something to drink?"

"I...uh...yeah. Sure." Wine? He's giving me wine? My parents never let me drink.

Gabriel crushes out his cigarette in the ashtray and then stands and heads over to the corner kitchenette. I take a moment to scan the room as I sink into the other chair.

The heat tightens my cheeks.

I hope I don't have to sit here for much longer. Else I won't be reeking of suds anymore.

Gabriel returns with a soda can. I take it with a nod as I purse my lips. Of course the provost won't give me alcohol. What the hell am I thinking?

I crack open the can and take a sip. "It's hot in here."

"We'll move in a moment."

I glance at him from under my lashes. He sounds like his mind is miles away. I guess someone like him spends a lot of time thinking about God, even though he probably has Him on speed dial.

I look down at the can, and do my best to shove away the unpleasant thoughts trying to infiltrate my mind.

"So, uh, I hope you don't mind, but I took some more initiative today."

"Hmm?" Gabriel says, his eyes still locked on the flames.

"You know my roommate, Jasper?"

Gabriel's head snaps to the side. His vague smile is frozen on his face, but there's no mirth in his eyes. "What about him?"

My tongue tangles.

What the hell?

"Oh, he...I mean...I was tutoring him. English. We had our first lesson today."

Gabriel's eyes flicker over my face. Why do I get the feeling he's trying to catch me out in a lie? I take another sip of soda. "That's... that's okay, right? You said—"

"Oh, of course, child." His smile thaws and even spreads a little wider. "I just hadn't expected you to begin so soon."

"Should I stop?"

"Not at all." Gabriel turns back to the fire. "That boy could use a positive influence in his life. You'll do him a world of good."

Just what the hell did Jasper do? I've got to get it out of him. Maybe Perry knows.

There's a faint knock from the hallway. I'm not surprised Father Gabriel didn't hear the first two—the sound is so muffled it could be lost in the crackle of a burning log.

"That would be our supper," Gabriel says, sounding downright cheery at the concept. He stands and extends an arm as he calls out, "Come!"

I know I shouldn't stare. I know it's wrong to even have a single thought about Gabriel's body. But it's impossible not to.

For one, I hadn't expected him to be so well built. His biceps strain against his shirt sleeves, and his forearms are corded with muscles. Now his hands look proportional—his meaty palms and thick fingers a testament to a strong, fit man.

I hurry over to the table, desperate to keep my curiosity in check. Gabriel follows. I hesitate about which of the two seats to take until Gabriel pulls one out for me.

Why does this feel like a date? Then again I wouldn't know what a date was if it hit me on the head.

I thump into the seat, and drag it under the table. With my hands on my lap and my head down, I feel like I'm waiting for him to start a sermon.

Instead of cracking open a bible, Gabriel takes his seat opposite me and lays his serviette over his lap.

The antechamber's door opens. I turn on automatic.

When I see who's standing in the doorway, my blood runs cold.

CHAPTER FOURTEEN
TRINITY

Reuben enters Father Gabriel's apartment with a large, covered tray in his burly arms. At first he stares at something only he can see, but as soon as he notices me, it's like I'm the only person left in the entire world.

I've never had someone look at me like this before.

It's unnerving.

And provocative.

Every nerve ending in my body switches on.

That look must only last a second, but it feels like an eternity that Reuben and I lock eyes. Then he drops his gaze, and it's as if I've ceased to exist.

"Thank you, child," Gabriel says as Reuben sets down the tray between us.

Reuben lifts the lid and goes to put it down on the counter in the dinette area. "Do you need anything else, Father?" he asks in his deep, melodic voice.

Gabriel waves at him. "That'll be all for now, child. Come back later to collect the dishes."

Reuben turns to leave, and Gabriel stands to dish up food from the set of small dishes on the tray. I'm watching Reuben's back so I don't notice at first Gabriel is dishing up for me.

"You're looking a little thin, Trinity," Gabriel says. "Though I'm sure the past month has played havoc with your appetite."

"What?" I look down at my plate. There isn't room for another pea. "Wow...that's a lot of food."

"Your mother used to lose weight whenever she was upset. I can't remember how many pies I brought to your house, hoping to get her appetite started."

I don't remember any pies.

Reuben's walking even slower than before, as if he's listening to our conversation. It makes me want to yell at Gabriel to shut up. I don't want Reuben to know anything about me. He made it clear he thinks I'm up to no good. He'll use anything he can against me.

Even my dead parents.

"My first class was a success," I rattle out.

It was the first thing I could think of, and the worst choice of words. Today was the furthest from a success. Hopefully Gabriel isn't exactly going to interview Jasper about my teaching skills any time soon.

"Is that so?" Gabriel returns to his seat as Reuben slips out the door.

It's as if the provost had already forgotten Reuben was here. I'm not surprised; despite his size Reuben makes less noise than a cat, especially on these carpets. Is he one of the kids that have been at Saint Amos for so long he's just another gear in the machine?

"Well, it's still early days, of course, but I really do think teaching is something I'd like to do."

Gabriel takes a sip of his wine. Where my plate is practically splitting under the weight of all the food he piled on it, there's oceans of white china between his servings. I've never seen a chicken breast look so lonely before.

"You should attempt a full class during summer break."

I almost drop my fork. "Yeah. I'll look into that." I gulp at my soda and try to think of something to change the subject again.

My only intention is to score brownie points. But if I'm not careful, I'll have agreed to run a summer class for half the school before dinner is over.

"Does the school host anything fun during summer break?" I ask before shoving a fork full of food into my mouth.

Gabriel shakes his head, and then frowns up at me. He tuts quietly.

"That's right. I must have forgotten to mention it. Saint Amos is closing over summer break. First time in almost five years, actually."

Closing?

Closing!

"Closing how?" I sit back in my seat. He wasn't wrong about my appetite—it comes and goes with my mood. I never eat when I'm uneasy, and for some reason his announcement fills me with dread.

"The students are leaving." Gabriel chews on a piece of chicken for a moment, looking thoughtful. He washes it down with a sip of wine and then puts down his cutlery. "We have extensive maintenance work to undertake. Several sections of the building will be cordoned off. It's just safer to send the students away until we reopen in the fall."

I put my cutlery down too. "Where are they going?"

"Some of our students are going home, or visiting extended family. The rest will be boarding at Sisters of Mercy in Devon."

Those that don't have homes.

"Like me?"

He nods. "Maybe you'll like it so much you decide to stay."

I swallow down more soda, but my mouth is still dry.

I've been codependent my entire life. I didn't have a choice, really. Not with parents who refused to send me to a regular school. The thought of what Father Gabriel's telling me sets my heart to racing.

"But I can stay here if I want?"

"Not during the break, but if you decide to return with the other students..." he spreads his hands, that absent smile of his not shifting one iota.

Then he pushes away his plate in favor of nursing his glass of wine. He takes a few sips as I try to get back into my meal, but it's impossible with him watching.

After a minute or so, he stands and goes over to the fireplace. He keeps his back to me as he lights a cigarette and takes a long drag.

"I'm not pushing you away, Trinity." He turns, smoke jettisoning from his nose. "I just want you to be happy. You're not happy here."

I hastily swallow. "But I am, Father. Really, I am."

"Don't lie to me, child." He puts his head to the side, his smile turning hard. "I know it can't be easy, a girl—*woman*—like you—" he points at me with the hand holding his cigarette "—surrounded by men."

What the hell am I supposed to say to that? It feels like a trap, like he wants me to admit I can't make it. That I want him to treat me like the friend I thought I was. That I need him to make an exception for the poor little girl who just lost her parents.

"I know these boys too well." He runs his fingers through his hair, takes another drag. His exhale obscures the fire for a moment. "So many troubled youths beneath this roof, Trinity. It would turn your hair white to hear their stories." He reaches out and flicks his cigarette ash into the ashtray.

"I know it won't be easy," I say as I slowly get to my feet. I hesitate, and then join him by the fire. "But..."

Lord, why is this so difficult to say?

"You're all I have left."

He glances at me for a second before his eyes go back to the fire. "You know that's not true, Trinity."

My chest fills with molten lava.

This again?

Really?

My hands are in fists, but it seems there's no way I can possibly unfurl them. If my feet weren't rooted to the spot, I'd storm out of here.

Why the fuck did I even come?

He *always* does this. He turns things around and makes it seem like it's your fault. That it's always been your fault, and you were too stupid and too egotistical and too—

vain

—to realize it.

"You know what?" I whirl to face him. My dress feels like a cheese grater against the inside of my wrists. "I *should* go to Sisters of Mercy. In fact, why don't I just go there right now since it's obvious you don't want me here."

I don't wait for his reply. My dress scrapes against my legs as I charge for the door leading out of this hell hole.

It's not just his cigarette smoke giving me a headache. Tears are waiting to fall.

Father Gabriel can say what he wants, I'm not biting.

My parents *believed*.

In God.

In the church.

In Father Gabriel.

Their lives—and subsequently, mine—were formed around the concept God is love. They say he notices when a damn swallow falls, but he couldn't be bothered to save two cherished members of his flock?

I don't give a fuck about me—God and me, we've never really been on speaking terms—but my parents deserved better than having their brains smeared over the tarmac because they hit a patch of ice.

I jerk at the door handle, but somehow Gabriel locked it when I wasn't looking because it won't open.

A hand appears, grasps mine, draws my fingers away.

I snatch it back. "Let go," I snap.

I try the door again. Gabriel slings a hand around my waist and drags me back.

"Let me go!" I shriek.

He lifts me bodily, and I start kicking and screaming like I'm possessed.

I'm vaguely aware Gabriel's trying to get me to calm down, but I can't stop fighting him.

I won't.

I'm a bottle of soda someone's been shaking and shaking and shaking.

Gabriel's just popped open the tab.

"I can't let you go," comes Gabriel's voice as I pause to draw breath. "Our holy Father won't allow it, child."

"Fuck you!" I beat at him with my fists, and he finally releases me when I land a blow to his midsection. "Fuck you, and fuck your God!" I stagger, stab a finger toward him. "You weren't there. He wasn't there. Never. Not once!"

Gabriel rushes forward, and I try to block him. But he's obviously had practice at calming down hysterical members of his clergy. He side-steps easily before wrapping me in his arms and squeezing the life out of me.

My legs become weak and rubbery. Soon, they can no longer hold my weight.

We sink to the carpet. My ragged sobs and Gabriel's heavy breathing as he resists my struggles are the only sound for a moment. This close, he smells of red wine and cigarettes and a woody cologne.

There's a crash.

I hiccup in fright and turn to the door.

Reuben's standing there, shoulders bunched and hands held in blades. There's a look of such avid determination in his black eyes that I shrink away.

Inadvertently seeking comfort in Gabriel's arms.

"I heard…" Reuben cuts off.

"Everything is under control," the provost says.

Bitter words line up on my tongue, but I can't say anything with these hitching lungs of mine.

"Please, child." Gabriel's voice is tight, but calm. "Just take the dishes and leave. This does not concern you."

There's a clatter of crockery and cutlery as Reuben cleans the apartment.

Gabriel and I are still on the floor, and the fact has a wave of shame rolling through me. I turn and burrow my head against Gabriel's chest, and let a month's worth of anger, and hurt, and fear pour out of me.

So what if Reuben sees?

So what if the whole world knows how weak and pathetic I am?

It doesn't matter.

Because *I* don't matter.

If I did, then I'd still have my parents. I'd still be happy.

But I don't matter to anyone anymore.

Not even God.

CHAPTER FIFTEEN
ZAC

I sit up in bed and stare at the shadow of the man who's just stepped into my room.

"What are you doing here?" I ask.

Rube doesn't reply immediately. Instead, he moves about my room, hunting in the dark. Seconds later, a match flares and he lights the single candle on my desk.

My apartment is one of the smaller ones on the fourth floor of the east wing.

Reuben shouldn't be in this wing. He has a single student room on the west.

Light takes its time to seep into the shadows. Reuben sits on the corner of my bed, his profile cast in stark relief by the candle.

I don't need much more than a desk and a bed, so that's all there is this room. I'm fortunate enough to have an en-suite bathroom, but it's nothing more than a toilet and a shower.

"She was with him tonight."

There's no question who he's talking about.

Cass calls him Old Scratch, or Lucifer when he's feeling snarky. Reuben never addresses him by name, except if he's speaking to someone outside of our group. Then he uses the provost's full honorifics.

Apollo's terms of endearment are multitudinous. I think he commits several hours a week to thinking up new ones, in fact.

We're all obsessed with the past. We all suffer the same sick compulsion—to exact our revenge. We all pretend we have some form of control over ourselves.

Over each other.

"He fucked her?"

Rube snorts. "Dinner. And then confession."

"Confession?"

"He knows her parents. She said he's all she's got left."

My bed creaks as Reuben rocks forward, then back. Forward, then back.

"He kept touching her."

Shit.

That's why he came busting in here when he knows better than to expose our relationship like this. What he saw must have seriously unhinged him.

"Tell me."

Rube puts his head in his hands. "Holding her like she was his motherfucking child," he whispers.

I slide my hands under the blankets. At night, when the temperature drops, the pain in my ankles worsens. I draw my legs into a cross-legged seat and rub at the tendons, willing away their wretched ache.

"And she let him, Zac." Rube's whisper gains strength. "She let him put his sick, filthy hands on her like it meant nothing."

Christ, now my wrists are starting to ache too.

I need to cut this short. Rube's intensity gets to me sometimes. Makes it hard to stay focused. And I need to stay focused. My brothers depend on my stability. If it weren't for me, they'd still be scattered to the winds.

I brought us back together.

I forged their white-hot hatred into malleable steel.

I'll be the one to lead the charge on that fateful day. The one Cassius accused me of wanting to postpone.

Nothing could be further from the truth.

But I know what life is like. It's when you think you have everything under control that it all implodes.

. . .

FOR THE LORD watches over the path of the godly, but the path of the wicked leads to destruction.

"WE HAVE to get rid of her," Rube mutters sullenly. "Let's do it tonight. Me and you. I know what room she's in—I checked."

Fuck. I surge forward, going onto my knees on the bed, and grab hold of Rube's shoulder. "Listen to me."

His muscles turn to stone under my hand.

"Reuben, listen to me."

Eventually, he turns to face me. Slowly, reluctantly, but he turns.

"We can't kill her."

"Yes we can," he states in a dead monotone. "It'll be easy."

"It'll draw attention to us."

"But she'll be gone."

"Rube. You're not listening."

"Better she's gone than she's with him."

Jesus, I'm losing him.

I get up and go to stand in front of him. He tilts back his head. I'm casting deep shadows over his face. "We don't know all the facts, Reuben. Remember the facts. They're important. More important than feelings." I press my hand to his chest. His flesh beneath his shirt is surprisingly warm, despite his cold heart.

"She doesn't know what he's going to do," Rube says. "Better she's gone, before she finds out."

I let out a sigh, and sink down in front of him. "We'll get rid of her, but without exposing ourselves. Without risking everything. Isn't that better?"

Rube's *humph* sounds doubtful. I need to call in reinforcements. We can't risk Reuben going rogue.

"Let's meet with the guys. We'll figure this out together."

When he doesn't respond, I grab his wrists and start massaging them. A second later, he catches hold of me and does the same. I grimace in pain before I can control my features. His hands are strong, and he knows exactly where it hurts.

"What's to figure out?" Rube says. "If we can't kill her, then we'll make her life unbearable. She won't have a choice. She'll have to leave."

His black eyes catch the light as he finally makes eyes contact with me again. If anyone saw him right now, they'd be convinced he was possessed by the Devil.

They'd piss themselves if they knew how right they were.

"No one comes to Saint Amos out of choice, Rube."

He studies me for a moment before his lips turn up into a cold smile.

"We did."

CHAPTER SIXTEEN
TRINITY

"What's wrong with you?"

I don't bother answering Jasper, just like I didn't bother getting undressed for bed last night, or showering, or even washing my face.

What's the point anyway?

"Hey, are you sick or something?"

"Sure," I mumble back. "Let's go with that."

Jasper mutters something under his breath before stomping out of the room. Thankfully, he closes the door behind him—I don't know if I have the energy to go after him and close it.

Minutes later, the prayer bell sounds.

I don't regret anything I said last night. I should...but I don't.

I can't remember how long I spent in Father Gabriel's room, in his arms. I know at some stage he lit a cigarette. That smell drove me out of myself just long enough to get to my feet and finally make it out of his room.

I walked the halls for a while. Half lost and panicking, half not giving a fuck if I ever found my way again.

But I eventually arrived back here in this little cubbyhole of a room. I climbed onto my bed, rolled myself in my blankets, and fell into a dreamless sleep.

That was a century ago. Or mere minutes.

Time is something that happens to other people.

The bedroom door opens, thumping against the wall.

I don't even flinch.

"You're sick?" Sister Miriam says from the doorway.

I consider the consequences of being as rude to her as I was to Jasper.

Not worth it.

"Yes," I mumble.

"Do you have a fever?"

"Yes."

Shoes clomp over the tiles. An icy hand clamps over my forehead. This time I do flinch, and I even manage to scramble up and move away from that hand.

Sister Miriam studies me for a moment. "You've been crying."

No fucking duh. Did my swollen eyes give it away?

"Come. Get up."

I shake my head. "Please, I'll go to class. I just...I just need to sleep for a little longer."

"You *will* get up *now*. You *will* wash. You *will* eat breakfast with the others."

I wish I could spontaneously burst into tears right now. I'm not sure if it would help, but I've got to believe even someone as cold-hearted as Sister Miriam might be moved by the sight of tears.

Fuck, who am I kidding? Anyone who works in a place like this has got to be immune to shit like that by now.

I'm sure that's the only way people stay sane around here.

I obviously took too long to answer her. Her mouth twisting into a sour grimace, Miriam darts forward, catches hold of the shoulder of my dress, and drags me out of bed.

"That wasn't a request, Miss Malone."

Miss Malone.

She hauls open my closet and takes down one of the hangers. The next moment, I'm clutching a brown dress to my chest.

It's not as thick as the one I'm wearing. This is normal fabric. Still stiff, but in a way that suggests it hasn't been through the wash enough times to be soft.

A new dress, made just for me.

It should make me happy, even superficially, but instead all I can think about is how ashamed I was last night. Sitting there in a heap on Gabriel's floor.

Did Reuben tell anyone?

Does someone like him even have friends to gossip with?

Miriam draws back the sleeve of her habit to check a dainty wristwatch. On her, it looks like the string on a roll of salami.

"You have half an hour. Plenty of time to wash up and get down to breakfast." Her eyes narrow. "I'll know if you don't show. I'll know if you don't eat. Don't test me, Miss Malone. You'll regret it."

I scowl after her as she leaves. I believe her—after all, she knew I was playing sick.

Jasper.

He must have said something to her.

I'm going to *kill* him.

Fuck his grades. I don't care if he fails. In fact, I hope he has to repeat the entire year. Maybe then he'll think twice about snitching on someone.

I head for the showers, but I don't make it all the way. A few yards from the door, I can already hear the commotion inside. I don't know how many boys are in there, but even one would have been too many. Is night the only time I stand a chance to shower alone?

This is such bullshit.

I go back to my room and flop down on my bed. When the bell rings for breakfast, I lay there for a few seconds before my brain wills my body into action.

Self-preservation in action.

I drag off my old dress and slip into the new one. I *really* need a shower, but I'll wait until tonight. In the meantime, the smell of washing powder on this dress smells will have to do.

The fabric is baggy around my boobs and too tight around my hips. It's so uncomfortable that I stand for a good minute seriously considering wearing the old, scratchy dress. At least it was baggy all over.

When I get down to the dining hall, everyone's already seated. Sister Miriam is stalking down the aisles, head poking forward like she's making sure no one's thinking dirty thoughts.

Or is she looking for me?

I hurry over to the tray table and grab the lone tray sitting there. As soon as I turn around, I spot Jasper.

Because he was watching me with a concerned look on his face.

Holy crap, was I *that* rude to him? Or does he know I got into a heap of trouble with Miriam? That latter seems more likely, especially since he moves aside and beckons me over with a flick of his wrist.

"Thanks," I mumble as I slide onto the bench beside him.

He studies me for a moment and then shrugs. "Nice dress."

"Fuck off."

His eyebrows go to his hairline, but he doesn't reply. Perry's sitting opposite us on the bench, but he doesn't even look up from his tray.

I hear Sister Miriam approach from the other side of the room.

Clomp, clomp.

Grimacing faintly, I peel the plastic wrap off the tray. "Ew," I murmur, using my spoon to poke at the beige gruel slopped in my tray.

Normally, there's something different in each of the little hollows—a piece of toast, scrambled eggs, oatmeal.

Not today.

Today it's all oatmeal. And it looks gross enough to be from last week's batch.

"Running low on donations or something?" I mutter, glancing over at Jasper's plate.

My spoon sags.

Jasper's tray is full of the usual—in fact, it looks like he even got a fucking breakfast sausage.

What the hell?

"Maybe they ran out?" Jasper whispers.

Clomp, clomp.

I heap some of the disgusting oatmeal onto my spoon and toy with it for effect as Miriam comes up behind me. There's a tug on the back of my dress, and suddenly my boobs fill the bodice.

"We'll need to take more measurements," Miriam says, as if I'm not surrounded by a table full of boys. "Come see me this afternoon."

I'm blushing so hard I don't even hear her walking away.

"Here," Jasper says.

I glance at him. He's holding out his sausage on the end of his fork.

When I look up at him, he drops his eyes.

"Not hungry," I say, pushing away my plate.

I stand and go over to the far side of the room, ignoring the eyes surreptitiously following me. I pour myself a cup of coffee, hesitate, and then double the amount of sugar I normally do.

I'm sure I'm going to need the energy today.

On the way back to my seat, I spot movement across the room.

Of course.

My day wouldn't be complete without someone filming me for no apparent reason. It's blatantly obvious he's got the lens focused on me —it tracks me as I cross the room.

I thump down into my seat and point at him, leaning sideways to Jasper. I keep my voice low even though Sister Miriam left the hall minutes ago.

"Who is that?"

Jasper frowns as he looks up. "Think his name's Apollo."

Perry turns in his seat and comes back with a nod. "Yeah. That's Apollo. Why?"

"Because I'm sick of him filming me." I stand and dust my hands. "And I'm sure Sister Miriam won't like it when I tell her what he's been doing."

"You're gonna tell?" Jasper frowns up at me.

I put my hands on my waist and glare down at him. "*You're* lecturing me about snitching?"

The hall goes silent.

My cheeks instantly turn red.

But I hold my ground, even when Jasper frowns in confusion. "I didn't say anything. Father Gabriel asked us where you were before he started prayers this morning." Jasper throws out a hand to encompass every student in the school.

Even Apollo and his damned video camera.

"He asked the whole school, and when no one said they'd seen you, then he asked me specifically." Jasper snorts and leans back, scooping up a heap of scrambled eggs with his fork. "I ain't gonna lie for you."

I deflate a little at that. I guess I should have realized Jasper wouldn't snitch, but I hadn't thought Gabriel would ask after me either.

I sink back into my seat and mutter out a low, "Sorry."

"Yeah, well, fuck you," Jasper says. He stabs his fork toward me again. "Now eat the fucking sausage."

I stare at the oily sausage, and then up at him.

You know what? Thank *fuck* my tray was the last one and all I got was prison gruel. I'm glad I couldn't go shower this morning because the place was infested with boys.

We've been through this little dance, the Universe and I. It seems to forget that even if it knocks me down, I'll pop right back up again. A little like punching fog, and a lot like punching a balloon.

I slide the sausage off his fork and bite carefully into it. It's not great, but anything's better than the gruel.

"And if you don't want to eat crap, get here sooner," he mutters.

"Yes, Mom."

My skin goes cold when I hear what I said, but it gets a chuckle from Jasper and a snicker from Perry, and I don't want to ruin that.

How long will it take before a single phrase like that doesn't stab icicles through my heart?

Another month? A year?

Maybe never.

However long it'll take I can handle.

Because, honestly...how much worse can this possibly get?

CHAPTER SEVENTEEN
TRINITY

Despite its awful start, my day seems to take a good turn. I made progress with Jasper today. Heck, we might even be able to get along after all.

I'm still buzzing on that high when I get to my first class. English—taught by the very severe and very dry Sister Sharon. I never knew someone who could suck the fun out of literature as much as she could. But I'm determined to get through the lesson with a smile on my face.

Until I see who's sitting in my chair.

"Cassius, please return to your usual seat," Sharon says.

I'm pretty sure I would have remembered if the handsome sociopath of a hallway monitor was in my class.

Nope. Definitely a first.

"I don't think she'll be able to see over my head," Cassius says. He sounds one-hundred percent genuine in his concern, but there's a gleam in his eyes that makes me wonder what the hell he's up to.

Surely he should have graduated last year already? He looks at least a year too old to be in my grade.

I stand at the front of the class, gripping my books like a lifeline as I wait for the situation to resolve itself.

"I suppose you're right," Sister Sharon says. She turns to me and then points to the seat in front of Cassius. "Take a seat Trinity. You're holding up the class."

Me?

I narrow my eyes at Cassius, and in response he slides an inch lower in his seat, props his elbow on the table, and leers at me like I'm a pork chop he's been salivating over since his last meal. Feeling overly exposed in my ill-fitting dress, never mind every eye in the class watching me again, I make my way to the seat in front of Cassius and sit down.

Try to sit down.

At the last moment, there's a flash of movement under Cassius's desk. The chair isn't there anymore.

Of course Sister Sharon had turned her back on the class to write something on the board.

Of course I lose my balance and land on my ass with a very comedic 'oomph' while my books and notepad go flying.

Of course everyone starts laughing.

And, of fucking *course*, Sister Sharon looks back as Cassius rushes over to help me up.

"Quiet!" Sharon whacks the edge of her desk with her wooden ruler. Then she turns shrewd eyes on me. "When you're ready, Trinity, I'd like to start class?"

The fall must have knocked out my senses, because I don't even struggle when Cassius kindly grasps my elbow and helps me to my feet. Or when he slides the chair under my ass like he's seating me for a dinner date.

"New Girl's a bit of a klutz," he says, loud enough that everyone can hear.

I glare at him.

His fingertips trail along the back of my neck as he moves around his desk and takes his seat.

I sit stiff and unmoving for the first half of the lesson, afraid that even the slightest movement will bring undue attention to myself while hoping that sitting still will make the back of my neck stop tingling.

I don't succeed at either.

"Turn to page eighty-four of your textbooks."

I glance around and spot my English textbook laying on its back beside me on the floor. Thank the Lord Sharon didn't see it there. She hands out knuckle raps if you dare to dog-end a single page in your textbook. Imagine what she'd do if she saw—

As soon as the book is in my hands, I know something's wrong.

A spike of dread shoots through me when I turn it over.

What the hell?

This isn't my textbook. Mine was a grubby second-hand copy—this one's squeaky new.

I risk a quick glance over my shoulder.

Cassius is slouched in his seat, his long legs stretched out in front of him, ankles crossed. He has a textbook propped up on the desk in front of him.

That's my textbook.

"Trinity?"

I spin back to face Sister Sharon. I open my mouth to apologize right off the bat for whatever she wants to charge me with, but then her eyes move down and land on the textbook.

"Have you forgotten how books work?" she asks sweetly, and my stomach sinks like a rock dropped down a well.

"No, Sister."

"Then open it."

Something tells me that's not a good idea.

I should tell her it's not my book, that Cassius switched it, but it's obvious he's one of her favored students. Plus, I never got around to writing my name in the front.

Screw it. I'm not gonna let this guy ruffle my feathers. My ass is still aching from my fall—I think I bruised it—and I don't want him to think any of this shit affects me.

WWJD, right? He'd turn the other fucking cheek.

But I can't move. I'm terrified.

Sharon's eyes narrow to slits. She walks over and uses the tip of her ruler to flip open the cover.

I stare down at a photo-realistic drawing of Brother Zachary. Then I tip my head up and gape at Sister Sharon as my cheeks catch fire.

Why?

Why would Cassius do this to me?

"Wow," comes a breathy whisper from behind. "That's downright blasphemous, little slut."

"I didn't draw that!" I scoot back my chair and jump up. "Sister, I swear this isn't my textbook."

Thwack!

Everyone in class except Cassius flinches when her wooden ruler slaps down on the book. Sister Sharon has good aim—she manages to cover Zachary's penciled ass and the cock he's got shoved in my ass.

"I could come up with better excuses in my sleep," Sister Sharon says, her wrinkled lips pursing with disgust.

I half-turn to glance at Cassius.

He's sitting there with his elbows propped on the table, his head in his hands, mouth open with shock like he doesn't know exactly where this book came from.

"Sit!"

My ass thumps into the chair.

"Hand out. Flat on the desk."

I turn wide, pleading eyes to Sister Sharon but my hand's already moving over the wooden desk. She uses the tip of her rule to flip closed the textbook, and then taps the far side of my desk.

"Here."

My hand slides to the spot she selected. I close my eyes and drop my head, stifling a gasp when she brings her ruler down on the back of my hand.

Thwack.

Thwack.

Thwack!

It's like she's trying to beat the sexual deviancy out of me. I keep my head down even when I hear her walking away. Then I glance back at Cassius without lifting it.

There's no mistaking the satisfied gleam in his eyes.

"Why?" I mouth to him, blinking back tears of pain. I slide my hand back and cradle it in my lap as I wait for his answer.

"Eyes up front!" Sharon slaps her ruler on the edge of her desk, and the whole class sits up, me included.

When she turns her back again, I'm already anticipating the warm breath on the side of my neck, and Cassius's smooth voice in my ears.

"I don't like you, New Girl," Cassius murmurs. "I think you should go back to where you came from."

"Fuck you." I sit forward so I don't have to listen to him anymore.

A hand knots in my curly hair. Cassius wrenches my head back. I'm so shocked, I don't even gasp.

His lips brush the shell of my ear as he whispers. "I'm just getting started. If I were you, I'd find a new school."

I SPEND the rest of the lesson silently seething as I try to ignore my aching knuckles and scalp.

As soon as the bell rings Cassius swaggers past me and out the door.

I scoop up my things and hurry after him.

Words are going to be said. Possibly even yelled. I won't stand for this and Cassius is going to know it in the next five seconds.

"Not so fast, Trinity."

I skid to a halt by Sister Sharon's desk.

"Sister?" I do my best to look humbled and not like I'm on my way to attack someone in the hallway.

She perches on the edge of her chair before taking a piece of paper from her drawer. Bowing her head, she starts writing. "This behavior is unacceptable."

I open my mouth but she doesn't allow me to speak.

"You've caused enough disruption by joining my class so late in the year—I won't stand for further theatrics."

I'm being outright bullied and she thinks I'm trying to get attention?

"When is your next lesson with Brother Zachary?"

A cold dread seeps into my bones. "Why?"

"I ask the questions," Sharon says. Her pen scratches on the paper as she signs whatever she was writing with a violent flourish.

"Right now."

"Good. You will take this letter—" she looks up and folds up the piece of paper she was writing on "—and you will hand it to Brother Zachary the moment you set foot in his class."

She holds out the paper. It's not even in an envelope. But as if she can read my mind, she adds, "It's for his eyes only."

This can't be good.

My fingers are numb when I take the paper from her. I turn and head for the door.

"And Trinity?"

I pause, biting the inside of my lip.

"If you disrupt my class again, there will be severe consequences."

My heart's still pounding in my throat when I make my way down the hall.

Instead of confronting Cassius about his prank, I slink down the hall and pray no one notices me. I clomp down the stairs and stand in front of Zachary's classroom door.

A student hurries toward me from the other side of the hall, and for a moment I'm convinced he's a messenger about to make my day even worse.

Instead, he pauses about a yard away from the door and watches me intently. "You going in, or what?"

Shit, I didn't even recognize him. It's Simon—a kid from my psych class. I step back and let him go ahead of me while I try and gather my courage.

But it's a lost cause—I'm rattled.

There's no denying I have a target on my back. But who put it there? And *why?*

<hr />

ZACHARY LOOKS up from his desk and then down at the paper I'm holding out. It trembles ever so slightly. He takes it from me, the class falling silent behind me when he opens it. Two of the students from my English class are also in psych, but I'm positive the rest of the class already knows about what happened in English.

Did any of them see the drawing?

I'd almost peeked at the letter when I was standing outside, but then I thought back to that stained glass window I'd seen on my first tour through Saint Amos.

That big eye in the sky.

Always watching.

Omnipotent.

Anyway, I don't want to know what it says.

Ignorance is bliss, right?

Zachary folds open the letter and scans it. He closes it up and slips it into his desk drawer. Then his eyes fall to the textbook I'm crushing against my chest.

I'd forgotten all about it, but as soon as his eyes settle on the hardback cover, the drawing inside flashes through my mind like a still from a porno film.

I imagine, anyway. I've never seen one. I've never had access to the Internet without parental supervision. The dirtiest book in the library I was allowed to use was Pride and Prejudice.

"The book," Zachary says evenly, when I don't make a move.

I hand it over reluctantly as my cheeks grow hot.

Zachary flips open the front cover and goes to turn the page. His hand freezes and then drops to the bottom of the page.

"Surprisingly accurate," he murmurs just loud enough for me to hear.

My ears start to buzz. "What?"

He flips the cover closed and sits back in his seat. Slowly shaking his head, Zachary studies me with magnetic eyes. "What are we going to do with you, Miss Malone?"

"It's not my book," I say.

He cocks his head. "You stole this from someone?"

"What? No!"

"Then how did you come to be in possession of it?" His eyes narrow with irritation.

The name is on the tip of my tongue, but I can't say it. Which is ridiculous—if Zachary and Sister Sharon knew what Cassius had done, he'd be the one facing off with Zachary right now.

He'd be the one about to be punished.

He'd...

No, nothing would happen to him. It's obvious Sister Sharon has a soft spot for him, and I'm pretty sure I saw him visiting Zachary on my first day here. It was only a glimpse as we passed in the hallway, but I'd recognize those blue eyes anywhere.

I could try and accuse him, but I was the outsider.

The outcast.

No one was going to believe anything I said. It burns like righteous fire inside me, the fact that telling the truth would only get me into more trouble, but I'm not stupid enough to believe I'm capable of convincing these strangers.

Maybe I'll go talk to Gabriel. If anyone would believe me, he would.

So I drop my gaze and hang my head like I'm overwhelmed with remorse.

"Take your seat," Zachary says.

When I reach for the textbook, he lays a hand on it to stop me. "We'll discuss this after class."

In a weird, hallucinogenic moment, I think he's talking about the drawing. What was there to discuss? The drawn-on expression of ragged bliss on my face as he pounds me from behind? The fact that I'm bent over this very desk?

Or how the longer I think about the drawing, the more I can't stop thinking about what it would feel like, being with him.

I don't think I'm going to make it to the end of class.

CHAPTER EIGHTEEN
ZAC

God damn it, it had been almost impossible to keep a straight face when I'd seen what Cassius had drawn inside that English textbook.

I hadn't wanted to risk a face-to-face meeting this soon after our last one, so I'd sent out a group text to my brothers early this morning. I hadn't mentioned much about what Rube had said, just that our goal today was to make Trinity's life pure hell.

I should have known Apollo and Cass would take it as a challenge.

I'd left the details up to them and, looking back, that might not have been the best decision. I've already caught a few whispered rumors about something happening at breakfast with Trinity. And I know she was absent from prayers this morning, although I'm not sure if my brothers had anything to do with that or not.

I'll get their full reports later this afternoon.

At least I made sure to tell Reuben not to go anywhere near her. I don't trust him in his current state of mind. This close, with so much at stake? It would be too easy for him to unravel.

I throw myself into my lesson like I always do, but I'm distracted.

Cassius's drawing is to blame.

Her shapely thighs and plump ass. Curls bouncing around her naked shoulders.

In the drawing, I have both hands on her hips, leaving her perky little tits free to bob.

I'd had every intention of holding her back after class and putting the fear of God into her...but that picture had roused something that had lain dormant inside me for a long, long time.

Maybe it was her innocence. From the way she keeps blushing, or how she's always hiding behind her books to shield her body from inquisitive eyes, it's obvious she's inexperienced.

Shy, and secretive, and naive.

But with just enough backbone that, for a moment, I'd thought she would rat out Cassius. But then she'd chickened out and had taken the blame like a good little soldier.

I need a clear head right now. I can't afford to be distracted by what I think her ass would look like while I fucked her from behind.

Those types of thoughts are what lead to acts of deviance and perversion in the first place. This is more natural than the ones I'm normally obsessed with, but regardless.

She looks relieved when I don't say anything as she passes my table after the bell rings at the end my lesson. And when she glances back over her shoulder, her frown makes me wonder if I'm being too soft.

That, or she's wondering about my response to the letter.

I thought I'd been casual as fuck, staring down at that drawing, but maybe I hadn't.

I'd hoped to join the boys in their fun, but I can't be as close to this as I'd wanted.

One of us has to keep a level head.

CHAPTER NINETEEN
TRINITY

I'm famished by the time lunch comes around. I head for the dining hall as quickly as I can. While the day had been sunny for the most part, gray-bottomed clouds are scooting in from the horizon. Every time one of them passes over the sun, the temperature drops a few degrees.

The fact that the smell of stew makes my mouth water is a testament to how hungry I am. There are about thirty students in the hall when I arrive, most seated with their trays in front of them.

I hurry over to the tray table, already reaching for one of the covered trays when something catches my eye.

A bright pink post-it has been attached to one of the trays nearest the edge of the table.

TRINITY MALONE

The tray is isolated by now—obviously no one dared touch it.

I pick it up and grimace.

More gruel.

Gray. Pasty. Disgusting.

The other trays are heaped with vegetable stew and fat slices of chunky bread spread thick with butter.

This. Is. *Such*. Bullshit.

I take my tray and make a beeline for the kitchen. I hurry up to the first cook I spot and thrust out the tray with its blatantly pink sticker. "What is this?"

The cook—a guy that could have been my age or a year younger—gives me a condescending scan before sneering at me. "Your food," he says.

"Why don't I get stew?"

"Because we don't make special food around here."

I frown at him. "Special? What are you talking about?"

He dismisses me with a flick of his hand and then pushes me aside with his shoulder. I start after him before someone calls out a few yards behind me. "Orders from the top."

I turn to another cook. "I don't understand." I put the tray down on a nearby stainless steel workbench. "I don't eat anything special. I just want normal food like everyone else."

"Well, we got told you're vegan and have these—" the guy shrugs, working his shoulders for a second "—lactose-gluten-sodium allergies and shit." He points at the tray. "That's pretty much all we got that you can eat."

"But...I'm not."

He shrugs and turns back to peeling potatoes.

"Can't I—is there any normal food left? Even just some bread?"

"Not for you. Not unless our orders change."

"Okay, so who?" I storm up to him, stabbing a finger at the floor. "Tell me who gave the order."

Another shrug. "Ask Apollo. He's the one who came and told us."

Apollo?

The guy with the video camera?

What. The. Actual. Fuck?

It couldn't be a coincidence.

What if Sister Miriam's the one who told me to film you in the first place?

But that doesn't make any sense. None at all. Sister Miriam can pretty much watch me all the time. More so than Apollo can, if she wanted. I mean, she literally stripped me down in the laundry room to take my measurements.

Another prank then? I'd thought breakfast was my own bad luck, but maybe someone had taken off the post-it at the last minute, seeing it was the only tray left uncollected.

Or maybe he wanted to make *sure* I got another serving of gruel.

Why?

Why the hell was I being targeted like this?

My mind scrambles as I head back to the dining hall, leaving my disgusting lunch behind. I'm starving, but I'd rather pass out from hunger than be subjected to a prank like this.

I meet Apollo as he's coming back inside the kitchen. He's wheeling a much smaller trolley than the one he uses for the students. There's still one wide, covered tray on it that looks similar to the one Reuben brought to Father Gabriel's room the other night.

"Hey!"

He's walking backward, dragging the trolley after him as he pushes open the door with his back. He smirks at me over his shoulder. "How ya doing, pretty thing?"

"Who told you I couldn't eat normal food?"

His smirk turns into a grin. "I don't kiss and tell."

"I knew it," I say, stabbing a finger at him as I pass. "You made it up."

"You gonna tell on me?" he calls.

My hand is on the door, but I don't push it open. I stand there for a second, listening to the sound of the trolley wheels squeaking. Then a pair of sneakers coming closer.

Apollo comes into view from the corner of my eye. He leans against the wall near the hinge of the door and crosses his arms over his chest.

"Because you can go rat me out if you want, but it won't change anything."

"I'll get to eat proper food again," I snap.

"Maybe. Maybe not." He sighs and leans his head against the wall too, scratching at his forehead with his thumbnail. There's a mark there, under the hair hanging in his eyes. A star-shaped scar. An old sports injury maybe?

"Wouldn't it just be easier to leave? I mean, this place sucks ass. Why the fuck would you want to come to school here anyway?"

I gape at him. "What the hell does it matter to you where I go to school?" I take a step closer and poke a finger in his chest. "I don't need your permission to be here."

His smile becomes a grin. "You're cute when you're mad."

"Fuck you!" I blurt out. "You'd better stop—"

My only warning is the sudden stutter of his eyes as he catches sight of something behind me. I spin around, already clamping my mouth closed.

Too late.

I'd been so caught up with yelling at Apollo I hadn't spotted Sister Miriam coming into the kitchen.

"Sister, he—" I point behind me, and even turn a little to make it clear who I'm accusing.

Don't ever turn your back on an angry nun.

She grabs my ear and yanks so hard I swear it almost comes off. I yell and shoot to my tiptoes so my ear doesn't tear free.

"Enough," Miriam snaps. "Enough, enough, *enough!*" The last word booms through the kitchen like a bomb going off.

Where there'd been the idle clatter of pans and cutlery, everything cuts off. The handful of people inside the kitchen are all staring at me.

Then Sister Miriam does the unthinkable.

She drags me out of the kitchen and through the dining hall...by my fucking ear.

Tears streak down my cheeks from the pain and humiliation, but I already know that whatever's coming next is going to be a thousand-fold worse.

This is what happens when you fight back, Trinity.

Should've eaten the goddamn gruel. But no. Suddenly, you think you deserve a slice of normal.

Wrong.

So very fucking wrong.

No one in this place is your friend. They'll never be your friend. Even Gabriel's already trying to get rid of you. Maybe you should pack your things and start walking.

The forest will be more hospitable than this place.

CHAPTER TWENTY
TRINITY

Thankfully, Miriam doesn't drag me all the way by my ear. A few yards outside the dining hall, close to the small prayer room, she releases me.

With a flick of her arm, she consults her little watch and then glares at me for a second. Her eyes move to the prayer room. She points. "You stay in there until I come for you."

When I don't move, she grabs me by my collar and drags me bodily through that little arched door. I stumble when she shoves me inside and catch my knee on one of the chairs. Whimpering, I turn as she starts closing the door in my face.

She pauses when there's little more than her face showing. "Best you pray to God that I've cooled down before I come back, else you won't have a strip of hide left."

She bangs the door in my face.

I cup my ear, massaging at my itchy, stretched skin where it meets my scalp with one hand and rubbing my knee where I bumped my leg with the other.

"Are you all right?"

No.

No, no, no, no, no!

Come on!

I spin on legs that feel like they've turned to rubber. A big shape unfolds from the small chancel and slowly turns to face me.

Reuben.

I swallow an angry sob and move back, fumbling behind me for the handle. After everything that's happened today, the only logical conclusion is that I'm about to die.

Terror traps a broken scream in my throat when I don't find the handle. When my fingertips brush blank wood. I don't dare look around, because then he'll pounce me and do God knows what to me.

Maybe bash my head on the floor till my skull cracks open.

Fuck, he could probably crush my head between his hands if he wanted.

"Please."

Wood.

Wood.

Brick.

"Don't."

Reuben ducks his head, and slowly replaces his rosary.

Brick.

Wood.

Brick.

Where the *fuck* is the door handle?

I have to risk it.

I glance around, all the while my skin crawling with invisible tarantulas.

He's still standing by the pulpit. He hasn't moved closer. My heart thumps in relief, but I don't stop looking for the handle.

"Let me show you," he says, and steps closer.

I let out a small squeal of panic and turn my back fully so I can find the damn handle.

But there's nothing there—just smooth wood.

I'm locked inside with a psycho.

My stomach plummets to hell.

"Where's the handle?" I yell, turning back to him. He's closer now, but not like the first time I saw him here. He's taking his time, edging forward as if he knows there's no rush.

"I can show you," he says calmly. "But only if you promise to calm down."

"Sure. I'm calm. See?" I sweep out my arms and then hug them to my chest. I step back as far as I can, practically disappearing into the corner of the small room as he reaches me.

"Why are you so scared of me?"

Because you're psychotic!

"I'm not. It's Miriam. I don't want to be here when she gets back."

"You'll get in trouble if you run away."

"I don't care!" I hastily lower my voice. "I mean, she knows where to find me. And I really have to pee. I'll get her outside."

"You haven't prayed yet."

Fuck. *Fuck!*

He's just standing there.

Liar. He won't open the door for me. It was just an excuse to get closer without me bolting. I glance to the side. I can make it over the chairs. Scramble to the front of the room. We'll chase each other around in circles until Miriam comes back.

But what if he catches me before she returns?

What will he do to me?

Fear of the unknown drives icy panic through me. I shiver once, hard, and then I can't seem to stop.

"Are you cold?"

"Please just open the door."

He shrugs. Then he pushes his hand against the wood, close to where the handle would be on the outside. The door sinks inward a little, and then bounces open a crack. There's a little rift where he slides in his fingers, and then he pulls it open.

I race for the opening, knowing I won't make it, but not willing to stand there and accept my fate.

Reuben presses the door closed in my face. I freeze, standing an inch away from the wood, too frightened to move.

His palm slides down the wood as he lets out a long breath through his nose. He moves closer until his clothes brush against mine.

Blood roars in my ears. It drives heat into my cheeks and constricts my lungs.

"You should pray."

"Okay," I manage breathlessly. "I'll pray."

"Ask God for forgiveness."

"I will." Forcing a swallow, I add, "I'll do it when I'm done with Miriam. Outside."

"You'll do it now. Inside."

This close, his smell is everywhere. Something floral, something rich, something woody. Masculine, but soft at the same time.

"Okay." I turn, assuming he'd step back so I head over to the pulpit.

Isn't this what you do when you're held hostage by a crazy person? You humor them, keep them talking until the cops come.

I have no idea where Sister Miriam went or how long she'll be away, but if I can keep up this pretense...

At first he doesn't move. With his hand on the door behind me, he's close to boxing me in. Admittedly, he's not the ogre I first thought him to be. He's tall and broad, but he's not a steroid-junkie.

I'd probably have thought him seriously attractive if I hadn't been so terrified of him.

Weird, how I've met so many handsome guys over the past few days. And in a place like Saint Amos? That's bordering on freaky.

"Here. This will help you focus your intent." Reuben lifts his rosary from around his neck and slips it over my head.

That's where the smell is coming from. His rosary is made from rose-wood. The sweet smell envelops me as soon as he slips the beads over my head. But there's something else mixed in there. His own scent. He must stroke the beads while he prays.

And I'm guessing he prays a lot.

My fear fades a little, even though I know it shouldn't. There's no guarantee that because he regularly prays to God that he won't hurt me.

But it makes it easier to believe he might have a conscience. Threatening me is one thing, but actually physically hurting me? That's crossing a line. One he might not be able to because of his beliefs.

I clutch that thought as I slip past him and stride over to the pulpit. It's only three yards away, so it's still like he's right behind me when I sink down onto the pillow laid in front of the chancel.

Resting on my knees, I put my palms on my thighs and duck forward. Hopefully I look like the real thing.

But as I'm kneeling there, the smell of Reuben's necklace

getting stronger and stronger, his presence growing until it fills every inch of the room...I start feeling more and more like a phony.

I've never prayed. Not once.

Sure, I've recited the Father's Prayer. I've read the bible. I've sat in church more often than I can count.

But I've never prayed.

I never felt that connection my parents and Father Gabriel claimed to have.

I was always acting.

Reuben knows it.

The last thing I want to do is make him angry. Should I stand? Give him back his necklace?

Fabric rustles behind me.

He exhales somewhere close behind before sliding his hands onto my shoulders.

I risk a peek. He's kneeling behind me. "What are you doing?" I whisper.

Another breath. It warms the back of my neck where my hair's been scooped up into an attempt at a bun.

"I'm praying for you," he says in his sonorous voice.

"Why?"

"Because I'm guessing you don't know how. And trust me, you need all the help you can get."

SISTER MIRIAM COMES to fetch me sometime later. Reuben never lifted his hands, and he never said another word to me again. I'd slipped into a trance while energy moved between us.

I'm not being new age about it—I *felt* it. My entire body came alive at his touch. Every disastrous thing that happened up to that point had melted away.

I was at peace.

I felt loved.

I'm convinced he actually managed to contact God on my behalf.

That, or he's some kind of god himself.

When Miriam comes for me, I'm not frightened anymore. Not of him. Not of her.

Not of this place, or my future, or my past.

I'm ready to face whatever she has waiting.

She notices that when I leave the prayer room.

But it doesn't change anything.

I guess around here nothing ever changes. Rules are rules. I misbehaved and for that I have to be punished.

I just wish it wasn't her handing out my penance.

CHAPTER TWENTY-ONE
ZAC

"This isn't working is it?" Apollo says as soon as I get within earshot. "Why isn't it working, Zac?" He was pacing, thumbs hooked into his belt, but as soon as I'm in the crypt's sunken center, he sinks into a chair and starts jiggling his leg.

He's not the only agitated one. Reuben is perched on the edge of his seat, meaty hands clasped and dangling between his legs. Cassius is smoking a blunt, but with an intensity that belies his slouched body and deadpan expression.

"I don't know," I mutter. I snatch the blunt from Cass's fingertips just as he's about to take a drag, and give it a hefty tug. "But she's fucking testing my patience."

Apollo snorts.

Between the four of us, I'm the rock. It takes a shit load to piss me off or deter me. Weather-beaten, but still standing.

Because, long before the Brotherhood, there was only me.

Then came Apollo. Then came Reuben. Then came Cassius.

Even back then, we had no notion of revenge. For us it was all about survival. Every day was a silent victory.

Every hour.

Every fucking second.

This girl is getting under my skin. Anyone in her position would have been out that door in ten seconds flat.

"She's a fucking masochist, that's what she is," Cass says. "But you were right. She didn't say a word about me to anyone." He sits forward, imitating Reuben. "She didn't, right?"

"Not to me." I shake my head and take another drag. Then I have to smile, because it's fucking rare either of us gets the chance. "That drawing though…"

Cassius's face lights up with a grin. He leans across and taps Apollo's chest with the back of his hand. "Bro, you should have seen it."

Apollo looks up at me. "You still got it, right?"

I nod. "Some of Cass's best work." I study the blunt between my fingers. "She's stronger than we thought. Braver. We might have to change tactics."

I take a last hit of the joint. It's almost down to the filter, but I offer it to Rube like I always do. I'm already retracting my hand on automatic when he takes it from me.

Apollo's jiggling leg freezes. Cassius turns to stare.

Reuben studies the joint, and then eviscerates the last quarter-inch of weed. I almost dart forward and retrieve it before he inhales the fucking filter too.

He drops it to the floor and crushes it out under a massive shoe.

When he exhales, Cassius and Apollo disappear behind the smoke cloud.

"She's not brave, she's just stubborn," Reuben says. He shifts in his seat before glancing hesitantly in my direction.

"What do you mean?"

"I know you said I shouldn't go near her—"

I'm on my feet in a second. "What did you do?"

"Nothing." Reuben spreads his hands. "She came to me."

"What? Why?" Apollo demands.

"Doesn't matter," Rube tells Apollo before turning back to me. "I didn't do anything. I just…prayed with her."

"Rube…" My voice is dangerously low. "What did you say to her?"

He shakes his head. "Nothing. But I saw she was more scared of me than Sister Miriam."

"If she's so scared, then why hasn't she ratted us out?" Cass demands. "I mean, all she has to do—"

"Shame. Denial. Fear of the consequences. I could go on." I take my seat, sitting back and spreading my legs. This isn't comfort, but when the four of us are together it's like I've come home after a long day. These brief meetings in the crypt are our versions of Sunday lunch.

Out there, we're just a bunch of kids.

In here, we're motherfucking assassins.

Unfortunately, Trinity Malone only sees us as we are outside these walls.

"Textbook behavior," I add.

Every eyebrow twitches at this—even Reuben's.

"So what do we do? The girl's not budging," Apollo mutters, sitting back and crossing his arms over his chest.

"That's just it…" I swing my leg up, resting my ankle over my knee. "We've been treating her like a girl. Like a delicate piece of glass we don't dare break."

Cassius chuckles. "I can break her for—"

"Cass!"

His eyes flick up to mine. "What? She suddenly so fucking special or something?"

"That's a bit hypocritical, don't you think?" I ask, tilting my head. We've been down this path of reason before—Cassius always ends up in the fucking bushes.

"She's a slut anyway," Cassius says.

I don't even bother looking at him.

We've all got twisted world views. But we also have an excuse. We never got to see the world as other kids did. Our crayon drawings didn't have rainbows and stick-figure family portraits. Ours—if we'd ever had any—would have been black and red landscapes crosshatched with repressed pain.

Cassius thinks everyone's a closet slut, and would fuck anything that moves if I didn't reign him in.

Apollo is a full out voyeur. He'd rather film someone masturbating than actually have sex with them.

Reuben will probably die a virgin. Kind of.

Me? It's best if I became a priest and swore celibacy for the rest of my life. Because unlike my brothers, there's only one thing that actually brings me joy.

They'd crucify me in a heartbeat if they ever found out what it was.

"She'll break," I say, shifting in my seat.

Reuben's staring at me so hard it's like he's digging through my brain with his fingers. If anyone's got me figured out even a little, it's him. But I'm hoping—dear God, I'm hoping—he knows better than to say anything.

Apollo sighs. "I guess if we keep pulling her hair long enough, she might—"

"I'll send her to the Hag," I cut in. My eyes cut to Cassius. "That okay with you?"

Cassius shows me his teeth. "Pics or it didn't happen."

"Why would I be there?" I ask calmly.

"You could be, if you wanted." Reuben cuts me off. "She's a girl. Wouldn't be appropriate for you to punish her yourself."

Cassius is already nodding furiously before Reuben's done talking. "But he can watch, to make sure she receives her penance, right?"

Reuben nods.

I swallow. Hard.

This was exactly what I'd been trying to avoid.

From the first day I'd had Trinity in my class, I could tell she wasn't brittle like the countless other children who'd crossed my path the last few years.

I knew this would come to outright violence. The kind of pain and hardship people rocked in the Old Testament.

And, secretly, I'd hoped the girl would meet my expectations. Because, besides this bunch of misfits, I've never met someone I could truly regard as my equal.

She's looking to be a strong contender.

It will be a pity to break her.

"Bro, I want details," Cass says through a devilish chuckle. "I mean, blow by fucking blow." He sits forward, eyes shining. "Hear me?"

Cassius isn't a sadist.

He is, however, sitting on the fence between sociopath and psychopath.

I nod, and drop my eyes as I get to my feet. "I'll make the arrangements."

Cass lets out a laugh, clasping hands with Apollo.

Reuben watches me, silent and forever judgmental.

I guess I'm being naive thinking he doesn't have some inkling about my own dark heart. He was by my side for months before the others showed up. We're all brothers, but he's my twin. We mirror each other's darkness in different ways, but we emerged—reborn—together.

CHAPTER TWENTY-TWO
TRINITY

S ister Miriam leads me to the first floor of the main building. We pass several administration offices until we reach one right at the end of the hall.

There's a window. A desk. An office chair. A wooden cabinet and an old-school telephone with its receiver resting on the cradle.

It stinks of cigarettes in here, which is surprising because I didn't take Sister Miriam for a smoker. Perhaps she received a visitor that did? Was that what she was busy with while Reuben was praying for me?

She says nothing as she walks up to the wooden cabinet.

I stand in the middle of the room, not moving a hair, hoping to delay the inevitable.

As if.

She finally turns to me, a strip of leather in her hand. Broad, maybe two inches. So stiff it barely moves as she steps closer.

"Close the door."

"Sister—"

"Close the door!"

My eyes squeeze shut at her yell. I spin around and go to close the door.

When I turn, I notice a second chair. Now the cigarette smoke makes sense.

Brother Zachary Rutherford is here, smoking a cigarette. There's a low table beside him, an overflowing ashtray, and a pack of filter-less cigarettes.

He takes a drag of his cigarette, his eyes never leaving mine.

"Over here, child," Miriam calls.

"What's he doing here?"

"Making sure I do my job," she says stiffly.

From the sound of her voice, she's about to take out a week's worth of irritation on my ass.

Lashes.

In front of Zachary.

I'd beg, if I thought it would do any good. Fuck, I'd go down on my knees and pray.

I still have Reuben's rosary. Its smell has been with me all this time, but it's suddenly lost its calming effect.

"Move."

I shuffle over on wooden legs.

"Hands here," she says, using the stiff strip of leather to point to an empty space on the desk.

I press my palms to the table. I'm facing the wall, my side profile turned to Zachary.

"Feet back."

I swallow hard and scoot my feet back a few inches.

"More."

Now my ass is sticking out.

Hot, shameful tears fill my eyes. I try to blink them away, but they just end up rolling down my cheeks.

I squeeze my eyes shut when Miriam flips up my skirt. I'm convinced she's going to tug down my underwear, but possibly to spare my modesty, she doesn't.

There's silence. Then I hear Zachary dragging on his cigarette, the dried tobacco leaves crackling faintly as they burn.

Thud.

Pain thumps into me. I gasp in surprise, vaguely proud I didn't scream.

Thud.

That wasn't so—

Thud.

I yelp in pain. Choke on a ragged sob.

Thud.

My legs go out. The pain of my knees cracking on the wooden floor is nothing compared with the dull aching throb on my ass.

This is hell.

Sister Miriam is the Devil.

She loops her arm under my waist and drags me back to my feet. "Can you stand, or does Brother Zachary need to hold you up?"

"Stop," I manage in a breathless whisper. "P-please, just stop!"

"Six more, child." There's a sudden catch in Miriam's voice. "You can do this. But you have to stand."

I manage a nod.

Thud.

I can't help it—I let out a wretched howl of pain. I'm in danger of scraping my nails off on the desk.

What could I possibly have done to deserve this?

I can end this, though, can't I?

If I tell Miriam it wasn't me.

I'll tell her to fetch Gabriel. He'll vouch. Tell him I've been set up.

Thud

Another howl, this one stronger than the last. Somehow that helps with the pain. I'm panting now; loud, ugly sounds only an animal can make. My cheeks are wet with tears. My face scrunches up as I fight the urge to collapse on the floor.

Thud

My ears start buzzing.

My legs give out.

Miriam's talking, telling me to stand.

But I can't.

I have nothing left.

An arm hoists me up. I think it's Miriam again, and that must mean she can't hit me again because—

Thud.

It's Zachary.

I can smell his slightly-sweet brand of cigarettes.

All I have to do is say his name.

Cassius.

Say it and this will stop.

She'll ask why? Why him?

I don't know.

They hate me.

Him, Apollo, Reuben.

They hate me.

But I can end this.

Nothing can be as bad as this. What will they do? More pranks? More bullying? I don't give a shit.

End this, Trinity.

Thud.

You can end this now. You just have to—

Thud.

I let out a whimpering mewl. The arm that had been supporting me tightens. The world spins on its head, and then I'm staring up into Zachary's jade eyes.

There's something strange gleaming in them, but I don't understand it.

Thought, reasoning—not possible.

There's just pain.

It eats through me like a slow-burning fire. Like the dried tobacco in Zachary's cigarette. Ebbing and flowing but ultimately moving deeper inside me.

"Take her to her room," I hear Miriam say.

Zachary's chest rumbles against my side when he replies. "Thank you, Sister."

Miriam's voice is tight. "Make sure she puts on the salve."

That fire moves through me, consuming me. It leaves behind nothing but ash.

Zachary takes me out of the room. His chest pushes and retracts against my body. Sometimes his breath touches my face, but mostly it doesn't.

I sometimes hear voices, and sometimes just the steady thump of his feet. With every step, my body grows more and more numb.

My eyes closed moments after we left Miriam's office. I can't remember how to open them again, even when a door creaks and a strange darkness falls over me.

Zachary puts me down on something soft. On my side.

I think he lifts my skirt, but I'm not sure until something skims over my sensitive flesh. I whimper and try to move away from that touch.

"Shh," he murmurs.

The surface under me dips.

A bed.

There's the sound of a lid being opened. The strong menthol tickles my nose.

"This will hurt."

I suck in a breath as frozen fire streaks over my tender skin and I try to move away but he grabs my hip to keep me in place. Every stroke is like hot air on coals, stoking the fire buried deep within. Bringing it to the surface. I'd have started sobbing, but I'm spent.

So I lay there and somehow endure the agony.

I wish I could pray.

I wish there was someone who would listen.

I know it wouldn't change anything, but wouldn't it be nice to know you're not alone?

I'm alone.

Even here with this sadistic fuck of a man who watches while a girl is beaten black and blue and then carries her somewhere dark and secret to hurt her some more....

Even here, with him, I'm still alone.

The bed shifts.

His hand slips off the back of my neck. There's the sound of a lighter flicking. I expect cigarette smoke. But this is something else.

Pungent. Foreign.

The bed dips again.

"Open."

Something dry pokes at my lips. I part them. "Inhale."

I'm past the point of fighting this. So I do what he says and hope this is the last of it because I can't take anymore.

I'm broken and used. A grubby porcelain doll with a cracked face, left to rot in the debris of an abandoned building. Once a treasured toy, now a spider's nest.

The smoke makes me cough. But I take another drag anyway. Then again. Again. The pain is still there, but it's distant now. And fading.

No, that's me.

I'm fading.

Fingers brush my temple. A stray curl tickles the side of my ear. I let out a long breath, and my body finally relaxes.

"Who are you, Trinity Malone?"

My head thumps along with that distant pain. Something new worms its way into me. Something warm and fuzzy and...

Nice.

"No one," I murmur.

"What are you doing here?"

"Nothing."

I want to fade away completely. But he keeps asking me questions I'm compelled to answer.

"How do you know Gabriel?"

"He's my friend. My *best* friend."

There's a long pause. So long, I almost do slip away. But then those fingers come back and touch the side of my face, tracing the outline of my jaw.

"I'd really hoped that wasn't the case," Zachary says.

The bed moves as he gets up.

I'm dimly aware this might not be my room. That I'm lying on a strange bed with my underwear around my knees and the back of my skirt hitched up. My hands tremble as I reach behind me, but Zachary snatches them by the wrists before I can adjust my clothing.

"You're leaving. I'll arrange a cab for you in the morning," Zachary says. "Just give me an address."

I laugh at him. "Fuck you."

I hear the deep breath he takes, and that makes me regret what I said. But there's no address I can give him. I don't have anyone else. I don't have anywhere else.

There's a burst of dull pain as he yanks my underwear up my legs. "Sisters of Mercy it is."

Hands slide under my waist. The world spins as he scoops me into his arms. Every thumping step he takes chafes my skin with fire.

We go down a flight of stairs, and then along a hallway. We're back on my floor, headed for room 113. He barrels through the door and drops me on the bed.

On my back.

I flip onto my side with a hiss, tears pricking at my eyelids.

"Remember, Trinity, you chose the hard way," Zachary says from the doorway. He tosses something my way, and it thumps against my tummy. Then he's gone, my bedroom door slamming shut behind him.

I fumble for the cold, hard object pressing against my stomach.

The salve.

I wrap my fingers around it and curl into a ball.

I don't cry, because there's no point. Whatever I smoked dulled the pain enough that I can probably fall asleep. But sleep doesn't come for a long time, because I keep replaying his last words to me.

You chose the hard way.

Just remember, Trinity.

You chose the hard way.

CHAPTER TWENTY-THREE
ZAC

"Morning, Boss."

I look up and frown at Cassius. It takes me a few seconds to move after the shock of seeing him at my door so early in the morning. "The fuck you doing?" I hiss, lurching across the room, hauling him inside, and shutting the door quietly behind him.

First Reuben, now this? You'd swear everyone had a fucking brain aneurysm this week with how they've been acting.

"How'd it go?"

"You couldn't wait?" I swipe a hand through my hair. "This is far from fucking circumspect."

"Circumspect," Cassius repeats under his breath, his eyes moving away from mine. "Smells dank in here. You still got that fatty around?"

"Cassius, you have to leave!" I hurriedly lower my voice. "No one can see you in my room."

"Why?" He drags a finger over my desk as if inspecting it for dust. "They'd just think we were fucking."

He's immaculately dressed this morning. Could be the cooler weather—those same clouds that keep threatening are gathering force—that made him put on his blazer, but there's no possible explanation for his perfect tie.

I grab the sleeve of his jacket and twist the fabric, using that grip to turn him around. "Look at me," I snap when his eyes slide away from mine.

"Relax, Boss." He drawls.

I hurriedly release him and step back. "How are you feeling, Cass?" I ask warily.

We start a dance, him and I. He moves to the left, I slide to the right. Round and round we go, where we'll stop, nobody knows.

"Honestly? A little left out." He sends a sparkling smile my way. "See, the last time we spoke, you laid out this brilliant fucking plan—" he waves a hand "—like you always do, and I was legit salivating to hear how it all played out."

He stops and pulls open the top drawer of my desk. I let him—I have nothing to hide from my brothers. If we still felt the need to keep secrets after the shit we went through then we'd be more fucked in the head than any psychology handbook could explain.

"You didn't call. You said you'd call." Cass looks up and lifts out the half-finished blunt I'd stowed away last night. "Feels like I got stood up."

"She got her lashes. I gave her a way out, she didn't take it. What more do you want to know?"

Cassius sinks down on my bed and lights the joint.

Gritting my teeth, I lurch forward and snatch it from his lips before the flame can touch the paper. "This hall gets foot traffic in an hour. The smell won't be gone by then."

"You know what doesn't get traffic?" Cassius leans back on my bed, propping himself up on his elbows. "My fucking dick. Not once since we've been here. I have needs, Boss. There's only so much wanking one dick can—"

He cuts off when I slam my drawer shut, the joint tossed back inside. "Stop acting like a fucking kid," I snap.

"Yeah?" He sits forward in a rush. "You know I don't have this mental fucking switch I can just turn off like you fuckers." He rests back on his elbows again. "You *know* that."

I study him for a second, and then lean to the side to turn the digital alarm clock to face me. "Fine," I say through a sigh. "Move over."

I hesitate, and then check the clock again. Then I lean over and snag the joint from my drawer, lighting it in one go. If I keep my door closed a little longer and open the window, most of the smell should have dissipated before the staff start moving around.

"So she walks into Miriam's office—"

"WILL you tell that bedtime story to me every night?" Cass says, beaming up at me with a goofy grin. About halfway through the retelling he settled down onto my bed, head resting on his hands.

"Sure," I say through a chuckle. "But now you have to get out of here." My eyes move to the digital alarm clock. "Because this really is the worst time for us to have to try and explain shit."

"Yeah, yeah." He pushes up onto his elbows, but then he pauses. "Hey, Zac?"

I pause, rendered frozen by the hesitation in his voice. "What?"

"If you were fucked in the head, do you think you'd know it right away?"

My hackles rise, but I do my best to keep my expression disinterested. "Like, if you went insane?"

"Yeah, sure. Like that. Do you think you'd know?"

I bring up my leg, but I put it down when I realize I was going to start rubbing my ankle. "It depends. If you're schizo, then probably not. Because it's so real to you, and you'd commonly start to disassociate."

"So your friends wouldn't pick up on it either?" he adds.

We've all learned a few things about the human mind. While I find it fascinating enough to possibly get my Masters in it one day, the Brotherhood approach it like other guys might football. Something we're all familiar with, and it passes the time.

"Depends on the level of the delusions you suffer. Bipolar, that's a different story. Relationships are the first to suffer, because you're not exactly antisocial. Borderline—"

"I almost fucked her."

My head dips forward before I can straighten my neck. "Her...Trinity?" My eyebrows shoot up to my fucking hairline.

After I *specifically* fucking forbade him from—

"It was before you said anything. She just got here." Cassius scrapes his nails over his buzz cut. "Before we knew she was...important."

I force myself to take a deep breath. "But you didn't, right?"

He stays quiet.

"*Right?*"

"I almost did."

"But you didn't."

"No."

"Then we're fine."

I didn't say he was fine. He wasn't.

None of us were.

"I'm sorry."

"You didn't know."

"Yeah, but, fuuuck. I *almost*..."

My skin goes numb. I wasn't listening right. I thought he was feeling guilty about my command not to try and sleep with Trinity before we'd figured out if she were a threat or not...but that wasn't it, was it?

"Cass."

"Yeah, I fucking know." He sits up in a rush. "Jesus." He scratches at his scalp with his nails.

I put a hand on his knee. "That doesn't mean you're..."

What the fuck am I supposed to say? He almost raped her, and I'm supposed to tell him everything's okay? I might sound like I know shit, but I don't have a fucking clue if this means he's a cunt hair away from becoming a serial rapist or if he's as frustrated as the rest of us.

Would anyone know?

Is the brain truly that predictable?

Now that we have the vague approximations of blueprints from deviants like Gacy and Bundy, can human nature honestly be read like a fucking deck of cards?

"Let's...we're just taking this one step at a time, all right?"

That was our motto back then when we were holed up in that cold, rat-infested basement.

One day at a time.

Dawn was our alarm clock. The Universe's equivalent of a reset button. When dawn crept in through those gap-toothed boards and ran a slow scan down the dusty floor where they kept us...it was a new day.

A day filled with possibilities.

And always, a day filled with horror.

CHAPTER TWENTY-FOUR
TRINITY

A bell sounds. I peel open my eyes with difficulty as I shift a body weighing ten tons.

What time is it?

What *day* is it?

I'm dimly aware a lot of time has passed since Zachary laid me on my bed. The pain woke me up a few times since then, but I only stayed awake long enough to nurse my bruises with ointment. Surprisingly, no one's bothered me. I guess Miriam had no choice but to give me a sick day.

I lie here in the dark, wincing as I fumble for the jar. I screw open the lid and scoop out some salve.

It stings going on but not nearly as much as yesterday. My bruises are healing but my pride is still battered and blue.

It seems so stupid not telling them about Cassius's drawing. I can't fight against the certainty he'll do something even worse if I rat him out. After all, what's stopping him from sneaking into my room and finishing what he started?

I'd love to know what I did to earn this. I mean, I've heard of hazing but does everyone really go through this when they arrive here?

I've heard of bullying too, but nothing like this.

I set down the jar on my side of the desk. There's barely enough moonlight coming in through the window to make out Jasper's body humping up the blankets on his bed.

I really, *really* need to pee.

I don't even bother sitting on the edge of the bed. I go straight to my feet, grimacing when my skirt brushes over my underwear.

Lord, this hurts. The worst I've ever gotten from Mom was a slap on my rump with her bare hand when I threw a tantrum. I think I was like ten or something.

Dad never laid a hand on me. He'd wanted to once, but my mother had stopped him. I can't even remember what I'd done wrong.

It's pretty late though, right? If Jasper's here and asleep, then it has to be sometime after ten.

Pretty sure I'm the only one awake on this floor. Which means I'd have the bathroom all to myself.

It's gonna hurt to go shower. But at least I'll be sure no one's going to walk in on me. And maybe the hot water will soothe out the pain.

I take out some pajamas, clean underwear, socks. I ease open the door and check the hallway before stepping outside.

Then I hesitate.

I thought Father Gabriel would come see me yesterday, but the only person I saw was Jasper. I could go there now. To Father Gabriel's room. I could tell him what happened.

Everything.

He said I'm safe here, and look what's happened? I've been bullied and falsely accused without a say in the matter.

Would he honestly let that happen?

———

A FEW MINUTES LATER, I'm standing in front of Father Gabriel's door. It takes every ounce of courage I have to knock. I'm still not convinced I can tell him everything, but I'm craving his comfort. I need someone to hold me and tell me everything's going to be okay.

Like a toddler with a boo-boo. Real mature, Trinity.

My knock sounds too loud in this broad, empty hallway.

But obviously, it isn't loud enough because there's no response.

I try again.

My hand goes over the doorknob. Locked.

Ha. So much for him trusting his things are safe. I guess that only applies to orphans like me who don't have anything valuable to steal.

I step back, bristling with a sudden anger.

I'm about to give the door the finger when movement catches my eye.

Reuben walks down the hallway. I stiffen, and like the idiot I am, I don't even think of fleeing.

"He's not here," Reuben says.

"Yeah, I figured."

"He'll be back tomorrow."

"You his PA or something?"

There's not a hint of what he might be thinking in those black eyes. "Or something," he says. "You should be in your room." His eyes dart down to the clothes bundled up in my arm. "What are you doing up here?"

I'm not big on lies. My mother had a good nose for them, and she'd catch me out every time. It was easier to tell her the truth. But lies come easier when you're dealing with strangers. The past few weeks have been a learning curve for me.

I'm fine.

No, I don't need to speak to a counselor.

Yes, I've said my prayers.

I'm still the furthest thing from a conman, but I'm pretty sure I sound convincing when I say, "Father Gabriel said I could use his bathroom so I don't have to share with the boys." I cross my arms, lifting my chin as I mentally dare Reuben to see through my lie. "But he forgot to leave me his key. Do you have one?"

The faintest smile touches Reuben's generous mouth. "I wish I did."

"Well, then, it's pointless us standing here, isn't it?" I put on my iciest expression and swing around to leave.

A hand closes around my shoulder and turns me back. I wince as my skirt shifts against my sensitive backside. But I smooth away the pained look before Reuben can notice.

"You should be careful around him," Reuben says.

"Father Gabriel?" I laugh. "You know he's a bishop, right?"

"Not anymore." Reuben dips his head, and the dim lighting in the hallway casts pools of shadows in his eye sockets. "And even if he still was, titles don't mean anything around here."

"I'm sure the *provost* thinks different." I snatch my shoulder away from his fingers and take a quick step back.

He doesn't try and touch me again, but his eyes fall to my chest instead.

Ugh. Why are men so disgusting? They see anything with boobs, and they can't seem to think straight.

I whirl around and hurry down the hall as fast as my sore ass allows. Just before I take the stairs, I glance back over my shoulder.

The hallway is empty.

Reuben is gone.

CHAPTER TWENTY-FIVE
TRINITY

My footsteps echo hollowly as I head for the closest shower stall. I stopped to use the restroom on the way here, and everywhere I went it was like walking through a frozen world.

There's a strange hush in Saint Amos this late at night. As if the building itself is sleeping too.

Or waiting.

There's a chance Reuben might still be stalking the halls. Heaven knows what he was doing on Father Gabriel's floor to begin with. Maybe him and Cassius work in shifts. But I'm pretty sure he has better things to do than stalk me.

I force a smile.

It doesn't help.

I shiver, and look over my shoulder.

A quick shower, and then back in bed. There's no way Sister Miriam will let me take another day off—I'm going to need all the restorative sleep I can get. I wish I had more of whatever it was Zachary gave me to smoke. It worked tons better than the salve.

It was weed, wasn't it? Because I'm pretty sure you smoke crack through a glass pipe or something.

I turn on the shower.

Icy water splashes down, making me squeal in surprise and snatch away my hand.

The water becomes lukewarm, then hot.

Yes!

I pull my dress over my head with a wince, and toss it on the floor. My dry clothes are stacked on the far side of the cubicle wall. Close enough that I don't have to walk naked across the whole room to dress, but far enough so they don't get wet.

The shift is next. I step out of my undies and give them a quick inspection. No blood on the back—guess I'm just bruised after all. I wish there were a mirror in this place, but they're as sparse as they were back at my house.

With a hard swallow, I try and prepare myself for the coming pain.

There's a noise behind me.

I whirl around, covering my breasts as I scan the empty room. I should hurry, unless I want some random boy walking in on me.

The right side door swings open causing my breath to catch in my throat.

No.

Reuben enters the bathroom.

No!

I snatch up my clothes and hurriedly slip into my underwear as I yell, "Hey! Get out!"

He doesn't even slow down.

"I swear, I'll scream!"

The door opens again. My eyes flit over to it as I grab my top and tug it over my head.

Cassius swaggers into the room, his eyes already on me. Where Reuben is staring at me like an obstacle he plans walking straight through, Cassius is mentally peeling back the clothes I'm throwing on with trembling hands.

Reuben stops a foot away from where the tiles begin. Just standing there, staring at me. *Through* me. Cassius joins him. "You're right, Rube. She's definitely not supposed to be here."

What the hell is going on?

Cassius steps closer. "You could get in all sorts of trouble being outside your room this late at night." He yanks away my sweatpants before I can tug them up my legs.

Right, because he's the fucking *hallway monitor*.

Oh my God. What's wrong with these people?

"Now what are we going to do about this transgression?" He takes another step, and I throw my hands up.

"Touch me and I'll scream."

"Do it," Cassius says. "No one can hear you. Not down here."

I back up, flinching when my back touches the wall. It's way too cold through the thin fabric of my vest "I'll tell Father Gabriel about this. And about the drawing." My eyes flicker to Reuben, but he could have been watching clouds moving across the sky for all the emotion on his face. "And I'll tell him about what you did on Monday."

Cassius cocks his head. "Compulsive liar much?" He leans to the side, grabbing hold of the edge of the tiled cubicle wall. Then he slowly starts unlacing his shoe.

I bare my teeth at him, inching to the side. If he moves closer and Reuben stays where he is, then I could squeeze past them. I'm not an athlete, but I'm sure I'm faster than them.

Would have been splendid if you'd been all soaped up and naked, don't you think? Like trying to catch a greased pig. Except you've got clothes on, Genius.

Cassius straightens and toes off his shoes. Then he pulls his shirt over his head.

Even in my panicked state, I can't help but notice his slim, perfectly proportioned body. Porcelain skin—not even a freckle to mar it. A dusting of hair trails from his chest down a flat, hard stomach and disappears behind his trunks.

"Reuben, can you move?" a voice calls out. "You're blocking my shot."

Reuben twists around, revealing Apollo. He's standing by the bench, his video camera trained on me.

My eyes want to pop out of their sockets.

"What the hell?" I breathe.

Cassius unbuttons his slacks, the rasp of the zipper drawing my eyes back to him. "Since you can't seem to take a hint, you little hussy, we've decided to stop being so fucking subtle."

"You're not supposed to touch her," Reuben says, turning disapproving eyes on Cassius.

Cassius throws him an irritated look which melts away as soon as he focuses on me again. I'm crowded into the corner now, a steaming waterfall between us.

"Please," I say, lifting my hands again. "Just let me go."

"Oh, we *want* you to go." Cassius shows me his teeth, but he's not smiling. "That's the fucking point. But you seem incapable of putting two and two together."

He steps out of his pants.

His black form-fitting trunks leave nothing to the imagination. I've never seen one before, but I'm pretty sure he has an erection. To my virgin eyes, it looks abnormally long and thick.

Panic transforms into anger.

How dare they? How fucking *dare* they? Honest to God, do they really think they'll get away with this? That I won't say something?

Without thinking, I scramble up the low wall. The adrenaline pumping through me puts wings on my feet, because I didn't even know if I could get over—and then I'm landing on the other side with a slap of bare feet.

I race for the door.

Apollo drops his video camera and chases after me.

Blood sings in my ears as I grab the door handle and wrench it open.

But there's someone blocking my way.

I bounce off Zachary's chest and land with a pained yelp on the floor. I'm up a second later, turning around and stabbing a finger toward Cassius.

"He...he was going to—to—"

Apollo skids to a halt, raising his hands like I'm pointing a gun.

Cassius turns to face the door, props his elbow on the cubicle wall, and rests his chin on his palm. "Christ, Zac, what took you so fucking long?"

None of the guys look like they've been caught assaulting a female student.

None of them even look remotely guilty.

Which means...

I turn, my eyes going wide. My heart's about to explode in my chest.

Zachary steps into the bathroom and closes the door behind him.

Then he locks it.

CHAPTER TWENTY-SIX
ZAC

What *took* me so long? I came as soon as I got his fucking message. I scan the room, taking a snapshot of the situation. Trinity tries to dart past me, but I catch the back of her vest and haul her back.

That vest and a pair of white panties is all she's wearing.

I sling an arm around her throat and put her in a lock. Not enough to choke her. Not even enough to cut off oxygen to her brain. Though I should have if I'd known how much trouble she'd be.

"This wasn't what we agreed," I drag Trinity forward with me despite her struggles. She sinks her nails into my arm, but even when she draws blood I barely feel it.

The ache in my wrists and ankles though? That's another story. That shit's been keeping me up at night. Getting high is the only thing that keeps it at bay lately.

When she starts gasping and gagging like I'm actually strangling her, I slap her ass. She yelps, whimpers, and goes still. I expect her to start bawling like a little girl, but her only response is a hitched breath.

"I told you to keep her contained until I arrived."

Cassius waves a hand at the shower cubicle. "Container." Then, he leans over and turns off the water. "In which she was contained up until a second ago."

I shake my head through a long-suffering stare. "Where are the ropes and—?"

At this, the girl lets out an indignant gasp and starts struggling again. Another smack on her ass shuts her up as abruptly as the first time. Her knees give out, but I just drag her up again.

"And the gag?"

She screams.

I haul her up against my chest and clap a hand over her mouth. No one lives on this level and the walls are thick, but we can't risk someone hearing the commotion.

How could we possibly explain away any of this?

Apollo moves closer. He holds out some cable ties constructed into a set of handcuffs. "No one uses ropes anymore, Zac," he says, rolling his eyes as he cuffs Trinity's wrists in front of her while I keep her mouth shut with my hand.

My ankles and wrists ache in protest at that comment, but I don't challenge him. "And the gag?"

Apollo shrugs.

"Here," Cassius says, jogging up to us. What the hell happened to his clothes? "Nothing like some used panties to shut a girl up."

Trinity struggles in my arms, whimpering against my hand.

Not exactly hygienic, but there are worse things in life.

Much, *much* worse.

I ball up her stale panties and shove them into her mouth.

She spits them out.

I give Cassius a deadpan stare. He rolls his eyes at me and steps toward Reuben, gesturing at his crotch. Reuben lifts his arms like he's being frisked while Cassius yanks off his belt.

He takes Rube's belt, plucks Trinity's panties from the floor, balls them up, and shoves them back into her mouth.

Then he uses the belt to keep them in place, tightening the buckle at the back of her neck.

Apollo comes back to the group, face forlorn. "I broke my camera," he whines.

"I'll buy you a new one," I say, without looking away from Trinity.

"Hmm," Cassius murmurs as he presses himself against Trinity. "Do we have to leave right now, Boss? Couldn't we have a little fun with her first?"

"Cut it out," I snap.

Astronauts can see his hard-on from the fucking moon. I cock my head toward him, making eye contact with Reuben. "Thought I told you to keep an eye on him?"

For once, Reuben doesn't stay quiet. He shrugs. "We were waiting for you."

The *fuck*?

The last thing I need is Reuben crushing on this chick. She's already done possibly irreparable damage to our brotherhood—which I'll make her pay dearly for—but this is a knock we don't need.

Apollo comes closer, his broken camera dangling from his hand. He starts studying Trinity like he's never seen a girl before and then steps back with a grimace. "Can we at least clean her up before we go? She really needs a shower."

Trinity widens her eyes at him.

Was that what I was smelling? My nose wrinkles before I can stop myself.

"Yeah. Just a quick wash," Cass murmurs close to my ear.

When did he come up behind me? He's got cat's feet sometimes, the evil shit.

Trinity shrieks behind the gag and yanks herself free. I wasn't holding onto her all that tight—where the fuck would she go, anyway? The door's locked.

She stumbles, probably not expecting to get free so easily, and goes to her knees with a muffled yelp.

"Don't you wanna see what's under there?" Cass is right against me now, whispering into my ear like the fucking devil himself. Another inch, and his dick will be poking my leg.

I shove my shoulder back, pushing him away. "That's not why we're here."

Trinity scrambles up, spinning around to glare at Cass and me. She frowns furiously at us as she works to loosen the belt with her bound hands.

I'd caught a glimpse of her ass when Miriam was giving her those lashes yesterday afternoon. It took every ounce of self-control I could muster not to get more than a semi. Especially when her sweet howls of pain echoed around me. When I'd taken her to my room after I'd specifically not lit a candle. But it hadn't been fully dark yet so I'd still gotten a fantastic view of her bruised ass when I'd put on the lotion.

I'd had just as much difficulty stopping myself from squeezing that ass. From slipping off my clothes and having her bare skin flush with mine.

"It's two in the fucking morning," Cass says. He's moved closer again. "No one's gonna come."

Before Trinity can loosen the belt, Reuben steps up behind her. He slides an arm around her waist and snags the cuffs, pulling her hands away. She freezes, eyes wide and sparkling with fear. He hooks a finger into the cable ties and shifts his grip so he's keeping her close with the same arm.

"We can't, Cass," I say in a low voice. "It's…"

Wrong.

Stupid.

Juvenile.

Reuben strokes her neck. At least, that's what I think he's doing. I lean back a little.

What the fuck?

He tugs, and a red rosary slips out from behind Trinity's vest. He nestles it carefully between her breasts.

Fuck, that's his rosary, isn't it? He *does* like her.

This is the last thing we need.

But who the fuck am I to deny us the things we so desperately need?

"You have five minutes."

Cassius darts past me, slapping Apollo's shoulder as he passes. "Rube, bring her!"

Trinity's eyes are bugging out of her head. She'd been keeping perfectly still while Reuben rearranged her jewelry, like a small fluffy animal trying to camouflage itself from a predator.

Only one problem.

There are four of us, and only one of her.

She can't hide. She can't even run.

She'll have to endure it. Which could prove to be a dear lesson for her.

We've had many such lessons and they've only made us stronger.
We'd be making her stronger too.
She catches my eye, and her skin pales.
Why?
I guess it's my smile.

CHAPTER TWENTY-SEVEN
TRINITY

This can't be happening.

It's not real.

This is all just another prank. They're going to shove me under the showerhead, maybe wet my hair. A little roughhousing. That's it.

They wouldn't *dare*.

Would they?

A shiver chases through me, spilling goosebumps over my skin and hardening my nipples under my thin vest. Reuben tosses me over his shoulder like a sack of potatoes, knocking the air from my lungs and leaving me momentarily stunned.

By the time I recover, I'm already in the shower cubicle. The shower's already on, steam churning into the air.

Too hot. It's too fucking hot!

Someone's chuckling under their breath. It's fucking terrifying.

I wriggle and scream into my gag as loud as I can when Reuben grabs my hips and sets me back on my feet. When I try to run, Zachary catches me with an arm and shoves me back. Cass grabs my cuffs and reels me in like a fish.

Water hits my hands, then my arms. It's not as hot as I'd thought, but it's warmer than I like. I struggle furiously, but that makes the plastic ties cut into my wrists.

That shit hurts, so I stop.

I could vault the wall again, but what would that help? I saw Zachary lock the door. The key is in the pocket of his slacks and—

I peek around at the sound of a belt buckle. Zachary unhooks his belt. His penetrating green eyes catching mine when he looks up.

This *is* real. This *is* happening. They don't give a fuck about the consequences.

My knees sag.

I'd have landed on my ass if Cassius hadn't caught my elbow and steadied me. "Aw...You done fighting?" he asks. "I was enjoying that."

"She knows it will be over sooner if she doesn't resist," Zachary says as he steps out of his shoes. He slips his shirt over the top of his head without bothering to undo the buttons.

There's a tattoo on his chest.

A coiling serpent. Fangs bared, ready to strike.

Oh my fucking God.

He steps out of his pants, baring white cotton boxers as plain as my own underwear.

Reuben steps away, turns his back, and slips off his own shirt.

This isn't happening.

I shriek into my gag and try to jerk free from Cassius. Pain slices through my wrists, and a tiny rivulet of blood races down my arm. Water hits it, turning it pink and then invisible in a flash.

Apollo hangs back. He's still chuckling, but he seems content to stand back while they...

Wash me?

Shame bursts through me. My chest tightens painfully.

"You're hurting her," Reuben says.

My eyes fly back to him. I'd been watching Apollo, trying to plead with him. He doesn't seem willing to participate, so it's worth a shot, right?

But staring at him means I can't keep an eye on the other three.

An arm slips around my chest. Cassius drags me against him and a hard length presses into the small of my back.

I don't want to look, but I have to. Else how will I spot my chance at escape?

Zachary's still smiling. I think it's the first time I've ever seen him look anything other than dead serious. "Take off the gag. We don't want to waterboard her."

Expert fingers manipulate the buckle at the back of my neck. The belt slips loose before he plucks it away. I spit out my underwear and haul in a sweet breath.

Relief only lasts a second.

Cassius pushes me forward. Water cascades over my head.

Blinded by the water, with Cassius's arm still securely around my waist, I don't stand a chance.

I can dimly make out Zachary with his dark smudge of a tattoo. He grabs a bar of soap and lathers it in his hands as he moves closer.

Cassius shoves me forward. My bound hands stick out on instinct, slamming into Zachary's chest. I puncture him with my nails, but he doesn't even flinch.

While I'm still spitting water out of my mouth, he shoves his hands under my vest and starts washing me.

I gasp, twisting to try and get away from his hands. But they're everywhere—my stomach, my breasts, my armpits, my back.

That's when Reuben steps up to us. He's easily an inch taller than Zachary, but he doesn't push him aside. Instead, he grabs the back of my neck and my arm, holding me still for Zachary.

"Please," I whisper, forcing myself to look at Zachary.

When we lock eyes, an electrical current surges through me. There's no sympathy in his eyes. Not even a trace of pity. He's enjoying this.

Is it my fear or my humiliation that gets him hard?

"You had your chance," he says. "You could have been out of here this morning already."

I open my mouth to tell him I'll leave, but then Cassius turns off the shower. There's a moment's crystallized silence, broken only by the *plink* of a water drop hitting the wet tiles.

Zachary tilts his head a little, daring me to speak. When I say nothing, he slides a hand over my breast and squeezes.

Hard.

I suppress a gasp, and will my eyes to stay on his.

Begging did nothing. Neither did threatening to rat on them. But maybe showing them I still have a backbone will make them think twice about taking this too far.

Zachary's eyes narrow.

He doesn't like that I'm defying him.

Another hand grazes up the back of my vest, tracing my spine. I break out in goosebumps, my nipples going hard again.

Terror dulls into something else.

He was right—the less I struggle, the faster this will go.

My breath hitches when the hand sliding down my back slips behind my underwear. Soaked from the shower, everything clings to me. I grimace when Cassius tugs down my wet underwear to my knees.

Hot breath tickles my ear. "Who'd have thought you'd be such a dirty girl?" Cassius asks. "You should be thanking us, you know? Working so hard to get you clean."

Reuben releases me. Maybe it's because I'm standing still now. Maybe it's because he knows—like I do—that there's no chance of me escaping again. "We can protect you," he says, making absolutely zero fucking sense.

"Shut the fuck up," Cassius snaps. He moves back a little, and his voice changes direction. "Why don't you go stand there by Apollo?"

I shiver at the sudden loss of heat. Without the shower on, the air is cooling rapidly. Reuben steps back, but he doesn't leave.

Zachary starts washing me again. The sensation of his soapy hands gliding over my skin makes my insides squirm.

It should be in fear, in revulsion, in anger.

But something else is blooming inside me. Something hot and tingly. It builds deep between my legs like a well that's slowly filling up with rainwater.

Zachary must sense something, because his smile fades. "She's clean enough." His eyes flicker away from mine. "Let's rinse her."

Cassius does as Zachary commands.

I flinch when hot water hits my back and then gasp when Cassius's hand slides down my tender ass and slips between my legs.

I lift onto my toes.

Now the only sound is the thumping water.

He cups my pussy.

Like an animal catching scent of its prey, Zachary's nostrils flare. His gaze skims down my body, settling on the hand between my legs.

His voice is low and so, so deep. "Cass...don't."

Cassius turns off the water, but he keeps his hand where it is. "I want to know if you're wet for us," he murmurs into my ear.

My eyes flutter as I try to stand even taller. My legs start shaking. I worm my fingers up Zachary's chest. Grabbing onto his shoulder, I tighten my grip until he looks at me.

I blink furiously, lick my lips, and mouth, "Please," at him.

That was the wrong thing to say.

"Well?" he murmurs, his breath stirring against my wet skin. His voracious eyes flicker up to Cassius. "Is she?"

Cassius groans like he's in pain. There's the unmistakable sound of wet fabric sliding against skin. His warm, hard cock presses against my thigh.

I whimper and dig my nails into Zachary's shoulder muscles. "Don't." The word comes out like a bullet. "Don't do this."

The hand between my leg clenches. I gasp and stagger forward until I'm flush with Zachary's hot, dry skin. The move should have dislodged Cassius's hand, but he moves with me.

Now I'm sandwiched between him and Zachary.

I've been appealing to the wrong person. He's obviously in charge, but it's as if he's been derailed.

Or maybe he's okay with this.

The thought makes me sick to my stomach.

So why are there electric tingles skating over my skin?

Is it because I've never had a hard body pressed against mine, never mind two? Because I've never looked up into eyes as intensely hungry as Zachary's? Or had a man touch me the way Cassius is touching me now?

In a normal situation, I'd have dated any of these guys in a heartbeat.

But normal isn't what got me to Saint Amos.

In this room, normal isn't a part of anyone's vocabulary.

We're all fucked in the head. I should be repelled by these men, but their presence is like a magnet to my leaden heart.

The wickedness of this sick, twisted moment feels so fucking right.

My eyelids grow heavy. I lean in, fully expecting Zachary to close the distance and kiss me.

A hand slithers over my ass and wedges between Cassius and me.

And then squeezes.

I yelp with pain. My eyes fly open.

Grim desire gleams in Zachary's eyes, now so dark green they could be black. His lips part as if he wants to say something.

Someone rattles the bathroom door.

I jump. Everyone spins to face the door.

Another rattle, this one harder than the last.

Then quiet.

Behind me, another drop of water plinks onto the tiles.

"Time to go," Zachary says.

"Yeah, no shit." Cassius withdraws, leaving me stranded on the tiles.

I start shivering. Reuben happens to glance at me as he slips his shirt over his head. He moves up beside me and drapes the towel I brought with me over my shoulders.

"How we gonna leave without someone seeing?" Apollo asks, hugging himself as he looks from me to Zachary.

"One at a time." Zachary looks back at me, and then his eyes move to Reuben.

"Bring her."

CHAPTER TWENTY-EIGHT
ZAC

My mind's reeling. I don't know who rattled the door, but thank fuck they did. Shit was about to get out of hand, and in a big way.

I was so close to losing control, I can still taste mint in my mouth. That would always happen back then when I lost myself in the moment.

We all found ways to deal with the shit we went through. I absorbed everything like a sponge. But there was no one to squeeze me out. That shit stayed inside me and festered into something dark and perverse.

I thought I had a handle on it.

Fuck, I think we all thought that until this girl arrived, all pure and innocent and shit.

Like dropping a mouse into a pit of hungry vipers.

"What are you waiting for?" I click my fingers. "Bring her."

Reuben blinks like he's coming out of a trance. Then he scoops up Trinity and throws her over his shoulder.

I take my keys out of my pocket and toss them to Apollo. "Make sure the coast is clear."

He nods and hustles outside with his broken camera under his arm, leaving the door to swing closed behind him. I happen to look at Cass, and we lock eyes for a moment. I don't expect guilt or remorse. Most of us aren't capable of expressing those emotions anymore. What I don't expect is the brief flash of uncertainty.

I give Apollo a few seconds to check the hallway, and then beckon the guys after me as I make for the door.

We don't encounter anyone else on our way to the exit. Whoever had tried to enter the bathroom had disappeared. Maybe one of the younger guys had wet their bed or something. That kind of shit happens a lot around here.

Apollo's waiting for us at the door leading to the northern grounds. Soon as I give him a nod, he runs to the crypt.

I wait a few seconds, and then slap Reuben on the shoulder not currently occupied by the bound and gagged girl we'd almost fucked in the showers.

Trinity lifts her head anyway and glares amber daggers at me.

Fuck, but she's beautiful, even with Reuben's belt between her teeth. Probably *especially* because she's fucking gagged.

In class she'd been meek and submissive—the perfect prey. But she showed me her teeth tonight, if only for a moment. It had roused the animal in all of us. Self-control, morals, revenge—for a few minutes nothing existed except our new toy.

Will I ever get to play with her again?

I grab her chin and brush her skin with my thumb.

Not a chance. It's too easy to lose control around her. Too easy to make a mistake. We haven't gotten this far for someone like her to fuck this all up.

Reuben breaks that brief contact as he steps forward and breaks into a trot. Cass and I stay behind, waiting for him to get clear.

"Ever wonder what'll happen when Rube gets mad?" Cassius murmurs as he squeezes into the doorway beside me. "I mean like really, really mad?"

"Like when he comes face to face with his Ghost?"

Of course I've wondered. That imaginary scene of chaotic violence has been the focus of some of my best jerk-off sessions.

"Yeah. Like that," Cassius says before jogging across the grounds.

I follow after a beat.

Reuben is only a few yards from the crypt entrance when we arrive. When he throws open the door, there's nothing but pitch black beyond. Apollo hurries forward and holds open the door for me, giving me a mock salute when I step through.

He doesn't follow us inside.

His job is to make sure we aren't disturbed.

REUBEN'S ALREADY HALFWAY down the library's easternmost aisle when I reach the basement level of the crypt. Cassius trails him, toying with Trinity's hair as they walk. People come down here so rarely there's a layer of dust over everything. That's why we make sure to tread where we least suspect someone will notice our footprints.

Over the months and years we've been enrolled at Saint Amos—and especially after I got my first set of keys as a teacher— we've managed to carve out a space of our own. Back here, far out of sight, we've arranged a few of the bookshelves so it looks as if the library ends a few yards short.

The ground floor of the crypt is for short meetings. This place, on the other hand…it's our nest. A sacred space no one knows exists. The only way in is through a gap hidden by a drape.

Reuben stands there now, holding Trinity's upper arm.

Now that she's back on her feet, Trinity seems to be a touch calmer than before. Or it could be the books. They have a calming effect on us too. The same hush seems to fill every library in the world fills this one too.

"Go ahead," I tell Reuben as I grasp Trinity's other arm. "We're right behind you."

He shrugs his shoulders, pushes aside the thick drape, and miraculously makes himself disappear into that dark sliver.

Cassius follows, and then sticks out a hand for Trinity. She resists a little at first, and then throws me a furious look when I make the kind of soothing sounds you use to calm a skittish horse. With a chuckle, I feed her through the gap, Cassius pulling her from the other side.

Unlike us, she goes through easily.

Too easily.

If we don't pay attention, she could escape.

Good thing Apollo's keeping watch upstairs then.

REUBEN TURNS on the lamp as I slide through the gap. Warm orange light suffuses the nest. From Trinity's wide eyes and stiff form, I'm guessing she didn't expect anything like this.

The space is as large as the library is wide, which is about ten yards, give or take. We've split our nest into two areas—a pseudo living area with sofas, chairs, and tables, and a makeshift bedroom.

Thankfully, since we all have private rooms in the dormitory, no one notices if we don't sleep in that wretched building, especially if we make sure we're back inside before first light.

The bedroom area is separated by another stolen drape. At the moment, it's tucked off to one side, baring the layers of mattresses and blankets and pillows that make up that side of the room.

A true nest.

And I guess Trinity's mind comes to the worst possible conclusion when she sees it.

She shrieks through her gag and races straight for the gap in the bookshelves. I catch the first thing I can, and yank her back by a handful of wet curls.

Reuben takes off his shirt, staring at the damp spot she made with no expression. He grabs a fresh shirt from the pile neatly stacked on one of the numerous bookshelves we used to create this space.

We moved out most of the books from this side of the wall and replaced them with bottles of sacramental wine and hard booze, cartons of cigarettes, porn magazines, and whatever else we felt we couldn't keep in the dorm.

I haven't been down here in close to a week. I'm not sure when last one of my brothers was either. We've been avoiding this space, and each other, so we wouldn't risk exposing ourselves.

We were so close, too.

I tighten the fist in Trinity's hair.

So fucking close.

I turn her to face me, and then wrench open the belt keeping her gag in place. For once, she doesn't spit out her panties immediately. Instead, she watches me with wide, bright eyes as her lips tremble an inch apart.

"The next time you run, I'm taking you over my knee. Do you understand?"

She hesitates, and then nods.

Cassius is close—I can feel his body heat. From the sounds of things, Reuben is pouring us shots.

I could use one.

I could use a blunt even more, but that's Cass's department. "Roll us one," I tell him. He moves away, taking his warmth with him.

I stick a finger in Trinity's mouth, hook her underwear and yank it out. She licks her lips and grimaces, but then smooths her face.

"You're hurting me," she says.

"What's your point?"

Something flickers in her eyes. Fear? Panic? It's gone too fast for me to make out.

I can't imagine what she's thinking. Luckily for her, she's not going to be wondering about anything for much longer.

CHAPTER TWENTY-NINE
TRINITY

This place looks like a psycho's version of a man cave with all the dirty magazines and alcohol lying around. The sofas have seen better years—most have been duct-taped to stop the stuffing from coming out.

Then again, it is clean, if untidy. No rat droppings or cockroaches anywhere.

And not a single mote of dust.

A stark contrast with the library I walked through to get here. I can't believe this place was here the whole time I'd been teaching Jasper. I didn't have a clue. Which I suppose is exactly what they made sure of.

Zachary still has a hand in my hair. His tight grip stings, but the ties around my wrists hurt more.

There's no way in hell I'm giving up on running out of here because he threatened to smack my bottom. Draw me over his knee? He'll have to fucking catch me first, won't he? Do they honestly think I didn't notice how difficult it was for them to get inside this place?

Especially Reuben.

I'll be out the door before they make it to the stairs.

Except for Apollo, who's obviously guarding the door upstairs.

But everyone's on edge right now. It shows in their eyes. I need them to let down their guard. I do my best not to let Zachary in on the fact I'm watching Reuben pouring alcohol into some mismatched tumblers and glasses.

Let them drink and be fucking merry.

Soon as they're not paying attention, I'm out of here.

Zachary inhales a huge breath. His eyes haven't left me once since I tried to run out. And that was my first mistake. I should have waited for the right time. But I'd seen this place, and I'd panicked.

Do they sleep in that mess behind the curtain?

Like...together?

It looks more like the kind of playpen you'd have rowdy sex in than somewhere to sleep. And while there aren't any rats out here, I wouldn't be surprised if there were fucking snakes in there.

Zachary tugs at the plastic ties around my wrists, and my eyes dart to him.

Was I staring? I've got to keep myself in check. I can't give them even a hint about what I'm thinking.

"What do you want from me?" I ask, hoping to distract him. Hoping to get some actual answers. They owe me that much after what had nearly happened up there. After what they'd nearly done.

Zachary holds out a hand. Cassius—who'd been busy rolling a weed cigarette on a nearby coffee table—looks up like they'd legit had some kind of telepathic conversation. He moves to the bookshelf separating their man cave from the library and opens a tin.

I almost don't hold my ground when the lamp's orange glow bounces off the switchblade he hands Zachary.

This is it.

This is why they brought me here.

They're a bunch of serial killers, aren't they? They hide out here and carve their way through whatever student they decide no one will miss.

Holy mother of God.

Is that what happened to all those students who Father Gabriel had told me disappeared in the woods?

I'm shivering. My skin is hot and cold at the same time. Zachary is staring at me, but I can't take my eyes off the switchblade. He drops his hand and flicks it open like a fucking professional.

My stomach drops straight into hell.

His hand darts out. I can already feel the blade sinking into my stomach. My eyes squeeze shut on instinct, and then flutter open a second later when there's no immediate pain.

He flicks the blade through my ties, releasing me.

My fingers tremble as I massage life back into my wrist.

Thank the Lord.

This will make it so much easier to escape.

He clicks his fingers as he points at the sofa furthest from the exit. "Sit."

"I'm not a dog."

He tilts his head. The orange light plays havoc with his eyes, turning them into surreal, gleaming orbs.

"Then don't make us tie you up like one," Cass says through a sneer.

I turn to frown at him.

In a flash, his fingers are around my throat. "Although you'd look real pretty in a collar."

Zachary lays a hand on Cass's arm, and he instantly releases me. Afraid he'll touch me again, I hurry over and take a seat where Zachary pointed.

"You didn't answer me," I say, making sure to use a neutral tone of voice.

Zachary drags a wooden chair to the space in front of my sofa. He seats himself at leisure, as if he's got all the time in the world.

"What makes you think you're in a position to ask questions?"

Reuben walks up to Zachary and holds out a short, thick tumbler. Amber liquid swirls around in it as it exchanges hands. Zachary throws it down his gullet and hands the glass back to Reuben.

I can't believe this is my psych teacher. Granted, I'd only had a handful of lessons with him, but I'd never thought he'd so much as touch a glass of alcohol, never mind sling it back like that.

Dad would have a nightcap before going to bed. I can still see him now, seated at his small desk in the corner of the dining room, a shot of brandy in one hand, the other slowly turning the page of his favorite bible. He would only ever have one glass.

Except when he returned from his missionary work with Father Gabriel. Then he'd drink like Zachary—tossing back shot after shot like he'd kept count of every nightcap he'd missed and was balancing the scales. Then he'd stumble off to bed and sleep for a day.

Mom said it was jet lag, and made her bed on the couch.

Then everything went back to normal.

Kind of, anyway.

"Answer him, honey tits," Cassius says. I flinch as he collapses onto the seat next to me. He has a glass too, but his still has alcohol in it.

"You want from me," I say.

Cassius sniggers.

"Information," I add hurriedly, willing my cheeks to cool down. "Else you'd have gotten rid of me already."

A bold claim. They could literally have brought me down here to finish what they started. But I know it's not that. Doing all sorts of dirty things to me in the shower hadn't been their intent when they'd trapped me inside there.

"We're just passing the time," Zachary says.

It can't be true, but there's nothing on his face to suggest otherwise.

How do they do it?

"I don't think so." I shake my head, and wrap my arms around my chest. It's not exactly warm down here, and I'm still only wearing my undies and a vest. The leather under my ass is deliciously cool on my tender rump, but it's freezing against the back of my thighs. I make a point of looking around their man cave. "You've got much better ways to spend your time."

Keep them talking. Learn something. And wait for your chance to run the hell out of here.

It's not the best plan, but it's *a* plan. A plan I can hold onto with dear life until something better comes along.

Cassius laughs and takes a sip of his drink. Then he produces a weed cigarette from his cupped palm and holds it out to me. I glance down at it, frown, and shake my head as I suppress a shiver.

"Here."

I look up. Reuben's holding out a big-bottomed wine glass with about an inch of alcohol inside. "This will warm you up."

He's definitely the member of this group I'm most uncertain about. While he gives off the kind of vibe that makes me want to climb over a wall to get away from him, he's the only one who hasn't hurt me or even threatened to yet.

Him and Apollo.

I take the glass from him and attempt a smile that probably comes out more like a grimace. "Thank you," I murmur as I take it from him.

He nods and disappears into the bedroom.

Cassius offers the cigarette to Zachary, who lights it and takes a deep drag before turning his attention back to me.

"How did you become friends with Father Gabriel?"

That's what they want to know? I shrug and bring the glass up to my nose. Whatever's in here is strong enough to make my eyes want to start watering. Maybe I should have taken that weed cigarette from Cassius instead. At least I wouldn't be hurting.

"He's my priest." I glance away, happen to spot a very dirty magazine, and hastily look back at Zachary. "Was, anyway."

"That's it?" Zachary takes another drag before passing the weed back to Cassius. "You said he was your best friend."

"He was, for a while." It's strange as fuck telling these near-strangers about my life. "Why are you so interested in him, anyway?"

Without warning, Cassius leans over and tweaks my nipple through my vest. I jerk to my feet in surprise.

He says, "We're the ones asking the questions," before I can get a word out.

Zachary clicks his fingers and points back at the sofa.

I want to throw my glass in his face. Not just the contents, the actual fucking glass.

"What changed?" Zachary asks in the same tone of voice he used a minute ago.

"He left our parish."

"Why?"

"He didn't say."

Zachary's jaw ticks, tensing like he's about to pounce on me. I crowd back into my seat, wishing I had something to protect myself with. I glance at Cassius, but he's staring down at the tip of the cigarette as if he's never been so fascinated by coiling smoke in his life. Zachary sits forward so quickly that I flinch. The contents of my glass swirl, almost spilling. His eyes go to the glass, and then back to me lightning fast.

"Drink it."

I hold it out. "I don't want—"

"Drink it!" His booming voice fills the room.

My hand shakes as I bring the glass to my lips and reluctantly pour everything in my mouth.

Cassius laughs when I start coughing around that fiery liquid as it sears its way down my throat. Then he snatches the glass from my hand and sets it down on the floor beside his arm of the sofa.

I wipe my chin with my fingers, and stare down at my thighs. My veins show up like tiny blue rivers under my skin.

Not sure how this is possible, but I keep forgetting I'm surrounded by crazy people.

That plan I had? A crock of shit.

I'm not getting out of here alive.

They're just toying with me.

The worst part is I'm starting to hope they'll at least take their time.

No one wants to die.

CHAPTER THIRTY
ZAC

T*hump.*
    Thump.
Thump.

I try to ignore my pounding heart, but it fills every inch of my awareness.

Calm down.

Thump.

Thump.

Thump.

At best, I'd considered Trinity just another poor soul who'd somehow managed to get a ticket on the worst ride boarding schools in West Virginia offered. At worst, she was one of those crazy-eyed lackeys who follow Gabriel around like they couldn't wait for their cup of blue Kool Aid.

It had never crossed my mind that she knew him.

Not as the provost of Saint Amos, or the ex-bishop of Redmond.

That she knew *him.*

The horrific twisted demon possessing his corrupted body. A sinister entity we'd finally tracked down after years of searching.

She knew the *Guardian.*

REUBEN BROUGHT HER A BLANKET. He even tucked her in while I finished the blunt. Cassius immediately started rolling another joint. I had another shot of whiskey. That, with the weed, pushed my savage fury down to a level where I could communicate again.

"Why did you come to Saint Amos?" I ask.

Trinity glances up at me, eyes widening. "I didn't have anywhere else to—"

"Why?"

"My parents. They're—they were killed in a car accident."

"When?"

"About a month ago." Her eyes are bright, but no tears. Is she lying? Wouldn't make any sense if she was.

Rube takes the seat beside her. Framed between him and Cassius, her feet not touching the ground and her hair drying into wild curls, she looks like a little doll.

Cassius lights the blunt this time, takes a pull, and holds it out for her. She glances across at him and then down at the hands in her lap. The cuffs left bright red welts on her fair skin. I try not to look at them.

"This isn't me being polite," Cassius says.

"I don't want any."

"I could give a shit," he says, turning to her and leaning in. "Smoke it."

We know how this works. We've done it many times before.

It makes me sick to think of the things we've done to get to this point. Trinity should be on her knees thanking God we've already figured out torture isn't as effective as the more subtle means of interrogation.

The weed will make her chatty. The alcohol will make it more difficult for her to lie. Plus, it reduces her flight risk. Trinity takes the blunt from him and hesitantly takes a drag. Then another. She coughs, hard, and tries to give the blunt back. Cassius grabs her wrist and forces the filter against her mouth. "One more." When she complies, he murmurs, "Such a good little girl," into her ear.

She swoons when she sits back, and our eyes lock through a haze of dank smoke.

"Gabriel's been here for years," I tell her.

She nods, and then shrugs. "I didn't have anywhere—anyone else."

"What about foster care?"

"I almost had to." She nods a few times. "Because I couldn't get hold of him. But then he finally got back to me." She lifts limp hands and drops them again. "Brought me here."

"How long was he your priest for?" Cass asks.

She leans to the side, studying him for a moment, and then hurriedly straightens when this brings her into contact with Rube's shoulder. He's watching her as intently as I am. He looks like a fucking psychopath—hands on his thighs, back straight.

He tucks a stray corner of the blanket under her leg.

"Ten, twelve years?" She cringes away from Rube as if she wants to burrow into the stuffing. "I'm not sure. Maybe longer."

"When did you first join his church?"

"Gabriel's—?" She breaks off and frowns, shaking her head. "Maybe eight years ago?"

I glare at her. "You said you knew him for ten years."

"Or twelve," Cassius supplies unhelpfully.

She shrugs. "He was friends with my dad for a while before we moved to Redmond. That's when we joined his church." She slumps a little. "What is this all about? Why do you—?"

"Pour her another drink."

I wasn't even looking at him, but it's Rube who stands to fulfill my order. Trinity waves a limp hand.

"I really don't want—"

My eyes slide to Cass. "Tell Apollo to search her room. Make sure she's not hiding anything."

Cassius is on his feet in a second, loping to the exit like a panther that's finally spotted something to pounce on.

"Hey!" Trinity sits forward, her tits bouncing behind that pathetic film of a vest. "You can't do that!"

"We can do whatever the fuck we want," I growl.

She stands in a rush and charges after Cassius, and I'm less than a beat behind her. I grab her shoulder, hauling her back. Her vest rips as she twists to knock away my hand. Then she's fumbling with herself, trying to cover her bare naked breasts.

"Ooh, can it wait?" Cassius croons from the exit, his voice moving closer. "Her roommate might spot him—?

"That fucking queer?" I snap. "Jasper won't say a word. Trust me." My eyes never leave Trinity's, not even to look at her tits.

"Fuck," Cassius mutters, and then there's just the swish of the drape.

Trinity tries to draw the torn halves of her vest back over her chest, and flinches when I tell her to stop.

"How close are you with Gabriel?" I ask, stepping up to her. She moves back until her shoulders collide with a bookshelf.

"We're...friends."

"He ever fuck you?"

Her eyes go wide, and color instantly suffuses her cheeks. "What? No! He's...he's my fucking priest."

"Was," comes Reuben's voice. He thrusts out her glass, now half-filled with whiskey. "Now he's nothing."

"He's still my friend," she says, ignoring the booze. "He's never done anything to—"

"So he's never touched you?" I close the distance, snatching the glass from Rube's hand on the way.

"No!" Her eyes sparkle with anger.

I grab her chin, force it down, and tip the glass against her lips. "Drink."

She turns her head, spilling whiskey down her throat and bared breasts.

"I'll lick that off later."

At this, her body goes rigid. That same light sparkles, but this time it's not anger. It's not even fear.

Weed's really good at several things. It makes you chatty. Happy. Hungry. Horny.

This little thing in front of me must be so fucking confused right now with her body throwing so many conflicting signals her way. I want to believe her.

"I saw you with him," Rube says as I steer the glass back to her mouth and wrench open her jaw. "You're more than friends."

She doesn't get a chance to reply, because I'm pouring whiskey into her mouth. This time, she catches it. Swallows it. When she coughs, some it sprays on my face.

I tear off what's left of her vest and use it to wipe my face.

She starts crying.

Those big fat crocodile tears insult me.

I jerk her forward and bring the flat of my hand down on her ass with a solid thump. Her tears cut off in an instant. She sniffs, still trying to cover her tits, but no longer being pathetic about all this.

"We never—I'm not—" She chokes on whatever she'd been going to say and hangs her head.

"But you want to," I say.

Her eyes dart up, still brimming, but she blinks away the tears before they can fall. "No."

"Of course you would." I slide a hand to the small of her back and draw her with me as I move to the couch. She comes with me, unresisting but unsteady. "Handsome fuck like that." My stomach churns, but I swallow down the bile that comes up and keep going. "You must have imagined what it would feel like?"

"No," she lies, her voice barely a whisper.

I sink onto the couch and draw her down with me. She takes her original seat, and glances warily at Reuben when he comes to sit beside her. He holds out her glass, and she lets out a forlorn little sigh.

Finally, the fight is over.

That last shred of resistance drains from her body. Her eyes dull to sullen gold as she drops the arms she'd been using to cover her chest. We don't look. Right now we couldn't be bothered with her tits. It's her mind we've been trying to lay bare.

She was right. We didn't bring her down here to fuck her. We came down here to interrogate her.

Torture never works.

Victims will say anything to get the pain to stop.

Weed and alcohol, though?

The combination leaves them helplessly compliant.

She lets Rube feed her the last inch of whiskey. When she shudders as the booze hits her throat, her convulsion reaches me through the seat cushion. Before I can stop myself, my hand's around her throat. I push her back against the couch, and she lets me. There's not even a sliver of fear in her eyes—just hopeless abandon.

Do your worst, Zachary.

Snuff out my life like the others. Why not? What else could I possibly tell you that you don't already know?

But then it hits me.

It's not what I need from *her*.

It's what *she* needs from *us*.

If she honestly thinks this friend of hers is the pure, innocent priest from her past, then we need to set her straight. It's a pity, having to break something so pretty...but at least the four of us will be there to pick up the pieces.

"How do you want him to fuck you?" My voice comes from far away as I start to disassociate from the moment, from what I'm about to do.

Her pulse quickens under my thumb.

"Like in the drawing," she says. Her lips curl up into a faint smile. "The one Cass—Cass's—ius drew."

"You can call him Cass," I murmur, leaning close, applying a little more pressure on her throat. She squirms a little, her eyelids flickering. But she's been numbed to everything—panic included.

It's better this way.

I know from experience.

Rube's hand enters my view. He fixes the rosary around Trinity's neck, positioning the crucifix just-so between her heaving breasts. Then he trails his fingertips down the center of her body.

Her stomach convulses at his touch, fluttering like a butterfly's wing.

She giggles.

I flinch at that innocent, happy sound as it wrenches me back into the here and now.

My hand tightens. I shove her back hard enough to dislodge Rube's hand and to recapture her attention.

"Did he ever touch you?" I ask again.

"*No,*" she gasps. "*Never.*"

"Good." I sit back, releasing her throat and flexing my fingers.

Rube lays a hand on her stomach, and it nearly covers her belly. "You should be thankful," he says.

Trinity rests her head back, slowly bringing a hand to her throat. She strokes the faint marks I left behind as her eyes move to Reuben. "Why?"

Her voice is thick now, her tongue sluggish as it forms the word. I guess she wasn't lying when she said she doesn't drink. She's minutes —perhaps even seconds—from passing out.

"He would have defiled you," Rube tells her mournfully. "Just like the others."

CHAPTER THIRTY-ONE
TRINITY

"...Take it to...drinks it all."

I open my eyes to orange-tinted darkness. It feels like someone's standing on my head. They may, possibly, be the same culprit who rubbed grit in my eyes. I push onto my hands and glance around.

I'm in their bedroom. This should alarm me. Terrify me, in fact, but I can barely think straight through the sullen *thud-thud-thud* of my head.

Orange light slices a line across the myriad blankets and pillows scattered about. I blink at the silhouette a few times before I recognize it.

Apollo comes over to me, stepping in and around the mattresses like he's walking a minefield. He crouches beside me and holds out a steaming cup. "Coffee," he explains. "Cream, two sugars. That right, pretty thing?"

I can't even.

I nod at him and accept the cup. Thankfully, my ass barely hurts anymore, so I can sit up in a cross-legged seat as soon as he disappears out of the room.

After a quick check to make sure there are in fact no snakes around, I drag a blanket over my shoulders. It's absolutely freezing in this place, and no surprise—it's not as if the library has heat.

The guys talk in hushed voices for a few seconds, and then there's utter quiet.

I spill coffee into my lap when Zachary calls out my name.

"Trinity? Join us."

I consider ignoring him.

Then I remember his warning. I don't need another hiding, thank you very fucking much. Juggling the coffee cup, I somehow manage to drag a blanket over my shoulders without spilling a drop. Then I make my way to the other side of the man cave.

They're all seated, Reuben and Cassius on the same couch I was on, Zachary still in his chair—although it's been pushed back closer to the bookshelf now—and Apollo on a badly worn armchair on the other side.

They all look up when I enter, making me freeze.

"Are you hungry?" Reuben asks.

Am I—?

I glare at him.

Do these freaks think they hit some kind of reset button when I went to sleep? What the hell is wrong with them? They've assaulted me, kidnapped me, *and* interrogated me, all in a matter of hours.

What. The. Actual. Fuck?

I still don't even know why. It has something to do with Gabriel, but Lord knows what.

Something inside me snaps. I storm forward, coffee sloshing dangerously close to the rim of my cup. "No, you sick fuck, I'm not hungry!"

I expect one of them to say something, maybe to try and calm me, but they keep staring like they paid good money for this show.

Setting down my coffee on the closest bookshelf, I keep the blanket closed with one hand and use the other to point at Zachary.

"You think you can just go around doing whatever the fuck you want? Well you're wrong! You can't."

Zachary settles back in his seat and crosses his arms over his chest. Is that a smile ghosting his lips?

"Someone's going to notice I'm gone. You realize that, right?" I scan the other faces one at a time. Apollo with his mop of unruly hair. Reuben with his ten-yard stare. Cassius who—

He's fucking *leering* at me. "Who's gonna notice you're gone, my little slut?"

"Stop calling me that!" I charge forward, emboldened by their apparent lack of giving a shit. I make to punch him on the shoulder, but nothing close to that happens.

Instead, he's on his feet pulling some kind of ninja move that has me draped over the back of the couch and him bending over me.

No one stops him.

Cass's hand slides under the blanket, grabbing at my breast. Reuben's rosary falls out and dangles from my neck.

"How did you sleep?" Reuben asks, as serene as fuck. Contorted like this, I can barely breathe. The fact that Cass keeps groping me isn't helping.

"Okay!" I shriek. "Please."

"Let her go," Zachary, by contrast, sounds exhausted.

"God damn it, Zac!" Cass pushes away from me, but not before he squeezes my ass with both hands. "Stop giving me fucking blue balls."

"You're doing it to yourself," Zachary replies. "Now sit. Both of you."

"Yeah, right over here," Cass says, showing me his teeth as he drags me around the couch.

I end up on his lap, despite my protests. He seems to remember Zachary could get me to stop fighting with a slap on my butt, so it takes three of them before I sink onto his lap and don't bolt straight up again.

It's not exactly the most comfortable seat. Does he *always* have a hard-on?

"Where are your things?" Zachary asks.

I glower at him for a second, and then remember how futile it is to resist, protest, or fight back. "What things?"

"Trinkets and keepsakes and shit like that," Apollo fills in. I glance up at him, but his eyes are on the camera in his lap. He seems intent on either fixing it, or taking it apart piece by piece.

"I don't have things like that."

"You didn't bring any with you?" Zachary asks.

"No. I don't *have* things like that." I cross my arms, mimicking him, and shrug. "What, is everyone supposed to have a whole bunch of junk for no reason?"

"Things of sentimental value?" Zachary says. "Most, yes."

"All I found was this," Apollo says, leaning over and picking up something off the floor beside his armchair.

I would have stood if Cass hadn't slipped an arm around my waist and clucked at me like I was seconds away from receiving another smack. So I toss my hair and try and make it seem like I don't give a fuck that they've taken the only thing I brought with me that wasn't clothing or shoes or underwear.

"It's a bible," I say stiffly. "In case you were wondering."

"An old translation," Zachary says, stretching to take it from Apollo. He flips it open, and I tense...waiting for the photo to fall out.

After how they'd grilled me about Gabriel, what would they say if they saw the photo of him and my father? It might spark the kind of reaction that ends in violence.

But nothing falls out. Either they've already found it, or I jammed it so hard between the pages that they'd have to open it to the exact place to take it out.

I can only hope they've been too busy to check.

Zachary hefts the thick volume in his hand. "I prefer these. The newer translations are too... polished."

"They've taken out all the good shit," Cass agrees. "All that fire and brimstone."

"Strange how many things are open to interpretation," Zachary muses, as if to himself.

"Mis-interpretation," Apollo says. The camera comes apart in his hands, and he stares at the assortment of pieces now littering his lap.

"Not everything."

I turn to Reuben, and swallow when I see him staring at me. When he reaches for me, I instinctively close my eyes. They pop open when his fingertips brush my breastbone. He lifts the crucifix dangling around my neck and rubs his thumb along the wood. It releases a sweet, heady scent that makes me squirm on Cass's lap.

Which, in turn, makes his erection even harder.

"Enough!" I snap. I yank the crucifix from Reuben's finger and turn to glare at Zachary. "Tell me what the hell I'm doing here."

Now my head's thumping like a bass drum. I press the heel of my hand against my temple, wincing, but I don't break eye contact with Zachary.

He sits forward, resting his elbows on his knees and lacing his fingers together. "You, Trinity Malone, are going to help us take down a sex trafficker."

I laugh, because what the hell else am I supposed to do? "Me? How?"

Zachary goes on as if I hadn't spoken. "They called him 'Guardian'." His jaw ticks. "You know him as Gabriel."

There's a beat of silence where even my heart stops beating.

Zachary gives me a grim smile. "Sorry. *Father* Gabriel."

MY COFFEE'S GONE cold in my hands. They gave it back to me a few minutes after they'd started telling me their story.

Apollo begins.

"My parents got shot when I was six. Mugging gone wrong kind of thing. I'd been an altar boy for like a month before that happened. Somehow, I ended up at an orphanage in Redmond instead of foster care.

"Not that I minded. I thought it was kinda cool. Had a lot of friends to play with. I was there for like a year before it happened."

He pauses, and starts collecting all the bits and pieces in his lap and putting them on the floor, arranging them around his bare feet.

"One of my teachers told me I'd done so well in class that he was taking me out for pizza." Apollo lets out a sardonic laugh. "Fucking idiot I was, I believed him. That's how easy it is to get a kid into your car. Fucking pizza, man."

He sniffs, and drags his hair out of his face. It flops back again, but he doesn't seem to notice. Zachary lights something. I first think it's weed, but then cigarette smoke billows into the air between us. They start passing it between them, each taking a drag or two before passing it on.

"We drove for hours. What it felt like, anyway. I started getting cranky. He slammed my head into the dashboard so hard I passed out." Apollo scratches at the scar on his forehead like he can still feel that pain through the years.

And here I'd thought it was an old sports injury or something.

"When I came to, I was tied up in a basement." He starts arranging the various mechanics of his broken camera around his feet in a halo.

It feels like someone's pouring cold water down my spine. He takes a deep breath, and glances up at Zachary.

Zachary nods at him.

Apollo looks at me.

That icy water freezes, and my entire body goes stiff.

"I had two Ghosts. They'd come every Saturday and Sunday, alternating like." He sticks out his fingers and twists them back and forth. "Never saw each other, but they timed their shit so well, they had to have wiped each other's cum off their dicks more than once."

My mouth fills with saliva. For a moment, I'm convinced I'm going to puke. Cass takes my wrist and urges my cup to my mouth.

I take a sip. "Ghosts?" The word slips out before I can stop it.

Apollo's eyes dart up. His foot starts tapping. "Yeah, Ghosts." He points at Reuben. "He came up with it."

"It's what we called the men who visited us," Reuben says. I glance at him, but he's still staring at Apollo. "We never knew who they were, or how long they'd stay. They weren't supposed to speak to us."

"But some of them couldn't shut up," Cass says.

I look at him over my shoulder. His blue eyes could have bored a hole through my head. "I got there a few months before Apollo arrived," he says.

"Where? In the basement?" I glance over at Apollo. "The same one?" Apollo seems to have forgotten I exist. He's busy with his camera again.

"Yup," Cass says. "Now snuggle up, honey tits. It's my turn."

CHAPTER THIRTY-TWO
ZAC

I need another blunt, but I light a cigarette instead. We know we don't smoke less when we share, but it's been a habit of ours for years already. Back when we first met, it took a lot for us to share anything, even our names.

Trust becomes addictive. Dangerously so.

Cass drags Trinity against his chest, arranging her like a sleepy kid—her head on his chest, her legs folded to one side. She lets him, but I think that's because she's in mild shock.

Or just really hungover.

"I was a handsome little shit, even back then," Cass starts. He toys with Trinity's hair, winding her curls around his finger as he talks.

It's surreal, listening to them. Stories spooling out like snagged threads from their tangled hearts. I've only ever heard snippets. Partial retellings whenever we'd discovered a new clue that led us deeper into the web of lies the Guardian had spun to keep his enterprise hidden from prying eyes.

"They must have been watching me for a few months already. I recognized the car they used when they finally snatched me. Broad daylight, the fucks. But they knew what they were doing. Where I'd be, at what time. That's I'd be alone."

Cass smooths a hand down Trinity's head, and it looks as if she burrows against him. "I lived in a small-ass town back then. The kind where your kid could take the bus from elementary school and you knew he'd get home safe and sound."

She shifts, tilting back her head, and shakes her head.

"But I didn't, did I?" Cass says as he tweaks the tip of her nose. "It was one block from the bus stop to my house. A five-minute walk. That day, I never made it home."

Trinity widens her eyes. Cass paints the outline of her lips with a fingertip.

"I didn't make a fuss. The minute I saw the car, I already knew what was happening. I don't know how, but I just knew. I tried to run, but they had one of their guys on the sidewalk ahead, and he just grabbed me and shoved me into the car."

Cass stops touching her. He looks away, his head dropping and his eyes clouding with dark shadows.

"They injected me with something. Knocked me clean out." His head snaps up, and he points straight at me as he grins. "I woke up next to James. You remember him?"

I don't say anything. Cass has the floor now.

He turns to Apollo, then Reuben. "You guys remember James? Fucker with the crazy eyes?"

I almost laugh.

I'm sure if we had to ask Trinity, she'd say we *all* have crazy eyes.

"Anyway." Cass waves a hand. "I had a shit ton of Ghosts. Didn't even bother keeping track." He bestows her with his radiant grin. "Guess I've always been a good lay." He winks at her, making her shy away from him.

None of us bat an eye when Cass glosses over his abuse. It's how he deals with his shit, just like we all have our little quirks and idiosyncrasies.

To each their own.

Trinity peeks at me without lifting her head. "How many boys did they...?"

"We're not sure." I shrug as I take a pull of my cigarette before handing it across to Cass. "Things were erratic. I assume on purpose."

"And the others? What happened to them?"

I push the inside of my lip against my teeth and chew on the skin. "That's not the question you should be asking right now."

Her brow furrows. She pushes up and away from Cass, making him groan theatrically. Then she carefully slides off his lap, as if worried he'll claw her back.

He won't.

As much as he likes to make out he was the furthest thing from a victim, he *did* suffer. He was the prettiest of the bunch. We all were— that's why they kept us for so long. Other boys would come and go, but our Ghosts seemed incapable of letting us go.

Fuck that, who am I kidding?

Of *disposing* of us.

Cass won't be feeling frisky for a while. He'll start acting out like he always does when he's forced to recall his past. But he drew the short straw, just like Apollo.

We try to be fair to each other. As fair as we can be without turning into complete and utter pussies.

"The Guardian. He wasn't a Ghost?" Trinity asks.

The cigarette, having traveled all the way around our circle, comes back to me. I tug at it before killing it in the ashtray.

"Not to our knowl—"

"Of course he is!" Apollo cuts in. Trinity jumps at the sound of his voice and turns wide eyes to him. "Just because he never touched us, doesn't mean he didn't..." He throws up his hands.

I wait him out to make sure he's finished. "To our knowledge, no."

"So how do you know he's involved?" Trinity's voice rises an octave higher.

"Because everything always leads back to him," I tell her. Then I sigh and sit back, running my hands through my hair. "The four of us—" I swing out a hand to encompass my brothers "—we lived together in that basement for years. Boys would come and go, but we'd stay behind. Some of the Ghosts started talking to us. We started piecing things together."

"Then we escaped," Reuben says.

I point at him. "Then we escaped." I exhale into the silence as Trinity leans forward with an expectant frown.

"And then?"

Traces of smoke from deep in my lungs wreathe my words. "And then everything went to shit."

CHAPTER THIRTY-THREE
TRINITY

It's inappropriate to laugh after what Zachary said, but I have a hysterical need to giggle.

Then it went to shit?

"I don't understand," I say, carefully swallowing down any mirth that dares to bubble up. "I mean, did they catch the Ghosts? How does that lead to Gabriel? None of this makes sense!"

Zachary shakes his head. "None of the men who molested us were ever arrested by the FBI or the police. Not. One."

I hug myself, and burrow deeper into my blanket. "Why? Didn't you have enough evidence?"

"Oh, we had evidence—" Apollo begins, but he cuts off when Zachary throws a hard stare his way. I guess his turn to talk is over.

I haven't heard Zachary's story yet, or Reuben's, but I'm already at the point where I want to tell them they're making this up.

And even if they're not, there's no way Gabriel could be involved in something like this.

No *fucking* way.

"Two arrests were made," Zachary says calmly.

"That's it?"

He nods once. "There was a trial. The suspects were sentenced to death."

My eyes go wide. The blanket creaks in my hand as I tighten my grip. "As in...the death penalty?"

Another nod. "They'll be executed next month." There's that tick again. He clenches his jaw as if he's suddenly aware of it, and swallows. "The investigation was closed a long, long time ago. According to the feds, they found everyone involved."

"Tell her about Gabriel," Reuben says. "She has to know."

Zachary holds up a hand. Licks his lips. I've never seen him this unsure of himself, and it makes panic flutter deep in my belly.

Earlier, they seemed convinced Gabriel was, *what?* Some kind of kingpin? The guy responsible for all their pain and suffering.

Zachary opens his mouth, but he can't seem to produce words.

For some reason, that terrifies me.

A hand lands on my shoulder. Reuben turns me to face him. It's unreal, seeing such deep pain on such a young, vital face. He could have been the poster boy for a high school football team.

"I'd always beg my Ghost to tell me why he was doing what he was doing." Reuben slaps his palm into his chest. Apollo flinches. "Why *me?*"

My mouth goes dry and goosebumps race over my flesh.

His black eyes trap me like tar.

"He said I should ask the Guardian. That he could explain it."

I'm hanging on every fucking word, but Reuben's struggling with this as much as Zachary was. His wide chest rises and falls as his breathing becomes slow and deep.

"I told him—" Reuben burrows a hand into the top of my blanket. I don't fight him—by now I know what he's looking for. He takes hold of my crucifix and rubs the wood. It seems to calm him, because a level of tension leaves his face. "I told him I didn't know who the Guardian was. That I only saw him. So he told me—"

His voice grows thick. Rosewood hits my nose how hard he's rubbing that crucifix.

"Rube," Cass whispers from behind me. "Bro, you don't have to—"

"The Guardian said we were the cure." Black eyes pin me. "That the Ghosts had a sickness. We kept their symptoms—those urges—at bay, so they could do their jobs." His breath hitches. "So they could preach the Word of God without being plagued by their desires."

My mouth falls open. Without thought, I lift my hands and wrap my fingers around Reuben's fist. My chest closes rendering speech impossible, but there's nothing I could have said anyway.

Nothing.

"When they were done—" He pauses to swallow. "When their visit was over, they would meet with the Guardian and confess their sins."

Reuben's hand trembles inside my fingers.

"And he would bless them, and make them pure again."

He lets go of the crucifix, taking back his hand and slowly putting them face down on his thighs.

"Until their urges came back, of course," Zachary says.

My heart fucking bleeds for these boys. I rub a palm over my collarbones, willing it to go inside and easy the ache they caused.

"Then the whole sick cycle would start all over again." Cass leans close, sliding his hands over my shoulders. "All with the help of your BFF."

I shake my head, and it frees a tear from my lashes. "No," I whisper. "Please. I'm sorry about this. What happened to you. It's...it's fucking wrong and disgusting." I haul in a breath and stand on shaky legs, turning to look at them. "But Father Gabriel didn't have anything to do with this. I *know* him. He's a *good* man. He's always been there for us."

Four stony faces watch me.

"Please. Believe me. It's not him. He's not your Guardian."

Fabric rustles behind me. I whirl around as Zachary gets to his feet.

"We thought you'd say that." He cocks his head and slowly scans me up and down. "And you're right. We don't have any proof. Not a—"

Reuben sucks in a breath, but keeps quiet when Zachary holds up a hand.

What had he been going to say? Surely if they *did* have proof, they'd tell me?

"Not all miracles are divine, Trinity." Zachary slides a hand around the back of my neck and draws me closer. I move on wooden legs, too entranced to even think of resisting. "But you? I swear on my life you were sent by God Himself."

"What?" Is all I can manage.

"That proof? *You're* going to find it for us." His hand tightens cruelly, wrenching a gasp from me. "You're going to bring it to us. And together we, us five..." He comes close enough to kiss me, for his commanding eyes to fill my world.

"We'll make him give us the names of our Ghosts."

I don't want to know what comes next. Cold dread is already spreading through my limbs, going for my heart.

"And then we'll catch them." His brushes a curl from my face. "And we'll inflict on them every wound, every pain, every bit of shame they inflicted on us."

My heart bangs against my ribs. "Okay."

"And then we'll kill them." His eyes don't change in the slightest.

"Okay."

Behind me, three voices chant one word in unison.

Amen.

I should be horrified at myself.

But I'm not.

I'll prove to these damaged, tortured souls that Father Gabriel is the kind and loving man I know him to be.

And if, somehow, everything they say turns out to be true?

Well, then, I guess I've signed a deal with the devil.

A-fucking-men.

To Be Continued...

THEIR WILL BE DONE

Theme Song

Scorpio — POUR VOUS

Playlist

Oh My God — HELLYEAH

Heathens — CORVYX

Something in the Way — AT SEA

How Far Does the Dark Go? — ANYA MARINA

Kvrt in Space — FRANHOFER DIFFRACTION

King Night — SALEM

A Conversation with God — KING 810

Amen — ΔAIMON

CHAPTER ONE
ZACH

I flick on my indicator and make the turn into Redwater's main street. My decade-old SUV rattles every time I strike a rut in the road. I'd have to buy a new one soon—this battered car was part of my persona as Zachary Rutherford, a kid from a low-income home who dragged himself up by his bootstraps, worked two jobs while he got his Bachelors, and couldn't be happier with the menial wage Saint Amos pays first-year teachers.

If I were to cash in all my assets, I could probably *buy* Saint Amos. And in a few weeks, my wealth is set to triple.

Another clank. This time it's internal and it comes as I hit another rut. Probably the shock absorbers. The roads around here chew through them.

It's risky, heading out today. When I left my brothers, the atmosphere was taut as a bowstring. If I'm gone too long, they might fall on Trinity like a pack of wolves. I'd have stayed, but I always go to town on Saturday. It would seem strange for me to stay at the school, especially this close to break.

I snort at the thought.

This is the first time I've even *considered* going off-script.

All because of one girl. A girl I can't get out of my mind since the day she showed up at my class. Even more so after our time in the shower. After we had her trapped and helpless in our nest. She thinks we're humoring her. Letting her decide which side of the battle line she wants to stand.

My lips twitch, but I smooth them before they can twist into a grimace.

With Trinity in the picture, everything's changed. Now I'm no longer just driving into town to buy Apollo a new camera, a few cartons of cigarettes, and to empty out my post box.

We'd originally planned to kidnap Gabriel. Apollo found an abandoned wood cutter's hut in the woods—a place straight out of the sixteenth century. We were going to do whatever the fuck it took to retrieve the names of each and every Ghost Gabriel handled, and find out who it was that he reported to. Because we know the Guardian had a superior.

And then we'd kill him.

We'd have done it over summer break, while Saint Amos was closed for repairs. No one would have missed him, and by the time the police were notified, we'd already be away on our killing spree.

The timing was perfect.

Everything had been perfect...until Trinity arrived and put a wrench in the works. That's what I'd thought, anyway. Now it turns out this unexpected development might work in our favor.

There'd always been a chance Gabriel wouldn't have handed us the information or that, under torture, he'd give us any bullshit just to make the pain stop.

But since Trinity's so fucking adamant Gabriel is a true man of God, we'll make her *prove* it. And in doing so, she'll inadvertently get us everything we need.

I park outside a photography store, ducking to look through the window. Then I take a piece of paper out of my pocket and glance at Apollo's horrific handwriting. I can't even remember how many cameras I've bought him over the years. He's as clumsy as he is introverted. Today's shopping run is going to be pricey, but it'll be worth it. Because one thing is for sure. Once we have the information we need, Gabriel becomes expendable.

My brothers and I agree fully that inflicting even a fraction of the pain and suffering he orchestrated over the years is the least he deserves.

That we deserve.

And Trinity?

I'll let my brothers decide what they want to do with their new toy—keep her, or discard her.

CHAPTER TWO
TRINITY

A rough shake, accompanied by an even rougher, "Hey!" drives me out of a deliciously tangled dream. I knock away Jasper's hand and scramble into a sit, clutching my blanket to my chest like he was trying to cop a feel.

But that had been Cassius. And a dream.

"What?" I squint up at him with scratchy eyes. "What is it?"

"Where were you last night?" He's still standing, forcing me to crane back my head to look up at him.

I turn my back to him. "None of your fucking business," I mutter.

He grabs my shoulder again. "You can't do shit like this."

"Shit like what, Jasper?" I yell, twisting around to face him. I kick off my blankets, glaring at him so hard he actually takes a step back and drops onto the edge of his bed. "What do you think I did that's so fucking wrong?"

He fidgets, smoothing his hair with a palm. "If the hallway monitor catches you outside your room at night, you get lashes. And I'll get them too."

I briefly consider telling him that I'd been with the hallway monitor. But then I remember Zachary's moss-green eyes, and the way he'd stared at me in the shower like I was an ice cream sundae and he was a self-destructive diabetic with a craving for cherries.

"Yeah?" I cock my head to the side. "Do they hurt, those imaginary lashes you keep getting on my behalf?"

I shouldn't be baiting him like this, but dear Lord I was enjoying that dream, and the blissful sleep that came with it.

Apollo and Cassius snuck me back here just before dawn. I made sure not to wake Jasper, watching him like a hawk as I'd changed into my pajamas and slipped into bed. And unless he'd woken up just after I'd gone to shower, how else would he know I was gone?

"Do they hurt—?" He cuts off with an angry sound and stabs a finger toward me. "You know what? Fuck you. Do whatever you want. But I swear, if I get punished again when you fuck up, then—"

I sneer at him. "When did you ever get...?"

Jasper stands, turns to the side, and tugs down his boxers. Mustard-colored bruises mar his skin.

My stomach turns over before logic can take hold. "You're lying," I tell him, standing to get my clothes so I have an excuse to get the hell out of our room. "Those look old, anyway."

"I got them the first day you arrived because you went to class without your school uniform."

"I didn't have one!" I whirl around to face him, thrusting out one of the dresses that miraculously appeared in my closet the day after Ruth took my measurements.

While Apollo watched.

My cheeks catch flame. I hope Jasper takes it as anger and not... something else.

"Think that matters?" he mutters.

"You want to know what I think? I think *you* did something," I say, walking closer until he's leaning back to get away from me. "Something bad enough to get you stuck with a roommate. And now you're trying to blame me for it."

This shuts him up, but from the sulk on his mouth, it won't be for long.

I huff and pause a moment to rub at my temples. There's still a faint headache lurking from all the weed and alcohol I consumed. "Where do I get painkillers from?"

He smirks at me. "Go fuck yourself."

"Asshole." I storm out, heading for the restroom. I hear him calling after me, but I ignore it. Probably just trying to blame more shit on me. The fucking nerve.

I find the closest restroom and change in the stall. After washing my face in the basin, I spend a few minutes trying to sort out my hair.

No luck—it will need another wash before people stop confusing me for a clown. My gaze tracks to the small window on the side of the restroom.

What time is it?

I bundle my pajamas against my stomach. The only laundry hamper I know of is the one in the showers, but I'm sure as hell not going there. I'm sure it's full of naked boys. And the only naked boys I want to see are a select few who I'm pretty sure wouldn't be caught dead in that place again.

I'm still blushing at that thought when I let myself back into my room and shove my dirty clothes under my bed.

"Idiot," Jasper mutters from his bed. He's lying on his back, a dog-eared copy of *Metamorphosis* propped on his stomach.

"Jerk," I snap back. I tug at the hem of my school dress and flounce out of the room.

My stomach keeps alternating between a hungry pit and a maelstrom of bile and stomach acid. Apollo had murmured something about coffee to me when they'd been sneaking me back inside, wrapped in a blanket with nothing but underwear beneath. If it hadn't been for them, I'd have peed myself at the thought of having to get back to my room without someone seeing me.

So coffee. Possibly breakfast.

Oh Lord. Do I have more gruel to look forward to?

I pause in the hallway, a hand on my stomach. I have to stop thinking about that or I'll fucking puke.

I'm used to the hallways being empty around here. It seems the only time there're lots of activities is in the morning when all the boys rush to go shower before pray—

Wait. Did I miss prayer?

I peek down the hallway and spot a boy heading toward me, hair wet and a towel dangling from his shoulders.

"Sorry?" I call out, stepping into the hallway.

He takes me in with a frown. "Yeah?"

"Were there prayers this morning?"

"It's Saturday," he says, frown deepening as he moves past me.

I throw up my hands at his retreating back.

I RISK A PEEK OUTSIDE. There's not a cloud in the sky and, judging from the position of the sun, it's early. I should have checked my schedule. Were the weekend activities even on there?

Opening the door wider, I step outside to catch some sun on my face before heading for the dining hall.

I'm not the last to arrive—there are a handful of trays still left on the table. Including mine—bright pink post-it still intact.

TRINITY MALONE

I GRIMACE before I notice there's a little heart above each of the I's in my name and then a butterfly starts fluttering around in my stomach. I grab my tray and turn to look for an empty spot.

On cue, the snickers begin. I spot a few gaps, but every time I get near, they miraculously close up.

Not all miracles are divine.

Assholes.

There's something different about the boys today, but I'm too busy trying to ignore their awful giggles to figure out what it is.

Movement draws my eye. Apollo's waving at me through the kitchen door's window.

A second butterfly joins the first.

Zach said he'd send for me to discuss what they wanted me to do next. Is that why Apollo's calling me? I hadn't thought it would be so soon. I'd hoped to get my head straight by then.

I swallow and walk across the dining hall.

I haven't had a chance to process the past twenty-four hours. I've never felt this conflicted in my life. I want to hate those guys—hell, *of course* I hate them—but after hearing their stories...is it any wonder they're so fucked up?

But what about Father Gabriel? The stuff they told me about him? I can't even begin to process that.

Zach told me Father Gabriel would be back tomorrow.

Apollo pushes open the door when I get close, and beckons me inside with a charming, lopsided smile.

"Hi," I say, fumbling with my tray as I push a stray curl behind my ear.

He cocks his head and leads me to a steel door. Daylight streams in when he opens it. I step into a courtyard that smells of damp bricks. There's a concrete table and four stools in the center.

There's a sickly pot plant in one corner, and another steel doorway opposite. Someone left their boots next to that door.

"Where does that go?" I ask, digging the edge of the tray into my stomach and trying not to look like a complete idiot.

"You don't have to wear your uniform on weekends," Apollo says, his back to me as he pulls out a packet of cigarettes and lights one. I look down at myself, close my eyes, and curse inwardly.

That's what was different about the boys. They were wearing normal clothes, not their usual drab brown.

Is that what Jasper was trying to tell me?

I *am* an idiot.

"Still have to get used to things around here," I murmur, heading for the table so I can put my tray down.

"Why bother? Not like you're going to be here much longer."

My tray clatters onto the table. I turn to Apollo, mouth gaping. "What do you mean?"

He points to one of the stools. "Sit. Eat."

"No." I cross my arms over my chest. "Tell me what that's supposed to mean."

Instead, he smokes his cigarette and stares at me through a gap in his blond hair. Did he wash it? I bet *he* has his own bathroom. "Sit."

I sink down, wincing when the icy concrete touches the back of my thighs.

"Eat."

Glaring at him doesn't work, so I let out a huge sigh and tear the plastic wrap from my tray.

Someone cut my toast into the shape of a heart. I look up at Apollo, deadpan.

He grins with one side of his mouth, blowing cigarette smoke my way as he drags his hair out of his face. "For the shit food I made you yesterday," he says.

I grab a piece of toast and start nibbling on it. "Please tell me what you meant." Maybe good manners will help me get through to this guy because being rude sure as hell didn't.

He puts his foot on the stool opposite mine, the table now between us. Taking another drag of his smoke, he leans his elbows on his raised knee, studying me for a few seconds before speaking.

He holds up two fingers. "We got two scenarios here."

I frown at him.

"First...we're right, you're wrong." He shrugs. "When it all comes to light, shit's going to go down. Big time. This place—" he flicks his fingers up, taking in Saint Amos towering above us on all sides "—will probably get shut down. Feds would ransack it. Everyone gets arrested. Etcetera, etcetera."

A chill shivers down my spine. I'm so convinced they're wrong about Father Gabriel I never even considered what would happen if, by some slight chance, they turned out to be right. I couldn't stay here. I'd be back in foster care until...when? I'm finished school? Then what?

Lord, but it's difficult to keep eye contact with Apollo. Paired against Zach and Reuben and Cassius, he seemed almost forgettable. But with his hair out of his face, his high, sharp cheekbones are more distinct. And his mouth? It's impossible not to watch him every time he takes a drag of his cigarette.

Eyes, Trinity. Eyes!

My gaze snaps back to his eyes. The crinkle in the corner of each tells me he knows exactly what I'm thinking.

My cheeks grow warm.

"And what if I'm right?" I blurt out before biting off another mouthful of toast.

Apollo tilts his head, and his hair slides back into his face. "Even if it's not Gabriel, Gabriel knows who it is." He shrugs, drags at his cigarette, and walks around the table to me. "And you'd probably go running your mouth if you think we'd hurt him, so...we'd have to make sure you didn't do anything like that."

I'm so shocked at what he's insinuating. I don't move when he brushes his fingertips down my jaw. "I wouldn't do that," I whisper.

"We're not exactly trusting of strangers. Nothing personal, pretty thing."

We.

All those years they spent together in that basement. I can't even imagine the bond that created between them. I'm guessing it goes far beyond hatching a plan of revenge. They're not just buddies—they're brothers.

"Please, you *have* to believe me." I widen my eyes as I turn to face him.

There's uncertainty in his eyes. But there's something else there too. I can't be sure, but I'm hoping against all hope that he wants to believe me.

"It's not me you have to convince," he says, his lips curling into a smile as he takes another drag of his cigarette.

His fingers trail down my throat. He traces the outline of my collarbone, sending a flurry of shivers through me. Toying with the top button of my dress, his smile hitches up. "Lunchtime, a day like this?" He tilts back his head and looks up at the patch of sky. "Everyone's gonna picnic in the field." He stands and goes to kill his cigarette in the pot plant. "No one will miss you until tonight." He walks over to the kitchen door, pausing with his hand flat on the steel.

"We'll fetch you in an hour. Wear something pretty," he says around a smirk.

"Wait!" I call out before he can disappear inside.

He steps back, waiting.

I scrounge up every ounce of courage to ask, "Do you guys have a private bathroom?"

CHAPTER THREE
TRINITY

If anyone ever wanted to conduct a study on the effects of blushing, I'd be the perfect candidate. In the past half an hour I don't think I've stopped blushing even once.

I'm in a room in the east wing. It's nothing like the one I have to share with Jasper. It's three times the size, and it has its own en-suite bathroom where I'm currently standing buck naked and terrified that someone's going to walk in on me.

Reuben, to be precise. Since it's his room, he accompanied me up here. I think he's in the small study-cum-dining area of his apartment, but his carpets are too thick for me to hear if he did move about.

Steam fills up the shower cubicle, turning the frosted glass white. I slip inside that heavenly cloud, and the water draws a deep sigh from me as it cascades down my body.

There was no way I was going to have lunch with Zac's boys while I still had traces of sticky alcohol over my breasts and crazy person hair. So I brought my clothes up here and slipped into Reuben's room while Cassius watched the hallway to make sure no one spotted me.

Apparently, I could get into a lot of trouble being on this floor. More so if I'm discovered inside someone's room.

Lathering rosemary-scented shampoo into my hair I try and squeeze every last drop of indulgence from the most blissful moment I've had in the past month.

For a few minutes, there's nothing but me, the warm water, and that delicious scent. It should smell like Reuben, but on me it smells different.

I'm glad it's his bathroom I get to use. I'd have refused if it was Cass's, and it would have felt really weird to use Apollo's. Strangely, despite how big and scary he is, Reuben feels…safe.

It must be amazing having someone like that in your life. Someone who can knock the teeth out of anyone who dares look at you funny. I'd never be scared again. Not wrapped in his strong arms.

My hand slides down my hip, and I hesitate, biting down on my bottom lip for a second. I peek behind me, but I can't see the bathroom door through the glass and steam.

Skimming lower, my fingers brush against my clit. A thrill flutters through me as my eyes slide closed. It should have been Reuben's black eyes that appear, but instead all I can see is Zachary. His solemn expression, that almost permanent crease between his brows.

I took it for severity, but now I know it's some kind of anger. Anger hardened into a diamond over time. But diamonds aren't pretty when they first come out of the ground. They're rough and murky looking. To sparkle, they have to be polished.

I doubt Zachary will ever let anyone close enough for that to happen. He or any of his brothers.

Sinful bliss flashes through me. I haven't done this in ages, and the guilty pleasure of it makes me bite down even harder on my lip. What do they do in that lair of theirs? Drinking and smoking like they own the place. Do any of them ever slip behind that curtain to do what I'm doing?

Alone.

Together?

Fuck.

A tiny moan escapes my lips. I'm so close I can almost—

There's a knock on the bathroom door.

"Trinity?"

I gasp and flinch away from my throbbing clit. Reuben's deep voice sends a tremble through me that congregates deep in my belly.

"I'm done!" I call out in a cracked voice. "Be out in a sec."

He says nothing, but I can imagine him frowning at the door, perhaps considering coming in to make sure I'm okay.

It wouldn't be the worst thing in the world. I've never considered what type of guy I would like—honestly, I've never met enough for that to ever have been a consideration, but out of all Zach's brothers, Reuben strikes me as the sanest. Sure, he's a bit hot and heavy with his bible, but on him that kind of zealous fervor seems pure and right.

Maybe because that's the only kind of crazy I understand.

I rinse, turn off the faucet, and dart out of the shower to grab a towel and wrap it around me.

After I've dried off and draped Reuben's rosary around my neck, I slip into one of my own dresses. Mom would have thrown this one out a long time ago, but I'd kept it because it was the prettiest thing she'd ever bought me.

Father wasn't always a priest. They married young, and tried for years to have a child. Father eventually turned to religion, expecting answers from God for why Mom kept having miscarriages. I guess they ultimately found their answer, because a year or two after my father joined the clergy, Mom became pregnant with me and carried to full term.

She bought this for my sixteenth birthday, but I never got to wear it. The moment my father saw it on me, he sent me back to my room to change.

They had a huge fight that night, and Father left without bothering to stay around for cake.

The cream-colored dress has lace at the bosom and on the hem, and because she always bought everything at least a size too big, I'd grown into it since I last wore it. I'd put it on when they were sleeping and twirl around in front of the mirror, pretending I was just like all the other girls I saw in church, or walking down the street. Girls whose parents let them wear makeup and jewelry and high heels.

I don't have heels, but this dress doesn't need them. It comes mid-thigh and clings to me like a second skin. I saunter out of the bathroom all casual like, pretending to focus on untangling my hair as if I wear stuff like this every day, even when my heart feels like it's going to pound out of my chest.

Reuben is busy texting on his phone. He glances up at me as I walk across the room. My stomach somersaults at his double take.

"Ready?" he asks. I nod, keeping my eyes away from him in an attempt to cool down my cheeks.

It doesn't help, of course, but I have no right to complain. I know this dress is trouble—that's why I chose it.

While I'd been rifling around in my closet wondering what clothing best suited a date with the devil—or four of them, in this case—I'd realized something.

They've been controlling me like a puppet. They wanted me gone so they bullied me. And if I'd had a choice, I'd have left. They want to turn me against Father Gabriel, and expect *me* to prove that he's not a pedophile.

I guess alcohol does put hair on your chest, because I'm done being their marionette doll.

I'm wearing this dress because that means Zach's brothers—and hopefully Zachary himself—will be so distracted that, for once, I'll have the upper hand.

It's not the best plan, but it's *a* plan.

What could possibly go wrong?

CHAPTER FOUR
TRINITY

When the Brotherhood had invited me over, I'd expected to meet them somewhere inside the dorms. I get that they can't be seen together or it would blow their cover, but I didn't realize we'd be going back to their man cave.

I'm sitting in Zachary's wooden chair. It's hard and too high—my feet dangle unless I point and touch my toes to the carpet. The guys are sitting on the big sofa staring at me like they can't decide whether to kill me or fuck me.

Apollo just makes Reuben look even brawnier by comparison, especially since Reuben's biceps are almost bulging out of his t-shirt.

"Where's Cass?" I ask, shifting in my seat.

"He'll be here soon."

"And Zachary?"

"Gone to town," Reuben says. Apollo immediately elbows him in the side. "Shut it!"

"What?"

"She doesn't need to know that."

"Why not?"

Apollo frowns at him in reply before they turn their gazes back to me. I lick my lips and shift uncomfortably.

"Do you want a drink?" Reuben asks, standing before I have a chance to reply. He pours one for each of us and hands them out before sitting down again.

My nose wrinkles when I catch a whiff of the eye-watering booze in my glass. "What is this?" I ask, swirling it around.

"Whiskey," Apollo answers. "Not the greatest, but this far away from civilization it's this or moonshine."

"What's moonshine?"

Reuben chuckles wryly. Apollo snickers. Then both their faces go blank. "Fuck, you're serious," Apollo murmurs. He shakes his head as he lifts his glass to his lips. "God help us."

I frown at him, about to ask just what the hell that was supposed to mean when there's a snap of fabric behind me. I twist in my seat, facing Cass as he storms into the lair.

"We've got company," he says, and then his eyes fall on me. A smug smile replaces his frown. "Welcome back, my little slut." His eyes rove over me like a physical touch. "Damn. You look good enough to eat."

I drop my eyes and try to hide behind my glass as he strides deeper into the sitting area. I'm starting to regret wearing the dress.

"Guess who's back?" he says, stabbing a thumb over his shoulder.

"Not Zachary," Reuben says. "Not unless he left early."

"No, not Zachary," Cass says, deepening his voice as if trying to imitate Reuben. "Those other two fucks."

"Again?" Apollo sits forward in a rush, dragging his hair out of his face. "Christ, you'd think they'd have better things to do."

"You going to stop them?" Reuben asks, putting his empty glass on the ground.

"They're already headed down here." Cass grabs his hips, twisting to face me. "We should gag her."

Reuben's already on his feet. I throw up my hands, miraculously still holding onto my tumbler. "No. No gagging. I'll be quiet."

"Can't take a chance," Cass says, shaking his head as he goes over to the bookshelf and rifles through a pile of clothing. He whips out a bandanna and twists it into a thick rope like he's done this a thousand times before.

I'm on my feet a second later, my glass tumbling out of my hand and landing silently on the carpet. "No, please, Cass."

"Grab her," he says through his teeth.

I make a dash for the exit, but a thick arm slings around my throat and drags me back. "They won't be long," Reuben says, almost kindly, as he turns me around for Cass. "But they can't hear you."

"I wasn't going to—"

Cass shoves the bandanna between my lips and ties it off behind my head. Then he pats my cheek and draws me out of Reuben's grip.

I'd been willing to hear them out.

But this?

It's obvious they'll never trust me, so what's the point in trying to change our fucked up dynamic? I've gotten myself enmeshed in their plans, and the only way out is along the path they've chosen for me. I hate them for not letting me choose. But why did I expect any different of the big bad world my parents kept warning me about?

"Put her in there." Cass points to the bedroom. Apollo grabs my wrists and starts dragging me across the room.

I shake my head and dig in my heels.

"Relax, Trin," Cass says.

I'm one-hundred percent focused on Apollo, but I can practically hear Cassius rolling his eyes at me. "Your virginity is safe." He lets out a dark chuckle. "For now."

My enraged shriek comes out as a manic moan.

"Shh," Apollo says, hauling me the rest of the way. Reuben holds the curtain back as Apollo pulls and Cass pushes. I end up tripping the last yard and falling on hands and knees inside their soft, dark sleeping pit. I scramble up in a rush, my fingers tugging at the gag.

Reuben's hand closes over mine. He's just a shape in the dark, if a *massive* shape, but his presence calms me. He doesn't try and shush me, or drag me, or do anything. He just gently guides my hands away from the knot at the back of my head until they're in my lap.

Two more shadows slip inside and merge with the darkness.

Despite the blood singing in my veins, I can hear them breathing.

And then the muted sound of fabric rustling. I sit up straighter, and Reuben's hands tighten around mine. It should have calmed me, but now I can feel his pulse, and it's racing.

Who the hell is coming?

"HERE?"

"Further back."

"But this is where we—"

"Want someone to find us again like last time?"

I sit up straight, my lips going slack around the gag. What the hell are Jasper and Perry doing down here? Did they follow Reuben and me when we slipped into the crypt? Do they suspect something?

It's only when Reuben starts stroking my knuckle with the pad of his thumb that I realize I'm gripping him hard as I can. I try to ease up, but my fingers refuse.

If they discover me down here, it will put an end to everything. Is that why Cass gagged me? He can't honestly think I'd make a noise and attract their attention—I could have done that any time in the past few hours I've been alone in the dorm. But since I'm past the point of complaining about their treatment, I sit and bear it.

At least until this fucking gag is loose. Then they'll get a mouthful.

A thump rattles a bookshelf a few yards away, back in the sitting area. Crap, what was that? Are they fighting? Fabric rustles, this time not nearly as muted as before.

If my eyes were to go any wider, I swear they'd pop out of my head.

They can't be doing what I think they're doing.

Can they?

Reuben peels open my fist and laces his fingers through mine. Something brushes my leg, and I turn my stricken gaze on Apollo who managed to move right up beside me without making a noise. Then again, I hadn't been focusing on them, had I? Apollo takes my other hand, mimicking Reuben.

Do they think I'll try scratching my way out of here or something? I shift on the layers of blankets and mattress beneath me, and squint in the darkness, looking for Cassius.

Maybe he thinks Apollo and Reuben have me taken care of, because I can't spot him in the shadows even though my eyes have adjusted to the dark.

Outside, Jasper and Perry start kissing. From those desperate sounds, it seems this tryst of theirs is long overdue.

More rustling.

A stifled moan.

Mother of God, I can't stand this. My brain seems very eager to fill in the blanks of what's happening. In my mind, those two boys are doing some very, very naughty things to each other.

I shift again, and then freeze.

No, this can't be happening.

Are those sounds turning me on? It can't be. It's more likely the fact that Zach's brothers have my hands clasped like kids on a first date.

The weirdest first date imaginable.

But there's definitely something happening between my legs. I'm starting to feel slick and tingly. Even my underwear's becoming damp.

There's another thump, a harsh indrawn breath, and then a deep moan.

Guess Jasper and Perry couldn't care less about keeping quiet—they think they're all alone in the abandoned library.

Oh my God! Jasper and I went through a whole lesson with him knowing he'd done this very thing just a few yards away? The pervert! Is that why he couldn't concentrate?

I flinch when a hand slides around the front of my throat.

Damn it. When did Cass move behind me?

Outside the lair, Jasper and Perry break into a furious, grunting rhythm. I can't make out if they're in pain or ecstasy. Probably a little of both.

Cass's other hand glances over my knee and up the inside of my thigh. I twist my shoulders, trying to get away from him. Reuben and Apollo tighten their grip on my hands.

I freeze.

No.

Bastards!

They weren't holding my hands because they were damn well sweet on me. They're keeping me still for Cass.

I grunt at them through the gag. Definitely not loud enough for Jasper and Perry to hear—although I doubt they'd notice a bomb going off—but I still end up with Cass's fingertips digging into my throat.

His hand starts moving again, inching toward my center.

Outside, books rattle on the shelf as the boys' pounding grows slower, but harder. I hear a muffled, "Fuck!" but I have no idea who said it because right now I have problems of my own.

Cass's fingertips slide under my dress and skate over my hipbone. He hooks a finger over the elastic of my underwear and tugs it down an inch. The hand around my throat travels up until he's cupping my jaw. He tilts back my head until I'm staring up at the silhouette of his head and shoulders.

"Lift your cute little ass so I can take these off," Cass murmurs into my ear.

What the fuck?

I start struggling, but that somehow translates into me agreeing that he can yank off my undies and leave them tangled around my knees. I buck, and that's when Reuben and Apollo grab my hips and shove me back onto the floor.

Panting into my gag, I toss hair out of my eyes and try to think of my next move while ignoring the fact that my body thinks this is all above board.

Lips brush my cheek as Cassius rains soft little kisses over my face and neck. There's a tug at my underwear before he groans into my ear. "You're fighting pretty damn hard for someone who's already wet," he says.

Heat washes over my face and sinks into my cheeks. I don't think I've ever been this humiliated in my life.

Outside, there's one last thump, and a groan to rival the one Cassius just let loose in my ear.

Another drawn-out, "Fuuuck," and I'm sure it's coming from Perry.

Frantic motion, skin on skin.

A deep sigh.

My mind is going haywire. The more I try and keep it blank, the more it fills with graphic images of what they're doing out there.

"Yes. *Fuck*," Jasper grunts.

Goosebumps break out over my skin, and I have no idea if it was that outburst, or Cass's teeth grazing the back of my neck.

Another thump.

Then a breathless, "We have to go," from Jasper.

"Not yet," Perry says, and my chest tightens how frantic he sounds. "Please, Jay. Just five more minutes."

They start kissing again. Cass's hand is less than an inch from the hot, throbbing mess between my legs.

"I'll fuck you first," Cass whispers in my ear. "Then Apollo, then Rube. Hopefully you'll be stretched out enough for him by then."

My body shudders, and Cass chuckles low and deep in his throat.

"Damn right you should be scared. I don't think you can handle him, my pretty little slut. Not that you have a choice, of course. Not if he ends up splitting you right down the fucking middle."

There's a soft, angry growl from Reuben.

"Wait!" Perry's voice makes me stiffen in surprise. "Did you hear that?"

"Let's go!" Jasper whispers furiously. Metal clinks against metal and fabric rustles. "Quick, before—"

A whistle pierces the air.

I gasp behind my gag. Zach's brothers fall back, releasing me.

Zachary's voice cuts through the air like a whip. "You two!"

"Shit!" Jasper hisses right over Perry's panicked, "Oh, *fuck!*"

"What on God's green earth are you doing?" Zachary bellows.

Again, we're all holding our breath. Waiting for the other shoe to drop.

Jasper yelps.

"Come here!" Zachary yells.

Off to one side, further away than he had been before, Perry starts crying. "Please, Brother, we were—"

"I know *exactly* what you two were doing."

My blood runs cold at the sound of Zachary's voice. Before I can stop myself, I'm hugging my arms over my chest. I don't ever want to hear him speaking to me with such frigid anger.

"Sister? It's Zachary. I'm sending Jasper and Perry to you." His voice moves away. "Twenty each. No, I'm afraid I have other matters to attend to. And no dinner for either of them."

I almost swallow my tongue when I hear the sound of the curtain hiding the lair's entrance being whisked away. Reuben and Apollo are on their feet a second later. Orange light blooms around the edges of the curtain shielding this side of the room, and then cuts a slice through the darkness when Zachary throws it back.

"What the fuck?" he demands in a deep growl that makes my hackles rise.

"I can explain—" Cass begins.

Zachary points back to the living area. Cass cuts off and steps into the living area without so much as a backward look.

Then he points to Reuben and Apollo. They follow Cass.

Zachary stares down at me, his face unreadable.

Without taking his eyes off of me, he tilts his head to the side and calls out, "Go get my things."

CHAPTER FIVE
ZACH

When I move forward, Trinity leans back like I'm gripping a blood-stained ax. I hold out one hand, then the other, showing her I'm in fact unarmed.

Fucking savages.

I knew this would happen. Which makes me a bigger idiot than they are. Luckily, those two queers were so busy fucking they probably wouldn't have noticed if Armageddon came and went. It's sad that I have to perpetuate the school's canon on homosexuality, but just like the fucked up car I'm forced to drive, some things are an intrinsic part of my persona. I can't break out of character yet.

Except here, in our nest.

I'd decided to cut my trip short after all. It's a blessing in disguise that Jasper and Perry agreed to sodomize each other down here—Miriam will be so caught up in giving them lashes that I'm sure she won't notice I'm back an hour early.

They gagged her again. I'm not surprised. In fact, I'd honestly expected her to be hogtied and deflowered already.

As soon as the gag is off, she scowls at me. "What's so fucking funny?"

I briefly close my eyes and let out the chuckle I'd been suppressing. "You should be thanking me," I tell her.

I try to help her up, but she shakes off my hand with a muttered curse. She stands, and then hurriedly tugs at something around her knees.

Her panties?

Jesus H. Christ.

I hold out my hand. "Give."

She looks like she might disobey, but then her shoulders sag and she hands over her underwear. I scan her as I untangle the fabric. For once, she's wearing something that fits, but that pale, clingy dress is like a red flag to a bull.

"Nice dress."

She doesn't look at me as she slips past to go out. "What, this old thing?" she mutters.

Underwear finally untangled, I go to fold it and stop.

It's soaked.

I turn a little, frowning after her as she disappears into the living area.

Why, I believe our little Trinity has a crush on us.

SHE'S SITTING stiff as a board in my chair, hands placed just so on her lap and her eyes down. But I can see her watching me through her lashes as I go to put her underwear in one of my tins. I had no intention of keeping it, but it will drive her mad knowing she'd left evidence of her presence down here.

Cass is gone. Probably hoping I'd cool off before he comes back with the things I bought in town.

"Twenty?" Apollo says. "That's a bit harsh, isn't it?"

"Second offense," Reuben says before I can open my mouth. "Should have gotten thirty."

"No one can stand thirty," Apollo says, sounding aghast. He flicks his head, tossing his hair from his face as he looks my way. "That Miriam's got a good arm."

"What is she doing here?" I ask them.

Trinity replies. "I'm here to talk."

I turn, my eyebrows quirking up before I can school them. "You came down here after I expressly told you not—?"

"We fetched her," Apollo says, sounding bored. I'm sure, without his camera, he's about to die. "Made sure no one saw. Right, Rube?"

"Right." Reuben stands. "Drink?"

"Double." My eyes are still on Trinity. "And for her too."

"I don't want—"

She cuts off when I shake my head, and drops her gaze back into her lap.

Such a pretty thing. Is that why Gabriel brought her here? I'd been thinking about it all of last night. Relocating Trinity to Saint Amos was a risky move for the Guardian. So risky, I'm still trying to figure out why he'd do it at all.

If he was in fact such a close family friend, then there's a strong possibility she might have seen him interacting with a Ghost from their church.

We're not a hundred percent sure how he chooses the Ghosts he works with. We assume they're all clergy members, but from a different diocese, or all from the same? I'd expect there would be nothing tying them together except Gabriel, and that he'd keep his distance.

Bringing a remnant from his previous life here, to Saint Amos, is not keeping his distance. Maybe he thinks he's safe now, after all these years. But he's never been reckless.

Until now.

Until Trinity.

But why risk everything...for *her*?

Unless his plans for her are short-term.

Because the only reason I can think Gabriel would bring Trinity here is because he knew she wouldn't be staying. So where is the poor orphan girl headed?

My thoughts go to the worst possible conclusion.

Trinity isn't here to finish out her senior year. She's here to meet someone very special. Perhaps a *few* somebodies.

My gut tells me Gabriel is planning on introducing her to her very own Ghosts.

CHAPTER SIX
ZACH

I sit in Apollo's armchair, and he sits beside Reuben. Trinity's barely touched her drink, but every time I make a point of looking in her direction, she does at least take another sip.

Gabriel's back tomorrow. There's nothing we can do—short of breaking down his door—to speed up this process. And if that had been a possibility, we'd have done it by now.

There's time to kill. I should be grateful for the diversion Trinity affords us.

Cass arrives with my things and sets down the bags alongside the back wall of the library. "Two cameras?" he asks a moment later.

"Couldn't make out your handwriting," I say, directing my voice at Cass, but staring at Apollo.

But he's so busy scrambling off the sofa, I don't think he even notices. I drop my eyes and let out a soft chuckle as I drain my whiskey.

It's taken us years, but we're finally starting to find joy in the little things.

"This is the one," he says, snatching the offending box from Cass's hands. "But I'll keep this as a spare." He tucks both boxes under his arms and looks about to leave.

"Sit down," I tell him, holding my glass out for Reuben.

He comes and takes it, but instead of going to refill, he stops beside

Trinity's chair, his back to me. "Finish," he says quietly, tapping a fingernail against her glass.

She cranes to look up at him, and slowly swallows down the rest of her glass.

Well, that's one mystery solved then. I shouldn't be surprised it's him that she fancies most. When Reuben looks at you, it's like you're the only person in the world.

I think that's what his Ghost liked most about him. It's one thing controlling a little kid who can't fight back, but controlling someone like Reuben? He'd always been stronger and bigger than the rest of us. Our rock.

That's the funny thing about erosion, though. It weathers mountains. Reuben's Ghost ground him to dust over the years. If we hadn't escaped when we had, there'd have been nothing left of him, just an empty shell.

But what will Trinity do when Reuben realizes he doesn't need to save her anymore? Because that's around about the time he loses interest in people.

"This all you could get?" Cass asks.

I don't have to look to know what he's talking about. My trips to town are like Christmas around here because I always come back bearing gifts. Cass's comes in a few dime bags that cost a fuck load more than a dime these days.

He opens the seal on one and takes a deep sniff. "Jaysus," he mutters, grimacing. "You tell him he has to cure his stuff longer than a fucking day?"

"I'm not getting into a debate with your dealer, Cass."

Trinity glances from Cass to me to Reuben to Apollo, her eyes flickering around like a nervous dragonfly.

"Did you know Jasper was gay?" I ask her.

I smile when she flinches at the sound of my voice and turns her wide, amber eyes on me. Rube brings me my drink and then hers. This time, she takes it without looking at him.

"No." She lifts a shoulder, sipping absently at her glass. "But some things make sense now."

"Like what?"

She takes a tiny sip of her drink. "Perry told me Jasper hated girls."

Cass snorts as he moves over to the sofa. He sinks down, nudging Apollo aside with his elbow. Apollo's so busy starting up his new video camera and going through the settings, he doesn't even seem to notice.

I tap a fresh cigarette from my pack and light it, standing to a crouch to hand it over to Reuben. All while Trinity tracks me with that dragonfly gaze.

The lacy bodice of her dress keeps catching my eye. Not because of the perky tits they barely cover, but because I keep wondering why she wore it. For someone who doesn't seem comfortable in her own skin, exposing so much of it must have taken courage. Courage I didn't think she had.

Does she think we'll start salivating over her to the point where we let slip something important?

I look away when Reuben hands back my cigarette.

My paranoia knows no bounds. And although I'm fully aware of how fucked up my mind is, I can't stop these intrusive thoughts any more than I can stop breathing.

Something else I was considering last night as I lay sleepless in bed. What if Gabriel brought her here because he knew his time was short? What if he suspects—or *knows*—who we really are? What if, this entire time, he's been tracking us as carefully as we've tracked him?

There's nothing in this nest of ours that would give away our true identities, but the mere fact that we know each other, that we've kept in contact...

Paranoia.

We barely resemble the kids we once were. There's a box of hair dye in one of the bags. Colored contacts in another. Cass's Ghosts loved his long hair, so it was the first thing he did when we escaped—shaving his head. We're no longer grimy, malnourished, basement-pale boys full of bruises and sores.

Still, from the day I arrived here and shook Gabriel's hand, I couldn't get rid of the feeling that he'd stared at me just a second too long.

Like he'd recognized me.

She could be telling the truth.

Or she could be a spy. He could have brought her here to infiltrate us, spread dissent, find out how much we know.

My fucked up mind is dead set on the latter.

CHAPTER SEVEN
TRINITY

Alcohol seems pretty good at calming my nerves. I'd been shaking when Zachary arrived, but not anymore. I guess it's also because I only have Zachary and Reuben's attention on me at the moment. Cassius is rolling more weed, and Apollo hasn't looked up from his camera yet.

Zachary doesn't speak again until Cass is done and the weed has passed around a few times. I don't bother refusing. I've never smoked before—weed or cigarettes—but I can understand why people do it. Once my lungs grow used to the hot smoke, the sensation is utterly delicious.

"This tastes different," I say, and instantly wish I'd kept my mouth shut.

You're not here to make friends, Trinity. You're here to figure out how the hell you're going to get yourself out of this mess.

"That's because it's absolute shit," Cass says. He quickly lifts a hand, palm out to Zachary. "Not that I'm complaining. I'd take ditch weed over no weed any day."

"Damn right you will," Zachary mutters, sounding more playful than serious.

His armchair is at an angle to mine, so I have to turn my head to look at him. I risk a quick peek now, trying to see his expression.

He's staring at me.

I quickly face forward, blushing.

"Give me my seat back," he says through a sigh. I bolt up off his seat, standing idle in the middle of their ill assortment of chairs and sofas like I'm showing off a new fashion line, before my brain starts working again. I sink into the armchair he'd been sitting in, squirming on the warm leather. Zachary takes my chair and spins it around on one leg, straddling it and laying his arms across the back before resting his chin on them.

It's the most relaxed I've ever seen him, but he still looks ready to pounce.

"You'd make a shitty poker player," Cass says.

"No I wouldn't," I snap back, hurriedly looking away from Zachary.

"Yeah, you would." Cass sits forward, ducking his head as if he's trying to imprint his statement on me. "Your face is an open book. Large print edition."

This makes Apollo and Reuben laugh, and puts a scowl on my face. Which I quickly smooth away.

Shit. I guess subterfuge isn't on the menu until I'm sober again.

Idiot.

I shouldn't have smoked or let Reuben bully me into downing my drink. Why do I feel like I have something to prove to these guys?

Everyone's attention is on me again. So I try and move it away. "You never told me your story," I say to Zachary.

Just his eyes move. "My *story*?"

"You and Reuben." I wave a limp hand. "The basement? How'd you end up there?"

Everyone stops moving. Even Apollo, who I'd thought wasn't listening.

Cass sits back and crosses his arms over his chest as he lets out a low whistle. "Presumptuous little slut, aren't you?"

My cheeks heat up again, but I force myself not to look at him. I keep my eyes on Zachary as he stares deadpan back at me. He takes a deep breath, and lets it out as a soft sigh before pushing away and straightening in his seat. "Our story," he repeats quietly, looking down as he smooths his jeans over his legs. "Our *story* is none of your fucking business, little girl."

My chest closes up, squeezing my heart like a fist.

"I just—"

"Gabriel will be back tomorrow," he cuts in. "How about you start focusing on that instead of sticking that pretty nose where it doesn't belong?" He stands without waiting for my reply.

I drop my head, willing myself to disappear into the armchair. I hadn't meant to be nosy. I just want to understand what I'm dealing with. I get that it's probably a horrible subject for them, but Apollo and Cass had told me theirs without biting my head off.

Maybe that's why *they* spoke up yesterday, and not Reuben and Zachary.

Holy shit...what did Zachary and Reuben go through?

I hug myself and risk peeking at Reuben through my lashes. He has a hand flat on his chest, his eyes boring into me. I hurriedly look away and on instinct reach for the rosary around my neck.

Then I freeze and look back at him.

His rosary. I've had it this whole time. Should I—?

"Keep it. I bought him another one," Zachary says.

I jump at the sound of his voice.

Dear Lord. Whatever nerves I had, they're shot again. Keeping cool around these guys is impossible. It's like trying to keep an eye on four moving targets. I'll just have to get used to the fact that they'll always have an advantage over me.

Strength in numbers, I guess.

I drop the rosary I'd been about to pull over my head.

Zachary hands a slim case to Reuben, and he stares at it for a few seconds before opening it. He lifts out a dull black rosary and slips it over his head. Then he tucks it away under his t-shirt.

They're all in casual clothes today.

Zachary is wearing a button-up shirt, pale blue, and jeans that look like he bought them at a thrift store. In fact, all the guys look like they got their clothes from the Salvation Army.

I'm assuming it's on purpose, seeing as Zachary just bought a brand-new laptop. Then there're the two video cameras...

Either he's rich, or he has a ton of credit card debt. I guess if you're planning on offing someone, you wouldn't really care about your finances.

"Do that later. I need you to set this up." Zachary leans across and hands Apollo the laptop.

Apollo flicks his hair out his eyes as he looks up at Zachary, and then gives a grim nod.

Zachary takes out a much smaller box and goes back to his seat. He toys with it as he watches Apollo remove the laptop's packaging and start it up.

I tip my glass against my lips and look down in surprise. It's empty. I hurriedly wrap my fingers around it, trying to hide the fact, but I'm too slow.

Reuben gets to his feet.

"In a bit," Zachary says as if he's reading Reuben's mind. "We need her to focus."

My throat moves as I swallow. With Zachary handing things out to the guys, there'd been an almost festive air inside this strange lair. For a moment, I'd forgotten where I was. Who I was with.

These are not normal people, Trinity. Your life is the furthest thing from ordinary right now.

I drop my head and snort quietly to myself. Like I'd ever had a claim to being normal.

"Gabriel has a laptop," Reuben says.

I start fidgeting with my glass. "Okay."

"It's hidden somewhere in his room."

I nod and glance at the other boys. Cass is smoking what's left of the weed, leaning an elbow on the armchair and slouching like he's waiting for his photoshoot to begin. He's wearing a white t-shirt made of flimsy fabric that drapes his body like silk. If it weren't for the hole in it, I'd have thought it was an expensive designer piece. But the hole is big and ugly—it definitely didn't ship like that.

Apollo's still busy with the laptop. His long fingers fly over the keyboard, his shoulders hunched and his hair hiding his face.

Zachary toys with the box while his eyes search me.

"So you want me to steal it?" I ask, when it seems Reuben's done talking.

"Of course not," Zachary says through an impatient sigh. "We need you to clone the hard drive."

I frown at him. "I don't know how—"

"It's easy," Apollo says without looking up. "Zach will give you the drive. You just plug it into a USB slot and it'll do the rest."

I nod, my eyes going to the box Zachary has. I'm not going to ask what a USB drive is—I'm hoping it will be one of those self-explanatory types of things.

"How am I supposed to sneak that into his room?" But then I hold up a hand, briefly closing my eyes. "How am I even supposed to *get* into his room?"

Zachary gives me half a smile. "You're a bright girl," he says, his smile turning sarcastic. "I'm sure you'll figure something out."

I clench my jaw as I tap a finger against my glass. "Why do you need me? Couldn't one of you just—?"

"You're so convinced he's a saint," Zachary says. "Time to prove it." He tosses the box to me.

I fumble it before opening it up and taking out a thin device barely longer than my thumb. "So I just plug this in," I mumble, turning it over in my hands. "After I sneak into his room and track down his hidden laptop."

"You have until Wednesday."

I look up at Zachary. "Why Wednesday?"

His smile is anything but merry. "Because by then, I would have lost my patience with you."

CHAPTER EIGHT
ZACH

Trinity gets up to leave. I scan her body as she does, and she folds in on herself like an origami swan. "Where do you think you're going?" I ask lightly, shaking out another cigarette.

"I have the thing," she says, holding up the thumb drive. "I know what do to. Surely I can..." She trails off before glancing at the exit.

"Leave?" I finish for her, getting slowly to my feet as I drag at the cigarette. "Now why would we let you do that?"

Her mouth opens, but she says nothing. Instead she grabs the blood-red crucifix around her neck.

Reuben would have preferred to have his rosary back but he needs to learn to let go of things. The crucifix is a start. A *good* start. I could never get him to abandon it. But all it took was a desperate soul and he handed it over like it was nothing.

Although I suppose he expected to get it back.

We all have to learn some hard lessons if we're to piece together the remnants of ourselves. Reuben has to understand that his past isn't encompassed in that cheap trinket.

We're his past.

Trinity flinches when I grab her wrist.

I drag my eyes down her body again. She looks up and meets my eyes, but there's uneasiness in those amber irises. "I think you should dance for us," I tell her.

"W-what?" she splutters out, her mouth lifting into an incredulous smile. "No."

"Fucking *fantastic* idea," Cass says.

"I can't dance," she says through a laugh. "And even if I could..." Her eyes dart around before she puts her hands on her hips and tries to look casual. "There's no music."

"You don't need music," I say, drawing her closer.

She steps back hurriedly, pulling her wrist free and letting out a huff. "I'm not dancing." Her eyes flicker over my brothers. Then they flash back to me and narrow. "Not unless I get something in return."

Cass whistles through his teeth. Apollo even stops messing around with the laptop long enough to look up at her with wide eyes and a slack mouth. Reuben snorts and rubs his jaw like he's trying to hide his faint smile.

I tilt my head at her. "Do you really think you're in a position to bargain with us?"

"Hang on," Cassius says through a chuckle. "Let's hear her out. What's your offer, Trin?"

She replies without taking her eyes off me. "I want to know how you factor into all of this," she says. An absent wave of her hand takes in my brothers, then the packages against the wall. "You're older than them. And a teacher, which means you've studied at college, right?" She steps close, until the rose-scented wood of her rosary beads tickles my nose. "And you're rich. So how did you wind up in that basement? How did you become a part of this?"

My eyes narrow. She gasps when I grab her jaw and squeeze dimples into her soft flesh. That sound ripples through me like a stone tossed into a pond. My cock starts paying attention for the first time today. I want to force her to her knees and make her swallow every rock-hard inch of me until she passes out from lack of oxygen.

I resort to fisting her hair instead, keeping her head in place. Fear turns her amber eyes a sullen bronze.

"For a dance from someone who can't even dance?" I sneer at her. "I don't think so."

There's utter silence from my brothers. Are they holding their breaths like she is?

I force a smile. "How about you dance, and I'll consider *not* giving you five lashes for being such a presumptuous little slut?"

Cass snickers at the fact that I'm using his words, but I ignore him. Trinity is all I'm interested in right now.

She would be pissing herself if she knew how deadly it was to attract my full attention.

Her face pales. "Lashes? Just for asking—?"

"Six."

Her lips begin to tremble.

I shrug, tilting her head back another inch as I close the distance between us. "We could demand worse things from you," I murmur. My hard-on presses into her stomach, and her eyes flare wide. She tries to arch away from me, but I release her jaw and press my hand into the small of her back. "Dirty, *sick* things." I grind into her even harder.

She shudders against me.

"Fine," she says through her teeth. "One dance."

My eyes fall to her lips. When she licks them, I almost kiss her just to taste her mouth.

Instead, I push her away and drag at my cigarette as I sink back into my seat. Then I click my fingers at her and again at the spot between us.

"Get to it then."

She moves to the center of the room, and hesitates before looking over at Reuben. "Can I have another drink?"

Reuben doesn't bother confirming with me first. Now that our business is done, I'm not anyone's boss anymore.

We agreed a long time ago that we couldn't all lead the charge and drew straws to determine our hierarchy.

Just because I drew the short straw doesn't mean I dominate them twenty-four-seven. By now I know when to step back and let them have their fun.

Our blessed Keepers knew that too.

It was their responsibility to feed us, shelter us, keep us hidden. And, most importantly, to make sure we didn't escape.

Keeping us tied up all the time damaged our young bodies.

Bruises became welts.

Welts turned into sores.

I still have kinks in both my ankles where the constant ligature of a too-tight rope altered my bone structure.

They were also instructed to keep our spirits up. Most of our Ghosts liked it when we fought back. But you stop fighting when you lose hope and our Keepers eventually figured that out.

So they made sure there was always a sliver of hope. Just enough to cling onto until our Ghosts' next visit.

Once a day while we ate, they'd let us out of our bonds. In that hour we'd search every inch of our cage, just in case a Ghost had dropped something, or we'd missed something the thousand previous times we'd searched.

Apollo found a rosary one day. Reuben recognized it as the one his Ghost would wear. We drew straws to see who would keep it.

Rube lost.

Trinity folds her hands in front of her as she waits, making an obvious effort not to look at any of us. Which is probably a good thing, because even Apollo's put away his toys to watch. And if she can't feel Cass's hungry gaze already peeling off that flimsy layer of fabric...

She takes the tumbler from Reuben and downs it in a rush. Her face scrunches up as she fights not to cough. She nods at him and hands back the glass.

"No music," she says softly, as if to herself.

"You're boring us," I tell her, my chair creaking as I shift my weight.

She throws me a panicked look and quickly starts swaying her hips.

"Slower, little girl."

I love the way her eyes flare when I call her that. But as if she picks up on the fact, she smooths her expression and instead closes her eyes.

A minute later, I bark out, "Enough."

She stops, her eyes fluttering open as she whirls to face me. "What?"

"You're terrible," I tell her, shaking my head. "Cass, give me your belt."

Her eyes go wide. She holds up her arms, one palm facing me and the other to Cass as he stands and starts taking off his belt. "No. No! I can do better. I just have to—"

"Here, I'll show you," Reuben says.

My lips quirk up. God, he certainly took long enough. He's a clever fucker, but he's so damn cautious you'd think he was simple.

I light another cigarette. Cass lights a joint. We pass them to each other as Rube gets up. Trinity takes a hurried step back when he looms over her, but then he grabs the back of her neck and hauls her back.

He slides his hand down her shoulder, her arm, and over to her hip. Then he takes her waist in both hands and swivels her hips in a figure eight.

"Loosen up," he grumbles in his deep voice.

"I'm trying," she mutters back, staring up at him like she's wondering when he plans on snapping her neck.

"Close your eyes, if it helps," he suggests calmly. "Pretend I'm one of those boy band idiots you girls are always crushing on."

I'm smiling full out now, and it has nothing to do with the whiskey-and-weed concoction wreaking havoc on my brain.

Reuben and Cass were the only two of us that had something resembling a normal childhood after we escaped the Ghost House. I'd fought to keep us together, but we were all from different states. Rube and Cass went to foster homes in West Virginia and Georgia, Apollo back to North Carolina, and I stayed behind in Virginia.

It took years for me to find them again.

Reuben ended up in a foster home with three other girls, which we'll never let him live down, especially seeing as he never fucked any of them. Although I doubt it ever crossed his mind. He became their big brother, and that's the persona he stuck with. And he did such a good job, that foster family almost ended up adopting him.

It was practically a done deal until something triggered an episode of psychosis. He destroyed that family's home and badly injured two of his foster sisters before the police arrived to restrain him. He landed in juvie for a year before being spat back into the foster system. Months went by before I could track him down. A lot of money exchanged hands before I finally got him relocated to Saint Amos.

Times like that, I honestly wished I'd had parents I could turn to. Having legal guardians to sign off on legit paperwork would have been so much easier than all the palm-greasing I did. But my parents were long dead, and after we escaped from the Ghost House, I no longer trusted *anyone* except my brothers.

Luckily, money can buy just about anything.

"Good," Reuben says. "Now your shoulders. You have to dance with your whole body."

"It's really hard without music."

"You don't need music," Rube says.

On cue, I tap my thumb against the back of the seat.

Thud.

Thud.

Thud.

Rube glances up at me, and gives me a ghostly smile. "All you need is a rhythm."

Cass and Apollo pick up the beat, Apollo with one of his rings against his glass, Cass tapping the back of the tin he keeps his weed in.

And Trinity starts to dance.

Her hips sway, and her shoulders undulate to the slow, steady beat we create.

"That's it," Rube murmurs. His head hangs low, his lips brushing the top of her head. "Do you feel it?"

I expect Cass to make a snide comment—he's got a fifth-grader's sense of humor—but when I look over at them all I see is a most familiar hunger.

That's how our Ghosts would look at us, a sinister voice hisses.

My jaw clenches.

No. This isn't the same. That was a sick, contaminated lust. This is pure and natural.

That's what he said about us. That's what we were.

Pure. Innocent. We were the cure for our Ghost's perversions. Our lot in life was to ease their suffering—a sacrificial offering to appease their depraved hedonism.

And they accepted us time and time again.

I falter on the beat, but Cass and Apollo don't even notice. Taking my cigarette with me, I stalk into the bedroom.

There the darkness swallows me, shields me, comforts me.

But my respite is brief and bittersweet.

That's what she is. Pure. Innocent. Is she our cure?

I try to block the voice, but clapping my hands over my ears does nothing.

You know what you have to do, don't you? To her, to them.

I go to the back of the room and lift up the corner of a mattress.

Killing Gabriel won't make the pain go away, Mason.

Not for you, not for them, not for her.

When I don't find what I'm looking for, I clamp my lips over the filter of my cigarette and shove both hands into that cool dark as smoke burns my eyes.

"Looking for something?" Cass asks, sinuous as a fucking serpent.

I rock back on my heels and snatch my cigarette from between dry lips. "Where is it?" I grate out.

"If I can't have my smack, then you can't have your—"

I spin around and grab him by the throat, pressing him into the solid wall. He chokes, and then chuckles into my face. "That shit's unhygienic as fuck," he says hoarsely.

"Where. Is. It?"

"You don't scare me, Boss. Never have, never will."

I can barely see anything in the dark, but there's a glimmer of light where his eyes are.

I bring my cigarette up, instantly mesmerized by the red glow on his wet corneas. He blinks, but he doesn't close his eyes.

"She's messing with all of our heads," Cass whispers. "Let's get her out of here. We don't need her."

"*You* need her," I counter, bringing that glowing ember closer to his eye. His cheek lights up faintly but he doesn't even bat a fucking eyelid.

"Do we?" He shrugs and lays his hand casually over the stiff arm pinning him against the wall. "I thought we didn't need anyone."

"Just tell me where it is," I say through my teeth. I hate how my voice shakes, but I'm past the point of being able to control it.

"That shit's like slapping a fucking Hello Kitty band-aid on a gunshot wound," he says. His voice drops low. "Come on, Zach."

He's right, and that makes me feel even more pathetic for allowing myself to be caught between shame and guilt and utter desperation. "I just need—"

"I *know* what you need," Cass cuts in quietly. "And I told you before, all you gotta do is ask."

His hand slips off my arm. Fabric rustles. Then he grabs hold of the hand holding my glowing cigarette. "Just not the face, bro. That's my moneymaker."

I clamp down on a near-hysterical bark of a laugh as I let him guide my hand down.

"We should try for a smiley face. Nirvana style. What do you say?" His voice is tight, light, steady.

I don't know how the fuck he so easily accepts my breakdowns.

"Fuck," I grate, squeezing my eyes shut so I can't see that tempting glowing ash. "Cass, no."

"Come on, you pussy. I've had worse."

"Fuck off."

"Jesus, the tension's killing me," he says through a grin I can hear but not see.

So fucking easy for him. For them. I should never have drawn the short straw. Rube would have made a better leader than me any day. Any of them would have. But it was me. So I had to man-up and fucking lead them.

"You know it's the worst part, right? The waiting? You fucking know it, Zach. So just do it, you cunt."

He guides my hand lower and closer, until my knuckles graze his bare skin where he's hiking up his shirt. I trail his skin with the pad of my thumb. My chest is so tight I can barely breathe, and what little air does come in feels like I'm sucking it from a fucking chimney.

Hot. Full of ash.

"Fuck," I say again, trying to ignore the erection straining against my jeans. Pain and pleasure—I've never had one without the other.

"Cass—"

"Just fucking do it," he grates.

My thumb skims over a puckered burn mark. Then another. Another.

"There." He sounds as breathless as I feel. "Right there."

"Christ."

My lungs fill with powdered brimstone as I press the tip of the cigarette into his flesh.

He stiffens, letting out a short, soft gasp. Then he shoves me so hard I fall back and land on my ass. I'm anticipating the boot heading for my stomach, but that just makes the impact ten times worse.

My breath rushes out in a pained grunt I can't possibly keep quiet. I roll onto my side, curling up as he kicks me again. Then he's gone, orange light blooming against the back of my eyelids before the room goes dark again.

I open my fingers and let the crumpled cigarette fall out. Then I bring my hand close and lick off the streak of ash smeared over my palm.

The almost constant ache in my wrists and ankles fades away as I lie there listening to Apollo tapping out a beat for Trinity as she dances for Reuben.

Tap. Tap. Tap.

Sounds like the leaking pipe in the back of the basement, doesn't it, Mason?

The pain makes it easier to push away the voice.

And that's always been the case, even back then.

Tap.

Tap.

Tap.

CHAPTER NINE
TRINITY

I t has to be the weed. Or the booze. *Something's* doing weird, weird shit to my brain. That bit in a Disney movie where a magical light zooms around the heroine and lifts her up? That's me right now. It feels like I'm suspended inches from the floor, a glittering aura whirling around me.

In my wildest dreams I would never have imagined anything could feel this good. This...right.

Reuben's got one hand around the back of my neck, the other at the small of my back. Using his hands and body, he guides me.

Moments later, faint noises in the background clamor for my attention but they sound wrong and violent so I push them out of my mind.

This...this is the complete opposite.

"See?" Reuben murmurs into my ear. "And you thought you couldn't do it."

I wasn't about to tell him I'd danced before. A *lot*. My mirror had been my only audience, and my worst critic. For all I know, I probably looked a right idiot back then as I swayed to my own quiet humming.

I'd really hoped to use my feminine wiles to strike a deal with these men, but I guess I still have a lot to learn about the art of seduction.

Also, dancing for an actual audience is much harder than watching yourself in a mirror. So much so, I hadn't even known where to start.

Reuben saved me.

This whole time I'd had my hands at my side, limply moving along with my arms. But as soon as Reuben's breath brushes my skin, I suck in a breath and force myself to reach out and touch him.

My fingers trace the outlines of his perfectly sculpted muscles. I tilt my head back and open my eyes. They flutter and then go wide in surprise.

Reuben's glaring at me.

He stops moving, and snatches my wrists together in one meaty hand. "What are you doing?" he demands in a low voice.

"I was just...I thought we were..."

Movement draws my gaze away.

Cass storms out of the curtained area of the room, a hand on his stomach like he's sick. The snarl on his face sends a chill through me, but as soon as he looks up and sees me, it disappears.

My mouth opens to ask him what's wrong, but by then everything's moving too fast.

"Enough of this bullshit foreplay," he grates out, whipping his hand away from his stomach. He points straight at me and advances so fast that I wheel back from him with a stifled yell.

He grabs my arm before I have a chance to get away, and throws me into the armchair I'd been sitting in.

I gasp—more in shock at how fucking strong he is than in actual pain. Then he's on top of me, straddling my waist and yanking my dress up my legs.

Cool air caresses my upper thighs as he hikes my skirt up my hips. Since my panties are still in Zachary's tin box, there's nothing to shield me from the dark lust gleaming in his eyes.

"Stop!" I yell. I start bashing at him with my fists, but he knocks my arms away with a flick of his hand, the other going to his belt.

"Keep singing that pretty song, little blackbird."

The hair on my arms stands up straight. His voice is low, rough, and has an English accent, like he's mimicking someone.

What. The. *Fuck?*

The button on his jeans pops open with a twist of his hand.

I scream, my fists turning into claws. He grimaces, now straining to keep back my attack while working his fly. I buck my hips to try and shake him off, but that just makes him laugh.

Why is no one stopping him?

Mother of God—are they just going to watch?

I obviously put up too much of a fight. Cass grabs my hair, wrenches back my head, and slaps me.

A shock wave coruscates through my skull. My vision swims with tears. My face goes numb. I blink hard, sending those tears down my cheeks.

I watch in dumbstruck silence as Reuben rips Cass off my lap and throws him against the wall like he weighs nothing. Zachary appears by the curtain, but his head hangs low, and there's a strange set to his mouth.

My Disney movie has just turned into a horror show.

Reuben's got Cass against the wall, his arm pressed to his throat. Cass's face reddens, but he doesn't fight back.

He's fucking *grinning* at Reuben.

Reuben's muscles bulge beneath his shirt as he uses his arm to shove Cass a couple of inches up the wall.

But there aren't any blows exchanged. He's just restraining him. Zachary lumbers over and tries to pull Reuben off. Reuben doesn't even shift.

A cool hand slips around my wrist and tugs. My neck feels stiff as I turn to look at Apollo. I'm dimly aware that I'm exposed, but my hand's shaking too much for me to successfully pull down the hem of my dress.

"Let's go someplace else, yeah?" Apollo says, smiling so calmly you'd swear he hasn't noticed someone was about to get murdered. "Come on. I wanna show you something."

When I don't move, he dips his head a bit and then presses a quick peck to my slap-stained cheek. "There. All better now."

Again he tugs at my wrist.

Somehow I stand.

He leads me out of the lair just as I hear the thump of flesh on flesh and hear Cass groan in pain.

What. The. Fuck?

BRIGHT SUNLIGHT BATHES my face when we leave the crypt. Apollo hangs back at the doorway, his hair shifting as he checks left and right.

There's no one in sight, but he still seems hesitant to leave the shadows and step into the light.

Vampire.

I laugh at the ridiculous thought, and Apollo throws a concerned look at me over his shoulder as he starts toward the dormitory.

"Okay there, pretty thing?"

I giggle at him.

"Sorry...it got a bit rough in there," he says. We're walking at a brisk pace, his fingers handcuffed around my wrist. "They'll calm down. A few punches and they always do. Like Fight Club, right? And shit, how was that cinematography? Did you know Cronenweth deliberately underexposed the actors' faces to force the audience to pay more attention in each shot?"

I say nothing, instead willing the world to stop bobbing up and down so hectically. I couldn't have had more to drink than yesterday, but yesterday I'd had a good long nap before I'd attempted to walk anywhere.

Now I feel like everything I've consumed today has only just kicked in. I feel like I'm walking on a trampoline an inch off the ground. And every time I shift my eyes even a little, the world blurs.

"I'm drunk," I announce.

"That's the spirit," Apollo replies without slowing. "Nice day for it, too."

I finally find it in me to pull back. "No. I mean...*really* drunk." I sway as soon as we come to a halt, and he steps forward to steady me by slinging an arm around my waist.

"Easy there," he says and then starts walking again. "There's nothing to it, see? You just keep your eyes on something that's not moving. Like the bell tower. Can you see it?"

My head tilts back.

Fuck, that's a big building.

"Yeah."

"Good. Just keep looking at that. I'll make sure you don't step on any snakes."

"Snakes?" My head bobs forward, and I stumble as the world takes a slow somersault. "Fuck."

"Sorry, bad joke. No snakes. *Holes.* That's what I'll keep an eye out for. Just holes."

"Holes," I agree, tilting my head back again. "Who rings the bell?"

"Not a hunchback, that's for sure."

I giggle like a fucking idiot at that. Cool shadows replace the sun, and I sag in relief. "Made it."

"Not yet, pretty thing. Should I carry you?"

I snort. "You can't carry me."

"Bitchy much?"

The world spins around me. I'm looking up Apollo's face, his victorious grin partially hidden behind a few locks of hair.

"You jus' call me a bitch?" I demand.

"Keep your voice down," he says. "And yes. Because you're being one."

I snort again. "You're a...you're an asshole. You all are."

"Quiet," he warns in a low voice, his hair shifting as he glances left and right. My teeth click together as he starts up the staircase. "Or I'll take you back to your room."

I hesitate, my head bobbing against the crook of Apollo's arm as he hurries up the stairs with me. My room? Jasper might be there? I grimace. I'm too drunk to deal with him. Or not drunk enough.

"Here," Apollo says. He sets me down and props me against the wall like a broom as he fishes in his pockets. He takes out a bunch of keys. The keychain used to be a furry cat face. Now it's grubby as fuck. While he looks for the right key, I start to slide down the wall. He props me back up with an absent tug on the shoulder of my dress and then herds me inside the room.

"Hey! I've been here before!" I head for the closest chair.

"Sure have."

When I sit down, I see he's leaving. "Hey, where are you going?"

He pauses at the door, turning to me. But then he closes the door without answering.

And locks it.

I sit up a little straighter and stay conscious, remember that I'm too drunk to give a shit, and pass out on the couch.

CHAPTER TEN
ZACH

My jaw pulses, the heat emanating from within a stark contrast to the ice pack pressed against my bruised flesh.

"Shit, man. We can't let anyone see you like this," Apollo says.

"No fucking shit," I snap, squinting over at him. I click my fingers at the tumbler he's supposed to be filling for me, and he hesitates only a second before filling it with whiskey.

"Is this going to mess with the plan?"

"I don't know, Apollo," I tell him through gritted teeth. "How about you ask Cass the next time you see him?"

"Man, you can't blame him for this."

I slam my fist into the arm of my wooden chair. "The fuck I can't."

"Here." Apollo hurries over with my glass. I drain it and hand it back.

"Just give me the fucking bottle."

"Yeah, right," he laughs, skipping back and snatching the bottle away like he honestly thought I was in any state to tackle him for it.

Besides the two solid kicks Cass got in earlier, he punched me in the jaw, the groin, and my fucking kidneys. *Twice.* Because by that time, Reuben had hurried off to check if Trinity was okay, not giving a fuck who survived the fight.

Cass has always been like a fucking rat in a corner. You wouldn't think he was even capable of throwing a punch, and then you're lying on your back wondering why the stars had come out in the middle of the fucking day.

All because I'd held back.

Because I'd thought Trinity was still in the room.

Watching. *Judging.*

I thump the wood again, wishing the arm would break and growling when it doesn't.

"She's done." I shake my head and point at Apollo as I breathe through a wave of pain. "Too much fucking trouble. Tomorrow, you take my car, you throw her in the trunk, and you fucking—"

"What, Zach?" Apollo cuts in with a snort, shaking his head at me. "We tell Gabriel his girl child wandered into the woods and got *et* by bears?" His lips twitch and he smooths his fingers over his mouth as if he could wash away his words.

A dark smile slowly spreads over my face. "I knew you weren't just a pretty face."

CHAPTER ELEVEN
TRINITY

I wake up to the sound of muffled voices and intense nausea. Pushing up to my elbows, I scan my dark surroundings to try and figure out where I am. This can't be my room. There are too few lumps in the mattress. The sheets are too soft. And it smells like Reuben, not mothballs.

Reuben.

Shit, I'm in his room. His *bed*room.

And I need to puke.

I slide off the bed onto wobbly legs. The room is so dark that I hit my knee against the side of the bed as I head for the glowing outline of the door.

It opens before I can reach it. Reuben's silhouette blocks out almost all the light.

"Bathroom," I say in a tight voice.

He grabs my shoulder and herds me out of the room. Everything's a blur until I reach the bathroom, where all I can focus on is the toilet.

Thank God he opens the lid for me, because I barely bend over before I puke.

Fingers brush my temples, drawing my hair away from my face. A large, cool hand caresses the back of my neck as I puke out my guts, stomach lining, and a lung.

I finally rock back on my heels. Reuben's holding out a washcloth for me.

Deliciously warm.

I wipe my face with it and stand on shaky legs. He points to the basin. There's a bottle of mouthwash there, the sink already filling with more warm water.

"We'll be outside," he says, turning to the doorway.

Apollo moves aside as Reuben approaches.

I clean myself and the bathroom as well as I can and try to ignore the fact that I still feel tipsy. When I step into the living area of Reuben's room, the smell of coffee hits my nose.

I still can't believe seniors get an accommodation like this if their grades are good enough. I guess Father Gabriel really wants me to work my way up from the bottom.

Apollo brings me a cup. "Cream and two sugars."

I can't help but smile. It's sweet that he still remembers how I take it, although the day he saw me putting in sugar I'd given myself a double dose.

Hell, I probably *still* need the energy. Maybe this will become my regular serving from now on.

"What time is it?" I ask, glancing around. The lights are on and the curtains are drawn, but it doesn't feel like it's night time yet.

"Five," Reuben says. He's sitting on one of the two couches that make up his living area. "Come sit."

His quiet command makes my hackles rise. I glance at Apollo with raised brows, but he just gives me his usual lopsided smile. "We need to talk," he says. Then he goes and fetches another two cups of coffee, handing one to Reuben before sitting down beside him.

Thank God. I'm not sure if I would dare to sit beside any of them after what happened in the library. My chest goes tight just thinking about what Cass had tried to do.

Suddenly the coffee doesn't taste as nice.

I sit on the fabric couch and hurriedly tug down my dress when it inches up my leg.

"Cold?" Reuben asks, already standing before I can answer. He disappears into his room and comes back with a wool blanket that he hands to me without a word.

I throw it over my lap and give him a grateful nod.

"Zach wants to get rid of you," Apollo says.

My sip of coffee goes down the wrong way. I cough and almost tip the entire cup over me. Thankfully it only spills on the blanket, else it would have burned me through my dress. I quickly put the mug down on the coffee table. "Excuse me?"

"You're causing disruption," Reuben says.

"Disruption?" Great, now I've turned into a parrot.

Apollo waves a hand. "Don't worry, we talked him out of it. But shit's still a bit tense right now."

Really? I thought Cass trying to fuck me on the armchair was a normal day for these guys.

I pick up my coffee again. It's instant, but it's warm and sweet and I need all of that right now.

"You should keep out of his way until you've cloned that hard drive," Apollo says before taking a noisy slurp from his cup.

"Zachary's my Psych teacher," I say dryly. "I have a class with him."

"Then get it done tomorrow."

I sit forward, frowning hard at Apollo. "How the hell—?"

"It's for your own safety, Trinity," Reuben says. "If Zachary says you have to disappear then—"

"Then the three of you will do what he says like the good little soldiers you are, right?" Of course I regret the words the moment they leave my lips, but I blame the headache and the lingering taste of bile in my mouth.

Oh, and don't forget the scratch marks Cass left on my inner thighs. I don't have to peek under my skirt to know they're there. I can feel them throbbing in time to my headache.

Reuben drops his head and lets out a heavy sigh. A humorless laugh huffs from Apollo, disturbing the surface of his coffee as he brings it up for another sip.

"How will you do it, huh? Mince me up into burger meat? Hit me over the head and bury me in a shallow grave there in the cemetery?"

Apollo purses his lips. "Hadn't thought of that." He shakes a finger at me. "That's a good one."

I glare at him. "You *can't* get rid of me. Gabriel will find out, and he'll start looking around. He'll find you—all of you—and then..."

I don't know what happens then, but I know they've been trying to avoid it for years so it's as good a threat as any.

Apollo stands and heads for the kitchenette. There're a microwave and a kettle and a few odds and ends on the counter. He brings back the device Zachary had been toying with earlier and holds it out to me.

"Do it tomorrow, soon as Gabriel's back."

"Yeah, I'll just invite myself to his room, ask him where his super-secret computer is, and copy everything while he pours me a drink or something," I mutter sourly as I snatch the box from Apollo. "Great plan, guys."

"It'll take like five minutes to copy. This shit's high tech," Apollo says as he sinks back into the seat beside Reuben. "And we'll help you."

"How?" I sip at my coffee as he and Reuben share a look.

"We'll create a diversion," Apollo says. "You get yourself into Gabriel's room, we'll do the rest."

I open the box and take out the device before weighing it on my palm. "How am I supposed to sneak this in?"

Reuben lets out a long-suffering sigh and gets up, putting down his mug as he passes the coffee table en route to me. "Give," he says, holding out his hand.

I pass over the device.

"Sit forward."

I do as he says, but with a frown for Apollo. He just shrugs, quirking an eyebrow at me as if he has no idea what Reuben's doing.

Reuben crouches in front of me, one of his knees clicking. He pulls down the bodice of my dress and slips the device between my breasts. Then he uses his thumb to smooth the fabric over my breastbone.

I look down. And then up at him.

"If he's the saintly priest you say he is, then he won't be staring hard enough at your tits to notice it," Reuben says.

"I can't wear this dress around Father Gabriel." Just the thought makes my cheeks heat up. Which is weird, because Reuben's touch hadn't.

"He's not going to find it." Reuben stands, putting his crotch directly at eye level. I hurriedly sit back and bury my face in my mug as I take a sip.

"Why are you helping me?" I ask quietly, glancing between them. "Why not just get rid of me like Zachary wants?"

At this, they share another look. Apollo drops his head, avoiding eye contact. Reuben doesn't say anything.

"Why?" I ask. "Tell me."

"Because we're all coming undone," Reuben says.

"And as much as Zachary likes to think getting rid of you will help, it won't," Apollo adds.

"Only one thing will," Reuben says.

"What?"

"Finding our Ghosts," they chorus, faces deadpan.

APOLLO LEAVES first to check if there's anyone in the hallway. As I wait for Apollo to come back, I peek at Reuben standing in the doorway. He's resting his shoulder against the jamb, arm barring my way as if he's worried I'll bolt out before the coast is clear.

"Thank you for helping me," I say.

He glances at me and then does a double take. I stiffen when he reaches for me, but it's only to slip the blanket off my shoulders. "They'd ask questions," he says with an apologetic shrug. "Else I'd let you keep it."

I don't know what comes over me. Maybe it's the alcohol that's still flowing through my veins or surviving Cass's attack with my virginity intact.

More likely it's the simple fact that Reuben's always been kind to me. Taking into account how his friends treat me, I'm starting to think it's something I shouldn't take for granted.

I step forward, go onto my tippy toes, and immediately realize my mistake when I pucker my lips a good two inches from his jaw.

I forgot how tall he was. Other than kissing the side of his neck, there's no other way to express my gratitude.

My cheeks catch fire. I sink back to my heels, dropping my gaze as I pray for the earth to swallow me.

A hand slips around my waist. Before I have a chance to protest, Reuben presses me to the wall beside the door.

I lift my legs and wrap them around his waist, if only so I won't hit the floor if he decides to let me go.

But he doesn't drop me.

He pins me to the wall with his body and uses his hands to smooth my curls out of my eyes.

"I wish you weren't part of this. You're too innocent to be mixed up in this shit. But then I wouldn't have met you," he murmurs.

My heart twists as he comes close enough for me to feel his breath on my lips. "And I can't imagine not having met you."

His lips crush mine.

I have time for a gasp, but then I'm swept under. His commanding lips fight mine, urging me to open and let him in, but I'm so terrified that I'm doing this wrong, that I taste gross, that he'll stop...

He makes a sound deep in his throat. Somehow, my body takes it as a signal. Resistance flees. My lips part to let him in and it's like stepping into the middle of a raging river. In an instant, I'm swept under.

Electricity courses over my lips as our kiss slows.

Seconds—*centuries*—later he pulls away, grabs my ass in both hands, and slowly lowers me to the floor.

I swoon like some corseted lady from the eighteenth century about to succumb to a fainting spell, and lean against the wall before my legs can buckle.

"You two done? Because we gotta go." Apollo's standing about a yard away, a deep frown creasing his brow.

Did he see everything?

I press the back of my hands against my hot cheeks. "Sorry," I murmur, yanking the hem of my dress down my legs and dropping my head as I hurry out of the door.

Behind me, Reuben lets out a throaty chuckle that does sinful things to my insides.

I BREATHE a sigh of relief when Apollo and I arrive on my floor and I see the hall is empty. The last thing I need is another run-in with Cass.

"Thank you for walking with me," I say.

"You gonna kiss me too?" Apollo asks dryly.

I stop to frown at him, but he just keeps walking. Is he jealous because I was nice to the only person who's treated me like a human being?

I push back my shoulders and hurry after him, catching his shirt sleeve. "You make it sound like I go around kissing boys at random."

"You don't?"

"Reuben's been super nice—"

"Super *nice?*" He glances at me, his face expressionless. "I can be super nice too, you know."

I stop walking again, my mouth working as I try to find words. "Jealous much?" I call out after him.

He spins around, eyes darting this way and that before narrowing and settling on me. "Would you keep it down?" he says, shaking his head. "We're trying t' be circumspect."

I lick my lips. "Sorry."

"Yeah, fuck, me too." He waves at my closed door and then frowns hard at me as he walks past me again, heading back the way he came. "Dinner's in an hour." Disapproving eyes scan me. "I'd suggest you wear something less conspicuous."

CHAPTER TWELVE

TRINITY

At the sound of the dinner bell, I swallow down a surprised yelp. I'm in the restroom washing my face after changing into jeans and a sweater. Not because of what Apollo had said, but because every time that dress moved against my skin I would either think about Cass or Reuben. And that would either make my skin crawl, or give me goosebumps. And not always in a logical order.

I must have had a meltdown of epic proportions if I can't keep straight what's supposed to feel good, and what definitely should feel bad.

I emerge from the restroom and immediately hang back as students stream into the hall from their rooms.

When the bulk of them have disappeared down the stairs, I merge with the remaining few headed for the dining hall, doing my best to ignore how they keep looking back at me like I'm some creature everyone thought went extinct with the dodo.

Extinction's starting to look really good.

FOR THE FIRST time since I arrived at Saint Amos, there's a queue to get into the dining hall. I crane to see past the boys instead of falling in line.

My mistake.

"Follow me."

I flinch at Apollo's voice. He's headed in the opposite direction of the dining room. With a casual glance back in my direction, he beckons me to follow with a cock of his head.

My choice is to follow him or to go stand in a long line while everyone stares at me.

Apollo leads me outside the building and then around the back. We end up at the back door of the laundry. He takes out a set of keys and unlocks the door, ushering me inside with a hand on the small of my back.

Then he unlocks a metal door set in the side of the room beside one of the massive steel basins and leads me into the small courtyard I was in earlier today.

Seems like a century ago.

He closes the door behind us. "See, I can be nice too," he says right by my ear.

A cluster of candles illuminates the concrete table and the two silver domes on top of it. A jug and two glasses stand to one side of the serving dishes, beads of water condensing on the side.

"Couldn't risk bringing any wine," he continues, snagging my wrist as he walks past, tugging me after him. Then he slips something out from behind his belt. "But I got something to keep us warm."

He flashes me a silver flask, takes a sip, and then hands it over.

I wave it away. "You did this for me?"

"The candles give it away?" he says through a playful smirk.

I smile, but then immediately school my expression into disinterest. I bet he expects a kiss for going to all this effort.

Well...it's kind of romantic, what with the candles and everything. I push away the thought, ignoring the heat creeping onto my cheeks.

I really *am* a blasphemous little slut.

"Well? What d'ya think?"

"It's lovely, thank you."

There's a mischievous sparkle in his eyes. Is he planning something, or is it just the candlelight?

Apollo offers me the canteen again. This time I don't say no.

DESPITE HAVING INVITED me out here for what I assume is some kind of date, Apollo doesn't say another word until our plates are empty. Dinner is accompanied by crickets chirping in the dark corners of the courtyard while cutlery scrapes against crockery.

Apollo grins at me as he collects our empty dishes, and tosses his hair from his eyes with a flick of his head. "I'll be right back," he says before disappearing into the kitchen.

I tip the flask against my lips, clearing my throat after the fiery liquid scorches its way into my stomach as I consider my next move. I could use this time alone with Apollo to my advantage. He must know how Zachary and Reuben ended up in the basement. Can I persuade him to tell me?

Apollo comes back with two bowls and sets one down beside me. I snag his jeans before he can move away. He wears them baggy, but thankfully they're not falling halfway down his ass like some of the boys I've seen in the mall.

"Why don't you come sit here?" I pat the stone stool closest to me. He hesitates, and then sets his bowl next to mine before taking his seat.

He studies me with a small frown.

I have zero experience in seduction, but I guess there's a first time for everything. I dig my spoon into my chocolate mousse and raise it to his lips.

He just keeps staring at me.

My cheeks grow warmer the longer he leaves me hanging. By the time he moves, I feel like I'm melting. But thankfully he eventually ducks forward and cleans my spoon.

"Rube's not a nice guy," he says as he leans back and brushes his hair from his face.

"I didn't say anything about—"

"People assume a lot." He points at me. "People like you." He points at the bowl of mousse and opens his mouth for another serving.

I resist the urge to jam the spoon down his throat. "I'm sorry I'm so transparent. And you're right. I *do* think Reuben is a good guy."

He chuckles at me. "That's because he's been practicing being nice for years now."

"Well he's definitely got the hang of it," I say, another heaped spoon accompanying the statement. My heart thumps a little harder. "How did he end up there anyway? Was he kidnapped too?"

"He didn't exactly wander in off the street, now did he?"

I frown, but I don't get a chance to speak.

"Listen, pretty thing. There's something you have to understand about us. We're not just a 'bunch of friends.'" His air quotes are rife with condescension. "Something happened to us in that basement." He quickly lifts a hand, as if expecting me to interrupt him. "Over and above a bunch of pedophiles repeatedly sticking their dicks in us."

My skin grows cold at his callous words.

"They broke us, Trin." His voice becomes thick and rough. "Broke us into a million fucking pieces. But we picked ourselves—each *other*—up."

His sorrow cuts the nerves to my hand and my spoon tinkles when it hits the side of the bowl. Apollo takes the spoon without missing a beat.

"I reckon we got some of those pieces mixed up when we picked them up." He scoops out a spoonful of mousse. I half-expect him to eat it, but instead he brings it to my lips.

We stay like that for a beat, him staring into my eyes as I get sucked right back into his.

Eyes as deep, dark, and dismal as the bottom of a well.

I eat the mousse. He keeps talking.

"So when we put the pieces together, we got a bit of each other too." He frowns hard as the mousse starts to melt in my mouth. "Does that make sense?"

I nod, because it does.

It makes so much fucking sense it scares me.

It explains why they're so close. The horrors they experienced, they *shared*, wove them together like a rug. Those strands, strong in their own right, became even stronger.

He scoops out more mousse and brings it close, but not close enough.

I lean in a little.

"We're not friends. We're brothers. A brother*hood*. And the only way you're weaseling your way in is if we let you." Apollo smears mousse over my mouth with a flick of his hand.

His eyes drop to my lips.

I reach up instinctively to wipe it away but he snatches my wrist and draws it into his lap. Then he ducks forward and sucks the mousse from my lips.

Heat floods my body.

I try to lean into what I think is a kiss, but he drops his mouth to my chin, then the side of my jaw, then my ear.

"There's something else you should know, pretty thing."

I freeze at the sinister tone in his voice. He moves my hand deeper into his lap, until I brush against something long and hard.

He nips my ear. "We'll never be jealous of each other, because we *always* share our toys."

CHAPTER THIRTEEN
TRINITY

I'm staring up at the ceiling later that night, toying with my curls as I try to make sense of the day, when Jasper slips into our room.

I've spent a lot of time over the past few weeks awake while everyone else was sleeping with thoughts swirling around my head like water going down a drain.

It never gets any less frustrating, especially when I know sleep could whisk me away to peaceful oblivion for a few hours.

"Hey," I greet him, going onto my elbows.

Jasper walks stiffly over to his bed, kneels on the mattress, and lowers himself down with his back to me.

"Everything okay?" I ask. Pretending not to know what happened to him is as difficult as straight-up lying.

"Fucking peaches," he mutters back.

I wince in sympathy, and then I'm glad it's dark and he's not facing me because I'd probably have given myself away.

My ointment is still in my top drawer. Should I leave it out and hope he notices it, or did Miriam give him his own bottle?

Twenty lashes.

Should have been thirty.

No one can survive thirty.

Fuck.

"I know you got lashes," Jasper says.

I sit up straight. "What—why would you think that?"

"For the drawing," he says without turning to face me.

My heart is suddenly beating too fast. "What drawing?"

Jasper maneuvers around until he's facing me. If it wasn't for the moonlight streaming through our tiny window, I wouldn't have seen him rolling his eyes at me.

"The one of Rutherford banging you."

I say nothing as my cheeks start to warm up.

I'd forgotten about Cass's prank. "Yeah. So what?"

"He likes it, you know."

"What, the drawing?"

"Beating people," Jasper says through a world-weary sigh. "He gets off on it."

He...*what*? I've heard some strange things before, but that? It doesn't make any sense. And Zachary might be cold and calculating, but...a sadist?

"I don't think he—"

"He loves beating people as much as he hates gays." The whites of Jasper's eyes shine in the moon's silver glow. "If you don't believe me, try telling him you're a lesbian. You won't be sitting for a week."

Jasper turns around again.

Even if I could speak, what the fuck am I supposed to say to that?

I need air.

I'm already in my pajamas—yoga pants and a tank top—so I grab my threadbare dressing gown from the foot of the bed where it keeps my feet warm in this ice-box of a room, shove my feet into the fur-lined boots I use as slippers, and shuffle out of the door.

For a while after dinner there was quite a lot of traffic in the hallway. Boys coming and going, laughing and roughhousing. But now all the doors are closed, and the passage is quiet.

Cass came by about half an hour after I'd gotten into bed. It was the first time I'd heard him call 'lights out' since I've arrived. I'd almost peed myself at the thought that he would slip into my room, but I guess he wouldn't risk it in case Jasper was there.

I use the restroom before heading back to my room.

I feel sorry for Jasper. It sucks that he and Perry ended up in a place like this, where their relationship is considered a cardinal sin. I wish I could tell him Zachary doesn't feel that way.

Maybe Jasper and Perry can be open about who they are when they leave Saint Amos. I've never had an issue with other people's sexuality. If you love someone, *truly* love someone, then things like gender shouldn't matter.

That's the one thing I'd admired about my parents. You could tell they were wholly devoted to each other. They weren't passionate lovers or anything like that—I've only heard them making love once, and it only lasted a few minutes. But they spent every moment they could together. I guess my mother's miscarriages brought them closer together. They happened way before I was born, but I'm sure they played havoc on the marriage. Luckily they tried one last time before she had a hysterectomy, else I wouldn't be here.

To hear them tell it, God was the one who saw them through those dark times.

I think it was love. A love so strong, it could survive anything. I guess I shouldn't be surprised that they chose each other—and God—over me the night of the accident. I was never included in that love triangle, because I was never as devoted to their faith as they were.

Not for lack of trying. But no matter what I did, it never felt right.

Father Gabriel would often try to rope me into conversations about God when he came to visit. He was subtle about it, and I give him credit for that. But even he could never convince me.

I still went to church, of course. I still prayed when everyone else did.

Gabriel's coming back tomorrow.

The thought makes my pulse beat a little faster.

What do I do if I find out everything the Brotherhood's been telling me is bullshit? Would Gabriel still take me under his wing after I doubted him? Or would he act like he did all those times I came right out and told him I didn't believe?

I can't handle seeing that disappointment in his eyes again.

Not now. Not after everything.

I walk past my room door without pausing.

I don't know if I can risk hurting my only friend. I need to make up my mind about Zachary and his brothers *before* Gabriel gets back.

There's only one way I can think to do that.

I push back my shoulders, take a deep breath, and start down the stairs.

CHAPTER FOURTEEN
ZACH

I lost control today.

It's the girl.

Trinity has a talent for tearing down the walls I've meticulously built up around my dark heart. When she's around, I can't forget how fucked up I am.

Because of her, I lost control. Now the darkness doesn't soothe me like it should, nor does the joint I just smoked envelop me in its usual mind-numbing fog.

I feel sick, but not in a physical way. Times like this, it's as if the disease in my mind is actual cancer, slowly spreading through my neurons.

Infecting. Weakening. Killing.

What will happen when my sanity is gone? When there's nothing left to hold onto? When I can't slow down the clock?

The things I did today were supposed to give me more time. But instead of resetting that fateful countdown clock chiming out the minutes till my next breakdown, everything I did today sped it up.

Hurting Cassius.

Our fistfight.

Punishing Jasper.

That last one I'm particularly pissed about. It should have been

Miriam, that steward of righteous repentance, doling out his punishment. But I thought it would tame the demon clawing its way up from hell through my body, so I did it instead.

I struck him over and over again, punishing him for something I don't consider a crime.

There's a faint noise from outside.

Have one of my brothers returned to our nest? They know better than to disturb me when I've gone dark.

Something could have happened. Something important.

Or maybe they're in as much need of solitude as I am right now. Rube comes here for the quiet sometimes. Just sits on the couch and stares at nothing as he rubs his thumb over his rosary.

Not his anymore.

But does that change anything?

I have to get up and confront whatever—whoever—it is, but I don't trust myself yet.

Maybe I never will.

Orange light from one of the lamps on the other side of the partition spills through.

Something's wrong.

My brothers know the dark soothes me. They might dare to come close, but they wouldn't risk provoking me.

I rally myself, calling back the tendrils of my mind from the far-away places they drift to when I don't keep them contained. It takes effort, and time.

By then, I can hear soft noises as the invader starts hunting. Tins rattle. Clothes rustle.

I push into a sit and hang my head between my knees for a moment. The cool air slides against my bare back as I breathe deep and try to center myself before standing.

I head for the edge of the curtain, the padded floor masking my footsteps, and zone in on the sound of a tin rattling. Sliding a finger behind the curtain, I part it far enough to see a sliver of the room beyond.

My chest tightens painfully.

I'm suddenly too aware of the slow *thump-thump-thump* of my heart.

She shouldn't be here.

I shouldn't go out there.

She's a blast of warm air to the glowing coals of my mind, and everything around us is mere tinder.

But I guess I like the flames, because I slip out of the dark anyway.

I've *always* liked the flames.

CHAPTER FIFTEEN
TRINITY

There's nothing here. I thought they'd have hidden things between their clothes and porno mags and booze and cigarettes.

But there's nothing. Nothing!

Everything here has a purpose. Not a single object is decorative or sentimental.

It's fucking creepy.

I guess it was stupid of me to think they'd leave anything incriminating lying around.

I'm just about to leave when I spot the corner of a book sticking out under a heap of clothes.

My bible.

I pull it out, running my palm over the cover as I trace the embossed letters with my fingers.

I'm about to open it and take out the photo of my father I'm hoping is still inside when the hair on the back of my neck stands up.

"Find anything interesting?" Zachary asks, his voice inches from my ear.

I spin around with a strangled gasp, clutching the thick bible to my chest like a shield. But it falls from nerveless fingers when I see his face.

He catches it absently before it can hit the floor, and sets it down on the shelf behind me.

Dead eyes the color of pond algae regard me for long moments before he leans forward and rests his palms on the shelf. First one hand, then the other, boxing me in.

It's strange seeing him bare-chested in a pair of jeans. It feels wrong. A *sinful* kind of wrong. But when I try to look away, my gaze darts to the tattoo on his pec before I can force myself to look up at him. The combination of that sinister tattoo and his dead eyes is chilling.

"I was—"

"Lost?" he rasps as he narrows his eyes. "Browsing? *Spying?* Tell me if I'm getting warmer."

I'm trembling inside. His proximity, his intensity…it's too much. I can barely breathe. But instead of bowing my head and begging him for forgiveness, I shove my nose into the air and glare up at him.

"I'm taking you on your word about all of this," I say. I lift up a finger. "You couldn't give me a shred of proof. But I'm willing to give you guys a chance, anyway."

"Liar." He lets out a long sigh that shifts strands of hair against my face. He ducks down, leaning in until his nose is almost brushing mine. "If you believed us, you'd be snug in your little bed right now, not wandering around sticking your nose where it doesn't belong."

I have to cleave my tongue from the roof of my mouth before I can speak. "Fuck you! I *do* belong here."

We frown at each other.

"I mean, I have every right to be here. I have every right to ask questions. You can't expect blind faith from me."

He throws back his head and laughs. When he looks at me again, my body goes cold. That crazy laugh didn't add a single degree of warmth to his dead eyes.

"Do you honestly think we live in a world where you have rights?" He arches against me, pressing me into the ridge of the shelf. I wince, but quickly smooth my face.

Don't show a flicker of what you're feeling, Trinity. Cass says they can read me like a book? Well it's time I closed the goddamn cover.

"Of course I have—"

"Wrong," he cuts in, grabbing my jaw. "This is the real world. And in the real world, you're not special, Trinity." His eyes grow hooded. "None of us are."

I grab his wrist. He's too strong for me to pull him away but at least this way I can feel his pulse.

It should be racing, like mine.

But it's dead calm.

Fear worms deep into me and starts squirming around in my intestines like a fat snake.

I didn't expect anyone to be here. I could have sworn they'd said it was risky staying out here. That they all went back to the dorms at night. But I guess he couldn't go back reeking of weed and booze like he does. Or with that purplish bruise on his jaw. He's in no state to be seen outside of these walls.

And I'm not safe down here with him.

"I should leave," I say.

"You should never have come." He ducks lower, his glare pinning me like a butterfly to a corkboard. "Tell me, little girl, why *did* you come?"

He'd see right through me if I lied. And honestly, how much worse could I make this?

"Because I don't trust you. Any of you." I swallow hard and muster up every bit of courage I have left. "But you can change that. Tell me. Tell me everything."

His lips quirk into a dark smile. "Everything?" he murmurs.

He tucks a curl behind my ear before trailing his fingers down my jaw. It shouldn't, but that touch sends a thrill down my spine.

It could be fear masquerading as something else, but I have a feeling it's not. I'm trapped in the lion's den and instead of looking for a way out, I'm poking the fucking lion.

I *know* Father Gabriel isn't capable of hurting anyone. But that doesn't matter to the Brotherhood, does it? I've been drawn into their war, despite my protests.

I don't have a choice but to fight but I'm going to make sure I'm on the right side of the battle line first.

"You couldn't handle hearing what happened to us in one day, never mind the *years* we spent down there," Zachary says.

"We? It's always *we*." I poke him right between the dripping fangs of his snake tattoo. "I want to know about *you*. I want to know what kind of person *you* are. How else can I trust you?"

He laughs. "You want to know what kind of person I am, Trinity?"

The only warning I have is the darkness shadowing his eyes as he scans my body.

Zachary grabs me, spins me, shoves me.

Hard.

I tumble over the arm of the couch, barely stopping myself from bouncing onto the floor. Expecting him to pounce on me—perhaps even try what Cass tried—I scramble into a sit. But he just stands there watching me, his chest heaving like he went three rounds with the world champion.

"I used to think I was a good person, back when I was a kid." His hands curl into fists and then open again as he steps closer. "Thought I'd become something great. Astronaut, doctor. The usual shit kids fantasize about."

In my fantasies, I was a ballerina. But my parents made it clear that the only career they approved of was me becoming someone's wife and, eventually, someone's mother.

It didn't faze me that much. I was probably too short to be a ballerina anyway.

Zachary moves to the front of the couch. And I stay right where I am, because for the first time since I've been pressing him for information about his past, I'm actually getting what I want.

So instead of bolting, I pull my legs into my chest, hugging myself as he stands in front of me.

Does he like towering over people? My neck's already aching from craning up to look at him.

"So what happened? What changed?"

There'd been a faint smile on his mouth. It fades as his hands slowly unfurl again.

"You really want to know?"

I nod.

He inhales deep and lets out everything as a long sigh through his nose. "There's something I want, too."

His smile returns.

I wish it hadn't.

It makes my stomach coil.

"But you're not going to like it."

CHAPTER SIXTEEN
ZACH

No one's ever shown such interest in my past. My brothers already know everything, and we're not exactly the type to sit around a campfire trading anecdotes. Not any that touch on the basement, anyway.

So what is her ulterior motive? Why is she still here?

"Deal?" It says a lot that I'd give her a chance to back out.

She nods.

It's possible Trinity doesn't fully comprehend what she's agreed to. Not because she's dumb—far from it—but because she's literally that naive.

"Get up."

She stands, her eyes not staying on mine longer than a second before flickering away.

She *should* be nervous.

I move behind the couch and pat the headrest. She visibly steels herself, lifting her chin and pushing out her chest before following.

When she's close enough, I grab her hips and shove her into the back of the couch. My cock stiffens at her surprised gasp. It's still a long way from being hard, but just the thought of what I'm about to do to her sweet, innocent little ass has my body readying itself.

"Hold on."

She hesitates and then spreads her arms, digging her fingers into the headrest's cushion.

"Like thi—?"

I grab her dressing gown and yank it off her shoulders, letting it pool by her feet. When I grab the waistband of her yoga pants she tries to move away, but a shove to the small of her back keeps her in place.

"Do they have to come off?" she asks in a tight voice.

"Obviously." I yank down her pants, baring her panties. My fingers itch to delve inside her underwear, to touch her...but that's not what we agreed.

I could have left her pants around her knees, but instead I draw them down all the way to her feet. I slip off her boots and slide her pants off, tossing them over the back of the couch.

When I touch the elastic of her panties, she stiffens. "Please," she murmurs. "Leave them on."

I should have ripped them off, but I fight back the urge. That thin film of fabric is inconsequential. If I want to admire my handiwork, I can do that when we're done.

"Spread your legs."

When she doesn't obey, I kick them open for her. I run a hand over the curve of her ass and then up her plump cheek, massaging the flesh beneath.

She shifts again. "What are you doing?"

I'm not about to educate this girl on the intricacies of spanking. "Is that your first question?"

She shivers under my hand as she gives her head a violent shake.

My cock stiffens even more.

I take off my belt, willing myself to move slowly so I can warm up her cool flesh and bring enough blood to the surface.

It's surprisingly difficult not to rush this part. The anticipation of hurting her is making me salivate.

I fold my belt in half and then again. I move close to her, my now straining cock brushing the curve of her ass as I reach around and press open her jaw with my fingers.

"Bite."

"Don't I get to ask my question first?"

I slap her ass with the flat of my hand.

She lets out an indignant yelp and glares at me over her shoulder. I hold up my hand, showing her my reddened palm, and her scowl fades a little. She opens her mouth and accepts the belt when I shove it between her pink lips.

"Face forward."

Usually, I wouldn't be bothered if she was making eye contact or not but I can't pretend she's a meek sub if she keeps glaring at me like that.

"This, then your question."

When she doesn't say anything, I smack her ass again.

"I need a yes, little girl."

Her shoulders stiffen, but she doesn't protest the name-calling. Maybe she's finally starting to accept just what a fucked up deal she's struck with me.

Soon, she'll be begging me to stop, and this will all be over. Questions unanswered, I'll send her back to her dorm, a newfound fear embedded inside her.

Deep, *deep* inside her.

CHAPTER SEVENTEEN
TRINITY

W hat the fuck have I gotten myself into? Trading slaps for intel? You'd swear I'd been dropped on my head as a kid. From the third floor.

My ass is already throbbing from the two smacks Zachary delivered. Fuck knows how I'm supposed to survive more.

But that's not what's bothering me the most about this. If I didn't know any better, I'd swear this was turning me on.

Which is ridiculous, of course. What the hell is sexy about having a belt shoved in my mouth? Or the way I'm drooling around the leather? Or the fact that I'm standing here in my underwear, waiting for him to start spanking me?

But if this is what it takes to get the answers I need—

My teeth sink into Zachary's belt as a hard slap thumps onto my ass cheek. I'm so surprised, I don't even cry out.

Whipping my head around, I stare at him with shocked eyes. I reach to take the belt out of my mouth so I can tell him he's hitting me too hard, but I don't get very far.

I catch one glimpse of the dark lust in his hooded eyes before he grabs the back of my neck and pushes me down again.

The next time his hand connects with my ass, I scream.

When I start squirming, he tightens the grip on my neck.

Slap. Slap. Slap!

I yell out wordlessly and grab his wrist, trying to pull his hand off my neck so I can straighten.

He steps back, and I stagger to my feet.

I snatch my yoga pants from the back of the couch. He doesn't stop me. My breath hitches as I try to ignore the stings on my backside.

"Fuck!"

"All right there, little girl?"

I grimace at him. "That was five," I tell him breathlessly. Well, technically it was seven, but I have a feeling the first two didn't count.

"So ask your question."

I lick my lips. "How did you end up in the basement?"

A massive erection bulges behind his jeans.

How can anyone enjoy hurting someone else? Even though I said yes, this is just…it's fucked up.

I guess Jasper was right. Zachary *is* a sadist.

He cocks his head a little. "Too vague."

I frown at him as I slide a cool hand behind my underwear. My skin feels hot to the touch, and stings when I touch it. How much will it hurt putting my pants back on? For now, I keep them bundled against my stomach.

"Who took you there, to the basement? How did they catch you?"

"That's two questions."

I grind my teeth. "Who took you to the basement?"

A fond look crosses his face. "My parents."

"W-what?"

"Is that your next question?"

"N-No. But…you have to explain. I mean…your *parents?*"

He surges forward, grabs my hips, and flips me over. I claw at his arms as he tries to pin me but somehow, he gets a hold of my wrists and holds them against the small of my back.

When he kicks open my legs again, my stomach bottoms out.

"No, wait!"

"So many questions, little girl," he says, his voice barely altered from the strain of keeping me in place. "Looks like we're going to be here all night."

There's no belt in my mouth when he slaps me. My teeth clamp down on instinct, and I bite the inside of my bottom lip. A trickle of blood seeps into my mouth.

I let out a Hollywood-style scream that's part rage, part agony.

"Jesus fucking Christ," he mutters, shoving away from me.

I hurriedly spin around, ready to fend him off if he tries to pin me again.

"Get the fuck out of here," he growls as he bends to pick up his belt from the floor. He loops it through his jeans and buckles it up before pointing at the exit, one eyebrow quirking up in a silent command.

My mouth works for a second before I find words. "No, but—"

"You obviously don't have the stomach for this shit," he says, stepping so close that his erection brushes my belly. "Get. The. Fuck. Out."

I keep my ground, but barely. Every molecule in my body wants me to flee, but my mind keeps spiraling in on those two words. I won't be able to sleep until I know more.

His parents.

His *parents?*

I swallow hard and force up my chin. "We had a deal."

He huffs mirthlessly through his nose. "There's a fine line between bravery and stupidity."

"I'm not being brave or stupid," I snap back. Without taking my eyes off of him, and while trying to ignore the fact that my hands are shaking, I grab the front of his belt and start unbuckling it.

He drops his eyes, watching my fingers work. Then he studies me through dark, thick lashes. "The fuck are you doing?"

"We had a deal."

"Not with a belt. You're nowhere near ready for that kind of punishment."

For some unfathomable reason, my insides pulse at the way he says that word.

Punishment.

I wasn't sure before, but I am now. This thing he's doing to me? This is turning me on. I don't get it—I don't even think it's *possible*—but nothing else can explain the way I'm tingling down there. When I move, I can feel how wet I'm becoming.

"It's so I won't scream," I say quietly after another hard swallow. "Unless you want to use my underwear again?"

His eyebrows draw together. "Tempting, but no."

Before I can move away, he grabs my bottom lip and tugs it down. "Something to bite down on works better."

I nod as if I already knew this and pull his belt free from its loops. I fold it like he did, and hold it an inch from my lips. "Ready when you are."

He lifts his head as he closes the distance between us, his dick now pressing hard into my soft flesh. I try to ignore it, but it just stokes the fire already building in my core.

His hands slide around my back and down to my ass. I wince when he starts massaging my skin. Then my eyes fall closed.

The soothing pressure eases the sting and sends delicious ripples through my body.

When his breath warms my face, I look up at him. He's watching me.

Hungry.

Angry.

But sad.

So sad.

And I need to know why.

I wedge his belt between my teeth and slowly turn around in his arms.

His hands trail down my curves. He hooks a finger behind the elastic of my underwear and tugs it down to the crease where my ass meets my legs. Then he steps back, leaving cool air to circulate over my exposed skin.

I brace myself against the back of the couch and bite down on the belt.

Slap.

Air hisses past my teeth as I suck in a pained breath. The sting that follows his slap is immediate and brutal.

Slap. Slap. Slap. Slap.

Tears prick at my tightly-closed eyelids, and I scrunch up my face with the effort of not yelling out or letting those tears fall.

Fingers brush my jaw. I reluctantly open my mouth and let Zachary take the belt from between my teeth.

"Your question."

I try to focus on anything but the pain, but it seems impossible to ignore. "Hold on," I murmur, my breathing picking up pace.

"Now, little girl." He caresses my ass, sending fiery licks of pain over my skin. I hiss and try to move away, but there's nowhere to go with me sandwiched between his body and the back of the couch. "Now."

"Your parents," I say through my teeth as my fingers dig into the couch. "Why would they send you to the basement?"

It's the first thing I can think of. The first logical thought of the thousands floating aimlessly through a mind that's coming undone from this exquisite pain.

Zachary's hand pauses. He squeezes me, and I go onto my tippy toes as I gasp at the pain.

I don't understand this. I've had ten lashes, but they were nothing like this. They hurt more, but this...this is a different kind of pain. It has all these layers to it I don't understand. I feel like crying, but not because it hurts, but because...

Because *Zachary* is hurting, and I can feel it.

I can *feel* his pain.

"Good question." Zachary starts massaging my ass again. "And I don't know if I have the right answer for you."

"What? That's not—" I cut off when his fingers stop an inch away from my entrance. Until now he'd been keeping well away from the hot, tingling mess between my legs.

"I'm not sure if it's the right answer, because I can't look inside their heads," he says.

He squeezes me, and I barely hold back a moan of pain.

"I'm not asking you to psychoanalyze them," I say, having to force the words through the pain.

He makes a soft noise in the back of his throat that could have been a stifled chuckle. "Aren't you?"

"You would have asked them. They would have given you some kind of answer. What did they say, when they took you down there? What reason did they give?"

He lets out a laugh that turns my insides into a frozen mush. "It was my punishment," he says. "See, I was a very naughty boy." He shifts behind me and his jeans brush my skin. The rough fabric sends a flurry of hot tingles through me moments before his hard dick presses into my crack, forcing my cheeks apart.

My breath catches.

If he wasn't still wearing his jeans, he'd be inches away from—

Taking what doesn't belong to him.

Which he could have done if he'd wanted. Is he holding himself back, or just toying with me?

"What did you do?"

Another laugh. Thankfully, this one isn't as chilling as the one before. "Sure you can handle another question?" He strokes my bare skin with his fingertips. They trace eight lines down my ass, and then converge less than an inch from my sex.

My face heats when he slowly pulls me open. My lips part reluctantly, soaked through from the twisted desire that's been coursing through me the entire time he's had me pinned against this couch.

"I said, are you sure you can handle another question, little girl?"

"Yes," I blurt out, immediately squeezing closed my eyes. "I mean... if you don't hit me as hard. Maybe." Fuck, my heart feels ready to explode from my chest.

He chuckles quietly as he folds over me. "It's sweet that you think I'm capable of mercy." He grabs my wrist, bringing the folded belt up to my mouth. "Open."

And, against all reason, that's exactly what I do.

CHAPTER EIGHTEEN
ZACH

I'm barely touching the ground and every breath I take is helium. If Trinity looked around and saw my face, she'd be screaming as she ran out of here.

Which is why I slide my hand over the back of her neck and hold her in place. That way, she can't see the sick lust on my face.

I slip a finger behind the hem of her panties where they're gathered just under the curve of her ass. This time she doesn't plead with me to keep them on. I tug them down to her knees, baring her smooth, shapely legs. I take a few seconds to admire the blurry red handprints on her ass before I start warming up her flesh again.

She shifts as if considering bringing her legs together so I tighten the grip on her neck as I kick them open even wider. This stretches her panties tight between her knees, and that's when I notice the near translucent patch in the fabric.

My cock hardens painfully behind my jeans.

I could unzip my fly and be inside her in seconds, burying myself balls deep inside her tight little pussy.

Except that wasn't the fucking deal.

My fingers dip lower, almost touching her. Her body stiffens, but she keeps still. Keeps her legs open.

I bite the inside of my lip as I give her body one last scan. Then I bring my palm down on her ass with all my strength.

The sound of her shocked yell reverberates deep inside me.

I'm in agony—suspended in ice, drowning in fire. Without conscious thought, I zip down my fly and take out my cock. I stroke myself, keeping my hand on the back of her neck as I inch my dick closer to her wet pussy.

She must feel the warmth coming off my body, because she stiffens again, as if expecting another blow.

Christ.

Her heat coats the crown of my dick as I ram my fist down its length. The pain makes me harder. Makes me want to fuck her even more. To spread her open and drench myself in her juices.

She makes a sound behind my belt. It sounds like a plea.

It takes long seconds for me to realize she's shaking. That she's no longer pressing back against my hand, resisting me. She's limp, draping the back of the couch like she doesn't have the strength to hold herself up anymore.

And then I hear her sniffs. The stifled sob.

I shove my cock back into my jeans and move to the side. Her eyes are squeezed shut, her cheeks bright red.

"The fuck is it now?" I ask roughly, ripping my belt out of her mouth. "Finally decided you've had enough?"

As soon as the belt is out, she moves away from me, her hands shaking as she yanks up her underwear. She lets out a string of mangled words.

"Sorry—don't—happening—shouldn't—stop."

I watch her as she tries to put on her yoga pants. When they're halfway up her legs she turns away from me, surreptitiously wiping at the inside of her thigh as another sob wrangles its way out of her mouth.

"Hey." I grab her elbow, but she twists her arm out of my grip. I frown, and this time I grab her waist and drag her up against me. "What's going on?"

"I'm sorry," she says, her lips trembling. "I don't know why that happened."

I stick my hand between her legs, wiping at the slick wetness on her thighs. "This?" I ask roughly. "Are you embarrassed about this?"

She covers her face with her hands, shrinking in on herself like a wilting flower. I make an angry noise in the back of my throat. "You asked for this," I tell her as I yank her yoga pants up the rest of the way. "Don't play coy now."

She rips her hands away and struggles in my arms, but I refuse to let her go. "It was supposed to hurt," she says. "It wasn't supposed to... why did it...*what the fuck's wrong with me?*"

The last is a yell. She glares up at me before her face crumples and her mouth starts quivering again. "What's wrong with me?" she whispers.

"Nothing, my girl." I wipe away her tears with my thumbs as I cradle her face in my hands. "Absolutely nothing."

I stare into amber eyes that demand more from me. But what the fuck am I supposed to say?

She wanted answers, I wanted release. We made a deal. How the fuck were we supposed to know it would turn out like this?

But now, staring into her eyes, I guess I had it wrong all along.

This wasn't about her. It wasn't about me. It was about *us*. All of us. The Brotherhood. The Ghosts. The Guardians.

It was about the basement.

She can't believe what happened to us.

No one can be that cruel.

That perverted.

That sick.

It can't be true.

But it is.

Trinity Malone couldn't accept the truth so she tried catching me in a lie.

A slow, hard ache starts up in my ankles before spreading to my wrists.

I trace the bottom of her lip with my thumb. "I disobeyed them," I tell her quietly.

She blinks, trapping a tear in her lashes. "What?"

"You wanted to know why my parents were punishing me."

Her eyes widen ever so slightly.

"I went somewhere I wasn't supposed to. Saw something I shouldn't have."

My chest closes up. I take a deep breath, but it barely fills my lungs.

She doesn't say anything. Doesn't push me for more. Perhaps she thinks I'll tell her to leave if she does.

Those bright, amber eyes just watch. Not perversely curious, like the policemen who'd taken our statements after we'd finally escaped. Not pitiful, like so many of the parents in the foster homes we'd ended up in.

Just watching.

Waiting.

I manage another breath, this one even shallower than the last. My erection has faded completely, and my skin prickles hot and cold. I move my hands to her shoulders, and she tenses under my hands when I grip her tight.

Her lips move like she's biting the inside of her cheek.

I want to kiss her, which is weirder than fucked up because I *never* want to kiss anyone.

"The basement was in my house."

Her lips move, but no sound comes out.

"My parents were the Keepers." I try to swallow, but I can't. I try to keep quiet, but it's as if she's pulling the words from me. "Gabriel paid them to look after the boys. The Ghosts would arrange times with them. They kept it all a secret, but I started noticing things when I got older. Tracks in the driveway. Strange smells."

Trinity scans my face and presses her hands against my bare chest as if she wants to feel my heart beating.

She won't, though.

"I stole their keys one day. Said I was going to a sleepover. They drove me to my friend's house, but I came back, and I waited until it was dark. Until they were asleep.

"They found me down there in the basement. A silent alarm had gone off. I should have run away, but I couldn't just leave them there." My voice trails away, thickening. I doubt she hears me when I add, "I couldn't leave my brothers there."

Her fingertips dimple my flesh. Still searching for that elusive heartbeat?

No, Trinity. There's nothing for you to feel.

My black heart stopped beating a long, long time ago.

CHAPTER NINETEEN
TRINITY

I'm already awake when the bell for Sunday service rings, but I lie there for a few seconds before getting up. Tomorrow it will be a week since I arrived in Saint Amos. After almost eighteen years living a life where nothing ever happened, these last few weeks are ridiculous in comparison.

I like to think that I'd have preferred to live a boring life, but then I wouldn't have met the Brotherhood. They're the most interesting people I've ever met but they're also the most fucked up people I've ever met.

I stifle a yawn.

Guess I'll have to take the good with the bad.

Jasper pushes into a sit and presses the heels of his palms into his eye sockets.

When he gets up, I stare up at him in astonishment. "You're going to mass?"

"Why wouldn't I? You're going. Rutherford's going. *Everyone's* going."

Because your ass probably hurts worse than mine and those pews are fuck hard?

I frown at him as he grabs his clothes and exits the room. I'm starting to think he's becoming a little obsessed with Zachary. I get being pissed off with him, but this?

Screw it.

My mind's way too fucked up to figure out what Jasper's up to.

I grab one of the two dresses I used to wear to church on Sundays and head to the restroom to wash my face.

Jasper's sitting on the edge of his bed lacing up his shoes when I get back. Guess he didn't bother showering again. I can't blame him—I wouldn't want the other kids seeing my bruised butt either.

I took a quick peek at my ass in the restroom mirror after making sure there wasn't anyone else in one of the stalls. Surprisingly, it isn't as bruised as it feels. Was it because Zachary kept massaging it while—?

Oh no, Trinity. *Hell* no. Your thoughts will remain pure as freshly fallen snow today.

"Want to walk together?" Jasper asks.

"Uh...sure," I manage while battling my shock. Dear Lord, I don't think I can take any more surprises today. I already feel like I'm walking a razor's edge.

Jasper stands, wincing faintly, and then sticks out his hand.

"What?"

He glares at me.

I cringe back when he darts forward and tries to grab my hand. "What are you doing?"

"I'm not going to rape you," he says, rolling his eyes. "Just...give me your fucking hand."

As soon as I give it to him, he hauls me up from the bed.

Halfway down the hall I eventually find my voice. "What's up, Jasper?" I try for casual, but I have no idea if he falls for it.

"Shut up and look like you're in love with me or something."

I barely suppress a snort. Everyone in Saint Amos is on the fucking spectrum. Must be the stuffy air in this place.

Jasper's palm sweats against mine, and he keeps shifting his grip as if he's not sure if he's holding my hand right. We draw more than a few eyes on our way down to the church, and no wonder. He's wearing a thousand-yard-glare that could incinerate anyone who happened to cross his view, and I'm alternating between trying to make myself invisible and keep an eye on Jasper to make sure he's not about to jump out a window—with me in tow.

By the time we get to the chapel, there's a small group of boys tagging along behind us.

You'd think it couldn't get more awkward than this, but then Perry enters the picture.

Jasper stops short. I glance at him and immediately turn to see what he's looking at with a face that suddenly turned to stone.

Not what. *Who.*

Perry's standing under one of the trees dotting the lawn between Saint Amos and the chapel. He *was* heading our way, but as I watch he slows down. A second later he stops, watching us with owlish eyes as Jasper heads for the chapel again.

"Aren't you going to—?"

"Don't be an idiot," he mutters, tugging me after him. I give Perry a timid wave, but he either doesn't see me or decides not to draw any more attention to himself because he doesn't wave back.

I couldn't be happier when we step inside the chapel's cool shadows. I aim for the pew closest to the door but Jasper tightens his grip and hauls me down the aisle like this is our own shotgun wedding.

I guess morning prayers aren't compulsory for staff but Sunday mass is because today the pews are crammed full.

I spot all four members of the Brotherhood as Jasper hauls me down the aisle. Apollo is on the other side of the church in the second row, nestled between a bunch of men I assume all work in the kitchen. Cass and Rube are sitting with the students.

Judging from the way they're staring at me, the fact that my roommate is holding my hand doesn't sit well.

I should probably mention to Jasper that holding my hand isn't going to make anyone believe he's suddenly into girls. What it will do is get him into a ton of shit for dragging me around like he just bought me at a slave auction.

We sit in the second row behind the teachers with Zachary less than a yard to the left. It feels like he's the only one in the entire church who hasn't been watching me since I walked in.

Somehow, that makes me more nervous than if he'd been staring like his brothers.

The bruise on his jaw is barely noticeable now. I'm sure if it was still visible, he wouldn't have dared to show his face this morning.

I wince when my ass hits the pew. Although Zachary's spanking didn't bruise my skin as much as I'd thought it would, it still hurts like hell. Especially on these hard seats.

Jasper must be in agony.

I glance aside at him and then hurriedly look straight ahead. He's glaring so hard at Zachary I'm surprised my Psych teacher's hair hasn't caught on fire.

Although it seems Zachary isn't paying him any mind, I know for a fact he's aware of us.

Both of us.

Thanks, Jasper. All I wanted this morning was to remain invisible.

I was exhausted when I got back to my room last night. My ass hurt, my head hurt...my *heart* hurt.

Yes, I'd been digging for answers, but I hadn't expected to unearth a rotting corpse.

A few more kids rush in and hurriedly find seats. A reverential hush fills the chapel's vaulted ceilings. Timing his entrance perfectly, Father Gabriel walks in a mere second after the first bored whisper reaches me from the students seated behind us.

My lungs turn to concrete.

Gabriel looks just like he always does, but now that familiar smile gracing his wide mouth seems fake as margarine. His eyes aren't keen and inquisitive anymore—they're cunning and shifty.

It's like that optical illusion. Once you see the rabbit, you can't see the duck anymore.

As soon as he catches sight of me, Gabriel's gaze strips me bare.

It's just your imagination.

There's no reason for him to suspect anything is different about Trinity Malone, daughter of Keith and Monica—devoted parishioners of the Redford Missions of Love church.

I'm starting to sweat.

Gabriel's eyes release me when he takes in the rest of the crowd, and I sag in my seat.

"Good morning, children."

There's still no proof to Brotherhood's claims, but logic doesn't reign in my mind anymore.

Is it because you want them to fuck you? Is that why you don't need proof anymore, you blasphemous little slut?

My mouth turns sour.

Father Gabriel starts on a sermon that sounds like so many others I've heard over the years. I find myself studying the side of Zachary's face until I catch Gabriel looking at me.

Adrenaline spikes through me, leaving me tingling and panicked as it recedes. For the rest of the sermon, I keep my eyes locked on Gabriel, but he never once looks in my direction again.

His sermon feels like it lasts for hours. Hours I spend debating my position in this invisible battle raging between the Brotherhood and Father Gabriel.

Finally, we end in the Father's Prayer and begin communion. In Redford, only a handful of people would go up—those that wanted to partake.

I guess they do things differently here. Here, everyone partakes. And as more and more people file out of their pews, I get the feeling it's compulsory.

Gabriel and Zachary make just the right amount of eye contact. Their exchange seems as normal as the one before and after. Gabriel glances up from his paten of bread and locks eyes with me.

He says nothing as he holds out the body of Christ. I lean forward, open my mouth, and let him place the bread on my tongue.

"It's good to see you again, my child."

I stay silent, too scared my voice will shake if I return the greeting.

It could be the play of light on his face, but I swear he frowns at me before smoothing his expression.

The sip of wine he gives me from the chalice tastes like ash.

―――――――

"YOU COMING?" Jasper asks when I don't take his hand.

"Not yet."

He scowls at me, sends a withering look Zachary's way, and stalks out of the chapel like Satan is nipping at his heels.

I stay in my seat, watching Gabriel through my lashes. Instead of immediately exiting the stage like he does after morning prayers, he weaves through the loitering students and staff clasping a hand here, patting a shoulder here, murmuring, "Child this, child that."

When it becomes obvious he's ignoring me, I stand up and make my way to the aisle. I'm dimly aware of Zachary from my peripheral view. He's still seated, head bowed over a standard-issue bible as if he's contemplating the word of God before heading off to breakfast.

Gabriel is talking with Sister Miriam when I come up behind him. Miriam sees me and frowns, but I stand my ground. Gabriel turns with a small frown between his thick, dark eyebrows. When he spots me, his face lights up.

Then he turns back to Miriam. "If you'll excuse us, Sister."

Miriam nods, but from the way she adjusts her habit as she leaves, it's clear what she thinks about me interrupting their conversation.

"Are you well?" Gabriel asks, reaching for me.

I sidestep his hand before I can catch myself, and instantly regret it when his smile fades and his frown returns deeper than before.

"Is something wrong, child?"

"Of course not, no," I blurt out. I can't seem to stop wringing my hands. "But, if you're not busy, I'd like to, I mean, could we talk?"

"Certainly." He reaches for my elbow as if to steer me somewhere private, but I step back again.

"Dinner. Um...could we have dinner again?"

His frown deepens. "Are you sure everything is okay?"

I'm itching to get away from his x-ray eyes. I've never been able to lie to him, and I don't think that will ever change. "Tonight?"

"I'm afraid I already have plans with—" He waves away whatever he'd been going to say. A broad smile replaces his frown, and I hate the fact that it makes me feel warm inside.

"I would love nothing more."

"Thank you, Father."

He watches me with that same enigmatic smile as I strut away on stiff legs.

I don't dare look up until sunlight hits my face. The relief I was expecting doesn't arrive. I could be looking over the side of a cliff.

Why does it feel like I've just set a date with the Devil?

CHAPTER TWENTY
ZACH

Fabric whisks. Cass slips into the lair, his eyebrows twitching when he sees me on my chair, smoking a cigarette. I guess he expected me to be sulking in the dark, fighting my demons.

"Didn't get enough of me yesterday?" he asks, face pinched tight as he walks past and sticks his head into the bedroom. Making sure we're alone? "And here I thought we were trying to be circumspect."

"We set up this place for a reason. No one would think to look—"

"Might as well install a fucking revolving door at this rate." He comes back in my direction and snatches the cigarette from my lips before I can take another drag.

Ash scatters onto his jeans as he collapses on the couch, draping himself over the cushions like he's desperate to show me just how few fucks he gives.

I click my fingers, demanding he returns my cigarette. He whips his head around to study me as he drags hard at it, and then hands it back.

Just before I take it, he pulls away his hand. "This about the girl?"

I retract my hand, lean back in my seat, and shake loose a fresh cigarette for myself. "You got to make things right."

He turns around to face me and lies back with his head propped up on the arm. "The fuck I do." He hikes up his leg and then crosses an ankle over his knee so he can toy with the hem of his skinny jeans with the same hand holding the cigarette.

I stopped buying them new clothes months ago. But it doesn't matter what Cass puts on, it always looks good. Even old shit like those jeans.

Who knew…maybe when this shit was over, he'd grow out his hair and get a few headshots. He'd easily make it as a model, and preening in front of a camera would be the perfect fodder for his ravenous narcissism.

As long as they never asked him to take off his shirt, of course.

"You scared the shit out of her," I state, deadpan as I tug at my cigarette.

Puffs of smoke spout from Cass's mouth as he laughs. "Thought that was the plan."

I slam my fist into the arm of my chair. "You fucking idiot."

Cass flinches, but recovers in a flash. He considers me for a second before leaning over to flick his cigarette into the cup on the floor by the arm of his couch. "*I'm* the idiot?"

"Who do you think she trusts more? A bunch of strangers on the far side of borderline, or the family friend who's been in her life since she was in diapers?"

Cass's face hardens at this. He despises it when I bring up the fact that the four of us are more than a little broken. He opens his mouth, but I cut him off without waiting to hear what he comes up with this time.

"We're not trying to get her to leave anymore, or have you forgotten? We need her on our side."

"We don't need her," he says. "We don't need any—"

"You're right. We don't."

Cass glares at me suspiciously.

"We don't need her," I repeat as I lean forward and rest my elbows on my knees. "We could go back to the original plan." I flick my wrist and purse my lips. "Wait for this place to clear out. Hope we can grab Gabriel before he gets the fuck out, and then hope we can break him." I spread my hands. "Sure a lot of wishful thinking in that plan, but it's the best we could come up with, remember?"

Spots of anger spring up on Cass's pale face. "She's going to fuck this up."

"She will." I nod.

He shakes his head, laughing through another exhale. "Unless I grovel for her forgiveness, right?"

His bitter words send a rush of heat through me, but I don't call him out for them. It's how I know I'm getting through to him. The harder he fights, the closer he is to giving in.

Like a cornered rat.

It's how he copes. Unlike the three of us, Cass never could switch off his mind. He's too intelligent for that. It would be like trying to dam the Amazon river with a handful of matchsticks.

So he fought.

Tooth and fucking nail.

He fought so hard that his Ghosts would be injured trying to get to him. And that made us happy. We started cheering him on—silently, of course. Even back then we knew we had to keep our Brotherhood a secret. Even as kids we understood that secret would keep us safe.

So Cass fought. Sometimes he'd win, sometimes they'd overpower him. It went on for weeks, until one of them stuck a syringe filled with heroin into his arm.

"She *will* fuck this up," I say again. "But only if she's not a hundred percent on our side."

"That'll take more than a half-assed apology to—"

"Which is why you're going to make it count."

Cass's scowl pins me. "She won't let me near her, you know that."

"I also know how persuasive you can be."

I'd meant it as a compliment, but for some reason it just makes more angry spots flare up on his cheeks.

We sit for a few seconds smoking our cigarettes, silent, brooding, waiting each other out.

"What's so fucking special about her anyway?" he asks.

Did I hear that right?

I get up and crouch beside him to kill my cigarette in the cup by his couch. When I look up, his iridescent blue eyes glue me to the spot.

I wasn't just blowing hot air up his ass. When he wants something —really, *really* wants something—it's as if the Universe aligns to give it to him.

Even if it's just an answer to a question I'd rather not give.

"I never said she was."

"You didn't have to."

"You're delusional." I start to stand, but Cass grabs my arm, and not gently either. His fingernails bite into my flesh as he tugs me closer.

"What happens when you have to choose between her or us?"

A hard frown creases my brow. "That's never going to happen."

Cass's expression clears. He releases me. "Yeah, let's hope it doesn't," he says as he gets to his feet. I stand too, and he pushes past me to get to the door. "Because it looks like you've already made your choice."

"Cass."

He slips out the curtain.

"Cass!"

I could have gone after him, but then I'd seem desperate. Falling onto the couch, I sit stroking a thumb over the marks his fingernails left in my arm as I let the latent warmth from his body soak into mine.

He's full of shit, but that's nothing new. Of the three of us, his walls are the tallest and the strongest. No one's ever broken through them. He doesn't let his guard down for anyone, not even his brothers. But that wasn't a requirement for joining this war. Every war needs soldiers, and those soldiers need ammunition.

Rage.

Hate.

Vengeance.

In this case, we each had to bring our own. But me and Rube and Apollo? We're weak, flickering candles compared to Cass.

He's the motherfucking sun.

CHAPTER TWENTY-ONE
TRINITY

After breakfast, I spend a few hours at the tiny desk in our room catching up on my homework. Jasper is there for a while, reading a book, and then he disappears without a word. I decide to close the bedroom door behind him, just in case someone—*Cass*—decides to pop in for an unannounced visit.

I wish more and more every day that I had a damn key.

A few minutes before the lunch bell gongs, I hear a soft sound by the door. I whip my head around to stare at the folded paper someone pushed under the door.

The hair on the back of my neck stands up as I wait, but thankfully the door stays closed.

When my heartbeat goes back to normal, I stand and fetch the note.

SHOWER?

The words all are in capitals, stiff and boxy.

Reuben.

He's letting me use his bathroom again. Which is so sweet, especially with tonight's dinner in mind. I guess now would be the perfect time to go—everyone else would be in the dining hall, eating. If I hurried, I might still make lunch once I was done, but I'd happily trade a meal for a private shower.

Plus, I'd get to see Reuben again.

The prospect does strange things to my tummy and I have to push away the thought so I can figure out what I'll be wearing to dinner tonight.

I KNOCK QUIETLY on Reuben's door. Why does no one except Father Gabriel answer their doors in this place? After a third knock I try the handle, eager to get out of the hall before someone spots me.

The handle turns.

The door opens.

I let out a relieved sigh when it opens and quickly slip inside. The apartment isn't massive, but the minimalistic decor makes it seem pretty spacious. How do students get apartments like these? What does Cass's room look like? Zachary's? Apollo's?

"Hello?"

No answer.

I head for the bathroom and then hesitate. Is it weird that Reuben's not here? Maybe he's sleeping. Or studying with headphones on.

"Hello?" I push open his bedroom door and step inside, biting the inside of my lip. I should be in the shower already but damn it I'm too fucking nosy. I know so little about Reuben that I can't bear to pass up a chance to poke around.

After all, it's obvious the Brotherhood doesn't keep *anything* in their lair.

I go through Reuben's closet and find nothing but clothes. Only some books and a lamp on his desk. Notepads inside the drawers, all filled with school work. Something starts nagging at me, but I'm too busy snooping to give it any thought. He could be back at any minute. For all I know, he just stepped outside to make a call or smoke a cigarette.

My eyes move around the room until they settle on the bible on Reuben's nightstand. When it falls open in my hands a hard shiver courses through me.

Phrases in every sentence of every verse on every page have been highlighted.

I flip through, going faster and faster until I can't make out anything but an orange blur, but still the odd phrase leaps out at me.

Subject to your masters

Sells his daughter

Lay with him

Great plague

Fiery lake

Seek death

Know that I am God

There's a noise from the living area.

I snap the bible closed and hurriedly put it back on the nightstand, trying to adjust it the way I had found it. Then I grab my clothes, and dart out of Reuben's room, fully expecting him to be standing there.

But thank the Lord, he's not.

I release a noisy sigh, press a hand to my hammering heart, and let myself into the bathroom. After stripping down and folding my dirty clothes in a neat pile, I set Reuben's blood-red rosary on top of everything. I'm not sure how many times wood can get wet before it starts warping or something but I'd rather not risk damaging it. Plus, I'm sure the water will eventually wash away its glorious smell.

The hot water feels *sinfully* good. I start lathering my hair, eyes squeezed shut so I don't get shampoo in them. I'm just about to start rinsing when a hand slithers over my shoulders.

Reuben.

I bite the inside of my lip, half-mortified, half-jumping out of my skin with excitement.

I start to turn around, but then his hands sink into my hair and begin rinsing out the shampoo. It hurts when his fingers tangle in my wet hair, but my body still sparks to life—skin tingling, lips quivering, core tightening.

"Mmm, that's nice," I murmur, leaning into his touch.

Once my hair is rinsed, his hands slide down the back of my neck, returning to my shoulders. Strong thumbs sink deep into my flesh, applying pressure right on the precipice between pleasure and pain.

I groan at how magnificent it feels. At how *right* this moment is. It's as if wild electricity sparks between us. If I hadn't been drenched, I'm sure my arm hairs would be standing on end.

"Thank you for letting me use your shower. I really needed..." My words trail away as his hands move lower. He uses the flat of his hands to gently push me forward. On instinct, I put out my hands, bracing myself against the wall.

His knuckles dig into the flesh alongside my spine as he starts working his way down my wet skin.

One hand stays at the small of my back, working the muscles above my hips, the other slides down my ass.

Over the bruises Zachary gave me.

My breath catches at the faint thrum of pain he brings to the surface as he strokes my skin. Did Zachary tell Reuben about our deal last night? Apollo says they tell each other everything.

He squeezes my ass cheek.

I can't help but groan at the deep-seated pleasure that pain forces into my core.

He lets out a strange sound, as if he's holding back a groan of his own.

There's a muted splash as he moves closer. Now both hands are on my ass. My heart stutters as his fingertips sink lower and lower.

"Wait."

He stops.

"I'm not...I don't think I'm ready for...for that." My cheeks heat up at the admission. He must think I'm some kind of cock tease, letting him touch me and then pushing him away when—

His fingers wreath deep into my hair and he uses that grip to tilt my head back. Water streams over my face, some going up my nose. I splutter, starting to struggle, and then his mouth closes over mine.

Suddenly, the fact that I could drown doesn't matter anymore. Eyes closed, heart thumping, I melt against him.

He tastes like toothpaste and something sweet—soda?—and his lips massage mine so expertly that I barely notice when he draws me against him again.

Until I feel his hard-on, of course. I gasp into his mouth, my eyes flickering open. Water pours into them, forcing them shut again.

This is ridiculous. He's going to drown me.

"Let's get out," I whisper through his kisses, blubbering like a fish half the time.

In response, he reaches past me and turns down the faucet. Not all the way—water still patters over my face—but it's more a gentle drizzle than a cloud break now.

His mouth is on mine before I can blink the water out of my eyes.

Lips so warm.

Slippery.

Demanding.

Holy hell, how can anything feel this good?

I lose myself to him. My lips open on cue when his tongue slides over them, allowing him deeper inside. He moans against my lips, and my core tightens painfully at that urgent sound.

His hands coast down the front of my body. He squeezes my breasts, and rolls my nipples between his thumbs and index fingers hard enough to make me flinch.

Then he slides his fingers down my tummy. His kiss slows, and with it, his movements.

He presses harder against me, until I start aching deep, deep inside. His hands converge above my pubic bone, resting there for an eternity as he draws every ounce of resistance from me with a hard, languid kiss.

My arms had been dangling at my side. When I reach up to touch him, he grabs one of my wrists and instead urges my hand behind my back, between us, close to his cock.

Then the other hand.

I claw into his thighs. Does he want me to touch him? How do I—?

He grabs my wrist again, slides his hand over the back of mine, and meshes our fingers together. Then he drags my hand up his thigh, over his trunks, and up his stomach.

The fingers of his other hand are still just above my aching center. But when he urges my hand down his stomach and behind his underwear, those fingers sink down too.

I touch his cock the same moment he touches my clit.

I convulse, shuddering uncontrollably as a whiplash of heat and electricity surges through me. I break away from his kiss, my head digging into his shoulder as I arch away from his body.

But he refuses to let me go. He starts massaging my clit—hard and achingly slow—as he curls my fingers around his cock.

He rains kisses against the shell of my ear, using his teeth to toy with my earlobe as he starts pumping his cock with my hand, his fingers wrapped tight around mine.

"Fuck," I whisper, arching again as his fingers press even harder against my clit.

What the hell am I doing? I barely know this guy, and here we are, probably seconds away from fucking? I didn't think my first time would be in a shower. But, God, this feels so fucking right.

He moves my hand up and down his smooth, hard cock, speeding up as his fingers start strumming my clit faster than before.

My mouth falls open, but then I choke on a spray of water. He abandons my clit just long enough to turn off the water, and then dives back between my legs. But this time his hand sinks down lower than before. His fingertips sink between my lips, and he strokes all four fingers over my entrance.

I shudder hard, a broken gasp spilling out of my open mouth.

He groans, low and deep, and then I don't feel his underwear brushing against my hand anywhere.

Shit.

This is happening.

Fuck!

I'm terrified, but ecstatic at the same time. If just this feels so fucking good, I can't imagine—

His lips touch mine, demanding another kiss. I turn my head, and he devours my lips and tongue as if he owned them the second he saw me.

My eyes flicker on the cusp of opening as he applies a hard pressure on my clit and starts rubbing his palm against that nub of nerves.

"Fuck." I moan hard against his mouth, and move his cock down with my hand. I'm still jerking him off, but now his crown can't be more than a few inches from my entrance. I'm too short though. I have no idea how this would even work if I wanted—

"We'd need a stool for that, peaches," he says.

My heart plummets into my stomach when my eyes fly open and I see Cass's face an inch from mine.

I open my mouth for a scream, but he's too fast. In a second, he's flipped me around and pinned me to the tiled wall, one hand over my mouth the other on my throat.

My teeth can't reach him because he keeps his hand cupped. My nails don't seem to leave any marks on his wet, naked skin.

It was a trap.

That was what was bugging me earlier. I'd flipped through page after page of Reuben's handwriting, but I'd been too idiotic to connect the dots.

"Would you calm the fuck down?" Cass says, tilting his head and frowning as if I'm working on his last nerve.

So it's easier for him to rape me? I belt out an enraged—if muffled—scream and try to knee him in the groin. He twists away like all of this is second nature. Then he's up against me with the wall of his body, pressing me to the wet tiles.

"What, suddenly my dick isn't good enough for you anymore?" he growls. "And here I thought I'd do something nice for you."

Astonishment turns my bones to jelly.

He studies me for a second, and then slowly peels his fingers from my mouth. "Jesus, I'd have been fucked off with you if you'd gotten me in the nuts," he mutters.

"Nice?" I say, my voice violin-string tight. *"Nice?"*

He slaps his hand over my mouth again. "Keep. It. Down," he growls through his teeth.

I almost try and knee him again, but I have a feeling that would be the worst way to handle this fucked up situation.

He removes his hand again and steps back. I twist my legs and slap an arm over my breasts in a lame attempt at modesty as I start shaking. Not that it actually matters. His hands were all over me. *Almost* inside me. And I—I was—I'd had his…

His eyes slide down my wet skin. "You cold?"

"Sure. Let's go with that." I circle him warily as I move to the frosted glass doors.

I can't believe I let him touch me. I can't believe I almost let him *fuck* me.

I step onto the mat outside and reach blindly for a towel. Cass shifts as if he wants to get out too, but I lift my chin and widen my eyes at him.

"Don't you dare," I whisper furiously. "Don't you *fucking* dare."

He rakes his fingernails over his buzz cut, eyes narrowing. Then he brings up his hand and licks each of his fingertips, popping them out of his mouth one at a time. "Hate me all you want, your cunt is crushing *hard* on me."

"Get out."

He shrugs and slowly gets out of the shower. Unbidden, my eyes dart over his body as my mouth sets in a furious, trembling line.

Mother*fucker*.

Then I see the burn marks scattered over his muscles. I thought I'd felt something when my fingertips had skimmed his abs but I'd been too lost in his kiss.

Cass grabs the other towel and slings it around his waist. "So you wanna fuck in the bedroom or on the couch?" he asks as a wicked grin slides onto his mouth.

"Get out!" I stab a finger at the door.

He chuckles as he leaves the bathroom, but the sound cuts off as soon as I kick the door closed behind him with a strangled yell.

I should be shocked. Terrified even. But I'm just *fucking* angry.

How dare he?

How fucking *dare* he?

The worst part is, my body hasn't caught up yet. I'm still aching inside, and the more I move about trying to get my wits about me, the worse it gets. I feel like I'm going to implode.

Fuck.

I glare up at the ceiling, bite down on my lip, squeeze closed my eyes, and shove a hand between my legs.

But I wrench it away before I touch myself, shame worming through every inch of me.

I deserve this frustration for being such an idiot. Priests remain celibate all the time. Nothing to it.

I dry off and dress, and as I'm about to leave the bathroom, I hear Reuben's apartment door opening.

Thank God. At least I don't have to face him. My hand is on the door handle when I hear voices.

"What are you doing here?" Reuben asks.

I freeze, straining to hear through the door.

"Lady Malone needed a shower. I'm her escort."

"Your hair is wet."

"And?"

"Why is your hair wet?"

"I had a shower too."

My chest clenches so tight, I can barely breathe.

"Alone?"

"That would be wasting water," Cass says through a laugh. "It was her idea."

I bolt out of the bathroom. "He's lying!"

Reuben turns his frown onto me. He's wearing jeans and a tight-fitting sweater. Standing next to each other like that, it's ridiculous to think I'd confused Cass for Reuben. They're close in height, but Reuben's almost twice his size.

Oh, you knew, you blasphemous little slut.

The immoral, sinful, hedonistic part of me I always suppress figured it out right away, but the bitch kept silent until it was too late. Until I was so caught up in—

"So you didn't shower together?" Reuben asks, glancing back at Cass.

"No. I mean, we did, but—"

Reuben drops his gaze. "You should leave. I'm busy with an assignment."

"It wasn't my idea. He tricked me!"

But he walks into his room without a backward glance. Somehow, it's worse that he closes the door quietly and doesn't slam it. Disappointment always hurts so much more than anger.

"Shall we go?" he asks, quirking an eyebrow at me. He's wearing a smug smile, arms crossed over his chest as he leans back on one foot. The epitome of someone having a rip-roaring good time.

"Asshole!" I throw him the finger, glaring at him as I storm over to the door and let myself out.

Everyone around here is crazy.

As I walk back to my room, my dirty clothes bundled against my chest, Alice in Wonderland plays on repeat through my head.

We're all mad here.

We're all mad here.

We're *all* mad here.

CHAPTER TWENTY-TWO
TRINITY

"Come."

My heart flutters uneasily at Gabriel's command. I tug at the waist of my dress before letting myself inside. The dark, long-sleeved dress—a creation that would have better suited Wednesday from the Adams family—sits tighter than I like it. I even considered opening some of the buttons that run down the front, but I was afraid I'd end up looking like an eighteenth-century prostitute. Mom bought the dress for me about two years ago and I guess I've filled out since then.

The smell of cigarettes and wood smoke wash over me as I open the second door leading into Gabriel's living area.

He's wearing a button-up shirt tonight, sleeves rolled up to mid-arm, and a pair of dark slacks.

"Good evening," he says, turning from the fire to greet me.

I smile and lift my hand to wave.

He comes over, spreads his arms, and draws me into a hug. When I don't hug him back, he hurriedly steps back and releases me.

"Is everything okay?"

Wet concrete pours into my stomach. "Yeah, of course," I manage, although my voice is anything but steady. "I'm just a little tired. I haven't been sleeping well."

"When would you like to eat? Sister Miriam mentioned that you weren't at lunch today, so I'm guessing—"

Is he keeping tabs on me?

He cuts off as if I'd asked the question out loud.

I guess if anyone's going to notice I'm missing, it'll be Miriam. And I'm much easier to spot than one of the hundreds of boys in this place.

You're jumping at shadows, Trinity.

"I'm okay." I force myself to move closer, pretending to warm myself by the fire. I'm already starting to sweat, but if I keep my distance, he might become suspicious. I can't have him wondering if I have an ulterior motive for being here tonight.

Someone slipped another note under my door a little less than an hour ago. It wasn't Cass's handwriting, thank God. I assume it was Zachary's.

Keep him busy until eight.

You'll have 15 min alone.

Good luck.

It's half-past seven. I should have asked for supper if only to pass the time, but I can't eat when I'm this nervous.

The drive is hidden behind the elastic of my underwear. The dress's fabric is too thick for it to stand out, but to me it feels like a massive, ticking bomb you'd have to be blind to miss.

"How was your...trip?" I hazard. It's as good a question as any right? I have no idea where Gabriel's been the past few days, so—

Checking in on the children he has holed up in a basement somewhere of course—*children like Zachary and Reuben and Apollo and Cass. Maybe the Keepers in his newest hidey-hole fucked up and he had to go sort some shit out. Or maybe he brought some new Ghosts through for a tour of the premises.*

These are the bunk beds our little sex slaves sleep in. Here are their chains. This is where we feed them, but only if they've been good little boys.

Jesus *fuck*, Trinity. What the hell is wrong with you? You're here to prove Gabriel is innocent, or did you forget?

Still, I hear myself blurting out, "Where *did* you go?"

Gabriel lets out a soft laugh. "Nowhere interesting. I had a last-minute meeting with the construction company fixing up this old place." A rueful smile touches his mouth. "I truly hope their estimate is accurate. I can't have them gutting the school's finances."

Repair estimates and finances? Pointless. I have to get him talking about something personal. So I ask him the first thing that pops into my head.

"Were my parents good people?" I ask.

He frowns at me, and then slowly sinks into his chair. His eyes never leave me as he nips at the tip of a cigarette from his box and draws it out with his teeth to light it.

"Sit, child."

I obey without thinking. Thankfully there's already a chair near my ass else I'd have ended up on the floor because I obey without thinking.

"Would you like a drink?"

I nod. Gabriel sits forward in his armchair, twists to the side, and pours out two glasses of wine. One is little more than a splash in the glass, the other is close to the brim.

The sissy inside me wants to refuse his offer, but I push aside Trinity the Wimp just as she starts yelling about how wrong this is.

"Why didn't you attend Father Quinn's counseling session?" Gabriel asks.

I had just brought the glass to my lips, but I snatch it away again. "He told you?"

Father Quinn replaced Gabriel when he'd left Redmond. I'd never liked him—he stank of Fisherman's Friend sweets because he somehow thought it would cover up his halitosis.

I don't remember much about the week after my parents were killed. I *do* remember hearing words like "shock" and "therapy" bandied around everywhere I went.

I'd also forgotten that he'd offered counseling. More than once.

"I couldn't talk to him," I say truthfully.

"Can you talk to me?"

I look up. He's watching me with a most familiar look in his warm, brown eyes.

Patience.

Sympathy.

And with the wholehearted belief that whatever sins I had committed, we could overcome them together.

How the hell can a man like this possibly be involved with Ghosts and Keepers?

I almost want to tell him everything, just so we can have a good laugh about it and the world can go back to normal.

But I know my life will never be the same again, so does it matter what degree of fucked up I land on?

We're all mad here.

No, we're all fucked up crazy here.

"Trinity?"

My eyes snap back into focus. I take a tiny sip of wine, and then another because I barely tasted the first. It's not as brutally sour as the one the Brotherhood poured for me.

"I don't know how much you can help," I say hesitantly before taking another sip. "You weren't there at the end."

Gabriel looks down, and shadows darken his eyes. For a heart-wrenching moment, I think I've already blown my cover and pissed him off. I fully expect him to toss me out of his room. Instead, he lights himself another cigarette.

"You don't smoke, do you?" he asks.

"No."

"You're right to sound disgusted," he says through a faint laugh. "It's a disgusting habit." A thick plume of smoke jettisons from his lips. He sips from his glass, and then sits back in his seat, his eyes on the fire.

"I often wonder if they would still be alive if I'd stayed at Redmond," Gabriel says.

The wine glass clicks against my teeth as I turn to face him. I hurriedly lower it into my lap. "Why would you say that?"

"The same reason you wonder if you'd be dead had you been in the car with them." He drags hard at his cigarette, his voice tight as he speaks without expelling any more smoke. "One of Satan's many games, keeping us fixated on the past." Finally, he empties his lungs and then takes another sip of wine. "So easy for him to slip in without you noticing when you're so busy replaying events over and over to see if there ever would have been a different outcome. Like a spider crawling in under the door."

The longer he speaks, the tighter my chests grows. I've never heard him talk like this. His sermons are dry—all repetition and loosely connected anecdotes taken out of context—but this?

If this is how his conversations went with my parents, then no wonder they'd stay downstairs for hours after I'd been sent to bed. Our house had thick doors. Even with my ear pressed to the wood, all I heard was the murmur of low voices.

"Your parents are dead, Trinity. That's not something you can change or control. What you *can* control is how you feel about it."

"I'm angry," I say, without waiting for him to ask.

"At them, or yourself?"

I squirm in my seat. "Both." Then I shake my head. "No. Just myself."

"Because you didn't go with them to church?"

I nod.

"And why is that? Why *did* you stay at home that night?"

I run my finger around the rim of my glass. It's practically empty, but there wasn't much of it to begin with. I don't dare ask for more. I need Gabriel to see me as the same girl I was when he left Redmond— sweet and innocent and naive. Definitely not the undercover spy I turned into.

"We had a fight. They left without me."

"What did you fight about?"

My cheeks warm-up, and I know it's not from the heat of the fire, or the sip of wine.

"Something stupid. Something really, *really* stupid."

Silence settles between us. The fire pops, shooting a spark onto the hearth. It pulses like a dying heart before it fades to nothing.

There's a distant rumble. Is it starting to rain?

"No one alive is a good person, Trinity."

My eyes snap to him.

He smiles faintly, but without looking at me. "You asked if your parents were good people."

Suddenly I don't want to know the answer. Instead, I absently sip at my wine before remembering it's empty.

Gabriel holds out his hand. I give him the glass. This time, he fills it. But when he passes it over, he doesn't let it go straight away.

We lock eyes over that forbidden wine, and I can see his hesitation from the way he frowns at me.

"It's probably better if I don't—" I begin, releasing the glass.

"They shouldn't have treated you like that," Gabriel says. His warm brown eyes are cold now, a muscle in his jaw ticking.

My heart claws its way up my throat.

Oh my God.

He knows.

He fucking *knows*.

I ONLY REALIZE I've gulped down a mouthful of wine when it scorches the back of my throat. I blurt out a hoarse, "How did—?"

But Gabriel doesn't let me finish. "The way they confined you?" He glances away as he shakes his head. "Keeping you from the world like you were a sin?"

What the hell is he talking about?

His gaze touches me again, hot and livid, before jumping back to the fire. "I never wanted that for you, child. I told them time and time again that you had every right to lead your own life, but they refused to listen."

"My...parents?"

"An immune system must be exposed to bacteria and viruses for it to build a resistance against them." He waves a hand in my direction but without taking his eyes from the flames. "They left you defenseless."

Why is he so upset? Did bringing up my parents hit a nerve? I know he was close to them, but—

"If no one's good, does that mean everyone's bad?" I ask.

He turns to me, blinking as he focuses on my face. "We are all born into sin. Only through confession and penance can we cleanse our souls."

"I haven't confessed in a long time."

"Not since your thirteenth birthday."

I swallow hard, and wish I could look away. Mom made me do it. She made me climb into that cubicle and confess my sins to Father Gabriel.

"Don't let such silly things plague you," he murmurs, a ghost of a smile coming back to his mouth. "There are worse things in the world."

Worse than having to admit you'd been discovered touching yourself? Worse than feeling such overwhelming shame at your changing body that you swore never ever to even *look* down there again? And you've kept that promise ever since.

So worse, maybe, but not for me. Not back then.

Except, quite possibly, this moment. Because all that shame just came crashing back like a fucking tsunami.

"I should go," I mumble, wine sloshing up the side of the glass as I push to my feet. "You're busy, and—"

He's on his feet next. He grasps my wrist, and gently takes away my wine. "I'll never be too busy for you, Trinity. Please. Sit."

But my body feels like it's constructed from rusted metal.

He urges me down, but instead of taking his seat again, he goes to stand in front of the fire. His body blocks the heat, and for that I'm grateful. But it also blocks the warm light. I feel lost in his shadow.

"There's something you should know, child," Gabriel murmurs. "Something I've been meaning to tell you since you got here. I probably should have told you a long time ago."

Gabriel turns to face me. With his face in shadow, I can't make out anything in his eyes. But his voice is low and deep when he speaks again, filled with...what? Regret? Shame?

"It's about your father. I—"

A cell phone rings. I yelp at the unexpected sound, and Gabriel lets out a soft chuckle that sounds forced. "Sorry, dear. Let me just take this."

The fuck? No!

I whip my head around to stare at him as he walks away, already putting his cell phone to his ear.

My eyes latch onto the big wall clock hanging beside his window.

Eight o'clock.

Right on time.

CHAPTER TWENTY-THREE
ZACH

"I'm starting to think you don't like me anymore." The mischievous gleam in Cass's eyes belies the questioning tone in his voice.

"What tipped you off?" I pull the rope tight and give it a yank for good measure.

Cass gags theatrically before slipping the noose off his head. "I'd say forcing me to fake my own suicide, but we both know it goes back further than that."

We laugh. It's sad that we both sound genuinely unfazed.

I sent Reuben and Apollo to watch Gabriel's hallway. They'll message me as soon as he leaves his room. Then they'll keep an eye on both stairwells to make sure Trinity isn't surprised half-way through her scavenger hunt.

"Ready?"

"To die? Yeah, I guess. I mean, I'd hoped for another few years or so, but fuck it." Cass sends a toothy grin my way and climbs up on the chair. "Tell Mom I love her and Dad that he's a cunt."

We chose to stage this shit show in his English class. He hates Sister Sharon anyway, and I don't agree with her disciplinary methods, so it's a win for both of us. It's been difficult doing all of this with nothing more than the glow of a cell phone screen to work with, but we didn't want anyone to happen to look out a window and see a fluorescent lamp shining in a classroom that should only have souls in it tomorrow morning.

"May I state again, for the record, that there were easier, less lethal ways to create a diversion?"

"Cass—"

"I mean, we could have pulled the fire alarm—"

"Dorm doesn't have one," I cut in.

"Or flooded the bathroom—"

"Then I'd have to phone Miriam, not the provost. Keep up, Cass. It's this or broke. Why the fuck else would I be calling him, and not one of the other staff?"

"I could snap my neck, you know."

I snort at him. "I doubt it. But just in case—" I hold out my hand, and he glares at me before clasping it. "I can't say it was a pleasure knowing you, but at least we both know you'll be happier in hell."

"Damn straight I will," he says, showing me his teeth as he holds onto the rope and rocks the chair back on its legs. "Lucifer had me at succubus."

I check the time on my cell phone. "Thirty seconds."

"Jesus, just make the call," he grumbles as he slips the noose around his neck again. "Gonna take the old geezer like a century to get down here, and that's if he doesn't break a hip on the way."

I hop onto a nearby desk and peer out one of the small windows set into the top of the wall. "Fucking storm's turning the lawn into a swimming pool."

"Hope fuck face can swim."

"Making the call," I say, ignoring Cass's bored voice behind me.

I time his answer with my feet landing on the floor. "Gabriel! F-Father. Please, hurry!"

"Zachary? What's—?"

Cass starts making gagging noises. I whirl around, waving at him to stop.

"It's Santos!" I yell. "He said he's going to, to—shit, father, he says he's going to kill himself!"

Cass starts choking again. This time, he mimics sucking a giant dick to accompany the suggestive gagging sounds.

I wave him away and hurry out the door before Gabriel can overhear.

"Did he tell you where he was?"

"English. Sharon's class. Uh, room 2C."

"Are you nearby?" Gabriel's voice rises several octaves. I hear a door slam and his voice grows choppy, as if he's started running. "Can you see him?"

"No! I'm in the garage. I just got his text. Father, I'm not going to make it!" I tamper down a near-hysterical urge to start laughing. I've never pulled a prank before, but I understand why kids do it. The adrenaline rush is insane. My heart's hammering so hard it feels like it's denting my ribs.

"Call Brother Timothy! Tell him what's happened. I'm on my way." I hear his feet hitting the ground, and it feels like he's stomping over my chest.

I end the call with a trembling thumb.

It's now or never, Trinity.

Now or never.

CHAPTER TWENTY-FOUR
TRINITY

I watch open-mouthed as Gabriel disappears around the corner. I called out to him a few times, but I might as well have been mute.

Eight o'clock.

15 minutes.

Good luck.

Shit. What the hell just happened? I could barely make out anything from just hearing Gabriel's side of the call. But I know it was Zachary who phoned. The thought makes my hair stand on end.

There's no time for this shit. Start looking, Trinity.

I hurriedly close the door and race back into Gabriel's apartment. I don't bother with the kitchen or study area. If this laptop is filled with as much incriminating evidence as the Brotherhood says it is, he'd hide it somewhere a quick search wouldn't locate.

Damn it.

I throw open his closet and flick through his clothes. I search the bottom by his shoes and then I move onto his shelves. The scent of his fabric softener fills my nose as I worm my fingers all the way behind his sweaters.

Nothing.

I climb up on the shelves and burrow my arms between his luggage bags. I gag at the stink of mothballs coming off of them.

Nothing.

The clock back in the living area seems to have doubled in size. All I hear is that watch hand clanging through each second like a death knell.

Closet is a bust.

I haul open the drawer in his nightstand. A bible, a spiral-bound notebook, hand lotion, condoms—

I freeze.

Condoms.

Condoms?

What the fuck—?

There's no time, Trinity!

I slam the drawer shut, and try to will the sight of that black-and-gold packaging from my mind. I shove my hands under his mattress and shuffle all the way around the edge, grunting at how heavy it is.

Nothing.

I stick my head under his bed, and then crawl under when I realize it's too dark for me to see.

I try not to imagine that there's someone already under here, all the way at the back, reaching for me like I'm reaching for them.

Condoms?

Fuck it, concentrate!

Nothing. Bed's a bust.

I'm about to crawl out again when my hand brushes against something.

A thousand spiders burrow into my hair. I let out a strangled scream and have to force myself not to cannon out from under the bed, yelling.

It's just a bag, Trinity.

A bag *hidden under his bed.*

Jackpot!

I ruthlessly suppress the part of me that wants to wet itself and grab a fistful of the cloth bag, dragging it out with me as I crawl backward.

The closer I get to getting out, the more convinced I am that Gabriel is already standing in the room, waiting for me.

My heart is seconds away from exploding. I clear the last few inches and throw myself onto my back, clutching the bag to my chest like a shield in case Father Gabriel decides to pounce on me.

The room is empty.

No spiders in my hair.

Just condoms in the drawer.

I shove away the thought as I roll onto my knees and zip open the bag.

Gloves. A soft hat. A carton of cigarettes. A moleskin journal. Rolled up cables. A laptop.

A laptop.

I rip it out and flip it open. It doesn't look new, but since I've only ever used the library's clunky old desktop computers before, I wouldn't wager anything on my knowledge of this shit. But to compare it to the sleek, black machine Apollo was setting up yesterday? Yeah, this thing is ancient.

The screen is blank. I hunt around the machine, finger raised, until I spot the power button.

I stab it.

The machine remains dead.

Tick-*fucking*-tock, Trinity.

I drag my fingers down my face and stab the button again.

Nothing.

Dad had a laptop too. Never used it, but heard him swearing at it all the time.

Dead battery.

Battery died.

Gotta plug it in.

Cables.

The cables!

My hands are shaking so hard that I drop the bundle of cables twice as I scramble over the floor to the nightstand.

There's a lamp on it—has to be a power outlet nearby.

Tick. Fucking. Tock.

I yank the nightstand away from the wall, rip out the lamp's plug, and shove in the laptop's charger.

What time is it? How long has this all taken?

Don't look at the time, it'll only slow you down. They always get it wrong in the movies. Always looking back to see how far they've run, then—BAM! Dead.

Don't die, Trinity.

I fumble with the other end of the charger, but I can't get that tiny plug in that teeny little hole.

Stop.

Breathe.

Calm down.

Now try the fuck again.

It clicks into place.

"Fucking hallelujah." My voice sounds hoarse and broken.

I stab the power button. The screen switches from black to gray.

"Oh God, please. *Please.*" I hike up the side of my dress and fumble in my underwear for the drive.

It's not there.

I spin around, my eyes going wide. No. No! Did I drop it? Did it fall out while I was wriggling around under the bed?

PING goes the laptop.

My heart's about to give out, but then my fingers brush the plastic cover. It shifted, but it's still there.

The laptop's whirring, but nothing else is happening. How slow is this thing?

I can't stop myself.

I turn and look at the clock.

It's five past eight.

I deflate like a balloon, my shoulders sagging as I let out a relieved sigh.

What the fuck are those condoms doing in the drawer?

I squeeze my eyes closed. What did Apollo say about this device? Did the computer have to be on all the way, or just powered up? He said I didn't have to do anything, just plug it in, but *when*?

I guess it doesn't matter. Sooner rather than later, right?

My fingers have turned into foot-long sausages. I drop the cap and spend several billion tick-fucking-tocks trying to get the stupid fucking drive into the stupid fucking slot.

When it finally slides into place like a greased pig, I glare at it.

No wonder people throw computers and shit against the wall. I'm stinking of sweat, never mind those fucking mothballs.

The screen starts spitting out letters.

Shit.

Shit!

Was this a virus or something? Was that the Brotherhood's plan all along? But then I actually read the messages, and calm down a little. The computers in the library would spout shit like this too. Checking this, allocating that.

Normal. It's all normal.

My gaze is inexorably drawn back to the clock.

Seven minutes past eight.

Fuck.

I drum my fingers against the laptop's plastic frame. The Windows logo pops up, accompanied by a too-loud set of chimes that I'm sure Jasper heard back in our room.

Christ, I'm breaking out in hives.

Ten past eight.

This is ridiculous. There's no way a computer can take this long—

A bright blue desktop pops open. Twenty or so folders and files scream for my attention.

I have no idea if the drive is doing its thing, but I can't be bothered with it right now. I have about three minutes before I need to shove this thing back in its bag.

Three minutes to prove that Father Gabriel is a good guy.

Three fucking minutes.

CHAPTER TWENTY-FIVE
ZACH

My timing was off. Instead of the five to seven minutes I'd thought it would take Gabriel to make his way down to the classroom. He gets here in three minutes.

Three fucking minutes.

Did he run track or some shit?

I think I'm hearing things when his shoes thump up the stairs. I barely get to the other end of the hall before he clears the stairs. My heart beats so loud in my chest, I'm shocked Gabriel doesn't first stop to investigate the sound.

He races down the passage, a dark shape against the shadows. I've left the lights off to make it seem no one's been here yet except Cass.

Hopefully, Cass heard him coming.

Muffled voices reach me. I make my way down the stairs, race across the downstairs hall, and then come up the other side where Gabriel entered.

By the time I skid to a halt outside class 2C, I'm panting.

I flick on the light, flooding the classroom white.

Gabriel is on the floor. The chair Cass had been standing on lies on its back a yard or so away.

"Father?"

Gabriel shifts at the sound of my voice, but he doesn't look up. My chest is so tight, I can barely breathe. I like to think that I'm intelligent and cautious, but I just realized I'm an impulsive fucking idiot.

Cass isn't moving.

With the lights on, the ligature marks around his neck are too bright, too red, too fucking real.

"Did you call Timothy?"

Of course I hadn't. Cass was supposed to tip over the chair *as* Gabriel walked in. He'd be hanging for seconds before Gabriel brought him down.

Unless he slipped.

Unless he actually did break his fucking neck.

Unless the sick fuck let him choke to death as he watched, because he's known all along about us, known we were watching, and he was waiting for just the right moment, the perfect opportunity to—

"Brother Zachary!"

I flinch, tearing my eyes from Cass's slack face.

"Call Timothy." Gabriel doesn't shout. In fact, he sounds calm as fuck.

My fingers are numb as I slide my phone from my pocket. I make the call, and speak the words, but it's as if it's all happening to someone else.

Gabriel lays Cass on the floor and starts doing CPR. When he presses his mouth to Cass's, something inside me snaps.

"Don't!" I snarl, falling to my knees beside Cass's limp body. I shove Gabriel away, dimly aware that I'm doing this all wrong, *so* fucking wrong, but I can't stop.

This wasn't supposed to happen.

I close my mouth over Cass's and breathe into him, feeling his chest rise under my palm.

Once. Twice.

Start compressions.

Ten.

Twenty.

Thirty.

Gabriel sits back on his heels. His phone is out. He's talking to someone, but fuck knows who.

It's all over.

He knows.

And I don't give a fuck because I'm losing Cass.

Already lost him.

Fuck.

Fuck!

"Stay with me," I yell before breathing into his mouth again. Once, twice. "Stay the fuck with me!"

My ears whine like a buzzsaw. Cass's chest feels too spongy under my stacked palms, like I'm pushing down on a mattress and not my brother's chest. I will the force of every push to draw air back into his lungs, to massage his heart, to do whatever the fuck it was CPR is supposed to.

"Breathe!" I yell.

Gabriel's hand comes into view. For a sickening moment I think he's going to pull me away, to tell me I have to stop, that Cass is already dead. But instead he simply grabs the edge of Cass's t-shirt and draws it down his stomach.

Covering the countless cigarette burns scattered over his skin.

Marks *I* made.

Pain *I* inflicted.

My cheeks are wet, and I know I shouldn't be crying for some random student in front of Gabriel, but fuck knows how I'm supposed to stop.

I'm sorry.

I'm so fucking sorry.

I wish I could take back every nasty word I ever said to you, every fucked up thought, everything.

Every-fucking-thing.

"Zachary."

I'm staring at my meshed fingers as I shove down Cass's ribs. Twenty-five, twenty-six, twenty-seven—

"Zachary!"

I look up Gabriel, my face twisted with rage, with pain, with defeat. His eyes narrow, and his mouth thins into a stern line. "Stop."

"Fuck you," I growl out.

Gabriel's eyes dart up to his hairline. "Brother Zachary—" he says, reaching for me.

"Fuck, stop," someone croaks. A hand slaps weakly at my wrist. "Stop!"

I sit back and end up falling the last few inches onto my ass. Cass rolls onto his side, wheezing and gagging like I'd stuck my fingers down his throat. He puts a hand on his chest where I'd been doing the compressions and moans like a gutted pig.

"I heard something give," Gabriel says quietly. "You might have cracked a rib."

Jesus fucking Christ.

I scramble up, whipping my hands through my hair. The skin of my face is cold, tingling, two sizes too small. "I'm sorry," I hear someone say. "I'm so fucking sorry."

"Go wait outside, child," Gabriel says.

Blood whines as it races through my veins. "Cass—Cassius, I'm so sorry."

"Zachary!"

My eyes dart back to Gabriel. His face is pale, his mouth a hard, trembling line. He points at the door. "You've done enough. Go and wait outside."

It feels like I'm dragging my legs through concrete to get to the door.

I'm barely outside a moment before I hear running feet. Brother Timothy shoves me aside when I don't move, and falls down beside Cass, a paramedic's jump bag dropping to the floor by his knees.

"Cassius, can you hear me?" Timothy demands, grabbing Cass's shoulders and shaking him.

"Yes, fuck. Stop that, would you? It hurts. *God.*"

I step back further and further, until I can't hear Cass's voice.

I broke him.

I brought him back, but then I *broke* him.

The fuck is wrong with me?

My shaking hands curl into fists as I turn and force myself to walk away. There's nothing more for me to do here.

Like Gabriel said, I've done enough.

I've done enough.

CHAPTER TWENTY-SIX
TRINITY

A green light starts blinking on the device. I should take it out and shut down the laptop so I can put it back under the bed, but I can't. I'm frozen to the spot—faced with an email my brain doesn't seem capable of processing.

DEAREST GABE,

I wish you had never left Redmond.

I know it's been months since we last spoke, and it seems I only ever contact you when I need something, but I truly hope you understand my reasons.

I know you are busy at the school, and you made it very clear that I shouldn't contact you again...but Keith needs your help.

We need your help.

Things have progressed to a stage where I'm not sure I can keep this marriage together any longer.

My intention is not to guilt you into replying. I understand that there's a chance you might not even see this email. But I hope you do.

You've saved my marriage countless times before. I hesitate to ask, but can you save it again?

Can you bring us back to God's glorious light?

We need you, Gabe.

Keith most of all.

Please.
Monica.

THE FIRE POPS, breaking me from my trance. I whirl around to look at the clock. Quarter past eight.

I press the laptop's power button. It starts shutting down as I yank out the drive and hike up my skirt to slip it behind my underwear again.

A noise reaches me from the passageway outside Gabriel's room. So faint, it could have been my imagination, but I'm not taking any chances. Whether the drive had enough time to copy everything it needed, I don't know.

I slam closed the lid and pull out the cable, shoving the laptop back in the bag before winding up the cord as I trace it back to the power outlet.

Was that a door opening?

My heart knocks against my breast bone. I'm seconds away from puking with nerves.

I break off the tip of my nail when I pull out the power cord. I kick the side of the nightstand, shoving it back against the wall with my foot.

Tossing everything in the bag, I zip it up and crawl under the bed.

I can't bear going all the way to the back.

You're taking too long!

Fuck. I crawl out again, jump to my feet, and spin to face the door on the other side of the apartment.

Then I remember to breathe, and let out a massive sigh of stale air.

I tug my dress straight as I hurry back to the fireplace, glancing back over my shoulder to make sure the bedroom is in the same condition I found it.

I hiss in pain when my ass hits the chair. Despite the cushioning, I felt that impact all through my body. I shudder as I try to ignore the pain, and gently shift into a more comfortable position.

What were you doing while I was gone, Trinity? Who, me? Just been sitting here the whole time. Sitting here, watching the fire.

God, my heart's pounding. I wipe the back of my hand over my forehead, and then use both hands to swipe the sweat from my hairline.

Crackle, pop, grumble.

Caught between a hungry fire and an angry thunderstorm.

Shit, it's hot in here.

I get up again, scanning the bedroom again as I pass. Dear Lord, I hope I didn't fuck this up. I open the window and stick my head into the wet, chilly air.

Better.

Lightning fractures the sky, and a few seconds later a muted crack rumbles around Saint Amos.

I check the clock.

Twenty minutes past eight.

Damn it! I could still have been going through his emails. It only took me a minute to find the one my mom sent. Father Gabriel —*Gabe?*—is super organized. His emails were all sorted into folders. Accounts, Personal, Redmond, Bishop, To-Do, Unsorted, Spam, Sent, Deleted.

Mom's letter had been the tenth one in the personal folder. I guess it says a lot that the entire folder only contained a little over thirty emails. But although Gabriel likes to pretend he doesn't have a personal life, judging from my mom's email, he's had his nose stuck in our family's affairs for a long time.

His *guidance?*

If she only knew the shit the Brotherhood was accusing Gabriel of.

Oh, wait. She'll never know. She's dead.

There's no warning. One minute I'm glaring out at the black thunderstorm—the next everything blurs with angry tears.

I push away from the window sill and stalk back to the fire. Trinity the Wimp is yelling at me to stop, but I shove her in a mental closet and lock the fucking door.

Wine sloshes over the rim of the glass when I rip it off the side table. I tip my head back and swallow it all down in one go. Then I pour myself another from the decanter.

I even stare at Gabriel's pack of cigarettes for a moment, wondering if they'd help suppress the sudden swell of immutable fury roaring through me, but I dismiss the thought.

Weed. That's what I need.

I drain my glass, and press my hand to the back of my mouth as I pause, waiting for everything to come right back up again. It's red wine —what a fucking mess that will make of this pretty carpet.

A bitter laugh bursts out of me instead. I consider drinking straight from the decanter but then I remember I'm not a fucking animal so I pour myself another glass.

"That's enough, child."

I gasp in shock, spilling wine over my hand and—*yup!*—ruining the pretty fucking carpet. Spinning around, I stare at Gabriel with a slack mouth as he comes closer.

He takes the glass from my hand and urges me into the chair before perching on the arm. His head dips as he massages the back of his eyelids and lets out a long sigh.

"What's wrong?" I blink up at him, my hand reaching for him before I can snatch it away again.

That doesn't go unnoticed. Gabriel's eyes latch onto my hand where I keep it pressed into a fist in my lap. The shadows on his face seem to deepen.

"I'll have to reschedule tonight's dinner."

For a second, I have no idea what the hell he's talking about.

"Oh, this?" I nod, licking my lips. "Yes, of course." My tongue feels like it's growing thicker inside my mouth. Starting to regret the wine now, even if it did put out the fire raging inside me.

You can soak shit in alcohol, but ultimately that just sets the stage for a world-class explosion.

"I know I allowed it, child, but you shouldn't drink in excess. Or at your age."

Irritation flickers inside me, threatening to ignite my earlier anger.

Yeah, and a celibate priest shouldn't have condoms in his fucking drawer, but here we are.

I think I'm going to puke.

I stand, making contact with Gabriel on my way up. In an effort to veer away from him, I stumble over my own feet. If he hadn't caught onto me, I'd probably have fallen into the hearth.

His hand is on my hip. Strong fingers dig into my flesh.

Into the drive hidden behind my underwear. He frowns, and moves his thumb over the device. I twist away from him, blinking furiously as I try to sober the fuck up.

"I have to go," I state, holding up a finger. "But can—may?—I use your bathroom first?"

He frowns hard, and reaches for my hip again as he gets to his feet. "What is that?" he asks.

"Bathroom!" I yelp out, and then hurry away from him. I saw another door leading off his bedroom—it's either a walk-in closet for the hundred-plus clerical robes he needs, or it's the bathroom.

It turns out to be a bathroom.

I slam the door shut behind me, and because of that I don't make it to the toilet. Instead, I puke into the basin.

This is a new record for me. The most I ever puked was that time Mrs. Brady undercooked the hot dogs at the church fete for handicapped people back when I was sixteen.

I half-expect Gabriel to come inside and hold back my hair like Reuben did.

But he doesn't.

I spend a few minutes making sure there's nothing left to come out, and then a minute more splashing cold water on my face.

Unfortunately, the purge did nothing to sober me up. I stumble out of the bathroom and have to hold onto the wall as I study the back of Gabriel's head.

He's at the window, staring into the darkness.

He turns his head a little, but then straightens again. "Do you need me to help you back to your room?"

My spine stiffens.

We need your help.

"No," I say icily, crossing my arms over my chest despite how that makes me sway. "I'm p'fectly fine."

Besides the slurring, of course.

"I like to think I'm blameless, child."

It takes me a second to focus on him. "Wha'?"

He sighs, closes the window and turns to face me. There's a cigarette in his hand, and he drags at it till the coal glows red as Satan's horns.

"You asked if your parents were good people. And they are, Trinity. Truly…they are."

He walks up to me, a sad smile on his face. "But they're not blameless, and neither am I."

His hand is on my shoulder. I don't like it there, but I don't want him to stop talking. "What are you sayin'?"

He takes another long drag at his cigarette. Although he ducks his head to blow out the smoke, it piles up between us and still hits my nose. "Why did you go through my things?"

My eyes widen. "I didn't. I promise."

He looks to the side, drawing my gaze with his.

The bag I'd shoved under the bed is on top of the mattress, contents spilled out. The laptop is open. Even from here, I can see the email program is open.

It didn't shut down properly.

He knows I read the email.

But is that *all* he knows?

"I'm so sorry." I press my hands to my face, trying to hide behind my fingers.

"Shh," he murmurs.

An arm slides around my shoulder and draws me close.

I shudder against him, my hands still covering my face. "I'm sorry."

"I understand. I left before I could answer your questions."

He strokes my head and for some reason that's all it takes for me to surrender. That, and the half a bottle of wine I'd guzzled before he got back.

For a ridiculously sweet moment, *nothing* has changed. I'm sixteen, and I've just admitted that I don't believe in God. At least, not in the same way my parents do. And Gabriel's holding me, just like this, letting me sob into his shoulder.

But the moment is only that—a single moment. Fragile as a wine glass. And it shatters as soon as he speaks.

"I would ask you not to judge me, but—" his lips quirk into a smile that's warm, but so fucking sad. "You're a better person than I am, so you would have every right."

I lean back from him, my fingers sliding down my face. He cups my face with one hand, the other at his side, a half-finished cigarette dangling from his fingers. His touch causes my legs to lose their strength. I throw my arms over Gabriel's shoulders, holding onto him to keep myself upright.

"I drank too much," I tell him.

"I know, but this can't wait anymore. If you don't remember in the morning, then I'll tell you again. I'll keep telling you, until you find it in your heart to make sense of it."

His words are starting to run together.

Shit! He's about to lay some heavy fucking shit on me, but what. If. I. Don't. Remember?

"Tell me." I grab the front of his shirt, tugging at him. "Tell me what you did."

Tell me about Zachary. About Reuben. Apollo.

Tell me what the fuck you did to *Cass*.

Tell me everything, you sick, perverted—

"Trinity. Child. Look at me." He uses his hand to lift my head. Then he grips my chin and squeezes. The brief pressure brings me back from lolling off into a violent booze-induced daydream where he's crucified at the stake like Jesus, and the Brotherhood are the ones piercing him with spears.

"I had an affair with your father."

CHAPTER TWENTY-SEVEN
TRINITY

I'm on hands and knees. Technically, *elbows* and knees. I'd staggered out of Gabriel's room what feels like centuries ago, despite him begging me to stay and talk. I might have told him I was too drunk, too pissed off, too over his shit to stay.

I dunno. I just hope I didn't swear too much. Feels wrong, swearing at a priest.

That's not important. *This* is important. I hold up the drive and study it with narrowed eyes. Have to give this back.

But it doesn't fit under the door.

My plan failed because this stupid thing is too big.

I slit my eyes and concentrate on wedging the slim drive beneath the door.

"What are you doing?"

I look up and then sit back on my haunches in front of Reuben like a puppy begging for treats. How'd he know I'd be here? Coincidence...or had he been following me?

I hold up the drive. "Givin' this back."

Reuben watches me for a second and then reaches past me to unlock his door. Grabbing my elbow, he hauls me up and drags me inside his room. The door closes silently behind us.

I open up my hand, the drive on my palm. "Here."

Reuben barely touches me when he picks it up, and then immediately walks away. "What, no thank you?" I call after him.

I frown and glance around his apartment as he disappears into his bedroom with the drive.

I start nosing around again, but there's not much to see. The single drawer by the coffee station has instant coffee sachets and spoons in it. The microwave is empty. There's a cell phone charging next to the kettle, but when I try and turn it on, it asks for a pin. I try a few random numbers before a massive hand reaches around me, removes the phone from my fingers, and then wraps over my hand.

"You've been drinking," Reuben says.

"And?"

I flex my fingers inside his fist, marveling at how big it is. He could crush my hand without putting any real effort into it.

I hope he doesn't. I like my hand.

"Why would you get drunk around him? Or have you forgotten how dangerous he is?"

I laugh and arch into Reuben. "Hold me," I say, and then try to maneuver his other arm around my waist. But it's too heavy and unwieldy, especially since he's not helping.

"Tell me what happened."

"We spoke. He left." I hold up a finger and glance at Reuben over my shoulder. "That was you guys, right? You did something? He shot right the fuck out of there. I had more than enough time to copy everything."

I have no idea if that's the truth, but I'm not sure how long Reuben will let me hang around if he thinks I'm a failure. He might even send me back to Gabriel.

I flinch at the thought.

Never. I will *never* go back there. Never speak to him again.

He had an affair with *my father*.

"You're shaking."

"It's cold," I say, and try to make myself stop. Then I turn around, ending up facing him with his arm around my waist, still holding my hand. "But you can keep me warm."

His eyes drop to my mouth, then my throat, then my breasts. Every place they pause, the skin there begins to pulse.

"You can't be here," he says, releasing me and stepping back.

I *should* leave. I know that. But I don't want to be alone right now. Being alone would mean I'd have to replay all the shit that just happened, and in my current state, I don't know what to do with that information.

Then again, would I really be better off here? I feel safe around Reuben, but what if Cass or Zachary stop by? I already know I can barely fend off one of them…if they were to gang up on me—

"You're right," I blurt out, pushing my curls out of my face as a wave of cold tingles washes over me.

This is the last place I should be.

There's no safe place in Saint Amos anymore.

Maybe there never was.

I have to get out.

Reuben turns to watch me when I walk past him. "Do you want to know what's on the drive?"

I pause mid-step and peer at him over my shoulder. "You—?" I point to his bedroom. "You found something?"

He shakes his head. "We'll only know tomorrow. But do you want to know what we find, if we find something?"

It feels like a loaded question, and something I'm definitely not equipped to answer right now. So I err on the side of caution.

"Sure. I mean, of course." I nod and head back to the door.

I open it.

A hand slams down beside my head, closing it again. My spine stiffens like someone rammed a pole through my body. "What…what are you doing?"

Suddenly I don't feel that drunk anymore. Maybe it's the adrenaline surging through me.

"I didn't know you liked Cass," Reuben says.

"I…"

I *don't*.

For some reason, I can't say it.

But I don't!

Still, you enjoy what he does to you. The way it makes you feel. You've always loved the idea of being a sinner, haven't you?

"I'm not upset," he says in the same monotone as before.

Always so calm, so centered. Makes me wonder what it's like when he loses control.

Like you did with Cass.

Shut up!

"I should go," I say again. "Probably can't have anyone see me here."

"Do you still like me?"

"Yes."

Fuck. Fuck!

I shiver when Reuben touches the side of my neck, but it's just to draw a curl away from my ear.

"So you can like more than one guy at a time?"

No.

Yes.

Maybe?

Trick question! I *only* like Reuben.

Don't I?

What about Zach?

Fuck.

Well? What about him?

"Do I have to?" I murmur, trying to find an easy way out.

"Yes." Reuben's fingers trail down and then caress the ridge of my collarbones. That light touch sends a shiver through me.

"Why?"

"We're too close. Have been for so long."

"If you really thought that, then you wouldn't have kissed me."

He turns me around and gently grasps my chin. "Kisses mean nothing." There's a strange hitch in his voice that belies the words. Because he *does* like me, or because someone told him that a long time ago and he still believes it? "I like kissing girls."

My eyes widen. "Oh," I murmur, heat slowly crawling up my face.

Can I be more embarrassed? I thought Reuben genuinely liked me. But if it's just something he gets a kick from...?

Fuck it—he *does* like me.

I'll prove it.

"Then kiss me," I say. "Kiss me and tell me it doesn't mean anything."

He cocks his head a little to the side, as if intrigued by my suggestion. Then he ducks, scoops me into his arms, and presses me against the door. Just like last time, my legs wrap around him like I've done this a thousand times before.

Blasphemous little slut.

I'm suddenly too aware of how close my core is to his body. Pressed to his stomach just above his belt, I can only imagine what it would feel like if he was to lift my skirt so the rough fabric of his jeans could rub against me.

Damn it, I *am* a slut. Is this because Cass got me so hot and bothered earlier? Or is it because when I feel like this, I can't think about other things? Horrible, *confusing* things.

Maybe a little of both.

"Are you sure?" he asks.

"That I want you to kiss me?" I frown at him. "Yes."

"I mean, are you sure you want to test me?"

My frown deepens.

He shifts his grip, pressing me harder against the door. Even through my skirt, that friction is enough to send a host of urgent signals through my body.

Now every part of me is paying attention—from my lips to my nipples, to my center, to my fucking toes.

"You shouldn't treat this like a game, Trinity." Reuben's black eyes harden with the same intense determination he'd worn the day we met. He traces the outline of one of my buttons and then starts popping them open.

"You're supposed to be kissing me," I whisper.

"I am," he agrees calmly. "But you never said where."

Good God, now I'm picturing him kissing my breasts, drawing my nipples into his mouth and teasing each tight bud with his teeth. I start trembling internally. When I grab onto his shoulders, he pauses in his methodical work, his fingers in line with my nipples.

"Are you okay?"

"Yes," I say breathlessly.

He lets out a soft, "Hmm," as if he's not one-hundred percent satisfied with my answer.

God, this is torture. I'm tempted to ask him to hurry the fuck up.

The last button pops open. He slides a hand behind my bodice and parts the two halves of my dress.

But not all the way. Just enough so that I can see the edge of my bra when I glance down.

Then he shifts his grip and holds onto me with one arm—one arm? —while he hunts around in his pocket for something. What is he looking for, a condom?

I know where to find some.

Did Gabriel sleep with my Dad? Well, he'd have to, probably, to consider it an affair.

Dear Lord, I can't handle this shit.

I lean forward, my eyes fluttering closed, fully intending to kiss Reuben just to put an end to the sour thoughts filling my head.

But he moves his head aside so I end up kissing his fucking ear.

I huff impatiently and press the back of my head against the door, glaring up at him as he carries on rifling through his pocket.

I cross my arms over my chest, moving my mouth to the side. "What are you looking for?"

"This."

He lifts a red rosary. My hands fly to my chest, but I touch bare skin. "How did you—?"

"You left it here."

My mind scurries back to the shower I took earlier today. "No I didn't."

He says nothing.

"I must have put it back on."

Still nothing.

"I put it on top of my clothes. It would have been the first thing I saw."

He quirks an eyebrow at me.

"It must have fallen off." I keep brushing my skin and then hold out my hand, palm up. "Whatever. Give it back."

His fingers close over the red beads. "It's mine."

"You gave it to me."

"But you don't believe. What's the point?"

My heart stutters at that. His commanding stare forces me to drop my gaze. What the fuck am I supposed to say to that?

The smell of roses hits my nose. He's rubbing the crucifix with his thumb, intensifying the scent.

I bite down on my lip. I'm such a jerk. It obviously means a lot to him, and I'm demanding him to give it back.

He tenses when I lay my hand over his. I slowly close his fingers over the necklace.

"You're right. There's no point. It's yours, anyway."

But then, as I'm holding him, staring into those pitch-black eyes, a wriggling worm of doubt starts working its way through my mind.

"Wait..." I turn my head, watching him warily from the corner of my eye. "I *know* I put it on my clothes. It...it wasn't there when I got out."

He watches me with the patience of a rock.

My eyes go wide. "You took it."

There's the tiniest flicker in his eyes.

"Oh my God!" I slap a hand into his chest and begin squirming against him so he'll let me go. "You were *watching* us!"

He lets out a soft grunt, grabs my ass, and slams me back into the door hard enough to rattle it.

Shock dips me in ice.

My hands are on his chest, fingers digging into his muscles, but I slowly retract them and hug myself instead.

He lets out a long breath through his nose and then slowly scans my face like he's looking for something.

I don't know if he finds it, but a moment later he slips his rosary over my head and tucks it behind the open halves of my dress. Then he slowly starts buttoning me up again.

"Why?" The word warbles out before I can stop it.

"Why did I watch, or why didn't I stop him?"

"Both!" The anger's coming back, but I force myself to swallow it down.

"I watched because I like you. Because you were enjoying it. Because I wanted to see what you look like when you come."

I should be flooded with horror or disgust. Instead, I stare at Reuben with morbid fascination.

I thought it was *him*. That's the only reason I allowed—

"And I didn't stop him, because I was pretending it was me in there, not him."

His words spear into through me like a blunt knife.

"What?" I belt out, thumping his chest with my fist. "That makes no sense!"

He grumbles faintly as he steps back and lets me slip to the floor. I'm breathing so hard you'd swear I ran a fucking marathon. "That makes no fucking sense, Reuben!" I yell, bashing my other fist into him.

He catches my wrist before I can get off another blow and then closes his arms over me, crushing me to his massive chest. I let out a strangled yell, but fighting him is pointless.

"Can I kiss you now?" he asks.

That knife twists, scraping over my bones and shredding my heart. It takes every ounce of self-control I still have, but I manage a hoarse, "No. Never." I clear my throat and force strength into my words. "Never, *ever* again."

Then I shove at him with all my might.

And he lets me go.

I don't look back when I leave, but I manage not to slam the door. I take two steps before the smell of his rosary hits my nose again.

I leave it hanging from his door handle, blinking back tears as I stalk back to my room.

CHAPTER TWENTY-EIGHT
ZACH

My heart almost explodes from my chest when I spot Cass sitting on the couch. I wasn't sure if he'd be here. A part of me wishes he wasn't. A part of me can't be more relieved to see him.

Cass looks up from the latest edition of *Pussy Pounder* as I slip into our lair through the narrow opening in the bookshelves. I can't wait for the day we'll have a space of our own with a proper fucking door. No, fuck that. No doors. Just an archway.

I know exactly where we'll go when this shit's taken care of.

Whenever I go into town on the weekends, I spend an hour or so at the local coffee shop. Their filter coffee tastes like the shit you scrape out of a gutter, but that's not why I go there.

Their Wi-Fi, although spotty, opens up a new world. For an hour, I can escape this shitty school and the decades-long path my brothers and I have been trekking.

For those few precious minutes, I go house hunting. It started as a mental itch I had. We have a game we play. Can't remember the last time we did, but since our answers are always the same, I have that shit committed to memory.

It's called: what would you do, if you could do anything?

Not highly original, but for a bunch of kids trapped in a dark basement who'd never played sports or gone to the mall or even asked out a girl to the prom...it filled a void.

We played it once or twice after we escaped, but it became painfully obvious that we'd be adults by the time we'd had our revenge.

What did it matter, then, what dreams we had as kids?

But those things stuck with me.

Apollo loves the ocean even though he's never set foot on the coast. Before he was taken, he'd watch surfing championships on television and imagine it was him slicing through those waves on some beach in Malibu. Honestly, I think he just secretly wanted to take photos of chicks in bikinis. But who the fuck am I to judge, right?

One day I went to town on a supply run, hungover as fuck after a night of blunts and whiskey, and I decide to get a plate of something greasy at the coffee shop. Only to discover they have Wi-Fi.

In this place?

Shocker.

I had one of Apollo's old laptops with me. He wanted me to send it in, because he swore the on-board graphics card was malfunctioning. I stopped listening after the fifth time he mentioned the driver and took it with me anyway.

They keep forgetting they don't have to repair shit. *Ever.* If it breaks, I'll buy them a new one. Money means fuck all to me.

So, hungover as fuck, I decide to get Apollo's laptop out of the car and go online while I'm waiting for my grub.

I'm guessing the laptop didn't shut down properly because as soon as it boots up, the browser pops open and loads the last website Apollo had been on.

A Youtube video of some surf competition.

Minutes later, I was hunting down coast-side properties in California where I'm guessing—probably incorrectly—that a guy can catch the best waves.

Then I found it.

Six bedrooms, five en-suite. An infinity pool overlooking the ocean. A garage big enough for as big a collection of classic cars as Reuben wants. A game room for Cass, replete with a fucking billiards table. Billiards, not pool, because he's snooty like that.

There's even a fucking dance studio with wrap around mirrors on the walls, perfect for Cass to admire himself in.

I haven't told them about the property.

I also haven't told them I put in an offer on the place on Saturday. I know I'll be getting that call sometime this week—my offer was ten grand above asking.

It's eating me alive, but I have to make sure it's happening before I break out the champagne.

And yeah, I bought champagne. Four bottles of the most expensive brand the liquor store stocked.

"Love the new look," I tell him, pointing at my neck. "Just give me a heads up if you're about to start reciting bad poetry, though."

He's wearing a black turtle-neck shirt and dark jeans. Sullen colors which match the smudges under his eyes.

"I could have died," he says, voice as dead as his eyes.

"I think you *were* dead for a few seconds." I wish there were a power outlet down here so I could brew some coffee. The only other alternative is alcohol or weed.

I choose the whiskey, turning my back to pour out a shot. Fuck the fact that's it quarter past six in the morning.

"But luckily, you've always been a stubborn sonofabitch." I glance at him over my shoulder when I don't hear the rueful chuckle I was expecting.

"It worked," I say.

Cass shifts a little, and then runs his palms down his legs. "Yeah?"

"She took the drive to Rube last night."

"So why aren't they here? Why aren't they going through his shit?"

"You know Apollo has to be in the kitchen before breakfa—"

"You think I give a fuck?" Cass yells.

I set down the bottle of whiskey and turn to face him. He's on his feet, hands bunched into fists at his side. But he's glaring at the floor, not me, as if he can't bear to make eye contact.

"Cass..."

"I risked my fucking life for that shit," he says, finally looking up. Eyes the color of dirty ice stab through me. "I don't care if you have to go drag that little cunt out of the kitchen by his fucking ball sack, you go and—"

"Christ, Cass, I'm here," Apollo says.

We both turn to him as he sidles in through the opening to our lair. He's wearing a baggy plaid sweater with an unraveling collar, sweatpants that have seen better decades, and a pair of tiger-striped gumboots. Judging from his rat tail hair and the damp patches on his top, it's started raining again.

He slides a backpack from his shoulder and collapses on the couch, then glances across at me and groans when he sees the bottle in my hand. "Don't we have coffee down here yet?"

"No power, remember? It's this or warm beer," I say.

"Fuck it," he grumbles, hiking up his sweater as he shoves a hand under the fabric to scratch at his ribs. "I'll get coffee later. Let's get this over with."

I take my usual seat and both me and Cass watch Apollo as he slips the drive into his new laptop.

"So what shit did you make up for Gabriel?" Apollo asks as he starts tapping the laptop's touchpad. "He ran out of there like someone had set his grandma on fire."

My eyes go to Cass, but he keeps his head down, using his thumbnail to push back his cuticles. "Does it matter? It worked."

"Yeah it did," Apollo says through a grin without looking up. "Looked real fucking spooked. That's—"

He cuts off and starts shaking his head.

"What is it?" I sit forward. "Apollo?"

"Shit," he mutters, his eyes flickering as he scans the screen. "There's nothing here."

"What do you mean there's nothing?" Cass growls. He grabs the laptop from Apollo, stabbing the down button as a glare slowly deepens on his face. "There's tons of shit on here."

"Yeah, but nothing useful." Apollo takes back the laptop, scowls at Cass, and then gets up and goes to sit in the armchair opposite us. "Just a bunch of crap."

"You couldn't have gone through everything so fast," I say, wincing around my first sip of whiskey.

Apollo lets out a world-weary sigh. "I'm using keywords and search strings. Either he's code-named the shit out of everything, or he's encrypted the important stuff." Apollo scratches his head and then gathers back his hair from his face. "I'll keep looking, but I have a feeling he's not keeping anything important on here."

"A feeling?" Cass sits back in his seat, crossing his arms over his chest. "How about you actually check first?"

"The fuck crawled up your ass?" Apollo mutters, sending a questioning frown my way before focusing on Cass. "I've done this hundreds of times. I can tell if someone's trying to hide shit."

"I'd feel better if you took a good, hard look."

Apollo lifts his thumbs from the keyboard, throwing me an exasperated look. "Zach—?"

"Do a manual search," I say. "It's the closest we've gotten to him yet. Maybe there's something you're missing."

"Oh, there's something missing all right. She only got like eighty percent of the drive. Guess she pulled out early." He glances up with a coy grin which none of us return, and then mumbles something under his breath as he goes back to the laptop. "And, he hasn't even bothered to clear his browser history in..." Apollo holds up a finger as he stares at the screen. "Forever. *Literally*, since the dawn of fucking time."

"Or he could have deleted just the shit he didn't want you to see, leave everything else, then it *looks* like he didn't delete anything," Cass says, lifting his eyebrows at Apollo.

"So either he's really fucking innocent, or he's really fucking guilty." Apollo sniffs. "Go figure."

"Apollo, take the laptop with you. Go through it today and make sure. Check every fucking cluster on that hard drive."

He mutters something sarcastic about "clusters" and snaps the laptop closed with ill grace. "Sure thing, Captain." He stands as he slings the backpack over his shoulder again. "But on the off chance I'm right—" a glare for Cass "—what the fuck do we do? If it's not on here, then he's keeping it someplace else."

I study him for a second, and then shrug. But before I can open my mouth, Cass cuts in. "We tell her it didn't copy anything. Tell her she has to do it again."

"I don't know if she can," I say.

Cass turns his glare on me. "Does it look like I give a fuck?"

"Dude, seriously, what's your deal?" Apollo demands, his hand tightening on the backpack's strap. "You have another wet dream about Zach and wake up with a sore ass?"

Cass rushes so fast to his feet, I'm already reaching to stop him going for Apollo. But he doesn't rush him—he just stands there, chin up and shoulders back, as if waiting for Apollo to throw the first punch.

Then he grabs the neck of his sweater and tugs it down.

I squeeze my eyes shut. It's instinct, something I've always done when I'm suddenly faced with a sight I can't—*or won't*—process.

But then I force my eyes open. Force myself to see.

I force myself to become a *witness*.

It'll come down to us versus them, if I get my way. My brothers feel different, of course. They don't want any of this shit going to trial. Their definition of justice is biblical.

An eye for an eye. A life for a life.

And they're convinced that each and every Ghost took a life.

The marks around Cass's neck are swollen and bruised. But he always bruised easily. The Ghosts liked that about him.

Easily damaged, but impossible to break.

Apollo gapes at Cass's neck, the unspoken question writ large in his wide eyes.

"She's going back, and she's getting what we need," Cass says through his teeth. "And this time, there won't be a fucking noose around my neck."

"I hear you, man," Apollo says, putting out a hand as he immediately switches into conflict resolution mode. "But don't you think we're putting a lot of shit on her shoulders? What if she can't do it?"

"She's a smart girl, isn't she? I'm sure she'll figure it out. She just needs the right motivation."

There's a heartbeat of silence before Cass pushes past me. Apollo watches him leave and then turns angry eyes on me.

"What the fuck happened?"

I hold my tongue. I'd been about to spout a whole monologue about how shit got fucked up and it shouldn't have gone down like it did. But none of that matters anymore, does it?

"I fucked up." I take my seat again. I study the glass in my hand and then toss everything into the back of my throat. "I fucked up, and Cass got hurt."

"Yeah, no shit." Apollo sinks down on the edge of the armchair. "Is he okay, though? Like, mentally?"

"I don't know. We haven't had a chance to talk."

I'd gone to his room last night. He hadn't been there. I'd eventually tracked him down in the infirmary, where a grim-faced Timothy was filling up an orange prescription bottle for him.

When I'd tried to catch up to Cass in the hallway, he'd shoved me out of the way without saying a word. I know when I'm not wanted. I didn't try and go to him again. I was hoping he'd have cooled off by now. Guess I was wrong.

I've been getting a lot of shit wrong lately.

"Does Reuben know?" Apollo asks quietly.

"No."

"I'll have to tell him."

"Obviously."

Apollo lets out a sigh. "He's gonna be pissed."

"Aren't you?"

"Yeah, of course. But what's done is done, right? Can't change anything. No reason to start yelling and shit."

I go over to refill my glass.

"Don't you have class?" Apollo asks.

I set the bottle down again. "Yeah. Fuck."

"Smoke a blunt," Apollo says, coming up behind me. He lays a hand on my shoulder and squeezes my muscle. "It'll help more than the whiskey. Want me to roll—?"

"Don't you have shit to do?" I snap. "Reuben, the data, breakfast? Sounds like a busy fucking morning."

Apollo withdraws his hand. The sigh he lets out as he leaves takes me back.

Fuck, it takes me back.

I'm losing my shit again, and he knows it. Cass probably knew it before anyone, but he loves playing with fire just as much as the rest of us.

But no one, *no one* likes to get burnt.

CHAPTER TWENTY-NINE
TRINITY

Instead of going to morning prayer, I hide out in a restroom stall staring at the freshly painted door. From the faint marks shining beneath the white paint, it looks like someone had gone to town on the thing with a Sharpie. Wish I knew what they'd written.

My appetite hasn't been back since I puked last night so I don't bother going to the cafeteria when the breakfast bell rings. Instead, I head back to my room and try and get in an hour's sleep.

The next bell rings me from a death-like sleep I don't remember falling into.

Time for class.

Thankfully, I only have Calculus and Sociology before lunch. It gives me half the day to work up the courage to find a way to excuse myself from Psych with Brother Rutherford.

Despite my nap, exhaustion weighs down my limbs and fogs my mind.

I had an affair with your father.

I. Can't. Even.

I thought I'd wanted answers from Gabriel, but I changed my mind.

Now that the shock's worn off, all I'm left with is a weird mix of disgust and anger. Not disgust over the fact they're two guys, but because Dad cheated on my mom. And with our fucking priest, of all people.

But that's not what's eating me alive.

If Gabriel is capable of having an affair, then what *else* is he capable of? And since he's openly admitted that he has sex with men...

I cover my face with my hands and rock forward on my bed. Class starts in a few minutes, and I'm still dressed in last night's clothes.

I came to Saint Amos to be with the man I thought of as a friend.

But I was wrong. There's nothing here for me. No friends. No support.

Come the weekend, when all the other students transfer over to Sisters of Mercy for spring break...

I'll be going with them.

WHEN I ENTER the dining hall at lunch, finally peckish for the first time today, I immediately regret my decision when I spot my tray with its pink post-it note.

TRIN

There's a heart over the I again. Thankfully, the actual food inside looks like everyone else's. If anything had been cut into the shape of a heart, I'd have bolted.

Jasper tries to get my attention, but I ignore him and head for the back of the room. When I walk past the kitchen doors, I spot Apollo through the window.

I ignore him too, even when he beckons me with a flick of his hand.

The Brotherhood has what it wants. I'm sure Gabriel's computer was stuffed full of all sorts of incriminating evidence. It's time they realized I'm not useful anymore and left me alone.

Apollo doesn't leave the kitchen or try and attract my attention again. I sit and eat my sandwich, pretending not to notice the way the boys around me stare as if expecting me to start doing somersaults.

Then Sister Miriam comes up to me, stopping right beside my bench during her usual rounds.

I pause mid-chew and look up at her as my mouthful of cheese-and-tomato sandwich dissolves on my tongue.

My stomach flips over when she hands me a folded note. "What's this?"

"It's a note, Miss Malone." Miriam's voice could have fixed our little issue with the melting ice caps.

"Thank you?"

But she's already gone. The boys around have me have all transformed into spotted barn owls. I'm itching to fold open the note and find out what it says, but then anyone at the table could read it.

It looks just like the notes the Brotherhood slips under my door. Same paper, same fold. Probably just a coincidence.

More likely, it's a note from Father Gabriel.

Gabe.

I twist my mouth to the side and shove the note into my pocket. The dress Sister Ruth made for me feels softer after it's gone through the laundry a few times. I'm grateful for the thick fabric now. It's been raining pretty much nonstop since last night, so the temperature inside the dorms has plummeted.

I leave the other half of my sandwich uneaten, and take my tray to the rack filled with empty dishes. I spot Apollo in the window again, but I pretend not to see him beckoning me.

Did they find something on that device? Is that why—?

No, fuck it.

Curiosity killed the cat, hung the monkey, and drowned Trinity Malone.

I'm done looking for answers.

CHAPTER THIRTY
TRINITY

I get as far as the prayer room down the hall from the cafeteria. Glancing around, I duck behind the pillars shielding the alcove's door and tug the note out of my pocket.

I apologize sincerely for my behavior last night. I was out of sorts, and I shouldn't have handled such a delicate matter the way I did.

Please join me for dinner tonight.

I am sure you have many questions.

I would like to answer them.

Gabriel.

My heart is thundering like a waterfall by the time I reach the end. Did Miriam read this? There'd be no way for her to decipher such a vague letter, but I'm still convinced she knows everything.

I had an affair with—

Fuck!

I crumple up the letter and hurl it away from me, tears blurring my vision. I storm off as fast as my whipping skirts allow, wiping furiously at my eyes as more tears build up.

Why can't I just be normal?

A normal girl, with a normal family, attending a normal school, with normal friends.

Is that too much to ask, Universe?

Rain batters my face. I glare up at the sullen clouds stretching from horizon to horizon. In their dull light, Saint Amos looks more like Dracula's castle than ever before.

I spin around and give Saint Amos the finger. Then I stalk over the lawn, heading for the classroom block. I'm early for my next class, but if a brisk walk through the drumming rain can't clear my head, nothing can.

I was going to skip out on Zachary's class. I'm pretty sure he wouldn't have reported me. But I can't bear the thought of being stuck alone with my thoughts one second longer.

Halfway down the slight incline, my shoe hits a patch of thinning grass and I slip in the mud.

I sit for a moment like that, rainwater soaking through my dress, before I push myself up and carry on walking.

Fuck you, Universe. I've had worse.

Don't have your notes, Trinity. Textbook's still in your room.

And so what? Let Zachary write me up for detention.

The rain should be steaming off my skin, that's how mad I am. But all it does is pound down, wet and relentless, until I finally step under cover of the eaves. I shove open the door and storm inside, heading for Zachary's class.

Breathing hard from climbing the stairs, I pause a second outside his door before going in.

I come to a stop as soon as I'm inside.

He's at his desk, hand cupping his jaw as he stares at nothing. When he looks up at me, the heavy frown on his face clears in an instant.

He gets to his feet, watching me expectantly.

"What?" I snap. "Did you also forget how to thank someone?" My skirts whisk around my legs as I storm up to him. "It's easy. You say, 'thank you,' and then I tell you to go fuck yourself, because it wasn't a pleasure."

His frown is back. "What?"

"The files." I wave my hand. "The things I copied. You got it back, didn't you?"

"Yes, but—" he begins, stepping around the desk.

"But *nothing*. The least you owe me is a thank you, and I'm still fucking waiting." I grab my hips and start tapping my foot. "Well?"

"Well *nothing*." He rushes forward, grabbing the side of my dress before I can move out of reach. "Did you even *find* his laptop?"

"Wh-what?" I splutter.

"How did this play out in your head, hmm?" He drags me with him as he heads for the door.

And then he locks it.

I go stiff a moment before the panic hits.

"Let go!" I yank at his hand, but he's holding on so tight I'd probably tear the fabric before I could peel off his fingers.

Instead of releasing me, he slams me into the wall beside the door. Even if someone were to look through the frosted glass, they wouldn't see either of us.

I open my mouth to scream, but he slaps a hand over my lips before I can get a sound out.

Fuck.

I try and knee him.

He kicks my legs open and wedges himself between my thighs, inadvertently hiking up my dress to a rather inappropriate height. When I go for his eyes with clawed fingers, he grabs my wrists and slams them into the wall above my head.

Fuck!

"Listen carefully, Miss Malone, because I'm only going to say this once," he hisses in my ear. "There was *nothing* on that drive."

I yell against his hand, but of course he can't understand me. And all my protest earns me is him slamming his body against mine and driving the air out of my lungs.

I collapse against him, wheezing.

"You're not listening."

I try and say "I'm sorry" through his hand. Some of it must come through because he eases up ever so slightly on my wrists and pulls back so he's not crushing me to the wall.

For some reason, my body responds with despair at the sudden loss of pressure. Like I somehow *enjoyed* the fact that he was suffocating me.

He puts his mouth by my ear again. "You seem to think you can just do whatever the fuck you want. Let me assure you, little girl, that's nowhere near accurate."

My eyes are squeezed shut, but he stays quiet for so long that I dare to open one just to peek at him.

He's watching me like a jungle cat.

"We need that data." He squeezes my wrists, grating the bones together. I mewl against his hand, nodding furiously to convey just how ready I am to listen and obey.

"You will go back to him tonight. Do you understand?"

Another furious volley of nods.

The fury on his face subsides a little. He studies me again, his gaze tracing every contour on my face.

"And you will bring it to us the moment you have it, not a minute later. Do you understand?"

I nod and then push a vehement, "Yes" through his fingers.

His lips quirk into a smile that's as cold as the ruthless gleam in his eyes. "Good girl."

It shouldn't, but even his backhanded praise sends a sensuous ripple through me. Perhaps it's just relief that he's decided not to slit my throat.

I squirm a little, trying to convey to him that I would be happy to comply even more if he stopped pinning me to the wall like a maniac.

His eyes grow hooded. Slowly, he slides his fingers off my lips. They settle around my throat, which isn't much better for my health, but at least now I can talk.

Which means I could try to persuade him that I'm on his side.

Their side.

It doesn't have to be true. Fuck it, it *definitely* isn't true. But I like to believe I'm getting better at lying. Or, at least, warping the truth to my advantage.

But first, I need to figure out why he seems dead set on the fact that I didn't do my job.

"I did what you said." I keep my voice soft and low, not wanting to provoke the beast that's only now starting to retreat. "I don't know why it didn't—"

"Think we give a fuck about your excuses?" he rasps. My eyes fly shut as he starts squeezing my throat. "We don't!"

"But I did everything you said." Despite my best efforts, frustration builds as I force my voice to stay calm. "I found the laptop under his bed, and I put the drive into the—"

"I don't want to hear it, little girl."

Boiling hot anger pours into me. I've had just about enough of everyone in my life telling me what the fuck to do. How the fuck to feel. What I can and cannot control. Which version of the truth they think they can get away with.

My father and I were never on the best terms, that's a given. He ruled our house with an iron fist, and I always resented him for that. But I obeyed, because it's what my parents expected from me. Because the bible said so.

Honor your parents somehow became shorthand for blindly obeying every single rule. For letting them tell you what to believe and how to behave.

They shouldn't have treated you like that.

No, Father Gabriel—fucking Gabe—they shouldn't have. But they did.

Everyone did.

Everyone still does.

Will it never end?

Or has it only gone on this long because I've let it? Because I submitted where a normal, sane human being would long ago have thrown off their shackles and stormed the plantation?

My veins thrum with sullen rage as Zachary carries on talking, his mouth an inch from my ear. "I don't care how you do it, but you *will* get us that data, and you *will*—"

My eyes fly open. "No!" I yell. "If you want it so bad, get it yourself!"

His fingers tighten even more as he grinds his hips into me. "Did you just shout at me?"

I freeze when his hard-on presses into my belly.

Oh my God. He's enjoying this!

I almost laugh at the thought. Of course he's enjoying this—his dick was twice this size when he was *spanking* me, what the fuck am I expecting? He gets off on other people's pain, so I guess humiliating them, torturing them, it's all the same.

"Gabriel's busy." I swallow and try not to let the feel of his cock distract me. "He told me so last night. He'll be busy this whole week."

He rakes his gaze over my body, and then glances to the side. Curiosity, of course, gets the better of me.

It's ten past one.

His class starts at half-past.

We both look back at the same time. He moves against me again, and this time it's obvious he wants me to feel his erection. My heart spasms with panic while my inner thighs contract with the urgent need to close and deny him access.

Dear Lord, all he has to do is dip down, and he could be inside me. If we were both naked of course. But he's wearing slacks, and I'm in this monstrosity of a dress, so—

"I know what you're thinking," he murmurs. His mouth twitches, and then he's biting down on his lower lip, drawing that tender flesh through his teeth. "But as much as I'd like nothing more than to fuck you against this wall, we both know this isn't how it happens."

A heatwave crashes over me. I let out a mangled, "What?"

He releases my throat, dragging that hand over my breast. He squeezes so hard that I yelp in pain, and then catches his lip between his teeth again.

"I've been thinking about it," he murmurs, crushing me with his body again. His hand coasts down my belly, and I feel him move his erection aside so he can burrow his fingers between us.

"Fucking you."

He wriggles his fingers through the folds of my dress. I quiver when he makes contact with my bare skin an inch above my underwear.

If he hadn't been pressing my wrists to the wall, I might have ended up on the floor. The lower his fingers move, the more strength leeches from my body.

"You know where it will happen, don't you?" His voice drops low. Rough, guttural. He barely sounds like himself. "In our special place, down there in the dark."

His mouth touches the side of my neck and despite everything, a shiver dances over my bones. He slides his lips over my skin, and then grazes my jaw with his teeth. I twist my head away, terrified at how hard my heart is pounding.

His lips follow, and he nips at my jaw again. A moan slips out of me before I can stop it, and in response he groans and dips down.

"That place where no one can find you. Where no one can hear you scream."

I gasp and jump onto my tippy toes when the crown of his cock presses against my underwear. A hard, aching throb pushes into me, almost as if he'd already broken through that flimsy barrier. He grabs my jaw and wrenches my head back to face him.

"And trust me, girl, we'll make you scream," he whispers, a malicious light dancing in his eyes. "Because it always hurts like fuck the first time."

He devours me.

When I close my mouth, he forces it open with his tongue. When I try to move away from his cock, he slides a hand over my entrance and squeezes me so hard that I whimper into his kiss.

"Christ, we're going to enjoy making you bleed."

Shock finally battles through the confused blur of emotions roiling inside me. I bite down on his lip and buck my hips against him as hard as I can.

I taste blood in my mouth a second before he falls away from me. Staggering to the side, I barely find my feet before his hand is around my throat again.

Lights dance across my vision as he slams me against the wall.

"I like it when you fight. Playing with dead things isn't any fun."

He laughs at me.

And then he kisses me.

Blood and mint-sweet saliva mix in my mouth. He shoves his hand up my dress. Before I can slam my legs shut, he strokes me through my underwear with his knuckles.

That feather-light caress is so at odds with his kiss that for a long moment I'm lost.

His kiss slows, but becomes harder. Somehow more urgent. He strokes me again, sending a deep ache through me.

Instead of pushing him away, I claw my fingers into his chest.

His breath hitches.

He rakes his nails against my inner thigh, leaving a trail of fire behind. I gasp and rear back, and whatever had been keeping me at bay snaps.

Zach steps back, dragging a hand over his mouth. There's a cut on his bottom lip, smears of blood around his mouth, but it doesn't look like he's bleeding anymore. He gives me a quick, condescending scan with his forest-green eyes, and then points to the classroom door.

"Clean up before someone sees you," he grates.

And I move to comply without a thought. With my back turned, I stop.

"No." I don't turn back. I don't look at him. If I see him, I'll falter. "I'm not your puppet anymore. I'm not *scared* anymore." I hear movement behind me, but I simply curl my hands into fists and refuse to let fear take root.

"Things have changed. I can't go back there again. Not tonight. Not ever. And if you contact me again...if you threaten me again..."

I swallow hard and force myself to turn around.

Zachary's watching me with a cocked head, face unreadable, body slack. As if his mind became disconnected from his body. It's the most terrifying sight I've ever seen but somehow, I push through.

"If you or any of your brothers come near me again, I'm calling the police. Or the church, or something. Someone."

Fuck it, Trinity, stay strong.

"Stay away from me. And stay away from Gabriel."

The last is as much a surprise to me as it is to Zachary. He straightens his head with a snap, eyes boring into me like a physical force.

"Or I'll tell him everything."

I should have led with that. Zachary's face slowly pales, but I know it isn't with fear.

It's anger, or rage, or a dirty-bomb of the two. I back up, and feel behind me for the door.

I turn the lock.

Then the handle.

I keep my eyes on him like I would a wild animal, just in case he decides to pounce on me before I'm in the clear.

The last thing I see before I close the door is Zachary's face.

He looks like he's seen a ghost...and he's planning to murder it.

I barely make it to the downstairs restroom. I puke into the basin, my stomach contracting so painfully, I'm shocked there aren't chunks of blood in the sink when I rinse it out.

It takes a few seconds before I can convince myself to look in the mirror.

My hair is mussed and my dress isn't sitting right. But it's the blood on my chin and around my mouth that makes me force down a dry retch.

Trust me girl, we'll make you scream.

I have to get the hell out of this school.

CHAPTER THIRTY-ONE
ZACH

Reuben doesn't bother to knock. It's not that he doesn't respect my privacy or any of that shit. The four of us never need permission to speak to each other, or even just to be in the same room. If we'd had to put up with pleasantries like that back in the basement, we'd all have gone stark raving mad.

"I came as soon as—" he begins.

"Sit."

He takes the foot of the bed, perching picture perfect like always. Straight spine, chest out, chin up.

I watch him for a second, and then reach over to my drawer and take out a joint I'd rolled just for this occasion.

"It's the middle of the day," Reuben says. "Someone could—"

"What?" I snap. "Ex-communicate me?" I glare at him from the bed where I'm sprawled on my back.

As part of my pious disguise, I took a room more befitting a first-year student than a teacher. That's Zachary fucking Rutherford for you. Groveling would-be priest who couldn't swat a fly.

I'm not scared of you.

But she sure fucking looked it. Trembling like a newly born foal. It had taken every atom of self-control I still possessed not to pin her to my desk exactly like in Cass's drawing, and fuck her into submission.

Monsters breed monsters.

Rube shakes his head when I pass the joint to him after lighting it up.

"I insist," I say, pushing the words through my teeth.

He could have argued. He might have won. Instead, he takes the joint, studies it, and hits it like a champ.

That's what I love about Rube. He knows when to say yes, and when to say no.

That's how he stayed sane with his Ghost. That evil motherfucker broke him over and over again. Eventually Rube stopped fighting. Every "no" turned into a "yes". He taught himself to submit.

We'd all have been a lot better off if we hadn't fought so hard. But then everyone except Cass would be as broken as him. Days like today I don't know how Reuben can stand to look at himself in the mirror.

He hands back the joint without making eye contact.

"She won't do it," I tell him before taking a drag.

"Why?"

"Because sometime in the last twenty-four hours, she decided we're full of shit and Gabriel's a fucking saint."

"She said that?"

"Pretty much." I study the tip of the joint, and then move my focus to Rube's face. He's staring at nothing again—most convincingly. "He got in her head."

Rube lets out a soft sigh through his nose before leaning back to dig in his pocket.

He exchanges a piece of mangled paper and his red rosary for the joint.

I read the note and then toy with the rosary while Rube helps himself to the rest of the joint.

She was lying to me. Not only is Gabriel not busy, he *asked* to see her tonight. I'm not sure I like this version of Trinity. It takes a special skill set to manipulate people with backbone. I don't think I have the energy to play that game.

"Guess we should have seen it coming," I say.

"So we're back to Plan A?" Rube exhales a plume of smoke.

"Not yet."

He looks across at me, frowning hard. "Then what?"

I wriggle my shoulders under me, pressing my head into my pillow. "I'll go."

"To see Gabriel?" Reuben sounds uneasy.

"She told me where he hid his laptop."

"How will you get in?"

"I'll figure out a way." I wave my hand at him. "Leave it to Beaver."

"Cass should go instead." Rube should have taken my glare as a warning, but he just keeps going. "He's got a reason to talk with Gabriel."

"So do I."

"Yeah, but—"

"He's sacrificed enough." Rube goes quiet, but I can sense he wants to say something. "What?"

"Cass. He was—"

"What, Rube?"

But Reuben shakes his head. "It doesn't matter. You're right—you should go."

I frown at him. "What were you going to say?"

He turns to me, a faint smile on his mouth. "We're getting close. Can you feel it?"

Is it the weed, or is he being weird on purpose? "Close to what?"

His smile inches up, but it doesn't grow warmer. "To the end."

I shove my hands under my neck and massage those suddenly tight muscles. "You excited or something?"

He takes a moment to consider. "Eager."

"For vengeance?"

His dark eyes latch onto mine. "You know what you'll have to do?"

I blink, thrown by his sudden change in direction. "What, tonight?"

He nods.

Yeah, I fucking know. I'll have to do whatever it takes. Just like Cass.

"Like you said, we're getting close. Can't fuck it up now, can we?"

He grabs my ankle and squeezes. I wince, but the pain I feel is ephemeral. He keeps his thumb there, digging into the sensitive spot behind my Achilles tendon. It doesn't seem intentional, but I learned a long time ago that Reuben does everything for a reason. He puts other psychopaths to shame.

"Then do whatever it takes, brother, and let's finish this."

GABRIEL'S DOOR IS OPEN. I stand in the hallway for a moment, my face slack and my body non-responsive no matter how hard I try to force it to move forward.

He knows you're coming. No need to postpone the inevitable.

I wrap my hands over my chest, grabbing my elbows as I step inside. No use going in like a warrior in a battle charge—I must be the epitome of calm-as-fuck Brother Zachary. I can't let my mask slip for even a second.

Not like it did last night with Cass.

I broke him.

But he's still alive.

For nothing.

We don't know that.

Shut the fuck up!

The argument in my head ceases. For now.

Let's get this over with.

I announce myself with a weak, "Father?" as I step through the antechamber and into his apartment proper.

I've only been here once before, and then too briefly to remember much. The fire is lit but smoking heavily, as if the logs he put on were damp.

The laptop isn't under the bed like Trinity said it would be. It's right in front of Father Gabriel on the four-seater dining table.

White light bathes his face and reflects off a pair of glasses I've never seen him wear. I know I didn't make a sound getting here, but as if he senses my presence, he looks up from the screen.

The jolt he gives when he sees me couldn't have been faked and suddenly I'm questioning every fucking thing that's led me to this point.

"Son," he says, hurriedly taking off his glasses and standing as he closes the laptop lid. "I'm so sorry, I didn't hear you come in."

Son?

I suppress a disgusted snarl before it can reach my lips. "It was open." And then I add a belated, "Sorry, I should have knocked."

"No, no." Gabriel moves around the table, lifting his hands. "It's perfectly fine. I was just..." He looks toward the fire. "Is it too warm? I thought with the rain it would be colder tonight."

He's wearing a t-shirt and jeans. With his glasses off, he could have been in his late thirties.

Keeps himself buff for a priest. Vain much, Father?

My eyes narrow as I study his back. What fucking game is he playing, pretending at some saintly priest who needs glasses to read and gets so easily caught up in his work he wouldn't notice the knife plunging into his neck until it was too late?

Now I'm wishing I had a knife on me. Wishing I'd crept up behind him and used it.

But I could never forgive myself for doing such a selfish thing. My brothers deserve to take his life as much as I do.

We made a pact.

Their vengeance is mine. Mine is theirs.

If we can't find the Ghosts, if we can't get Gabriel to confess and give up their names, then we agreed to kill him together.

Gabriel's voice wrenches me back to the present. "I'm glad you came to see me."

"It's about Santos—" I begin, eager to get this shit show on the road.

"Yes." He waves a hand to one of the armchairs. "Please, sit."

My skin crawls at the thought of being closer to him.

Coward.

I take the seat he offers and risk another glance around his room. With my back to it I can't see much, but at least I have a good view of the bedroom area from here. His bed looks roughly made. Did he just draw the sheets up and plump the pillows?

Was he sleeping before he decided to turn on his laptop? Or has he not tidied since he woke up this morning?

Perhaps he never went to sleep.

I'd love to know what happened here last night. What he and Trinity spoke about. What he said to turn her against us.

Or had we done that ourselves?

"I know this would have been discussed at length during your seminal training, but after last night, I feel you may need a refresher."

I frown up at Gabriel. "About what?" And then add a reluctant, "Father."

"Celibacy."

I look away, my lips writhing in an attempt to smile. I transform my bemusement into confusion so that when he turns to face me, he'll see nothing suspicious. "I don't follow."

Gabriel's face is anything but warm and kind. There's a hardness to his mouth, a chill in his eyes.

There he is.

Is our Guardian coming out to play?

I slide my hands along the arms of the chair and sink my fingertips into the cushion.

We stare at each other until he breaks the frigid silence. "When did you and Cassius meet?"

My eyelashes flutter before I can widen my eyes in surprise. I don't even have to fake it.

"When he enrolled?" I grimace inwardly when I hear my words come out as a question and not a statement.

Gabriel's mouth curls up at the edges. "This is a safe place, child."

A safe place?

My fingers dig deeper, and I let them. It's either that or they'll be digging into his fucking throat.

"What is it that you're insinuating—?"

He lets out a soft huff of a laugh, a sad smile touching his mouth. "God sees everything." He lifts his hands for all the world like he's preaching a sermon. "*I* see everything."

Cold shock flashes through me. I'm on my feet, hands balled in fists. Gabriel doesn't seem surprised by the sudden vehemence in my voice when I say, "And what is it that you see, Father?"

He steps closer, until there's barely a foot between us.

"I see a lonely young man who turned to a friend for comfort."

His hand lands on my shoulder, but I dip away from him and stumble back. My jaw clenches so hard, I don't think I could have spoken if I tried.

"It's something I've seen a hundred times, if not more. And while it's perfectly understandable, it's still a sin."

Is he talking about the basement? Back then we only *had* each other.

Where else could we have found comfort but in each other's arms? There was nothing wrong with it.

There *is* nothing wrong with it.

Nothing.

Gabriel follows me, face neutral but his cast with deep shadows.

Cunning, shrewd, *cautious*.

So careful not to reveal anything.

"I know you, Zachary."

And there it is, bare and naked. He knows me. Gabriel's known about us *all along*.

"Then you know I've known *you* for a long time too," I growl, no longer bothering to disguise any element of my true self. "So why do we keep playing these childish games?"

Suddenly, there's hesitation in Gabriel's eyes. And when I step closer, it's his turn to step back.

Dancing with each other.

Parrying. Attacking.

Like we've practiced this altercation in our minds for years.

I know *I* have. Why wouldn't he?

They say strangling is an act of passion. I can't agree more. I'm in love with the thought of snuffing out the Guardian's life with my bare fucking hands. So much so, my fingers itch to be around his throat.

He lifts his chin, his gaze wavering before his mouth sets in a hard line. "You don't know anything, child. You're dealing with malevolent forces you can't *begin* to understand."

Too fast, he grabs me. We're against each other but with bodies bristling—repelling each other like same-pole magnets.

"I know exactly what I'm dealing with," I grit out as I scour his eyes for the truth. For his *genuine* self. But before I can find anything, he grabs the back of my neck and digs his fingers into my flesh.

A shudder courses through me, and I hate myself in that moment more than I ever have before.

I used to think I was a sadomasochist. That I enjoyed both inflicting and receiving pain.

But that's not the case.

I simply *endure* pain in return for others allowing me to inflict it on them.

His hard grip rouses a sexual tension in me—not because I enjoy the pain he inflicts, but because I know that soon—so much sooner than I'd thought—he'll be at *my* mercy.

A mercy his Ghosts eradicated from me years ago.

"Don't act like you hate me," Gabriel murmurs. "I *am* you. And you are me."

"I'm nothing like you!" I yell. I fist his t-shirt in my hand. "I'll *never* be like you!"

He tsks me as he searches my face, a fond smile stretching his mouth. "I'll let you in on a little secret, child." He licks his lips, and on instinct I lick mine. "You can only hate yourself for so long. Then there's nothing left to do but forgive."

I should have seen it coming, but I'm so wrapped up in my own hateful thoughts that his mouth is against mine before I can push him away.

Though that contact is brief, the outrage of his unsolicited touch rips through me like an electro-magnetic blast.

"The fuck?" I stagger back from him, wiping my mouth with the back of a shaking hand. My disgust is mirrored on his face.

He tilts his head to the side and blinks slowly at me. "So you can fuck a man, but you can't bear to kiss one?"

He walks up to me. I fall back with a warning growl he ignores.

"It might feel like less of a sin, but trust me, son, it's not."

My back hits the wall.

Gabriel stops a few feet away, sliding his hands behind his back.

"God has already condemned us both to hell."

CHAPTER THIRTY-TWO
TRINITY

I should be in the laundry room doing chores, but with four days left till the end of term, I doubt anyone's going to lay down the law on a rainy Monday afternoon.

So instead I'm in my room, considering sneaking into the shower room.

I feel dirty after what Zachary did to me.

How he made me feel.

And while there's nothing I can do about my filthy mind, the least I can do is wash the feel of him off my body.

After what happened yesterday with Cass in the shower, though...

That delicious tightness and tingling had stayed with me for close to an hour, maybe a little more.

Today? It's been three hours since Zachary touched me, and I can still feel him stroking me through my underwear.

None of it makes sense, of course. I should be horrified—disgusted even—by what he did.

Scaring me like that.

Forcing himself on me.

I thought my heart had been beating with panic...but now I'm wondering if it hadn't been excitement instead.

Maybe if your life is as boring as mine, anything is exciting.

It's seriously messed up to think that my body is capable of confusing fear with lust, or pain with pleasure.

God, when did I turn into such a sexual deviant?

I realize I'm stroking my hip bone through my dress and hurriedly snatch away my hand.

Not going to happen, Trinity.

I wouldn't be able to bear the guilt. The shame.

Don't let such silly things plague you.

Gah, I knew it!

My mind keeps going back to Gabriel or Zachary.

Gabriel feels the need to answer my questions. About how my father was gay, or the fact that he cheated on my mom?

The Brotherhood will hurt me in the worst way if I don't find the data they're looking for. I may have bought myself some time today with Zachary, but how much?

There was an announcement about the end of term in prayer today, Jasper told me. The buses are arriving on Thursday morning to take everyone through to Sisters of Mercy.

Can I hide from both sides of this war until then?

I grab my pillow and shove it over my head, muffling a frustrated yell.

"Need a hand?" Jasper asks from the doorway. "I'd be more than happy to oblige."

I whip away the pillow and glare at him. "Fuck off," I snap.

He pushes away from the door with his shoulder. "Geez, what's got your panties in a bunch?"

"Nothing." I watch as he rummages in his side of the closet and pulls out casual clothes. "Hot date?"

Maybe he's meeting Perry. I can only hope he won't go down to the library again.

"Gross," Jasper says.

"Why gross?"

"Because I'm going to see Father Gabriel, you sicko."

"How was I supposed to know?" I call after him as he exits our room.

I shrug my shoulders into the mattress, wincing when one of the many lumps dig into my back. Why is he going to see Gabriel? Maybe he's going to confess about liking Perry. About the things they did.

Great. Now I'm reliving *that* saucy interlude in my head.

Is this what being horny feels like?

Maybe it's hormones or something. My cycle's due to start any day now...I always get a little cranky before. Except this time I'm craving Reuben's pecs, Cass's mouth, and Zachary's fingers, not pepperoni pizza.

Oh, Lord. I'm *still* hot and bothered. I throw my arm over my eyes, letting out a huff of annoyance.

For fuck's sake.

The worst part is, I know exactly what will help. But ever since Mom made me confess, it's been impossible for me to get myself off. Soon I was pushing away the urge the moment it arrived.

Not what I'd consider healthy, but there you go.

I'm rubbing my hip bone again.

Damn it.

I jump up and go close the door, peeking out into the hallway first to make sure there's no one around.

What I wouldn't do for a lock on this door.

I plop back on the bed and skim my fingers over my dress until I'm hovering an inch or so above my clit.

Then I wait for the shame to drive me back like it always does.

Except...it doesn't.

My fingers creep closer. My core constricts in anticipation the closer I get to my clit, as if more and more nerve endings spark into action.

I make a soft noise in the back of my throat when I finally touch myself through the thick fabric. It's so subtle, I can barely feel the pressure, but fuck it if anticipation isn't eighty-percent of the thrill.

Quickly I lift my knees, letting my dress slip down my thighs and pool at my waist.

I grab the hem of my skirt and tug it up my stomach—

"Am I interrupting?"

Are you fucking kidding me?

I sit up in a rush, cheeks glowing as I shove my skirt into my lap to cover my underwear.

Is it just me, or does Apollo's grin stretch even wider when I glare at him? "What the hell are you doing here?"

He stands to the side, one arm holding open the door, the other beckoning me with a flick of his fingers. "Come with me. I want to show you something."

"WAIT. WAIT!" I push the words between heaving pants. "You're going too fast."

"You gotta work on your stamina, Trin," Apollo says. I don't have to look at him to know he's wearing a fat grin. "We still have a flight to go."

"Do I look like an athlete?" I ask, straightening with a wince and forcing myself up the stairs after him.

He laughs as he disappears around the corner of the landing. I arrive a few moments later, blowing like a racehorse. Okay, maybe not that bad, but I definitely have a stitch. I guess I didn't have to run after him when he loped up the first flight of stairs, but he had me so curious I couldn't help myself.

He hasn't answered a single one of my questions. Hasn't told me where we're going. But I realized about halfway up the tight corkscrew stairs that we must be going to one of the towers dotting the four corners of the dormitory. That, or the bell tower.

I was kinda freaked out taking the stairs. While I won't go as far as to say Saint Amos is cozy and inviting, the dorms are a far sight homelier than this staircase. Here, there's nothing to dress the rough brick wall, and the only natural light comes from small square windows filled with thick panes. Of course, with the overcast sky, it's practically night outside already. That leaves the job of illumination to the handful of naked light bulbs sticking out of the walls every few yards. They're so far apart that I have to step through deep shadow to reach the next one.

Someone could break their neck.

"You made it," Apollo says, sounding genuinely surprised.

"Screw you," I mutter, and then stop talking so I can concentrate on getting air back into my lungs.

We're standing next to a thick wooden door that Apollo unlocks with a key from his pocket.

I half expect to hear bats take flight when the door swings inward.

The bell tower.

It's so much larger than I'd thought. The bell hangs a few yards away from where we're standing. A wide ledge circles it, opening to balconies.

"It's..."

"You should see it during the day. The view I mean. The bell's nothing special."

Apollo moves inside. When I don't immediately follow, he grabs my wrist and hauls me after him. "Come on. We don't want to be here when the bell goes off. It's super fucking loud."

He leads me past the bell to a much smaller door set off to one side. The metal door makes it seem like some kind of maintenance area.

The door opens to black nothingness.

Then Apollo turns on the light, revealing a tiny room with nothing more than a desk and a rickety-looking office chair, fabric unraveling on one corner of the cushion.

There wouldn't be enough room in here to swing a cat. Possibly not even a small guinea pig. Not unless decapitation was on its bucket list.

Less than a yard away from me is a blank wall.

Well, it *used* to be blank. Now it's covered with sheets of paper board glued together to form a massive canvas.

I step forward on automatic.

I'm dimly aware that Apollo's still holding onto my wrist, but instead of letting me go, he comes in behind me and shuts the door.

"This is everything," he says.

He's not kidding. The wall is covered with photos, news articles, and pink post-it notes. Lengths of blue string join seemingly random objects together, forming the type of web only a spider on LSD could make.

"There's so much...stuff," I murmur as I step to the side to try and find a starting point.

Apollo uses the grip on my wrist to lift my hand. He carefully forms my fingers until I'm pointing, and then moves my fingertip over the collage.

He stops a foot or so away from the middle. I'm pointing at an old photograph—color, but edging toward sepia and slightly out of focus. It's a school photo showing a small class of about twenty girls and boys dressed in school uniformed lined up on sports benches with two adults.

Behind them rears the majestic turrets of Saint Amos.

FRIENDS OF FAITH Children's Home
   CLASS OF 1991

MY HEART SINKS like a stone tossed into a deep well. It still hasn't hit the black bottom when Apollo says, "Recognize him?" and drags my finger to one of the boy's faces.

"I do."

But it's not the only face I recognize. I swallow hard and then glance at Apollo. He's looking at me, not the board. "Why are you showing me this?"

"They told me you don't want to help anymore," he says. "But I think you should."

I rip my hand out of his. "Zachary told you to bring me up here?" My voice is tight, my hands balling into fists.

"No." Apollo shakes his head. "He—they…" He lets out a long sigh and pinches the bridge of his nose before looking back at the hysterical matrix of evidence scattered over the wall. "They'd kill me if they knew this was here."

"*Kill* you? Bit dramatic, don't you—?"

"Don't tell them. *Please.*" He turns to me, grabbing hold of his elbows. "We're not supposed to keep stuff like this around."

"So why do you? Why is this here?"

"I had to put it all together so I knew it made sense." He waves a hand at the photos and clippings, shaking his head. "I mean, it's easy for them. They're all so fucking smart. They just keep this shit in their heads. You ask any of them which year the fire broke out on Rhode Island, how many orphans apparently died in it, they could just tell you straight off the bat."

Fire? Orphans? What the hell is he babbling about?

"Me? I get it all confused. So I made this. It helps me keep track. Helps it all make sense."

I find the clipping he's talking about.

14 DEAD IN FIRE

MY EYES SWIVEL back to him. "And it all leads here?" I ask, pointing at the photograph again.

"Yeah, in some way or the other." He runs his palms carefully down the wall, smoothing everything in his path. "I thought, if you saw this, you would know it's not just four guys talking shit. It's real, Trin." He cautiously moves closer. "Can you see how real it is?"

"Where did you get the photo?" I force myself not to look at it, even though I'm itching to snatch it off the wall and burn it.

"High school yearbook. Tracked it down in a library a few years ago."

"How old is he?" My voice is hoarse now. I'm barely holding back... what? Anger? Fear?

Apollo is right. This changes everything. This photo?

It. Changes. Everything.

"So will you do it?" he asks. "Will you go back and try again?"

"I don't know." I have to crane my head to look up at him when he steps closer still. "I'd need more time, I think. Or maybe I did it wrong. Zachary said—"

"He lied." Apollo's eyes narrow. "He wanted you to think you'd fucked up so you'd try again."

My mouth falls open. "That's—"

"Why I brought you here." He squeezes my arm. "But please, don't say anything. Not to anyone. Understand? No one can see this."

I nod mutely, wishing my skin would stop tingling where he touched me. Maybe it was our proximity, or my brain trying to cope with the next-level shit it had just been dealt...but suddenly I want nothing more than to kiss him.

He must see something in my eyes because his gaze drops to my lips a second before he ducks down and presses his mouth against mine.

Wanting and doing are two very different things, of course. No matter what I want, I shouldn't let him kiss me. I mean, what does that say about me?

Blasphemous little sl—

You know what? Fuck it.

I arch into him, tangling my fingers in his hair. If this is going to happen, then for once I'm going to be in charge of it fucking happening. No more being bullied. No more unwanted fingers in my yoohoo.

Apollo huffs out a laugh as we totter back from the force of my kiss. But instead of pushing me away, or laughing harder at my pathetic attempts at seduction, he slings an arm around my waist, hoists me up, and plops me onto the desk behind him.

The cold metal starts seeping through my dress.

But cold is the last thing on my mind.

I'm focused entirely on Apollo's mouth. But, also, how silky his hair feels as I twine it through my fingers. Then there's his intoxicating taste, and the way he urges my hips closer to his with both hands on the small of my back.

Okay, fuck it, my mind is going in fifty different directions. But just like that web on his board, everything leads back to him.

His kiss grows deeper. He slides his tongue into my mouth, cautiously curious, until I give him unrestricted access.

Then he kisses me so hard my core starts to ache, and I can't help but moan against his lips.

"Fuck, you taste good," he murmurs, a volley of hot pants brushing my skin as he pulls away. "I thought they were making that shit up."

Wait...*what?*

I shove him away. Stare open-mouthed.

He grins, rakes his hair out of his eyes, and pounces on me again without a word of warning.

They told him what I *tasted* like?

I thump a fist into his chest, but he just grabs my wrist and moves it off to one side without pausing his kiss.

It's ridiculous to attack him, especially since I'm still kissing him back. Fuck...kissing him back? I'm barely holding my ground. He's so passionate, so enthusiastic, my heart starts fluttering in my chest like a moth trapped in the tub.

But still I try and pound him with my other fist.

And then he snatches that one too. Now they're both at the small of my back, and he uses both hands to keep them there while he urges me forward, closer to the edge of the desk.

He tips his head forward, leaning his brow against mine. We're both panting, and this time it has nothing to do with climbing stairs.

"I could kiss you all day," he breathes, and then brushes his lips over my nose, my cheek, my ear. "But that bell's going to go off in a minute."

And then the craziest words fall out of my mouth. "Can we go back to your room?"

Hormones.

That's my story, and I'm sticking with it.

He grins against my mouth, and a happy huff caressing my lips. "I'd love to, but I can't. Raincheck?"

I nod, biting the inside of my lip hard enough that I'm surprised I don't taste blood.

He lifts me, twirling me around once before letting me slide to the ground, kissing me on the way down.

Then he herds me out of the tiny room, allowing me a precious second to stare at his media mural before he shuts the door and locks it.

When he turns, I force a wide smile onto my face and desperately hope he can't see through it.

That photo is going to haunt me. Those faces...

I push the thought out of my mind. It's pointless trying to understand, especially when the answer is but a question away.

Gabriel wants to see me? Well guess what...?

I *do* have questions for him.

CHAPTER THIRTY-THREE
TRINITY

I spend a good half hour fussing with my hair as I stare at my reflection in the restroom mirror.

Stalling.

Trying to convince myself that going to see Gabriel is for the greater good, even if I'm not sure I actually want him to answer my questions.

Eventually there's nothing left to do but to start climbing those stairs.

I'm so deep in thought that I don't notice his door is open until I'm about to walk through.

I pause.

Should I announce myself or just go in? He did invite me and I doubt he'd leave the door open if he didn't want me to come inside.

The antechamber's door is partially closed. I step up to it and touch my hand to the worn wood before I hear their voices.

Thank God I stop to listen.

"I'm nothing like you! I'll *never* be like you!"

I flinch and snatch back my hand. What is Zachary doing here? I back up, intent on turning tail and getting the hell out of here, but then I hear Gabriel's voice.

Compared to Zachary's outburst, his soft reply is barely audible. I move closer to the door and put my ear right by the crack.

"...only hate...for so..."

Speak up, damn it.

I move closer and push gently at the door so it swings a little wider. Zachary stands in the middle of the room, silhouetted by the fire.

There's a hand on the back of his neck.

"...nothing more to do but forgive."

I slap a hand over my mouth when Zachary twists away with a grimace on his face. Had Gabriel just tried to *kiss* him? I stagger back, but I can't bear to take my eyes away from them.

"So you can fuck a man, but you can't bear to kiss one?" Gabriel moves closer but Zachary retreats until his back is flush with the wall.

"It might feel like less of a sin but trust me, God has already condemned you to hell."

What the fuck?

My heart's in my throat as they glare at each other. The tension from whatever argument they were having before I arrived presses down like gravity on steroids.

I half-expect them to break into a fight, and the thought has my chest so tight I can't breathe.

My brain works overtime as I try to piece together what might have happened.

Is this because I told Zachary I wouldn't come back here? Did he decide to get the data himself? I turn, scanning the room through the door crack. The bed looks rumpled, and my stomach sinks.

Did they...?

Oh my God.

But then I spot the laptop on the dining table, lid closed, plugged in. I put a hand on my dress pocket. Apollo gave me back the drive just before we went our separate ways. He said I'd done everything right, but that the copy wasn't complete. Luckily, it wouldn't start from scratch—the device would check which files were already copied.

Five minutes, Apollo said.

Five minutes should do it.

I turn back to Zachary and Gabriel. They're both so tense, it's impossible to tell who's mad at whom. Seeing them side-by-side, I can't say which one would win in a fight. Gabriel has a good fifteen years on

Zachary, but he's much more muscular than the younger man. I know Zachary's strong but is he strong enough?

If they started fighting…could I slip in and copy the files while they were distracted? I could hide under the tablecloth—it almost reaches the floor.

That's a big if.

Especially since now they both seem to be relaxing a little. Weighing each other up.

I can't imagine what's going through Zachary's mind, facing his nemesis like this.

I'd be terrified.

I don't know if I moved at just the right moment, but something makes Zachary look straight at me through the crack in the door.

His eyes flicker, but that's literally the only reason I have to think that he saw me.

"You're right," he says, pushing away from the wall. Gabriel stands his ground as he comes closer. My lungs are about to burst how I'm holding my breath. "I'm a sinner, Gabriel. Just like you."

Oh, God. What is he doing?

Zachary grabs Gabriel's shoulder. Gabriel doesn't even flinch.

"I guess even penance couldn't change that."

Zachary makes as if to walk past Gabriel, his hand slipping from Gabriel's shoulder. The priest turns to follow.

Putting his back to me.

Crap!

Zachary must have come to the same conclusion I did. But now I'm too terrified to move.

Do it, Trinity. Do it!

Just a few yards, then you're under the table cloth. Gabriel won't see you—he's completely fixated on—

Zachary's eyes slide past Gabriel and his lips twitch with what I've come to recognize as suppressed anger.

Wondering why I'm not moving. Why I'm wussing out like the pathetic wimp I am.

Despite what Apollo thinks—what I *made* him think—I didn't come here to steal Gabriel's private files. I came to confront him about that photo, the one that's been plaguing me since I laid eyes on it.

But now it feels like stealing the files is the *only* reason I'm here. Like this was fated from the moment I set foot in Saint Amos.

Gabriel must have seen Zachary's gaze shift. He turns to look behind his shoulder.

Zachary snarls.

My stomach folds in on itself like a poor attempt at a souffle.

No. No! Don't—

Zachary grabs Gabriel's jaw and wrenches the older man's head back to face them.

And kisses him.

My skin goes ice-cold, but the jolt of panicked adrenaline that spikes through me is enough to get me moving.

I push open the door, slip through, and pause just long enough to close it again. Then I'm scampering silently over the carpet. I rush under the table cloth and almost knock my head against one of the table legs in my hurry to conceal myself.

I squat there for a moment, trying to muffle my too-fast breathing.

I shouldn't have bothered.

There's a soft sound a few feet away. Something whisking against leather, maybe.

I squeeze my eyes shut.

What the hell am I going to see when I emerge from this table cloth?

I push away the thought before it can debilitate me. I take the drive out of my pocket and uncap it, then steel myself with an unsteady breath.

One.

Two.

I slowly peek out from under the tablecloth. I'm close to the wall. Zachary and Gabriel were at least a yard or so behind me, to the right. I peer around the side of the tablecloth trying not to disturb it.

I see their legs and hurriedly retract into the safety of the tablecloth.

Shit. They're too close.

But I can't wait any longer. If I can slip the drive in without being seen, then I can probably just leave. Maybe Zachary can pull it out when—

He's done fucking Gabriel?

I squeeze my eyes shut.

Fuck it, Trinity. Focus.

When he's *done*.

Breathe in. Out.

Much better.

I duck out from under the tablecloth, letting it drape my shoulders as I go to my knees. The chair Gabriel was using is in my way, so I have to twist awkwardly to get at the laptop.

Would it work with the lid closed? It'll have to, because I can't open it. That's something Gabriel would definitely notice.

I peek up over the top of the table and almost immediately latch eyes with Zachary.

Oh. My. God.

My lips part as a quiet shock rifles through me like wind through a discarded newspaper.

Gabriel sinks to his knees in front of Zachary, who's propped against the back of one of the armchairs on the other side of the room, his back to the fire.

There's a clink of a buckle as Zachary yanks open his belt.

But his eyes aren't on the priest in front of him.

They're on me.

Hot and livid.

Look what you made me do, Trinity. Look what you fucking *made me do.*

Guilt wracks me. My hand trembles uncontrollably as I try and push the drive into the slot on the side of the laptop.

Gabriel wrenches down Zachary's fly. I force my eyes to stay on the laptop, but those two bodies are stuck in my peripheral vision. Even blurred, I still know what's happening. What they're doing.

The drive twists, falling on the floor. I almost don't catch the hiccup of frustration that claws up my throat. I drop down, panicked tears filling my eyes.

Zachary groans.

Even that sounds angry.

Look what you made me do.

I snatch up the drive and straighten, not bothering to duck my head anymore. Gabriel has his back to me, and he's so focused on servicing Zachary's dick that I doubt he'd notice if the rapture happened.

Despite my trembling fingers, I force the drive into its slot.

Zachary's next groan drags my gaze back to him.

This time, I can't look away.

His head moves back, mouth parting. His Adam's apple bobs as he swallows. Then he grabs Gabriel's head, his fingers sinking deep into the man's dark hair.

He grunts as he forces Gabriel to move faster over his cock.

All the time glaring at me from across the room, lips parted, his whole body moving with each furious breath.

His jade eyes glitter with hatred. But none of it's focused on the man giving him head.

Every ounce of that rage, that revulsion...that disgust...

Look what you made me do, little girl.

His eyes flutter as he lets out a deep moan. As if that sound triggers the memory, his promise fills my head.

Christ, we're going to enjoy making you bleed.

I DON'T DARE STAY any longer in Gabriel's room, so I creep out while they're busy. I can only hope Zachary manages to take out the thumb drive without Gabriel noticing.

It shouldn't have been possible, but somehow—despite everything—I manage to fall asleep a few minutes after I get back to my room.

And not only do I sleep...I dream.

In my dream, Zachary's stalking me down the halls of Saint Amos.

I know it's him because when I turn my head fast enough, I catch a glimpse before he ducks away behind a column or an open door.

When I try to run away from him, I quickly realize my top speed maxes out at a fast walk.

Which means it's only a matter of time before he catches up with me.

When I face forward again, Gabriel is waiting at the end of the hall for me. I come to a stop but the hallway keeps moving as if I'm standing on a conveyor belt.

Whether I like it or not, I'm headed straight for him. He opens his arms—a handsome, charismatic, modern-day Jesus with his short hair and dark eyes. His clothes flicker—priests robes, jeans, slacks—and then he's just wearing a loincloth.

His body gleams. Sweat? Oil?

A crown of thorns appears on his head.

They pierce deep. Draw blood.

A hot breath warms the back of my neck. I turn around. Now the hallway streams backward and it's Zachary I see. But I'm racing away from him, and he's reaching for me.

I'm a sinner.

I hear his voice even though his mouth doesn't move. In the blink of an eye, his face contorts into that of a maniac's—mouth twisted in a sadistic laugh, eyes wild—before smoothing into the mask of a saint.

Just like you, little girl.

Terrified, I spin around and start running away. The hallway zooms past in a blur.

Gabriel streams toward me. Dark, wet blood masks his entire face, the whites of his eyes too pure in contrast.

He tends to his flock like a shepherd. He gathers the lambs in his arms and carries them close to his heart—

I try to scream, but the sound stays lodged in my chest, burning.

Burning.

Gabriel's skin catches alight. He doesn't seem to notice. The only thing he cares about is holding me.

Comforting me.

Bringing me to the light. But if I so much as touch him, I'll be consumed in flames.

Zachary breathes on the back of my neck.

I spin around, body convulsing with horror.

He reaches for me, face flickering from saint to demonic sinner a thousand times a second, until it's nothing but a smudgy blur.

A hand clamps over my mouth, and muffles my terrified yell.

My eyes fly open.

A dark figure ducks down and slowly transforms into Apollo.

"Shh," he murmurs, putting a finger over his mouth. "It's just me, pretty thing."

I watch him with my heart thundering away in my chest.

He crouches beside my bed and puts his head close to mine, nuzzling the side of my throat.

But I can't shake the feel of Zachary's hot breath on the back of my neck, and that leaves me paralyzed.

"About that raincheck?" Apollo whispers into my ear.

CHAPTER THIRTY-FOUR
TRINITY

Maybe I'm still dreaming. I must be, because Trinity the Wimp would never follow Apollo anywhere in the middle of the night.

Never in a million years.

Right?

Because rational me knows that he's trouble, despite the cheeky grin he keeps sending my way, despite how he looks like he's bursting to tell me something juicy.

So I'm dreaming then. Which makes all of this much easier to process. Like when he says he hears someone coming, and suddenly presses me against the wall like we're in a spy movie and this is just an excuse for him to kiss me?

Well, don't think I don't know what he's trying to pull. His lips barely touch mine before I'm convinced this whole thing is an elaborate ruse.

But then I don't care anymore, because he's kissing me, and fuck my life, he's a good kisser.

We're partially hidden in one of the alcoves on the ground floor. I think he was leading me to the kitchen courtyard, even though I'm sure it would have been way too cold to be out in the open this time of night.

He barely gave me enough time to grab my slipper-boots, and all I've got on is a thin sweater and a pair of yoga pants that have started wearing out at the hems how I've stepped on them countless times before.

"I didn't hear anything," I murmur in lieu of a protest when he starts kissing my neck. "Are you sure there's someone—?"

He presses two fingers against my lips, silencing me as he grins down at me. "Nah. Just wanted to kiss you."

My tummy flips over at that. I bite the inside of my lip, and he must take it as a sign, because he ducks down again and captures my mouth with his.

When he kisses me, it's as if we only have seconds left to live.

His hands slide down my hips, caressing my ass through my thin pants. But he never squeezes, never gropes, never shoves anything anywhere. It's like he's exploring a foreign new land he's only ever heard of in fairy tales, and is determined to drink it all in.

But despite the fact that all we're doing is kissing, despite how I'm sure that's all he wants, my body responds to him like he's announced he's going to pop my cherry.

When his hands skim up my waist and begin exploring my breasts, my nipples instantly harden to tight buds.

He stops kissing me and leans back, staring down at my breasts like he's never seen a pair in his life.

Right—and he never looks through any of those porno mags in the Brotherhood's lair. As if.

His warm breath chases shivers through my body as he slips his hand under my sweater and scoops my breasts into his hands, weighing them in his palms.

My head falls back. I sigh as he strokes my skin and moan when he ducks his head and sucks one of my nipples into his mouth. But as soon as it disappears into his hot, hungry mouth, he pulls back and glances down the hallway like a double-agent sure he's been caught in the act.

"In here," he whispers, and drags me into the small prayer room where I first met Reuben.

I'm sure Reuben told them what had happened—they tell each other everything, after all—and my suspicion is confirmed when Apollo stops in his tracks and glances back at me with a sheepish grin on his face. "Is this cool?"

I don't know what comes over me. Maybe it's the fact that these four boys have been toying with me since the day I arrived. Maybe it's all the fucked up shit that's been circulating through my head the past few days.

It makes no sense, but suddenly I want nothing more than for Apollo to descend on me like a bird of prey on an unsuspecting rabbit.

I surge forward, grab his face in my hands, and kiss him as hard as I can.

In response, he circles my waist with his arms and spins me around and around until we bump into the altar.

He lifts me. My ass thumps onto the hardwood a second later. I wince into our kiss and he must suspect that he hurt me, because he darts back almost a yard and holds out his hands, palms out, like he's trying to fend off arrest.

"I'm so sorry. Shit. That was so stupid of me. Did I—?"

I'm almost fucking panting, and he has the nerve to run away? I shift closer to the edge of the altar and deliberately spread my legs.

He just stands there, looking like he's trying really hard to remember if he left the stove on.

So I beckon him like he's beckoned me so many times before.

That works.

He surges forward, smiling into our kiss. But then he deepens the kiss and urges me backward. I expect a hard wood floor beneath me, but he grabs one of the pillows reserved for pious knees and tucks it under me.

My heart wants to burst open at that simple gesture. When it seems everyone only ever wants to fuck you or spank you, someone giving you a pillow seems like the kindness of the century.

He lays on top of me, light and wiry compared with his brothers, but he more than makes up for it with passion. His lips scour mine, his tongue eager and demanding and gentle all at the same time.

When I start panting against his mouth, my body working overtime to try and process the delicious sensations he's wringing through me, his lips skate over my cheek and brush my ear, the side of my neck, my collarbones.

"Fuck," I murmur as my hands disappear into his hair.

I forgot how silky it was.

He grazes one of my nipples through my sweater, and I arch from the pillow. The fabric is already damp from his mouth, and when he moves to my other nipple, it grows cold in the tiny chapel's brisk air.

So I slide my hands over his shoulders, trying to keep him close so I can absorb the heat cascading from his body.

Which is when I feel his hard-on pressing into my leg.

And for the first time, that feeling doesn't freak me the fuck out. Instead, it flabbergasts me.

How can I do that to him? Does he really find me that sexy, that hot, that...fuckable?

I squirm under him, willing him to touch me somewhere other than my breasts. My nipples are already as tight as they can go—that pleasure turns into almost-pain.

When he doesn't move, when he keeps nibbling at my nipples like we have all night and he's existed without sleep for centuries...well, I guess I feel I just have to take charge for once.

I grab his hand and mesh our fingers together.

Somehow, he takes that as a signal to start kissing my mouth again. He presses our interlaced hands above my head, pinning me as he forces his tongue between my lips and steals my breath away.

Which is all fine and well, but his kisses are only aggravating the now heavy throb emanating between my legs. I clamp my thighs together, but that doesn't help.

So I open my legs again and wrap them around his waist.

That, *finally*, gets his attention.

Apollo stops kissing me. He pops up onto his hands like he's doing push-ups and stares down at me with a look akin to panic on his face.

"No, shit, Trinity..."

"What?" Wow, why is my voice so hoarse? "What is it?"

"We can't do that, pretty thing."

"W—what?" My head's spinning from his kisses, and it takes a second for me to realize what he's saying. "You don't want to...you don't want to have sex with me?"

"No."

And then it's as if he's stomping on my fucking ribcage.

My legs fall away from his body, my feet thumping on the altar's wooden floor. I pull away from him and immediately start wriggling out from under his body, my cheeks on fire.

I don't think I've ever been this embarrassed in my whole fucking life. And I had to tell Father Gabriel that my mother caught me masturbating in the bathtub, so the bar's pretty fucking high.

"Hey, wait now, I didn't mean it like that."

"No, really, it's fine," I mutter. I stumble to my feet, pushing him out of the way when he jumps up and tries to stop me from leaving.

"You don't understand," he calls out. "I can't!"

I come to a stop, head low and curtained by my disarrayed curls. "Can't, or won't?"

And then I wait for whatever vague, bullshit excuse he expects me to accept. Because that's how it is with the Brotherhood. They're so caught up in their own shit, they don't realize that the people around them have a right to know what's really going on in their heads.

Even if it's tragic. Or horrific. Or downright psychotic.

You can't trust a stranger. And they'd always be strangers to me until they actually started telling me the—

"It's...kinda complicated."

And there it is.

"Yeah, well, I've had enough *complicated* to last me a lifetime, thanks," I call out behind me without turning around. I storm to the little prayer room's door, fumbling for that special spot—

Apollo grabs my shoulder and turns me around. "But if you have a minute," he says quietly, "I can try and explain."

IT TAKES LONGER THAN A MINUTE, but fuck does he do a lot of explaining.

I sip at my hot chocolate as I peek at Apollo from under my lashes. He brought me to the bell tower after fixing me the drink so we could talk. He's wearing a puffy bomber jacket, and I'm cuddling into a blanket.

One of the things he told me was that he wasn't allowed to fuck me.

Girls, sex, money, clothes, parties, sports, movies, games—they were all distractions.

The Brotherhood had sworn an oath to each other. And nothing —*nothing*—was as important as that oath.

"So...none of you have ever really dated anyone?"

I'm more than a little tired. It's exhausting just *kissing* Apollo—having him explain the intricacies of the relationship between four friends who met in a sex dungeon when they were kids...

I'm too scared to tip my head to the side in case all that information pours out of my ears.

At least he made me hot chocolate. And it's fucking delicious. And at least, tonight, we can see the view. Which is fucking spectacular.

But the Brotherhood's personal life?

I. Can't. Even.

"I guess." He tugs at his cigarette and exhales a plume of smoke into the black night. "Although, Cass once brought home this chick—"

"Home? Where?"

He flicks ash from his cigarette. "Virginia. Zach rented us a house. We only stayed six months or so." He takes another drag. "But it was home while it lasted."

"How old were you?"

He lifts the hand holding the cigarette and squints as he scratches his head. "Shit. I dunno. Sixteen? Seventeen? Zach might have been nineteen already. But anyway, Cass was still getting fucked up back then, and when he went out to go score, he picked up this random chick. Think she was fucked on heroine too, I can't remember. Anyway, he brought her home, back to us."

My body goes rigid. I'm not sure I want to hear what happened to the fucked up girl. And Cass did drugs? It's like I'd need an encyclopedia to keep track of these guys.

"...and then she was all like, you don't have to pay me, I'll just take the dope—"

"But Cass tried to fuck me," I cut in. "More than once." I turn to look at Apollo. "Why do you let him get away with it?"

Apollo flinches, maybe because I sound so fucking bitter, but what? Am I supposed to be nice about the fact that Cass can assault me when his brothers aren't even allowed to touch me?

"He can't help himself," Apollo says.

I laugh. "Are you for real?"

"He has impulse issues."

I frown over at him. "What's that supposed to mean?"

"You take psych, don't you?" Apollo shrugs. "We all got our issues. Cass can't keep it in his pants. It's like he blacks out or something." He waves a hand, smoke trailing erratically behind his cigarette. "Zach can explain it better than me."

"So that's it? He has issues, so he can get away with whatever he wants?"

"Yeah, no," Apollo murmurs. "On that count, you're very fucking wrong." He stands. "Anyway, you have school tomorrow. You should get back to bed."

I stand and quickly drain the last of my hot chocolate.

"Just leave it there," he says, waving in the general direction of the cup as he walks past me. "I'll come fetch it tomorrow."

My eyes skip past him. The door he took me through yesterday is hidden behind the massive bronze bell. If I had X-ray vision, I would have been able to see that incriminating photo through the bell and the wall.

I hurry to catch up to Apollo. "Did you find anything?"

"Hmm?" He flicks the butt of his cigarette over the balcony and glances down at me a second before he slides his arm over my shoulder and hugs me closer. "Oh, yeah. Fuck. I totally forgot to tell you."

I stop walking.

He turns, frowning curiously as he faces me. "What now?" he asks through a laugh.

"What did you find?"

"You sound surprised. Did you think we wouldn't?"

"Apollo!"

He shrugs. "We found what we were looking for, Trin." When I scowl at him, he uses a thumb to smooth down my brows. "Sorry, but it's not my place to tell you."

"Then whose it is?"

Another shrug. "Speak to Reuben. Maybe he'll tell you."

"And if he won't?"

Apollo bops my nose with a knuckle. "Then I guess you'll just have to keep asking until you find what *you're* looking for."

CHAPTER THIRTY-FIVE
TRINITY

Reuben isn't in morning prayers. I wolf down my breakfast and hunt around the campus for him, but without being able to ask anyone where he is, it's no surprise when I turn up empty-handed.

Gabriel said he was the same year as me, but I haven't seen him in any of my classes. I could see if he's attending one of the others this morning. So I head out early to the classroom block and stalk the halls like a petite, poop-colored version of Death.

But either he has a free period this morning or he's playing hooky, because I don't spot him anywhere.

Cass looks up when I walk into English class five minutes late, and sends the kind of wolfish grin I've come to expect from him my way.

Because I'm late, Sharon gives me a rap on my knuckles that stings well into the rest of the lesson. It's impossible to miss how much Cass enjoys my punishment—I'd be shocked if he doesn't have a boner.

A few minutes into the lesson, a teacher comes to speak to Sister Sharon. She instructs us to read from our textbooks while she's gone before slipping out of the classroom.

"Morning, slut," Cass whispers into my ear before the door's finished swinging closed. "Hear you've been sticking your nose where it doesn't belong again."

I sit forward, crossing my arms over my chest and pretending to ignore him.

If I can't find Reuben, then the alternative is asking Zachary or Cass. But screw that, there's no way I'll be asking Cass anything.

I'll find Reuben, even if I spend all day looking.

———

THANK God it doesn't take me the whole day. A few minutes before lunch I pass the little prayer room. The hall is empty, so on impulse, I decide to slip inside and check for Reuben.

He's kneeling on one of the cushions, head bowed, hands meshed in prayer.

"Hey," I call out, and then do a double take.

Is that the same pillow—?

Nope. *Push that thought right out of your mind, Trinity.*

Walking closer, I brush my collarbones. Is it weird that I miss his rosary? I'd gotten into the habit of toying with it—I had to go back to playing with my hair instead.

I stand for a minute or so behind him, but he doesn't acknowledge my presence. If my business with him hadn't been so urgent, I'd have taken the hint and left.

But I have to know what they found. If they have actual evidence against Gabriel...

I go to kneel beside him, grabbing another cushion for my knees. I glance at him and then mimic his pose.

And I manage to stay that way for a whole ten seconds before my patience runs out.

"I'm sorry to interrupt you—"

"Then don't," Reuben says.

Wow. Cranky much? I shift on the cushion, glancing at him again.

His red rosary is tangled in his fingers, the crucifix dangling down between his wrists.

I have to get him to talk to me. If not him, then who? Zachary? Cass?

I'd rather poke a fork in my eye.

"I'm sorry about...the other night."

"Which one?"

At first I think he's playing it cool. He'd have to be, pretending my rejection didn't affect him.

But what if it truly *didn't*? What if he's moved on? Apollo said they all had complicated relationships with, well, relationships in general. Sex was even more complicated.

"I was upset, okay?"

Reuben stays silent.

"After what Cass did—"

"What's this got to do with him?" Reuben asks, finally straightening and turning to look at me.

"W-well, he tricked me." I frown up at Reuben. Even with both of us on our knees, he's a foot taller than me.

Just tell him, Trinity. What's the worst that can happen?

"I thought he was you," I blurt out.

Reuben frowns. "What are you talking about?"

"The shower?" My cheeks start heating up, but I forge ahead before I can lose my nerve. "I only let him touch me because I thought he was you."

Reuben watches me, expressionless, silent.

"My eyes were closed."

Nothing.

"Because of the soap."

You'd swear he was a marble statue, not a living, breathing man. Although I'm only guessing that he's breathing right now, because it's definitely not apparent.

"I just...you've got to see it from my perspective, right? You guys... you tell each other everything. Share everything. It's...kinda weird for me, okay? It feels like you're ganging up on me."

And then I stop, because honestly I've run out of words.

He tilts his head a little. "Don't good friends tell each other everything?"

"Not like that," I say through a laugh, but I cut off the sound prematurely.

How the fuck would I know? My best friend used to be Gabriel.

The thought sends a wave of shameful heat coursing through me.

I realize now I was the only one of us who thought that. To him I was his lover's daughter. A member of his flock, nothing more. I bet the only reason he ever spoke to me was at the request of my parents. They probably begged him to get me more involved in the church.

In God.

Reuben grabs my chin and lifts my head back up, forcing me to look at him. "I'm not angry with you, Trinity."

For some fucked up reason, that admission makes my heart flutter. "Oh. You just seemed—"

"But I wouldn't want to expose you to anything that makes you uncomfortable."

He releases me, and I wish he hadn't.

"I realize it's asking a lot, probably too much, for you to accept us the way we are."

Something in his tone makes my chest grow tight. "You mean…?"

He waits for me to finish, but I have to swallow down the lump in my throat first.

"You mean…you *want* to go out with me?"

The edges of his mouth quirk up.

He shakes his head, and grabs hold of one of my curls. His eyes shift to his fingers as he winds it around his digit. "It's not that simple."

I try and pull my hair free, but he's got it good and twisted.

I let out a confused chuckle. "But…then I don't—"

He pulls me closer. "And even if I asked, you'd never say yes."

"Of course I would." My eyebrows flinch into a quick frown. "That's what…I mean, I just said—"

He laughs, but without humor. "Are you sure?"

I nod, and then wince when the movement tugs at my scalp.

"No backing out," he warns, moving closer still.

My heart's beating faster the closer he comes. "Why would I want to?"

"Because," he murmurs, his lips brushing mine.

My eyes flutter closed and my mouth parts, fully expecting a kiss. "Because why?"

"I'm not sure you can handle it."

"Only one way to find out."

"I guess."

Oh my God, is he never going to kiss me?

"So do it." Find out, kiss me, whatever the hell. Just do it.

"And what about them?"

"Who?" My thoughts are already evaporating like fog.

"My brothers?"

"Fuck 'em." I murmur.

"That's just it, Trinity."

Despite it tugging my scalp again, I move back so I can look into his eyes. I don't like the tone in his voice. And when we lock eyes, I like the strange gleam in his even less.

"That's what? Stop going in circles. I know it's complicated." Suddenly, my mouth doesn't seem to have an off switch anymore. "Apollo told me. Sex, girls, whatever—too distracting. No relationships. But you're all big boys now, I'm sure you can multi-task." I lean in again. "Now are you going to kiss me, or what?"

He laughs and slides a hand around the back of my neck. But he still doesn't close the distance.

"So he told you everything, did he?"

"Yeah."

"Hmm. Then I guess you really *are* sure," he says. "Trinity Malone... will you go out with us?"

Yes!

"Yes!"

Fucking finally.

His eyes light up with a smile. He presses his lips to mine, but we barely touch before my mind finally catches up with me.

Will you go out with us.

Us.

"Wait..." I push away from him and hold up a finger. "Hold on. Did you say—?"

"I thought Apollo explained it?" Now he's looking...not upset, but maybe a little impatient. Or frustrated. Maybe he really wants to kiss me as badly I want to kiss him.

"I think, maybe, he might have left some stuff out," I say quietly, my shoulders sagging.

Reuben nods. "We're a package deal, Trinity."

My brain instantly rejects the thought. "But—"

He puts a finger on my lips. "That's why I didn't stop you when you left. It's always too complicated. Girls like things simple." His dark eyes flash. "We're not."

Understatement of the fucking century.

He stands and gets ready to leave, putting his rosary around his neck, buttoning up his shirt again.

Well fuck this. I'm not leaving empty-handed.

"Apollo said you found something in Gabriel's files."

Reuben pauses as if considering my statement, and then nods just once.

"Can you tell me what it is?"

He goes to his haunches in front of me and watches me for a moment as if he's trying to figure out how sincere I'm being.

"That's the thing with us, Trinity. You're either with us, or you're against us." He smiles, not unkindly, and traces my bottom lip with his thumb. "There's no in-between."

CHAPTER THIRTY-SIX
ZACH

My last student files out of the door seconds before Reuben steps into my class. I happen to glance up, and do a double take when I see him.

"What the hell are you doing here?" I widen my eyes at him as I hurry past to force the door closed faster than the hydraulic normally allows. "Did anyone see you?"

Reuben doesn't have a class with me, and I've made a point of not associating with him in the dorms. Cass being the hallway monitor gives us a little more leeway, but this...?

"You weren't checking your phone," he says, not even seeming apologetic for contravening our strict guidelines. "It's important."

"So what is it?" I ask, and then duck my head forward when nothing changes on his stony face. "Well?"

"Trinity came to see me. Wants to know what we found."

"And?" I cross my arms over my chest. "What did you say?"

"What you told me to." He shrugs. "But it's been hours. I don't think it worked."

"Of course it did," I tell him, pushing the words through my teeth as I head back to my desk. This was my last lesson of the day—I was on my way to pack up and head back to my room. I shove my handbook in my drawer and remove my cell phone. There are a handful of notifications on the screen—so many that most of them are crowded out. The last few are from Reuben. "So what's so urgent it couldn't wait?"

"We're running out of time for your games. Why can't we just tell her about—?"

"Why are you risking everything coming here to argue over something we've already discussed?" I shove the phone in my pocket and head for the door. "The decision's been made. Now get out before someone sees you."

I turn, my hand on the door handle, to see if he has any last words before we exit the classroom. His eyes narrow, but that's the extent of irritation he ever shows.

Reuben's like an iceberg, though—what you see on the surface is only a tenth of what's lurking below. If he looks this annoyed, he's close to a meltdown.

"We have until Friday," I tell him, my words exiting with a sigh. "Trinity will come around by then."

"But if we just told her—"

My hand tightens on the handle, but I force my voice to remain at the same level. "Then what, Reuben? She'll *trust* us? Trust requires proof, belief doesn't. You want her to trust us? I want her to have *faith* in us like she should have from the beginning."

"Blind faith?" he asks.

"Best kind there is."

He opens his mouth, possibly to carry on arguing, but cuts off when the door opens under my hand. I take a hasty step back so it won't crash into me, my heart doing acrobatics at the thought of who was about to walk in on Reuben and me.

Apollo's blond head peeks around the door, his eyes going wide when he sees me, and then wider still when he sees Rube. "Thank fuck I found you," he says.

"The hell are you doing here?" I whisper furiously.

"It's important, and you weren't answering your—"

I grab him by his shirt and drag him inside, closing and locking the door behind him. "Christ, what the fuck has gotten into you two?" I turn on them, but don't get a word out.

Apollo's very rarely serious, but right now he could be running for fucking president.

"What?" I bark out.

"I started searching manually through everything Trinity copied. I just found a bunch of emails," he says, voice wooden. His mouth twitches as he starts nibbling on the inside of his cheek. His eyes flicker to Reuben. "You're not going to believe this."

CHAPTER THIRTY-SEVEN
TRINITY

The church goes quiet when Father Gabriel climbs onto the altar. I'm sitting right by the door of the chapel, hoping I can be the first to get out of here at the end of morning prayers.

I still have no idea what I'm going to do. As much as I want—*need*—to know what the Brotherhood found, Reuben's words keep going through my head.

You're either with us, or you're against us.

But I can only decide which side I'm on once they tell me what they have on Father Gabriel. They could be bluffing. Trying to get me on their side so they can use me for their own nefarious purposes.

And then there's the other thing Reuben said. How they're a *package* deal.

He wasn't talking about their war, or their oaths, or any of that shit.

He was talking about me and him. Or…I guess…me and *them*.

Definitely not the sort of stuff I should be contemplating in a house of worship. I might just catch on fire and I doubt any amount of Holy Water could put me out.

The hall shushes as soon as Father Gabriel walks onto the stage. I study him as circumspectly as possible as he leads us through a prayer. Usually we go through announcements and read a bible verse before ending on the Father's Prayer and being dismissed. But this morning, everything feels like it's taking a thousand times longer.

So, like always, I zone out.

And I'm only wrenched back to the here-and-now when everyone inside the hall breaks out into cheers.

My heart pounds in response to the unexpected ruckus as I hurriedly scan the hall to figure out what I'd missed. Some students even have the gall to stand up, but they hurriedly sit when Gabriel lifts his hands to silence the crowd.

"The buses arrive at seven tomorrow morning. Please ensure you are ready to depart so we don't have any delays."

I sit back, shoulders sagging in relief. The last I'd heard, the buses taking us to Sisters of Mercy were supposed to arrive on Saturday—now they'd be here tomorrow. Three days early.

But that relief evaporates a second later.

What am I going to do?

I need to find out what the Brotherhood knows. I thought I'd still have a few days, but now…?

My mind is made up about Sisters of Mercy. I don't belong here anyway—I can finish my senior year over there. At least I can make some friends there.

But I can't leave without knowing.

Guess I'm going to have to bite the bullet. Much as I didn't want to, I'll have to track down Zachary and speak to him. I'll probably have to trade a few spanks for the info, but I survived those last—

"—nity Malone, please come see me after assembly."

Shock flashes through me. Did Gabriel just call my name?

A few of the boys sitting in the pew in front of me glance back in my direction.

Shit. What does Gabriel want with me?

Oh, right.

He wants to *talk*.

I cross my arms over my chest and hug myself hard, my mind like a kicked-over anthill as Gabriel runs through the last announcements.

I don't join in for the Father's Prayer, and that gets me more than a few scandalized stares from the boys around me.

Let them stare.

Gabriel knows I'm not a believer. It wouldn't surprise him in the least to hear I sat this one out.

When kids stream past me on their way outside after assembly ends, I consider for a full minute what the repercussions would be if I just left but I'd just be delaying the inevitable. Plus, Gabriel would never let me climb on a bus tomorrow without talking to me.

I wait for the majority of the boys to leave, and then make my way to the front of the hall, fully expecting Gabriel to be waiting in the small room just off the stage.

He's not.

So I head to the only other place he could be.

I'VE BEEN KNOCKING on a lot of doors lately. Would be excellent practice if I ever decide to become a missionary like my father.

There's a grim smirk on my face when the door opens.

I stand there for a second, speechless, before I lower my hand. If Gabriel had been here, I'd have expected him to ask me to come inside, not to answer the door himself.

"I wasn't sure if you'd come," he says. His eyes dart past me, and then he waves me inside his apartment. "Let's talk inside, child."

I scrape up every spare bit of courage I still have left after his miraculous appearance. "No."

He frowns. "I'm not going to talk to you out in the hall," he says, his eyebrows drawing together. "This is a personal—"

"You're right, you're not going to talk to me." I push back my shoulders and hold up my chin. He's so much taller than me, but somehow it helps. "Honestly, I think you've said enough."

He tilts his head a little, eyes flinching as if I caused him actual pain. My chest tightens at that, but fuck it. I'm not the one in the wrong here. Not even a little.

"I came because you're the Provost, and I'd probably get detention or something if I didn't. But I'm not here to talk, and I won't listen to anything you have to say."

Thump, thump, thump goes my heart in the sudden silence following my statement.

For a moment, I think he's going to ignore everything I said and just drag me inside anyway. But then his eyes drop, and he lets go of the door handle.

"I'm sorry you feel that way." His eyes fix on me again, studying me for a second as if wondering how far he can push my moratorium. "But I didn't mean to hurt you, Trinity."

I lift my chin a little higher. "By sleeping with him, or telling me about it?"

"I know what I did was wrong. I should have stopped it. No—I should never have let it happen in the first place." Again, his gaze drops. "But your father is a very persuasive man."

I go from an imperious glare to a confused frown. "What do you mean—?"

"I—" Gabriel's mouth tightens, and then he steps back. "Please. At least just let me close the door."

I shouldn't show him any quarter, but for some reason I do. For some fucked up reason, I step forward and let him close the door behind me. We stand in the small antechamber, both stiff and uncomfortable and looking away from each other.

"I should have stopped the affair before it began, but I was...weak. And every time I broke it off, all it would take was one email from Keith, and I'd be back."

I squeeze my eyes shut as my cheeks start heating. "Please stop. I don't want to know."

But he doesn't. He just keeps telling me things I don't want to hear.

"I told your mother we had to tell you, but she said it wasn't any of your business. And that hurt me, Trinity, because I believe you had every right to know."

My eyes flicker up to him, my mouth going dry. "Mom...*knew*?"

He nods. "Yes. It was...she..." Gabriel clears his throat. "Are you sure you won't—?" He twists to grab the handle of the door leading into his room.

"No. You said one minute." I hug my chest and try to will myself to leave. I guess it's morbid fascination keeping me here.

"It was her suggestion," he says.

An incredulous laugh tears through me. "Oh my God, do you honestly expect me to believe—"

"In an effort to keep their marriage intact, she suggested we—"

"No!" I yell out, lifting both hands to ward him off. "Fuck no. You are *not* trying to convince me that my mom has anything to do with this!" There's laughter in my voice, but it's far from pleasant. I take a step closer, stabbing a finger toward him. "And because they're both dead, I'll never be able to confirm or deny any fucking thing you tell me, anyway. So why not blame everything on her, right? Make it out as if my dad was the one who—"

I cut off with a disgusted sound.

"You're not fooling anyone," I whisper as my eyes start filling with tears. I step back, fumbling behind me for the handle without taking my eyes off Gabriel. I grab it, wrench it open, back up.

"Especially not me." I swipe at my wet cheeks, shaking my head as I scowl over at him.

He hasn't moved, hasn't tried to get another word in. And thank the Lord for that, because I might have physically attacked him if he'd tried.

I point at him again. "They were right all along." The world blurs, but I blink hard to jar those hot tears from my eyes.

"Who?" Gabriel demands evenly as he steps forward. His expression is neutral, but there's anger in those brown eyes.

I step into the hall, my lips twisting so hard I almost can't get the words out. But when I do, they echo down the hall.

"Burn in hell, Gabriel! You fucking burn in hell!"

CHAPTER THIRTY-EIGHT
TRINITY

W eed and cigarette smoke taint the air. I shouldn't be here, but I couldn't keep away any longer. My curiosity is stronger than my fear, and it's what compelled me to slip out of bed as soon as Jasper fell asleep.

It's what has kept me moving down the stairs and across the lawn and through the crypt.

It's what is keeping me here now.

I would have come sooner, but I told myself I'd wait. With each passing hour, the certainty that I had to come here, that I had to do this, grew and grew until I couldn't think of anything else.

I want to know what they found.

I want to know what Reuben meant.

I want to know...what it *feels* like.

And I'm hoping, dear Lord I'm hoping it will make the pain in my heart go away. Because after I yelled at Gabriel like that, it's as if someone's spent the rest of the day carving a hole in my chest with a red-hot poker.

Digging, and digging.

Fuck knows what they're looking for, but if it's sympathy or forgiveness...spoiler alert—they won't find any.

My fingers brush the drape disguising the entrance to the Brotherhood's lair. It's quiet out here—so quiet I'm starting to wonder if I'll walk into an empty room like last time.

Like last time? You mean when Zachary was here and he spanked you until you almost had an orgasm?

Yeah, fuck, like last time.

I didn't want to wander down here in my pajamas, so I slipped on one of my church dresses before climbing into bed. But now I'm regretting it, because the more modest of the two dresses hasn't come back from the laundry yet, and this one ends at my knees.

I feel naked.

When I pull away the curtain, orange light cascades into the dimly lit library. If someone is inside and facing the exit they could probably see my hand jutting through. But no one announces my arrival.

I haven't yet decided if I *want* them to be here, or if I want the place to be empty. I'll never have the courage to come back. But will I have the courage to stay if they're here?

When I sidle through that opening and come out on the other side, the decision is taken away from me.

The Brotherhood *is* here. And from the looks on their faces, they were expecting me an hour ago.

Zachary's on his wooden chair, Apollo lounging in the duct-taped armchair. Cass and Reuben share the couch like they have each time I've been here. A joint is making the rounds. This time, everyone takes a drag before passing it on. When it reaches Apollo, he stands and comes over to me with it, holding it out.

I take it. Study it. Smoke it.

It's strong enough to make me cough, and Apollo looks like he's holding back a smile. When I try to give it back to him, he shakes his head and his eyes move back to it, then to my mouth. A silent command for me to take another hit.

I'd only be fooling myself if I thought I had a choice in the matter, so I take another drag and hand it back. This time he takes it, hitting it on the way to Zachary.

He takes a last drag and then extinguishes the burning tip between his fingers.

Then there's silence.

Just four men watching.

Waiting for me to speak.

I step closer, hugging myself. It's colder down here than I remember. Probably because it's past midnight already. There's no heat down here —the room is brisk, despite their body heat.

"I want to know what you found," I say, staring at each of them in turn, but landing last on Zachary and holding his gaze. "I have a right to know."

Zachary laughs.

Just once.

Roughly.

And with not a trace of humor.

Suddenly the room is a lot colder.

"I can't argue with that," he says, and slowly gets to his feet. "In fact, I think it's downright impolite for us to keep anything from you anymore, right guys?"

There's a muted, "Right" from the others.

Impolite?

I sense danger in the air, and it has nothing to do with the way Zachary's stalking over to me like he has all day to pounce.

Something's happened.

Something's changed.

But what?

"So go on then." My hug intensifies, until I start losing feeling in my fingertips. "Tell me."

Zachary tuts me. "First, I feel we owe you an apology, Miss Malone."

I don't like the way he says my name.

I don't like it one bit.

"For what?" When I frown at him, a faint smile touches his mouth.

"For treating you so poorly. For withholding information. Withholding...our *affection*."

My eyes dart to Apollo, but he looks away. When I turn to Reuben, his face hardens.

What the hell is going on?

Maybe I *am* too late—a bottle of whiskey and several joints too late. The malevolence seeping out of these men feels like it's all directed at me.

Just your imagination.

Just your—

"So I think it's time we righted some of those wrongs, don't you?"

I shake my head. "Stop with the games. Just tell me what you found and then I'll leave."

Zachary snatches my wrist, moving so fast that I don't have time to step back. "No, see, Miss Malone...we *insist*."

CHAPTER THIRTY-NINE
ZACH

Trinity's pulse flutters like a hummingbird's heart under my thumb. She's not terrified, but definitely unnerved. I guess it's a good thing I went ahead and smoked as much as Apollo said I should. The last thing I want is to accidentally break this pretty little thing.

Not when there's still so much pain to wring out of her.

And pleasure, of course, but that has always been secondary.

"Cass," I call out. "Get ready."

Trinity's amber eyes open a touch wider. She tries to peer around me, but I move to the side and block her view. "Let's not spoil the surprise."

From behind me comes the sound of someone's belt being removed. The metallic clink of the buckle sends a rush of blood to my cock. She has no idea what's coming...but I can see she's already convinced herself she knows exactly what will happen next. Meanwhile, I'm getting a semi just from the thought of what we have in store for her.

I cup her face in my hand. "We made a deal a few days ago, do you remember?"

Her face turns a shade paler. When I take a step back, urging her forward, she digs in her heels instead. "No," she murmurs, shaking her head.

"You don't remember?"

"No, Zachary, please. I..." Her brow furrows, and she darts to the side to see past me again.

With another smooth step, I block her view. I grab her chin, wrenching her head back and forcing her to look up at me.

"That's not how this works, girl. You want something, and so do we."

She flinches at the pet name. "I've changed my mind. I don't—"

I dig my fingers into her chin, feeling her jaw move as she snaps her mouth closed.

"Of course you do. Stop denying it."

I'm holding her too tight for her to nod but I take the widening of her eyes as agreement.

"Good. No use wasting our energy on fighting." I turn my head a little. "Ready, Cass?"

"Yeah." He sounds too serious. Grim, almost.

Goosebumps break out on my bare arms, and it has nothing to do with the chill air down here.

We're used to the cold, my brothers and I. That basement was cold and damp and disgusting—so it's no wonder. Trinity's little dress doesn't seem to be keeping her very warm taking into account her trembling lips and cool skin.

But it could also be fright.

Because when someone behind me snaps a belt those bright, amber eyes dull, dread replacing her uneasiness. She even stops shivering for a second as she turns those terrified eyes to me.

Yeah, keep your eyes on me, little girl. Because if you happen to look down, you'll get an idea of just how much I'm enjoying this.

Which is exactly what she does. She rips her face out of my fingers, leaving red marks behind, and tries to peel my fingers off her wrist.

"Let me go," she murmurs. "Please, Zach, let me go."

"So now it's *Zach*?" I jerk her into me, grab the small of her back and grind my dick into her stomach. "And when exactly did we become such good friends?"

Something akin to a whimper escapes her lips. She starts struggling against me, another breathless, "No!" slipping out of her trembling lips.

"Jesus, is this happening or not?" Cass demands behind me.

Guess I go out of my way to be cruel sometimes, even to those who don't deserve it.

I grab Trinity's arms, fumbling with her when she tries to rip free, and turn her to face my brothers. She tries to step back, but I keep her in place with my body.

We don't have the kind of props and equipment down here that we had in the basement. No wire-framed beds with handy straps. No suspended rails and butcher's hooks.

But we have Reuben.

He's sitting on the couch, feet firmly planted. Cass is kneeling on the floor in front of him, buck naked.

When Trinity goes rigid in my arms, Cass glances up at Reuben and gives him a barely perceptible nod.

Reuben breaks eye contact, and his usually emotionless face turns to stone. He grabs Cass's upper arms and wrenches him forward.

Tonight, Rube will be our brace *and* our straps.

Cass folds over Rube's lap, burrowing his head into the couch beside Reuben's hip, baring his already bruised ass to Trinity.

"Who did that to you?" she gasps.

Aw, fuck. Ain't she the cutest?

Trinity hurries forward the instant I release her. While she falls to her knees beside Cass for all the world like a fucking mother hen, I walk past Apollo to fetch the belt he's holding out to me.

"I did," I say.

Cass lets out a soft grunt when my belt slams against his flesh.

Trin yelps in surprise and falls back, flashing me her white panties and a horrified expression as she scrambles away.

I expect her to start crying.

Maybe even run.

Instead, she bolts to her feet and shoves me hard enough to make me take a step back.

"Stop!" she yells, putting herself between Cass and me. "Stop hitting him!"

"Hear that, Cass?" I ask, absently snapping the belt as Trinity shows me her teeth. "She wants me to stop."

"Jesus, fuck," Cass groans, which is surprisingly articulate for him at a time like this.

I try to keep my eyes on Trinity, but it's impossible with Cass busy having a fucking apoplexy behind her.

She doesn't have a fucking clue. Not a single goddamn clue.

She's hurting him more than my belt ever could.

"Put it down," she says, holding out her hand. "Just...put it down."

It must be the weed, because I legit want to humor her, just to see how far this goes before she realizes what the hell's going on.

I can see why Rube likes her so much.

Fucking adorable, she is.

I haven't met something this innocent since my parents tossed Cass down those basement stairs, nearly breaking the poor kid's neck. That didn't happen again, of course, not after his first Ghost saw the scratch he'd gotten on his pretty fucking face.

Oh no.

After that, *nothing* touched his face.

Or Rube's.

Or Apollo's.

I wasn't there because I was pretty, so they felt they could hit me wherever the fuck they wanted. One of them even broke my nose.

Luckily, I don't scar as easily as Cass.

Luckily, mine wasn't the first nose the Ghosts broke in that basement, and by the time they broke mine, Rube had experience in straightening broken bridges.

"You think I want you to watch me belt him?" I ask Trinity, genuinely intrigued.

"I don't care what you want," she says. "Just give it here, okay?" She flicks her fingers, but doesn't look at the belt. Keeps her eyes on me. Like I'm a wild animal bound to attack as soon as she breaks eye contact.

I guess I am, at that.

Her eyes flicker when I hand her the belt. "Okay," she murmurs. Then she glances at Rube. "Now how about you let him go? Please?"

"Why are you sticking up for him?" Apollo asks as he collapses into his couch, a freshly rolled joint dangling from his lips. "Thought you had it in for him?"

"I didn't say that," she says, frowning briefly at Apollo before looking at me again. "Can Reuben let him go?"

I lean my weight back on one foot. "We're not done here yet."

"Please, Zachary. Whatever he's done...he doesn't deserve this."

The smirk falls right off my face.

She shakes her head, those amber eyes glowing with naivety. "No matter what he's done, you can forgive him. You're friends, aren't you?"

A soft laugh huffs out of me. "You think he deserves forgiveness?"

"Yes." She nods firmly. "Definitely."

"Fine. We'll forgive him. But on one condition..."

Her eyes become wary, searching my face as if she can try and spot where I'm headed. But if she hasn't figured it out by now, it's not gonna happen.

"What?" she asks reluctantly.

Apollo lights the joint. A haze of weed smoke fills the space between.

I smile at her as I lean forward. She flinches when I touch the belt in her hands, but since I don't try and take it away, she doesn't fight me.

"You take his place."

CHAPTER FORTY
TRINITY

I'm about ready to pee myself. Of all the possibilities I'd dreamed up, Zachary belting Cass while Reuben held him down and Apollo watched...

Yeah, that never came up.

I wince as Zachary tightens his grip.

I don't want him hitting Cass, but...I don't want him hitting me either.

At least, not with a fucking belt.

I don't know where I summon the courage, but perhaps it's because I've managed to convince myself that this is the lesser of two evils.

I move the belt to the side. "You can use your hand."

Surprise or irritation flickers in Zachary's eyes. He rips the belt out of my hand and grabs the front of my throat.

"You get the belt, or Cass gets the belt. It's that fucking simple."

He's not choking me, else I'd have fought him. Maybe I can still reason with him. "What did he do to you?" I murmur, trying to keep my voice for Zachary's ears alone. "Why do you have to hurt him?"

But this place is too small, because Cass hears me.

"What did I do?" Cass says.

Unwilling, my eyes drop to where he's still kneeling a few feet beside me. And no matter how hard I try, I can't look away.

It's not just that he's beautiful. And I mean, holy hell, he's the kind of handsome where if you saw him in a movie or in a magazine, you'd spend a good few minutes wondering about him. What his life was like, where he lived, if he had a dog, how much he was paid and whether that was a lot of money to someone like him.

Even naked, bruised, and wearing a condescending smirk, my stomach flips over at the thought that someone as gorgeous as him is speaking to me.

Me.

Trinity Malone.

A no-fucking-body.

Somehow, I hold his gaze. Hell, I even manage to study him a little.

Countless circular scars dot what would have been perfect abs. Pale, nearly invisible scars along his ribs and thighs. More burn marks there. Most so old and faded, it's no wonder I didn't notice them that day in the shower when they—

"I sinned," he says and sits back on his haunches, stretching his arms like a cat getting up from a nap.

Thankfully, he doesn't stand, else I'd have been able to see everything. Instead, his dick is hidden in the shadows pooling his lap.

"Sinned how?" I ask.

"I touched you without your permission. More than once." Cass's smirk transforms into a smile that's anything but repenting. "Apparently, I should be punished for shit like that."

My skin suddenly feels two sizes too small. I can't turn my head, so instead I swivel my eyes to look at Apollo. "You told them?"

He shrugs as he takes another pull on the joint. Smoke billows from his mouth, clearing to reveal a Joker-like smile. "We tell each other everything."

"I didn't mean—"

"Fuck it," Zachary growls. "Offer's just expired."

He rips the belt out of my hand and shoulders me aside. Grabbing the back of Cass's neck, he pushes the top half of his body onto Reuben's lap.

I stumble back before I can catch my balance. I don't know who would win in a fight between Cass and Zachary and I never want to find out. But there must be some unspoken agreement between them, because although Cass's muscles go taut as if he's resisting Zachary, he ends up right where Zachary wants him.

Which is when Reuben grabs hold of him again, holding him still.

"No, Zachary, please!" I reach for Zachary, but I'm too scared to grab him in case he *does* turn that belt on me.

"You had your chance," Zachary hisses.

Cass tenses when the belt whistles through the air. The crack of it meeting his flesh is too loud. Too violent.

My heart breaks when Cass's entire body ripples with pain. He's gritting his teeth—spittle dotting his lips as he grunts through the blow—

Crack!

And the next.

"Zachary!"

And the next.

"Stop!" I grab Zachary's elbow, but he shakes me off with a growl.

Crack!

"Enough!" I yell.

My brain is obviously misfiring, because then I do the most idiotic thing in the world. I slip between Zachary and Cass, turning my arms up so the belt would land on my forearms and not on my face.

Zachary freezes, arm upraised, a wild snarl on his face. "Move," he says.

"No! That's enough!"

When Zachary doesn't move, when no one tries to get me out of the way, I start babbling in self-defense. "I'm the one who said he has to pay, right? Well, it's enough. I forgive him. For everything. Okay? So... enough. It's *enough*."

Zachary slowly lowers the belt. "You don't get to decide the sentence."

"Of course I do." I straighten, reluctantly dropping my arms. "I'm the one who charged him."

"This isn't a fucking court, girl."

"I don't care."

Hooded green eyes study me for a long moment. "There're still two lashes left." His voice is rough, but his face is a wooden mask. "Move out the way, or you'll be getting them on his behalf."

I glance over my shoulder at a shaking Cass.

Tear tracks shine wetly on his cheeks. His skin is virulent red and purple now. Tiny dots of blood have come to the surface where Zachary's belt landed.

He won't last another two lashes. He'll start bleeding, and it will all be because of me.

I turn back to Zachary, swallow hard, and force my voice not to shake.

"Then I'll do it," I say, holding out my hand. It quivers a little, but when I concentrate, it stills. "Give me the belt."

Zachary laughs. "What, so you can tickle his ass? This is punishment, girl, not fucking foreplay."

"I'll hit him as hard as I can. I swear it."

Cass would never last another two lashes from Zachary's muscular arm, but mine is like spaghetti in comparison.

Lesser of two evils, right?

I narrow my eyes a little. "Reuben said I'm either with you or against you. No in-between. Right?"

"That's right," Reuben says.

"Well, I'm with you, Zachary." My eyes dart to Apollo. "Apollo." I glance behind me. "Reuben. Cassius." I turn back to Zachary. "I'm *with* you."

I duck forward and wrap my fingers around the belt.

"Now give me the damn belt."

CHAPTER FORTY-ONE
ZACH

I don't know who's more shocked out of the five of us. Trinity asks for the belt, and I give it to her. I fucking *give* it to her. I expected begging, perhaps finally some tears, maybe even her going to her knees and sucking me off in exchange for Cass's hide.

I'm *with* you.

And fuck, for a second there, I believed her.

I step back so that I don't lunge for her instead.

I almost forgot why we allowed this girl in here. Why we're humoring her.

Why is it so easy to forget that she's the enemy? It's not like it's news—I've known from the moment I laid eyes on her that she was some kind of trouble.

I just didn't realize how deeply enmeshed in all this she is.

But that all changes tonight.

When we're done with her, she'll be as broken as we are. Useless.

Trinity folds the belt in half and readies herself.

She thinks she can get one over on us? I know she's going to go easy on him, and we'll punish her for it.

That, and everything else she's done to us.

Luring Reuben with promises of romance and love and all that bull-shit. Acting all surprised when Apollo turned down her pussy.

I'll admit—we were idiots for not spotting the snake in the grass.

But we're wiser now.

We've caught onto her little games. Her little tricks.

She's in our territory now. Until we decide she can leave this place, she belongs to *us*.

And I, for one, plan on using her until she begs me to stop.

But I won't. No matter how hard she begs.

Because *they* never did.

Our Ghosts never let our curses or our pleas touch their cruel hearts. We thought it was because they were impervious to our pain.

Until it became obvious they didn't *have* hearts.

Guess they traded them to the Devil in exchange for fulfilling their sick desires.

Just like each of us has given ourselves over to the Devil too.

For a chance at retribution.

For revenge.

Tonight we seal that pact.

Tonight, Trinity becomes our sacrificial lamb.

I smirk as she lifts her arm, a mix of sympathy and utter reluctance on her face.

Oh, she plays her role so well. But I see right through her.

Trinity grits her teeth.

The belt whistles down.

Cass grunts and squirms against Reuben's grip.

A cloud of weed smoke creeps around me like a nefarious fog. Behind me, Apollo murmurs, "Fuck me," with the utmost respect.

My admiration is fleeting, and leaves me feeling hollow inside.

I watch deadpan as she strikes the final blow, only mildly surprised it doesn't make Cass come or bleed.

Then she hurls the belt away from her like it's a viper and spins on her heel.

Her cheeks are red. Her eyes bright, zealous.

"There," she says, pushing the word through her teeth. "It's done. Now tell me what you found."

Trinity Malone isn't the innocent little girl we'd all assumed she was.

Does that mean we won't enjoy breaking her?

Not at all.

It just means we don't have to hold back.

CHAPTER FORTY-TWO
TRINITY

I t's obvious Cass is in pain, but he's not acting like someone who's just been punished. In fact, the longer he stays as he is, breathing hard and holding onto Reuben's waist as if he'd fall over if he let go… the more I'm starting to wonder about all of this.

I know they were waiting for me, but why? Just so they could show me words have consequences?

And even after all of this…I have a feeling Zachary is still not going to tell me what I need to know.

"Zacha—"

He lifts a hand, the first two fingers raised, for all the world like a priest about to bestow a blessing.

"There was a file," he says. His lips part, but then he hesitates. "Apollo, you tell her."

"He hid it in the system directory," Apollo says.

Ice blows over my skin and settles deep in my bones. I'm dimly aware of Cass moving behind me, making soft, pained sounds as he dresses. I can't imagine how much pain he's in—I only got a handful of lashes from Miriam and I could barely stand the agony.

How long has Zachary been beating him? Why do Reuben and Apollo allow it to happen? Do they always watch like tonight? Does Reuben always hold him down?

Suddenly I don't want to be here anymore. Not surrounded by these four twisted men.

I thought I liked Reuben. Hell, I thought I could learn to *love* him, even, but not if he lets Zachary push him around like this. But can I blame him? I wouldn't want to be on Zachary's bad side either.

And that's not the only reason I want to leave. As much as the Brotherhood terrifies me...it's also the look in Apollo's eyes.

Sympathy. Pity. I'm not sure.

He feels sorry for me and I'm not sure why.

"Clever, but not clever enough. He encrypted it, renamed it, and hid it around a bunch of other system files so it would blend right in."

Apollo slips off the couch and stands to his full height. When he comes closer, I have to crane my head back to keep his gaze.

"See, he disguised it so well that I almost gave up. But I got a hunch. Ran a system check. Replaced all the standard files. All except a handful were overwritten. That file of his, it was one of them. One of the outliers, the ones that didn't fit."

"Any of this sound familiar, my little slut?"

I nearly jump out of my fucking skin when a hand lands on my shoulder. Cass's voice is right by my ear. I want to slap away his hand, but...it was because of me that he was punished. And more brutally than I'd ever have considered necessary. I could at least hear him out.

Hear *them* out.

Even though I just want to run out of here with my hands over my ears.

Because even now, after I'd yelled at Gabriel and told him I believed the Brotherhood...I don't *want* to be on their side. I want to be on *my* side. I want to live in a Utopia where there's no such thing as pedophiles and sex trafficking and men with psychological issues caused by the kind of trauma normal people can't even wrap their heads around.

I guess that stopped being an option after Lucifer was thrown out of heaven. Not that I ever believed in God and the Devil. It sounds like a story used to drive home common sense in a world where it's somehow not obvious that you should love thy neighbor.

But after meeting the Brotherhood?

I don't know if I can afford *not* to believe.

"What was inside it? What—?" I swallow hard to dislodge the knot from my throat. "What was he hiding?"

"We don't know," Reuben says.

His hand is on my shoulder too, now. Warm and big compared to Cass's smaller, cooler hand. But both grip me equally tight. Both hold me just as firmly in place.

"It needs a password," Zachary says. My eyes flicker to him as he steps closer.

Now that I'm surrounded by three of the four brothers, the room isn't that cold anymore. Apollo stands a little way off still, watching.

"I'm running a decryption program on it, but unless I get my hands on a server farm or some shit, it could take months to crack."

"So you don't know," I say, and the words come out with a laugh of relief. "It could be anything."

The hands on my shoulders tighten. Cass begins stroking the side of my neck with his pinkie finger.

Zachary takes my chin, but almost gently this time, tipping my head up. "We don't have to know what it says to know it's what we want. What we've been looking for."

I grab his wrist and slowly, carefully, pull his hand away from my face. "Gabriel's not perfect." I nod a little, glancing at each of them, even the two standing behind me. "But neither are any of us. We're all sinners, right?" I face Zachary again. "What if it's all in your head? Maybe it's time you stopped looking for ghosts in the shadows."

The moment the words leave my mouth, I know it was the wrong thing to say.

Zachary twists his hand, grabbing my wrist and tugging it down.

Before I can pull away, he's forcing me to grab his hard cock right through his jeans, his fingers folding over mine. He makes me squeeze him, and that only makes him harden even more.

"Does that feel real to you?" he says.

I try to pull away, but he just grips me tighter. I can feel him pulsing beneath my hand.

"Stop," I whisper.

"Never," he says, his lips peeling back in a snarl. "We'll never stop. Not for you, not for Gabriel. No one can stop us, Trinity."

He presses against me, sandwiching me between him and the men behind me. Apollo stalks closer, for once not looking like he finds anything about this situation remotely humorous.

"Not even your father."

I CAN'T FIGHT one of them. Definitely not four. Begging has proved useless. So, instead, I scream.

But that just makes them laugh.

And then everything goes to shit.

Reuben's hand slips around the front of my throat. The other, around my waist. He drags me over the floor and sits on the couch, pulling me onto his lap.

When I try and kick his shins, he wraps his legs around mine, pinning them to the couch.

And then drags them apart.

My skirt dips into that space, thankfully retaining some of my modesty, but that doesn't give me a shred of relief.

Not when I'm faced with three men who look ready to rip every last stitch of fabric off me with their fucking teeth.

When Apollo darts forward, I let out another useless scream. A scream he silences with a kiss as he climbs onto his knees beside Reuben

Now I can barely breathe, never mind fill my lungs for another scream. I tear my lips away from Apollo, but Zachary steps forward and grabs my jaw in his strong, unrelenting grip.

"That's not how it works, little girl. If he wants to kiss you, then you'll let him fucking kiss you."

I only realize he's holding a belt in his hands when he slaps it against his thigh. I jerk at the sound, and squirm on Reuben's lap in an effort to escape.

Again, futile, but there's no way I'm just going to sit here and take this.

Zachary said he'll never stop?

Neither will I.

But you wanted this, Trinity, a sinister voice croons inside my head. *You said you wanted to know what it feels like…? Well, you're about to find out.*

No, not like this! I wanted—

Flowers and romance and dinner dates?

Normal.

I wanted *normal*.

Zachary turns my face back to Apollo and releases me. Apollo's lips capture mine, his kiss going from tentative to violent in a matter of seconds.

My dress, full sleeves and a bodice that reaches my collarbones, opens with a zip in the back. So when Apollo tries to slide a hand behind the fabric, it's too tight for him to gain access. He makes a grumpy sound and shoves a hand between Reuben and me, hunting.

I feel every inch of that zipper coming down. And when I slap my arms over my chest to keep my dress in place, Cass grabs my wrists and wrenches me open again.

So I bite Apollo's lip. Not hard, I mean, I don't even taste blood, but—

"Fuck!" He jumps back, pressing the back of his hand to his mouth. "She bit me!"

I feel as much as hear Reuben chuckling.

"I don't think we've made ourselves clear," Zachary says.

My eyes are drawn reluctantly to him when he drags his chair in front of me. He uses his boot to urge Reuben's legs wider, in turn spreading me open even further. Then he sits down, his legs between mine and Reuben's, and leans in close.

"No one dragged you down here, girl." He puts his hands on my thighs and grips tight. "You came on your own. You'd probably like us to believe it was out of curiosity, but we know that would be a lie."

"What are you talking about?" It's not my imagination anymore. There's something they're not telling me.

Something they found?

My mind instantly goes back to the email I read. The one my mother sent Gabriel. Did they figure out Gabriel was having an affair with my father?

There's no way to stop my cheeks from growing hot, just like there's no way I can stop Zachary noticing my sudden humiliation.

His lips quirk into an unfriendly, one-sided smile. "There she is," he hisses. "Took you long enough."

"I can explain," I blabber out, immediately contradicting myself with a panicked, "I didn't know!"

This makes the Brotherhood laugh.

Cass sits beside Reuben and me, wincing when his ass touches the cushion. He sticks his hand under my skirt and trails his fingers up the inside of my leg. "Really expect us to believe that?" He lets out a huff of a laugh and then strokes a knuckle over my underwear. I squirm against Reuben, trying to get away from his touch.

Which is when I realize something that's been nagging at me for a while.

Reuben's got a hard-on. And every time I move, he gets harder.

Fuck.

"I didn't know!" My voice wavers. "Please, you have to believe me. I only just found out."

"And you didn't think to tell us?" Zachary says. His fingertips dig into my thighs as he leans close enough to kiss me. "Didn't think we should know?"

"Does it matter?" I shout. "Does it change anything?"

At this, they're silent. Zachary even draws back a little. I squirm again, but hurriedly stop when I realize that's a bad move.

Zachary drops his gaze to my lap. And then I can't help but shift because it's as if I'm stark naked.

He looks up at me without lifting his face, staring at me through thick lashes.

"It changes everything, girl."

CHAPTER FORTY-THREE
ZACH

Trinity doesn't like my statement. Oh, she doesn't like it one bit. But there's fuck all she can do about it, isn't there?

Fuck all she can do about *anything* right now. If there'd ever been a good time to stop this in its tracks...well, she flew by it about ten minutes ago.

My brothers are ravenous wolves and she's the little rabbit that sprung the trap. Me? I'm the hunter who *set* the trap, and that with only one purpose in mind—to catch something they can sink their teeth into while I watch.

Apollo rips down the front of her dress, exposing her perky tits to the room. To those rabid wolves.

And they descend on her every bit like a predator on prey.

My fingers slide off her thighs as I sit back in my seat and take out my cigarettes. I nip one out of the box and light it as Cass and Apollo duck their heads and consume her nipples with hungry lips and ferocious tongues.

Thick, warm smoke fills my lungs. Watching them, a surge of blood hardens my cock behind my jeans.

Trinity lets out a whimper of protest and tries to move away from their mouths, but there's nowhere for her to go.

"Stop!" Her yells don't exactly fall on deaf ears. In fact, Cass and

Apollo both look up at each other when they hear her. With perfect timing, they grab the sides of her dress and yank it down to her hips.

That's when she really starts thrashing.

But with Reuben holding onto her throat, his other muscular arm strapping her waist, she can only wriggle around like a fish on a hook.

Between the three of them, they urge her dress out from under her hips and down her legs.

I lean forward and snag it, slowly dragging the fabric over her knees. That's where it gets stuck—with Reuben's legs twined around hers, I can't take them off.

Lucky for me, I have a knife.

When I flick it open, she freezes. Her pale stomach trembles as she holds her breath.

"You're not fooling anyone," I tell her.

I lean forward, running the sharp tip of the knife over one hipbone, then the next.

Cass groans softly in the base of his throat, and shifts as if the hard-on trapped behind his jeans is giving him grief. That or his bruised ass. Probably a combination of the two because he enjoys pain as much as I enjoy inflicting it.

With her dress tangled around her spread-apart knees, only her panties on, she looks like a doll sitting on Reuben's lap. His thick thighs are twice the size of hers. That arm of his looks capable of snapping her in half if she so much as breathes wrong.

It's impossible to miss Reuben's dick either. Still trapped behind his jeans, that massive ridge looks like it's trying to nestle into her ass crack. No way she can't feel it. No way she can't realize where that dick is destined to burrow itself as soon as we're done playing with our supper.

My cock wants to bust a seam trying to get out of my jeans at the thought.

And tonight, he can't back out either.

We have two cherries to pop.

My knife hitches against the hem of her underwear and then travels straight down between her legs. From where I'm sitting, I have the perfect view of her cunt—if she wasn't wearing these panties.

Trinity sits absolutely still, lips parted, eyes hooded as if in resignation. I pause right above her clit—nothing but a film of fabric between her and the knife. Holding the tip there, I smile at her and slowly drag at my cigarette.

"You keep telling us to stop, but this wet pussy is singing a different tune."

Her tits quiver when she dares to take a breath. "Please, Zachary. Don't do this."

"You've changed your mind?"

She swallows and dares to shift. I guess Reuben's getting harder by the second. That comfy lap ain't so comfy anymore.

"Yes. I...wanted this but not anymore. So please, let me go."

"You're a good liar," I tell her. "One of the best I've met." I glance at Cass, then at Apollo. "Go on, boys." I cock my head at her cunt. "Check for yourselves how badly Trinity doesn't want this."

Cass wastes no time, and Apollo's only a beat behind him. They trail their fingers over her thighs while she starts kicking up as much as a fuss as she dares with my knife tip held so close to her clit.

Their fingers trace the plain hem of her underwear before they each sink a hand behind that filmy fabric. They're both staring at her, as if daring her to look at them, but she's staring straight at me.

She holds her composure for a second longer, and then her lips start trembling again.

"No, no, no, please, stop, stop!"

But they just keep going.

Their fingers inadvertently lift the fabric up as they pass, sending the tip of the knife slicing through.

Her scandalized gasp could either be for the naked blade now teasing the fuzz above her clit, or those fingers sliding over her wet folds.

Because, from where I'm sitting, I can see she's soaked right the fuck through.

Betrayed by her own depravity.

Just like us.

CHAPTER FORTY-FOUR
TRINITY

I'm light-headed. Confused. Scared shitless. Naked but for my useless underwear, I've never felt this exposed.

Or this turned-on.

As soon as Cass touched me earlier, it was like he'd turned a switch in my brain. Not the part that does the thinking—ha, if only—but the part that controls my body.

Now it's on automatic.

I can't control the way I clench deep inside when Cass and Apollo touch me. Or how tingles ripple through me when Zachary scrapes that knife over my underwear.

And now?

I have their fingers smearing my pussy with juices that leaked out of me because somehow—*some-fucking-how*—it appears that I'm actually enjoying this.

I moan in protest, trying to shift back from their fingers. But that only digs Reuben's dick deeper against my ass.

"No, please, God." My moans turn into whimpers when Cass and Apollo dip their heads and start teasing my nipples with their teeth. While their fingers are still stroking my wet pussy.

"Fuck!" I yelp as Cass bites down hard enough to leave faint marks on my breast.

A warm, sweet breath rifles the hair by my ear.

If Zachary hadn't moved the knife away at just the right moment, I'd have it sticking an inch out of my fucking stomach right now, because without any warning, Reuben sits up straight.

The grip around my throat lessens, but only a little, and then I realize why.

He's unzipping his pants.

"Reuben, no. Please. Please!" I squirm furiously now that there's no knife pressed to my fucking clit to stop me.

Zachary lets out a muffled laugh around his cigarette. Cold metal presses against my thigh.

Snick, snick.

Heat flashes over my skin as Cass and Apollo yank off my underwear.

Now there's nothing shielding me from their eyes. Or the warm, hard, cock Reuben releases from his pants a second later.

"P-please," I murmur, blubbering like a little girl as I start to struggle.

"Ssh," he murmurs into my ear. And then kisses my earlobe. The side of my jaw. He slings his arm around the front of my throat, and drags me against him as he sinks back on the coach.

He brings his legs together, and for a second I'm convinced they'll let me close my legs.

Maybe even let me go.

I mean, fuck, they can't actually do this, can they?

But you want them to, don't you? More than anything in the world.

I shove the traitorous thought from my head. I said no a dozen times. I've yelled, I've screamed, I've begged. Why the fuck—?

Because you love this.

You're loving every fucking second of it.

"No," I whisper furiously.

Apollo and Cass drag Reuben's jeans down his legs and then hold me down while he takes off his shirt.

Now it's just flesh against flesh.

While Zachary's untangling my dress and tugging it off my ankles, I squirm on Reuben's naked lap.

And that's when I realize how wet I am, because I can feel it.

And I'm guessing Reuben can too.

He lets out a low rumble deep in his throat that I feel as much as I hear. Zachary just pulls Reuben's jeans away when I start kicking. Almost absently, Zachary catches my ankle and tucks my leg behind Reuben's.

And just like that, I'm trapped again.

Zachary's cigarette is gone—fuck knows what happened to it. Cass and Apollo are both struggling out of their shirts.

My breath hitches. I start panting, soft and shallow.

Zachary grabs my chin and yanks my head to the side. Forcing me to stare straight into Reuben's black eyes.

His warm breath chases a shiver through me a second before he kisses me.

It's fucked up, I know.

It makes zero sense.

But I kiss him back anyway.

Maybe it's a form of escape. Because when my eyes flutter closed, I can't see the others anymore. And in this moment, no one else is touching me. I can almost convince myself that it's just Reuben and me.

Our first night together.

Just a guy and a girl—

Until Zachary's hands land on my knees. I know it's him, because he's the only one who would grab me hard enough to bruise.

He urges my legs open, for a moment fighting not just me but Reuben too.

I think Reuben won't let him win, but I'm always wrong when it comes to the Brotherhood and this time is no exception.

Reluctantly Reuben opens his legs, in turn dragging mine open too.

Cool air licks over my wet pussy, and I shudder at the sensation. Reuben's kiss deepens, his strong lips bruising mine. I mewl against his mouth, digging my fingers into his arm as I try and pull it away from my throat.

Cass and Apollo descend on my breasts again. This time they use their lips and their teeth. Kissing, sucking, nipping, biting. I start writhing on Reuben's lap and, if his legs hadn't been open, I'd probably have smeared him with my juices. But I'm suspended over the gap between his legs.

And when I feel Zachary's body heat warming my knees, and force my eyes open, I realize why.

Zachary smirks at me for a second and then reaches between my legs. "You'll have to open a lot wider, girl," he says.

The back of his hand brushes my pussy as he reaches past me. I gasp and shift against Reuben, breaking our kiss.

He lets out a low grown a second before I feel the tip of his cock brush my pussy.

I go rigid, frowning as I try to look down to figure this all out.

Zachary's got a hold of Reuben's cock in one hand. And when I look up at him in utter shock, his smile slips away.

Without letting go of Reuben's cock, Zachary goes to his knees in front of us.

Reuben groans again, and shifts under me. Suddenly, his cock is right against my entrance.

My body sparks alight. I gasp, my nails sinking into Reuben's arm as I try to get out of the way but Cass and Apollo grab my thighs, keeping me exactly where I am.

Zachary uses his other hand to grab Reuben's wrist, urging the man's fingers between my legs.

A furious throbbing starts up deep inside me as Zachary shows Reuben where to touch me. How to smear my juices over my pussy until I'm drenched and dripping.

Then he guides Reuben's cock back to my entrance. Together they part me. Someone's finger—fuck knows who—slips inside me.

I gasp as my body goes rigid.

Cass and Apollo stroke my inner thighs, building a crazy hot friction over my skin. I hear zips being pulled down.

For my own fucking sanity, I know I shouldn't...but I do. I look.

They take their cocks out and start stroking them with expert hands and fingers.

I choke back a sob. "Please..."

But this time, I don't know if I'm begging them to stop...or to just end my fucking misery.

The ache inside me is unrelenting. I keep clenching tighter and growing wetter until I'm drenching Reuben's cock and Zachary's fingers.

Reuben nuzzles against the side of my neck, bites my earlobe, and murmurs, "Kiss me."

And I turn. And I fucking kiss him.

Because, obviously, I've lost my fucking mind.

Zachary rubs Reuben's cock through my folds faster and faster, his thumb dipping inside me on each pass. Teasing me until it feels like I'm already coming undone.

Hands grab my wrists. Cass and Apollo urge my nails out of Reuben's muscles. And I let them, because Reuben's kiss is melting every last shred of resistance.

My fingers brush the softest, warmest skin. I hesitate, almost recoil, but then I feel a mouth on my inner thigh.

Oh fuck.

No.

What?

My eyes flutter open and I dare to peek down as Reuben's tongue slips into my mouth.

Zachary's shirt is off. Possibly his pants too—my eyes are blurring with lust and passion and whatever crazy spell they've put me under.

Zachary kisses the top of my knee. My inner thigh. When he leans closer, his body heat sends an electric ripple through me.

I gasp into Reuben's mouth as Zachary grazes the sensitive flesh of my inner thigh with his teeth.

Working his way up.

Closer.

Toward my exposed pussy. My bared clit. All the while stroking me with the dripping-wet crown of Reuben's cock.

So when Apollo and Cass urge me to grab hold of their dicks...

They groan in tandem as I wrap my fingers around them.

Hard. *Fucking* hard.

And just how Zachary guides Reuben's cock over my pussy, they show me how to touch them. How fast to stroke them.

I'm aching and throbbing and panting like a fucking animal before Zachary's mouth even comes close to my pussy.

When he holds Reuben's cock out of the way and swipes his tongue over the entire length of my pussy, I buck against his mouth like a woman possessed.

Yeah, fuck, I *must* have the Devil inside me right now.

What the hell else is there to explain why, when Zachary reaches the top of my pussy and flicks his warm, wet tongue against my clit, I force myself against his mouth hard enough to make myself come?

I'm so lost in my own climax, I barely notice that I'm gripping Cass and Apollo hard enough to make one curse me, and the other come.

Warm cum trickles down the back of my hand when my eyes flutter open a second later.

Cass eases my fingers off his dick, muttering something about keeping me the hell away from him. Apollo, on the other hand, ducks forward and steals my mouth from Reuben. Then he makes my hand move harder, faster.

"Fuck," he murmurs, breaking off our kiss.

And then he leans back from me, a wicked grin sliding off his face as he urges my movements to slow. His gaze flickers to Zachary, and then down to my pussy.

Another silent command.

One I understand when Zachary ducks down and sucks my clit into his mouth.

I gasp as blissful agony shoots through me. I shove a hand in Zachary's hair, only realizing a second later that it's still covered with Cass's cum. But then nothing matters anymore, because I'm pushing Zachary's mouth harder against my clit as I buck up to meet him.

While Apollo uses my hand for his own pleasure. His groan comes seconds before he does, and then that hand is coated with his cum too.

Zachary nips me with his teeth, and another climax comes charging toward me. A gasp rattles through me as I arch my back, fully expecting another spectacular orgasm to tear through me.

Instead, he moves his mouth away and shoves a finger inside me.

"She's ready," he says.

He looks up at me, and for possibly the first time ever, a genuine smile spreads his lips.

"This will hurt more than anything you've ever felt," he says. "But you're going to bear it, because he fucking loves you. Hear me?"

My heart stutters a beat.

Reuben relaxes the arm he's had slung around my throat the past eternity and instead grabs a breast, squeezing it mercilessly in his strong hand. I whimper, turning confused eyes on him.

"I'm sorry," he murmurs, and then nuzzles his face into my hair. "I should have said something."

"You...?"

I can't even.

It doesn't make sense.

We've only...like...

I go limp.

I can't fight this anymore. It would take another three of me to even try. I just don't have it in me.

"Hmm," Zachary murmurs and then goes back to his knees. "I liked it better when you were fighting."

Then he slaps the inside of my thigh with a hand. I gasp, but barely flinch.

"You come once and you're useless after?" he says. "That's not good enough, Trin."

He ducks down, scraping his teeth over my skin hard enough to leave behind ridges. I squirm, but that's all I have the energy for. "Where's your fight. Where's that spunk?"

"All over my fucking hands," I say, holding them up. "And your hair."

There's a moment, this crystallized silence, where it could have gone either way.

I don't know if I'd have preferred us to all laugh it off.

I didn't get a choice.

Zachary snarls at me. "Want me to pity you, slut?"

A cold shiver races through me. "No, I—"

He grabs my face hard enough to bruise and then yanks at his belt.

"Zachary," comes Reuben's voice from behind me.

"You'll thank me later," Zachary says to Reuben as his belt clatters to the floor.

"Zach—"

"You might want to bite down on something, little girl," Zachary says, his eyes on me. But then he looks past, to Reuben. "Hold her down so I can open that pussy up for you."

CHAPTER FORTY-FIVE
TRINITY

My scream does nothing to stop them. Apollo grabs my hands and holds me down so I can't fight. And Reuben just opens his legs, exposing my pussy for Zachary's cock.

My eyes blur with frightened tears, but I blink them away before they can fall. Zachary wedges his knees between Reuben's legs and leans closer, one hand slipping past us to grab the cushion beside Reuben's head.

Zachary's breath stirs the fine hairs beside my ears when he leans in and I turn away. But then strong fingers make me face him again.

Reuben. The fucking traitor.

Zachary's eyes dart down to my lips. "Want me to kiss you like I love you too?" he murmurs.

He ducks down, his lips brushing mine. No more than the faintest tease.

If I could have turned away I would have, but Reuben's keeping me in place in every possible way—chin, body, legs.

I feel the couch cushions sink down a little as Cass returns from wherever he went to. His fingers trail over my thighs. A second later, so do Apollo's.

Reuben shifts under me, and suddenly his cock is pressing against me again. He groans softly as he grabs his cock and smears it through my pussy, again coating himself. The tip of his thumb slips inside me, and then his cock is pushing against my entrance.

I don't know if Zachary somehow knows what's happening down there, or if they're all psychically linked, but when I gasp as Reuben pushes against me, Zachary kisses me.

Hard.

Passionately.

And yes, like he fucking *loves* me. But in his own twisted, fucked-up way.

It's nothing like he's kissed me before. It feels wrong, but the kind of wrong that makes me wonder why I was trying to stop him in the first place.

Any of them.

Cass and Apollo's fingers stroke over each side of my pussy, and then pull me open even more. I push up into Zachary's kiss, breathless as I try to kiss him back as hard as he's kissing me.

He makes a surprised sound in the back of his throat a second before his tongue forces its way into my mouth.

And then his cock brushes over my clit. He dips down, wetting himself on my arousal, and then comes back, massaging me with the tip of his dick as he tongue-fucks my mouth.

Reuben releases my jaw and instead grabs one of my breasts, squeezing me so hard I whimper against Zachary's mouth.

"Jesus fuck," Zachary whispers, briefly breaking our kiss. "If you had any idea how badly I want to hurt you."

My eyes flutter open.

"Then do it," I say.

I don't know where it comes from, the sudden bravado that rushes through me.

Maybe it's the brief flash of admiration that flickers deep in Zachary's moss-green eyes. Maybe it's the fact that, even for a second, it feels as if I have all four of these men at my beck and call.

Reuben strokes his cock over my pussy and tests my entrance again. And as I'm staring up into Zachary's eyes, panting from our violent kiss, I understand what he meant. Why he wanted to fuck me first.

Because when Reuben pushes the first inch of his cock into my pussy, I let out a low, agonized moan.

He immediately pulls out, stroking me as he nuzzles the side of my neck. All while I stare up at Zachary as if to defy him, only to realize it doesn't work like that.

As much as Reuben wants to make love to me, he can't, because it would hurt me. And he can't hurt me.

Zachary knows it.

If I want to fuck Reuben, I'd have to fuck one of them first. I bite down on my bottom lip as wild thoughts rage through my head.

Slut.

Whore.

Sinner.

But I push them all aside.

I keep forgetting, I'm not normal.

I'm *special.*

Zachary's eyes drop to my mouth. I bite down harder on my lip, and let out a small moan.

"Christ," he mutters. But instead of kissing me, he nips at my chin. "Don't just give it to me, little girl." He kisses me once, hard, and leans back as he starts stroking his dick. "I want to *take* it."

So I give him what he wants.

When he drops his hips and touches his cock against my pussy, I start struggling.

It comes easily enough, because I'm fucking terrified.

Not just of him.

I don't know what will become of my life, even if I miraculously don't go through with this.

So I fight him.

When his shoulder comes close enough, I sink my teeth into him. And I get a slap on my pussy for that, which makes me whimper in pain.

And that makes him even harder.

So he slaps me again, groaning as I buck.

"Finger her," he snaps, his eyes only briefly darting up to Reuben.

Two thick fingers tease my opening. And then Reuben shoves them into me.

I arch off him, a gasp rattling in my throat that Cass leans forward and snatches with a kiss.

Fuck my life.

I moan into his mouth as Reuben slowly starts to finger me.

A hot mouth presses to my pubic bone. I'm convinced it's Zachary's but when a tongue tentatively licks my clit, I realize it's not.

Apollo.

My body melts against Reuben under their attention. Reuben fucking me with his fingers, Apollo massaging my clit with his lips and tongue and mouth. Cass stealing my breath with a kiss.

My eyes flutter open the second Cass breaks away.

Zachary's sitting in his chair, stroking himself as he watches me being devoured, a look of utter contentment on his face.

But the spell breaks when a climax thunders toward me. I claw my fingers into Apollo's hair, forcing him harder against my clit, but Zachary grabs his shoulder and wrenches him away.

"Stop."

Reuben's fingers tug out of my tight, dripping pussy. Zachary slips between my legs, drags his fingers through my slit, and licks my juices from his fingers.

"You're wet enough," he says as he leans closer. He puts his mouth by my ear.

He pushes my head aside with his, and Reuben's lips catch mine in a slow, gentle kiss I can feel all the way down to my toes.

Zachary's cock touches my clit and drags down.

He stops against my entrance, and eases himself in the first inch as his breath paints hot lashes against the side of my neck.

"Jesus, you're soaked," he says.

I manage a mewl in response.

Then he goes in another inch. I gasp into Reuben's mouth, and he starts kissing the corner of my mouth instead.

"Don't hold back. I want to know how much I'm hurting you."

A breath rattles through my throat as he eases himself in another inch. I grab hold of his shoulders, and then sink my nails into his flesh.

He hisses through his teeth.

And then slams into me.

I scream, because *fuck* it hurts.

And then I fight, because I want him out.

But he holds me there, pinned on his cock, and pants against the side of my neck.

"So fucking tight," he whispers. "Jesus."

A sob chokes me. I try and move, but I'm pinned between him and Reuben.

"P-Please," I manage.

"Does it hurt?"

"Yes!" I hiss.

"I'm not even in all the way," he says. And then he forces another inch inside me.

Tears slip down my cheeks as I gasp out in pain. Fingers slip between us and touch my clit and then pleasure wars that pain.

Reuben begins massaging my clit as he kisses the side of my neck.

Caught between them, I slowly start to come undone.

Zachary pulls back no more than an inch, and then thrusts into me hard enough to jar a hoarse yell from me.

Reuben's fingers speed up.

I'm clinging so tightly to Zachary's dick, I'm surprised he can move at all. But he does. As soon as he's filled me with every inch of cock, he starts fucking me hard and deep.

Every thrust rips a new yell from me. Powerful at first, and then hoarse and broken.

Reuben massages me even harder.

I'm howling now, scratching at Zachary's chest like a caged animal.

Because that is exactly what I am.

Trapped between them, I have nowhere to go. No way to stop him fucking me, hurting me, making me bleed.

And as he picks up speed, as his rhythm smooths, Reuben bites the side of my neck, and Zachary captures my lips for another kiss, I come.

I fucking come so hard I can't even scream.

And Zachary fucks me through my climax and beyond. I'm still coming down from that impossible high when he grabs my hips and thrusts into me the hardest he has yet.

His cock pulses as he empties himself inside me, bruising my hips with his fingertips.

I don't even have time for a breath. Zachary pulls out of me with a ragged gasp, the last spurt of his cum warming my skin as he comes over my clit.

"Fuck her," he says, not even bothering to look at me. "Get in there and fuck her while she's still bleeding."

Reuben shifts under me. I have time for a breathless, "No!" of protest, and then I'm being split open all over again.

Zachary grabs my hair in a fist and yanks me forward for a violent kiss as Reuben buries himself balls deep in my bleeding, aching pussy.

I might have died. It's entirely possible. Because I remember kissing Zachary, and then suddenly I feel like I've gone to heaven.

I've never felt such mind-numbing pleasure. But the pain is too intense for me to enjoy it.

At least, that's what I think.

But then someone's strumming my clit again, and...

"I'm going to come!" I whisper against Zachary's mouth.

He steps up, his dick bouncing angrily, already erect again as he steps aside for Cass.

"What...?"

Cass goes to his knees. Sits forward. And closes his mouth over my clit.

I throw my head back and gasp.

"Am I hurting you?" Reuben whispers into my ear.

I somehow manage a whimpered, "Yes."

"Should I stop?"

"No!"

"Good," he growls. "Because I can't. You feel too good. So fucking good, my love."

Something invisible squeezes my heart. "Fuck me harder."

"But I don't—"

"Fuck her harder!" Zachary barks out.

Reuben growls deep in his throat, but he obeys. Grabbing hold of my hips, he shifts forward until he's right on the edge of the coach. Cass scrambles back as he wipes his mouth with the back of his hand. By the time Reuben's done arranging me and I look up, Cass is stroking his dick and looking about to come again.

Reuben spreads my legs, reaches past me, and grabs Cass's head. He jerks the man forward, forcing his mouth over my clit. "Fuck his mouth," Rube commands quietly in my ear. And then he puts his hands on my hips and moves me against Cass's lips.

Fuck, but it's too much.

I begin to unravel.

Reuben swipes a hand over my pussy, opens me with his fingers, and rams his cock into me. I buck forward, but he grabs my hair and yanks me back. Keeping me caught between his cock and Cass's mouth, he starts fucking me slow and deep.

It fucking hurts like all hell, and then it doesn't anymore. But still I'm whimpering and mewling because the pleasure is just as agonizing as the pain was.

When I come, it's with a hoarse yell. Reuben grabs my ass and yanks me against him, driving his dick as deep inside me as it can possibly go. Cass follows us, his tongue lapping against my clit.

I shudder as my climax plays out, my fingernails leaving crescent moons in Reuben's thighs. He fills me with his cum, and it leaks out of my pussy when he starts pulling out.

I grab the back of his neck and turn my head to kiss him.

"Stay inside," I whisper just before our lips touch.

So he does.

He stays inside, filling me even when he starts to soften, as Cass keeps licking me and licking me and licking me.

We're still kissing, both still panting, when I feel myself about to come again.

But Reuben doesn't capture my cries this time. The mouth on my clit disappears, and instead I'm staring into the bluest eyes I've ever seen.

As Apollo tears me apart with his tongue on my clit, Cass snatches my breath away with a kiss.

CHAPTER FORTY-SIX
TRINITY

I should feel different. Why don't I feel different? Sure, there's still a faint ache deep inside me, but mentally, I'd have thought I'd feel...

Like a woman?

I shrug off the voice and tug in a deep breath. I'm nestled against Reuben's chest and stomach, his arm draped over my waist. We're using Apollo's lap as a cushion while he's propped against a heap of pillows. Cass and Zach are somewhere nearby too, but in the dark I can't quite be sure *where*.

They brought me in here after they were done with me last night. After I couldn't take any more pleasure or any more pain.

My eyes are grainy, and my body's sore. I don't know if I slept for hours or minutes.

I don't dare wake the Brotherhood but I need to get the fuck out of here and figure things out.

Also, I need to pee.

I carefully slide out from under Reuben's arm and creep naked into the living area of their lair. There I find my dress and slip into it as quietly as I can. Thank God Zachary didn't decide to cut it off me along with my underwear.

I hunt around for my shoes. One of them ended up under the couch.

Having to go to the bathroom almost becomes a non-issue when I stand and see Zachary leaning against a nearby bookshelf, watching me.

"Christ," I whisper, putting a hand on my pounding heart. "You scared me."

"Leaving already?" he says, and goes over to a packet of cigarettes tossed on one of the empty shelves. There's a metallic click. A puff of smoke. He still has his back to me.

"I need the bathroom," I tell him. Then I hesitate. "I'll be back after."

Tobacco ignites with a faint crackle as Zachary inhales. "What makes you think we want you coming back?"

My heart stutters. "What did you say?"

"You all had your fun." He turns, exhaling a plume of pale smoke. "It's time for you to fuck off." He comes closer while I'm still trying to process his words, and grabs my chin. That touch hurts more than it should—they bruised me all over last night.

"When the first bus to Mercy leaves this morning, you'll be on it."

I start to shake my head. "Why—?"

Zachary shoves his body against mine, driving me back.

A pained gasp rattles out of me when I thump into the bookshelf, but my lungs seize up a second later when something cold, sharp, and all too familiar pricks the side of my jaw. "Shake your head again, and this'll go straight through your fucking cheek," he says.

My body goes rigid. I swallow hard, my mind reeling as I try to think of something to say.

I thought I'd seen Zachary angry before, but the rage burning in his eyes has nothing on that.

The knife slides down the front of my throat, over the front of my dress. I squeeze my eyes shut when his hand goes up under my dress.

"Look at me, Malone."

My eyes flutter as I reluctantly force them open. The tip of the knife scrapes the inside of my thigh as he brings his hand up...and up...and up. Then it's touching the most sensitive part of me, a breath away from slicing me apart.

In sheer panic, I glance at the curtain separating this room from the next. If I screamed, would they—?

"I know what you're thinking," Zachary says. "But I'm in charge, not them. If I say you leave, they'll agree."

My skin tries to crawl off my body as I slowly pull my gaze back to Zachary. Cold, dead eyes watch me for a second.

"Why?" I murmur, not able to stop the tears welling in my eyes. "Why are you doing this?"

"Because you and that fucking priest take us for fools," Zachary hisses. The knife pricks my skin, but doesn't break the surface.

It doesn't have to—I know Zachary wouldn't hesitate to slice into me. I can see it in his eyes.

"I don't understand," I say.

I saw what Zachary did last night. He has to be bisexual to some extent to have done what he did last night. So why is my father and Gabriel's relationship such a sticking point with him?"

I search his face, trying to find meaning in his words. "You can't blame me for what my father did. It was his choice. I had nothing to do with it."

Zachary's eyes narrow to slits. "Back then, maybe. But now? You expect me to believe this is all a coincidence? You arriving here just before we're ready to strike?"

I frown hard at him. "What does that have to do with—?"

He leans into me, snarling. "I know who you are. Nothing you say is going to change my mind, little girl."

Who I am? He's always known—

"If you're not on that bus when it leaves, I'll come find you, and I'll make you bleed."

He smiles.

Claps a hand over my mouth.

And drags the tip of the blade down the inside of my thigh as I whimper in sudden panic.

"Only this time, I'll use my knife."

CHAPTER FORTY-SEVEN
TRINITY

I barely have enough strength in my legs to drag me up the stairs, but somehow I make it all the way to the fourth floor of Saint Amos. It's still early—the sun hasn't even risen yet—but already I hear the distant sound of doors opening.

Saint Amos is coming to life.

But I'm dying.

It has nothing to do with the shallow cut on my thigh. It was the fear that came after. It has drained my spirit to the point where I'm wondering if I'll live to see sunlight again.

I could have gone to my room. Climbed into bed. And fallen asleep...possibly forever. But I came here instead. I came back to Gabriel.

I know he'll take me back because that's what he does. It's his job to forgive people.

Sometimes, he even does it on behalf of God.

Maybe I should confess. Serve penance. Maybe then my life won't be so fucked up anymore.

Makes sense. This was all my fault. I went there. I slept with them. What did I expect? That I'd wake up to breakfast in bed?

No, I hadn't expected that. I'd *hoped*.

But Zachary made me realize something I should have realized a long time ago.

The men down there in the back of that library? They are mentally unstable. I'd be too if I'd suffered like they had. I don't blame them for that.

But they need help.

I stop outside of Gabriel's door, lift a fist, and bang it on the wood. Then I lean against the wall beside it as the world takes a slow tumble.

Am I in shock? If Zachary had pushed that knife less than an inch up, he would have—

"Trinity, what are you—?" Gabriel cuts off with an angry sound. "Who did this to you?"

Oh.

Right.

The bruises on my face.

The cum stains on my dress.

The blood trickling down my leg.

He's wearing sweatpants and a t-shirt. Glasses resting on top of his head. He looks like my father sometimes did on Saturday mornings when he slept in and would come downstairs at ten o'clock in the morning for his first cup of coffee.

Gabriel and my father had a lot in common, come to think about it.

I straighten, hug myself. Stare at Gabriel.

"There's…"

He holds out a hand. Wants me to come inside. I look past him, into the small, dimly lit antechamber. Past that, to his room.

No fire this morning.

A suitcase, packed.

Ready to leave.

But I thought he was staying? That's what the Brotherhood's entire plan hinged on.

"Please, child. Come inside. I'll make you some—"

"There's something I need to show you," I say.

Gabriel's gaze searches my face. "What is it?" His voice is low.

I swallow hard, and wish I could look away. But his brown eyes have mine trapped, his face blank. "It's…"

His voice is clipped when he says, "Speak, child."

"It's in the bell tower, Father."

CHAPTER FORTY-EIGHT
TRINITY

My heart's pounding like a bongo drum. Father Gabriel holds out a big bunch of keys he'd taken out of a drawer in his apartment and glances at me over his shoulder.

He doesn't say anything. He just frowns, and puts the key in the lock. But when he turns the key nothing happens.

Because it was already unlocked.

He opens the door. A slash of light paints the blank wall inside. Gabriel steps inside, turns, lifts his hands. "What do you want to show me?" he asks.

I rush into the small room and slap my hands on the bare wall.

"It was right here. Pictures, photos, articles." I turn, and stab a finger into his chest. "About you. Everything. It all leads back to you!"

He grabs my wrist and twists my hand. I yell out in pain, my body moving to the side on instinct.

As soon as I yell, Gabriel releases my hand and takes a hurried step back, the metal desk rattling when he backs into it. His fierce expression dissolves into shock. "I didn't mean to hurt you."

I scramble away from him, my back slamming into the wall.

This can't be happening. Where the fuck did it all go?

They'd kill me if they knew.

Shit...Did the Brotherhood find out about this room and take everything down?

"Why did you bring me here?" Gabriel has a hand on his heart, but not clawing at it like he's having a heart attack or something. Just...flat. Like he's counting his own heartbeats.

"It's gone," I murmur. "They took it."

"Who? What?" He looks around. "Trinity, talk to me. Tell me what happened." He steps closer, reaching for me, his eyes darting to my legs, to the blood. "Tell me who did this to you."

But I can't. I mean...what the fuck am I supposed to say? Yeah, so, there's this bunch of guys, they say you're a criminal mastermind. And they have evidence, which was all here, but now it's gone.

I'd sound like a lunatic.

"You can trust me, Trinity."

His one hand connects with my shoulder. Then the other. He squeezes my muscles, ducking down so our eyes are level.

"You can tell me anything."

"What other sins have you committed?" I ask quietly. "Besides fucking my Dad, obviously."

Gabriel's face hardens. "That's between God and me, child."

"You said I can trust you, but I won't. Not until you tell me everything."

He releases me, steps back. His eyes narrow as he studies me. Then he takes in the room again, turning as he crosses his arms over his chest. "I don't know why I thought things would be different," he says, so quietly I step forward on instinct to hear him better.

"What things? Are you talking about you and my dad?"

"I thought I could...explain."

"He cheated with you on my mom and you expect me to *trust* you?"

Gabriel runs his hand over the dusty metal desk, and my gaze follows the trails he leaves behind right to the marks my butt made when Apollo set me down on the edge.

Gabriel outlines that heart-shaped smudge in the dust as if he can see into the past.

An invisible hand grips my throat, and not nearly as kindly as Zach or Reuben ever did.

"Dear child..." he murmurs. "There's so much you still don't know. So much I have to tell you."

And then he opens one of the drawers.

The screech it makes drags ragged nails down my back.

Tell me? What the hell does that mean? Is this...is it about the Brotherhood?

No. He'd never tell me if he was guilty. No one in their right minds would.

"So tell me," I say.

I step closer.

Gabriel reaches inside the drawer and comes out holding an envelope. He glances at me from the corner of his eye, his back still turned, and frowns. "Is this what you came here to show me?"

He holds up the envelope.

TRIN

THERE'S a heart over the I.

Tears blur my vision.

Suddenly I don't want Gabriel to see anything. I want him to keep talking. But when I lean forward to take the envelope, he moves it out of reach.

His brown eyes dart over my face, hunting.

"What is it?" he asks.

I have no way of knowing, but the second he asks that question, it's as if I can see right through the fucking envelope.

"A photo." I lick my lips. "It's a photo of you."

He tilts his head a little. There's even a hint of a smile on his mouth. "Of me?" That smile stretches. "I hope they got my good side."

I laugh, but it sounds like I'm seconds away from losing my mind.

Or maybe I have already.

Gabriel lifts the envelope a little. "May I?"

My head nods, but it's as if someone else is doing it for me. My eyes move, but not because I ordered them to.

I watch, frozen in place, as Gabriel opens the envelope.

Takes out the photo.

The coy smile he'd been wearing melts away. For a second, his face could have belonged to a corpse.

Then his gaze flashes up to mine. "So young," he murmurs.

He tips up his chin, staring down at the photo a second longer. When his eyes lock with mine again, my body goes ice-cold.

"Who left this here?" he asks.

I can't move, let alone speak.

Gabriel comes closer, glancing between me and the photo, eyes slowly narrowing. I stifle a gasp when he grabs my jaw, tilting my head back so he can stare at me at just the right angle.

His eyes widen a little.

"So much of your mother in you, isn't there?"

My stomach drops.

"And to think," Gabriel says, his mouth breaking into a fond smile, "She swore to Keith and me that she'd never have children."

He turns the photo to me, drawing my eyes.

Middle row, two from the left. A young Gabriel Blake, hands behind his back, stern expression on his face.

"But then she fell pregnant. A boy, did you know that?"

Middle row, four from the left. A young Keith Malone. Solemn, bleak. But so were all the kids in that photo.

My eyes fly back to Gabriel.

"She didn't keep that baby though. Or the next. But she kept you, Trinity." Gabriel's eyes move back to the photo, and my gaze follows. "She kept you, because you were special."

Middle row.

Three from the left.

Inches shorter than the boy to her left and the boy on her right.

A young, pretty Monica Stevens.

My mother.

So petite looking there between Gabriel and Keith.

"Do you know why you were special, Trinity?"

A tear breaks free when my eyes shift so I can look at Gabriel. Again, premonition fills me with a cold, frigid dread.

Don't say it.

Don't say it.

DON'T SAY IT!

But he does.

"Because you're mine," he whispers. His grip on my jaw tightens. "And I wouldn't let her."

To Be Continued...

DELIVER US FROM EVIL

Theme Song

everything i wanted — BILLIE EILISH

Playlist

Dangerous — SON LUX

Ma And Pa — LONDON TEWERS

See the Light — SOFA SURFERS

Temple Priest — MISSIO

Repeat After Me — KONGOS

Serpent of Old — SEVEN LIONS

Lake Of Fire — NIRVANA

Poacher's Pride — NICOLE DOLLANGANGER

Joan of Arc — IN THIS MOMENT

I t's amazing, the things you don't notice the first—or the hundredth —time around.

She kept you, Trinity. She kept you because you were special.

When I first came to the bell tower with Apollo I never noticed the stale, chalky smell inside this small room.

Do you know why you were special, Trinity?

Gabriel is a handsome man, especially with his warm brown eyes. But I never noticed the spots of bronze in his eyes before.

Because you're mine.

I never noticed his shaggy eyebrows. The shape of his nose. How similar his eyes are to mine. Suddenly, it's impossible *not* to notice.

I wouldn't let her.

Gabriel—my *father*—scans my face like he has so many times before. But this time, there's hidden meaning in his gaze. He's not checking to see if I've finally found God. He's staring at his daughter's face. Picking out his likeness, or perhaps my mother's.

He brushes his thumb over my lower lip. The intimate gesture sends a surge of panic through me that freezes me solid.

But only for a moment.

Then self-preservation kicks in.

I shove Gabriel away and whirl around, bolting out of the tiny room. But I barely take two steps before he grabs my hair and yanks me back.

I fly into him, and we both crash backward into the wall. He slips an arm around my waist and drags me back. When I realize he's taking me further into that tiny room, I put everything I have into my struggles.

I grab the door frame as I pass. Gabriel makes an angry sound in his throat, then he rips me free with a hard tug that leaves behind some of my fingernails.

I scream again, as loud as I can.

He throws me away from him, and I catch a glimpse of the enraged snarl twisting his face before I hit the wall.

Bright pain lances through my head.

Gabriel crouches at my side, face disturbingly blank even after our scuffle. I groan and try to sit up, try to move away, but that makes my head hurt even more.

He touches the side of my face. "I didn't want it to be this way. I wanted to tell you. I wanted you to know the truth. But they fought me on it. Both of them. Said it would confuse you."

Gabriel shakes his head, breaking eye contact for a second. "I should have fought harder, child. I should have insisted. But..."

When he looks at me again, there's something terrifying in his eyes. Despair.

"I loved them, Trinity. Both of them. I know it's impossible to understand, but it's the truth." His voice goes hoarse, and he runs those same fingertips down my cheek. "I did it for them. And I'd do it again."

He smiles, but it's faint and more sad than happy. "They're gone now. It's just us. But we can start again. Me and you. We can be a family again."

He wants me to be his daughter? If I could have, I would have laughed in his face. How the hell can he think I'd want a sick, perverted man like him for a father?

But I can't even stand, let alone argue. "Please, just let me go," I whisper. "I won't tell anyone."

He grabs my shoulder, squeezes it. "Shh." He shakes his head. "It'll be perfect, you'll see. Now you wait here. I'll be back with something to help you sleep. And when you wake up, it'll be a new day. A new life."

It's amazing, the things you don't notice.

I'd always thought that tiny spark, that delightful little gleam that Gabriel got in his eyes was a kind of righteous joy.

Now I see it for what it truly is.

Madness.

Gabriel leaves, locking the door with a finality that makes my skin crawl. I have to get out of here before he comes back. But there's no way I can open that door and this room has no windows.

My heart starts knocking in my chest.

I'm trapped.

CHAPTER TWO
RUBE

I open my eyes to darkness and cigarette smoke, a combination that never fails to give me heart palpitations.

Triggers come like a thief in the night. Ambushing my mind, my body. I've stopped fighting them because I'll never win. Same reason I stopped fighting my Ghost.

As if my sudden panic wakes him, Cass fumbles a hand down my arm. "Jus' Zach," he murmurs, still half asleep as he laces his fingers through mine. He squeezes my hand, and then he relaxes, already asleep again.

In the basement, sleep was our oblivion. I was always exhausted and Cass was fucked on heroin more often than not, so it was easy for him to slip away with me.

But I'm wide awake now.

Trinity is gone.

I shake loose Cass's hand, tugging on my shirt as I step out from behind the curtain.

Zach is sitting in the armchair, smoking a cigarette.

Darkness and smoke.

"Where is she?" My voice is still raspy from sleep.

"Probably halfway to Sisters of Mercy by now," he says, and then takes a long drag at his cigarette without looking up at me.

"She left without saying goodbye?" I inch closer as I wait for his response. Because I'm pretty sure it's going to piss me off. And if that's the case, I might go for his throat.

I consider myself calm. Reasonable. I think things through a hundred times before I act on them. But when I'm triggered it's like a switch inside me flips. All that calm, all that reason...it's decimated by rage. Like a town flattened by the shock wave of a nuclear bomb.

Zachary can trigger me at will. He's had that power ever since I found out who he really was. I couldn't reconcile the fact that he'd been living a normal life above us while we hunkered in the dark waiting for our next visit.

I spend a lot of time dredging up memories of the Utopia that had existed above us. Replaying them. Wondering if the sounds I'd so often heard were made by him. A patter of fast, light footsteps—was that Zach on his way to school? A faint thump—Zachary sitting down in front of the TV, eating a PB&J sandwich while he watched Sesame Street? Sometimes we'd hear voices, but only if the Keepers shouted. And then the words were usually unintelligible because they'd made sure to soundproof the basement as much as possible.

All except one. A name.

Mason.

"Didn't want to wake you," Zachary says.

I have no way of telling if he's lying. He's had years to perfect the art of twisting the truth.

Fuck. Why did I let myself sleep that deeply?

Because I was happy for the first time in a long time. And it felt good. And it felt safe. And I let my guard down.

This is what happens.

"And she said she's going to Mercy?"

We can fetch her when we're done with Gabriel. I know a few of the sisters who work there. Shouldn't be too difficult to find her if she wants to be found.

Zach takes another drag before replying. "She's an orphan. Where the fuck else would she go?"

So callous. But I knew him when he was still vulnerable. When he was still human. The first week he was down in the basement with us, he'd been crying for his mother. Begging his father to open the door and let him out. That he didn't belong down there with the 'other kids.'

He eventually realized he wasn't special. Not to them, not to us. He was exactly like the 'other kids.'

We'd been planning escape long before he arrived, but we were suspicious of each other because we were each treated differently. Cass had a regular dose of drugs to keep him warm and fuzzy while abominable things were done to him. Sometimes he even seemed to be enjoying it. Apollo only had two ghosts, and they only ever spent time with him on the weekends. Zach and I? Our Ghost treated us like scum. We were kicked and bitten and had foreign stuff shoved in us all the fucking time. We were tools—objects of pleasure for a sick man. Sometimes he would visit us together, make us watch what he did to the other one. Or he'd take us away to one of the upstairs rooms. Play us against each other. We'd get treats when we were alone with him, while our brothers in the basement starved.

That shit really messes with your head.

Other boys came and went. So many we didn't bother finding out their names. Weak, shattered, hollow. Nameless shapes in the gloom, some of who never made a sound, despite how brutally they were used.

Some who, after a few days or a week, would stop moving altogether.

We don't know why they brought the boys there to die. Not until we'd escaped, anyway. Then it became so clear.

A lot of things became clear after we were free.

But that would never have happened without Zachary. We wouldn't have been able to get out of there without his help. He knew the layout of the house. He knew his parents' schedule. And he had a solid plan. But it would take four, possibly even five kids to pull it off. He sat and watched. Chose us, because he saw strength and resilience.

If Zachary hadn't come to the basement, we'd have died there like the other boys.

If we hadn't been there, Zach would never have escaped.

Everything happens for a reason. Trinity's arrival only strengthened that belief. She came to Saint Amos—to us—for a reason. It wasn't a coincidence.

I thought it was a sign from God. A reminder that there was more to life than revenge. That love *could* exist in a void. Until we discovered who she really was.

She wasn't a Godsend.

She'd been sent by the Devil.

There's movement at the partition—we woke Cass. He moves aside, letting Apollo into the room.

"She's gone?" Apollo asks. The disappointment in his voice hits me harder than it should. Apollo has changed so much since Trinity arrived. I don't know if the others see it, but he's started interacting more, not just sitting quietly in the corner absorbed in whatever toy Zachary lavished on him. When Zachary isn't around, he starts talking about what we'll do after we've found our Ghosts and ended them, as if he's obsessed with starting a new life.

Before, he'd been drowning in the past. Trinity had brought him to the surface. Had breathed life back into his cold, dead mind.

"Yeah," Zach says, "and we should get going too."

How often he's sat like that. Slightly hunched, cigarette dribbling smoke from one end as it dangles from his fingertips. He's lost weight again. It happens when things come to a head. He stops eating, and his body takes sustenance in any form it can—even if it's from his own flesh.

He locks eyes with me. Green to my green.

Green...but outsiders only see black. My Ghost liked my eyes. Forced me to keep them open. Forced me to watch. And then told me how pretty they were when I cried. So, like Cass shaves his head, I hide behind colored contacts. I've worn them for so long, so religiously, that I hardly notice them anymore.

"Now how about we get a move on?" Zach stands and crushes out his cigarette in the designated mug.

"First, coffee," Cass mutters. He doesn't seem that pained that Trinity's gone. I guess she was just a piece of tail to him. It's easy for him to pick up girls. He simply has to look in their direction and smile.

"I'll bring you some," Apollo says. "I need to grab my stuff."

"Yeah, me too." Cass stretches. "I'll walk with you."

Zach turns on them with narrowed eyes. "The fuck you will. We're sticking with protocol until Gabriel's tied up in that fucking cabin. Got it?"

Apollo nods, even dropping his gaze. Cass scoffs and gives him a dismissive wave. "Fine, whatever." But there's a shift in his eyes I've seen too many times not to know what it means.

The moment they're out from under Zach's watchful eye, they'll meet up. They might even walk together anyway, despite what he says. Because although he's taken command, Zach doesn't control us.

I guess, after going through what we did, we'll never let someone have that much say in our lives.

Apollo and Cass leave, and I make to go after them, to warn them. Because they might not like it, but Zach's right. We have to be careful. If Gabriel slips through our fingers again...

But a hand catches my arm, squeezing my bicep hard, almost cruelly.

And I have to let the other two go.

I glance over my shoulder. Zach's face is stone.

"Gotta run some things by you," he says.

Code for "I need you." Always has been.

So I stay.

We smoke a cigarette together. We have a shot of whiskey. And we listen to each other recite exactly what we'll do to our Ghost the day we find him.

W here the fuck is Apollo? I'd have stuck with him after we left the library, but he said he needed to take care of some shit. I thought he was being literal—I wasn't hanging around for that. But that was ages ago, and he's not answering my calls.

I need to make sure he's okay, and that's pissing me off.

I *hate* needing things.

Sleep.

Sex.

Coffee.

Sleep replaced the heroin. Coffee replaced the adrenaline. And sex replaced...Huh. I guess it didn't replace anything. I suppose my brothers need things too, but they're not addicts like me.

The least I can do is fucking own that shit.

Denial's for pussies.

I could slip into the kitchen and make myself a cuppa. That wouldn't raise too many eyebrows for Cassius Santos, the Hall Monitor. After, I'll track down Apollo and find out why he ditched me.

The kitchen's pretty bare. Can't even find a kettle. Looks like everything's been locked up for the big exodus. Guess then there's less stuff to dust off when everyone gets back after summer break.

One of the kitchen guys comes out of what I assume is the pantry with a bag of what could only be potatoes and calls out, "Hey, man," when he sees me.

I walk over. "Hey. You seen that blond guy who works here?"

The kitchen guy frowns. "Apollo?"

"Yeah, him."

Kitchen guy shrugs. "Nah, man. He was supposed to be here to help me with this shit." Kitchen guy cocks his head to the bag of potatoes.

"'Kay. Thanks."

"You tried his room?"

"Yeah," I call back without looking around. Idiot. Why wouldn't I have—

"Bell tower?"

I stop walking. Turn back. "Bell tower?" Why am I suddenly in a modern-day remake of the Hunchback of Notre Dame?

The kitchen guy puts down the sack of spuds. "Yeah. He goes up there to smoke a spliff."

Well fuck me sideways. And here I thought I knew all there was to know about twinkle toes.

"I'll take a look. Thanks, man."

Kitchen guy nods. "If you find him, tell him Dave says fuck him." He shakes his head, picks up his sack, and heads off to wherever bags of potatoes are destined during summer break.

It takes me a few minutes to find the stairs leading up to the tower. Another few minutes to climb them. And Christ, I'm fucking done when I reach the top.

Really gotta quit smoking.

But the little shit's not in the tower either.

"Fuck."

I pull out my phone, try and call him. It's probably a lost cause, seeing as he didn't answer before, but—

I hear it ringing.

Not through my phone. I actually hear Apollo's Nirvana rip off ring tone rocking it out somewhere nearby. I look to where the sound is coming from, and it feels like every hair on my body is stretching for sunlight.

There, barely visible behind the mass of the bronze bell, is a metal door.

It's standing ajar. Beside it, smeared on the stonework, is a bloody handprint.

Ice coats me from head to foot, and then I'm running.

Running so fucking fast.

But I know I'm already too late.

CHAPTER FOUR
APOLLO

I'm going to miss this view. I hope there'll be enough time to sit up here and smoke a last joint before we leave Saint Amos forever. I could bring the crew here when we're done. We could all sit up here and stare out at the forest.

Because we *will* find Gabriel.

He *will* tell us where to find our Ghosts.

And then we just have to go and kill them.

I fill my lungs with sweet forest air. I'll miss this old stack of stones too. Probably the only one who will. The others hate it here. Always have.

I like gloomy places. Even the basement—but only when there weren't any Ghosts around.

And the forest.

Shit, I'm going to miss that forest.

But I have to get going. When I move, keys jingle inside my pocket.

Did Trin find the envelope? I didn't want to put it in her room in case Jasper found it before she did. Now I'm worried she didn't come up here again after I cleaned out the place. Or, if she did, that she didn't check the drawer. Shit. Maybe I should have left it out in the open.

Trin didn't mention anything about finding the photo, and I have a feeling she would have. Maybe give me a knowing look or something. A kind of a thank you.

The photo means a lot to her. I wish I knew why.

I've stared at it so many times over the years, I have it memorized. Especially Gabriel's face. He was young back then. He looks so innocent in that photo, if a bit of a prick. Guess that's no surprise. Maybe that's how she'd prefer to remember her father. Innocent.

I saunter over, glancing at the view as I try to drink in every leaf on every tree.

I unlock the door and push. It swings open, then gets stuck like there's something in the way.

The hell?

I push against it, shove a little harder. There's a groan.

My eyes go wide, lungs tight and hot and bursting.

I squeeze in through the gap and stare down at Trinity. It takes me way too long to process what I'm seeing because there's blood down there and blood makes me feel like gravity has stopped working.

I grab onto the thin edge of the metal desk behind me, holding on, trying to stay rooted to the floor so I won't float away.

Her eyes are open, but she looks out of it. Concussed maybe. I've seen it plenty of times. Ghosts playing too hard with their toys. Sometimes they break them and those toys don't always heal.

"Trin." My voice comes from far away.

Shit, man. Keep it together. She needs you!

But there's blood pooling on the floor by her head. More on her legs. She's still wearing the white dress, and her skin is so pale. The red looks neon against all that white.

Focus on her eyes, man. Look at *her*. *Help* her.

I push away from the desk. Start rambling. "Hey. It's okay. I'm here. Trin. Trin! Can you hear me? I'm here, pretty thing."

She groans again, her eyes fluttering closed. I get closer. See all that blood is actually her dark hair. Only a little blood. A small splash. Almost less than the streaks on her thighs.

We did that.

No. Can't be. I saw blood yesterday, but not that much. Not enough to make me float away.

I touch her shoulder, scoop a hand under her head. Help her sit up.

Got to be careful with a possible head trauma. So, *so* careful.

"Hey, you there?" I ask. "Can you hear me, Trin?"

Her mouth moves, but no sound comes out. Is that good or bad?

"I'm here, pretty thing. You're safe now. Everything's fine."

Best thing ever—someone telling you shit's fine. Even when it's not, it doesn't matter. Because you give them hope, right? Would have been like those other kids if we didn't have hope. The ones that came to the basement to die.

"'Ming," I think she says.

"Shh. Don't speak, okay?" I can carry her, but not down all those stairs. Not without jarring her. And that can't be good.

Gotta get help.

I take out my phone.

Shit! Cass has been trying to reach me. I must have forgotten to take my phone off silent this morning. I turn on the ringer now. Then I go to call Cass.

"Coming," Trinity says, and this time I hear her fine. But it's too late, because her eyes are already wide, her lips peeling open in dismay.

Maybe if I'd understood sooner, Gabriel wouldn't have had the upper hand. But he works out. Stays fit.

I don't. Hate getting sweaty. Hate feeling tired and stiff.

When Father Gabriel comes at me from behind, slings an arm around my throat, and puts me in a chokehold, there's nothing I can do about it.

Sweet fanny fuck all.

I swat at him, try and scratch out his eyes, but he dodges like a snake.

Trinity watches, eyes brimming, lips distorted. Angry, scared. But just sitting there like a broken doll propped up against the wall in some filthy playhouse.

I finally make contact. Scratch his cheek.

But the light's fading. I can't fend him off much longer. And once he's rid of me...

"They're coming for you, you piece of shit," I manage through a collapsing windpipe. "I'd run. Run fucking far."

God, it takes everything I have to say those words. Not just physical effort, because taking a nap right now is all my body wants to do.

I'm giving up everything we've tried so hard to conceal. No vote. No consensus. But I can't let him take her. And I know that's what he's going to do after leaving her here like this. Probably had to go fetch some ropes, or a carpet to roll her up in like those old spy movies.

Life is more important than revenge. Trinity's life especially.

I don't care if she's Gabriel's daughter.

I don't care if she was sent to spy on us.

I care too much about her for that shit to matter.

My brothers might never forgive me, and that's fine. I can handle that. But I'll never forgive myself if I didn't do everything in my limited power to protect her.

"They? They who?" Gabriel says. It sounds like he's trying not to laugh. Like he thinks I'll say anything to drop his guard.

"My brothers. They're coming up the stairs. You're trapped."

"Brothers? You don't have any brothers." He laughs outright now, so hard his chest shakes. That vibration goes through me. Fills me.

The Guardian wasn't one of the sick fucks who took turns offloading their unrighteous perversions on us. He never touched us.

But he orchestrated everything.

The feel of him so close against me, it's worse than cleaning out the fucking grease trap.

It turns my stomach, gives me the shakes, and just when I think I'm about to puke...

It flicks a switch.

I'm useless, a victim. Then suddenly I'm not. Because all that rage, all that horror, all that shame and humiliation and pain rises up in me like a motherfucking tsunami.

And wherever it goes, it leaves devastation in its wake.

I let go of the arm around my throat. It clamps tighter. Lights sparkle in the darkness that's eating away ten times as fast at the edges of my sight.

I clasp my hands. Throw back my arm. Drive my elbow into Gabriel's stomach.

He makes a soft sound that sends a puff of ashtray breath against my face. His grip relents, but not enough. So I do it again. Then I stamp on his toes.

Fighting like a fucking girl, but still fighting. That's what counts.

He folds forward, and I push back, shoving him against the edge of the metal desk. It must catch him somewhere painful—his hip, his ass, his kidneys, I don't fucking know—because he yells out and loses hold of me.

I swing around and throw a punch. It lands solidly on his nose.

Blood gushes.

I start floating away.

Gabriel comes at me, teeth shining red through the blood. And all I can do is stand there as he rams into me. Drives me over Trinity's legs and into the wall.

She's lying on her side now, and I can only hope I didn't hurt her. Trample her pretty legs, or bruise her beautiful skin.

Gabriel takes hold of my hair, twists it, rams my head into the wall. And then steps back as if to check out his work. The darkness comes, and with it some flashing lights. Pain is there, but distant, because I'm already fading. I slide down, my legs refusing to keep me up.

He puts a hand to his nose, coating it with blood. Looks stunned that there's so much of it. Then he's crouching, poking a needle into Trinity's arm.

I want to tell her it's going to be okay. That we'll find her, somehow. That we'll make Gabriel pay for whatever he's planning to do with her.

Somehow.

But he's already scooping her up. Her head lolls back, and I know it's not because he might have broken her earlier, but because he set her mind free and it's flapping away like a bird.

That's something at least.

Whatever he does, she won't mind it one bit anymore. That's how that shit works.

Maybe I'll tell her now, when I leave my body.

Because there's nothing else left for me to do now but float away.

Float away and never come back.

CHAPTER FIVE
CASS

That bloody handprint feels like an accusation the closer I get. A blatant stamp of the Universe's disapproval. I slam into the metal door, and barely manage to catch hold of the handle to stop it flying inward.

Inside, Apollo's phone rings a last time before going silent. I hope that means that I'm not too late. But that glaring smear of red says otherwise.

Need to calm down. Need to get control.

But as soon as I'm inside and I see Apollo crumpled up against the wall, fury obliterates what little control I had left.

My hand shakes as I lift my phone. It's already locked again, and now it doesn't recognize my fingerprint, beeping impotently at me once, twice, fucking five times before it unlocks and lets me dial.

I go to my knees, trying to be gentle when I thumb back Apollo's eyelid. Left, then right. No fucking clue if anyone's still left behind those pupils though. I pat his cheek. He comes around with a groan. His head tips forward, but I push it back with fingers on his jaw, but gentle. Could be gay for him that's how tender I'm being.

"Gabriel?" I ask. Meanwhile, my phone rings in my ear then goes to voice mail. I redial. Why the fuck isn't Zach answering? "He did this?"

I mean, who else, right?

But how? *Why*? That's what I need to know.

Apollo's eyes roll around in their sockets as he tries to focus on me. He eventually gets out a pained, "Trinity."

I frown, huff out a laugh. "Yeah, no. Try again. Gabriel, right?"

"He's got Trinity."

My blood turns into a raspberry slushie.

All that shit I was spouting about denial? Well, I guess I'm a pussy after all. I couldn't have given less fucks when I found out Trinity had left. There was even a whole good-riddance vibe in my head. Because obviously she couldn't handle the four of us. We were too much for that pretty little slut. Who wasn't a slut after all, and I guess that goes a far way in explaining why she bolted in the first place.

But now?

Christ fucking Jesus.

I was bullshitting myself at a master level. Because if I didn't give a fuck, there'd be no way I'd be outright getting heart palpitations at the thought that something bad might happen to our little girl. And that makes no sense, because we were just having a good time. I don't do feelings. I don't—dear God—do relationships. There's no way you can date someone like me.

So why do I feel like someone's gone and dug up my future grave, poured lighter fuel over my corpse, and set it alight?

The phone goes to voice mail. I call Reuben without missing a beat.

Apollo's eyes flicker, about to close.

"Nuh-uh," I tell him, gripping his jaw harder. Next I'll be putting my nails in him. "Tell me what happened."

He winces, but whether that's from whatever blunt trauma he experienced or my grip is difficult to say. I won't call him an outright pussy, but he's never been able to handle pain, or blood, or any of that shit. Despite what he claims when we get pissed and rage about the deliciously dark shit we'll do to our Ghosts, I know he'll be the one standing outside, keeping watch. Or digging the grave. Or something that doesn't include binding, torturing, and killing.

It's not that he can't hurt a fly. He swats them all right. But he only does it hard enough to daze them, and then tosses them out the window.

"Apollo!" When he doesn't respond, I try, "Trevor!"

His eyes go wide. He winces again. Mumbles, "He took her."

"Yeah, you said that already, Christ. *Where* did he take her? Did he say anything? Does he know?" Too many questions, but I can barely stop myself from yelling at this point.

"He...I dunno. Didn't say where." Then he closes his eyes, and I'm convinced he's about to start crying.

"Cass?" Reuben's voice legit makes me flinch.

I turn away from Apollo, letting go of his head and glancing around the tiny room as I talk to Rube. "Yeah, buddy? We got a serious fucking problem on our hands."

CHAPTER SIX
ZACH

I'm headed to Gabriel's room when I get the call. I shouldn't even have checked who it was—my mission is set in stone. I must find Gabriel before he leaves Saint Amos.

We know he's staying behind to oversee the repairs to Saint Amos. Him and him alone. Which is perfect, because by the time they figure out Gabriel's missing, we'll be lost in the woods. Even if they send out search parties, the chances of them finding that decrepit hunting lodge is slim to none.

Reuben is on his way to the admin offices. We want to make sure Gabriel doesn't have a chance to escape if he happens to catch wind of his own death. Fuck, for all we know, he has a direct line to Satan and Old Scratch sends him prophetic messages every now and then.

Cass and Apollo are probably disobeying me and having a joint together somewhere. They take things like summer break too fucking seriously. It pisses me off, but I can't really blame them for acting like the kids they are.

My phone rings as I step into Gabriel's hallway. I hurriedly take it out of my pocket to silence it, cursing myself for being idiotic enough not to have done that already. When I see it's an unknown number, my curiosity is piqued. Only a handful of people have this number and none of them would phone from an unknown number.

I hurry back down half a flight of stairs before answering, fully expecting to hear Gabriel's voice on the other end of the line. Not that he's one of the handful. But the feeling's impossible to shake for the precious second before an old lady says, "Hello. May I please speak with Mason Price?"

It takes another second before I can answer. "Speaking."

"Mr. Price, it's Beverley from California Key Realty. Is this a good time?"

I stop breathing. My back's against the wall, and I use it as support to slide down until I'm hunkered in a crouch.

I force myself to take a breath.

"No time like the present," I say, and even manage a faint chuckle. "What can I help you with, Beverly?"

I STARE at my phone for a few minutes after the call ends. My fingertips are still tingling. My chest still feels too tight. But for the first time in a long, *long* time, those feelings bring relief—even joy—and not anxiety.

It's done.

It's fucking *done*.

We got the house.

Soon as it's out of escrow, it'll be ours.

There's a grin on my face, and I can't seem to shake it. Fuck, I don't even want to. I draw in a huge breath as I stand, and for a moment it feels like I'm still rising, like a fucking balloon some sweaty kid lost at the fair.

Christ. Why am I so surprised? In this economy, with my generous offer? But I *am* surprised. Fuck it, I'm shocked. Because honest to God I thought the Universe would send a last fuck-you to the four boys it's been such a motherfucking cunt to all these years.

Nothing's ever been easy.

Getting out of the basement.

Trying to keep us together. Focused.

It's been hard fucking work all the way.

I can't remember how many times I've wanted to give up. How often I've wanted to let the Universe win.

But then I'd think of them.

Of my brothers.

And I'd find my second wind. I'd get the strength I need to tell them we need to push on. And they'd rally. They *always* rally.

I shove my phone in my pocket and head for Gabriel's apartment again. But my euphoria starts fading the closer I get. My steps become reluctant.

About a yard from his door, I slow down. Then stop.

This means everything to them, to me…but I can't stop thinking about the house. I'm even getting fucking feels about it. All I want to do is spill my guts to them. I'd call them, but it has to be in person. I want to see their faces light up as I tell them about the infinity pool and the dance room and all those big fucking windows. Light everywhere. The coast so close you can taste salt in the air.

Fuck.

I rake fingers through my hair.

Fuck!

He's one man, Gabriel, but suddenly I feel like I'm facing off against an army. And it's just me this time. I don't have any of them. Yeah, I'm only supposed to find out where he is. Track him until we've got everything in place to grab him. But it's suddenly too real. And, at the same time, surreal.

I'm walking into a nightmare, when I should be heading for the life of my dreams.

That house is everything we've always wanted—

I close my eyes, shake my head.

What the hell am I thinking? Of course they won't be happy. This—I open my eyes and glare at Gabriel's door—*this* is what they want.

What *I* want.

What we've *always* wanted since that first repulsive hand touched us. Since that first voice whispered to us that everything was going to be fine, as long as we play along.

It's just a game. You like games, don't you, Mason? Can I call you Mason?

My skin crawls at the thread of unwanted memory, but I'm too agitated to push it away. So it slithers in deeper, grabs hold of my conscious mind.

I fold my fingers around Gabriel's door handle. Open the door. It should be locked, but it isn't.

This game, I call it hide and seek. But we'll be playing it a little differently, okay?

My Ghost's voice raises goosebumps on my skin. I grit my teeth and step inside Gabriel's apartment. The next door is standing open. I swear I can hear sounds coming from inside.

I'm going to take this chocolate—you see it?—and I'm going to hide it. You like chocolate don't you, Mason? You must be hungry. If you find the chocolate, then you can eat it.

My heart hammers inside my rib cage like a fist trying to break down a door. I slink to the side, pressing my back to the wall.

There's a clatter from inside Gabriel's room.

Fuck. He's here. I have to leave. Go wait by the stairs. Watch him. Send a message, let my brothers know—

Now close your eyes, Mason. Close your eyes so I can hide the chocolate. Good boy. Keep them closed. I'm hiding it now. Good boy. Keep them closed. Give me your hand. Yes, good boy. Now I want you to find it. Go on. Don't be scared. Put your hand in, Mason. There. You feel that? Feels good, doesn't it?

Nausea wells up so fast, so bitter, I taste bile in my mouth before I can swallow it down.

The world swims, and for a second I'm convinced I'm back there in that room. My first night with my Ghost. Playing hide and fucking seek with a sicko.

I cataloged them all. My Ghost, their Ghosts. They're all saved neat and tidy inside my head. Their voices, what their aftershave smelled like, the size and shape of their dicks. Any rings, or freckles or scars on their hands. Those that showed their faces? They'll be the easiest to find. But we'll find them all.

Each and every last one of them.

Keep them for as long as it takes. Until *we're* satisfied.

And then burn them at the motherfucking stake. A sacrificial offering to the God who abandoned us, left us to rot in that basement with those demons.

My phone trembles as I bring it out of my pocket. The memory retreats. Finally have my body under control again. Sticking to the plan.

But before I can back out, something slams closed inside Gabriel's room. Thankfully, instinct takes over. I throw myself against the wall, crowding into a corner by the small key table. Holding my breath, closing my eyes.

He swarms right past me.

I catch a whiff of his aftershave as he disturbs the air, and like I always have, compare it to the database inside my head.

Unless he's changed what he wears, he's not one of them. Not one of the men who abused us.

Gabriel leaves his apartment in a rush, not bothering to close the door behind him. I wait for my arms and legs to stop quivering, and then slip out of the room and follow him down the hall.

I start to type out a message, but then I hesitate.

I almost lost control back there. Teetering on a knife's edge. Me. Them. I'm good at bringing myself back from the void, but they aren't. It's their one weakness.

I'll follow Gabriel, see where he's going. If he looks to be leaving, then I'll let them know. Then we can take him down.

I lick my lips as I wait for him to hurry down the first flight of stairs, then I follow him.

Silent.

Wary.

I'm always thinking of traps. Still not entirely convinced he doesn't know exactly who we are. That's my paranoia of course. Not as easily turned off as old memories.

You feel that, Mason? It feels nice, doesn't it? Oh, you're such a good boy.

GABRIEL GOES to the bell tower. And that makes no sense, but I follow him anyway. I follow him all the way up the stairs and then hang around out of sight behind the first twist in the stairwell.

What's up there? A big fucking bell. Is this part of his provostial duties or something? Does he have to ring the bell to signal the end of term or some shit?

I still feel sick. My skin feels oily. I could use a shower to wash that debilitating memory off me. But I'll watch Gabriel first.

My phone's still on silent, so it vibrates furiously when someone calls.

Cass.

But I can't take it now. I need to listen. I need to be a few steps ahead when Gabriel comes down again.

And then he does. But something's different. His footsteps sound heavier than before. Little details like that don't get past me. I was on full alert back in that basement...I don't think I've ever gone back to normal.

I sneak down the steps as fast as I can, and it's too easy to stay ahead of him, silent like this. Because he's moving slower. Carrying something, maybe. Something heavy enough to slow him down. It's driving me mad trying to figure it out, so I just fucking stop with the mental gymnastics. I concentrate on staying ahead, keeping the sound of his heavy footsteps within earshot.

I slip into a nearby alcove when the stairs exit on the top floor landing. I'm sure the shadows are hiding me, but I'm quivering with adrenaline when Gabriel finally shows.

What?

No.

I blink, hard. Then again.

Is that...?

I watch Gabriel walk past with Trinity in his arms. If I ever had any doubt they were father and daughter, seeing them together eradicates it.

Same dark hair. Same nose, even. His is slightly larger, of course, and there's a fan of blood leaking from it that makes me think Trinity must have put up quite a fucking fight.

I follow as soon as he has a big enough lead on me. I expect him to go to his room seeing as it's only one hallway to the left, but instead he takes the stairs.

My phone vibrates again, but I don't bother checking. I know I should be calling my brothers and updating them on the situation, but there's a question that plays on repeat in my mind, crowding out all other thought.

Why is she still here?

Why is she still here?

Why *the fuck* is Trinity Malone *still* here?

CHAPTER SEVEN
RUBE

When I squeeze into our lair the first thing I see is Apollo on his armchair with a washcloth pressed to the back of his head, wincing as he stares at nothing. Cass comes out of the bedroom like he heard me struggling to get in but for once he isn't wearing a look like he's about to tell you the punch line of a joke. He looks grim and serious and it scares the living shit out of me.

"Tell me everything."

But it doesn't help when they do, because they don't know all that much. Apollo got knocked out before Trinity said anything useful.

"And Zach?" I ask, still standing near the exit, barely moving.

Cass drops his gaze. "No answer."

"What if he got him?" Apollo says, and from the frown that flashes over Cass's face, he's only stating what we're all thinking. "He was supposed to keep tabs on Gabriel's room. He could be—"

"Cass, go check."

"Should we really be splitting up right now?" he asks.

I'm about to tell him to go check anyway, but he's right. Even though we have a huge school to search, splitting up will leave us vulnerable and exposed.

The trick is working out where Gabriel will go. We have to get into his head and figure out his plan.

The fact that Trin had been lying there, waiting for Gabriel to come back...that makes me think she surprised him. Perhaps they fought over something. That room is so far out of the way—maybe that's where they'd been meeting all this time.

The thought makes my heart calcify.

We'd trusted her.

But Apollo said she was injured. So things must have soured between her and her father. Now he's taking her away, but where to? Where in Saint Amos could he—

"He's leaving," I say, already turning on my heel. "We have to get to the road, try and stop him."

"How? We'll never make it!" Cass calls after me, but I'm already sprinting down the library's main aisle.

They'll either follow me or go look for Zach. We shouldn't split up, but I know deep down Gabriel's leaving. We'd only be at risk if we tried to stop him. I can take him on my own, unless he has a gun. But if he had one, he'd have used it on Apollo.

Not every criminal runs around wearing a pistol on his belt. Not like in the movies. I've known plenty of bad people in my life, and not a single one of them would even know how to fire a weapon.

I do. We all do. But we don't keep guns on us because we know there's a chance one of them might go off. And who the fuck knows who'd be at the receiving end of that bullet?

Guns are too easy to use, and too difficult to keep hidden. Especially around a bunch of boys still struggling with the fact that they're men.

The exertion of the sprint hits me when I'm halfway across the lawn. I circle around the side of the dormitory, heading straight for the road.

We don't know how long Apollo was unconscious for, but the sun's barely warming up the land yet. It feels like everything's *just* happened.

I can't bear to let her slip away. Not a second time.

When my legs and lungs start burning, I push harder.

And I'm rewarded for my effort. Despite my heart clanging like a race horse's in my chest, despite the fact that I'm breathing fire, I make it in time.

I turn the corner.

I see the car.

Gabriel's car.

I'm in exactly the right place to watch him drive off, a shadow slumped beside him in the passenger seat.

He doesn't notice me because I'm yards away. If he did, I doubt he'd care.

Because I'm too late.

I ran too slow.

I didn't give it my all.

My legs collapse. My teeth clack together as I go down.

I'm still there, staring at the last place I saw them, when Cass runs up to me. He's out of breath, muttering something about stairs and smoking, and then his hand is on my shoulder.

I slap it away. I'd stand and face him, but I can't.

Muscle failure is a bitch.

"Gone?" he asks, but it's more a statement than a question.

Fucking gone.

And I was so close. If I'd pushed a little harder, if I'd thought just a little faster...

Cass helps me up. The ground feels spongy as we head back to the library. Something catches my eye.

I turn.

Zachary's standing on the front steps of Saint Amos. The big doors are open wide—Gabriel must have left that way. Zachary turns and disappears into the blackness without a word.

And then it all comes together.

I'd be mad, but I've got nothing left. I burned up everything in the useless sprint over here. It'll take time for my tank to refill.

I don't say anything to Cass, and I probably should. But sometimes it takes me a while to process things.

Like the fact that we were just betrayed by our brother.

CHAPTER EIGHT
TRINITY

It was all a dream. Saint Amos, the Brotherhood, Ghosts and Keepers and Guardians. Nothing but a nightmare. Sure, it makes no sense, but how else do I explain waking up in my old room back in Redford with groggy memories of photos and men with knives and losing my virginity in a library with four psychopaths?

My core aches when I try to remember details of the dream though. How they used my body for their own pleasure until they were spent.

Until *I* was spent.

I've had sexy dreams before, but nothing like that. Nothing that intense, that...vivid.

I force myself to picture the Brotherhood's faces.

Zachary with his intense green-eyed stare and that serpent tattoo on his chest. Apollo with his long, sandy-colored hair and light-brown eyes. Cass—mouthwateringly handsome, but those blue eyes so heartless. And Reuben. Black eyes and such a kind heart.

I sit up in bed, staring around blearily at my room as I scratch my tummy. Daisy wallpaper. French-pane windows. Pastel pink curtains.

My body is stiff, my muscles sore. The itch is what woke me, I think, but it's hard to remember more than that.

I tug down the sheets and stare at myself. I'm still wearing the lacy white dress. There are a few spots of blood on it. More blood on the inside of my thighs—dried, smeared. My neck feels stiff. When I touch the back of my head, I find a bump on my skull. It should hurt, probably, but it doesn't. Not really.

The aroma of onions trickles into the room, wiping out my own stink of sweat and dried blood. There's a distant thump. Someone's in the kitchen.

Mom? Dad?

Awesome. I should go say hi.

Somehow, I make it to the top of the stairs, even though it's like I'm walking on clouds. From here I can only see a slice of the kitchen floor —I still don't know who's making the noise. The smell of cooking is intense now. I should be hungry, but instead I feel empty inside. Hollow, like a chocolate Easter egg. But in a good way.

I don't know why, but everything's good. And if it wasn't, I'm pretty sure I wouldn't give a damn anyway.

I cling onto the railing as I make my way downstairs because my legs feel kind of unreliable. Cigarette smoke comes to me in between the breakfast smell.

Wait. That's not right.

Dad's not allowed to smoke inside the house. He didn't even do it when Mom went to the shops.

Where *is* Mom?

She died in a car accident.

I falter halfway down the stairs.

Oh my God. They didn't both die. All this time, Dad's been living in our house in Redford while I was sent from pillar to post. While I had to bear the shame of being stranded in a school full of boys, an orphan girl who no one liked. No one except the Brotherhood.

Why would he do that to me? How *could* he?

The thought is visceral, but with no emotions attached. In fact, I don't feel anything. Except for a sudden itch behind my neck.

"That you, child?"

Dad called me that. Child. Like I was one of the kids in church. Maybe he got it from Gabriel.

I clear the stairs. I can see in the kitchen now.

There's a man by the stove. He has his back to me. There's a whole fog of smells now—bacon, onions, cigarettes, coffee, burned toast.

The man turns, smiling fondly when he spots me.

I'm convinced it's Dad, even though I know he's dead. So convinced that I see him there, right there. So convinced that, when my brain tries to interject, to correct me, I write it off as the fact that he's got a big Band-aid over his nose, and his face is a little puffy, and that's why he doesn't look quite like Dad but just enough that it *must* be him.

Dad beckons me closer with a spatula as he turns and starts dishing up food onto the plates standing ready on the kitchen island.

"Is this a dream?" I ask him through numb lips. Might as well make sure, after all.

"Would you like that?" he asks. And it's not Dad's voice at all. It's Gabriel's.

"Dunno," I say, but actually, I don't care.

Unsteady legs take me deeper into the kitchen. I stand next to a stool, but I can't even imagine how much effort it would take to get up.

Gabriel puts the pan back on the stove, dusts his hands, and comes around the island. His damaged face should scare me, but instead it intrigues me. I feel like I should know how he was hurt, but I can't seem to find the memory. He slips his fingers under my armpits and lifts me onto the stool like I'm a toddler.

"Morning, daughter," he murmurs, close to my ear, before he walks around the island and takes his seat on the opposite side. "Sleep well?"

When he slides my plate over, I try and pick up the fork propped on top of a piece of blackened toast. My fingers can't seem to get it right though.

Something is wrong.

With this setup.

With me.

"Hasn't worn off yet," Gabriel says, as if talking to himself. He takes a bite of his food and then points his fork at my plate. "You're probably not hungry. Should I put it in the microwave?"

The fork drops from my fingers, and he chuckles at me as he comes around to my side again. He pushes away the plate and grasps my chin with his fingers, turning my head to face him.

"How are you feeling?" he asks, staring deep into my eyes.

"Not feeling anything."

He smiles. "That's good." He drops his gaze, and it takes me a second to realize he might be staring at my body. I think I should care about that, but I don't. Not even when he rubs his hands up and down my arms like he's trying to warm me up. "You're so dirty. We'll have to get you cleaned up after breakfast."

He cups my face in his hands, wiping a strand of hair from my cheeks with his thumb. "You look just like her. It's uncanny."

Is he talking about Mom? Where is she, anyway?

"Where's Mom and Dad?" I should know the answer, but I don't. Another memory that refuses to come when called.

His smile fades a little. "Don't worry about them. We'll get along just fine on our own." He goes back to his side of the island.

I watch as he eats while my stomach grumbles quietly to itself. It probably means I'm hungry, but the thought of putting food in my mouth isn't in the least appealing. There's a soft pattering nearby, and I turn to look at the kitchen window. A gust of wind blows rain against the panes, smudging the world outside.

It's difficult to tell the time of day with the sun hidden behind the clouds, but I'm sure it's not breakfast time. Closer to midday, perhaps even past. And we're all the way back in Redford, a trip that takes hours, but I don't remember a single moment of it.

And then I do.

The bell tower. Gabriel has a needle. Apollo tries to stop him but he can't. It hurts going in but then my fear, my resistance, it all melts away into warm, cotton candy nothingness.

After that, there's only bits and pieces floating around in my head.

A long car drive tainted with the stink of cigarette smoke.

Stopping in front of my old house.

The overwhelming conviction that everything was right with the world, and I was exactly where I belonged.

"What did you give me?" I ask him. Not angry, not even scared.

Gabriel studies me over the brim of his coffee cup for a moment, and then takes a small sip before setting it down.

"Heroin," he says. Then he gives me a small, secretive little smile. "You'll love it. Your mother did."

"YOU MUST BE GETTING COLD," Gabriel says as he starts washing his breakfast plate in the sink. I'm still where he put me, and I have a feeling I'll stay here until he decides to move me again.

"No," I tell him, and quite truthfully. It feels like I'm wrapped in a thick, invisible cocoon. I don't even feel air moving against my skin.

"Let me just finish up here, then we'll go get you cleaned up and into something warm."

He's so nice. Always thinking of others.

"I loved them both, you know," Gabriel says, turning to me as he flicks soapy water off his hands. "It probably sounds strange." He smiles, laughs softly. "How can you possibly love two people?" Wiping his hands against his jeans, he deepens his smile as he comes closer. "But truly, I did."

He holds out his hand.

I take it.

It's still a little damp, but so warm. His grip is tight as he pulls at me, urging me to slip off the stool and follow him upstairs.

"We met at Saint Amos. Of course, back then, it was called Friends of Faith." He clicks his tongue. "Horrible place. Horrible." Sighs. "Better now, after the church took over. The new administration was a breath of fresh air."

He opens the bathroom door, pulls me through, and lowers me onto the closed toilet seat. I sit there and watch as he turns on the tub's faucet.

"Bubbles?" he asks, holding out a bottle of purple liquid.

I shrug a little. "Sure."

He tips some in and bubbles boil up and start spreading like a plague.

"You probably think I'm a hopeless romantic." Gabriel toes off his shoes and goes onto his knees on the carpet in front of the bath. He sticks a hand in the water, agitating it so more bubbles form. "But truly, I was in love. I believe we all were." He pauses. "That's why we named you Trinity. Because you were *our* child. All three of us."

I nod. Love is a wonderful thing.

He catches sight of the movement from the corner of his eye. "Have you ever been in love?"

"I am."

He frowns a little at this. "Really? With who?"

"The Brotherhood."

His frown deepens. He sits back on his heels, putting his head to one side. "I don't follow."

I shrug. "Weird. I know. But I am." Talking is easy. Once I get going, I can't seem to stop. "I'm not sure about Zach. He scares me. But I love Reuben. And Cass. And Apollo. Different, but the same, you know?"

Gabriel reaches over and turns off the faucet, his eyes not leaving mine. When he speaks, it's slowly and carefully, like he wants to make sure I understand every word.

"You mean you *like* them. You were friends with them?"

"No. I slept with them. All of them."

The slap comes out of nowhere. I don't even realize it's happened until after. Suddenly, I'm facing the wall by the bath, and there's a fierce tingling ache on the side of my face. I turn back to face Gabriel, working a jaw that feels rusty.

White spots pop up on his cheeks. He turns back to the tub, twisting open the faucet so hard it squeaks.

"A whore," he says quietly as if to himself. "Your father said this would happen. Said you'd take after your mother."

I lift a hand to my cheek. I should be insulted, but it feels like I'm watching this all play out from the back of my mind. When my body moves, it's like someone else is doing it. When I speak, I'm hearing those words for the first time. "But I love them."

Gabriel swipes a hand through his hair, leaving a clump of bubbles on the side of his head. They start popping, and I swear it sounds like a hissing snake.

"She could have had her pick," he says, shaking his head. "Any boy at that school would have been happy just to have her look in his direction." He nods fiercely, whipping up more and more bubbles. "But she chose my Keith. Always wanted what she couldn't have, your mother."

His head snaps around. He looks me up and down, a disgusted sneer pulling at his mouth. "You're filthy," he says, in much the same tone of voice he's been using the whole time. "I hate filth."

"Is it because of the basement?" I'm dimly aware that I shouldn't be saying this stuff. That I should be keeping quiet. But my mouth's on automatic. Words spill out before I can filter them. "Because maybe if you'd cleaned the boys more, you wouldn't hate filth. It's psychological. Must be. You hate yourself for what you did. So you hate whatever reminds you of that place."

Gabriel stops with the bubbles. He doesn't look at me as he sits back on his heels, hands dangling over the side of the tub and dripping water and bubbles. Then he leans over and closes the faucet.

After the last drop falls, the bathroom is quiet but for the faint hiss of the bubbles.

He clears his throat, but it doesn't make his voice any smoother. "What basement?"

"The one you kept the boys in."

He whips his head to face me, eyes wide. "I don't know what you're talking about," he says, but his words sound so hollow, I wonder why he bothers trying to lie.

"You kept them there for years. Four little boys. More, I think. But those four were special. You kept them the longest."

Gabriel tries to stand, but there's something wrong with his legs. They tangle, and he ends up sitting on the edge of the bath. The whites of his eyes gleam, his eyebrows almost at his hairline.

"I don't know what you're talking about," he says again. Voice hoarse now, but still so rehearsed.

My fingertips start tingling. At first, I think it's because I'm scared. Terrified even. At least, I should be, somewhere deep inside. It only makes sense.

But then I realize it's the heroin wearing off.

Can't let him know, though. I have to take whatever advantage I can get, even a tiny one. So I make sure not to move. I try and keep my breathing at the same steady pace. And I continue talking.

"Apollo."

Gabriel's lips part suddenly, as if he's about to object. But he says nothing. Just sits there on the edge of the bath, gripping the porcelain with white-knuckled hands.

"He's the one that broke your nose."

His eyes flinch. He shakes his head. "I don't know what—"

"Cassius."

Gabriel's chest moves as he takes a deep breath. He suddenly seems to break out of whatever spell he'd been under. Standing, he steps closer, towering over me.

His expression is neutral as he slides his hand under my armpits and lifts me onto my feet.

And I let him.

Because if I try to fight him now, there's no way I'll win. And then he'll know I tried to trick him. I can't take a chance like that—I don't know how many I'll get. Right now, he's preoccupied. I've pushed him off course.

"I guess they probably changed their names or something," I say.

I expect him to deny it again. But this time he's silent. I guess he's trying to ignore me, but I can tell from the aggression in his movements that what I'm saying is hitting home.

The way he tugs at my dress to get it off. How his face contorts when I do nothing to help or hinder him. The way he draws back, as if startled by the fact that I'm not wearing underwear.

I have to use everything I can.

"They cut my panties off with a knife," I tell him. Lying is so easy. Maybe it's something to do with the residue of the drug floating around in my brain. I have no idea how they work, but it's as if it's annihilated every single filter I've ever had.

"Trinity." His voice is unsteady. He steps back, watches me. "Stop."

"Why?" I tilt my head to the side. "I thought you like this kind of thing."

His eyes go wide again. "You don't know anything," he whispers furiously. "You're a child playing with—"

"I thought you liked children," I say. It's becoming more difficult to keep my voice neutral. Emotions are coming back. Shame. I don't want to be standing naked in front of a priest. In front of a man I once thought of as my only friend.

But I also don't want to stay here, with him. I don't want to find out what he planned to do with me here, alone in my old house. The fact that he keeps comparing me with my mother, a woman he claims to have loved, when I can see only hate in his eyes.

"What are you insinuating?" He takes another step back. He's almost at the closed door now. Can I drive him out completely?

I put my head straight again, fight every cell in my body not to cover my chest or twist my legs. "I'm saying I know about the children you kept in the basement. The ones you hired out to those men."

I step forward.

His back hits the closed door. His eyes go even wider, and they start searching my face, frantic. What are you looking for, Gabriel? A sign that this is a nightmare, and not real life?

Trust me, that wish never comes true.

"I don't know what you're—" he says hoarsely.

"And they know about you." I stop walking because I can't bear to be closer right now. My skin feels like it's crawling with insects. Hundreds of them. The kind with little hooks all over their legs. And those legs, those hooks, they keep snagging on the fine hairs all over my naked body.

"No," he whispers, giving his head one shake. "No, you're wrong. You've got it all wrong."

And that's when the cold hits me.

I don't know how those boys kept the cold out, because I can't. I've never been able to. It's like I was wearing a blanket, and some invisible hand snatched it away.

A shudder ripples through me so hard that my teeth clench.

Gabriel looks at me. At my trembling body. And I guess he realizes what's happening. Something switches on in his head. Or off.

Because where I was convinced—*convinced*—he was about to tell me everything, perhaps even break down in a fit of conscience—

Gabriel throws back his head and laughs. Just once.

He grabs me.

On instinct, I struggle.

But I guess he's had a lot of practice dealing with unruly kids, because he kicks my legs out from under me and tips me to the side in one smooth motion.

My shin slams into the side of the bath, but that barely slows me.

One minute I'm standing, the next I'm under a sea of hot water and bubbles. My gasp of shock has me choking, my throat burning as water goes where it shouldn't.

I fucked up.

I pushed too hard.

I thought I was ready, but I clearly wasn't. My struggles are weak and pathetically ineffectual against Gabriel's strong arms.

He easily holds me under the water. When I reach up and try to gauge out his eyes, all I'm really doing is brushing his face with my fingers.

I manage to close my mouth. Hold my breath. It hurts like nothing I've ever felt, because my lungs still want to expel the water that went down my windpipe. And I'm trying to suppress those convulsions best I can.

Pain flickers red hot inside me. Building. Building.

My eyes are open, and they burn too because the water's too hot.

I don't know how long I can hold my breath, but it already feels like it's been too long.

My limbs are so heavy. My body weighs a fucking ton.

I can't even reach Gabriel's face anymore. So I try and grab onto his shirt.

Can't hold on.

Hands slap into the water.

My body convulses on its own, this time I can't stop it, and my lungs empty themselves. It takes forever, but then it's over in a heartbeat.

Only pain and emptiness left now.

And the faint sensation of his hands on my shoulders, holding me down.

CHAPTER NINE
RUBE

"Anything?" Apollo asks quietly as soon as he spots me. I'm sitting on the couch, Trinity's big white bible on my lap. I was reading it, but not with enthusiasm like I usually do. More just paging through, hoping for a sign that she'd read it too. A dog-eared corner. Some notes in pencil.

But there's no trace of her on here.

Maybe she never even opened it.

Which means I have nothing to remember her by.

"I'd have told you," I say, closing the bible and letting out a sigh.

It's been hours since I watched that car drive away. I've been waiting for a contact of mine who has an in at the Bureau to run Gabriel's plates and see if he comes up anywhere. But it's as if they disappeared off the face of the planet. For all I know, they switched cars as soon as they hit Redwater.

I rub my eyelids.

Zachary's been MIA. I saw him last at the front entrance of Saint Amos, a fact I reluctantly laid out to my brothers as we began piecing together what had happened this morning.

None of them reacted like I'd expected when I told them what Zach had done. Cass just stared, and Apollo let out a rueful snort like I'd told him he lost a bet he hadn't been expecting to win anyway.

I don't even know if he's still here at Saint Amos. We'd know when we go to the garage. And that'll be soon, because we have to leave.

That much we've decided on at least.

But where do we go? Anywhere past Redwater could be taking us further away from Trinity, from Gabriel. And we'd have no way of knowing.

We tried everything. Searched every record of Gabriel and Trinity's in the admin office. All we found were dead ends. Gabriel had cleaned house.

I don't blame Zach for hiding. I would too if I got a message like the one I sent him earlier.

WE WILL NEVER FORGIVE YOU

I didn't have to ask the others. I know they feel the same. Apollo's chewed his nails to the quick. I'm surprised Cass hasn't passed out from oxygen deprivation from chain-smoking.

They're fucked.

We're fucked.

And Zach did nothing. He just stood there and watched. For all we know, he helped Gabriel carry Trinity to his damn car. Maybe even wished him well as Gabriel sped off.

"Might as well head to Redwater," I say, standing. "Nothing more we can do here."

"I'll get Cass," Apollo says, turning.

I go to put Trinity's bible on the coffee table, but then hesitate.

I should take it with.

If we find her, I want to give it back to her.

Not if. When.

When.

When.

"What were you reading?" Apollo asks.

I frown at him. "Nothing specific."

"I mean..." Apollo rolls his eyes. "Read it to me." He lifts his shoulders.

"You want me to read to you from the bible?" I know my frown is deep, but Apollo looks hurt at my expression.

"Well, yeah." He flicks his hand. "Wanna know what it says."

I turn my head a little to the side. "It's the bible," I repeat. "It says a lot."

He crosses his arms over his chest. "Never mind then," he mutters and heads for the door. Apollo's never once shown an interest in religion. Spirituality, maybe, when he's high. But that's always been a more Universal Mind thing.

I didn't even stop for a moment to think what he and Cass are going through right now. How losing Trinity, then Gabriel, then Zach, affected them.

I clear my throat, and Apollo pauses by the door. Quickly scanning the page, I pick the first verse that stands on its own.

"Moreover, brethren, I would not that ye should be ignorant, how that all our fathers were under the cloud, and all passed through the sea. And were all baptized unto Moses in the cloud and—"

Apollo cuts me off with a wave of his hand. "Stop, stop. What use is that?"

"What were you expecting?" I ask, sitting back, closing the book, and putting it down on the cushion beside me. "A map?"

"Something inspiring," he says. "Not random—" He waves his hand again. "Forget it. I'll go find Cass and meet you at the garage."

I shake my head, letting out a long sigh as he closes the door behind him. Something inspiring?

I should have flipped to Revelations instead, read him chapter twenty verse ten.

And the devil that deceived them was cast into the lake of fire and brimstone, where the beast and the false prophet are, and shall be tormented day and night for ever and ever.

Maybe knowing that God had special plans for our Ghosts once they passed over would have *inspired* him.

My apartment door bursts open.

Apollo stands there in the doorway, hair disheveled, eyes wide.

I'm already on my feet, ready to attack whoever's behind him. But he just grins at me, claps his hands.

"I love that fucking book!" he yells, pointing at Trinity's gold-trimmed bible.

"What—"

He waves away the question, beckoning me to follow him. "We have to get to town, now!"

"Apollo, what—"

"I know how to find her, Rube!" His grin is infectious, especially paired with the exact words I've been waiting to hear all day.

I know how to find her.

CHAPTER TEN
APOLLO

"Wifi password," I bark out at the first waitress I see.

Her head moves back as she gives me a filthy stare, then she clicks her tongue. "All right," she says. "Settle down." Still frowning, she points with her chin. "Where you sitting?"

I'm about to frisk her for the damn password when someone's shoulder brushes mine. The waitress turns from me, and her frown dissolves instantly.

Should've listened to Rube. He told me to let Cass go in first. Nothing loosens lips like Cass's face.

"Hey, darlin'," Cass says, slipping in front of me. "We're outside, table twelve. Can't pass up a chance to watch that glorious sunset, now can we?"

I don't even know what accent he's putting on. But it doesn't matter, because it works. He's barely done speaking before the waitress is fumbling in her apron. "We got these paper thingies now," she's saying, her eyes glued on Cass as she rummages around. "They're changing it like every day."

"I hear you," Cass says. He sticks his arm around his back and pushes me away with his fingertips.

I guess he can't work his magic when I'm glaring at his conquest from behind his shoulder and willing them to get on with it. I grit my teeth, but I back off and go back outside.

Rube looks up as I thump down on the wrought iron chair. We chose a spot a little away from the rest, although this time of day, the town is pretty quiet. Everyone looks a little tired, like the drove of students they must have had in this place earlier today exhausted them.

Redwater's only diner is a nice enough place, but I'm itching to be on the road and headed toward wherever Trinity is. And that waitress back there has my hands tied.

Rube had to hot-wire Sister Miriam's old Ford to get us here. No idea why she left it behind—maybe she went on the bus—but it saved us because Zach's SUV wasn't in the garage. We'll have to switch cars before we leave here, of course. Rube's been eyeing an old truck parked next to the liquor store that has dust on the windscreen. If we can get it to start, then hopefully it won't be missed before we're far enough along to where we need to go.

Soon as I figure out where the hell that is.

"Coffee?" Rube asks.

"Yeah. Can we get something to eat?"

He frowns, and then nods. "But no lobster."

With Zachary gone, we only have a handful of cash between the three of us. We never figured a day would come when Zach wouldn't be there, swiping a card for whatever we needed.

How naive.

I still can't get over what he did, even though I kinda expected something like that to happen eventually. He's never been on board with Trinity. He's been treating her like the enemy from day one. And we went right along, because he laid it out so logically that it only seemed right.

I guess we've trusted him for too long.

Cass saunters back a minute later with a piece of paper dangling from his fingertips. I snatch it from him before he even has a chance to sit down.

I snort when I see what's written on the back. "She gave you her number?"

Cass shrugs, lounging in his chair like he was born without a spine. "Told her I wouldn't call."

Reuben rolls his eyes and then watches me type in the password.

It's one of those generated ones that are supposedly so secure. But the more random a password is, the easier a hacking program can crack it. It's passwords made out of words or phrases that are the hardest to crack. That's why Bitcoin wallets are usually protected with a seed phrase—a string of twelve random words that are easy enough to remember, but near impossible to crack without the use of a super-computer.

That's why I know for a fact that the password to Gabriel's secret archive is some kind of phrase. My program's still trying to crack it, but I doubt it'll happen any time this century.

Soon as my laptop connects to the diner's wi-fi, I start looking for Trinity.

The world dissolves as I hunt through every database I can access.

Baptism.

Reuben laughed when I told him. We all laughed. Because it was so damn basic, we should have thought of it hours ago.

Trinity was baptized. Had to have been. Catholic parents and a priest as a family friend? No way around it.

And parishes keep baptism records. They have all kinds of useful shit on them like parent information, addresses, stuff like that.

I have Trinity's date of birth from the admin file. Her parent's first and last names too. But the rest of the file was empty. There were a few notes sent to Social Services requesting more info, but I guess their turnaround time is longer than she's been at Saint Amos.

All I need to know is which parish keeps her records.

I hop around the Internet, finding bits of information to add to my search.

Someone shoves a cup of coffee my way. I drink it down without tasting it, but fully appreciating the jolt of caffeine. A plate of food arrives, and it smells damn tempting, but I'm already down the rabbit hole so it grows cold beside me.

The light changes. Hues shift. Streetlights come on. The temperature drops.

And then I have it.

An address.

I look up. Cass and Rube are staring at me. "Well?" Cass says. "Tell us."

"It's not much." I grab a fry off my plate, swallow it down despite how cold it is. "But it's a start."

CHAPTER ELEVEN
ZACH

I'm driving down the I-44—going too fast and giving way too few fucks. The joint I'm smoking helps. The bottle of whiskey in the glove compartment I sip at every now then, that helps most of all.

I never thought it would be this hard walking away from them. Or, in my case, driving away. Never thought I'd feel compelled to go back to them. To her.

But I am. And it is.

I hit the joint again. Tasteless. But I guess that happens if you keep smoking the same shit over and over.

No it doesn't.

I could have stopped Gabriel. If I didn't want to get my hands dirty, I could have called my brothers, warned them. *They* could have stopped him.

But I didn't.

They said they'll never forgive me for that.

Fuck—*I'll* never forgive myself for that.

A part of me was grateful he was leaving. And that part of me managed to take control long enough to sit back and let him walk away. But the rest of me? Numb, because it felt like I was losing something more important than my charred and blackened soul.

"That's because I *am* more important."

I glance in the rear-view mirror. A jolt goes through me when I see Trinity sitting in the back seat.

"What the fuck are you doing here?" I peer at her over my shoulder.

She's wearing the same lacy white thing she did when we took her virginity. Except now it's freshly laundered and her curls bounce around her shoulders like she's just come out of the salon.

And her lips are red.

Like the Whore of Babylon.

"You should watch the road," she says, an easy smile tugging at those cherry-red lips.

I smile back, glance at the road.

And almost lose control of the car as I swerve out for a truck. It blares its horn at me, the near miss rocking my now stationery rental like Trin and me are fucking in the back seat.

I turn around. She's not there anymore.

When I straighten and look ahead, she's standing by the hood of the car with her back to me. A gust of wind toys with her curls as she looks over her shoulder and beckons me with a crook of her finger.

I fumble for the car door, my composure shattered by the fact that I almost died. That I almost got Trinity killed.

Impossible. She's with Gabriel.

But that doesn't change the fact that when I walk up to her, when I grab her arm, when I turn her to face me, she's as real as I am.

I press her against my body, testing the theory. But there's no mistaking the way her hips press into the tops of my thighs. Her breasts into my ribs. And she makes a sound, a protest to my manhandling, as if I'm hurting her.

So delicate, like a dandelion. One breath and she'll scatter.

But I won't let her. Not again. The parts of my brain that held me frozen on Saint Amos's front steps aren't here right now. Maybe they clocked out after the deed, I don't know.

I grab the back of her neck and I kiss her right then and there on the side of the road.

Hard.

Relentless.

Forgetting how easy it was to break her. How much I enjoyed it.

"Here?" she murmurs against my mouth. "Right here?"

I don't know what she's talking about until she pulls back and climbs onto the hood. Spreads her legs.

Black underwear, which is wrong, because that's not what she was wearing. But maybe she changed, right? Girls like her don't go around commando.

My dick's out a second later. Too eager, but I can't help myself. I have to be inside her again. Feel her suffocating me. Milking me.

I thrust into her pussy with enough force to make her cry out.

Her fingers bite into my shoulders. "Harder," she says.

Her curls bounce. Her mouth forms a perfect 'o'. A car comes past, hoots at us. I give it the finger without looking. And then I yank down the top of Trinity's dress so I can draw one of her nipples into my mouth.

This isn't right.

Fuck it. I'm sure plenty of people have fucked on the highway.

No, this isn't right.

It's the way she rocks into me. So steady, so perfect. Like she gets paid by the fuck, blow jobs extra.

And that's not her.

That's not Trinity.

But I fuck her anyway, because it feels almost as good as the first time.

Maybe even better—this time there's no strange uneasiness floating around in my head. Because back then, with her, it wasn't just sex, and I still don't know why.

People fucking. Sometimes consensually. Sometimes not. That's all sex is to me. All it will ever be.

But it wasn't that way with her.

It's ridiculous, and pathetic, and stupid, but that doesn't change how it *felt*.

Like it meant something.

Like it would mean something every single time.

Except now.

This feels different.

Empty.

Fake.

I slap her thigh, but I can't feel that sting on my palm. She cries out though, and that helps. I fuck her harder, until her moans of pleasure become yelps of pain.

A normal man would stop. Maybe even apologize.

I'm not normal. Not even close.

Her pain is my pleasure. Nothing about that will ever change. She tenses around me, resisting me now. And that arouses me more than it should. More than what's moral or acceptable.

When she starts begging me to stop, that's when I finally feel a climax approaching. But it's taking too long. Like it's just out of grasp.

I pull back, wanting to kiss her again. Trying to capture something of the first time.

But the face of the thing I'm fucking is no longer recognizable. It's still wearing the dress, but that fabric is dirty and tattered. Stained with blood and cum. The dead thing's face is bloated, disfigured, brutally beaten.

I push away from it, a yell trapped in my throat, but my dick is stuck inside it.

It's drawing me closer, arms wrapped impossibly tight around the back of my neck.

Its puffy, scarlet lips pucker as if for a kiss.

And then I'm coming inside it. The feeling goes on and on. Hollowing me out. As if it's not my semen I'm ejaculating, but my organs, and my bones, and my flesh.

My eyes fly open, a horrified gasp rattling deep in my throat. I push into a sit, clamping a hand over my heart. I can feel every violent clang as it pumps adrenaline through my body.

Jesus.

My body's stuck in some corporeal purgatory between Heaven and Hell. A dopey kind of pleasure from coming on the sheets. A skin-crawling horror from the memory of what I was pumping my load into.

I stumble out of bed, and almost crash into a wall I didn't expect so nearby.

Where the fuck am I?

Then my memories settle, and I'm back in the real world.

A motel room on I-44. I'd driven until I'd almost fallen asleep at the wheel, and then driven some more until I'd found a place to crash that wasn't my rental car.

Christ, that dream. No, that fucking *nightmare.*

I hit the shower before I'm even fully awake, washing the dream and the feel of decaying pussy off my dick.

I almost puke, but manage to choke it back.

Then I slide down the wall and curl into a ball, letting the water pound onto the top of my head until my scalp feels numb.

Until *I* feel numb.

It doesn't help. Body and mind, they're two separate entities.

I wish I could say the basement taught me that, but it didn't. *Mom and Dad* taught me that. They believed in discipline of the corporal kind. Mom with a wooden spoon. Dad with his belt.

I wasn't a naughty kid, I was high maintenance. Energetic. And they weren't. When I wanted to play outdoors—they'd lock me in my room. I'd end up breaking things, and then they'd punish me, even though I knew they had enough money to replace anything I ruined.

Only years later did I figure out what the problem was. I had ADHD, and an acute sensitivity to sugar. They never gave a shit about what I ate in between meals. And they'd keep replacing the sweets I ate. Maybe they didn't realize how bad it was. How it fueled my disobedience.

I guess I'm partly to blame. I never told them how it made my muscles ache and ache and ache until I had to move. Until I ran in circles, or threw things, or bounced on the bed.

My young body was a hormonal shit show. I either couldn't concentrate, or couldn't stop concentrating. Especially when I was punished. It was like my brain was working overtime to figure out why I invited pain.

It took years for me to realize that I was inviting it because I *did* enjoy it to some extent.

Because when they punished me, I wouldn't let any of the hurt show. And that confused them. And their confusion brought me great, great pleasure.

I was in my teens before I figured out that I enjoyed causing people harm. Emotional or physical, it didn't matter. They were the same thing, but experienced at different frequencies.

Cass was the one responsible for that epiphany. He claims the basement turned him into a masochist but I think he was probably one all along.

When Cass ran out of dope or wanted something different to tune out to, he sought out pain. The others refused to give it to him. Me too, at first. Back then, my brothers didn't know about my darker side. The side that wanted to inflict suffering.

And I resisted him, until he goaded me past the point of no return.

Somehow, he'd figured out my secret.

So I hit him, just like he wanted. But a lot harder than he'd anticipated. I'll never forget his gasp of pain, and the shock in his eyes. Watching the confusion on his face as he tried to figure out what had happened? It felt fucking amazing.

That's when things changed. When I began to understand who the mind inside the body was. Me. My soul.

My brothers led me to that discovery, each in their own way...and I'm grateful.

But I still betrayed them and they deserve better.

That's why I left. Because my brothers deserve a life without me.

But not like this.

Not while the thing they—*we*—so dearly want has been taken from them.

I know they'll never forgive me. I knew before I read Reuben's message. But I don't need their forgiveness.

I need them to accept my help this one last time.

When the water turns cold and I start to shiver, I know it's time to get out.

I leave that place feeling like a dick for not cleaning up, but I couldn't stay a second longer.

I can't believe it's taken me so long to realize it, but I've been heading in the wrong fucking direction this whole time.

"BLACK COFFEE," I say as soon as the waitress behind the counter looks up at me. I immediately break eye contact, but I see her watching me for a second longer before she goes to get my order.

Because I look like shit.

I didn't dare stop again, so I've been relying on caffeine and sheer willpower to keep me awake. It's been a rough road, like trekking up a crumbling mountain track, and I'm sure the downhill's even worse. But hopefully, by that time, I've found them again.

I didn't bother calling. Knew they wouldn't pick up. But technology has its perks.

The coffee arrives, and I blow on it to cool it faster. I order a sandwich—not because I'm hungry but because my body needs fuel.

I could have carried on driving to California. Set myself up in a hotel until the transfer papers for the house were signed. Until they gave me the key.

But then I'd have resigned myself to a life of misery. Probably a short one, at that.

They don't need me...but I need them. It's painful to admit, but I've had more than enough time to come to terms with the fact.

I detoured soon as I located their phones. I'm surprised they didn't ditch them...but I guess they weren't expecting me to come back.

Fuck, *I* wasn't expecting me to come back.

I stick a hand down the front of my shirt and fish out Trinity's crucifix. The wood feels smooth, almost oily, between my fingers. I lift it a little and squint through what looks like a clear gem stuck near the top as the smell of roses fills my nose. The Virgin Mary peers back at me, resplendent in front of her golden halo. Face serene. Like she knows everything's going to be just peachy, as long as I have faith.

I found it on the floor a few steps from Saint Amos's front doors, right after I'd locked eyes with Reuben. The clasp was bent—must have fallen off her neck as Gabriel carried her out of the building. I meant to give it back to Rube, perhaps put it somewhere he would find it, but then all I could think about was leaving.

Found it in my bag when I was pulling out clothes to change into. Hung it around my neck in case I lost it, because one thing is for sure... I will find my brothers. And when I do, this is going back to Rube.

My coffee is almost finished before my food arrives. But I don't complain, because I need the break, and I wouldn't have given myself that luxury.

My brothers are nowhere close to Saint Amos like I'd thought. They're in some small town in Virginia. I'm guessing they have a lead on Gabriel. Makes me want to find them even more, and I hate it. But revenge really knows how to get its claws into you. And fuck, does it latch on.

Was that way with my parents, too.

First week I was in that basement, my sadistic little mind was having a fucking field day. Oh, the beautiful, brutal things I did to them in my head. Holding them at gunpoint. Forcing them to do despicable things to each other. Thoughts of their fear, their humiliation—it kept me going for a while.

I'd keep banging on the door, begging them to let me out. Pleading with them. Trying to convince them that I wasn't one of the others.

Yes, I wanted my limited freedom back. But more than that, I craved the pain I knew I would inflict on them soon as I was free. Vengeance for hurting me. For hurting all the boys they'd kept in that dark hell.

To this day, I can't believe those tortured souls had been under my feet all that time. That I'd been living mere yards away from so much pain and suffering.

Some part of me still believes that's how my mind came to be so fucked up. That, unknowingly, I'd absorbed all that abuse through the pores in my skin. Like radiation, it began poisoning me.

I pay my bill. Leave.

The rental reeks of cigarettes, but I couldn't care if they kept my entire deposit because of it.

All I care about is one thing—getting to my brothers.

What happens after I arrive, that's up to them.

"Trinity."

"Trinity!"

I'm cold. So cold compared to the warm hands on my body. Behind my neck, between my shoulders. Pushing me onto my side.

I retch. Throw up. I choke on the water and bile burning my nose and throat. It hurts a lot, but at least now I can breathe.

Hands on me again—so warm—helping me up. A towel to cover my nakedness.

Those hands guide me down a passage and into a room.

Halfway across the soft carpet I recognize where I am. A bedroom, but not mine.

Mom and Dad's.

I'm still in Redford.

Oh God, I miss them so much. The smell in here, although stale, pushes pins through my heart. But why is everything still the same? It's been more than a month. Surely someone would have bought the house? Moved in? Made it their own? Why is it still exactly the same as the day I left?

I shiver, and then try to resist when the hands lead me to the bed.

I was never allowed in here.

It was *their* room. They made that very clear.

I never once ran in and clambered over them to wake them up when I was a little girl. No snuggling between them if I had a nightmare.

Because I was a good girl. I obeyed them. Even now, even though they're gone, I feel like I'm disobeying them.

But when someone pulls away the sheets, revealing a warm nest I can burrow into, I go. No hesitation. Because I'm tired. I'm hurting. And I'm so cold.

As I slip between sheets that still smell like my parents, I hear a voice. Mom's. Not singing—she never sang—but reciting a prayer.

...hallowed be...

Oh, right. I know this one.

I burrow into the bed, cringing as my wet hair makes my cheek itch. I'm not clean enough to be on these sheets. I can still smell myself. But there's lavender too, and that makes me think about bubbles and that makes me want to climb out of bed and run away.

But I'm too tired.

...give us this day...

So I stay where I am, curled into a ball, trying to warm up. I cough, and clear my throat, and try to get rid of the awful feeling inside me. The rawness where water went but shouldn't have.

...forgive us our...

I lie there even when someone gets in behind me and holds me. Even though I know who it is. Even though I know what he's capable of.

I'm even fucking grateful, because he's so warm, and I'm so cold.

...lead us not into...

I lie there in his arms until I fall asleep. And I'm still there when I wake up.

But I only wake up a long, long time later after he wakes up. After he brushes hair from my face and kisses my cheek. Only after he squeezes me tight and whispers, "Morning, daughter."

...deliver us from evil...

Now I'm not tired anymore. I'm not hurting as much. I *am* scared. But I'm also angry. And I want out.

...thine is the kingdom...

My mind races as he snuggles his face into the back of my neck, as if he's smelling me.

...the power and the glory...

This is not my new life. I'm getting out of here, whatever it takes.

...forever and ever.

Amen.

CHAPTER THIRTEEN
TRINITY

I think Gabriel has fallen asleep again. I guess it's tiring, holding someone captive. But he should be used to it though.

The thought leaves a bitter taste in my mouth. I shift a little, then pause, waiting for his reaction.

Nothing but a soft breath against the back of my neck. His arm is still slung around me, his fingers dangling over my hip.

It would be so easy to stay here. Although I don't feel as shit as I did when I woke up on the bathroom floor after he tried to drown me, my body is still weak. I haven't eaten in...days?

So easy just to let it happen.

To go somewhere else inside my head.

But that's not what *they* did. Those four boys in the basement fought back. They stayed strong, and they found a way out.

But they were four.

I'm just me.

So easy to feel sorry for myself right now. To think it's useless. That I'd make Gabriel angry and he'd try to hurt me again.

Even though right now he's peaceful. Almost like the Gabriel I used to know and love. But he won't stay this way. I'll say something and it will trigger him to the violence, and he'll try to hurt me again.

I gently grasp his wrist and lift it. Slow. Easy. I keep it suspended as I carefully wriggle to the side.

The tendons in Gabriel's wrist go tight. He murmurs something inaudible as he tries to hold onto me in his sleep.

I freeze, eyes squeezing shut, and send a prayer to any higher power who might be listening.

Our father, which art in heaven.

Hallowed by thy name.

The prayer becomes a mantra that cycles over and over in my mind as I slowly make my way to the edge of the bed. As soon as I'm clear, I put his hand down on the sheets.

The instant I let go, he turns over, dragging the bedding with him. Leaving me exposed and naked on the far side of the bed.

I slip out and stand hunched over, my heart thudding relentlessly in my chest. With his back to me, I don't know if his eyes are open. They can't be—why would they?—but that doesn't change a thing.

Deliver us from evil.

All I need is for him to stay exactly as he is. Lost in whatever perverted dream he's having right now.

I back up out of the room, hesitate at the threshold, and then pull the door closed as I creep into the hallway outside. I'd have locked it, but the key's gone.

I know I shouldn't be wasting a millisecond, but I can't run into the street naked. And it will only take a few seconds to put on clothes. Just pants and a shirt. I won't even bother with underwear or shoes.

That's the plan, anyway. But when I step into my room, it's as if the world does a somersault around me.

I freeze.

It looks like a tornado went through this place.

My closet doors are wide open. Everything inside them has been dumped on the floor or on the bed. Little ornaments—the kind of knick-knacks you accumulate when you're young—are everywhere. Some shattered. Tears and scuffs on the wallpaper where he threw things against the wall.

Was he looking for something? Or did my accusations really piss him off that much?

Move, Trinity! He could be waking up any second now, and you're just standing there? You've established he's a nut job—now how about you get on with escaping?

I force myself deeper into my room, but it's like I'm in a trance. There's so much chaos in here I can't find anything.

I pick up a jacket that doesn't have a zipper or buttons—pointless.

A scarf.

That goes around my neck, because, well, that's where scarfs go.

I find leggings. Pull them on. They're not fully opaque, but they're better than nothing.

Finally, the last piece of the puzzle. A sleeping shirt. Picture of a grumpy cat on it. Something about needing coffee. I tug it over my head as I turn to head out the room.

Gabriel's standing by the door. Chin down as he watches me. Hands opening and closing at his sides.

Panic slices into me like frozen razor blades. I wrap my arms over my chest and take a step back. "I was getting cold," I say.

He's wearing only a pair of sweatpants. I hadn't even realized that when he was in bed with me. I don't think I've ever seen him bare chested. I had no idea he was so muscular. So strong. No wonder I couldn't fight him.

He lifts his chin. "You have to accept the things you cannot change." He turns his palms to face me, arms still at his sides. "I'm your father. That's never going to change."

His body fills the doorway. I can only get out if he comes closer. It's that or jump out of a second-story window. There's a tree outside—I could maybe catch hold of a branch.

That's a big maybe.

How badly would it hurt if I missed the tree?

Maybe I can try and find out what Gabriel wants. I mean, I could be over-thinking this. What if he just wants to take me to the mall, watch a movie together, eat some take out?

As long as I don't mention the Brotherhood, or the basement, I should be fine. Even now, he looks calm.

"I…"

Lord, why is this so difficult?

He puts his head to the side, waiting. Always so patient.

"What are…we doing?" Another swallow. "Here, I mean?"

He frowns, glances around. Then he reaches out and straightens a framed picture I drew when I still believed in unicorns and how *awsum* they were.

"I've always liked this house," he says. "Spent much more time here than I should have."

His eyes fix on me again. I don't know how I could ever have thought those brown irises were warm, or comforting. Now they look cruel. Calculating, even. "They left it to me, the house."

"Don't you have a house? Why don't we go there instead?"

I don't know if it's better being here or in a different place, but we'd have to be in a car, on a road, out in public to get there. If I can convince him—

"My house?" Gabriel purses his lips. Shakes his head. "No. My house is no place for a little girl."

Ghostly fingers crawl up my back and start toying with my hair. That's what he thinks of me? A little girl? Does he even know how old I am?

It sickens me to think about it, but maybe that's the only card I have to play right now. He keeps calling me daughter—maybe I can count on his paternal instincts to get me out of this jam.

"I'm kinda hungry," I say, putting a hand to my stomach. "Can you make me something to eat?"

The kitchen has knives. Pans. Several objects I can use to hurt him with. It's also closer to the front door, which has a lock I can turn from the inside without needing a key.

If I can get to the front door, I can get out of the house. I can run down the driveway and scream at the top of my lungs. The neighbors would hear. They'd have to look out their windows. And they'd see me running like a lunatic—

"No."

My shoulders sag a little. "But I'm—"

Gabriel's eyes narrow. "Do you really think I don't know what you're trying to do?"

Fuck.

Fuck!

I try and look innocent. "Really, I just want some—"

"You've been bad," he says, stepping closer.

Yeah, come closer, you fucking creep. Close enough that I can run around you and out of the room. Down the stairs. To the front door.

I wish I'd thought of that yesterday. I'd been a few yards from the front door. But I'd been so doped up on heroin, I hadn't even thought about it.

No. I'd been convinced my father was in the kitchen cooking breakfast.

Ha, ha, ha. I guess he was.

"Slut like you, you don't deserve to eat."

Oh Lord. It's all coming back to me now. The things I told him when we were in the bathroom. Boy do I regret that plan.

I need to turn this around.

I wish it didn't have to come to this, but I can't think of any other way of doing that.

"Father, please."

There's a flicker of something in his eyes.

"Please, I'm sorry." Denial isn't the way to go. But confession might just work. "I sinned. I know that now, I see it. I just…"

I drop my head. The tears that come aren't all that forced. I've had a lot of practice with feeling sorry for myself.

I've been doing it my whole life.

I pitied the fact that I had such strict parents. That I could never do all the fun stuff other kids did.

Then I pitied myself because I'd been orphaned by a random twist of fate. That God had let two of his sheep die. Then came Saint Amos, and oh boy did my pity party turn into a rager.

Now this.

I used to challenge the Universe. I'd shout "What else you got?" in my head when I was feeling particularly downtrodden.

But I've met a group of men who could have pitied themselves day in and day out. I can't believe how weak I am, compared to them. How little it took to defeat me.

The attention of one man, when they've had to withstand many.

Two days, when they lasted years.

So yeah. I think I can suck it up and play pretend for a while.

"Will you help me, father?"

Gabriel's chin lifts a little higher. "Help you?" His voice is faint. He frowns, opens his mouth. But I cut him off with a sob that's not at all feigned.

Every cell in my body is screaming at me to stop, but this is the only way.

That's how you overcome fear, right? You face it.

I walk up to him, stumbling over the things scattered over the floor, and I put my arms around him, and I hug him hard.

When I close my eyes, I can almost believe it's my first day at Saint Amos, and he's just arrived outside my room.

The familiar smell of his fabric softener, his aftershave, him...wafts up to me. When he wraps his arms around me so tight.

"Please, father." Another sob. "Help me find the light."

His chest expands as he inhales, and I shiver when he kisses the top of my head.

"Of course, child," he murmurs.

Hands find my face. He draws back my head and stares down into my eyes. His smile is wide, and warm, and genuine. It shouldn't, but it lights a candle inside me.

He strokes away a tear with his thumb. "Come. Let's eat."

My body is ten pounds lighter as he grabs my hand and laces my fingers with his. I float behind him, barely touching the ground as he leads me down the stairs. I force myself not to look at the front door as we pass it, and my body complies.

A gust of wind slams raindrops hard against a nearby windowpane. And then he turns away from the kitchen.

My hope shatters like a glass trinket hitting a stone floor.

The hand around mine is suddenly too tight. He's pulling me a little too hard.

"Father—"

I cut off with a pained sound as he yanks me after him. "You want to find the light?" he yells, glancing back at me with wild eyes. "I know just the place." He turns again, and my heart sinks deep into the churning depths of my stomach when I realize where he's taking me.

I kick back, scream.

He pulls at me until I'm close, and then grabs me. Slaps a hand over my mouth. All the while still walking toward the door at the end of a long passage.

Hidden away like a nasty secret. Even the keypad beside the door is flat and discrete. You probably wouldn't see it unless you were close.

Gabriel keys in a combination—so fast, I only catch the first two numbers, 4 and 2. When he opens the thick door, the smell of damp earth and crawling things slams into me.

He slaps a hand against the wall, and the basement light flickers on. It's not much—a bare bulb that only seems to solidify the shadows into something more sinister than before.

Gabriel brings me in front, an arm around my waist to keep me tight, a hand over my mouth to keep me silent. He forces me down the stairs one at a time. I struggle as much as I can, despite the fact that we could both take a tumble and land up with broken necks.

Especially when the sagging metal frame of my old single bed comes into view. Because then I know a broken neck is the only winning hand in this game.

I'd wondered about the lock on the basement before—the pilot light is down here, so we'd be stuck if he wasn't around to light it again if it ever went out. But who was I to question Dad's wisdom? His quirks and his rules? How could I, when Mom didn't?

I've never been down here before. Hell, I wasn't even allowed in the passage back there. The space is surprisingly small, until I realize the walls are soundproofed. Someone closed up this space on purpose. Turned a massive basement into a much smaller, more intimate space.

Someone? You know exactly who did this.

But my mind rejects the thought.

My old mattress is still on that rusting bed frame. There's even a sheet over it, but its moth-eaten and stained.

And then I see my old potty trainer.

And then I see the ropes still attached to the bed frame.

I start kicking up my legs, twisting and wriggling, but it doesn't help. Gabriel holds me with ease. His voice doesn't even sound strained when he speaks.

"No better place to look for the light," he murmurs into my ear, "than down here in the dark."

And then...then I see the video camera.

CHAPTER FOURTEEN
TRINITY

I wish I knew a bible verse by heart right now. Or lots of them. Then I could choose the perfect one. Something Old Testament about going to hell for your sins.

Probably wouldn't have helped. I mean, Gabriel's a priest. He knows the bible back to front, and not one verse ever swayed him toward the light.

He shoves me away from him. My hands fly out and barely catch me against the plastic sheet lining the floor.

I scramble onto my back, ready to kick out if he comes close.

The room is small, claustrophobic even. The bed takes up most of the space. If I can distract him, I can try and get past him and up to the stairs.

Like I haven't tried that before.

"What do you want?" I try to keep my voice calm in case he lunges at me to keep me quiet. Or maybe it doesn't matter down here with all this soundproofing.

I've certainly never heard sounds coming from the basement. Or had I dismissed them as my imagination?

Gabriel lifts his hands, showing me his palms. As if he wants me to trust him.

What a joke.

"You said you want to find the light." His voice is tight and unsteady, like he's barely keeping it under control. "Many boys have found the light down here."

I shake my head before I can stop.

"You don't believe me?"

"Dad would never—"

Gabriel's bitter laugh cuts me off. He walks up to me, dodging effortlessly when I kick. Then he grabs me by the hair and hoists me to my feet, shaking me mercilessly.

His other hand grabs my chin, turning my face and forcing me to look around the small room.

"Who do you think built this place?" he hisses in my ear. "It wasn't me, child."

If I could shake my head, I would. The things he'd said after I hobbled up to his room at Saint Amos and told him I had to show him something in the bell tower...

But my mind rejects what he's telling me.

"No," I murmur. "Dad was a good man. A holy man. He would never—"

"Your *dad*?" Gabriel croons, mocking me. He's becoming unhinged again, like he did back in the bathroom.

"I'm sorry," I blurt out. "I'm sorry, Father, I didn't mean—"

He shakes me into silence. "Always blameless," he whispers as he drags me close against him. "No one ever suspected. Not even you."

Of course not. Why would they? My dad kept to himself and both my parents were quiet people. But they loved the church. They loved people. I never heard them say a bad thing about anyone. Oh, they'd fight behind their closed bedroom door, but I wasn't idiotic enough to believe they had a perfect marriage. Dad was gone a lot and Mom didn't like staying home to look after me. She never said it, but I could see she missed him when he wasn't around.

When I was younger they'd sometimes go away for a week or two, but that stopped as soon as I hit puberty. It was Dad who told Mom to stay at home. He probably thought I would lure a boy back home or something. He seemed to think I was a whore as much as Gabriel did.

I always thought he was strict because of his faith, but maybe he was actually trying to protect me from people like him? Deviants and pedophiles who would see me in a short skirt and obsess about what they could do to me if they had me to themselves?

Somewhere hidden. Somewhere secret.

A dark, soundproofed room like this.

"Please," I whisper. "Please stop."

I can't let him destroy my past. It's all I have.

"Forgiveness requires confession, child," Gabriel says, his lips brushing my ear. He shakes me again, kisses my temple. "Only through confession can we be cleansed of sin."

"P-please."

"I told your mother that so many times. But she wouldn't listen, just like you."

My heart stutters in my chest.

Mom knew?

Oh Lord, who am I kidding? Of course she knew. But logic doesn't ease the pain of realizing my mother kept Dad's secret.

I stab my elbow into Gabriel's stomach.

I get lucky. He's distracted, and I manage to hit him hard enough, and in just the right spot, that I knock the air from his lungs.

He doubles over with pain, his grip releasing just enough for me to wriggle free.

I make a dash for the stairs, for the door, for freedom.

My foot lands on the first stair, and then Gabriel kicks it out from under me. I fall face first, my chin slamming into the wooden step. Blood leaks into my mouth from the cut my teeth sliced into the inside of my cheek.

But I'm already scrambling up, ignoring the pain, ignoring the sound of Gabriel's furious breathing behind me.

I don't reach the door.

Halfway up the stairs, Gabriel latches onto the back of my sleeping shirt and *tugs*. I go flying down the stairs, missing all of them. I land on my back on the plastic sheeting with a loud *crump*.

Air gushes out of my lungs. I roll onto my side, groaning as a dull ache spreads through my body from the impact.

When I force my eyes open, they fix on Gabriel's loafers.

He grabs my hair and drags me over the floor. My scalp is on fire where he's pulling, hurting more the harder I fight.

The bed squeaks when he throws me down, and I scream in panic. I try to roll off, but he slaps me so hard I see stars. There's a violent yank on my arm, the rough kiss of a rope, and then I'm bound.

Like he's done this a thousand times before.

I start sobbing with frustration, fear, desperation. "P-please!"

"That's it," he says, voice menacingly low. "Keep begging. That's just how he liked it."

What. The. *Fuck?*

I kick and lash out, but it's as if Gabriel is made of steel. He doesn't even blink when I rake my nails through his skin hard enough to draw blood.

"Help!" The yell burns my throat.

I was right about the soundproofing. Gabriel doesn't give a fuck. He grabs my foot and lashes it to the bedpost.

My toes catch his chin, sending his head snapping to the side. There's a hush, a pause as he straightens his head.

His brown eyes resemble those of an animal head hanging above some redneck's fireplace.

There empty. Dead.

He grabs my other foot, lashes it down. I try and untie the knot on my left hand while he's busy, but it's so tight I don't make any progress by the time he's done.

And then he climbs on top of me, straddling my stomach.

Terror pours ice through my limbs. I go stiff, panting as tears leak from the corners of my eyes.

He grabs my chin, his fingertips biting cruelly into my jaw. Then he snaps my head to the side like he can't bear looking at me anymore.

A giant sob wracks me as he ties off my last wrist. He settles back, crushing my stomach with his weight, and studies me.

My head is still to the side, and I don't dare look at him. Instead I squeeze my eyes shut and start praying.

Our father, which art in heaven,
Hallowed be thy—

"Look at me."

—name. Thy kingdom come.
Thy will be done, on earth as—

"Look at me!" he roars.

His fingers wrench my head to face him, but I keep my eyes squeezed closed. It's stupid, it's fucking juvenile, but it's the only way I can defy him now.

I'm not going to lie here and take this.

"Trinity." His voice is soft now, sinister. "Open your eyes."

"Fuck you."

A slap sends white spots dashing through the black behind my eyes.

"You like it, don't you?" he rasps. "The fight. The struggle. The *pain*. Got that from your whore mother."

My eyes fly open. I stare up at him in shock. "How dare—"

He slaps me again. "Is this the only way you'll let me in? Is this what it will take? Because I've done worse." His voice catches. "I've done so much worse for so much less."

My heart thunders in my chest. What the hell is he talking about? His shoulders move back, hand raised for another slap.

"No! Stop! Please!"

He pauses, but his hand stays up.

"I don't know what you mean. Please..." A sob cuts in, I force it down best I can. "Just...just talk to me, Gabriel."

Pathetic, trying to reason with a mad man. But my head aches, and my cheek's on fire, and I can't take anymore. I'm so close to surrender, I can already feel his hands on me.

His chest rises and falls, exaggerated. His hand drops, but barely an inch.

"Please. Just talk to me. Tell me..." I have to swallow hard before I speak again. "Tell me what you want."

"What I want," he repeats woodenly.

His hand falls to his side. His eyes move off me, staring at nothing. Or maybe only something he can see.

"Yeah," I manage. My voice rebels, but I push out the words anyway. "Let's talk, Gabe. Just you and me."

His eyes slide back to mine.

I squirm under him before I can control myself because that blank face of his ratchets up my fear a thousand notches.

"So you can use me like he did?" he murmurs. Shakes his head. His voice drops to barely a whisper. "My fault. I let him use me. I let him control me..."

The hand he'd been about to hit me with curls into a fist. But instead of slamming into my face, he leans on it, putting his head close to mine.

He stares into my eyes from an inch away. I can feel his breath on my face, still a little too hard, too hot, from our struggle. My flesh writhes beneath my skin like I have a thousand worms burrowing through my body.

"It was his idea." Gabriel laughs, sending a puff of warm breath over my lips. "But no one will ever believe me. Know why?"

His eyes skitter over mine, searching. I keep my face neutral. Try and keep my eyes locked on his.

"Why?" I manage.

He draws back a little, and then his eyes fall to my lips. "Because he's a clever fuck, that's why."

Gabriel taps my temple hard with a finger. "Always ten steps ahead of me."

My entire body vibrates how hard my heart's beating. "I'm sorry," I murmur. "He shouldn't have used you."

"No!" he agrees, breath painting my lips again. His eyes are locked on mine now, so intense I can almost feel his pain. "No, he shouldn't have. Not if he loved me like he claimed he did. But you know what, Trinity? I realized something a few years ago." He glances away for barely a second before his eyes are back on mine again. "Still can't believe it took me so long, but I realized, of *course* he didn't love me. He's not capable of love. He'd just pretend. Just like he'd pretend to be normal."

He grabs my chin, shakes my head. But not violently this time. Almost gently.

"Had everyone fooled, didn't he?" He smiles, bitterly, cruelly. "Me. You. Everyone."

My head sinks into the dirty mattress when he pushes back to sit. He drags his hands down his face and then slowly climbs off me.

Relief floods me with heat, then cold. I don't know what to say. I feel like I'm walking a tightrope, and one wrong word could send me plummeting to my death.

Literally.

But I don't need to. He's gone off on a tangent, and I'm merely his audience.

"I was such a fool back then," Gabriel purses his lips. "I was so infatuated with him, his plan sounded…logical. If his urges, his *compulsions*, only became worse when he repressed them then he had to find an outlet for them."

My skin grows cold. I swallow hard, and then force myself not to fixate on Gabriel, or the words spilling out of his mouth. Instead, I tug surreptitiously at the knots lashing me to the bed, trying to find a little give in them. Something. Fucking anything.

"We tried everything, Monica and I. Sick things. Things you couldn't wrap your head around. But it was never enough. The two of us? We were never enough for him."

He points at the bed, and I freeze. But he's so far lost in the past, I doubt he even sees me anymore.

"I'd strap her down for him. *Hurt* her for him. Ropes, whips, knives. We'd fuck her raw, but it was never enough for him."

My guts twist as I glance down at the mattress I'm lying on.

Lord, don't let this be the same one they—

My eyes flutter closed as I will my nausea to settle down.

"It became a game, in the end." Gabriel walks up to the bed, stares down at me. When he reaches out and grabs a lock of my hair, curling it around his finger, I do my best not to pull away or puke. "But Keith always won."

My body sags.

I'm not getting out of these knots. I doubt I'm even getting out of this basement. Not after I see the look in Gabriel's eyes.

Defeat.

He knows there's no coming back from this. You can't tie up your daughter in a basement and still expect her to love you.

If that's even what he was after. It's night and day with him. Like a faulty switch that keeps dimming and brightening a light even when you're not touching it.

"You're crazy," I say quietly. Not with malice. Just stating a fact, that's all.

Gabriel smiles as he huffs out a breath through his nose. "Yes." He agrees through a sigh. "I am." Then he releases my hair. "But not always. Not at first." He points at himself. "He made me like this. With his tricks and his games."

He's nodding over and over again, like he's stuck. "*They* did this to me."

"You can't keep blaming him. He's dead."

At this, he throws back his head and laughs.

The sound is more terrifying than when he was on top of me, slapping me into submission.

"Oh, God." A last laugh. "Yes." Another sigh. "They both are. They are so very fucking dead." He dips his head a little. "God answers our prayers in his own way," he says, placing a hand over his heart. "It only took a few thousand of them before he answered mine."

I grit my teeth at him. "It's karma. It's what happens if you're a bad person."

His face turns to stone, but he doesn't try and stop me.

"Think you'll get away with it? You won't." I lift my head, pushing my chin out at him. "And I hope God punishes you. I hope you die a slow and horrible death. Because that's more than what you deserve for what you did to those boys, you sick fuck!"

The silence that comes after my pronouncement seems much too quiet, like the walls in here are still soaking up every stray sound wave.

Gabriel tilts his head to the side. Takes a step closer. "You still don't get it, do you?"

I cringe away the closer he comes, but there's nowhere for me to go. Tied spread-eagled to this bed, I can't do anything to protect myself.

"I had nothing to do with those kids. Nothing!" He points a finger to the side, then stabs it into his chest. "He blamed everything on me. He set me up when I told him I'd take you away from him. And he couldn't have that, could he? Oh no."

Gabriel gives his head a furious shake.

"You were the only reason Monica stayed. You were the glue that held your dysfunctional family together. Monica wouldn't leave him, because he told her he would hurt you if she tried."

My ears are singing. Not hymns, but dirges filled with despair.

Gabriel lets out another bitter laugh. "And that was my fault." He lunges forward, grabs the front of my shirt in a fist. "I'm the reason you're alive. I'm the reason he had something he could use to control her with. To control *us* with."

His other hand cups my cheek. "He used you to turn her against me. And when I threatened to expose him, he made it look like *I* was the one who arranged everything. All those boys, for all those sick men? Me!"

My mouth is open. My eyes wide. But I can't digest the information flooding my mind.

"He found a film of a young boy." Gabriel's eyes are wide, his face sickly pale. "He made us watch it. Me and Monica. Told us *that* was what he needed. *That* was the only cure for his sickness. Just one boy. One boy, and he wouldn't prey on anyone else again."

"N-No, pl-ease," I manage, but sobs cut up the words.

"Who do you think it was, found that first boy for him? Hmm?" He leans close again, twisting the fabric of my shirt. Pushing me hard into the mattress. His fingertips dig into the side of my face as he forces me to look at him.

"Who do you think brought him down here, to the dark?"

"N-No..."

"Wasn't me," Gabriel whispers furiously. "I refused. I told her I'd have no part in it."

"Please."

"But she loved him so fucking much. More than life itself. More than that boy's life."

He shakes my head. Twists. The fabric is cutting into my flesh. It feels like it's compressing my lungs.

Or maybe that's fear.

Panic.

Denial.

"He didn't last very long down here in the dark. Keith said it was because he didn't have any friends to play with."

I close my eyes.

Our father, which art in heaven.

"But there wasn't enough room down here, was there? Monica tried to reason with him. Not enough room for another boy, Keith. Where would he sleep?"

Give us this day, our daily bread.

"So they had to find somewhere else. A bigger house. Someplace out of the way."

And forgive us our trespassers, as we forgive those who trespass against us.

"And they did. They found a lovely, big old house out in the country. A place no one would suspect. And they had to, because Keith had found himself some friends. Believers of his cure."

And deliver us from evil.

"Nice big house. With a nice big basement. And then the boys could have friends to play with. And there was more than enough space to put them, when they were dead."

"You're lying," I whisper. "Mom had nothing to do with this. She couldn't have. She's not—"

"Oh, you'd be amazed, child. You'd be fucking amazed." Gabriel releases my shirt and absently smooths the fabric down over my chest as he stares into my eyes.

"Who do you think washed all that filthy money they earned?"

"No. They didn't have money. We weren't rich. You're lying!"

Gabriel's lips quirk up in a smile. "No, you weren't rich. Monica was clever. She made sure not to raise any suspicions. But as soon as you were eighteen, they were going to disappear."

He stands, leaving behind the ache where his fingers had been gripping my face.

"But then God struck them down. Now they're in hell, Trinity. Right where they belong."

"And what about his friends?" I ask, my voice hoarse, broken. "What about the boys?"

"Dead. They hid them well. His followers...?" Gabriel shrugs as he purses his lips and glances away. "They'll find other cures." Then his eyes are back on me, fiery and determined. "But God will seek them out, one by one, and he will strike them down."

"How can you be so sure?"

"Because I've been praying, Trinity." A smile crawls onto his face. "I've been praying for each and every one of them."

CHAPTER FIFTEEN
RUBE

"This is it?" Cass says through a mouthful of smoke. He tips back his head and then shakes it as he flicks away the butt end of his cigarette. "What a dump."

"Still can't believe this didn't come up before," Apollo says. He's got his hands in his pockets as if it's cold outside, but the sun is shining and I'm in short sleeves.

Could be the damp. It must have rained here last night, because the ground is still soggy in some places.

"Too close to home," I tell Apollo. "He made sure nothing led back here."

I head for the church, leaving them standing on the sidewalk.

Cass strays away down the road and Apollo hurries after him. Maybe Cass is worried he'll run into a priest. His hatred of the clergy borders on psychosis.

I let myself in and wander down the aisle toward the chancel. The nave is empty, which is no surprise for a Friday morning.

There's a sister near the altar, replacing some of the gutted-out candles. She turns when she hears my footsteps and does a double take.

"Can I help you?" she calls out, hugging herself and grabbing hold of the blatant crucifix around her neck. Seems this is one of the dioceses that don't require sisters to wear habits. But the big cross was still a dead giveaway.

"Morning, sister…?" I stop a few feet away, keeping my distance and hoping it'll help ease her mind.

"Vicky," she says reluctantly, giving me a small nod.

This isn't the greatest neighborhood, but why is she so spooked?

"Reuben." I lift a hand to shake, but she ignores it, instead watching me with wide eyes as if willing me to get to the point.

Chances were slim to none that anyone would hand over baptism records to a non-relative.

We'd stopped off at the mall on the way here and picked up fresh clothes for me. Not really something we could afford, but we all looked like a bunch of degenerates in our Salvation Army getups.

I bought a pair of dark jeans. Thankfully, it's warm outside, so I didn't have to get a jacket. Instead, I'm wearing a branded athletic shirt that looks a lot more expensive than it was, thanks to their 50% off sale. A little deodorant to mask the smell of new clothes, and I was set.

Ask, and ye shall receive.

"I'm sorry to drop in unannounced like this, but I only just got the address and, well…" I throw her a sheepish look. "I just couldn't wait to see it."

"See what?" Vicky asks, but at least she's not holding herself rigid anymore.

"The chapel." I glance around. "She wasn't lying. It is beautiful. And I think we'll just about be able to fit everyone in."

"Excuse me?"

I glance at her from the corner of my eye. "The wedding party?" I wave at the rows of pews. "I think we'd just about be able to fit everyone in."

"Wedding? Here?" Vicky's eyebrows dart up. "When?" She shakes her head.

"Our wedding." I let my voice get a little deeper.

Vicky takes a step back.

I immediately hold out a hand. "I'm so sorry, but are you sure you're booked here?" I look at the ground, my jaw bunching. "I knew that wedding planner was full of—" I cut off, and hurriedly make the sign of the cross, ending off by lifting the metal crucifix around my neck and kissing it.

Another purchase, since Cass said the black crucifix Zach got me was 'too intense.'

I turn back to Vicky, who's wide-eyed now.

"I'm sorry. My fiancée tossed out the last wedding planner we had, so we have a new one, and I didn't like her from the get-go but…" I lift my hands, shrug. "You don't want to mess with a bride-to-be."

Vicky shakes her head. "When is the wedding?"

"In three weeks," I tell her. "Wedding planner was supposed to call. I just stopped by because I was convinced from the way Trinity described this place that it might be too small for all the guests."

Vicky holds up her hands. "Trinity?"

"Malone." I move my chin to the side. "Daughter of Keith and Monica?"

Vicky puts a hand over her mouth. "Oh my…I…" She shakes her head. "I didn't even know she was old enough too—" But then her jaw clicks shut. "I'm going to check the register straight away."

I let her walk a few paces before following. She leads me back through the nave, to a small office beside the foyer.

"If we decide not to get married here, would you send her baptismal records over to Father Kennedy? I'll give you his email address."

"Oh, we don't keep electronic records," Vicky says. "But I can always fax the certificate through to him."

I take my phone out, put down her details as a new contact even though the certificate is useless to me. I need the record the parish keeps where they note the parents' names and, usually, an address. It's a long shot, but right now it's all we have.

She motions to a chair, and we sit in stuffy silence as she opens a big ledger and makes a note of the impending wedding in three weeks.

"Where were you baptized?" she asks, peering at me over her glasses.

Some things you don't lie about. "I wasn't."

The temperature inside the room drops a few degrees.

"Do you have any of the documents with you?"

The sudden chill in the air spreads right to my lungs. "Documents? Like my social security number?" I reach for my wallet, but she shakes her head.

Ticking off on her fingers, she starts up, "I need your Freedom to

Marry letter, your dispensation form, your civil marriage license, and the information for marriage form."

Christ.

I almost cross myself again hearing that list.

"Guess I have another wedding planner to fire," I murmur, as if to myself. "Is there still time for me to get those, or do we have to post-pone? I hope not. I've already lost the deposit on a cake because the previous planner had the dates wrong. And don't even get me started on the flowers. Did you know that, apparently, peonies are only beau-tiful if they haven't opened all the way?"

I'm not an actor like Cass. Hell, even Apollo could have done a better job convincing this woman that I'm a groom in a pickle. But I got the gig because any sister of the cloth would be too shocked Cass didn't catch flame when he walked into the chapel to deal with him, and Apollo...well...he gets distracted sometimes.

Also, I had sisters. Which apparently makes me the closest thing to a wedding expert we have.

Thankfully some of my frustration comes through because, even though I'm not Catholic, Vicky softens a little to my plight. "No dear. If you go down to the courthouse today, you should have everything you need in a week or so."

"Can you..." I stop for a second, make it look like I'm calming myself. "Can you please just check if you *do* have Trinity's records? With my luck, I've come to the wrong church."

"Oh, you're in the right place," Vicky says, mothering mode now fully engaged. "But it's a good thing you ask, because some of our records were destroyed in a fire a few months ago."

And there it is. That's why she was so uneasy seeing a stranger in the chapel. There's a shadow in Vicky's eyes that wasn't there before.

She goes over to a metal filing cabinet and opens it, her back to me. "What is her date of birth?"

I check on my phone, give it to Vicky.

I'll be pushing it if I ask, but it's burning me up. No pun intended. "A fire?"

At first I don't think she's going to answer, but then she lets out a sigh and closes the cabinet. I already have my suspicions before she starts talking, and when she's done, they're confirmed.

"Terrible thing," she murmurs. I can't help but notice she's empty-handed as she adjusts her glasses and takes a seat. "The police ruled it as a botched robbery or something." Vicky purses her lips. "Father Quinn was here that night. He often stayed late. Said he liked the quiet in the chapel. He lived close to the railway tracks, so I understand why."

"Father Quinn?" I say. "Trinity never mentioned him." The next almost sticks in my throat, but I force out the words as smoothly as I can. "She only ever spoke about Father Gabriel."

Vicky lights up like a billboard. "Oh, Gabriel." She nods a few times, a smile deeply etched on her face now. "Yes, they were close. He loved the Malones." The smile fades a little. "But no, he'd left years before that. Father Quinn took over the flock from him. Good man, if a little...studious."

An introverted priest? Downright unnatural.

"So Father Quinn was here when they broke in?" I nudge her, seeing as she's no doubt still daydreaming about Gabriel. I get it, the guy's good looking. But if she knew a shred of what his rotten heart was capable of, she'd be shitting herself right now.

"Yes." She drops her gaze, takes off her glasses. "They came in, shot him, searched the place, and then..." She shrugs. "They said it wasn't arson. The police. Said a candle had fallen on some papers. But this isn't the eighteenth century." She laughs a little, but it's sad and hollow. "It's not like Father Quinn sat here reading by candlelight."

I let a little silence pass. But I have to be on my way, because her empty hands mean I was right.

"So...those records?"

She looks up and blinks like she forgot I was sitting here. "Oh. Sorry. No." Shakes her head. "They must have been—"

"Destroyed." I cut in. "In the fire." I rub my eyelids as I let out a heavy sigh that's not nearly as much acting as it should be.

"It's okay," she says. "I know Trinity. We can recreate the records. Most of the congregation still lives around these parts. Miss Langley was there. I know that for a fact. She comes to all the baptisms and first communions."

"Miss Langley," I reply, nestling that bit of information in my head. I'm not exactly planning on canvassing the town, but who knows what a name could—

"She babysat for Trinity," Vicky says, beaming as she gets lost in a past that I'm guessing was much more bearable than the present. "Not often, of course. Just when her parents went out of town."

My hackles rise up like a motherfucking rebellion.

"Out of town?"

"Oh, Trinity didn't tell you?" Vicky cocks her head a little.

"She...doesn't talk about them very much." And thank fuck I can even think clearly at all with how my mind is scrambling.

"Yes, of course." Vicky's brow creases. "Terrible thing, that."

A lot of terrible things happen around these parts. If I didn't know any better, I'd tell her to go looking for the Indian burial ground this town was built on.

I mentally plead with Vicky to carry on talking.

For once, the Universe is on my side.

"Her father was a missionary," Vicky says. "Her mother went on one or two missions with him, but then she stayed at home after that. The missionary life isn't for everyone."

Oh no, it most definitely isn't.

"And Miss Langley sat for them?"

"She did. If I can get another two or three witnesses, then I can have those records ready by next week." Vicky looks proud of herself, and I almost feel sorry that her hard work will be for naught.

"Well, I do hope you find her."

"Won't be that hard," Vicky says with a laugh. "She's Trinity's next-door neighbor."

I HAVE to stop myself from jogging back to the car. Cass and Apollo are already inside, Cass at the wheel.

What the hell were they expecting? That I'd come running out with a file under my arm like they're the getaway car?

I slam the truck's door, turn to Apollo. "Find Maude Street." Then to Cass. "I have the address to her old house."

Cass puts the car in gear, staring at Apollo in the rear-view mirror.

I don't know why we're all so strung out, but I can feel the seconds streaming by as Apollo searches.

"Turn around," Apollo says. "Then take the first left."

Cass stomps on the gas and throws the car into a wide arc that leaves tire marks on the road. I squeeze my eyes shut, wishing I'd told him not to rush. But maybe it's a good thing. If Vicky calls the police and sends them to Maude street, they might get there before we do.

I don't know what we'll find there, but something's telling me we have to hurry.

"Faster," I tell Cass.

He doesn't say anything, but he skips the next light regardless of the fact that it's been red since it came in sight.

I guess it's a good thing this is a quiet part of town and there weren't any cars on the road. The only one in sight, in fact, is a white Hyundai.

But I don't think it would have mattered.

We're on a mission from God.

CHAPTER SIXTEEN
TRINITY

The urge to start feeling sorry for myself is back, and twice as strong as before. Honest to God, I don't know how the Brotherhood did it. I've been tied to a rusty bed in my family's basement for what feels like days, and I'm about ready to lose my mind.

The rats don't help. I can't see them, only hear them, and that makes it worse somehow.

Gabriel turned the lights off before he left. Something about the dark helping me find the light I was so desperately seeking.

I should have known he had me figured out. I mean, he'd told me so himself. I'd never considered myself an optimist, so I guess I'm just naive then. A hopeless romantic—

Gah!

I cut off the thought with a grimace. That's what he'd said when he'd been talking about my parents. And God he'd even sounded a little lovesick.

Which makes *me* feel sick.

I test the ropes again, rattling the metal bed frame, but they're as tight and unyielding as the previous thousand times.

All this time I was living right above this room, and I had no idea.

Rattle. Squeak.

He's coming back. And soon. He doesn't have to—I'm sure he thinks I'm pretty secure—but it was the way he said those words.

You should pray, Trinity. Pray to God for forgiveness.

Forgiveness? How fucking *dare* he? I don't believe for a second he wasn't a key player in this whole thing. Of course he'd try and shift the blame—he'll die a horrible death in prison. And it's not like my parents can testify against him.

Rattle, rattle, SQUEAK.

I stop moving. That last squeak sounded different. Like something was giving.

Rattle, rattle, rattle, rattle, rattle—

The part of the bed frame designed to hold the mattress collapses under me. Pain dashes through my wrists and ankles as I'm suddenly suspended limb from limb in the air. I gasp, let out a breath, inhale deep. When I squirm, my butt barely brushes the mattress under me.

Fuck.

My wrists ache and burn where the ropes are cutting into me. My left hand especially—there's a dull, thumping ache coming from the base of my thumb, as if the sudden tensing on the ropes did some serious damage.

As soon as I can breathe through the pain, I start shifting again, tugging at the ropes.

I'm loathe to try with my left because it already hurts so much. I go around again. Right hand, right foot, left foot. Nothing. The bed's posts are still rooted to the spot. Nothing seems to have changed except the fact that I might have a dislocated thumb.

My left hand aches even more, as if thinking about it aggravates the injury.

Huh. Houdini would pull off a famous escape like this in the blink of an eye. But those were all tricks. Wasn't he double-jointed or something? He could put his shoulder out of its socket and—

My eyes swivel to my left hand. In the dark, I can't see anything.

Oh God.

No.

Can I?

It's already hurting so much...

But what if I managed to dislocate my thumb? Then I could slip my hand out of that rope, right?

I squeeze my eyes shut, trying to build up some courage.

My thumb is probably already pretty malleable. All I need to do is pull it through the noose. It'll hurt, duh, but maybe not as much as earlier. And the pain is—

Pretty fucking unbearable. And the agonizing ache is only getting worse the longer I linger on this stupid plan.

But it *is* a plan.

And it might even work.

And then I'd be free, no longer hanging here on my strings waiting for the puppet master to return.

I don't even know what he went to go and do. Is he trashing another room? Oiling himself up? Lying in my parents' bed and—

Fuck! Those thoughts are not in the least helpful.

Breathe.

You can do this.

Oh Lord, I hope I can do this.

I grit my teeth.

I hold my breath.

And I slowly start pulling on my left hand.

The pain in my thumb immediately intensifies a million-fold. I start shaking internally, my body fighting with me to stop the torture, but I can't.

I won't.

I keep picturing the Brotherhood. Determination gleaming in their eyes. The things they'd say to me right now if they knew I was considering defeat.

But the pain gets worse, and the rope isn't budging. Pain wells, and with it comes a wave of frustration. I pull harder, the tears that brim and then leak down my face not even blurring my vision. Or maybe they do, I can't tell in the dark.

"Ah!" The yell doesn't echo. This small chamber is too well insulated.

But as I yell, I jerk on my arm as hard as I can.

Agony bursts into my hand. For a second, I'm convinced I've torn off my thumb.

I scream twice, first at that jolt of pain, and then again when my hand drops onto the mattress below me. I drag my hand onto my chest, cradling it against my chin as I let out a ragged sob. I start panting through my mouth as I try to get a handle on the pain.

That hurt more than the lashes I got from Miriam combined with Zachary's spanking.

I force my breathing to slow. Imagine the pain leaving my body with every exhale.

My hand's hot and throbbing, but eventually the pain recedes enough that I can think past it.

With the restraint freed, my shoulder is on the mattress now.

I laugh when I realize I have to try and untie the knot around my right hand with a hand that now sports a dislocated thumb.

Oh Lord, how I laugh.

But then I stop. And I grit my teeth.

And I push through the pain.

Somehow, using my other fingers, tearing off nails, wailing through the pain, I manage to loosen the knot.

My face is wet with tears. I think I've chewed a hole in the side of my cheek, but after what feels like eons of struggling and trying to ignore the red-hot pain in my hand, both shoulders thump onto the mattress.

Time's slipping away, but I allow myself a few minutes to just lie there. Regaining my strength. Trying to get back my composure.

When I sit up and start working on my legs, there's a burning conviction inside me.

I don't care what it takes—Gabriel's going to pay for this.

"I got a bad feeling about this," Rube murmurs. "Something isn't right."

"Like the fact we're still in the fucking car when we should be in there?" I say, rapping on the window with a knuckle. "Yeah, bud, I feel you. All sorts of fucking wrong."

Rube throws me a glare. "We can't just barge in there—"

"Guys, come on. This isn't helping." Apollo grabs my headrest and pulls himself closer, nestling between the sedan's front seats.

We swapped out the liquor store's truck for a silver VW someone left unlocked in a driveway. That was about an hour ago—whether it's been reported stolen yet is anyone's guess.

"What's not helping is us sitting here like fucking spectators. I'm getting out."

"Wait. Just fucking *wait*." Rube opens his door and climbs out of the car. It's a testament to how big he is when the shocks let out a creak of relief.

I'm relieved too, because I was itching on the inside like a fucking junkie.

My love affair with heroin is an on-again-off-again thing. I've always been careful with my dosages after getting out of the basement—I started chipping straight away without even knowing it was a thing—

but I've been through stages in my life where I've used religiously enough to get strung out.

That's how I feel right now.

Strung out.

Long overdue.

Except my drug of choice isn't black tar.

It's her.

Trinity fucking Malone.

And she's in that house. I can feel it. Right there, close enough to see if she was standing at a window, while we're over here in this piece of shit car, sitting around like we're scoping out the place for a fucking home invasion sometime next week.

I've been patient. We went with Rube's plan at the church when I was all for locking whatever nun was creeping around the place in the bathroom while we rooted around in their files.

From what Rube tells us, that would have been futile. No trace of Trinity was left in that place.

But now?

Now we're sitting here with our thumbs up our asses while Mr. Cautiously Careful out there triple-checks God knows what.

I climb out the car, ignoring Apollo's bleated, "Wait, Cass!"

He climbs out a second later anyway, so what the fuck?

"Counting the tiles on the fucking roof?" I ask Reuben.

He doesn't even bother to scowl at me. "He knows we're here."

"Impossible."

"He could have seen the car."

"Then he would be out the back door already, no pun intended."

"That wasn't a pun."

I grind my teeth at Mr. Cautiously Careful AKA Sir Correct-me-if-I'm-Wrong. Which I never could, because he never was.

"That thing you're feeling?" I tell him. "It's the earth revolving on its fucking axis. She could be—"

I stop.

I'd been about to say dead, and I don't know why. Gabriel wouldn't kill her—she's too valuable. She's what led us here in the first place. And he had to have known that, right?

That's why he took her. Why he's using her. Maybe that shit about him being her father was purposefully planted on his laptop for us to find. He knew we'd assume the worst.

But fuck. You start going down that rabbit hole, and you end up as knotted as a pair of horny dogs.

"We do this now, or we don't," I say, glancing at Apollo. "The longer we stand out here, the—"

"You're right," Rube says.

And thank fuck for that, because I was close to smacking him upside the head. I start forward, but his voice stops me. "Get back in the car. We'll circle the block. Maybe we get in the back way, or through a window."

I turn to him and stare him down. He's about the same height as me, but I know I'll be the first to kiss dirt in a fight.

But that doesn't matter.

Because he's *wrong*. We can't wait anymore.

She's in there, and she's in danger. Fuck, Trinity being within a foot of Gabriel is more than I can stand thinking about. Even if she is his daughter, I know a perverted prick like him wouldn't think twice about sticking it in her.

They've been alone so long already, I'm sure he's done it a couple of times.

Usually I can control myself. I don't get angry, I get snarky.

But this? The thought that right now he could be—?

"Fuck this," I snarl.

"Cass. Please."

I stop, but only because it's Apollo and the poor guy honestly wants to help. It kinda sucks that he's always so nice about it. Always seeing every side of the argument. He should have been born a few years earlier where he could have run free with his hippie friends, protesting the Vietnam war and getting fucked on acid all the time.

"Just...wait. Would you?"

So I wait.

I wait for hours, days. A fucking eternity.

I wait while Reuben and Apollo start discussing what they'd do if they couldn't find an open window. Should they break it, hope no one hears?

Oh wait, Rube thinks he saw someone. What's that? Another person walking down a street in Suburbia? The fucking horror. But no, he was mistaken, it was just some old lady pruning her rose bush.

And then I wait some more, because now they've moved onto conflict resolution. What if Gabriel has a gun? Nah, Rube doesn't think so. Not all bad guys have guns or some shit. But Apollo's not sure. Now *he's* Mr. Fucking Careful.

I can't.

I can't take it.

This waiting. This supposing and assuming and fuck ton of maybes. Not while Gabriel's doing God only knows what to my blasphemous little slut.

This time I don't warn them. I just turn and walk away.

Apollo makes to grab me, but I dodge him. And then I storm the fucking castle gates like I have an army at my back.

Because I do.

They'll come. Rube and Apollo will be right behind me.

And we're going to rip Gabriel a new asshole. And then shove foreign objects up it until he bleeds. And then give him a blood transfusion so he can cling to life…only to suffocate him with a pillow made from his own skin.

Yeah, I've been thinking about it. A lot.

Maybe I'm not that calm after all.

But fuck me, I'm good at hiding it.

I stalk up to the door, and I lift a hand to try the handle.

A grin tugs at my mouth when it turns and the door swings open.

But that smile dissolves a second later when I see Trinity standing in front of me. Wide-eyed, face bruised, clothes rumpled, hair disheveled, mouth peeling open like she's about to scream.

And that's all I see.

Just her.

Because fucked up as she is, *ruined* as she is, she's so fucking beautiful I can't believe I've been without her for so long.

My *drug*?

Fuck that shit.

She's the blood in my veins. She's what makes my heart pump, and my organs work, and my skin glow.

And she's right in front of me. Like a prayer God answered without me having to even get on my knees and utter a single word.

I'm swelling. Bursting with happiness.

Fuck that—with joy.

And here I thought that was only possible when I was high.

We found her.

She's ours.

The world is suddenly a better place. A place I might decide to live in a little longer than I'd planned.

But then Trinity's gone.

Someone's tackling me from the side.

And I realize it was all a trick.

Gabriel used her as bait.

And I fell for it.

My shoulder hits the ground first, and then the rest of my body, the force of the impact driving the air from my lungs and spittle from my lips.

Ha, *literally*.

So excuse the pun.

CHAPTER EIGHTEEN
TRINITY

4201. *Beep.*
4202. *Beep.*
4203. *Beep.*

I blink sweat out of my eyes and take a second to work my neck with my good hand. I don't know what's worse—hoping that I'll hit the right combination before Gabriel comes back, or wondering if I even have the first two numbers correct to begin with.

Nope! Can't think about that. Negativity need not apply.

4204. *Beep.*

4205. *Beep.*

Thump.

I freeze. If my heart wasn't pounding so hard in my chest, I might have been able to make out if that sound had been my imagination or not.

Thump.

No. It's not. Gabriel is back.

4206. *Beep.*

4207. *Beep.*

4208. *BEEP.*

My hand cramps up. Not from pressing numbers, but I'm guessing from the ropes and from the tugging. My left hand aches relentlessly at my side, but I ignore it as much as I can.

4209. *Beep.*

Thump.

Oh Lord, he's coming.

4210. *Beep.*

My heart's in my fucking throat. Every time I try to swallow, it bobs around like an ice cube in a glass of lemonade.

Fuck, why the hell did I have to think about that when I'm so thirsty?

Thump.

My hand shakes so much, I can barely punch the right numbers.

4221 *Beep.*

Damn it! I have to remember I've already tried that one.

Thump, thump, thump.

He's right beside me. Which room is that? I'm trying to picture the layout of my own house, but I can't.

4211.

Click.

Is it the dining room? The living room?

42—

Wait.

I focus on the light above the panel. It's flashing green now. Was it doing that before? Why do I remember it being solid red?

I grab the handle, and open the door.

It swings inward and bathes me in gray light. As I step outside and turn into the hallway, I figure out what room he's in.

Dad's study.

The room right above the portion of the basement I was just in.

No wonder I never heard anything. Dad kept that door locked.

I'm a fucking idiot. I thought my Dad was a God-fearing man with a fully functioning moral compass.

How could I have been so wrong?

The thought makes me nauseous, so I hurriedly stop trying to figure anything out. Instead, I focus on creeping down the hall as quietly as possible.

Quietly...but quickly.

The hall takes a turn and reveals the front door. It's only about two yards away. My heart kicks into overdrive again, and then I'm running.

It's fucking idiotic, but I can't help it. I can't stop. It's too close, and I'm too scared.

So I run.

And then I slam into the wood as I'm fumbling for the lock. It turns, the tumblers clicking loudly as they slide back into the door.

I twist the handle. Step back so the door can open.

Behind me, someone starts running.

Thud, thud, thud, thud, THUD!

The door is open.

But I can't go through because someone's standing there.

Cass is standing there.

What the hell is Cass doing here?

He opens his mouth as if he's about to say something. But he never gets the chance. Someone crashes into him, sends him tumbling over the rose bushes lining the front drive.

Cass becomes Zach. Tall, grim, panting.

A second of frozen time. Then I surge forward, delirious with thoughts of escape. Hardly believing my luck.

He'll save me.

Wrap me in his arms.

Hold me tight.

But none of that happens. He doesn't drag me out of harm's way.

Zach surges forward, and then shoves me. Hard.

I crash into the door. My scream is little more than a choked gasp of pain as my injured hand is trapped between my body and the door.

Zach pushes past me. My head slams against the wood. Sparks flash and pop in front of me as I sink to the ground.

And then he's gone.

My conscious mind drifts, losing track in a deluge of pain and confusion.

There's a loud clap in the living room, like a car backfiring. There was a young couple down the road who lived here a few years back. Their car would do that sometimes. Always scared the shit out of me.

Grunts and roars from the living room. Then another clap, this one louder than before.

Then legs swarm past me. I tip my head back despite the pain.

Reuben. Cass. Apollo.

They all look down at me, but only as they pass. Then they move on, deeper into my house.

It's weird having them here.

Weird being back.

I should show them around. But I have to clean my room first. What'll they think of the basement? Maybe I shouldn't show them that. They wouldn't like it.

I'll show them the picture of the unicorn. It'll make them laugh.

Awsum.

"Hey, pretty thang."

I force my eyes open, catch sight of Apollo's face. He's pale, eyes jittery. "Everything's just fine, hear me? You're safe now."

And I believed him.

Lord, I *believed* him.

CHAPTER NINETEEN
ZACH

Christ, where are my brothers going in such a hurry? I'm too far away to see who's driving—all I know is that Reuben was inside the Redford Missions of Love church for a few minutes, and then came out empty-handed but with a speed to his steps I haven't seen in a while. Not full out running—I guess he didn't want to draw unwanted attention, but it was obvious he was on the move.

When they slam on the gas and throw the car into a U-turn, I almost think it's because they spotted me.

But I doubt it.

It seems they have other things on their mind.

I give them a lead before following.

We drive for a few minutes, headed downtown. Our route takes us past a mall, and then almost back the way we came before heading downtown again.

Are they being paranoid? Retracing their steps?

Or are they struggling to find their way in a strange town? Ha, if Apollo's the one navigating, then we're all in for a few more U-turns.

Eventually, we venture into the suburbs. Perfect little houses on their perfect little lawns. Two and three bedrooms, mostly. Some double stories here and there.

Where are we headed, boys? I can't for a second believe Gabriel would live in a place like this.

Trinity.

I start looking around a little harder. Driving a little slower.

Is this her old neighborhood? There was no address on the intake form at Saint Amos. I guess, by then, she was officially a ward of the state.

Or someone had fucked with her records.

My brothers turn down a side street. I park on the sidewalk, tracking them on my phone's app, because I have a feeling this is their last turn.

Seconds later they stop.

Then I'm out of the car and jogging down the opposite side of the road. Thank God I had the foresight to pack a hoody. I keep the hood pulled up as I jog. Paired with sunglasses, I'm hoping I'd look like another guy out on a jog, but I know it'll only take one longer-than-normal glance in my direction for my brothers to recognize me.

The people around here like their trees and shrubs. And not so much fences between properties. As long as no one looks out their window and spots me jogging over their freshly manicured lawn, I should be good.

My brothers' silver car is parked a few drives down, opposite side of the road. I slow down, slip behind a bushy shrub, and stretch like I've got a cramp. But all the while peeking at them through a gap in the foliage.

A minute later they get out of the car. Reuben first, his head turning all directions as if he's scouting for danger.

Then Cass.

Then Apollo.

But they just stand there, talking. Watching.

I peer down my side of the road. There are a few trees and shrubs I could use as cover, but I have no idea which house they're targeting. I could end up jogging right into their line of sight.

Reuben turns and looks straight at me.

I throw myself back, stumble over a fucking garden gnome, and land flat on my ass.

As I'm about to get up, I hear a door open behind me. I look back as an old lady walks out onto her porch. She scans her lawn, and despite her thick glasses—or perhaps because of them—sees me.

Shit.

I get up, trying not to bolt, and then stop when I feel a tug on my pants leg.

Christ, I've gotten my jeans hooked in a thorn.

The old lady's garden isn't quite as well kept as the others around here. Her roses, for instance, are the kind you'd expect growing wild around a mansion where neighborhood kids dare each other to knock on the door.

I yank at my pants, and that shakes the entire row of fucking roses.

If Reuben is still looking this way, it would look mighty suspicious.

So I fall into a crouch and do my best to unhook my jeans without rustling as much as a single leaf.

"Everything all right, dearie?" a thin, wobbly voice wants to know.

I glance up into a pair of watery blue eyes, and give the old woman the most charming smile I have. "Got a little stuck on your roses," I tell her through my teeth.

"They are magnificent, aren't they?" she wheezes, clasping her hands at her breast as if she's offering up a prayer to God for her killer botanicals.

Another subtle yank, and finally my jeans are free. But I don't stand yet, because that would put my head and shoulders above the rose bush. I don't want to reveal myself until I know what the hell they're up to. And the last thing they need is a distraction.

I glance around. I could head back the way I came, but Mrs. Nosy's yard is wide open but for this thorny hedge.

"Are you with the church?" Mrs. Nosy wants to know.

I stare up at her with a frown. Dressed in a hoody? In what world could I possibly—

But then her eyes move down my chest, fix on something there a second, and fly back to my eyes. Her smile brightens a little.

I look down too, to see what she finds so fascinating.

Trinity's crucifix. Blood red against my gray hoody. Impossible to miss. It must have come out while I was jogging, or when I landed on my ass beside her roses.

Mrs. Nosy beckons me with a frail hand. "Why don't you come inside, dear? I'll fix you a glass of lemonade."

I feel like I've stepped through a portal back to the eighties where old ladies go around offering cold beverages to any sweaty teen that happens to come within yelling distance of their whitewashed porches.

But my options are limited. If I break cover, my brothers could see me. If I go inside with the nice lady and let her pour me a drink, I could wait them out. Keep track of them on my phone. Fuck, I might even give them a call and see if they pick up.

Don't know what I'd even say if they did, but I'd think of something.

THE OLD WOMAN'S name is Langley, and she's a Mizzz because her husband died a long time ago.

I'm starting to think she had ulterior motives for the lemonade, especially when she puts down a plate of cookies too. I ignore them—I haven't touched refined sugar for many years. I don't plan on falling off that wagon any time soon, so I only take imaginary sips from the glass of lemonade.

"Are you one of the new missionary boys they told us about on Sunday?" Miss Langley asks.

I would have choked on my cold drink if I'd actually been drinking it. "Missionary boy?"

"For the mission to Ghana." Langley beams, which happens anytime she mentions the church.

Now I'm convinced this is Trinity's old haunt. It could just be this one biddy, but I have a feeling everyone around here is really serious about finding Jesus.

A priest like Gabriel really brings that out in a person.

I figure I don't have much to lose except having the cookies withdrawn—God willing—so I say, "Ghana." I look introspective. "God willing, Miss Langley, we'll be changing hundreds of lives in that village."

She clasps her hands again, her lips trembling. "Oh, you must be so excited."

"I am." I shift in my seat, nod my head a little. "But if it wasn't for Father Gabriel, I wouldn't even be here."

"Father..." Langley sags in her chair. "I miss him so much. He was such a good influence on you young ones."

Fuck, if she only knew. But I nod along, try and look as Catholic as possible, and even go as far as to toy with Trinity's crucifix.

"Actually, I've never met him."

Langley's eyes widen behind her thick glasses. "You haven't?"

"No. It was Trinity." I pick up a cookie, break off a piece. "She told me all about Father Gabriel."

"Trinity!" Langley lets out a long sigh as she sinks back in her chair. "How is she, the little lamb?"

"Oh, she's doing wonderfully."

"I'm so glad." Langley shakes her head as she looks out the kitchen window with its lacy curtains. "I was so upset to hear what happened. And right here, so close to home."

"The accident happened here?"

"Oh no, that was somewhere in town." Langley waves a dismissive hand. "I mean, for such a gifted child to lose her parents. So young."

"Gifted?" I sound incredulous, and Langley doesn't like that one bit.

Her eyes are narrowed when she turns back to look at me. "Father Gabriel always said she was a gift from God. Her mother couldn't conceive for many years." Langley shakes her head, clucks like a mother hen. "But then Keith and Monica found God, and He blessed them with a child."

Seems everyone knows everyone in this place. Hell on earth.

I don't know how to react to what she said, so I don't. Instead I finally take a small sip of lemonade and try not to think about how much sugar it has in it.

"Such a wonderful family," Langley says. She stares out the window again, a fond look on her face. "That child was always so sweet. A true blessing. Never once when I looked after her did she as much as make a fuss."

Looked after?

"Now I remember," I say, nodding and toying with another piece of cookie. "I was wondering where I'd heard your name. Trinity mentioned you."

"Oh, she did?" The old lady blinks rapidly. Dear God, is she fogging up? "How kind of her."

"Said you were her favorite babysitter."

Langley's eyes start brimming. She hurriedly looks away, and then seems to come to. "Oh, uh, you'll be needing that donation." She stands before I have a chance to ask her what the hell she's on about.

She disappears down the hall, and I take my drink and pour it down the sink. When she comes back in, I'm in my seat again, just putting the glass back on the table. Her already wide smile grows when she spots my empty glass. "Would you like another?"

"Oh no," I tell her, patting my stomach like we've just finished Thanksgiving dinner together. "Folks around here are too kind."

She giggles a little at this and starts writing out a check.

Like taking donations from the congregation.

She hands it to me, but doesn't let go. "Where is your little...the clipboard? With the—" she gestures vaguely "—with the place for me to sign?"

I pat my pockets theatrically. "You know, Miss Langley, I think I left it next door."

Her eyes almost goggle out of their sockets. With surprising speed for such an aging gal, she's on her feet, her head whipping to that same kitchen window as before. "Father Gabriel is back?"

And then it's as if her lemonade was spiked with fucking amphetamines. I'm standing a second later, ruthlessly suppressing the urge to run.

"What do you mean?" My voice comes from far away.

"Gabriel!" She turns to me, clasps her hands again. This time like she's begging. "Oh, I thought... I thought you just came from him. I was hoping he'd come back."

I want to shake her until her teeth rattle. "Back where? I don't—"

"Didn't Trinity tell you?"

My heart bangs into my breastbone as if to try and get me moving. "Tell me what?" I'm grimacing at her through my teeth, but she doesn't seem to notice.

"Father Gabriel. He moved into their old house. I guess the estate put it up for sale, but I never saw a board outside. And I'd have noticed —they're going up all over the place! Why, we had a young couple move in right across the road. Big house for just the two of them. You'd think they're planning to fill it, but I don't know. The woman looks closer to forty than thirty." Langley shrugs, as if the fact that she's rambling isn't having any effect on me.

It is.

I'm about to have a heart attack if she doesn't tell me what I need to know. "Gabriel is living next door?"

"Yes, yes he is. But he's hardly ever here. Still, so much better than living next door to a stranger, wouldn't you say?"

I don't say anything.

I turn and I run the fuck out of that house like the devil himself is breathing down my fucking neck.

They're here for Trinity, not Gabriel. Somehow, they got the address for her old house. That's why they parked down the street.

But if Gabriel bought the property, who the fuck knows what kind of traps he laid out for unwanted guests?

I run, and I don't stop.

I plow right through Langley's roses, ignoring the thorns that prick at my skin, and I race across the next-door neighbor's lawn.

But I'm too late.

Cass is up front, about to try and open the door. Fuck, maybe he's even going to try knocking first.

Reuben and Apollo? They're straggling behind, fuck knows why.

I'm closer to Cass than they are, but I'm still too far away.

All I can say is, thank God for Miss Langley's lemonade.

When I grit my teeth and push, I go a little faster. I clear the hedge separating me from Cass like an Olympic hurdler.

I crash into him just as the door opens.

Just in time to see Trinity's shocked face.

Just in time to see the shadow deeper in the house.

A man, lifting a gun.

Because of course he has a fucking gun. Why wouldn't he?

Cass and I go over another rose bush. He's yelling. I scramble up, dart back to the door.

Trinity is still standing there, blocking me. She doesn't seem to realize she's about to die.

It's better, not knowing.

As soon as I shove her out of the way, that gun is on me. Pointing at *me*. I know I'm already dead.

And the knowledge sits there like heartburn in my brain. It tries to overwhelm me, to render me useless through fear, but I shove it away even harder than I shoved her away.

I sprint down the passage. Three steps, and I'm there. Staring into a pair of brown eyes that should recognize me, but don't.

When I slam into Gabriel, the gun goes off.

But it's fine, because it doesn't hurt. I'm still moving, still fighting.

I herd him backward through momentum and rage. Pushing, pushing.

We end up in the living room a second later. His teeth are bared like a wild animal's. I'm snarling like a beast. We tackle each other, end up on the carpet. I get a blow to his head. He gets a knee to my groin.

And then the gun goes off again.

And this time…

This time there *is* pain.

It's vast and it's endless and fucking magnificent in its abundance.

But that's not fine, because now I can't fight anymore. And Gabriel…he's on his feet. He's running.

Thank you Jesus.

He's not running toward the front door. Toward Trinity or my brothers.

The cowardly fuck is running away.

Thank Christ.

I try to cross myself, but my body just lies there.

Body and mind. Two different things entirely.

I'm still here. I'm still conscious. But all I can do is watch and observe—paralyzed as, all around me, the world dissolves into chaos.

CHAPTER TWENTY
RUBE

I've never felt so torn in my life. My body is being sent in two different directions by a mind suddenly unable to prioritize. But I'm rooted to the spot because this is where Zachary is lying.

We're in Trinity's living room, judging from the couches and the dusty television set. But Trinity's not here. She's still in the passage by the front door.

That's where I want to be.

I caught a glimpse of Gabriel a second before he turned a corner and disappeared toward the back of the house. No doubt escaping through the back door we would have been covering if Cass hadn't been so fucking impulsive.

That's where I want to be too.

Instead I'm standing here, watching Zachary's blood soak into the carpet.

And then Trinity screams, and it's as if everyone's minds come back from wherever they'd wandered off to.

"He's getting away!" Cass says, but he's running toward Trinity, not Gabriel.

Apollo falls to his knees beside me, inadvertently soaking his jeans in blood. "Is he dead?"

I don't know.

I just don't fucking know.

"Call an ambulance," I tell Apollo.

But now his hands are full of blood because he was trying to stop it running out of the two holes in Zachary's torso, and that's freaking him out and he's gone and frozen up.

"Apollo!"

Brown eyes snap to me. "Yes?"

He can't be here. Not around all this blood. Like a fucking candle in a snow storm.

And I can't let Gabriel get away either.

It shouldn't be this easy to make crucial decisions, but it's as if there's no choice to make at all.

"Don't let him get away!" My voice is too loud—it booms back to us —but maybe that's what gets Apollo on his feet. I stab a finger down the passage. "Follow him!"

Apollo turns and runs.

"*Just* follow him!" I yell after Apollo's retreating back, with no clue if he heard me or not.

Then it's back to Zach because a glance behind me shows Cass is examining Trinity like he just got his Ph.D.

Guess neither of them is phoning the ambulance.

I fish my phone out of my pocket. There's a part of me that's sitting back and watching me operate, and it's gobsmacked that I'm still functioning. That I'm lucid. That my voice is legible when the 911 operator on the other end of the line answers my call.

But that's because they need me right now. My brothers. Trinity. They need me to be strong. I can freak out later, or not at all. I don't need to add fuel to this fucking inferno.

"I need an ambulance."

And then I go blank, because I guess a part of me isn't all that focused right now.

"2192 Maude Street," comes Trinity's voice. It's faint, but it's steady. That's my girl.

The operator starts talking me through emergency procedures. Applying pressure to Zachary's wounds to stop the bleeding. And I try. Fuck, I try. But his blood keeps seeping through my fingers. And it's eating into the carpet and heading for my knees.

I shift back like it's contagious.

Cass appears on the other side of Zach's limp body. He moves away one of my hands, using both of his to stop the flow of blood from the wound.

I mimic him.

And slowly the blood stops trickling through my fingers. I like to think I did that. That I somehow stemmed the flow.

But it could be that Zach's heart has stopped pumping.

CHAPTER TWENTY-ONE
APOLLO

Leaves and low-hanging branches whip against my face. Holy shit, did Gabriel run track or something? I'm struggling to keep up. He had less than a minute head start on me.

We're weaving our way through the dividing line sandwiched between properties. Not all of the houses have fences, but most of them do have trees and shrubs for privacy.

Gabriel obviously knows this area very well. He's pulling all the moves—throwing trash cans between us, rousing dogs who must have been distant offspring of Cujo.

All I can do is try and keep him in sight. Lucky for me, he's leaving behind a path of devastation. Broken branches, rustling shrubs, gates thrown open.

I chase him over a road, and then down a cement embankment.

And then I lose him.

I'm panting, bloody hands on my bloody knees as I scan left and right. The embankment led down to a storm drain, but there's no fucking way I'm going into that black hole.

I'm not an idiot.

I know he's waiting in there for me.

Shit!

I could go over the top. But if he's watching then he'll know what I'm trying to do. So should I stay, or should I—

Something slams into the back of my head.

I land on hands and knees, fire scraping over my palms as I skid over the cement floor.

Before I can scramble up, a foot hits me square in the stomach.

God! Again? Fuck!

I kick out, manage to catch Gabriel's shin. Not that it fucking helps —I could have been kicking a tree stump.

He takes a step back, and then surges forward again. Grabs the back of my neck. Hauls me to my feet.

I catch the crook of his arm when he goes to punch me, and that he wasn't expecting. But he recovers so fast, I don't even have time for some kind of counter strike.

He rips his arm free and shoves me like we're a pair of bullies marking turf in the schoolyard.

I slam into the side of the storm drain's massive mouth, banging my head.

There go the last of my fond childhood memories.

And that's when Gabriel whips out his gun. Which is round about the same time I put my hands up.

Oh God, the blood. I squeeze my eyes closed and try my best to remain fixed to the earth.

"Okay! I yield!"

And he laughs. The fucker actually laughs. There's a click from the gun, which I assume is him taking off the safety.

I'm supposed to know about these things, but I was so high when Zach took us for practice shooting. I can't remember a damn thing.

Instead of yielding, like I asked him so damn nicely, Gabriel grabs my shirt and rams me into the concrete wall again. Then he drags me around the corner. It's an overcast day, so there's no sharp line in the limbo between shadow and light. Just a dark haze.

All the better to rape you in, my dear.

Jesus, fuck, no.

I tilt forward to try and push him out of the way. The icy nozzle of a gun burrows into my forehead, urging my head back and back and back until it presses against the uneven wall behind me.

Christ.

I lift my hands, close my eyes. "Just make it quick, okay? And if it's all the same to you, I'd prefer it if you rape me after I'm dead."

There's another click, and that confuses the fuck out of me, because I know some guns have a hammer, but this one doesn't.

I open one eye, then the other.

Gabriel's lowering the gun.

But the moment I open my mouth to thank him, it's up again.

"Stay where you are," he says.

He wasn't going to kill me? Fuck me? Why? I mean, I'm grateful obviously, but confused. But there's no way in hell I'm going to antagonize him into shooting me. What good would that do anyone?

"Sure, yeah. I'll stay right here."

My hands are still up, and it's taking quite a lot of my concentration to ignore the smell of copper in the air. I should be fine, long as I don't dwell. Long as I don't look at my hands.

Gabriel trains the gun on me as he steps back.

Follow him.

Aw, fuck, Rube. I wanna, but he's going to kill me if I try.

Follow him.

"Hey, uh…"

Gabriel pauses. The hand around the gun tightens.

"I just want to know one thing."

He frowns at me. "Quiet."

I curl the fingers of one hand until just my index is up. "Just one. Please? Humor me? It's the least you can do."

Gabriel shakes his head like he's wondering which of the two of us have lost our minds.

Probably both.

"What?" he snaps, taking another step back.

"Why'd you do it?"

He stops. "Do what?"

"The basement. The kids. Us." I point at myself with my finger. "I mean…that wasn't cool, man. Seriously. Are you a psychopath? Because you're lacking all sorts of empathy."

Gabriel's lips lift into a snarl, and it looks like he's reconsidering letting me live. But fuck it. I mean…

"That's why you're following me?" Gabriel moves the gun a little closer as if he's pointing with it. "Talk to Trinity. I told her everything."

"Like how you chose us? Did you tell her that? Because I've always wondered about that. I mean, compared to Cass and Rube, even Zach, I'm not much of a looker."

Gabriel shakes his head as if he's got something in his ear. "I don't know why she chose you."

"She? She who?" Was it Zachary's mom? I never met the woman, but—

"Monica chose. She...she drew less attention than Keith. No one thought twice about her sitting in the park, reading a book."

Wait...*Monica*? As in Trinity's *mom*? But there's a look in Gabriel's eyes as if he's waiting to see my reaction. Playing me.

"Yeah, okay. Blame it on a dead girl." I nod a few times. "Clever. No one can prove you wrong."

Another snarl. "You want proof?" He steps closer and jams the gun against my chest.

If I'd been paying closer attention at that shooting range, I might have remembered how to take a gun off someone. I mean, I'm pretty sure that's something they cover.

But I didn't.

So I can't.

I don't dare try. Because his finger is curled around the trigger, and I have a feeling the smallest jolt will send a bullet straight into my heart. Ain't no coming back from that, not unless you're the Son of God. And I'm pretty sure he's come and gone.

"Yeah, proof would be nice," I tell him, barely moving my lips in case he sees it as a threat. "But only if it's no trouble. Don't want you going out of your way to prove your innocence or anything."

He narrows his eyes at me. His lips move. "Apollo."

"You got me." It's hard to be cheery when there's a gun digging a hole in your pec, but I fucking try.

"You worked in the laundry at Saint Amos." His voice is soft now, his eyes unfocused.

"It was the kitchen, actually. But you knew that already."

"Why would I?"

And it's fucking weird, in that second, I believe him. But I'm probably biased because my cause of death is so close I can lick it.

"Everything you're looking for is on Keith's hard drive."

If I had ears like a dog, they'd be pricking up right now. "Yeah? Where's that? Gomorrah? Sodom?" I can't help it. I kid around when I'm nervous.

The way Gabriel's jaw ticks, he's not amused.

"In the study. In the safe. Same combination."

"What, the study door and the safe?"

He makes an angry sound and steps back, shaking his head. "I don't care how he made it look. I didn't do it. None of it." Another step. He's brighter now, lit up by the faint gray light of the overcast sky.

But before he turns to leave, I say, "And what about that file on your hard drive? The archive you hid in the system files? Same combination?" I know it isn't. My password cracking program already went through the numeral-only phase.

"Archive?" He turns back to me. "It's one file."

My heart legit skips a fucking beat. "Same combination though, right?" I ask. "That also going to prove you're innocent?"

"It's password protected." He looks at the ground. "If you can open it, show it to Trinity." When he looks up, his eyes have a dark shadow over them that has nothing to do with the rain that's on the way. "Then maybe she'll change her mind about me. About them. About everything."

Un-fucking-likely.

"So what's the password?"

Gabriel's face turns to stone. "I don't know, child. I've spent years trying to figure it out." Then he shrugs and starts walking away. He glances back at me. "Promise me you'll show her."

Anyone with a shred of sense in their heads will tell you to never make a deal with the devil. But they've never faced a devil like Gabriel.

I guess he's had years to practice his poker face, because fuck knows I can't tell if he's bluffing.

And it's kind of a stupid request. I mean, why wouldn't I show Trinity? She's as much involved in this as any one of us.

"Promise me." He's stopped walking. Somewhere along the line, he put the gun back in his pocket.

I drag my fingers through my hair before I remember about the blood, but luckily it's dried already. It's still gross though, still makes me light-headed even thinking about it.

Gabriel's face collapses. "Please."

"Yeah, fuck. Whatever."

He grimaces, perhaps for my language, perhaps for my vagueness, but it's as good as he's going to get. And I guess he realizes that, because he turns and walks away.

Follow him.

But instead I slide my back down the concrete wall and sit on my ass, trying to process why the fuck I let Gabriel get away.

CHAPTER TWENTY-TWO
TRINITY

"...but I can't blame you. *I'm* pissed off at me."

Consciousness ebbs and flows, bringing with it a familiar voice. Who's Apollo talking to? He seems agitated.

"You weren't there. You didn't see the look on his face. How he spoke about you."

"Who?" I try to say, but nothing comes out. My lips don't even move. I feel like I'm caught on the edge of sleep. My brain is certainly foggy enough. And all I want to do is slip away again.

Apollo drops his voice, makes it raspy. "Promise me you'll show her."

My fingers twitch. My lips move. "Apollo."

But he's so caught up in what he's discussing with the other person in the room, he doesn't notice.

"If I can just figure out that password. But what the hell is it? He said the combination was the same for the study and the safe, right? But the study didn't have a lock. The basement had a lock...but we'd have to get back inside the house to check it out. And now that it's a crime scene, the fuck that's going to happen, right?"

Lord, maybe I should go back to sleep. I can't understand a word he's saying.

But then someone's holding my hand. "Trin, listen. I know you're in there somewhere. Can you wake the fuck up and explain this to me, please? Maybe you can decode the Gabriel Chronicles, and that would be swell, because Cass and Reuben are pretty pissed off with me. I need a win."

Mmm. Sleep. That does sound good.

"Come on, Trin."

How can I say no?

I force my eyelids open. They're heavy, fluttering like a downed butterfly. Too-bright light spears into my head. "Ow." I choke out hoarsely, squeezing my eyes shut again.

"Hey! You're back!" Another squeeze to my hand. "Fuck yeah." Something brushes my cheek. "Okay, so let me fill you in, right? I was chasing after Gabriel, and—"

"Apollo, enough." A shiver chases through me when I recognize that deliciously low and rumbly voice.

Reuben.

I force my eyes open to slits and move my head to try and find him.

He's standing opposite Apollo, on the other side of my hospital bed. As I catch sight of him, he wraps his hand around mine. So warm and tight.

"Welcome back," he says quietly. "I hope you had pleasant dreams."

"Course she did," another voice says, the speaker out of sight. "Because she was dreaming about us. Weren't you, darlin'?"

I have to tip my head forward to see Cass. He's lounging in a chair pushed to one wall, but he stands and comes closer when we lock eyes.

"What happened?"

The last thing I remember is taking Gabriel to the bell tower. How he found the photo. And then...him shoving me against the wall. I hit it hard—is that why I'm here? I shiver violently, and Apollo immediately tugs the thin hospital blanket at my feet all the way up to my chin.

"Body warmth will work better," Cass says, giving me a lopsided grin.

"Cut it out," Rube demands, throwing him a faint scowl. Then his eyes are back on me. "How are you feeling?"

"Heavy."

"Anesthesia," Apollo says. "It'll wear off."

Rube squeezes my hand. "They said you can come home tomorrow."

"Home?" My mind flashes back to that tiny, cramped room at Saint Amos. To the Brotherhood's lair where Zach shoved a knife between my legs and told me he'd fuck me with it if I showed my face again. I squeeze my eyes shut. "I don't want to go back there."

"Not *your* house," Apollo says through a chuckle, making no sense. "*Our* house!"

"He means our hotel room," Rube says dryly, but looking at Apollo, not me.

"It's where we live," he says, shrugging. "What else am I supposed to call it?"

"It's not home. Not even close." Cass runs his fingers over the top of my foot. "But it'll be a far sight better with you in it, that's for sure."

Anywhere's better than that horrible school. I smile at Cass. At Rube. At Apollo. I get another peck on my cheek from Apollo, and Rube starts massaging my hand. I lift my left hand, and stare at the mass of bandages over it. When Rube catches my puzzled look, he shakes his head and gives me a faint smile. "Dislocated thumb. But it'll heal just fine."

When did that happen?

He ducks down, presses his lips to my forehead. Whispers, "You'll heal just fine, Trinity."

I let out a happy sigh, but that beautiful moment only lasts a second. I wriggle a little to sit up taller, and crane to look around the room.

Someone's missing. Did Zach stay away on purpose? He's made it clear he hates me, so I wouldn't be surprised. But that hasn't stopped him hanging around with me before. Honestly, I'd have thought he'd have enjoyed being here, especially if there was a chance to see me in pain. That's what he gets off on, right? Pain?

But now that I'm looking, I notice an edge to the brothers. A grimness to their smiles. Shadows under their eyes. It's not the kind of concern you get from someone who bumped their head against a wall.

What aren't they telling me?

"Where's Zach?"

When their eyes drop in unison, so does my stomach. Right to the fucking floor.

It makes no sense. He hates me, and I'm terrified of him. But the thought that something's happened to him, it scares me more than that knife up my skirt ever could.

Because I know he'd hurt me...but never more than I could take.

Knowing that, I shouldn't have run off that morning and gone to Gabriel, but I'd thought Zachary would change. I thought being with him, with all of them, would make things different. Like I was sprinkling magic pixie dust on them.

I'm worse than a hopeless romantic. I'm a fucking *fool*.

No one's going to change just like that. And these men? Probably never. The damage done to them is too deep. It may have scarred over, but those scars are permanent.

Instead of trying to change them, I should accept them for who they are.

But something tells me my epiphany came too late.

"Where is he?"

"Let's not..." Apollo trails off.

Cass steps back, waving a hand. "You know what, we can chat about that later. You need to rest."

I turn wide eyes to Reuben, who's looking from Apollo to Cass with a blank expression. "Reuben? Reuben!"

He looks down at me. Strokes my eyebrow with his thumb. "It's too early to tell," he murmurs.

"What is? What do you mean?"

"You don't remember?" Apollo asks.

I stare at him, my voice rising to a shout. "Remember what? Tell me what's going on!" The last I direct to Cass.

He's watching me through his lashes. And then he blinks, like he's snapping out of a spell. "He took two gunshots to the chest. One barely missed his heart. The other...didn't."

Someone *shot* Zachary? My body goes ice-cold. "Oh my God."

Reuben squeezes my hand. "It's too early to tell if he'll pull through, Trinity, but the doctors are doing everything they—"

I pull out of his grip, grab the edge of the sheet, and do my best to get out of the hospital bed. "Is someone going to help me?" I demand through gritted teeth.

Apollo rushes around the bed, but Rube puts out a hand to stop him. I scowl up at Reuben with as much ferocity as I can muster, but before I can open my mouth to cuss him out, he bends and scoops me up off the hospital bed.

Now I'm floating through the air like an aerial dancer. Cass comes over, grabbing the IV stand and wheeling it after us as Rube heads out my hospital room behind Apollo.

I've never been in a hospital before, but I have a feeling I'm in one of the private wards because I was the only one inside the room and there's tasteful artwork on the walls we pass.

We go down an elevator, and when we exit, there's suddenly too much excitement and activity. I burrow back against Reuben, and as if they sense my sudden panic, Cass and Apollo walk in front of us like a shield.

I hear voices murmuring up ahead when we stop. And then Cass says, "Does it look like I give a fuck about visiting hours?"

Rube grumbles something I don't catch, and then we're on the move again. He takes me through two more doors, and then the air is filled with the mechanical beep of machinery and the whoosh of life support systems.

Apollo and Cass part, their faces grim.

Rube takes me right up to the bed as if he won't even entertain the thought of my feet touching the ground.

Zachary's chest lifts and falls in time with the massive machine on the other side of the bed.

He's pale and drawn, his cheekbones poking at his skin. Lips bloodless. Deep shadows under his sunken eyes.

My vision blurs. I blink hard, freeing my tears so I can see him again.

Apollo is talking to someone in the background. A nurse? A doctor? Their soft murmurs don't sound positive.

"Put me down," I say.

"We should get you back—" Rube begins, but I lift my unbandaged hand and lay it on his chest. Still not looking at him. Still focused on Zachary. "Please. Put me down."

I have so many questions, but that's not important right now. Right now, I'm trying to understand why it feels like the world is breaking down around me.

There's no way I could have imagined the things he did and said, but now it feels like it was all a bad dream. The man lying in this bed isn't capable of such violence, of such spite.

It's impossible, but I know it's true, and those conflicting thoughts make me feel dizzy and on edge. I want to shove away those thoughts and focus on my anger, but when I glance around the room, I see I'm not the only one struggling emotionally.

How can I be angry with him when he's dying? We can sort out our shit later.

I slide out of Reuben's arms and land on wobbly legs. He grabs me around the waist, keeping me steady as I lean forward and take Zachary's hand in mine.

"Hey," I whisper, and then clear my throat. "It's me. Trinity. You remember me, right? The little girl who annoyed you so much?"

But nothing changes. There's no quirk of his mouth, no twitch in his fingers.

I glance behind me and tilt my head back to look up at Rube. "Can he hear me?"

Reuben nods, his grim expression softening. "Of course he can."

I turn back to the bed. Move a little closer. I stroke my fingers down the back of Zachary's hand, careful not to nudge the IV drip. "Hey, so, the guys and I were wondering when the hell you're coming back." I try to laugh, but it doesn't come out right. "It's kinda lonely without you." My voice catches on "without you" and when I try and speak again, I realize I've gone mute.

Cass appears at my side. He slides an arm around my waist, just below Rube's, and squeezes me. "Yeah, you fucker. I mean, I get taking a vacation and shit, but this is costing us some serious dough." He laughs too, and it sounds so forced that my heart shrivels up like a dying flower. "Well, guess it's costing *you*."

Apollo walks around the bed, and he hesitates before reaching out and stroking Zachary's head. "You know we still have asses to kick, right? Can't do that if you're lying on yours."

There's quiet. Cass, Apollo, me…waiting.

Rube clears his throat. He hands me to Cass, and I miss his arms the second they leave my body.

When he stands over Zachary's bed, it's as if someone puts a stake through my chest and twists it.

Compared to Rube's strong, broad body, Zachary's looks so...fragile. Broken.

"What you did..." Reuben begins. "It wasn't right. You know that. We all know that. But I'm hoping it was one of those times you couldn't help it."

I turn a puzzled frown to Cass, but he closes his eyes and gives his head a shake, as if telling me he'll explain later.

Rube clears his throat again. Then he reaches out and lifts Zachary's hand before lacing their fingers together.

"But then you did something so brave, so selfless...we'd be dicks not to forgive you." His voice goes thick. "So if you don't want to come back because of what I said, just know that I was full of shit. I do forgive you, Zach."

"I forgive you too," Apollo says. He gives Zachary's head another stroke. "And I need you, man."

"I forgive you." Cass grabs his leg. "And you know I fucking need you."

Then they all turn to me.

But the words stick in my throat. And when I shake my head, tears spill out of my eyes and race down my cheeks.

They don't know what he did with the knife.

They didn't hear how he threatened me.

I can forget about what he did, but I don't know if I can ever forgive him.

"He saved your life," Apollo murmurs. "Doesn't that mean anything?"

"Apollo." Rube's voice is firm, his frown deep.

I glance at Apollo, then back and up at Rube. "What is he talking about?"

Rube points at Zachary's chest. At the two sets of bandages plastered over his skin. "One of those bullets were meant for you, Trinity."

"And one was meant for me," Cass says beside me.

And then it comes rushing back.

My old house.

Gabriel trying to drown me in the bath.

The basement.

Gabriel chasing me down the hall.

Cass at the front door.

When I look down at Zachary again, it feels like someone is wrapping barbed wire around my heart.

"I...forgot." I swallow hard and put my hands over my face. "How could I—"

"Concussion," Apollo supplies, and then shrugs when I look up at him with slitted eyes. "What? You asked."

I lick my lips. He saved my life. Possibly in exchange for his.

Only a cold-hearted bitch would hold a grudge against someone who sacrificed themselves for her.

"I forgive you, Zachary. And I need you too." I look up at his three brothers, and my next words come easy, because I've never spoken truer ones in my life.

"We all need you."

CHAPTER TWENTY-THREE
TRINITY
SIX MONTHS LATER

Water laps against the side of the infinity pool, merging seamlessly with the nearby ocean. It splashes against my body as I slap my arms down on the cool tiles beside the pool. I shiver at the contrast between warm and cold, and almost slip back into the heated water when a pair of bare feet pad into view.

I tilt my head back, blinking water from my eyes as I stare up at Cass.

"Water's perfect," I tell him.

But he just keeps standing there, watching me. If it was any other guy, it would have been creepy as all hell. But it's Cass, and with those stunning blue eyes staring at me, it just makes me feel like I'm melting inside.

"Are you getting in, or you just going to keep gawking?"

"Rube wants to see you," he says.

I stop paddling my feet, sinking a little lower into the water as a chill races through me. "Now? But—"

"No buts." He crouches beside the pool, his swimming shorts hiking up his legs. He's put on muscle in the last few months. Everyone except Apollo has, who flat out refuses to use our mansion's built-in gym for anything more than some light cardio when it rains longer than a day. "You promised."

"Yeah, bu—" I cut off, pressing my lips together. "God. *Now?*"

"Now, my blasphemous little slut," he says with a rueful grin.

I give him a half-smile, and let him haul me out of the water. His eyes rake over my body, taking in every curve. In the past, I'd have wanted to snatch up a towel and cover myself.

But the Brotherhood have taught me a lot of things. Being proud of my body is one of them.

How can I hate something they worship?

Cass leads me back inside the house, but not before we both glance back at the view. The crests of the waves are barely visible—fluffy white lines that chase each other across the pale shore. At night, the ocean sighs like a sleeping beast, and I've fallen in love with it as much as I have with them.

All of them.

The ground floor of the mansion is built for entertaining, but we've never had any guests. What we have is too special. Too unique. People would ask too many questions. Or they wouldn't understand, and try to become part of something they're not.

Cass veers off into the kitchen, and I pause at the foot of the broad, open stairs that sweep up to the first floor. "What are you doing?"

He comes back a second later with strawberries and a bottle of champagne. "Hungry," he lies.

"Bribing me won't work," I tell him, grabbing a strawberry off the tray and popping it in my mouth as we start up. "But I do commend your efforts."

He chuckles at that, but not as enthusiastically as he usually would.

My steps become slower the higher we go up. And then almost stop when I can see over the landing.

They're all there. Congregating. Waiting for me.

The second floor is reserved for the bedrooms, and the mini-theater with its massive TV and an assortment of day beds and recliners. My men spend a lot of time up here, watching movies, sports, reality shows. Soaking up the world they missed the last decade and a half.

Sometimes I join them. But most of the time I'm curled up on the window seat nearby, working through the pile of books beside it.

I missed out on a lot too. Tolkien. Dickens. Rowling. Harlequin. My men don't tell me what I can and can't read. Don't tell me how I can and can't dress.

For the first time in my life, I'm free.

Truly free.

Rube turns to face me, arms crossed over his chest. He's wearing a dark, short-sleeved shirt that looks painted on to his beautiful sculpted torso, and a pair of baggy sweatpants.

Those dark clothes, paired with his black eyebrows and black hair, make his green eyes pop.

I'll never forget the morning I woke up beside him, turned around, and saw his real eyes open for the first time.

I guess just like it's taken me forever to get used to Cass's longer hair. It's not as long as Apollo's but when he's in the mood Cass ties it up in a man bun that makes me start panting.

"Enjoy your swim?" Rube asks, but there's an edge to his voice like he's already planned how much I'm going to regret stalling.

Apollo sits forward on one of the day beds, an unlit cigarette dangling between his fingers. I don't let them smoke inside the house, and I guess he hasn't gotten around to heading outside to have it yet.

He's wearing three-quarter shorts and a too-big vest that shows most of his ribs and chest through the armholes. Cass's favorite pastime —besides watching celebrity cooking shows—is to make fun of his style. He doesn't seem to realize Apollo doesn't have a style—Apollo wears the clothes that are in his cupboard, usually whatever's on top of the pile he sees first.

As if thinking his name summons him, Cass steps up behind me, proffering the tray of strawberries as he presses a kiss to my ear.

"Ma'am."

I wave him away dismissively, but only after I've snagged another strawberry off the tray.

"Fine," I say through a sigh. "Where is he?" I ask, sticking out my hip and trying for all the world to sound like a cocky bitch.

Rube's head tilts and then he steps to the side, revealing the only non-reclining armchair in this space.

Zachary is perched on the edge of the seat. He's wearing a Gucci T-shirt that probably cost more than the couch, and a pair of tattered jeans.

He looks the same as he always has.

Weeks after we left Virginia and came to live in Dana Point in this mansion Zachary bought us, the others started transforming. Like butterflies fresh out of their cocoons.

Cass grew out his hair.

Reuben stopped wearing his colored contacts.

Apollo...okay, he hasn't transformed much. But he does spend a lot less time by himself than he used to. He and Cass go surfing together in the morning where in the past, according to Rube, he'd have gone alone.

But Zach?

Put him in a cable-knit sweater and a pair of loafers, and he's Brother Rutherford.

Which is one of the reasons why it's been six months, and Zachary and I still haven't spoken more than two words to each other.

Because *he hasn't changed.*

Not on the outside.

Not on the inside.

"I did enjoy my swim, thank you for asking," I tell Rube, now blatantly ignoring Zachary. "In fact, I think I'll go have a lie-down. All that splashing around tired me out."

I turn my back, slip past Cass, and head for the master bedroom.

"Trinity." Zach's voice stops me in my tracks. And fuck, I hate that he still has that kind of power over me. "Please."

The taste of strawberries goes sour in my mouth. "No." My back is still turned. "I'm not..." I want to say ready, but that's not the right word.

I hear fabric rustle. Zachary getting to his feet. I hear his bare feet on the floor as he comes closer. The moment his hands touch my shoulders, I spin around and shove him away.

There's a sudden tension in the room, like every one of his brothers is holding his breath.

"I said no." The words are barely a whisper.

Zach watches me, and then nods. He takes a step back, drops his eyes. "Okay."

I blink hard, and look away making sure I don't catch anyone else's eye.

No, he hasn't changed. He might act it, and his brothers might insist he has, but I know he's the same angry, spiteful person he was six months ago.

Sure, he's been going to therapy. But from what Cass tells me—which isn't a lot—he's only just started on a very long journey.

And in the meantime? He's pumping himself full of drugs so he'll be the kind of man we all want him to be.

Calm.

Peaceful.

But what happens when he stops taking his drugs? Will he be holding a knife up my skirt and telling me to fuck off again?

Yes, I'm grateful he saved my life. But he's the whole reason I was in that house to begin with. It's because of *him* that I told Gabriel everything I knew. He's the one that made me question everything I thought I knew. And when I had no answers, I turned to the only man I thought could provide them.

Gabriel.

His brothers think he's earned my forgiveness.

He hasn't.

Not even close.

But every time I try to explain it to them, I get tangled up in words and emotions. So I told them I wasn't ready. That I had things to work through before I'd let Zachary be a larger part of our lives than he is now. Because I can't deny them anything, but I'll be damned if I'll let him anywhere near my heart.

The sound of my damp feet is barely audible over my pounding heart as I head to the top floor. The entire level is reserved for the main suite. Bedroom. En suite bathroom. Massive walk-in closet. A small lounge. A wrap-around balcony with a hot tub.

I lied about going to sleep. I'm too wired for that to even be an option. But at least I can rinse my hair and get into some comfy clothes. My skin's pebbling after being in that warm pool.

When I step inside the black, gold-veined marble shower, it turns on automatically.

Apollo rigged the whole house with stuff like that. At night, my way is lighted with barely-visible downlights all the way down to the kitchen for a glass of water. When I step into the pool, the lights turn on.

I lose myself under the shower's rain setting, trying not to think about the looming argument.

It always comes when I say no.

Then my men spend days trying to change my mind. We fight. We make up. And the whole thing's forgotten for a week or two.

Then the cycle begins again.

I'm considering telling them Zachary has to leave.

But he provides for us. Everything we have, it's because of him. And they've moved on already. They truly forgave him in that hospital room.

It's just me.

Fingers skate down my spine. I spin around, gasping, for some reason expecting it to be Zachary.

But it's Reuben. Naked. Wet.

My eyes trail over his pecs. His washboard stomach. The thick cock in its bed of dark curls.

"What—"

He grabs my shoulders and presses me against the cool marble wall. Then he swipes hair out of my face, cupping my head in his massive hands.

I think he's going to say something, but instead he ducks his head and kisses me.

My arms are around his neck a second later. I press my body against his, savoring the feel of his naked skin against mine. He forces his tongue into my mouth, fighting me back when I resist him.

I know what he's doing. He's softening me up. Hoping I'll change my mind about Zach.

And since I like this game, I'll allow him to play it.

He slides his hand down my stomach and caresses my clit with the tips of his fingers. On cue, I spread my legs, inviting him lower.

But tonight he teases me. The only thing he deepens is his kiss, his fingertips feather soft as they stroke me.

Hot tingles spread through my core. I'm already becoming wet from his touch, and as if he's reading my mind, he takes away his hand and instead grabs the back of my neck.

I could kiss him for an eternity, but now that he's stoked a fire inside me, it's not enough. I need him inside me, filling me, ending the ache he forced on me.

But when I push him away, breaking our kiss, and I stare up into his mesmerizing green eyes, I already know what's going to happen before I open my mouth.

"Fuck me," I command him.

His eyes narrow. "Haven't you learned any manners yet?"

My men are big on manners lately. I can be as demanding as I want in bed, but I have to be polite about it.

But I was set up—again—and that makes me feel rebellious.

I'm ready with another demand, but Rube darts forward and catches my lips with a kiss.

This time he doesn't hold back.

It's fierce and it's controlling and it makes my legs weak.

And he uses that against me. When I sink down, expecting him to grab my ass and haul me up against the wall, he instead breaks our kiss and pushes me to my knees.

"What are you—" is all I get out before he presses his thumb and forefinger into my cheeks, opening my jaw.

And then his cock is sliding into my mouth, already hard, already salty with precum.

He grabs a fistful of my hair and moves my lips up and down his dick.

I would have resisted more, but God I love the sound he makes when I'm sucking him off. I look up at him, and a tremor races through me at the intensity in his eyes. How his jaw bunches like he's barely able to hold himself back.

But thank the Lord he does, because otherwise I would suffocate. As it is, I can barely fit more than half his cock in my mouth.

"We've given you more than enough time," he says, his voice as tight as the seal of my lips around his dick. "So why won't you listen to him? Why won't you even hear him out?"

I hate the fact that they're taking his side. I guess I haven't known them as long as they've known each other, but you'd think they'd demand he pay for what he did to me.

Slamming my hands into his thighs, I push away from him. Rube relinquishes the grip on my hair just enough so that I can choke out his cock.

"He's never even said he's sorry," I blurt out. "But you want me to forgive him?"

Rube's eyes narrow. "He's tried, Trinity. More than once."

I start to argue, but then Rube shoves his cock back in my mouth.

"Every time he wants to talk, you walk away. Or tell him to go fuck himself. Or decide you need a nap."

Oh my God. He makes me sound like a spoiled brat. But with each reprimand, his cock is being shoved into my mouth, so I have no choice but to shut up and listen.

"So when I'm done with you," Rube says, his voice dropping an octave lower, "You'll go out there, and you'll listen."

He tightens his fist in my hair.

It's taken him a long time to even dare to do anything that might bring me the slightest pain. He's refused to sleep with me ever since we arrived at this mansion. He keeps saying he doesn't want to hurt me again. It doesn't matter what I tell him. What his brothers tell him.

And I'm starting to think it has something to do with Zach. I know Rube's not childish enough to bribe me, but...It's as if he needs me to forgive his brother before he can even think of making love to me.

I'm not happy with the fact that I could be the one sabotaging my happiness.

Another twist. Sharp pain brings tears to my eyes that the shower's rain setting patters away.

"Do you hear me?" he asks. His voice is gruff, tight. He's getting close.

I nod, and even bat my eyelashes at him. Then I swirl my tongue as best I can around the tip of his cock, my core clenching at the salty taste of him.

He lets out a deep groan, and then thrusts hard into my mouth as if he wishes he was fucking me instead.

Don't we both?

When he comes a second later, I swallow what I can, but some of his load trickles out the side of my mouth while I'm choking it down.

He pulls out, his cock bobbing an inch away from my lips as he uses his thumb to scoop up the cum dribbling down my chin.

"Don't waste," he murmurs. I dart forward, drawing his thumb into my mouth and sucking it clean.

"Good girl." He strokes my wet hair, and for a second I think he's going to put his cock back in my mouth for another round.

I guess I deserve it.

As much as I hate to admit it, he's right. Ever since he came back from the hospital, I've been avoiding Zach. I refuse to listen to him, dodging every request he's made.

Honestly, I'm surprised it's taken this long for my men to call me to task for it.

Rube crouches, grabs my hips, and helps me to my feet. Then he smooths back the hair straggling over my face and kisses my forehead.

"When?" I murmur, closing my eyes. I'm pretty sure I can reschedule any date I set. More importantly, I'm hoping that if I do set a date, he'll finally do the one thing I've been begging him to for months now.

Make love to me.

He trails his fingers down my body, slides his hand between my legs, and tests me with a crook of his middle finger.

His breath is warm and sweet on my face when I look up at him, waiting for his reply.

But he's wearing a grim expression I don't like one bit.

"Now."

CHAPTER TWENTY-FOUR
ZACH

As soon as I realize my leg's bouncing, I lean forward and rest my elbows on my thighs, lacing my fingers together. I've got nothing to fidget with, so I toy with my fingers, meshing them together then moving them apart, as I wait in the small den adjacent to the main bedroom.

Our bedrooms are on the second level, but Trinity sleeps on the top floor, and everyone usually joins her up there.

Except me.

I was banished the moment I set foot in my own house.

My leg starts jittering again until I push away that negative thought.

A cigarette would have helped. A joint would have been even better.

Trinity doesn't like us smoking cigarettes inside the mansion. Despite the fact we outnumber her four-to-one, my brothers treat her word like law.

I don't understand it. Not one fucking iota.

There's no sane reason for us to bend the knee to a girl. Especially one as little as her.

But she's got everyone wrapped around her little finger.

Including me.

Not that I'm complaining. Trinity fascinates me. Despite everything she went through she only holds one grudge.

I've heard her admit to my brothers that she's forgiven Gabriel. Her parents.

But not me.

What gives?

Tonight is her last chance. If she won't hear me out, if she won't pass that same forgiveness onto me...then there's nothing left for me to do but leave. It would kill me to go, to abandon my brothers again, but I'll have no choice.

Maybe I'll still get the kids on weekends, who knows?

I drop my head, letting out a rueful huff as I watch my fingers work against each other.

Then come the footsteps.

When I look up and see her standing a few feet away dressed in a silk robe that does nothing to hide her exquisite curves, my heart pulses in my chest. I put a hand over it, wincing before I can stop myself. Ever since the surgery, it's been doing some strange things inside my chest.

My doctor says I'm imagining it.

I think he bought his degree.

Trinity's eyes dart to my hand, then back to my eyes. Her face is steel, her body rigid.

Rube comes up behind her, a towel wrapped around his waist. I'd have assumed they fucked in the shower, but from what the guys tell me, that belt cinching her waist might as well be a chastity belt. There's been nothing serious between the four of them since that day in the library back at Saint Amos.

Guess we all still have some issues to work through.

"Well?" she says, quirking her eyebrow at me. "I'm listening."

My hackles rise at her tone, but then Rube sticks out a hand, palm down. I force myself to take a breath, and then I stand, urging myself to stay calm.

"Where do you want to—" I begin.

"Right here. Right now." Trinity plants her ass on the couch opposite to the one I was sitting on, putting a small coffee table between us. Then she spends a few seconds rearranging her robe, as if she doesn't dare let me get a peek at her legs.

"Fine." I sit again, run my palms down my thighs, and wish my heart didn't feel like it missed every other beat.

And then Rube leaves. I stare at his retreating back, my eyebrows shooting up to my hairline.

So much for moral support.

"Can we hurry this up?" Trinity says.

I turn back to her, my lips thinning. But then I remember what Rube said before he went into the bathroom to talk to her.

Don't let her get in your head.

He doesn't know she's been in there since day one. Wasn't able to get her out back then, sure as fuck won't be happening now.

I start off the only way I know how. "I'm sorry."

She sniffs, crosses her legs, and stares out the window at the black ocean. There's a moon out tonight, so the beach glows under its pale light, but I'm sure she's watching the waves. They're hypnotic at night.

But nothing compares to her.

With her eyes off me, I have a rare opportunity to study her. Her dark curls, heavy with water, cling to the side of her neck. I want nothing more than to peel it away and lick up the beads of water it will leave behind.

With the apology out of the way, I can get onto the good stuff.

"I'm not going to defend what I did. Or try and reason with you. It was wrong. Dead wrong. And I shouldn't have done it. But I can't go back. I can't change what I did."

But she says nothing. Just keeps staring out the window.

"Trinity."

I bite my tongue, keeping back another prompt.

When she finally turns to me, her amber eyes are fucking luminescent. "That's it?" she murmurs. "I was wrong, I shouldn't have done it. *That's* your apology?"

I open my mouth, but she doesn't give me a chance to speak.

"You're right, Zach. You can't change the past. But what's stopping you from doing it again? Leaving them again?"

"I just said—"

Wait...*Them?*

That's what this is about? She's pissed because I left my brothers behind?

I frown at her, stand, hesitate. And she tips back her head to stare at me, as if daring me to walk away from the conversation.

Because that will be the end of it. Then I might as well keep walking until I'm out the fucking door.

I move around the coffee table, slow so she doesn't bolt. And she lets me sit next to her, which is the closest I've been since I shoved her out of the way of Gabriel's bullet.

"I was protecting them," I tell her. I reach for her, but she pulls back, eyes slitting warily. "I'd..." I trail off, and then it's my turn to look away because I'm not sure I can bring myself to tell her the next part. Not if I'm still trying to get her to trust me.

"You what? Thought they'd be better off without you? That they'd just go on with their lives?" She twists, facing me, her knees knocking against mine. Then she stabs a finger into my chest, ruthless, no concern for the scar less than an inch away.

"If that's the case, then you should never have come back because it's obvious you don't give a fuck about them."

I open my mouth. She cuts me off.

"If you did, you wouldn't have left them when they needed you the most. They almost got killed, and that's on *you*."

I can't take another stab in my chest, so I grab her wrist. But as gently as I can, only tightening my grip when she tries to tug her arm free.

"*You* almost got killed too," I tell her. "Or did you forget?"

My brothers told me she had a bout of amnesia when she came out of the anesthesia. According to them, her memories all came back. But she's acting like she has no fucking clue what almost happened back then.

If she had died...

Her pulse throbs under my thumb. Quick, strong. She's angry, but she's keeping it under control. I guess we've both learned some tricks the past few months.

Her eyes flick left, right. "We're alone now," she whispers fiercely, leaning in close enough to kiss. "You can drop the act."

My heart slams into my rib cage. Before I can stop myself, I'm grinding her wrist bones together.

She winces, and then a spark of victory lights up her eyes. "They'll believe anything you tell them, Zach, but you showed me your true colors. And I can't unsee that."

And then it hits me.

She's talking about the knife. What I said when I told her to leave.

I drop my head, huff. "Fuck," I murmur.

She huffs too. "Yeah, fuck." Then she pulls her hand out of my grip and gets to her feet. "I won't ever let you hurt them again. Not now, not ever. And if that means you'll always hate me, then you'd better strap in, because it's gonna be a bumpy fucking ride."

Trinity moves to walk past me, but then I'm standing, my body a wall she can't pass. She rears back, glaring up at me, mouth opening.

I don't give her a chance to speak.

She makes an angry sound when I grab her wrist and force her hand against my heart, pushing her palm flush against the thick scar left behind by my surgery.

"You're wrong about a lot of things," I tell her.

"Am I?" she mutters, trying to pull her hand away.

"You were wrong to forgive Gabriel."

She ducks her head, laughs bitterly. "Oh my God."

"You were wrong to forgive your parents."

Her head snaps back, her plump mouth distorting into a snarl. I don't try and stop when she slaps my face with her free hand, but then I grab it too, press that against my chest.

"And you're wrong not to forgive me."

"You don't get to decide who—"

"You want the truth? I told you to leave that morning because I couldn't stand the sight of you anymore."

She gapes at me, indignant, but far from incredulous. How she saw this coming, I don't know. I guess I got my point across better than I thought the morning Gabriel snatched her from Saint Amos.

"You make me sick, Trinity."

Hurt flashes in her eyes.

That tiny spark of pain reminds me of the beast I harbor inside my mind. The one that seeks out violence and chaos...and vulnerability.

That's all it takes.

Just one spark.

And I'm done.

I can never hurt her again. Never bring her pain again. Not like this. I wasn't going to carry on talking. I was going to leave her with those bitter words. But for the first time in my fucking life, I want to ease her pain. Even if it denies me the thing I've always craved so deeply.

But she has to understand.

I slam her hand into my chest. "Every time I looked at you, my heart would twist. Every time you came close, my skin would go cold." I manipulate her hand, bringing it up to my cheek. Not the one she slapped—that one's still stinging, but the other.

I press her knuckles to my flesh and will her to feel that chill.

"Every time we were together, the five of us, I felt like I was dying."

Slow realization turns her bronze-dark eyes to bright amber.

"So yeah, I told you to leave. I shouldn't have, it was selfish as fuck, but when I thought about how I felt around you...a sadist like me...I couldn't even imagine how you made *them* feel."

I glance past her, to where my brothers said they'd wait.

"So I made you leave. And I told myself I was doing the right thing." I shake my head, let go of her hands. "That we'd be better off if you were gone."

Her hands drop to her sides. The hurt is back in her eyes, but it's different. It doesn't fuel me like it should.

I clear my throat. Rake fingers through my hair.

"When I realized how wrong I was...that's when I came back. And it was wrong. I shouldn't have pushed you away from them, Trinity. It wasn't my decision to make."

She stares up at me, silent, barely blinking. Her chest rises as she takes a deep breath, but she exhales without saying anything.

"And what I've been trying to tell you..." I look down, reach for her hands.

I wait for her to pull away so I can turn and leave.

She doesn't.

Trinity lets me take her hands again. Does nothing as I lace my fingers with hers. As I pull her a little closer.

I clear my throat again.

"I'm waiting," she says.

I start to growl at her impatience, but I check myself immediately.

Swallow. Fucking breathe.

"I don't forgive you, Trinity Malone. I don't think I ever can."

Her eyes go wide. Her fingers tighten around mine. "What?" she says, but it's barely a whisper.

"I was broken before I met you. Broken, and selfish. And I was happy not giving a fuck about anyone but myself." I tug her the last bit, until her body's pressed against mine. "Then you came along, and you fixed me. You made me *feel* again. I'd promised myself I'd never be scared again. And then I met you."

I shake loose one of my hands, then the other. I finally get to peel the strands of wet hair from her throat, and run my thumbs down the side of her neck.

"And now I'm terrified all the fucking time."

She puts her hands over mine, her lips parting. "Zach, I didn't—"

"I love you, Trinity. But I don't think I can ever forgive you."

Her eyes are limpid, glowing.

I duck my head. Aim for her lips. And they part oh so fucking invitingly.

But then a finger presses against my mouth, hard enough to push my head back. My eyes fly open, and I glare down at her as she puts her head to the side.

"No."

A most familiar frustration rises inside me. "No?"

"I don't accept your apology." She shrugs. "That was a good start," she says, and then clears her fucking throat. "But it's not enough."

"Christ, woman, what the hell—" I start.

She puts her finger back on my mouth. "Nuh-uh."

I pull away. Bite down on my lip and pretend it's hers instead.

It doesn't work.

I want to rip her to shreds…and then plaster her back together with kisses. I'm trembling from the force of stopping myself lunging at her.

She puts that same finger to her own lips, purses them. Cocks her head again. Taps her lips once, twice, three times.

"What?" I growl, when she stays silent.

"You must be tired," she says.

I shake my head. "Not even a little."

"You should rest."

She takes my hands, laces our fingers, and leads us toward the bedroom. And then my heart does that thing I hate so much—twisting in place before thumping around like a tooth in a loose socket.

"Why didn't you just say you wanted to fuck?" I tell her as I leer at her ass through the silk robe she's wearing.

She stops dead in her tracks, and turns to frown at me. "Who said that's what I want?"

I blink, exhale hard. "What?"

She points at the bed. It's a king-size, covered with pillows and furry blankets. A girl's bed. "Sit."

I don't like the mischievous light in her eyes. "Or what?"

"Or you can leave, Zach." She quirks an eyebrow. "Forever."

At first I think she's dead calm about it, her face not even twitching...but then I see her hands. They're in fists at her side.

So I go over to the bed.

I sit.

And she smiles at me like I deserve a fucking treat.

Trinity turns her head without taking her eyes off me, and calls out, "Guys? I need a hand." And then, with a twist of her mouth, adds a reluctant, "Please."

CHAPTER TWENTY-FIVE
APOLLO

"Shut it, would you?" I whisper, waving a hand behind me. "I can't hear if you two keep yakking like that."

"You shouldn't be eavesdropping in the first place," Rube says.

"Aw, leave the kid alone," Cass says.

I turn and scowl at Cass over my shoulder. "Kid?" I'm almost two years older than him.

He smirks at me from where he's lounging in the hot tub. He practically lives in the thing. I'm surprised he hasn't sprouted scales yet.

I put my ear back to the crack in the sliding door. Rube pulled it closed when he came back a few minutes ago, and then scolded me when I tried to open it.

Zach and Trinity are talking so quietly, I can barely make out more than a word or two. It's driving me nuts.

"Apollo, chill," Cass calls out.

"Shh!" I hiss.

There's a splash, and the slap of wet feet on the deck. The balcony is covered in slats of wood that stretch all the way to the eight-seat hot tub. A yard away, the balcony ends with a glass railing so you can soak up the bubbles while staring out at the ocean.

I fucking love this house.

I've never loved anything as much in my life...

Okay, that's a lie.

"...forgive you, Trinity Malone. I don't think..."

I strain to hear more.

Screw this.

I grab the sliding door. "I need the—" I begin.

Rube lets out a low, "Not a chance," a second before Cass grabs the door and slides it closed all the way.

Right in my face.

"Come on, man. I won't bug them."

"Let them talk," Rube says. He's standing by the railing, leaning on crossed arms as he stares out at the ocean. He faces forward again as Cass splashes back into the hot tub.

"Come and get in," Cass says. "Knowing those two, this could take hours."

Hours?

I sigh, and stand for a few more seconds by the door. I guess Zach will tell us everything anyway when they're done...but how am I supposed to wait that long?

As I'm about to turn around, I hear something.

I'm right up against the door a second later.

"What?" Cass demands behind me. "What is it?"

I love you. But I won't ever...

I turn wide eyes to Cass, then to Rube, who's facing me now.

I creep away from the door like Zach and Trinity are the ones listening to us, and beckon Rube over when I reach the hot tub.

He frowns, but walks over anyway.

Cass glances up at him and then shields his eyes with a flat hand. "Dude, can you put on some shorts or something?"

Rube is still wearing the towel he came out of the bathroom with. "How about you stop looking?"

Cass rolls his eyes, and then trains them on me. "What did you hear?"

"He said he loves her." I step back, clapping my hands together in front of me as I wait for their response.

Cass rolls his eyes again and mutters, "Christ, finally."

Rube looks like he turned to marble. "He said that? You're sure?"

I nod feverishly. "I know what I heard."

Rube shakes his head. "You must have—"

"Jesus, Rube, don't put on that act. We all fucking knew it."

Rube's one eyebrow cocks up. "We did?" he says dryly.

"Fucking obvious from day one. She pushes his buttons just right, and he loves that shit."

And Rube doesn't argue, because I guess he did know. We all did, just like Cass said.

Zach's mental, but under all that repressed rage, and hate...he's just a guy. It's been brutal for us, even after we got out of that basement, and it fucked us up in different ways. Zach went on the offensive. He'd push people away the moment he saw them as a threat. To himself, to us—it didn't matter, because to him, we're one and the same.

I'm so fucking glad he was the one who said it first. Because holy crap, I've been wanting to tell her that for a while now.

Zach's not our leader anymore. We don't need that kind of structure. But maybe it was some kind of respect.

Unspoken, but unanimous.

I love that about us.

We have an unbreakable bond, the four of us. With Trinity...

I don't know if she'll ever be on the same level as us—mentally, emotionally—but we have the rest of our lives to figure it out. And I'm not going anywhere.

Now that Zach's told her how he feels...I'm pretty sure he's not going anywhere either.

"So you think she'll let him upstairs?" I ask them.

Cass rolls onto his back and sticks his toes out of the water, not bothering to humor me with a reply.

"Don't know," Rube says. He comes closer, grabs my shoulder, squeezes. "But that's her decision, not—"

"Guys!"

All three of us spin around to face the door. And I'm sure my heart isn't the only one that goes *thump* at the sound of Trinity's voice.

"I need a hand."

Cass lets out such a delighted chuckle, the hair on my arms stands up. He jumps out of the hot tub, streaming water over the deck as he races for the door. We shove and push at each other, jostling for pole position, but all it takes is a disapproving rumble from Reuben to make us stop.

We look back at him. Cass shrugs, mouthing, "What?"

Rube holds up a finger.

And then Trinity lets out a sulky, "Please."

Rube nods his head.

All it takes is elbowing Cass in the stomach, then I'm the first through the door.

CHAPTER TWENTY-SIX
CASS

"You called," I say, walking up behind Trinity and sliding my hand onto her shoulder. The black robe she's wearing does all sorts of delicious things to my fingertips, especially when I trace her collarbones through the silky fabric.

Zach is sitting on the edge of her bed, looking mighty out of place against the pale pink bedspread.

Rube comes up behind me, but doesn't pass. I guess he's waiting to find out what she wants, just like me. Just like Apollo.

And, judging from the frustrated look in Zach's eyes, he doesn't have a fucking clue what this is about either.

"This is going to get a little tricky," Trinity says, but without taking her eyes off Zach. But she puts her hand over mine, molding my palm over her shoulder. "Where do you think he's going to sleep?"

Apollo's about to say something stupid, I can see it, so I cut in with a quick, "It's a king. There's enough room."

"Is there though?" Trinity muses. She glances up at me, pouting like she's legit having to think about it.

Fuck, I could eat her whole right now. But rather than wolf my way through a delicacy like her, I'd rather take my time and slowly nibble my way over every inch of her.

"So what are you saying?" Rube says.

She looks over at him, and starts stroking the back of my hand. "I don't think he'll fit."

Jesus Christ, she's doing this on purpose. I don't care how innocent she sounds, she's got to know every single word coming out of her mouth is a double entendre. I mean, the guy's sitting on her fucking bed. She's wearing nothing but a silk robe. And I can practically smell how desperate she is for a fuck.

We've spent many nights in that pastel pink bed of hers—me, Rube, Apollo. Nothing more than some light petting and some serious kissing though. She's constantly leaving us with blue balls, and then walking around like she doesn't have a fucking clue how close we came to holding her down and just taking what she seems so ready to give.

I know it has to do with Zach. And I know Rube has this fucked up notion that he'll rip her in half with his giant dick.

If I thought it would make even the slightest difference, I'd have told them all to spend some quality time on PornHub and see how many cunts get ripped apart on there.

We can't break her any more than we already have...and I didn't hear anyone complaining back then.

But after all the shit with Zach getting shot, Gabriel getting away, and our last chance at revenge decomposing in its own shallow grave...I guess we all suffered a bit of a setback.

Hopefully, that shit's all settled now.

"Fit where, my little slut?" I ask her, sliding my hand down the front of her body and cupping a breast.

Zach's eyes move to my hand, then up to my face. I grin at him.

He's the sadist in the house, sure, but that doesn't mean I don't like fucking with him.

"On the bed," she says, as if it's painfully obvious what she was referring to. I give her tit an extra hard squeeze for that, and she lets out an indignant little gasp.

"Then he sleeps on the floor," Rube says.

I barely stop a laugh, glancing at him from the corner of my eye. Rube walks up and comes to stand beside Trinity. He crosses his arms over his chest, and then cocks his head to the chaise lounge pushed against the glass wall opposite the bed. "Or the couch."

"Hmm," Trinity muses. "Maybe the couch."

There's a long, drawn out silence. Then Apollo ducks toward Zach and whispers, "I think she wants you to go over to—"

"Yeah, fuck," Zach growls, standing in a rush. He comes close as he walks past, and gives all three of us a scathing glare.

I almost fucking giggle. It must be eating him up, trying to keep his temper in check.

I've been there to pick him up after each therapy session, and shit gets fucking real in those first few minutes as we fuck off out of Dana Point.

When Zach ratted on me to his shrink, telling the guy I helped him control his urges, I was dragged in there for a session or two myself.

Ain't fuck all wrong with me, so I refused anything more permanent, but I was happy to help out Zach.

Except, now I can't. I'm not allowed to be his pin cushion anymore. We'll never get to finish the smiley face of cigarette burns on my stomach.

The shrink was horrified when I lifted up my shirt, which I found hilarious...which Zachary didn't.

That was my last co-session with them.

So when he walks past and throws us a glare, it feels like it lands harder on me. Like I'm the one who said he has issues he needs to sort out.

Well...he *did* abandon us. And he didn't do fuck all when Gabriel took our Trinity away.

So yeah.

Therapy is his punishment.

And he can glare at me all he wants for thinking I'm a hypocrite.

But I do feel for him. I can't imagine what it's like, having to deal with our shit on top of the maelstrom of pain and suffering churning around inside his head.

So I grin at him.

That makes him huff and turn his back on us. Big mistake.

Don't ever turn your back on a wild animal.

Rube grabs the back of Zachary's neck and shoves him forward, pinning him down on the bed.

Trinity gasps. Apollo shoots forward. I barely manage to grab the back of his shirt and haul him back before he can interfere. When he turns to give me an incredulous stare, I shake my head.

We all have shit to work out with Zach. Trinity, in essence, opened the flood gates.

"You really think he deserves to sleep up here?" Rube grates, looking back at Trinity.

I'm shocked—and a little amazed—that her voice is calm when she says, "Yes."

Rube lets him go.

Zach scrambles up, turns, and Rube's hand is around his neck again. Zach lifts his arms as if he wants to grab Rube's wrist, but then he looks over at Trinity, and his hands fall down beside him as he lowers himself onto the edge of the bed.

Now I'm wishing Apollo had heard more than Zach apparently confessing his love for Trinity, because the fact that Zach's allowing this shit to happen? I'm guessing we missed some serious drama.

Although, "allowing" isn't quite accurate, judging from the expression on Zach's face. I'm guessing there's a hurricane brewing inside his head.

I feel sorry for him, I do. But it's about time he starts manning up.

"How about we use a reward system?" I say, and start stroking Trinity's shoulder again.

"I'm listening," she says.

Rube glances at me over his shoulder. "Reward for what?"

"If he's good, then he gets to sleep on the couch." I move my head beside Trinity's, like I'm the devil whispering into her ear. "If he's bad, he sleeps on the floor."

Zach clears his expression, and no wonder. I like whatever game Rube and Trinity are playing. I want in.

Who knows...tonight we could all be winners.

Apollo's lips tug into the wickedest smile I've ever seen on him.

Trinity steps forward, out of my grasp. And then over to Rube and Zach, gently moving Rube out of the way.

And the sonofabitch goes.

But I guess we'd be in just as much shit if *we* disobeyed Trinity right now.

She touches Zach's chest, and then points to the pink, padded headboard with its big rhinestone studs.

"Sit."

Zach's mouth twitches, but he manages to keep his expression neutral as he shifts back on the bed until his back is against the headboard. He grabs a handful of her pillows, and he's about to toss them over the side of the bed when Trinity clicks her tongue.

"Leave them alone."

He grits his teeth, but then he subsides, looking totally out of sorts amid the mountain of girly throw pillows. And then Trinity climbs onto the bed. And then she takes off her fucking robe.

"Hey," I call out.

She turns to look at me, eyebrows quirked up.

"What the fuck, woman?"

Now it's one eyebrow.

"Impatient, much?" Apollo mutters next to me.

"Yeah, obviously." I wave at Zachary. "How is this any kind of fair?"

Rube chuckles.

The motherfucker actually fucking *chuckles* at me.

"Do you want to sleep on the floor?" she asks.

I drop my gaze. Shake my head.

Trinity faces Zachary and slowly crawls over the bed toward him. He sits up a little taller, glancing over at us with a blank face before looking back at her. Like he thought he knew how this game would go, but now he's fucking clueless.

You and me both, buddy.

I feel like going off and having a sulk. I didn't sign up for a spectator sport. I love a good tennis match, but nothing beats actually holding the racket in your hands and slamming it into a fucking tennis ball.

But she doesn't care. Trinity knows we're all fucking salivating over her tight, curvy little body as it sways over to him.

She taps each of Zach's ankles, and he spreads his legs so she can kneel between them.

This is goddamn animal cruelty. Why the hell are *we* being punished?

She tugs at his belt, biting her bottom lip as she eases his pants off and down his legs. She doesn't even leave him with a pair of boxers.

I'm shocked he doesn't have a boner yet, because I'm already rocking a semi.

Oh, right. He's not wired like that.

That makes all of this even worse. This tease show won't work on him.

She retreats, taking his pants with her. Then she tosses them over the side of the bed.

"Apollo." She turns to look at the guy, and his face lights up like a Christmas tree.

He steps closer, and then pauses. "Yeah?"

Trinity lures him onto the bed with a crook of her finger, and then sits up on her knees when he gets closer. She looks up at him, for all the world like he's the sun and she's the head priestess of a sun-worshiping cult.

She runs her fingers through his hair.

Takes off his shirt. Helps him out of his pants. Then she pats his chest and turns to look at me. Beckons me.

I'm up on that bed so fast I get carpet burn from the fucking sheet. She doesn't have to help me out of my pants—they're off before I get within a foot of her.

Trinity looks down at my dick and then back up at me with rosy cheeks. For all the world like the fact that she's made me this hard is something she's struggling to come to terms with. Then she pats me on the chest.

But I dart forward and kiss her instead. Because fuck the rules—I'll go mad if I don't taste her right this second. She responds with a moan that makes my dick throb, and then pushes me away.

"Wait," she says through a laugh. "Just wait."

"Fuck, woman," I growl. "What do you think we've been doing the last six months?"

"Cass," Rube says, voice low.

My skin prickles in warning, and I sit back on my haunches like the good little pet I am because that's how desperate I am to ensure she'll let me stay on the fucking bed.

I feel so fucking whipped right now.

And I couldn't give a shit.

Is this what love is? Because, fuck, I'd never have thought it felt this good.

She calls Rube up next. The bed gives a little creak when he gets on, and I know I'm not the only one who flinches.

Come to think of it...if any one of us could break her, it would be him.

She tugs the towel from his hips, and then kisses each of his pecs while she stares up into his eyes. But when he reaches for her, she leans out of the way, shaking her head.

She takes Apollo's hand and leads him to the middle of the bed. She positions Rube at her left, me on her right.

When she finally turns back to Zachary, he shifts a little like he's wondering what's going on in her pretty head.

And damn it, so am I.

Right now I wouldn't rule out a circle jerk.

Then she turns around and offers Apollo her deliciously plump ass.

"Oh," he says. "Fuck."

I roll my eyes and start shuffling over to him. If he doesn't know how to fuck our precious Trinity from behind, then I'm going to show him exactly how it's—

A hand slams into my chest, halting me. I glare across Trinity's back at Rube. "Man, come on."

He shakes his head, and I swear he's suppressing a smile. "Do you want to end up on the floor?" he asks.

Douche bag.

Meanwhile, Apollo's murmuring, "Um," and stroking Trinity's ass like he's never seen a woman in his life before.

I feel physical pain right now. And that's because my cock is rock hard and I have nothing to stick it into.

Trinity reaches around and hands Zachary's belt to Apollo.

I shiver. Hard.

I'd been staring so hard at her perky little tits, I hadn't even noticed when she took Zach's belt off his pants.

Which, I'm guessing, was her plan all along. Because judging from the groan Zachary lets out, Apollo's suddenly stiff body, and an inhale that gives Rube even bigger pecs, none of them noticed either.

"Oh, Trin, no..." Apollo protests weakly.

So she slaps him with the belt. Not hard—I mean, he barely even flinches—but it's enough to make him reconsider his position on BDSM.

He pats her with the belt.

Christ. I can't even.

"She's supposed to feel it, jack ass," I tell him.

Apollo looks up at me, cringes a little, and whacks her again. This time at least hard enough to leave a faint mark.

She lets out a little sigh, and promptly lays her head on Zach's thigh, an inch away from his dick.

Which isn't so flaccid anymore.

"Do you want him to hit me harder?" she whispers, looking up at Zachary.

All he does is groan, and then shift like he wants to get off the bed.

Rube and I move in unison. We each grab one of Zach's shoulders and slam him back into the headboard hard enough to rattle it against the wall.

He sends us both an angry scowl, but settles down when Trinity moves a little closer, nestling between his legs like a sleepy cat.

From the way her head's positioned, I'm sure Zach can feel every breath on his dick.

God, and here I thought she was torturing us? Zach's got the best fucking view in the house, but he can't touch her, can't move...and worst of all, he's not the one holding the belt.

A powerless sadist.

I fucking love it.

And maybe that means I have a touch of sadism in me too, because I'm getting hard from the tortured look on his face.

Apollo belts her again.

Trinity puffs out a sigh.

Zach groans and presses his eyes closed.

"Watch," Rube says, his other hand going around Zach's throat.

I wouldn't call Rube violent—not in the slightest—but he does have a thing with necks. I don't even want to go there, because I don't know if it's something related to his time in the basement, or a kink he picked up along the way.

It's also the only thing that Zach seems to respond to. And maybe that's the sole reason Rube does it.

Thwack.

I stare down at Trinity, at the look of rapture on her face, and I know she's not faking. The moment I set foot in her tiny room at Saint Amos, I knew she was a freak.

I bust in there, and she looked up at me like I'd opened God's bedroom window. But I get that a lot. And that's not what did it for me. I knew the second I threw her up against that closet door that she was hot for me.

Not like she was one step away from spreading her legs or anything. It was more...subtle than that. It was the way she looked at my mouth, how her breath turned into a little pant. Like she was terrified of what I was about to do to her...but she couldn't wait for me to start.

She loved what the four of us did to her the day we took her virginity. She flourished under our hands and our mouths and our cocks like a fern unfurling after the snow melts.

Now she's here, eyes fluttering as Apollo leaves stripes on her ass, and it's perfect.

Everything about this moment is perfect.

I don't know how long it will stay this way...but I'll be praying every night that it's forever.

CHAPTER TWENTY-SEVEN
RUBE

I t's like I snap out of a trance when Trinity murmurs, "Stop."

Apollo lets up immediately. I don't think he got in more than eight or so shots, but every blow to Trinity's ass was torture for me, so I can't imagine what he was going through.

I wanted to stop him. I wanted to grab her and wrap my arms around her and then fuck up everyone who'd been watching and not helping her escape that belt.

But she *wanted* this.

And I don't know how I'm supposed to feel about that.

Apollo's chest rises and falls as he looks up at us each in turn, like he's also just waking up. He drops the belt and moves away, eyes widening when he sees his own hard dick.

Why is he so surprised? No mortal man could have heard the sounds Trinity made and not have a fucking hard-on. We're all hard— even Zach.

I expect her to start sucking his cock. She was teasing him the entire time anyway, she might as well. I'd be happy to watch.

But then she pushes up onto her hands and knees, and turns to look at me. Her eyes are a dark bronze, her cheeks flushed, her lips gleaming. She licks them, and I quickly focus on her eyes again, like she'd caught me watching porn.

"Do you want to fuck me?" she asks, voice breathy, unsteady.

I can barely speak but I manage to get out a rough, "Yes."

"How badly?" Another slow lick of her pink tongue over her gleaming lips.

"Very fucking badly."

"Want to know how much I want you?" she murmurs.

In that moment, it's as if no one else exists. Everything—everyone—else fades away as she leans closer.

We are all barely more than a foot away from her and Zachary. I can feel the warmth of her body. Zach's.

I take my hand off his throat, and he coughs—just once. But I'm still holding him back, away from Trinity, because if he lunges at her I might kill him.

Which makes no sense, because I'm not a jealous man. But I guess I've just learned the extent of my patience.

It's most certainly run out.

"Rube?" she whispers.

"Yes," I say, after clearing my throat. "Tell me."

She shakes her head. Turns her shoulder to me. And then she lies back against Zachary.

I can't stop the growl. And Zachary looks over at me like he doesn't like the sound of it.

Trinity lifts her knees and kicks up on the bed, so her ass is on Zach's stomach. His head is beside hers now, which means he can easily kiss her if he wants, but at least his cock is far away from her pussy.

That should make me feel better, but it doesn't.

It's still closer than mine is.

She glances away from me, to Cass, putting her finger in her mouth and chewing on it like she's suddenly shy. Perhaps she is, because it's only when Cass slides a hand over her knee and urges her leg to the side that she opens them.

Apollo lets out a groan. Trinity looks at him, and cocks her head to the side. "Swap with Rube," she says.

For a second I almost feel sorry for him, especially when his face crumples with dismay. But he had a solid view of her ass and pussy while he was belting her.

My turn now.

I'm in front of her a second later.

Cass urges her leg open a little wider, and Apollo does the same with her other leg.

Revealing the light fuzz of hair on her mound and the dark pink slit between her legs I'm dying to shove my cock into.

"Fuck," I murmur.

And then Zach slides his hands down her stomach. My eyes fly to his, my teeth gritted. But I can't stop him. He can do what he wants, unless Trinity says otherwise.

And thank God, she does.

She clucks her tongue. Apollo and Cass grab his wrists and wrench his fingers off her belly. He moves under her, pressing his lips into a line as if he can't bear to have her on top of him anymore.

And that makes Trinity giggle.

I hope to hear that sound every day for the rest of my life.

She slides her hand down her stomach, locking eyes with me again as she strokes her fingers over her pussy. Even without touching her, I can see how wet she is.

How badly do I want to fuck her?

More than there are atoms in the universe.

She lifts her hand and presses it to Zachary's lips. "Lick," she commands him.

And the greedy bastard does just that. And then groans like he's sipped ambrosia.

"See?" she whispers, dragging her fingers through her soaked pussy again. "That's how badly I want you to fuck me."

My jaw bunches, and my cock throbs. I grab it at the base, trying to hold it still, trying to throttle it into submission. Trinity's eyes flutter down, and I feel her gaze on my dick as if she's stroking me.

"What the actual fuck are you waiting for?" Cass demands. "Because if you don't have your cock inside her in the next second, it'll be mine."

"I don't want to—"

"Hurt me?" she cuts in. "Do you think it'll hurt more than the belt?" She glances up at Apollo. "Would you like to belt me again?"

Zach lets out a soft, "Fuck," like he can't even handle the thought. And from the way his cock starts bobbing, I'm thinking he won't be able to control himself much longer.

So I shift up the bed. I wrench Zach's legs aside, splitting them open as wide as Trinity's so I can get closer to her.

I lean over her, my hands brushing Zachary's ribs, and press my mouth to hers.

I should be happy with our kiss. It's fierce and ravenous...but my dick falls against her stomach, and the feel of her satin skin against my dick fills me with an insatiable lust.

It's not enough.

It will never be.

"Make sure she's really wet though," Cass says. "Don't want to rip her in two."

There's a laugh in his voice. I lean back, and look down as he trails his fingers over Trinity's stomach.

Her belly flutters at that touch. She gasps when Cass squeezes her clit, and then groans when he slides his fingers inside her.

My cock starts bobbing too, blood pumping furiously into the thick shaft. I grab it so it won't interfere, but when I see how Trinity's pussy starts dripping, I can't just sit here with my dick in my hands.

But before I can move, Apollo reaches over and smears her juices along her taint and over her back door. And the sound she makes at that has my cock throbbing in my hand like I'm seconds away from coming.

If she hadn't sucked me off in the shower, I'd probably be emptying my load all over her tits right now.

The torture is real, me sitting back and stroking my dick as Apollo and Cass finger fuck her inches away. And when they slide their free hands under her knees and drag her legs up alongside her chest, opening her up for me, it takes every fucking molecule of willpower I have not to thrust into her.

But she's so close.

Her body goes tight. Her eyes are closed, her mouth open. And when Zach's fingers glide around her ass, when he strokes her back door and then dips the tip of his pinkie finger inside her, Trinity comes.

With a growl I feel more than hear, I shove my hips forward. Not caring who or what I touch on the way, I force the crown of my dripping cock against her pussy, and then smear it through her slick, hot cunt lips.

She shudders, whimpers.

I look down, mesmerized how her pussy swallows the tip of my cock. Grabbing her ass, I lift her hips clean off Zachary's stomach.

She makes as if she wants to grab onto me, but then Apollo and Cass grab her hands and force her fingers around their dicks.

I'm not surprised when Zachary grabs hold of his own dick, taking advantage of the fact that no one is policing him anymore.

Cass happens to look over, and he sees what Zach's doing, but now it's like the four of us are sharing a secret. Because Trinity's head is thrown back on Zach's shoulder, and she doesn't seem to know what fucking planet she's on.

So we let Zach jerk himself off. And he and Cass and Apollo watch as I take my dick out of Trinity's pussy, smear it through her dripping folds, and then slap it over her clit.

She gasps, her body convulsing. "Oh God," she murmurs hoarsely.

Zachary groans, and then bites her ear. She turns to him, stares at him, openmouthed and lost as I slide my wet cock over her clit.

She's still stroking Cass and Apollo's cocks. And they're watching me tease her with my dick.

"Reuben," she moans, finally turning back to me. "Please." She whimpers, squirms in my hands. My fingertips sink into her ass as she wriggles around. "Please fuck me."

God, how am I supposed to say no?

I bite down on my lip, grab my cock, and guide it to her entrance.

"Christ," Cass murmurs. "Why the fuck is this so hot?"

"Because he's got a big dick," Apollo says breathlessly, "and her pussy's too fucking tight by half. He'll never get it in there."

I want to tell them to shut up, but I don't. Because every word ratchets up my own arousal a thousand-fold. Even the glimpse of Zachary's fingers moving over his own cock is making my balls ache.

"Is she wet enough?" Cass asks, and then swipes his fingers over her clit.

"She's fucking soaking my cock," I manage.

"Fuck, she is." Cass groans. "Beg him for his cock, my beautiful little slut," he says, reaching over and grabbing a fistful of her hair.

"Fuck me," Trinity says, turning to kiss the inside of Cass's wrist.

"Hard," Cass says.

"Fuck me hard," she says, her eyes shining with lust when she turns to look at me.

I force myself deeper inside her, her tight little pussy making every inch a struggle.

"Oh God, I'm so fucking close," Cass mutters through his teeth. He slaps away her hand and moves up the bed. "Open your fucking mouth, my little slut."

Trinity turns to him, eyes wide with shock. "What did you—"

He grabs her jaw, forces open her mouth, and rams his cock down her throat.

I squeeze her ass hard, and she yelps in pain, but the sound is muffled around Cass's cock. He fucks her mouth, a hand fisted in her hair, the other around her throat, pushing her into Zachary's chest.

Zachary groans, and I feel the aftershock of his body convulsing as it travels through Trinity's body right to my cock. Zach's cum hits her cunt, soaking my dick. I flinch at the unexpected heat, but it makes sliding into her a little easier. So I go in another inch while Cass forces his dick between her lips again and again.

Then she chokes. His load seeps out between her lips, but he doesn't take his dick out. He slams a fist into the headboard as his back arches, and rams another inch of himself down her throat.

She chokes again, and this time he pulls out. She splutters and gasps, dragging a hand over her mouth and giving him a death glare. "You fucking asshole!"

He taps the side of her face. Laughs. "Oh, sweetheart, I'm only getting started."

He looks over at me, a strange smile lifting the corner of his mouth. "We're all only getting started."

CHAPTER TWENTY-EIGHT
TRINITY

I thought I was in control.

I'm not.

I thought they were just pawns in my game, that I could move them about and give them orders.

They're not.

And the most fucked up thing about all of this?

I'm loving it.

Every lewd, hedonistic second of it.

Because I don't want to control them. I want them to take what they want, when they want it. As rough and as savagely as they want, as they can.

Apollo wraps his hand around mine, forcing me to stroke him harder and then slower. From his face, he looks ready to come too. And when he looks up, rapturous, it's as if Cass knows too.

"Ever had your dick sucked, Apollo?" Cass asks.

He shakes his head, lips parting.

And then Rube starts pushing his dick into me again. Just the tip, and that already stretches me. I moan, rocking my hips to try and get him deeper inside me, but Apollo and Cass are still holding me down. Spreading my legs for Reuben and making sure my pussy is as wide open as it can go.

"Open your mouth again, my little slut. You have another dick to suck."

I glare at Cass, because now he's talking in rhymes and sounding so full of himself I want to slap him.

And fuck it, I do.

He looks back at me, mouth open, and puts his hand on the mark I left on his cheek.

"You didn't just do that," he murmurs.

Everyone stops.

"Cass, I'm—"

But then he ducks his head and I can't get another word out.

I lose myself in his kiss, feeling Apollo's dick throbbing in my hand as I hang on for dear life.

Zach starts stroking my back door again, and my body starts to tremble. Cass pulls back, pushes open my jaw, and turns my head.

Apollo doesn't quite make it inside my mouth. He shoots cum all over my lips and chin, and then tries to pull back, biting his bottom lip.

So I dart forward and close my lips over his cock, fitting as much of him as I can into my mouth, and licking him clean.

He lets out a low groan, his fingers sliding into my hair, tugging me down another inch.

Hands grab my breasts. Squeeze. It takes me a second to realize it's Reuben. He wants my attention now, and I have no choice but to give it to him.

Especially when he drags me off Zachary, lands on his back, and puts me down on top of him.

My legs go to either side of his hips, and I drop my head when I feel cool air over my pussy. I'm spread open, perfectly poised for Zach and Apollo and Cass when Rube shoves the first inch of his cock inside me.

A hand caresses my ass. Slaps me—hard. I turn around, expecting it to be Zach...but it's Apollo.

I lock eyes with Zach, and he moves around me on his knees.

Rube pulls his dick out and uses the crown to massage my clit. And then he grabs a fistful of my hair and drags me down for a kiss.

Which sticks my ass right into the air.

So no surprise someone licks me from pussy to ass and then sticks their tongue inside me. I whimper into Rube's kiss, and he pulls back my head as if wondering what's going on.

I can't even look back. I have no idea who's tongue fucking me. And when a second mouth joins the first, I have even less of a clue who's doing what back there. But when Zachary comes into my peripheral view stroking his dick...

Well, it could only be Apollo and Cass back there.

One of them shoves a pair of fingers inside me. Fuck, for all I know, they each have a finger in there.

My mouth falls open, bliss quivering through me as Rube keeps rubbing his dick over my clit.

"Fuck, I'm getting close," I warn him. Them.

They don't listen.

They don't fucking care.

Whoever's fucking me with their finger, they start picking up the pace. Their hand thumps into my pubic bone, sending a violent pulse through me with each impact.

There's a mouth on my clit now. A tongue that keeps lapping against my entrance. Another finger on my back door.

When Rube tightens his fist in my hair and shoves my head to the side, my mouth is already open for Zach's dick.

Not because I was expecting Rube to force me to suck him, but because I'm gasping for air.

Rube uses his grip to slide my mouth over Zach's cock, keeping up a steady rhythm. Then he grabs one of my hands, leaving me balancing like a tripod, and wraps my fingers around his dick.

I've never had to multi-task like this before. I don't even know if I'm doing anything right.

But when a mouth latches onto my clit and starts sucking as his tongue flicks that sensitive nub, my climax speeds closer.

A second mouth licks my pussy as the pair of fingers ramming inside me slow...slow...stop.

"Fuck!" I pant out. "No! Don't stop!"

But they do. Apollo and Cass pull back, leaving me a shaking, shivering wreck seconds away from a climax.

And then I realize why when Rube wraps his hand around my fingers, and helps me guide his cock to my entrance.

He uses the tip to push apart my lips, and slowly sinks the first inch into me.

Zach moves to the back.

Hands grab my ass and gently urge me to part even more.

And then a second cock brushes my pussy.

"No!" If I could have looked back, I would have, but Rube's still got his fist in my hair. "No, you won't fit!"

Zach lets out a dark chuckle. "Exactly what you said," he says.

Then he drags his dick up and pushes it against my backdoor.

"No! Fuck!" I start struggling.

There's no way I can handle this. It's too much. Who the fuck was I kidding?

Rube grabs my head, brings me down close. "If you can take me, then you take him too."

"No, please!" I'm still struggling, and Zach's dick slips away from its target.

"Hold her down," he growls.

Immediately, I have a hand on each thigh. Apollo and Cass force my legs open wider, and one of them even wraps an arm around my waist, holding me steady.

Someone starts teasing my clit with their fingertips. I hear someone spit, and feel wetness on my skin.

Zachary tests that too-tight opening again with his dick. "God, you're fucking beautiful."

Teeth nip my ass.

I'm done trying to figure out who's doing what. I'm drowning in ecstasy.

Fingers touch my pussy lips, drag me open.

The arm around my waist forces me down, and Rube's cock thrusts into me. Fingers stroke my backdoor the second Zach's dick slips away, but it's only to spread some lubrication. Because then he's back, and he's forcing himself inside me.

"No, God, please!" I'm sobbing. Choking.

I feel like I'm bursting, but there's no pain. Just so much fucking pleasure I don't know what to do with it.

I let out a hoarse scream when someone comes on my back with a groan.

And then Rube drags me down for a kiss. Filling my mouth with his tongue, as my pussy is forced down onto his cock.

When I come, the world stops.

I can't breathe.

My body locks up.

And then the agony of pure bliss hits me. Warm wetness slides out of me as Rube starts fucking me. As Zach eases his cock in and out of my backdoor.

"Fuck her harder," Cass commands behind me. "I want to hear her scream."

And they hold me down so Rube can do just that.

And I do scream.

And then I cry.

And then I come again while I'm still recovering from my last orgasm.

But when Rube's ready, and I see his face tightening, feel his dick throb, I grab his face and I kiss him as hard as I can.

Because I'm theirs. Wholly. Truly. To do with whatever they please. To admire, to worship, to satisfy, to fuck.

All they ask is that I accept the fact that they all need me. Each and every one of them.

And I do.

Because I need them just as much.

I've finally found my real family. They're kind and loving and genuine.

Everything a family should be.

CHAPTER TWENTY-NINE
TRINITY

I'm met with the aroma of baking bread, coffee, and bacon when I walk downstairs. My mouth is already watering by the time I reach the kitchen and see Cass at the cooker.

"Smells incredible," I tell him, sliding onto one of the bar stools in the breakfast nook so I can watch him while he cooks.

I never knew he was such a keen chef. But he's a hedonist like me, and food is one of our weaknesses.

He turns, bathing me with a gorgeous smile as he takes me in from head to toe. "Morning, my beautiful mess," he says.

I laugh, not even bothering to disagree.

My curls are all over the place, the shirt I found on the floor to cover up my nakedness before coming downstairs happens to be Apollo's too-big vest, and I'm pretty sure I have at least five hickeys on my neck.

Don't forget the fact that I barely had any sleep last night. I'm surprised I'm not walking with a limp.

"This beautiful mess needs coffee," I groan, but Cass puts up his spatula in warning when I attempt to climb off my bar stool.

"What did I say about setting foot in my kitchen when I'm cooking?"

I quirk an eyebrow at him, but I stay where I am. I've had my ass pummeled with that spatula before, and I don't think I can handle that level of sheer eroticism so early in the morning.

Not without coffee.

Not while Cass is wearing my cooking apron.

He gives me an evil grin, as if he's reading my thoughts, and briefly abandons whatever heavenly dish he's cooking to make me a cup of coffee.

"Are you saying I'm not capable of pushing a button?" I ask dryly, as he sets down a cup in the espresso machine.

"You shouldn't have to," he shoots back. "Not after what we put you through last night."

I blush, and try to cover it up with my hands before he can notice. But he looks back just in time to see my cheeks turn red.

"Fuck, girl," he murmurs, "Don't make me come over there and give you something to blush about."

I barely stop a giggle from spilling out, instead focusing on the coffee Cass slides over the marble-top island toward me. He tosses the bacon and onions he was frying into a large bowl and starts stirring it as he sends me another lewd smile.

Oh God...is he making a frittata again? I take a quick sip of coffee to wash down the saliva flooding my mouth. And I'm not drooling over the food.

Cass looks like he just walked out of a photo shoot. I know he doesn't use product in his hair, so how can it look like he spent hours in front of the mirror teasing it into the perfect bed-head style?

Does it even matter that my apron has a pink unicorn on it?

No, it does not.

He rocks *awsum*.

"Now you let me get this in the oven, then I'm taking you upstairs and—" he begins.

"Breakfast will have to wait," Rube says from the stairs.

We both turn, Cass with spatula raised, me with my coffee cup by my lips.

As soon as Cass spots Rube, he switches off the oven and starts untying the apron. "What happened?"

Rube looks grimly at me, and then flicks his fingers. "Best if you see yourself."

My stomach lurches.

No.

No, no, no! I want to stamp my foot like a five-year-old. Can't I have a little bit of normal?

Cass and I follow Rube up the stairs to Apollo's room. It's kitted out with a double bed, and a computer station that—to me, anyway—looks like something out of the Swordfish movie.

The computer area is the only part of his room that's not chaotic. Everything else is partially submerged under magazines, surfing gear, or clothes.

"Do you ever let the maid in here?" Cass asks. He picks his way across the floor like he's walking through a minefield.

"She was in here yesterday," Apollo mumbles absently, and then pushes away from the table, pointing to one of three massive monitors.

Honestly, the only thing he's missing is a hologram projector.

"What is it?" I ask, standing in the doorway. I don't have a thing about untidiness...I don't like computers very much. The most time I've ever spent on one was when I was copying the files for them off Gabriel's laptop.

I guess maybe that's why I don't like them—they only remind me of bad things.

"It's an article posted a few days ago," Apollo says. "It's...uh..." he looks up at Rube, who nods. "It's about Gabriel."

I frown at him. "He made the news? Why would he do that? He's got to know the police are after him?"

He has Zachary's attempted homicide hanging over his head, a fact that I'm pretty sure was made clear when the police taped up my old house and then froze his accounts.

But it was like he disappeared into thin air after his discussion with Apollo. The police couldn't find a trace of him, and neither could we.

It's been months.

Secretly—*selfishly*—I'd hoped the guys had put everything behind them. That they were starting new lives and leaving their Ghosts and Guardians and all of that behind them.

Now this.

"He...kinda didn't have a say in the matter," Apollo says.

I roll my eyes. "What have I told you lot about being cryptic? It's just plain annoying."

Crossing my arms over my chest, I venture deeper into Apollo's room, until I'm standing beside Rube. He smooths a hand down my head, toying with a curl as I lean in to read what's on Apollo's screen.

VIRGINIA PRIEST FOUND DEAD IN TIJUANA

MY SKIN GOES COLD. "NO," I murmur. "Oh my God."

The article states Gabriel's body was discovered by hotel staff in his room in Tijuana, Mexico a day after he hung himself. What the hell he was doing there was anyone's guess.

I stop reading halfway through. Clear my throat. "Well...I guess that...ends it?" But when I look up at my men, they're all staring at me like they're waiting for the other shoe to drop.

"What is it?"

"You read that last bit, right?" Cass asks, pointing.

I decline to answer, instead I'm craning over Apollo's shoulder again.

The last line of the article sends a centipede crawling down my back.

The executor of Father Gabriel Blake's estate requests that any next of kin contact them urgently.

And then a phone number with a Virginia area code.

"Nope." I shake my head as I retreat. "Not interested."

"Trinity," Rube says, sliding his hand down my shoulder. But before he can grab me, I dodge away from his touch.

"Nope." I cross my arms even tighter. "Nope, nope, nope."

When I turn, fully intent on stalking out of the room, Zachary's barring my way.

God *damn* it! I hate it when they gang up on me outside of the bedroom.

"I'm not calling," I tell him, holding up my hands. "You can't make me."

"What if he left you something?" Apollo asks. "Don't you want to know what it is?"

"I couldn't care if he left me a private jet and some of Fort Knox's gold," I say, glaring at Apollo over my shoulder. "I don't want anything to do with him."

"He's your father, Trinity," Rube says.

"He's most *definitely* not."

"Whatever you don't claim goes to the state," Zachary says.

I turn away from all of them, instead staring out the window at the distant sea. It's idyllic out there which is bullshit, because nothing short of pre-hurricane weather will suit my mood right now.

"Including whatever's in that safe."

The sudden hush in the room after Zachary's statement isn't from us being quiet. It's the hush of breaths being held.

Shit.

I forgot about the safe.

But from their reactions to Zachary's statement, my men haven't. For all I know, Apollo's still been running his password cracking software every second of every day since they left Saint Amos. In fact, now I'm pretty sure they've *never* stopped searching for their Ghosts.

And I want to keep them from their truth because I'm too busy being happy?

I turn to Zachary. "Then go. You can take my social security card and claim whatever—" I wave at the computer "—it is."

Zachary shakes his head. "You have to be there in person."

"Yeah? And how would you know?" I have no right to be angry with him, but I need to channel this frustration—this fear—somehow.

"Because when I had to claim my inheritance after my parents died, I didn't want to be there either." He looks up, to the side. "But I'm glad I did, because at least we have a roof over our heads."

The bastard is guilt-tripping me.

And it's working.

I've contributed nothing to our home. I would have, obviously, but I don't have a penny to my name. No job. No inheritance.

But if Gabriel left me something...

"Fine," I snap. "Then let's go."

"What about breakfast?" Apollo calls out as we all stream out of his chaotic room.

"We'll get something on the way," Cass says over his shoulder.

"Aw, man. I was looking forward to that."

My stomach grumbles quietly to itself as I head upstairs to change.

Yeah, Apollo. You and me both.

CHAPTER THIRTY
TRINITY

I don't like this place. There's too much chrome and glass and expensive-looking art on the walls. Gabriel's executor—a middle-aged woman whose name I already forgot—has a habit of clicking her pen after every statement she makes, like a judge banging her gavel.

"And this is the last one. If you'll just sign here." She taps a line on the paperwork, as if I've been struck blind and can't notice the bright yellow post-it arrow stuck to the side of the page. And then clicks her pen.

Click.

I sign. Date. I slide the form over to Reuben. He signs as a witness. Dates.

The lawyer takes the paper back and then stands, going over to a cabinet with a keypad on the side. But not before she runs her gaze over my men.

I don't know how much she's figured out about our relationship, but the fact that all four of them accompanied me into the room probably gave her some clues. Then there were the hickeys I wasn't allowed to cover up with makeup. Four hickeys...four men...

She should know they're mine. And I swear, if she looks at them like they're a deep-dish pizza and she's just come off a fast, I'm gonna—

"Almost done," Rube says, sliding his hand onto my thigh.

I'm wearing a sunny empire-waist dress. I should feel like a doll, but

I don't. Which is weird, because it definitely felt like Cass was playing dress up with me. He always insists on dressing me and anyone else who doesn't have enough willpower to turn him down before we leave the house.

My curls are scooped up on top of my head, but a few straggle down around my neck. I'm even wearing a touch of lipstick and a slick of mascara, which is usually all they allow me to wear, makeup-wise. I was also denied underwear, but that's a battle I lost a long time ago.

Thankfully I managed to get away with a pair of mules and not high heels like Cass almost always insists I wear.

It's not my problem they're all at least a foot taller than me.

The lawyer comes back with an envelope.

She's already handed me the keys to my old house, which is the only thing Gabriel left me in his will. Apparently, he only had a hundred dollars to his name. He didn't own a car, or any shares or anything. No overseas bank accounts. Nothing.

Just the house which, according to the lawyer, had been transferred into his name less than a year ago by my parents' estate.

"What's this?" I ask her.

And for the first time today, despite my barrage of questions, she shrugs. "It was found among his things. It's marked for your attention only."

"Maybe it's the password," Apollo says.

I don't have to look around to know his brothers are all glaring at him.

Best way to keep a secret? Don't tell Apollo.

"Password?" the lawyer repeats.

I wave my hand, and then toss a curl over my shoulder as I stand. "Private joke," I tell her. Then I stick out my hand, all formal like, and wait for her to shake.

She does, but reluctantly, as if she's waiting for me to open the envelope.

Don't hold your breath, lady.

I turn to leave, when Zachary says, "Did he leave a note?"

Freezing, I stare at the door. Only a few more steps, and we'd have been outside. Free.

But not yet.

"Um...yes. But I can't disclose—"

I turn on my heel, my voice snippy with how desperate I want to be out of here. "I'm next of kin. You can disclose it to me."

The woman looks at my men, then back at me. "I...have a copy."

"That's fine." I cross my arms, giving my boobs a little perk that doesn't go unnoticed. When I take the folded paper she hands me, and head for the door, my men follow me without a word.

Outside in the Range Rover, I'm nestled between Zachary and Reuben on the back seat, Cass driving and Apollo sitting shotgun.

Someone lights a joint, but I'm too busy staring at the envelope in my hands to see who it is.

They read Gabriel's suicide note in the elevator on the way down, handing it silently to each other. Rube wanted to give it to me, but I ignored him.

I don't want to know what Gabriel said.

Judging from their lack of conversation on the topic for the next five floors until we hit ground level, it wasn't important anyway.

"Aren't you going to open it?" Cass asks.

I look up, catching sight of his iridescent blue eyes in the rear-view mirror. "Maybe. Maybe not."

I slip the envelope into my purse, and tuck it between Zach and me. He looks over at the touch, and then grabs my wrist. He holds me for a beat, tight and fierce, and then smooths my hand over his thigh.

"Home then?" Cass asks.

"I'm hungry," Apollo says.

"You ate like an hour ago," Cass sighs.

"So?"

"Christ. Fine. And I'm guessing you want a fucking taco? Where's the closest—"

"Take me to Maude Street," I tell Cass.

Beside me, Rube shifts on his seat. I keep looking forward, willing him not to ask me if I'm okay.

Because I'm not.

But maybe I will be if I can finally burn my bridges.

I told the lawyer that I didn't want the house. That she could sell it. I signed some papers setting it all up.

But I know what my men want.

And now, maybe, I can finally give it to them.

"The safe?" Apollo asks, turning in his seat and grabbing the head-rest. "We're going to look in the safe?"

"It's probably empty by now," Zachary says.

"Yeah, but maybe it's not." Apollo grins at me. "And we know the combination."

"Do you still remember it?" Rube asks me.

Of course I do. It came back along with everything else that happened that horrific day.

4211.

The same combination that opens the basement apparently opens the safe in the study. At least, that's what my men decided after deciphering what Gabriel said to Apollo.

I still can't believe Apollo let him go. Then again...I still can't believe a lot of the things that happened that day.

When we pull up to my old house on Maude Street, I almost wish I'd let Cass drive us to the nearest Mexican take-out instead. My stomach's in knots, and I know it'll only get worse when I'm inside.

I guess word got out about the shooting. Everyone who was home that day must have heard the gunshots. The screams. The ambulance arriving.

As we head for my house, I see a handful of For Lease and For Sale signs down the road. Even the one right across my house.

It's sad. I lived in this house for close to a decade, and the only neighbor I knew was my babysitter, Miss Langley.

I take the house key out of my purse. I stare at it for a second before inhaling deep, putting down my purse, and turning to Rube.

"Okay," I tell him. "I'm ready."

He climbs out of the car and helps me step off the Range Rover's running board.

Then all the other doors open, my men pouring out of the car and circling me like a bunch of secret service agents.

I hold up my hand. "I got this."

"You can't—"

I turn on Zachary. "I can't walk five yards without adult supervision?" I ask, sugar sweet.

His jaw bunches, but he doesn't say anything.

"Can't we just—" Rube says.

"Do you guys think it's booby-trapped or something? Is the whole place going to explode the second I open the front door?" I walk ahead a foot and then turn on them, arms on my hips. "Seriously?"

They have the decency to look slightly embarrassed, but that doesn't stop Cass from opening his mouth to argue.

"No." I lift a finger. "*No.* I'll be right over there." I point at the house. "You'll be close enough to hear me scream."

Ooh, bad choice of words.

"Scream?" Apollo says, practically going to his toes. Rube's hands curls into fists. Zachary's eyes narrow. And Cass isn't lounging against the side of the car anymore. He's standing at the ready.

"Just..." I let out an exasperated growl. "Just stay in the car, would you? I'll be out in a minute."

I turn and head for the house, not bothering to find out if they'll grant me my wish.

I get that they're concerned about my safety, but Gabriel's *dead.* There's no bogeyman ready to snatch me anymore.

But when will they realize that?

My hand shakes when I try and put the key in the lock, so I take a few long breaths before letting myself in.

I leave the door open, turn around, and give my boys a wave.

Only Apollo waves back.

Why do I have a feeling I'm going to pay for this when we get home?

A faint smile toys around my lips.

I should do this more often.

The air inside my house smells stale. There's still blood on the carpet where Zachary was shot. The furniture is still out of place.

But Gabriel must have come back at least once, perhaps after the investigation grew cold, because there's a hint of cigarette smoke in the air.

I pause at the foot of the stairs, and then hurry up them to my room.

It's still in the catastrophic state Gabriel left it in. I turn and take the framed drawing of the *awsum* unicorn from the wall, stare around at the place I called home, and head downstairs with a knot in my throat.

My heart starts beating a little faster when I lift a hand to open the study door.

It's unlocked, but that's no surprise. I heard Gabriel moving around in the study when I was creeping out of the basement, and then he came running. Guessing there was no time for him to lock the door again.

I step inside my father's study and stare around. It's a mess. All the furniture's been shifted around. Books—mostly theological encyclopedias and leather-bound bibles—have been tossed off the bookshelf and lay scattered over the floor.

How the hell am I supposed to find anything in this mess?

And then I see it. It stands out like a beacon, and I don't understand how he couldn't have noticed it.

There's a large leather-bound bible still on the shelf, snuggled between two thick books. It's white, and I already know the letters on front will be embossed in shiny gold.

My mother's bible.

Except...it can't be. Because I took it from her reading corner the night I left my home forever. But when I pick it up, it has the same weight. The same gold-trimmed pages.

I open the cover. There's a letter-sized safe inside, perhaps two inches thick.

4-2-1-1

There's a soft beep.

I go to my knees, laying the book on the carpet so I can open the little safe's door so I can look inside.

A floorboard out in the hallway creaks.

I spin around, my heart climbing up my throat, and stare at the study door. But no one emerges from the hallway after a few ridiculously long seconds.

Jumping at ghosts. Or is it shadows?

I swear, if one of my men come in here because they think I can't look after myself for one second...

There will be hell to pay.

I shake my head and go back to the safe. Open the door.

A stack of hundred-dollar bills. Three sturdy envelopes.

The first envelope has a small thumb drive in it. I take it out, tuck it between my breasts.

Should have brought my purse, but I guess my bra will do for now.

The second envelope has a passport and some folded papers inside.

I open the passport.

Frederick Dalton.

I frown at the passport photo.

Who the hell is—

There's another creak, louder, right behind me. I whirl around, a hand to my chest. My cheeks flush with anger. "I told you to wait in the..."

But it's not Reuben. It's not Cass. It's not Zach, or Apollo.

It's a middle-aged woman I've never seen before, and she's smiling at me.

Which is fucked up, because there's nothing friendly about the gun she's pointing at my face.

CHAPTER THIRTY-ONE
TRINITY

Scream, Trinity, scream!

But my lungs are frozen with shock. I've never had a gun pointed at me before—not one I was aware of anyway. It's more chilling than I'd ever imagined. So malicious. So...impersonal.

The fact that it's a woman holding it doesn't matter. Her eyes are as cold and heartless as the gun's gleaming exterior.

She's dressed in jeans and a faded suede jacket, boots up to her knees. With her auburn hair pulled into a tight ponytail and a large handbag hanging from her shoulder, she could have been just another person walking past on the street.

Instantly forgettable.

When my lungs thaw enough for me to consider yelling out for the Brotherhood, three men walk into the study.

One has his gun aimed at me. The other two have theirs tucked in their belts.

"Get up," the woman says.

I obey reluctantly, my mind churning with useless options. No way I can run past them. And the study only has one window—and it's closed. Maybe if there'd been a gun in the safe...

"Shoes." The woman holds out her free hand and clicks her fingers.

"You...want my shoes?"

It's like there's a swarm of bees droning in my head. The woman tilts her head, as if daring me to say no, and I quickly slip off my shoes.

"Toss them."

I'm so fucking confused, but I throw them in front of the man wearing a black hoody. The other two are wearing dark sweaters, one with the collar of a polo shirt neatly arranged around the neckline.

Hoody picks up my shoes and tucks them under his arm. The man with the polo shirt sticking out of his sweater walks up to me.

I stiffen, my hands going into fists. But he walks right past, crouches, and picks up everything I've left on the floor—the passport, the money, the bible-safe. Then he goes over to the woman and puts everything inside her handbag while she holds it open, her eyes not leaving mine for a second.

"We're going for a walk. If you make a sound, I guarantee you'll need years of therapy to get over what they'll do to you." She cocks her head to the three men standing behind her. "Got it?"

My skin slowly starts crawling off my body. I nod, swallow hard.

I could still scream, of course. My men would be here in seconds. But they'd be walking into a gunfight with nothing but their fists. There's no way in hell I'm letting any of them take another bullet for me. Not when it was my decision to come in here alone.

And I'd joked the front door was booby trapped? Lord, the irony.

The woman makes a show of sliding her gun inside her handbag, still pointing it at me but circumspect about it now.

Hoody moves behind me and grabs the back of my neck. Pushes me forward.

I don't know what horrifies me more—the fact that his hand is cool and dry, or the considering look in his eyes when he passed me.

This can't be happening.

Who the hell are these people?

They're obviously here on a mission—they didn't act surprised to see me here, or at the stack of money. And judging from their weapons, they came prepared.

Did Gabriel send them to search for the safe? Does that mean he's not actually dead?

The thought sends an internal shiver through me.

I need to find out what's going on.

"Who are—"

Polo Shirt moves so fast, I don't have time to get my hands up to defend myself.

If Hoody hadn't still had a grip on the back of my neck, I'd be sprawled on the floor from the brutal backhand Polo gives me.

My eyes water from the pain, and I lift an icy hand to my cheek, trying to soothe the heat.

The woman is smiling now.

Finally, something I recognize.

It's the same smile Zachary wore the morning he told me to leave Saint Amos. When he had a knife up my skirt ready to slice and stab.

Enjoying my misery.

Just like she is.

CHAPTER THIRTY-TWO
ZACH

"She's taking too long," I tell Reuben. "She should have been out already."

"I think she's just saying goodbye," Apollo says. He looks like one of those birds who prance around in front of the mirrors their owners hang in their cages. Constantly ducking down and then lifting his head as if he's trying to check out his own reflection.

He's trying to spot movement in one of the windows, just like us. Trying to stare through that dark slit of the front door Trinity left ajar, down into the passage.

We're playing a game: the first one to spot Trinity wins.

"I'm going in." I grab the door handle, but all it takes is a sigh from Rube to stop me.

"We should give her space."

"Last time we did that, she got herself kidnapped," Cass mutters.

"No, last time Zach chased her away with a knife, she went crying to Gabriel, and *then* he kidnapped her," Apollo says. "Get your facts straight."

My eyebrows aren't the only ones to quirk up at that statement. Apollo's usually the last to challenge any of us, but I guess he's just as concerned.

"Time?"

"Five minutes, thirty-nine seconds since she set foot inside," Cass says, twisting in his seat and giving me a long-suffering stare. "Forty... Forty-one..."

I grimace at him, and he straightens with a faint grin on his face, but I see it slide off in the rear-view mirror a second later.

"So...I have to use the bathroom," Apollo announces. "I mean, when nature calls...?"

We're silent for all of a second before we pile out the car like a bunch of clowns exiting a VW bug. Except we're driving an SUV, none of us have a big red nose, and I doubt any clown has ever looked as grim as us.

I'm through the door first, expecting a whole shit show of things... but not the sudden paralysis that hits me.

My body grows heavy. Time slows. I'm filled with the visceral sensation of my heart pounding in my chest.

Rube grabs my elbow, steers me inside with him. But my eyes have already locked onto the stain on the living room carpet.

Blood.

Not something I'm ever affected by, not like Apollo. I'm not squeamish in the slightest. But this is different.

It's *my* blood.

And Christ, there's so much of it. How did I survive? But I almost didn't, and that's what's rooting my feet in place. I'm dimly aware of Cass and Apollo streaming past me, heading down a side passage that leads deeper into the house.

"No. Shit! She's gone!" comes Cass's voice from down the hall. "I fucking knew we shouldn't have let her come in alone."

"Check upstairs," Rube says, his voice tight, too loud.

All while my mind slowly disintegrates into white noise. Rube shakes me, and then I'm up against the wall. He grabs my shoulders, his thumbs forcing my head up.

"No time for this," he tells me, and for once his words are fast, close together. "Need you to focus. Need you *here*. Not in the past. Got it?"

His voice centers me. Reigns me in. It gathers what's left of my mind and somehow contains it.

I lick my lips. Squeeze closed my eyes. "I'm here," I manage.

The pat he gives my cheek is more like a slap. Then he grabs the front of my shirt and hauls me after him. "We're checking the back!" he yells, aiming his voice up the stairs where I assume Cass and Apollo disappeared to.

Then he drags me after him.

The back door is standing open. We run through it. There's a wooden fence behind Trinity's house, but a section of it is gone. We go through it. We cut across someone's yard, dodging unruly bushes and low hanging tree branches, some of which are still swaying as if disturbed seconds before we arrived.

"There!" I slam a hand against Rube's chest as he turns to run in a different direction. I point.

His eyes go wide when he sees the van. But all he gets is a glimpse.

We run toward it, but we're too late.

The van pulls away with a screech of tires, and by the time we reach the road, it crests a small rise before vanishing behind it.

Unmarked.

No plates.

One in a million.

I already know we'll never find it.

Which means we'll never find Trinity again.

CHAPTER THIRTY-THREE
TRINITY

I flinch every time I hear a sound. Just for that second, I stop shivering. But then the cold leaks back, and I start trembling again.

Most of the sounds come from above.

Faint voices. Muffled footsteps. The scrape of furniture.

Hoody brought me down here, shoved me to my knees, and then abandoned me. I'm still wearing the gag he pushed between my lips the second the back door of the van closed behind us.

Right before he stroked my hair and told me what a pretty little girl I was.

I couldn't answer him, obviously. But I didn't want to. Because I think the woman left him in the back of the van with me on purpose. To remind me what would happen if I tried anything.

Now that I'm alone, now that my terror is starting to go stale, I can't keep kneeling here indefinitely.

I'm on a mattress placed on the floor. Its fabric is damp, and the air has a clingy chill to it.

There's a smell down here. One I don't like one bit. It's so foul that I start breathing around my gag instead of pulling air through my nose.

The sounds coming from upstairs aren't the only ones I hear. There are things in here with me. Small things. Scurrying things. Rats or mice. Their sharp little claws catch against the concrete floor.

It's hard to tell how long I've been down here. It feels like an hour or more, but I think I would have been a lot colder if that were the case.

Hoody tied my hands behind my back. When I fold down onto my heels, that puts my hands in reach of the knots around my ankles. I've already tried to undo the ropes around my wrists—they're much too tight. But if I got the ropes off my feet, I could at least walk around. Maybe find something sharp for the ropes around my wrists.

It feels like another quarter-hour goes by as I work at the knots. Blind, all I have to go on is a vague idea in my head. Eventually I start tugging as hard as I can on anything that feels like it might give way.

Sometimes I forget to breathe through my mouth, and then I have to fight down nausea when that smell hits my nose.

But finally—*finally*—something gives.

The knot loosens.

With a hard tug, I slip free. The soles of my feet prickle as blood rushes back into them. I have to fight back a sudden influx of thoughts about what would have happened if I'd sat here and waited until my feet turned blue, and then black.

I push up, swaying on the mattress, and then hurriedly step onto the floor. I test the knots around my wrists again, but they're still tight, and my hands are aching from untying my ankles.

I give one last violent tug, growling with frustration behind my gag, and somehow lose my balance.

If it hadn't been for the mattress, I'd have cracked my elbow against the concrete floor. But thankfully I land on something soft instead. I lie there for a second, wondering how the hell I ended up here, and then start to push up to my feet again.

But then I realize my hands are by my hips. Still bound, but...maybe, just maybe...

I roll onto my back, lift my knees to my chest, and loop my bound hands under my butt. It takes time—wriggling and swearing and sweating—but eventually I get my hands out in front of me.

I've chafed my wrists so much I smell blood in the air, but now that my hands are in front of me, I can take off my gag and my blindfold.

Shouldn't have wasted those precious seconds, though. It's so dark in here that it doesn't matter if I have a blindfold on or not. I can't even tell the difference between opening and closing my eyes.

But with the gag out, I have access to my teeth. And they can grip the nylon ropes a hell of a lot better than my fingers.

I'm shaking with cold by the time I get my hands free, but I'm so giddy with relief I barely notice.

I slowly turn around, blinking hard as I take in my surroundings. Maybe it's my imagination, but I think I'm starting to see faint shapes in the dark. Maybe there is a little bit of light down here after all.

I go slow at first as I start to explore. I don't want to bump my bare toes into anything, or knock over something that could make a noise.

But the more I explore, the more frantic my movements become.

Especially once I hit the first wall of the small basement I'm in.

CHAPTER THIRTY-FOUR
RUBE

"I need to get gas," Cass says.

I point. "Go down there."

"Oh my God, Rube, seriously. Do *you* want to push this thing? Because I—"

"Go down the fucking road."

An edgy silence fills the SUV's cabin. We're all staring out the windows, trying to spot a white van, a head of dark curls, the slightest thing out of place.

We've been driving around for almost an hour.

I don't want to call it—*refuse* to—but we all know she's gone.

Cass goes down the road I pointed out, but as soon as he reaches the next intersection he doubles back and heads for the gas station we passed about a mile back. He does it without a word, but making sure he doesn't catch my eye in the rear-view mirror either.

Guess I wouldn't be surprised if this got physical.

If the tension eating away at my insides is anything compared with my brothers, then there'll be nothing left of us come dusk.

We have to find her before then.

If the sun goes down before then, she'll be lost forever. That's all I can think. We have to find her before dark. Have to find her before dark.

I should be figuring out how to find her, not what will happen if we don't.

The moment Cass stops the car at a pump, I'm out of the door. I go inside the convenience store, buy a packet of cigarettes, a soda. Zach comes in behind me. He grabs some chips, a six-pack of ginger beer, and another packet of cigarettes. We don't look at each, don't speak. The clerk ringing us up keeps sending us a wary look through her lashes as if she's considering triggering the alarm behind the counter.

Cass is still pumping gas when we get back. Zach tosses his bag into the back seat and climbs up without missing a beat.

I head for a picnic table a few yards away, lighting a cigarette en route.

Grit crunches under shoes behind me, but I don't turn around. "It's Gabriel, isn't it?" Apollo says.

I grunt non-committally, and then turn to face him as I pass him my cigarette.

He shrugs before taking it. "I'm thinking he paid someone to put up that article online. Paid that lawyer chick to handle everything as if he was dead."

"No," I murmur, taking back the smoke. "It doesn't make any sense."

"He wanted her back. Couldn't find her. Knew this would get her attention. Seems pretty straightforward to me."

"Then he'd have taken her somewhere we couldn't find them in the first place."

Back then, when Zach was lying in that hospital bed with tubes sticking out of him, I was sure I'd lose it. So instead of fixating on how likely he was to die, I tried to put together the pieces of this fucked up jigsaw puzzle.

But too much of it didn't make sense.

Gabriel had evaded us for close to a decade. Then all of a sudden he pops up on our radar. All right, not *him*, per se, but a bread crumb. The first of many. An article anyone but us would have missed.

A missing child turned up five years after he'd been kidnapped walking home from school one day. Told reporters he'd been abducted by a priest. Turns out the guy was a bank manager, and little Stuart only thought he was a priest because he wore a crucifix and spoke about God a lot.

The kid's abductor made a run for it, and was never found, but that article sure as hell got our attention.

We visited the abandoned house where the kid had been kept. Then we broke in one night and took a look inside. Tried to figure out where Stuart had been held.

No surprise: it was the basement.

There were too many similarities in how it had been set up for it to have been a coincidence.

Mattresses, covered in dirty sheets, lying on the floor. Hooks dangling from the ceiling. Metal dog bowls for water and food. Metal sheets riveted in place over whatever windows there were.

And then there was the cold.

And the damp.

And rats.

That article, that *house*, eventually led to Father Gabriel. But before we could track him down, *he* came to us.

ORPHANAGE UNDER NEW ADMINISTRATION

A short piece. Barely news-worthy. But it made it into the paper, and it had his name in it, and that's how we located him.

We'd found the Guardian.

A man who moved around the country and set up basements like the one we were kept in. Like the one little Stuart had been found in.

A man who kept his record clean. A man no one would suspect.

A priest.

And because we knew so many of our Ghosts were men of the cloth, there was no doubt in our minds that we'd found the orchestrator of the biggest child sex-trafficking ring of this century.

But how could a man who was so cunning, so fucking intelligent and well connected, be *so* stupid?

He could have taken Trinity anywhere, and we'd have lost them.

But he brought her here.

To her old house.

A house that was in his name.

That same day, Apollo told us everything Gabriel had said to him in the storm drain. But it had taken weeks of cajoling before Trinity told us her side of the story.

She believed Gabriel was lying. He'd become unstable, not sure if he wanted her as a daughter or a lover or a friend. And she decided she couldn't trust anything that came out of his mouth.

But what if Trinity was right? Maybe Gabriel *had* become unhinged. He'd realized he'd made a mistake taking her home. So he decided to try again. And this time, he would make her vanish without a trace.

"...think? Hey, Rube? Are you listening?"

I come back to the present with a big inhale, and then shake my head. "What?"

Apollo's eyes dim a little. "I said we should find an Internet cafe or something. I can download some of my code off the cloud and do some digging around. I mean, we've got the van."

I take a last pull of the cigarette before crushing it out under my foot. Then I head back to the SUV without answering him.

Cass and Zach are already inside. Zach is in the driver's seat now, and Cass is working his way through a ginger beer after deciding he'd rather sit in my seat than Zach's. I move around to the other side of the car and climb in, kicking shit over to his footwell to make room for my feet.

One of those things catches my eye.

Trinity's purse.

Cass and I both see it at the same time, but he gets to it first. Grabs it. Flicks it open.

His hand is shaking when he takes out the envelope, and I'm about to snatch it from him and tear it open how he's struggling to get the paper.

"It's a letter from Gabriel," he says.

His pupils shift left to right as he scans the page.

"Fuck." He looks up and locks eyes with me. "Guys...*fuck.*"

CHAPTER THIRTY-FIVE
TRINITY

I'm about halfway through my search of the basement when my foot hits something in the dark. With a metallic gong I'm sure could be heard a mile away, a dog bowl flies away with a *clang, clang, clang* before finally coming to rest.

My foot's wet.

I think there was water or something in there.

Now the smell's stronger. I gag and shake my leg, trying to get the water off.

Hell, I *hope* it's water. I'm not so sure anymore.

I hold my breath for a moment, wondering if anyone upstairs heard the ruckus. Then I start moving forward again, trying to remember which direction I was headed.

The smell is so much stronger now.

Stagnant water, is all.

My foot touches another mattress. Unless my imagined dimensions of this place are wrong, I'm close to another wall. I'm guessing this mattress is pushed up against it.

I lean forward, but I don't feel a wall where I should. So step onto the mattress and stretch—

Something bumps my foot.

If I hadn't clapped my hands over my mouth, I would have screamed. In fact, I do still scream, but the sound is muffled.

I jump back, my heart clanging in my chest almost as loud as that dog bowl.

What the hell was that?

I wait for something to happen. A sound that indicates movement, perhaps. More rat claws maybe.

But there's nothing.

So I crouch down and grope in the dark until I touch the edge of the mattress.

My fingers brush the surface as I move them reluctantly forward.

I'm almost sure I can make out the incredibly vague, pale outline of the mattress. But if so, then there must be a big stain in the center, because that area is dark.

God, I wish there was more light down here.

I swipe my fingers left to right over the mattress, with no idea where I'd felt the thing on my foot.

But there's nothing there.

Probably because I chased it away.

And I have no idea if I'm relieved or grossed out by the thought that I touched a live rat with my foot.

I'm just about to stand when my fingers snag something.

I freeze.

It takes me a few seconds to figure out what I'm touching.

Hair.

I leap back.

My scream echoes back to me, but I couldn't give a fuck if everyone above me heard. I scramble away, tripping on the edge of another mattress and falling hard on my ass. Then I'm on hands and knees, crawling. I hit another dog bowl but this one's dry and doesn't splash me.

I'm half-sobbing, half-choking by the time I get close to the other side of the basement—arms outstretched as I search out the wall I know is getting closer.

But instead of hitting the wall, something slams into my stomach. I fold in half, gasping in pain, sobbing with shock, and grab for something to hold onto.

I ran into a bar of steel.

A railing.

Stairs.

I'm up them a second later. Now my sobs are tearing me apart. Bile vaults up my throat, but I choke it down with a ragged gasp.

My hands bang against something.

A door.

I slam my fists onto it.

"Let me out! Please, please!" My throat burns as I shriek out a string of desperate pleas. "Let me out!"

As if someone on the other side of the door hears my prayers, it swings open.

I fall forward, stumble, catch myself, and go hurtling into the light. I can't see a thing—it's just white, and there's shouting and movement.

I run into someone.

They grab me.

Is it Hoody? The man with the polo shirt under his sweater? Or the woman with the gun?

I don't care.

I don't care.

I swipe my hands over my face, push hair out of my eyes.

The man in front of me, the one I ran into, he spreads his arms.

Smiles.

I recognize that smile.

But I don't know how.

Because the man staring at me is a stranger.

CHAPTER THIRTY-SIX
APOLLO

"Trinity's dad faked his own death?" I murmur.

I'm still staring at the letter Cass passed me. He read it out, but I'm reading it again. I was hoping I could get something—anything —by the font or type of paper he used.

But it's a standard font in Word printed on ordinary, cheap, letter-sized paper.

Even the signature just reads 'Gabriel' with an indecipherable flourish that could be anything.

Cass blows a plume of cigarette smoke out of the car window. "It would appear so."

We moved the car to the far side of the parking lot a few minutes ago. We should have started driving already, but we don't know where to go. Which means we could be heading in the wrong direction, moving further away from Trinity.

"What if he's lying?" Zach asks, twisting in his seat to scan our faces.

"Gabriel? Why would he?" Rube sits forward a little in his seat. "He's dead."

According to Gabriel's letter, Trinity's father—Keith Malone—is still alive. And although he states it as a fact, he doesn't back it up with evidence.

"Then what about her mom? Is she alive too?"

"It doesn't say," Cass reminds me.

"Yeah...but..."

"Look, this isn't getting us any closer to finding them," Cass says. He flicks the butt of the cigarette out of the window.

"What will?" Rube asks.

Quiet settles down. I've been trying to figure that out the past ten minutes, and I'm sure everyone else has too. But we don't have any leads.

"We're assuming Gabriel took her, but what if it wasn't him?" Zach says quietly. And then puts his hand over Cass's so he'll stop tapping his nail. "He could have had someone else do it."

"But how would he know—" Rube begins, sighing as he speaks.

"The lawyer." Cass snatches his hand out from under Zach's and clicks his fingers. "She obviously called him when Trinity picked up the key."

"So? We weren't followed here," Rube says. "How would he know exactly when—"

Rube stops talking when Zach lifts a hand and points out his window.

We all turn to look.

"What?" I ask, peering at the house. The garden. The roof.

"There," Zach says.

And then I see it.

A For Sale sign.

But I don't get it.

"He's watching the house," Zach says. "Trinity's old babysitter said a young couple moved in across the road. No kids, but the house is big enough for a family of five."

"So they watch the house. Someone lets him know Trinity's arrived. He comes and snatches her? And then what? Where does he go? And why?" Cass shakes his head. "What does he—"

"We have to go back," I say. "Back to her house."

Zach opens his mouth as if to argue, but then closes it again. Cass and Rube look at him, then at each other. Like there's a telepathic conversation going on.

It's fine, I'll wait them out.

"He's right," Cass murmurs. "Everything leads back to that house."

"But the safe is gone," Rube says. "What else could there be?"

There's a beat of silence. Then Zach says, "It's not much..."

I grin at him. "But it's a start."

CHAPTER THIRTY-SEVEN
RUBE

My first and only foster family had a study in their house. One wall was lined with bookshelves and old, musty books.

One day when my sisters were all at cheerleading practice and I'd been left alone for the first time in my new home, I was climbing up the walls from boredom. I tried watching television, but it didn't hold my interest.

So I explored the house, peeking into rooms I'd only caught a glimpse of before.

The study fascinated me. It felt stale and unused—when I opened the door, dust motes shifted through stray beams of light shining in from the window. I felt like I was walking into a crypt.

I went over to the bookshelf and worked my way through the titles. Some of the books stuck together when I tried pulling them out.

Those I left alone, scared I'd damage them and get crapped out.

But some came out a little easier. Titles I'd later learn to recognize, but which were alien to me back then.

Alice in Wonderland.

A Tale of Two Cities.

Casino Royale.

Great Expectations.

I'll never forget the smell of those books. Or how, when I turned the first page of Alice in Wonderland, I wondered why on earth an adult man would own a book like that.

Since then, I've always been drawn to books. My interest moved to bibles when I decided to play the part of a pious kid on his way to becoming a priest as a way to get closer to Father Gabriel without rousing suspicion.

Very little of that interest was feigned.

I found solace in the pages of any bible I read.

Cass is right—there's no safe in this room anymore. But there is a treasure.

Seems Trinity's parents collected bibles. Mostly King James, but there's a Geneva here too. I crack them open, hoping to find a clue, but they're as barren as the big white one Trinity came to Saint Amos with.

It makes sense—you'd destroy the value of the book by marking it— but a cheap mass-produced King James is just as empty.

I guess the church was just a front for Trinity's parents.

We split up to search the house. Apollo found a door we assume leads to the basement, but it has a keypad. That combination should be the same one for the safe we can't find. But Trinity never gave us the code. Apollo's gone to look around the house and see if there's another way inside the basement—maybe through a hurricane door or something. Cass and Zach went upstairs.

I said I'd search the study. But there's nothing in here. I crack open one more bible, but it hits the floor a second later when I hear a *rip* from upstairs.

Apollo must have just come back inside already—he and Cass are in the main bedroom when I arrive.

We watch, silent, as Zach digs his fingers into the edge of the carpet and yanks up another strip, baring the hardwood floor beneath.

"Hey, Zach?" Cass asks quietly. "Whatcha doing over there, buddy?"

Zach spins around in a crouch, staring at us with a lowered head. Eyes bright, wide. "You don't smell that?" he spits out. He waves a hand. "It's all over this fucking place."

I step forward, sweeping out and arm and using it to herd Cass and Apollo behind me, out of the way. "Smell what?" I ask.

Zach rushes to his feet. He charges toward me, and I almost back up when I see the ferocity on his face. But then he goes right past us, shoves a hand into a closet that's standing open, and drags out a sweater.

He brings it to me, shoves it under my nose. "This," he hisses.

I turn my head away, but he follows with the sweater until I take a reluctant sniff at the fabric.

When I snatch it from him and take another whiff, his shoulders sag. "It's him."

Zach's eyes slide past me, fix on Apollo, then Cass. "Our Ghost lives here."

THE SOUND of ripping carpet fills the room. Cass joined Zach on the floor, and they've almost torn up everything. Apollo is by the closet, dragging everything out into a pile on the floor.

Zach has them believing they'll find another safe or something in here.

I'm sure someone with as many secrets as Keith Malone had tons of hidey holes...but even if they do find another secret place, I'm sure it will be empty.

I go through the nightstands. There's nothing of interest in there— bible, tissues, lip balm, lotion. A half-eaten candy bar still in its wrapper on what I assume is Monica's side, judging from the feminine scented lotions and creams, but it's turned white from age.

I almost don't pick up her bible. None of the ones I've found have proved useful yet—why would anything be different up here?

But just like some people can't walk past a rose bush without smelling the blooms...

The instant I lift Monica's bible out of the drawer, I know it's not like the others. For one, it's been read before. There are faint finger-prints on the cover, as if she handled it after putting on lotion or cuticle oil. When I turn the bible so the spine rests in my palm and focus on the gold-trimmed pages, there's a narrow section that's been rubbed off from use.

Behind me, Zach and Cass start discussing which side of the room they'll start tearing up the floorboards on.

I open the front cover. There's a short message in an elegant script.

The light shines in the darkness, and the darkness has not overcome it.
John 1:5

DEAR MONICA,
Let this book be your light.
Love,
Gabe.

I LET the bible fall open in my hands, hoping it will land where the spine was most often opened.

New Testament. The book of Mark.

No notes, no dog ears.

I start paging.

I reach the end of Mark. The faster I thumb through those near-transparent pages, the tighter my chest grows.

Then I skim ahead.

Luke.

The forty-second book of the bible.

I page furiously until I reach chapter eleven.

It starts a quarter of the way down the left page, in the first column.

Our father's prayer.

It's been underlined several times.

The word "forgiveness" was circled so hard it tore through the paper.

I snap the book closed. Turn.

My brothers are facing me. Zach is frowning, and as soon as his eyes dart down to the bible, he walks up to me.

"Luke eleven," I tell him, slamming the book into his chest.

And then I'm bolting out the room, down the stairs, through the passage.

4-2-1-1

The basement door unlocks. I shove it open, take a step.

But then the smell hits me.

I freeze.

I'm still standing there at the threshold, staring into a black void, when the others arrive.

"Fuck," Cass mutters somewhere behind me. "There a light or something?"

"Probably one down there," Apollo says. "But, like, you'd have to find it first."

"Anyone have a flashlight?" Zach's voice is tight.

"Got one on my phone," Cass replies absently.

But none of us move.

We just stand there, staring into the dark.

Which is absurd.

It's just a dark room.

A few stairs.

If Cass gives me his phone, there'll be light. Then I can go down there.

But it doesn't matter what logic my fucking brain throws at me, I override it every time with, "it's a fucking pitch-black basement."

Maybe I wouldn't have had an issue if Zach hadn't told me that this was where our Ghost lived.

Because then it would just have been a normal basement. A cavity at the bottom of a house. Nothing to it.

But it's not.

It's our fucking Ghost's basement, and that changes everything.

Apollo clears his throat. "So...uh...are we going down?"

"Yeah, course," Cass says, but as if he's lost in a dream.

"Why wouldn't we?" The words come out by themselves—I wasn't even aware I was going to speak.

My skin starts crawling. I take a step back. And as if that breaks the spell, Cass and Zach and Apollo all move back with me.

We press up against the wall, staring at the rectangle of night in front of us.

Cass fidgets in his pocket. Pulls out his phone. He turns on the light and shines it at the hole.

It's like it hits an invisible door someone painted black.

Fuck.

"Okay," Apollo whispers. "Look, it's just a room, right?"

He takes a step forward. Then another. I stare at him, taking in his long blond hair, his lean frame. He puts his arm out behind him. "Phone."

In that moment, I've never had greater respect for him.

And he doesn't even look back. Doesn't take even a second to see what we think. He just grabs the phone as soon as Cass puts it his palm, pushes back his shoulders, and heads for the darkness.

The second it swallows him, the three of us surge forward and cluster around the dark doorway.

"Apollo!" Cass calls out, like he's convinced Apollo's already been murdered.

"Yeah?" With the phone shining ahead, he's a starkly contrasted silhouette. The beam of light from the cell isn't as powerful as a flashlight, but it chases away the shadows long enough for Apollo to pick out a few shapes in the darkness.

Stairs.

Plastic flooring.

As soon as he reaches the ground, he points the light across the room.

"Mother of God," Zach murmurs.

"Nope," Cass says, sounding like he's about to get sick. "Try, Father of Hell."

CHAPTER THIRTY-EIGHT
APOLLO

I wonder if they can see how much I'm shaking? I'm holding Cass's phone as tight as I can, but there's nothing I can do about the way the light shimmies and shakes all over the place.

If my brothers weren't all standing there at the top of the stairs, I wouldn't even have thought about setting foot down here.

Yeah, it's just a basement, but come *on*.

It's as much a basement as we're a bunch of friends.

Every inch of this place is dripping sinister and oozing malevolence. I suddenly wish I had some kind of biblical training so I could exorcise this place and be done.

But instead I have to creep around and look for a damn light.

I find it, eventually. It takes me a lot longer than it should have, but that's because I can't stop looking at everything else in here.

The bed.

The teeny tiny little toilet.

The camera on its stand.

Especially the camera.

But I can't think electronics right now. This isn't the time to veer off on a tangent.

As soon as I spot the string for the light, I tug it.

Light blooms, but the way that swinging lightbulb makes the shadows dance and weave is giving me the heebie-jeebies.

"Okay, guys, it's safe!" I call up.

I don't dare turn my back, because I know how that ends. So I just back up a little as I wait for them to join me.

But they don't.

And when I finally have enough courage to look behind me, I see the terror on each of those three faces.

Crap.

Why the hell did I have to choose this moment to be so damn stupid?

"Really?" I purse my lips. "Just me then?"

"You're doing so well, buddy!" Cass calls out. "Just keep going."

I shake my head, throw them the finger, and go back to staring at the room. "What am I looking for?"

They don't answer, because I guess it's obvious.

A fucking clue, idiot.

But like…what?

Hair? DNA? Fingerprints?

Or stuff like whether the bed was chosen at random or for specific child molestation purposes?

The camera catches my eye again, and I realize why.

I know there won't be a tape or anything inside. I mean…*duh.*

But as soon as I make a beeline for it, Zach calls out, "Leave it alone, Apollo, the rest of the room is more—"

I throw him another zap. "You wanna micromanage me, then come down here and do it yourself," I yell up.

"There won't be a tape in there," Rube says.

"I know," I say, drawing out the last word. "But this is…"

I trail off, rolling my eyes. Every time I talk tech, my brothers' eyes start glazing over. Only Cass humors me every now and then, but I doubt even he would understand.

This camera is old. Like the eighties old. But it's in amazing condition, especially considering the fact that it's been in this damp basement for God knows how long.

I want to take it off its stand, but I'm sure there are all sorts of fingerprints on it. Luckily I'm wearing long sleeves today—I pull them over my hands and use them to pop open the cassette compartment.

"It's empty," I call out.

"Told you," Cass says.

But then I turn the camcorder around, and frown. Under the fat sans-serif type of the brand name, there's a slanted word in script. It has the eighties jagged feel to it, like ACDC's logo.

LIMITED EDITION

Right. Got it.

My brothers step aside so I can come out of the basement. Cass puts out a hand to stop me. "Where you off to in such a hurry?"

"Library. Or internet cafe, whichever comes first," I tell him. Then I hold up the camera for them to see. "Unlike the van, this thing is one in a million."

"How's that going to help us?" Rube asks as I start walking away.

"Don't know yet," I call back. "But I'll let you know soon as I figure it out."

CASS DRIVES me to the local library while Rube and Zach stay behind in Trinity's old house. I'm not sure that's the best idea, seeing as how Zach flipped out earlier, but I guess if they do rip the whole place apart it might end up being all cathartic and shit.

I don't really care.

I'm too focused on how this camera is going to help us find Trinity.

It doesn't look like the kind of tech that's been in use since the eighties. It looks like a camera you buy on eBay at a ridiculous price because it's vintage, barely ever been used, and has some of its original packaging.

I'm hoping it's unique enough to have left a trace I can find quickly and easily.

And if it's not? Well at least I'm keeping myself sane and not constantly adding to my rather inventive list of things someone evil could be doing to a pretty girl like Trinity.

Cass watches me over my shoulder, but unlike Rube or Zach, he doesn't ask me what I'm doing every two seconds.

I'm grateful for that. I never mind explaining shit, but right now it would just slow me down.

Instead, he lets me get into the zone, and once I'm in...

"You should blink," comes his voice.

I sit back, shake my head, focus on him.

"What?"

He points at his eyes. "You have to blink every now and then. Keeps them moist." He stretches out his arms, jaw cracking with a yawn. "Let's get a coffee and a smoke."

"Dude, I was right..." I shove my palms over my eyes and massage my eyelids. "I was in the fucking zone."

"Yeah, well, you're going to develop a hunch if you keep sitting like that. And I can't be seen hanging around with hunchbacks." He slaps my thigh. "Come on. Up and at 'em."

God.

I look back at the computer. I can't even remember what thread of a thought I was following before he so rudely interrupted me.

We've been here twenty minutes, and the only thing I've discovered so far is that this camcorder isn't as unique as I thought it was. They're all over eBay.

I follow Cass to a food truck, but I wave away his offer of a burrito with my coffee.

I need blood in my brain, not my stomach.

Cass is halfway done with his burrito and I'm halfway done with my cigarette when a cloud passes over the sun. I squint up, staring at the gray-tinged cloud and its now radiant halo of golden light.

"How did Rube figure out the code for the basement?" I ask Cass.

He shrugs. "Don't know. Said something about a bible verse."

"I know, I was there." I roll my eyes. "What does it say?"

"Fuck knows."

I pull out my phone. "Do you remember what it was?"

Cass stares into the distance, chewing ponderously. "Luke...something."

I give him a deadpan stare. "Really? Could you try harder?"

"Why?" Cass crumples up the burrito's packaging and overarm tosses it into a nearby trash can. "It worked."

"It's significant."

"Everything in that book's significant to bible belters," Cass says. "Literal needle in a haystack."

"That's not—" I cut off with a sigh. "Screw it."

I start searching.

inspiring bible verse luke...

Google autocompletes on that, so I give the first search term a try.

I tap on the first result, and it takes me to a bible website. I read the first verse of Luke chapter eleven.

It's a prayer. A common one because even I've heard it before.

I guess Luke's the forty-second book in the bible. Forty-two-eleven.

It was the combination to the safe, which is now missing, and the basement. What's the chance it's also the password used to encrypt the file on Gabriel's computer?

But it's not a pin number like the basement door...

"Library. Now." I call over my shoulder, already headed in that direction.

"I haven't had a smoke yet!"

"Save it!"

I have a feeling he's going to need one when we're done, anyway.

We race back to the library. I remote access my PC back in California and quickly add the entire prayer to my cracking program.

It takes milliseconds to parse.

The file pops open on the library's computer.

I'm wrong, though.

Cass won't need a smoke.

Neither of us will.

We need someone with a stronger stomach.

CHAPTER THIRTY-NINE
ZACH

"You ever wish you could wipe out your memories?" Rube asks.

We're in our Ghost's bedroom. Neither of us would even consider sitting on the mattress, so we're squeezed in beside each other on the blanket box at the foot of the bed.

I don't even have to think about it. "No."

"Not at all?"

We're smoking a cigarette. It's our third in a row—we've been putting them out on the carpet in a blatant show of disrespect.

It should feel petty, but instead it feels amazing. Like we're extinguishing each and every one on the Ghost's bare skin.

"No, because then they'd get away with it. All of them."

"So revenge is better than forgiveness?"

I turn to him, narrowing my eyes. "I'm sorry, did I miss something? The last time I checked you were going to gouge out his eyeballs with your thumbs and then piss in the sockets."

He looks away. "If we hadn't come back here..."

I inhale deep.

Oh.

That's what this is about.

"Rube, it's not our fault. It's not *her* fault. It's theirs. Whoever took her. They initiated it, not us."

"Would have had a hard time initiating anything if—"

I bang my fist on his thigh. "We're going to find her. And we're going to kill whoever took her, like we should have Gabriel."

Rube is silent for more than a beat, so I look up at him. He's frowning. "You don't think it was Gabriel?"

I spread my hands like a prophet. "You really think it was?"

"Everything points to—"

"Exactly. Everything *always* points to him."

Rube's frown grows deeper. When he speaks, it's slowly and carefully. "Yes, because he was the Guardian, and—"

He cuts off when I shake my head. "You know what. You're right. Maybe it would be better if our memories were erased because we always storm in without thinking things through. We're so consumed with rage, and hate, and revenge, we don't ever stop to just...*think.*"

"You believe Gabriel was set up?"

I lay my hands in my lap, palms up, one on top of the other. I've been trying to meditate and shit—my therapist recommended it—but the only thing that happens when I close my eyes is that I'm immediately transported back to the basement.

It's always been the case.

Which is why I get so little sleep. It takes a lot of effort to convince myself that I won't wake up with some guy's hand down my fucking pants.

"I don't know what to believe anymore," I tell him. "And I don't know where Trinity is. And I don't know if we'll ever find her."

I see Rube's shoulders sag in my peripheral view.

"Maybe they'll find something," Rube says. "Apollo's good with that shit."

"It'll have to be a fucking miracle they find." I shake my head again. "I don't think anything less is going to cut it. Not this—"

There's a shriek of tires outside.

We're up in an instant, storming to the bedroom window. It looks out on the street, to our SUV that's just pulled up into the driveway.

Guess there's no reason to be circumspect anymore. If anything, I *hope* we draw someone's attention. If they come for us, at least then we'll know who took Trinity.

Apollo jumps out of the passenger door, Cass a beat behind him. They race up to the front door.

Rube and I meet them halfway down the stairs. It's crowded with the four of us, but that doesn't matter.

Apollo's holding out his phone. "Watch it," he wheezes. "One of you—"

Cass snatches it. "Christ, Apollo, get some fucking exercise." Then he looks at me, at Rube. "He figured out the password. He opened the file."

"The one from Gabriel?" Rube asks, reaching for the phone.

Cass pulls it out of reach.

For a second, just one *weird* fucking second, I think he's screwing around with Rube. That if he tried to go for it, Cass would pull it away again. Like driving away from someone before they can get in the car. But just a few feet. And then you apologize. And then do it again.

"Rube, my man," Cass says quietly. Then he shakes his head. Looks at me. "I...don't even know if we can."

"Can what?" Rube growls, going for the phone again. This time Cass lets him take it.

"Watch it," he says. Crosses his arms. He and Apollo share a look, and then drop their gazes. "We couldn't."

"It's a video?"

They nod, still looking down.

Christ.

There's a mess of noise from the phone. Rube turns it on its side, lifts his chin a little. But he's holding it. He's watching it.

I shift a little, peering over his arm at the screen.

Darkness. Then a flash of light. Pale blue carpet. Neat, clean. Suggestion of furniture which quickly resolves into a dark blue chest of drawers painted with big yellow stars. There's a red toy robot on top, and a random assortment of He-Man action figures.

Jesus Christ.

But Rube says nothing.

And we keep watching.

The view pans to a bed. There's a little boy sitting on the side. He has tear tracks down his face and his red Spiderman T-shirt is damp with spilled tears. He's still hiccupping, and as the person holding the camera phone goes closer, he lifts a little fist and wipes it over his eyes.

"Hey, Justin," someone croons softly. "Don't cry."

The boy frowns hard at the person holding the camera. "I wuh-want my muh-m-mommy."

"Oh, I know. I know. She said she'll be here any minute now."

I glance up at Cass and Apollo. They're staring at us now, both wide-eyed, like they're waiting for us to shout Uncle.

The kid's not even in a basement. Yeah, I couldn't go down into the dark earlier, but he's in a bright and sunny room.

Pussies.

But then I hear Rube swallowing. I look back at the screen.

It's gone black.

My stomach clenches.

Light returns. It shows a slim figure walking away from the camera that resolves into a young, pretty woman.

Late twenties.

Dark, curly hair.

Bright blue eyes.

Freckles.

She goes to sit beside the little boy, and puts an arm around his shoulder. He cringes away, but she just ducks her head a little closer.

"Would you like some cookies and milk while you wait for Mommy?" she asks.

The little boy looks up at her, wary, and shakes his head.

"Are you sure?"

He drops his head a little. Sniffs.

She scoots closer. "I tell you what, Justin. Let's have a nap, me and you. And when we wake up, your mommy will be here."

Justin shakes his head. "I'm not tired."

"I know." She moves a lock of hair off his forehead, and looks straight at the camera. "But it will make the time go by so fast."

Rube clears his throat. "Is that Monica?" he asks, looking up at Apollo and Cass.

"Who else?" Cass says. Apollo nods.

Rube doesn't look at the camera again. "How does this help?"

Cass frowns. "Gabriel said Apollo should show this to Trinity. I'm guessing he told her Monica was involved, and she wouldn't believe him."

"Yeah, she didn't mention any of that to us," Apollo adds.

I'm looking at them too, but I can still hear what's going on. The rustle of fabric. The cooing sounds Monica makes.

Rube goes to turn off the cell phone, but I stop him. His head whips to look at me. "Really?" he murmurs. "You really want to watch?"

"It's not in a basement," I tell him.

"Does it matter?" His voice drops low and deep. "You know what's going to happen. Why the fuck do you have to watch it?"

"Because it's not in a basement!"

Apollo leans back from my yell. I rake my fingers through my hair and snatch the phone from Rube's hand. I move my finger over the time bar.

There's a brief snatch of Monica's voice.

...show my husband what a handsome boy you are, Justin...doesn't that feel nice...don't cry now...

"This didn't happen in a basement. This boy isn't one of us."

"And that makes it okay?" Cass begins, indignation rife on his voice.

"Just fucking listen to me!" I pause the video, hesitate as I check the screen, then hold it up Cass. "There. See?"

Cass glances at it, and then immediately looks away. "Jesus Christ, you're a sick fuck," he mutters, and his face goes a shade whiter.

"Not...fuck..." I grit my teeth. "Look past the fucking bed. Behind it. There's a window. See? The curtains are open."

"Yeah, sure, I believe you," Cass says, but only looking at me out of the corner of his eye, not at the screen. "First prize, Zach."

"Wait...are you saying..." Apollo reaches for the phone, but then plucks his hand away. "Is there like a landmark or something?" he glances at Cass, bumps him with an elbow. "We could use it to triangulate the location of the house." And then his face falls. "But this must have been taken years ago. What's the point?"

"The point is, she didn't bother trying to hide anything. She didn't pull the curtains. She used the boy's real name." I tap my fingernail on the screen, but then hurriedly lock the phone when the video starts playing again.

Everyone goes rigid, jaws clenching, glaring at me.

"Sorry," I murmur.

They don't need to hear that.

Fuck, *I* didn't need to hear that.

"She felt comfortable enough to shoot a video on her phone and not worry about someone finding it."

"It was password protected," Rube says.

"Yeah." Apollo might have been trying to sound cheery, but his words just come out all wobbly. "Want to know what it was?"

Rube and I look at him. He drops his eyes. "Forgive us our sins," he says, sounding much less happy than before.

I push past them, unlocking the phone again. I turn down the volume and head into the living room, then hurriedly detour and go into the kitchen instead.

I don't need to be sitting next to a pool of my own blood trying to work this shit out, that's for sure.

Cass follows. He makes me a cup of black coffee and sits opposite me as I watch the whole video.

It makes me sick to my stomach to the point where I want to go puke up everything I ever ate...but near the end, Monica picks up the phone again and takes it over to the bed. As she's arranging it on the nightstand—bright blue like the dresser, with a night light shaped like Mickey Mouse—there's a clear shot of the window.

So clear, you can make out the horizon.

I freeze that frame, take a screenshot. It's got Monica's left eye in it, near the bottom. Her face is tilted down, but she's looking at the phone.

Probably imagining her husband's delight when she shows him the clip.

That eye sure is beautiful.

If you don't look too hard.

Because if you do, then you can see pure evil coiling in the darkness of her pupil.

Forgive us our sins?

Bitch, not now...not fucking *ever*.

CHAPTER FORTY
TRINITY

Exodus, Matthew, and Ephesians say you must honor your father and your mother. They don't mention whether that still applies if your parents sold their souls to the devil.

"Who were they? Those boys you were with?" my father asks.

I guess I don't have to call him that anymore. I'm not his daughter. I should feel relieved, but instead I feel violated.

It wasn't my father who lived upstairs in that house with me and my mother.

It was an impostor.

A stranger.

But they made me call him Dad. And they made me obey him.

The impostor walks closer. Calm, collected.

My head snaps to the side when he backhands me. Pain blossoms on my cheek, and I see stars when my eyes squeeze shut involuntarily.

"Who were they?" he asks again, so quiet I can barely make out the words over the sound of blood roaring in my ears.

"No one," I manage, blinking back tears of pain and terror.

They tied me to a chair, Hoody and Polo, while the impostor and the woman watched. I'm in a den or a study. Plushly carpeted, thick drapes —drawn. It was gloomy inside until Hoody turned on a desk lamp.

There are lots of books on the wall here. A big desk. It looks a lot like the study Dad had at home.

No, not Dad.

The impostor.

He's standing in front of me, legs hip-distance apart. Casual, but ready.

For what? Does he expect me to be overcome by some feat of super-human strength, shred these ropes, and make a go at him? I don't believe in miracles.

I thought I didn't believe in God either, but on some level I must have faith. Because I know the Devil's standing in front of me, and if there's a Devil, there must be a God.

"Trinity, child…" The impostor crouches in front of me. "There will only be more pain if you insist on being uncooperative. Do you understand?"

"They're just a bunch of boys," I tell him.

"What were you doing with them?"

"What does it matter?" I yell.

I glare up at him, but the second our eyes meet, I drop my head.

I'm not brave enough to stare Satan right in the eyes. Especially when those eyes belong to the man I thought of as my father for close to two decades.

The impostor sighs as he stands. He turns to Hoody, and they walk to the study door. Even though their voices are low, I can hear what they're saying.

"You got their plates?" Keith asks.

"Zachary Price. Dana Point, California."

My heart starts pounding.

Shit.

I guess it doesn't matter what I say, the impostor knows they're not just some random guys.

"Find them. Kill them." Keith looks at me over his shoulder. I wasn't expecting a look of fatherly adoration or anything—he's never looked at me like that.

My entire life, I don't think I ever did anything that made him proud, or gave him a reason to smile. I just always thought that was the kind of man he was—severe, chaste, Old Testament.

But now it's all starting to click into place.

It wasn't that he didn't love me.

He didn't have to, because I wasn't his. But I'm sure even the parents of adopted kids feel more for their children than he ever did— ever could have—for me.

Because there's not a trace of emotion in his voice when he says, "Kill her too."

And then he turns and leaves, not even bothering to look back.

My mouth falls open. The woman who brought me here comes in front of me and holds out her gun. But it doesn't have the same menacing effect as before.

Keith Malone just shredded my life to pieces.

And now I'm going to die.

Finally, the fear comes back. It shoots through me like needles of cold steel. My stomach twists, and I start dry swallowing like there's something stuck in my throat.

This can't be happening.

This can't fucking be happening.

I struggle, but the ropes are tight. I scream, but that just makes the woman frown.

She curls her finger around the trigger. I close my eyes, holding my breath as I wait for the inevitable.

"Jess, wait."

A hand lands on the woman's shoulder. She looks at it, glances behind her. "What?"

"I'll do it," Hoody says.

"Christ, Nick, there's no time for that shit." She shakes him off, points the gun.

"You go on ahead. I'll catch up." Nick wraps his fingers around the hand holding the gun. She twists it, snarling at him with irritation, and it goes off.

I scream.

My body's stiff as I wait for death or pain...but there's nothing. Just my pounding heart and the ice-cold flash of adrenaline pouring through my body.

"Fucking retard," Jess mutters, but her voice is moving away. "I'm leaving in ten, with or without you."

My eyes fly open. There's a hole about an inch away from my left foot. I manage a choking breath, and then there's a hand around the front of my throat.

Nick uses his thumb to prop my chin up, forcing my eyes to his. "How many times do you think I can come in ten minutes, Missy?"

I cringe when he licks his lips.

"Let's go find out."

I FALL TO MY KNEES, but I'm up a second later, scrambling to get away. Behind me, Nick barks out a laugh and then shuts the door.

Locks it.

Pockets the key.

But I'm already on the other side of the room, grabbing the window sash and hauling it up.

The curtain wraps around my arm. I swat it away and lean out, lifting my leg—

The ground sways toward me.

But from a distance.

I hadn't realized it, but I'm on the third floor. And below me? A gravel path hugging the side of the house.

Oh Lord, I'll never survive that.

I spin around. Nick veers around the bed I clambered over, a filthy smile on his mouth. I look back at the drop. Swing my leg over the window ledge.

It'll hurt, but hopefully only a little. Then I'll be dead, right? No need for them to go after my men.

Except...I don't know if that's what will happen. Nick and Jess were given orders. Who am I to say they won't follow them to the letter?

Death by gravel is the coward's way out. And I'll be leaving my men clueless. For all I know, they'll walk into our house in Dana Point and Jess and her crew will already be waiting for them.

Bang.

Bang.

Bang.

Bang.

I can hear every future gunshot slamming home into one of my men's chests.

Just as Nick gets in arm's reach, I dodge to the side.

We're in a child's room, a boy judging from all the action figures and faded blue paint. Where is he now, the boy that used to live here?

I slam into the door, pluck at the handle. Yes, even though it's locked, because all I can hope for right now is a fucking miracle.

Locked.

Nick laughs again. I spin around, flattening myself against the wood. He's only got ten minutes with me. And I'm determined to keep playing this game as long as—

Nick lifts Jess's gun. Or maybe it's his own, who the fuck knows?

And then he shoots me.

CHAPTER FORTY-ONE
RUBE

"Is this seriously the fastest you can go?" Apollo yells as he thumps the back of Cass's headrest. "I thought you said this was a muscle car?"

"Do you even have a dick?" Cass yells back. "This is a fucking SUV. The muscle car is that yellow Mustang we left back in California, you idiotic, dickless—" he cuts off with a growl that comes close to competing with the SUV's engine.

We're headed south down the highway at a ridiculous speed.

I've never been an adrenaline junkie. Going this fast makes me feel sick, not excited. But I grit my teeth and I bear it, because the faster Cass goes, the faster we get to Trinity.

She has to be there.

It's our only hope.

I mentally urge Cass to push the SUV as hard as he can without blowing the engine, and I hold onto the seat with claws for hands, and I will the contents of my stomach to remain where they are.

"How far, Apollo?" Zach asks.

Apollo briefly relents giving Cass shit, and checks his phone. "Another ten miles."

"Go faster," Zach says.

"Jesus fucking Christ," Cass mutters. "Do any of you even know

what a speed limiter is? And that this car has one? And that, even if I
wanted—"

"Shut up and drive," I bark.

Then there's silence.

And fuck, it comes just in time. Else I'd have told them to find me
something to puke into.

"This is our turn off," Cass says just as we pass a sign for a shooting
range a few miles up ahead. He slows the SUV and puts on the indicator. "Christ, they weren't fucking around when they decided to go
remote, were they?" he mutters.

There isn't much to see—just another long road.

"We still don't know which house it is." Apollo holds up the
printout from the Redford library and starts looking through the
windows. "But it's got to be at least two or three stories."

"Sounds like we're looking for a mansion," Cass says dryly. He
catches Zach's eye in the rearview mirror. "Sound familiar, Mason?"

Zachary narrows his eyes, but then his face relaxes again. He nods
reluctantly. "Long drive, so the main house is far from the road. Lots of
tree cover."

He's describing the house we were kept captive in. A place that used
to be his home.

That silence comes again, but Cass breaks it this time after looking
first at Zach, then at me.

"How about you burn this one down too when we're done?"

———

JUST AFTER THE turnoff heading for the shooting range, signs start
popping up for ranches and plots. We drive until we find the first house
that fits our description, but since there are two kids playing in the
front yard, we drive past.

A few minutes later, something more fitting comes into view. We
park behind a small copse of pine trees—just far enough to keep in sight
without being spotted.

It's a three-story house.

It's remote as fuck.

If there'd been more than one of its type in this area, we'd have to have searched them all...but there isn't. The only other houses are a few one-level ranch-style lots, most of them closer to the road.

Despite what Cass demanded, we didn't come with an arsenal. We all have Kevlar vests on under our shirts, but only Zach and Cass are carrying.

I never handle guns, and this is no exception.

Apollo also declined. I have a hunting knife on me, Apollo a switchblade. But we're only supposed to be backup for Cass and Zach, and we're merely going in to scope the place and see if this is where Trinity is being held.

"You sure you want to go in there unarmed?" Cass asks, twisting in his seat and grabbing the headrest. "I mean, you could just wave it around. It doesn't even have to be loaded."

I shake my head.

The last time I touched a gun, I almost killed two innocent girls, and traumatized an entire family.

If I'd had a sliver of doubt left that I wasn't a normal kid, that day changed everything.

It was a Saturday. Pissing with rain. My foster parents had a lunch date with friends, and their four daughters had decided to stay at home and watch sitcom reruns instead of going with.

I don't know who bought the bottle of booze, but it was almost empty by the time I walked past and saw them passing it around. I wasn't going to rat them out—I was just going to take it away. Our parents had made it pretty fucking clear how they felt about underage drinking. I mean, the youngest was thirteen. No one that young should be drinking anyway.

But when I tried to take it away, they ganged up on me. Thought it was a game. They were drunk, and I guess they'd been eyeing me for the past few weeks, because they tried to get me to kiss them.

They even started taking their shirts off.

A normal kid my age would have gone with it. But they were my sisters, and it was wrong, and the harder I resisted, the more intent they became.

My brothers think I'm a pussy because I never hit on any of them. I can't even imagine what they'd say if I told them the truth about what happened that day.

Because it wasn't just kissing.

They tried to get my pants off. And that shit triggered me worse than anything I'd experienced since we'd escaped the basement.

I snapped.

Lisa was the youngest.

She was so beautiful. Long blond hair, bright blue eyes.

I was just trying to keep her back, all of them. I shoved her too hard, and she took a tumble.

Ha. *Took a tumble.*

She slammed into a glass coffee table, face first. She almost lost an eye. I didn't see her again after that, but I have no doubt the accident disfigured her.

So much blood.

And then the screaming began.

I had to keep them quiet.

I know what happens when kids scream. Adults don't like it.

Kids are meant to be seen, not heard.

I grabbed two of them, put my hands over their mouths. The third was unconscious on the floor. I don't even know how that had happened. If I'd done something.

Still don't.

And that's how they found us. My foster parents.

Me with an undone fly, their daughters half-unclothed, and I'm holding two of them tight so they can't scream anymore.

Blood.

Limp bodies.

The mother passed out.

Henry—my foster dad—was holding a gun. At first, I thought they'd just arrived. I couldn't understand why he'd carry a gun around with him.

But later, when the red haze receded and memories came flooding back, I realized they'd been there long enough to see what was happening and then Henry went to get his gun.

Because I was lost.

Out of my own body.

I didn't hear them begging with me to let their daughters go.

I just saw the gun. And then I tackled Henry to the ground. I pressed the gun to his head and pulled the trigger, but thank fuck the safety was on so nothing happened.

And I kept pulling that trigger until the police came and arrested me.

Zachary got everything sorted out, of course. Since no one actually died, and he'd offered to pay for Lisa's plastic surgery—and then some —the charges were eventually dropped.

"I'm sure," I tell Cass.

"Looks empty anyway," Apollo says. "Maybe we're too late."

We sit in silence for a moment, and then all flinch at the faint *pop* of gunfire.

"Shooting range," Zach says.

Me, Cass, and Apollo nod.

And as if that's the signal, we file out of the car and head for the house.

"IS THAT..." Cass points.

I nod my head. "A grave."

"Is there a..."

"We'll have to check later," I tell him. "Keep moving."

We're at the back of the property, headed for the patio doors. It's the first set of doors we found, and one of the sliding glass panels is standing open.

It's too quiet.

Surely there would be something. Voices, a radio playing, a television set. Unless, like Apollo said, we're too late.

Or this is a dead end.

Who's to say they even own this property anymore?

But the neatly dug grave out back gives me a shred of hope. We're too far away to see if it's empty or not, but there'll be plenty of time for that once we've gone through the house.

I hear a faint noise. Cass holds up a hand. We stop to listen, but hear nothing.

Could have been Zach and Apollo, going through the front.

But then I hear it again.

It's faint, but it's undeniably a gunshot. Me and Cass frown at each other, but we don't dare say anything.

"Shooting range," Cass murmurs.

I nod.

We keep moving.

Through an entertainment area. Down a hall. I see a shape, and tap Cass on the shoulder, pointing.

It resolves into Zachary, stalking down the other side of the passage like a cop in an action movie. We glance at each other, and then he nods and looks up.

Downstairs cleared.

Cass and I are closest, so we go up the stairs first. As soon as we turn to head down the hall, I hear a sound again.

A panicked sob. A choked breath. Fabric and clothes rustling urgently.

My heart's in my fucking throat, but Cass puts up his hand like he knows all I want to do is bolt forward.

I guess he also recognized the voice making those sounds.

Trinity.

CHAPTER FORTY-TWO
TRINITY

The pain is so intense, I can't even scream. It's as if the bullet knocked every atom of air from my lungs. I drag in a horrible groaning gasp and slide to the floor.

I reach up, but I can't bear to touch the hole in my chest. Instead, my fingers shake in the air a few inches away.

Somehow, through the violent buzzing in my ears, I hear Nick chuckle.

Then I'm flying up, the pain intensifying as Nick twists the grip he has on the front of my blood-stained dress. "Hurts, don't it?" he says. "Should be thanking me on your hands and fucking knees, Missy, 'cos now you won't feel anything else."

He drags me to the bed. Tosses me on the mattress. I let out a low wail as I hit the firm surface, as that jolt sends a stabbing agony through me.

Liar.

The bullet hit me just below my right shoulder, but my entire torso feels like it's on fire. I can't move that arm, and my body is as limp as a rag doll.

Nick climbs onto me, pushes the muzzle of the gun so hard into my temple that I'm facing away from him, to a window.

The muzzle bites into my flesh, the cold metal spreading through me. Then he rips my dress up to my hips allowing the brisk air to caress my bare skin.

A wave of dizziness hits me. It feels like I'm on a boat, and the waves are tossing me around. Then like I'm drowning. Except I think I am, because when I try to breathe, there's shit in the way.

I cough. Retch.

Thick, warm liquid spills from my mouth.

The air smells like copper.

Am I dying? The pain is so immense, it's impossible to comprehend. I'm aware that I'm writhing with it, that he's fighting my limbs so he can wrench open my legs, but that's all distant and possibly happening to someone else now.

Or to my dying body.

Which is fine, because I'm not really there anymore.

I'm floating to the window. Heading for the bright afternoon sun beckoning me through the glass.

Not scared of falling anymore.

Because I'm weightless now.

I can just float away.

Up into the clouds.

And then the pain is back, a spear through my chest. I suck in a ragged breath, and turn my head.

Nick has his hand on my chest. He's leaning his weight on the bullet wound, grinning at me.

I reach up, numb fingers trying to pry his hand off my chest.

But then his body is between my legs, holding them open. And he's looking down.

There's still something cold touching my face, but it's different now. I use my good hand, my left hand, to feel alongside my head.

It touches cool metal.

The gun.

Pain, but not in my chest anymore. Down there. Down where he's looking.

Let him look at my cunt, I don't care.

Because then he's not looking up. He's not seeing me fumble with the gun. Trying to pick it up.

He shifts, his hand digging harder into my torn flesh. I cry out, and he groans as if the sound gets him hard.

But I don't care, because now I'm holding the gun.

Pointing it.

It shakes.

Oh God, how it shakes.

It weighs thirty million tons.

I pull the trigger.

Where I expect him to go flying backward, he instead collapses on top of me. I cry out at the agony when his head slams into my chest. I try and push him off me, but I've only got one working arm and he's still wedged between my legs.

I let out a wail of frustrated agony, but thank God I'm taking a breath when I hear footsteps coming up the stairs.

It takes everything I have to lift the gun again. I sling my arm over Nick's back, gritting my teeth through the pain as I try and aim it at the door.

It's too quiet out there.

Is it Jess? She said she'd leave—how long was Nick busy with me for? And if she's gone, then who's coming up the stairs?

The impostor.

He's back.

I curl my finger around the trigger and blink sweat and blood out of my eyes.

The gun steadies.

Someone yanks at the handle. They rattle the door. Then a shot goes off.

Pop!

There's a thump, and the door gives in, handle distorted by the bullet.

A silhouette darkens the doorway.

I squeeze the trigger.

The clap of the gun is deafening. It falls from my hand onto the floor. The figure in the doorway leans to the side, and then slowly topples to the ground.

I killed him.

I killed my father!

Tears spring into my eyes, blurring my vision. I let out a choking sob and try to shift Nick off me. He won't budge, but then the bundle by the door starts moving.

A hand appears on the carpet. Thin. Delicate. Speckled with blood.

Jess.

I shot her.

But I didn't kill her.

"No, fuck," I whisper. My movements become urgent, but I still can't shift the fucking dead body off me.

A second hand joins the first. Jess drags the top half of her body into the room. She looks dazed—eyes wide and unfocused, lips slack—but as soon as she spots me on the bed, her eyes narrow.

Other than her hands, I can't see any more blood. But it's as if the bottom half of her body doesn't work anymore, because she doesn't stand, or crawl...she just keeps dragging herself over the floor.

I stick my hand in Nick's hoody pouch. Cigarettes, gum, a wallet. Useless shit.

I swallow hard, steel myself, and reach down.

My hand brushes smooth skin.

Lower.

I recoil when I touch his ass. If I could lift my head, I'd be able to see better, but there's a terrible lameness spreading through me.

The dizziness is back. It comes in waves, each higher than the last.

It would be so easy just to let one of those waves take me away. To let it consume me.

Because it promises no more pain. No more leaden terror.

Jess grabs onto the side of the bed. How did she get here so quickly? Or did I actually pass out for a second?

I reach down again, pushing away my disgust and horror at touching Nick's dead skin.

He must have pushed his pants down to his fucking knees, because I can't feel them. Even if he had anything useful in them, they're too far out of reach.

Jess grabs my right hand, tugs. Despite the dead body lying on top of me, she still shifts my arm enough to send a spike of pain through me. I sob, my breath catching. I wriggle furiously, even hoping that her grip might pull me out from under Nick.

She's grimacing at me, but her face is whiter than the walls. "F'kn 'tch," she says through her teeth. "F'kn kill you."

Metal drags over the fabric. She lifts Nick's gun, aims it point-blank at my face.

I don't even have time to close my eyes.

This bang isn't as loud as the first, but maybe that's because I'm already dying. I also expected this bullet to feel like the first. Like a blazing-hot punch, then a poker being shoved through my flesh.

But I just see red.

The side of my face is hot, then warm, then cold. And very wet.

I blink.

The world turns pink.

I blink again.

Jess slides to the floor.

Shapes move, too fast for me to make out. A weight is lifted. I hear voices, a yell.

Someone looms over me. My eyes are squeezed closed from the pain, so I don't know who.

For some reason, I'm sure it's Nick. That he's somehow still alive, and he's about to climb on me again. To finish what he started.

"No," I manage, slurring the word. "No."

Another wave of dizziness comes. The biggest yet. My face tingles furiously, my fingers ice-cold and numb.

I try to fight it, but I can't. It's too big, too powerful.

It lifts me up, so I'm flying, and then I come down the other side. But I just keep sinking and sinking.

And sinking.

CHAPTER FORTY-THREE
CASS

When I step inside the upstairs bedroom, my mind balks at what I see. So while I'm still pointing my gun, I don't have a clue what I'm supposed to be shooting at.

Shock makes my brain slow as fuck as I try to work through it.

There's a thick trail of blood leading from the passage outside into the bedroom.

A *kid's* bedroom.

The one from the video. Even still has the same furniture, except some of it's been moved around and the paint is faded.

The blood leads to a woman propped up all awkward against the side of the bed like she's attempting an advanced yoga pose.

She's a suspect. Definitely.

Then there's the big dude on the bed. But he's taking a little nap. Fuck knows why he decided to take his dick out first, but I'm sure my brain will get to that in just a sec.

Then I see her.

My little Trinity.

And then the gun pointed at her beautiful face. My finger squeezes the trigger without bothering to get me up to speed first.

Trinity recoils when the woman's head goes splat inches from her face.

The woman—kinda dead looking now, especially with the hole in the back of her head—slides down and sprawls on the carpet.

Trinity looks like she just got done auditioning for Carrie, and they made her do the scene with the bucket of pig's blood.

But then Rube's in front of me, and all I see is his back as he charges the bed.

He grabs the guy off of her and tosses him to the floor like a sack of rubbish. He goes to lift Trinity, but I manage to dart forward and catch his arm.

I shove my pistol against his chest.

If I could have spoken, I'd have told him to back off with his big fucking hulk hands so he doesn't break her. But my chest's all clogged up with panic.

Trinity's eyes flutter. Her blood is *everywhere*. But somehow, she's still got some left. It wells out of the crater in her chest, and then disappears into the already blood-soaked fabric of her dress.

I smooth her skirt down her legs as I study the wound.

I'm the furthest thing from a paramedic, but Apollo and I were the fixer-uppers back in the basement. I know a hole like that can't keep pissing out blood, or else Trinity's going to run dry.

The sudden high-pitched whine in my ears tries to compete with my pounding heart. And there's more noise on top of that. But I have no time to listen to any of that. I have to keep Trinity's blood *inside*.

I slap the flat of my hand over the wound and press.

Hard.

Her pained groan goes through me like a fork through the heart. But I can't let up. When it starts seeping through my fingers, I grit my teeth and I put my knee on her.

Her whimper sounds exactly like the kind a kitten would make while I'm crushing it between my bare hands.

"Fuck," I whisper. "Rube, call an ambulance."

But he doesn't answer.

At first, I don't know why. And then I hear it.

Thud.

Thud.

Thud.

I drag my head around.

My eyes shut on their own.

Christ.

Jesus *fucking* Christ. That is not how you use a gun.

"Rube." I swallow down bile. "Rube!"

Thud.

......

Thud.

I retch anyway. "Rube, Christ, call the fucking ambulance!"

Rube's knees creak as he stands. He lets out a blustery breath, sounding more animal than human. Something falls to the carpet, and I can only assume it's the gun he was using to cave in the man's skull.

I'm not going to be able to sleep for a week.

I keep my eyes closed until I'm facing Trinity again, and only then dare open them.

I think the bleeding has stopped.

Dear God, let the bleeding have stopped.

But she's passed out, and that's not good.

"Trin? Baby girl. Wake up."

"She's been shot," comes Rube's voice.

My skin goes cold. He's not even out of breath. He sounds...

Like he always does.

Maybe even a touch calmer than usual.

Shock, that's all. He's obviously in shock. Fuck, *I'm* in shock.

But I'm keeping her blood in, and that's all that matters.

Rube doesn't matter right now. What he was doing to the dead guy over there, that doesn't matter either.

My stomach convulses.

Nope. Keeping my puke *in*.

"I'm not sure of the address. Hold on." I only hear Rube's footsteps when he reaches the tiles out in the hall.

"Apollo!"

I jerk at his bellow.

"What's the address?"

2142 Maude Street, Trinity whispers.

My eyes fly open. But those white lips aren't moving.

Great. Just fucking great. Now I'm hallucinating?

Her chest isn't moving under my knee either.

What's worse? Suffocating, or bleeding out?

But no. Our girl's stronger than that. She can breathe with me on top of her, right?

I brush my fingers against her cheek, smearing around the blood on her face. Shit...I can't let the guys see her in this state. She looks like a medieval prostitute who applied her rouge by candlelight.

I snag the hem of my shirt. Wet it with saliva. Wipe it over her skin. That works. But God, there's a lot of blood on her face. I keep licking my shirt and wiping it off.

Her cheek is semi-clean. I move onto her forehead.

Is it just me, or is she slightly colder than a living person should be? Nope.

Not a chance am I starting to think shit like that. She's just having a little siesta. Lot of work, fighting off a big guy like that. I'm not hundreds, but I think she shot him in the head too.

I have to take her to a shooting range sometime. She's a fucking natural. Okay, admittedly, it was as point-blank as you can get. I'm sure he's got powder burn. Ha, ha—we'll never know. Rube caved in his fucking skull with the gun.

"How'd you get so much blood on you, babe?" I ask her.

You shot the back of that bitch's head off, Trinity says.

"Whoa, easy on the snark there, little girl. Who's the one plugging you up? I believe it's me. You keep up that attitude, I'll let you bleed out."

Oh no, Cass, please don't do that. I love you so much. I want to live so I can thank you for saving my life, Trinity croons.

"That's more like it." I swipe my damp shirt over her nose. "And don't worry, you'll have plenty of time to thank me for saving your life. Rest of your life, come to think about it." Soon as her nose is clean, I press the tip of my finger to it. *"Boop!"*

"Cass," comes Apollo's voice from the doorway.

Christ. Can't he see I'm trying to keep our girl alive?

"What?"

"C-ass." This time, there's a hitch in Apollo's voice. I stop trying to clean Trinity's blood-splattered face and glance over my shoulder at the door.

"Get up," says the man behind Apollo as he walks them inside. Dark eyes scan the room, taking in the partially headless corpse on one side, then the other body on the floor by the bed.

He's a handsome man, but unnaturally so. His nose is just too narrow and shapely. His cheekbones slightly too pronounced. Like he was good looking to start with, and then went under the knife a few times just for shits and giggles.

"I said, get up." He presses the muzzle of his gun so hard against Apollo's ear that my brother's head tilts to the side.

"N-No," I manage. "If I do, then she'll die."

"If you don't, then *he* dies."

Apollo's holding tight to the arm slung around his upper chest. His eyes are closed, but I really wish they were open so I could at least have a chance of communicating with him.

It's pointless, though.

He's not a fighter like us. He's the thinker. The philosopher. A true hippy who believes violence is never the answer.

Bet he's regretting some of his life choices now.

"You always a dick to strangers?" I ask him as I furiously try to think of a way out of this.

Could shoot him, of course. There's a gun on the floor. The dead woman must have dropped it there. But I can't move that far or Trinity will bleed out. Plus, Mr. Vain looks trigger happy enough to shoot me if I so much as fart without his permission.

My comment curls up his lips ever so slightly. And God, that pseudo-smile makes my blood run ice-cold.

"You don't know who I am?" He shifts his grip on Apollo, grabbing a fistful of his hair instead of the chokehold. He turns my brother's head to the side so he can stare at Apollo's face. "Trevor recognized me."

A shudder goes through Apollo.

No.

It can't be.

If this guy was involved with our captivity ten years ago, I would have remembered him. Which means he must be a new player in this fucked up game, but who? Is he Gabriel's replacement?

But doesn't matter. Whoever he is, he's about to kill one, if not all, of the people in this room.

Where the fuck are Rube and Zach?

Rube went into the hall looking for Apollo so he could get the address...

I lock eyes with the new Guardian. And it's as if he reads my motherfucking mind. I barely open my mouth before he turns and slams the door shut behind him.

But the lock's busted, so it pops open again just an inch.

"Rube! Zach! Help!" My throat burns how I yell, but fuck knows if they can hear me.

Pointless. They're already dead, Trinity says.

Christ, not now, babe. *Please,* not now.

Okay, fine, she says. *They're alive. They're just busy, right? Jerking off somewhere, having a puff, taking a dump.*

She's got a mouth on her, this one. I'll have to take her to task for it when we get out of this jam.

The Guardian sees the problem with the door the moment I do, though.

And that, finally, is when Apollo's balls decide to drop. Most of us had that happen during puberty. Nope...not him.

He slams his elbow into the Guardian's stomach.

Which, sadly, doesn't do much. It just makes the guy grimace and then pistol-whip him so hard he goes down like someone pulled the plug.

"Fuck you, you shit-eating cunt!" I yell.

The Guardian doesn't even look in my direction. I guess he's established I'm not going anywhere.

He walks over and picks up the chair by the dresser and jams it under the door handle.

Literally a second before something big and angry slams into it on the other side.

Fuck, we *both* get a fright.

The Guardian steps back, gun raised, and points it at the door.

He pulls the trigger. The shot goes off. A hole appears like magic in the center of the door.

Right where Rube's chest would have been.

The assault against the door stops. There's a heavy thump outside.

Not unlike a big body hitting the floor.

I'm starting to lose grip on reality. The world is shifting ever so slightly, like a roller coaster ride just starting up.

I look down at Trinity's ashen face. I don't know if she's still alive. I press my fingers to the artery on the side of her neck, but I can't feel anything.

"Get off her." The Guardian is closer now.

"Might as well shoot me," I tell him as I drop my head and look at him over the point of my shoulder. "Because that's the only way it's happening, you cunt."

"Hmm." He takes another step closer. "Sebastian, isn't it?"

The ground drops out beneath me. I shake my head, leaning back, trying to get away without taking my weight off Trinity's chest.

"Yes, that's right." The Guardian tilts his head a little, and his voice becomes husky. "I remember you. You were the little junkie."

He lifts his free hand, swipes it down in front of his face like mimes do. Happy/Sad. But his expression doesn't change except to become...hungrier.

"Always doped up," he says. "I'm not surprised you don't remember me."

"Guessing you had an uglier face back then," I tell him, but there's no strength in my voice.

Don't listen to him.

It doesn't matter.

All that matter is keeping—

"Not at all. But I had to change. You understand."

And then I do. Like a fucking lightning bolt hits my brain and implants the information there.

I look down at the dead body I'm leaning my knee on. Then up at him. "I don't see the resemblance."

He laughs and comes a little closer, but still too far away for me to attempt anything. "Why would you?" he asks, and then runs his hand through his hair like he's putting on the charm.

I want to throw up those fish tacos I ate seven weeks ago.

"She's not my daughter."

I narrow my eyes at her. "Right. She's Gabriel's. Guess she got her mom's good looks then."

Something touches his expression then. The faintest micro-movement around his eyes. A twitch of his lips.

"It was their idea, calling her Trinity," he says. His voice sounds a touch hollow now. "They thought we'd all raise her. The three of us."

His eyes hadn't exactly been cheery before, but they're dead cold now. He glances down at Trinity's body, then back up at me. "Monica would have aborted her like the others, but then that prick interfered."

As if my earlier revelation had taken up every bit of computing power, my brain fails to comprehend what he's saying.

The Guardian looks at Trinity again. "Her father was a pain in the ass, but he worshiped me. Do you have any idea the things people will do if they think you're a God amongst men?"

I open my mouth to say something brutal, but then there's a gun in my face. "It was rhetorical, Sebastian."

As his finger curls around the trigger, a distant wail catches both our attention.

Ambulance.

Police siren.

And that's not the only thing I notice. Apollo is picking himself up off the floor.

When the Guardian looks back at me, I show him my teeth. "Think you can get out of here in time?" I ask him.

His eyes narrow. He straightens the gun. His lips part, a particularly malicious gleam in his eyes as he starts to speak.

And then Apollo hits him over the head with the chair he quietly took out from under the door handle. When Keith Malone crumples to the ground, my body sags as if it wants to follow.

But I grit my teeth, gather saliva, and spit it on his slack face. "That was rhetorical, you sick fuck."

CHAPTER FORTY-FOUR
ZACH

At the top of the stairs, the hallway splits east to west. Rube and Cass head west, so Apollo and I take the east wing.

"Stay close," I murmur to Apollo. "And be quiet."

"You're the one talking," he whispers back.

I open the first door and we peek inside.

Crib.

Mobile with stuffed animals.

Gender-neutral geese dancing over the walls.

I start opening the closet doors to make sure no one's hiding inside one waiting to leap out at us. But the closets are empty. As in, there's not even a single diaper in sight.

This place creeps me the fuck out. It feels staged, like the owners moved out ages ago and the real estate agent set it up for an open house.

Who lived here? Where are they now?

"Next room," I murmur, backing up with my weapon still pointed, just in case someone appears out of thin air.

A gunshot sounds.

I spin around and face a locked door.

Apollo's not inside with me. Then I hear a key turning in the lock and my hair stands on end.

What the fuck?

"Apollo?" I run up and try the door handle.

Locked.

Christ. "Apollo!"

I know it wasn't him that locked me inside, but now I'm shitting myself wondering what happened to him. I bang on the door a few times, but that's not helping. I could shoot at the lock, but what are the chances of the bullet ricocheting and hitting me somewhere vital?

I start kicking the door, but it's sturdy as fuck.

"Apollo! What's the address?"

Rube.

"Reuben!" I yell. "Reuben, open up!"

But there's no response. What the fuck is going on out there?

Screw this. I step back, raise my gun—

"Rube! Zach! Help!"

I pause. That's Cass. But wasn't he just with Rube? What the—

Thud.

Thud.

The sound's coming from down the hall. Like someone's banging on something. I turn on my heel, scan the room. My eyes latch onto the window.

With every distant thud, my heart climbs another inch up my throat.

I shove my gun into my belt and hurry over.

I don't stop to think. I don't even allow myself to give the ground more than a passing glance.

My sight is fixed on a nearby tree. From what I saw before I looked away, there's a good yard of thin air between me and the closest bough.

But there's a gunfight going on, and my brothers are involved. I don't know who's on the winning side, or if there even *is* a winning side.

I bundle myself up tight, and then push away from the window as hard as I can.

My stomach slams into the bough. A stray branch scratches my face. I fumble, manage to get an arm slung over the bough, and hold on until I have my bearings.

I work my way to the main trunk and climb down. I drop down the last few feet, already running for the patio doors.

Something deep and dark and rectangular draws my eye.

A grave.

A *grave?*

I race upstairs, my legs almost giving out when I see Rube on the floor. I fall down beside him, and start panting as I hike up his shirt with a shaking hand.

Gutshot. Surprisingly little blood. Does that mean the bullet's still in there?

There's a crash from inside the room, but Rube needs me more right now.

Except...I don't have a fucking clue what to do.

A hand lands on my shoulder, trembling slightly. I look up into Apollo's face.

"Cass needs you," he says.

"But—"

"Go." He falls to his knees beside Reuben and starts ripping off a piece of his shirt. I stand on unsteady legs and half walk, half stumble into the room.

It's the one from the video.

But there's blood here now.

And three dead bodies.

Four if you count—

"No! Trinity!" I rush forward, but then Cass is in front of me, driving me back. "No!" I try and shove him, but he somehow manages to herd me away from the bed. My back slams into a wall.

The sound of police sirens and ambulances want my attention, but I don't give it to them.

Cass clasps my head in his hands, wiping my face, forcing me to look at him. "Hey, bud. Hey. Over here."

We lock eyes.

"I did everything I could, okay? I tried to save her, but she's gone. She's *gone.* You read me?"

My heart stops beating. "CPR," I croak.

"Got no blood left," Cass says. He's grinning, but it's the kind of smile you see on a corpse where the fleshy bits of the face have been picked clean by scavengers. "It just kept oozing out. Can't put it back in, can I? So that's that. But listen, buddy, listen to me, okay?"

There's a heavy drone in my ears, which makes complying difficult, but I nod anyway. My eyes dart to the side as I try to look past him, but he tightens his grip on my face and sinks his fingertips into my scalp.

"Look, the police are going to be here in like…fucking *seconds*. All right? Now we need to do something very important. And we gonna have to do it really fast."

He steps back. Points.

A dark-haired man lays sprawled on the carpet. There's a gun near his right hand.

"We got to take this motherfucker downstairs. There's this big hole outside—"

"The grave."

Talking is good. Not looking at the bed, that's good too. Doing something that gets me out of this room? Even better.

"Yeah, the grave." Cass pats my chest. "Good. So, you grab his legs, yeah?"

Cass backs up, still grinning like a fucking Jack-O-Lantern, and grabs the guy's wrists.

"Come on, Zach. Stay with me."

I keep my eyes down. When my vision blurs, I blink them clear.

"We can do this."

I nod, not trusting myself to speak. But as soon as Cass breaks eye contact, my gaze flies to the bed.

She looks so serene.

So pale.

So fucking dead.

I blink again. My chest feels like it's caving in. Tighter and tighter and tighter. I try and breathe, try to clamp my mouth shut, but then another set of hot tears races down my cheeks. The salt in my mouth triggers a sob.

"No, n-no," Cass says, voice wobbling. "Fuck you, *Zachary*. You're grabbing his fucking legs, and we're putting him in that fucking grave!"

I choke, wipe my face on my shoulder, and lift the guy's feet.

He groans.

Maybe a normal guy would have dropped him. I don't. I hold on even fucking tighter. Because he undoubtedly had something to do with the dead girl on the bed, and that means I owe him a world of hurt.

A spasm goes through the guy's body, and then he lifts his head. He looks at me, dazed, unfocused.

There's something wrong with his eye.

Outside, in the hall, someone starts sobbing. Big, heavy, *ragged* sobs.

It takes me a few seconds to work it out.

Time where I'm holding back the ephemeral agony gouging out my lungs and stomach. Time where I'm moving back, dragging the guy's stomach over the pale blue carpet. Time where I'm staring at that fucked up eye so I won't look up again and see Trinity on the bed and lose my shit.

The man twists in our grip. His strength is coming back. There's a wet slick on the back of his head. Splinters in his hair.

That's where the broken chair comes from.

"Doorway," Cass warns. "Take a left, bud."

I angle out the door.

Apollo's head is on Rube's chest. His blond hair shifts with every sob wracking his lean body. He's hugging Rube with his elbows, hands fisted in Rube's shirt.

The guy we're dragging begins fighting us. Cass's grin turns into a grimace. My arms are starting to burn from the weight, from keeping his ankles clasped when he tries to kick his legs.

He keeps bucking off the floor, forcing us to take his full weight instead of letting us drag him over the tiles. He sends a loathing glare at me over his shoulder, mouth twisted with frustration and fury.

And then I get what's wrong with his eye.

It happened a few times to Rube, and would always freak me out.

His contact has slipped. Like an eclipse, the dark lens creates a crescent from the lighter iris below.

I almost drop his legs.

But then I think he recognizes me too. And his face loses all color.

I don't blame him.

He knows what happened to my parents. Fuck, maybe he was even the one who found them.

Were they still in those chairs? No, wait...the chairs must have burned in the fire.

I honestly wish I could have stayed to see their faces.

See how they struggled to get free.

How their skin began blistering from the heat.

Fire cleanses.

It was the only thing that made sense. I was doing them a fucking favor. And, if it didn't work, then at least they'd already know what Hell felt like before they got there.

I walk faster.

The sirens are so much closer now.

"Hey, easy," Cass calls out.

So I rip the man's wrists out of his grip.

There's no time.

"Zach, wait!"

The man immediately flips onto his back and grabs a passing rail before I can haul him down the stairs.

We stop.

Stare at each other.

My Ghost's chest rises and falls, the action speeding up the longer I glare at him.

Trinity's stepfather.

Keith fucking Malone.

But he looks different now. Too different to account for age.

Plastic surgery then.

He really didn't want anyone figuring out he'd faked his own death.

Like Gabriel.

Like Trin—

Pain slices through me. My jaw clenches so hard the enamel on my teeth squeaks.

Cass stomps on Keith's hand. The man curls toward the pain, letting out a wordless yell.

I yank him down the stairs.

He tries to sit up, but his head still hits several of the stairs on the way down. Each time, he leaves a splotch of blood on the wood.

I angle him down the short landing, and then we go down the next flight.

Cass hurries after, stomping on his hands every time Keith manages to grab hold of something. He must already have several broken fingers—they jiggle around too loosely as we make our way downstairs.

Police lights paint the living room walls blue and red. Outside, car doors slam.

I grimace up at Cass. "Grab his fucking arms."

He does so immediately, deftly avoiding Keith's teeth when the man tries to bite him.

We hurry through the patio doors, Keith fighting us every step of the way. But Cass and I, we're filled with the Holy Spirit.

It gives us strength.

It guides our feet.

Keith gasps in pain when we drop him into the grave. It's only about five feet deep—I guess whoever was digging it didn't do all that well in school. But his body is cast in shadow when he rolls onto his side and coughs.

"Hurry," Cass says, a shovel already in his hands.

When the first spade of dirt hits Keith's face, he scrambles up and tries to claw his way out of the grave.

Cass slams his shovel against the back of Keith's head.

But not hard.

Just enough to send him toppling over. He lies there at the bottom, dazed, as we frantically pile more dirt over him.

I hear voices coming from inside. But no one's headed out back yet.

I guess there's enough to deal with inside.

We throw heaps of dirt around Keith's legs and torso, trying to weigh him down as much as possible. Keith comes to when dirt starts hitting his head again. He twists, spitting and cursing when a shovel of dirt hits his face. He pushes his hand down, face contorting as he tries to pull himself out of the dirt.

But maybe he's concussed, because he can't seem to drag himself free.

And then he screams for help.

I jump into the grave and stomp on his head. He goes still, and then starts shaking. I stay there, my foot on the top of his head, as Cass fills in more dirt.

Just before I climb out to help Cass, I crouch down and brush away dirt from his one eye. It trembles, but it doesn't open.

"See you in Hell, Keith Malone."

We shovel in as much dirt as we dare, toss the spades into the hole on top of him and then dart around the side of the house. We wash our hands and shake loose dirt off our clothes, and then enter through the front door.

As we step inside the living room, I see a pair of cops step out onto the patio.

A hand fumbles against my leg. Cass laces his fingers through mine. I look down, then up at his face.

He's staring after the cops, shoulders stiff, jaw bunched.

"If he's still alive..." Cass murmurs. Tears brim in his icy-blue eyes, turning them shiny as fucking marbles.

"Then we'll find him again." I squeeze his hand fuck hard. "And we'll dig him another fucking grave."

CHAPTER FORTY-FIVE
TRINITY

I'm blindfolded. Gagged. My hands bound behind my back. My bare feet scrape over an icy concrete floor as I shuffle around in utter darkness trying to figure out where the hell I am.

Panic ratchets up my heart rate to that of a hummingbird's.

I'm not alone in this dark.

I'll never find my way out.

Something follows me. I hear it crawling over the floor behind me.

Nails *scratch* on the concrete. Skin drags.

My foot slams into a mattress.

Before I can find my balance, I topple forward.

The bedding is wet and warm.

Someone bled here.

You, Trinity. That's your blood.

I push away the voice as I struggle frantically to stand. The thing crawling after me starts panting. Desperate as I am.

Finally I get to my feet. I surge forward, running as fast as I can.

Straight into someone standing in the dark. Strong arms catch me before I can fall. They drag me close, and hold me tight.

It should have been comforting, but I know who these arms belong to, and I don't want to be anywhere near him.

My scream gets stuck in my throat. It's barely a wheeze. Fingers tangle in my hair and drag my head back. My blindfold is ripped off.

There's a click.

Light blooms, sickly yellow, from the bulb dangling above us.

I'm in the basement of 2142 Maude Street, but it's larger now. The floor is covered with dirty, blood-stained mattresses.

And there's a small, curled up body on each. Their shadows shift and dance as the light bulb swings left and right.

Almost makes them look alive.

I stare into my father's face, and Keith Malone looks down at me without expression.

Nails scrape against the floor. Plastic sheeting now—no longer concrete.

The panting comes closer.

I try to move away, but Keith is holding me too tight.

"You should be dead," he says. "I told them to kill you."

Nick and Jess. Are they here? With Keith's grip in my hair, I can't turn around to look. I can't even see how close the panting, crawling thing is that was following me in the dark.

"I will have to rectify that, child."

Keith's head snaps back. His mouth opens, but too wide.

Much too fucking wide.

A long, serpentine tongue uncoils and slaps onto my upturned face. I try to cringe away, but he's keeping me rooted to the spot.

His tongue leaves a layer of slime on my skin as it slithers down my neck, like a slug working its way down my skin. With a tug, he pulls down the front of my dress. I try to collapse in on myself, to hide my nakedness, but I can't. Not with my hands still bound.

His tongue creeps over my shoulder like a blind, wet snake. Searching. Hunting over my naked skin.

I try to scream, but I can't draw enough breath. My lungs are too tight.

The panting thing reaches my feet. Ragged nails scrape over my skin as it claws its way up my body.

It's smaller than me, but it's angry.

So fucking angry.

It wants to hurt anything, anyone.

Its hands grab my skirt as it tries to lift itself. As it tries to climb higher. My dress slides down to my hips and threatens to go all the way down my legs.

All the while that tongue leaves sticky trails over my breast, a nipple, the hollow in my throat.

The panting thing catches hold of my wrist. Drags itself up. The exertion makes it breathe faster. Like a dog back from a run. Quick and hard.

The sound comes closer as it crawls up my back.

Hair snags in my fingers.

And then I know what it is.

Who it is.

It had been lying on the mattress in that pitch-black basement. Already dead. That's what I'd been smelling. A girl with short hair, or a boy with long hair.

Dead.

Alone.

There in the dark.

Keith's tongue finds what it was looking for.

The panting thing claws my face, tearing out my gag.

A slick tongue forces its way deep into the hole in my chest, going all the way through to my back.

The pain is excruciating.

A scream tears apart my throat.

Cold, dead little fingers creep over my face and try to seal my lips.

"Ssh, Trinity," the child murmurs in my ear. "Don't let the bad man hear you."

CHAPTER FORTY-SIX
TRINITY

My body jerks violently. I clap a hand over my chest, grimacing as I sit up in bed.

I dislodge two arms on the way. Apollo mumbles something under his breath as he turns and goes straight back to sleep.

Cass looks like he's still sleeping.

I shimmy out of bed as carefully as I can, and hurry out of the room. I pad down the stairs, take a left, and sprint into the nearest bathroom.

If the basin had been another foot away, I'd have missed it. I retch violently, repetitively, my eyes streaming with pain.

I shudder as I rinse out the sink, then my mouth.

Again.

That's the eighth night in a row.

I gargle half the bottle of mouth wash and stand at the foot of the stairs, staring into the dark.

But I don't want to go back to sleep. Not if that fucking thing is waiting to pounce on me as soon as I close my eyes.

I head downstairs and let myself out onto the patio.

The ocean sounds calm tonight. The crash and sigh of the waves are barely audible from where I'm standing.

I flinch when hands wrap around my upper arms.

"Same one?" Cass asks.

I had woken him.

"Yeah." I swipe my hair out of my face, put a hand over my chest. "It hurts more every time."

"Psychic pain," Cass says, coming to stand beside me and leaning his elbows on the railing. "Doctor said you're hundreds. That shit's healed."

I rub my palm into the scar just below my collarbone. "He also told me it wouldn't become infected, and it did. He also told me the scar would be barely noticeable." I turn to Cass and point at the dark, puckered mark on my skin. "This thing is visible from the fucking moon."

"Vain much, princess?" he says through a smirk, and reaches for me.

I step back. "I'm not kidding, Cass. It *hurts*. It feels…"

"Like it's happening again?" he asks, cocking his head. "You read those articles I sent you, right?"

I roll my eyes and go back to staring at the ocean. They've all been trying to help me through this, but I guess no one comes back from a near-death experience without a little emotional baggage. Me? I never pack light.

A scar.

PTSD.

So many triggers they have to line up.

I smile to myself.

I'm one of them now. The Brotherhood. Just as broken and fucked up as they are. All it took was getting raped and shot.

Kismet.

Cass slings an arm over my shoulder and draws me against his chest. He's wearing my pink robe, but didn't bother closing it up—his skin is cool and smooth and oh so delicious to touch. I slide my fingertips over his pecs and down his ribs, then circle his waist and squeeze him as I lay my head against his chest.

His heart thumps away quietly in his ribcage.

If it weren't for him, I wouldn't be alive.

Any of them.

But especially Cass.

I don't remember much of what happened in the blue room. My therapist said the memories might come back one day or never. I don't know if I want to know everything—my men already told me everything I need to know.

"Hey, I've got an idea," Cass murmurs into my ear. "Something to get you out of that pretty head of yours."

"We're not going to raid the fridge," I tell him, although secretly if he pushed me, I'd probably cave. I've already put on ten pounds—I'll be rolling around like one of those kids in Charlie and the Chocolate Factory if my men keep stuffing me with food.

"Not what I had in mind." Cass steps away from me and goes to the edge of the infinity pool.

He shrugs his shoulders. My pink satin robe slides down his back and pools by his feet.

Oh God, he was naked and I didn't even notice.

How could I not notice?

Because I was stuck in my head.

He takes his time getting in the pool, as if he knows how much it turns me on looking at his body. Every muscle is toned and lean, from his taut neck to his slim biceps, to his almost-eight-pack to his gorgeous ass.

"Is it cold?" I ask him, as he slips into the black pool.

"A little." He twirls around, sending ripples to all four sides. "Promise I'll keep you warm if you get in."

I glance up at the main bedroom's balcony. There are no lights on up there. Zach and Apollo must still be fast asleep.

"Five minutes," I tell him. "I don't want to be all groggy for the doctor's appointment tomorrow."

Cass holds up a hand, fingers spread. He watches me intently as I take off my vest and boxer shorts, and swims closer when I step hesitantly into the pool.

The water isn't as cold as I thought it would be, but I still let out a theatrical shiver when it hits my nipples.

"Oh, my poor baby girl," Cass murmurs, scooping me into his arms and spinning us around in the water.

He urges my legs around his waist, his hands lingering on my ass as we take another slow spin.

"You know that crap about how time heals all wounds?" he asks, putting his forehead against mine.

I nod, staring into his pale blue eyes.

"Well forget about that. You have us, okay? What we can't heal, we can easily make you forget." His lips brush my ear. My jaw. My cheek.

I turn, but he pulls back, teasing me with just a whisper of his lips before they're out of reach.

"Cass," I whine, tightening my thighs around his waist.

"Princess," he says, in much the same tone. "Don't be so demanding."

"I just want a kiss. But then we have to go to bed."

"And the demands just keep coming." He squeezes my ass with both hands, hard enough to make me draw a quick breath. "When will you learn?"

"Hopefully never." I try and chase his mouth, but he keeps moving his head away.

Just when I'm about to give up on our kiss, my ass hits the small island in the middle of the pool. During the day, there's a fountain that splashes into the pool but right now it's just a slab of stone.

Cass pushes me against the side, grabs my hair, and kisses me.

I melt against him, losing myself in the passion of his expert lips and forceful tongue.

He breaks off our kiss and then hoists me onto the edge before sliding his hands down the front of my body. Tweaking one nipple, then the other. Then his fingers glide down my stomach.

He's already wedged his body between my legs, but I spread them a little wider when he gets close.

"God, I fucking love it when you open your legs for me," he murmurs as he pushes up on his hands to give me a peck on the lips. "You're such a fast learner, my precious little slut."

He scoots me back, careful not to scrape my skin on the stone and reaches into the water to grab my leg. He lifts it, positioning my foot on the edge, kissing my knee as he stares up at me with a wicked gleam in his eyes.

"Cass..."

"What?"

"We shouldn't be—"

He slaps my pussy, and I cut off with a sigh.

"We should get back in bed," I continue hurriedly as he lifts my other leg, positions it on the other side of my body.

He ignores me, of course. He's too busy staring at my pussy. Giving my knee an absent, cat-like lick, he sticks his hand in the water and starts stroking his cock.

"We will, soon as I'm done with you."

"But the others—"

"Can have whatever's left." His eyes dart up to mine as he strokes my pussy with his fingertips.

"Fuck," I murmur, my eyelashes trembling as I fight for my eyes not to close. If they did, it would be much too easy to surrender.

This is wrong.

It's not written in stone or anything, but when there's anything more than kissing, everyone's invited.

But Cass has been tempting me ever since my last bandage came off. Luring me away, kissing me until I'm breathless, and then trying to get into my pants.

I've fought him off more times than I can count, and I'm fucking proud of that.

But tonight...

He strokes my pussy, sending tingles up my body. I tangle my hands in his hair as he plants tiny kisses on my inner thighs, his eyes never leaving mine.

Like he's daring me to tell him to stop. Fuck, I want to. Because this feels so wrong—just the two of us, out here in the dark but so very exposed. All it would take is one of my men waking up and wandering onto the balcony for a smoke, and they'd know what we did.

Alone.

When he spreads my legs even wider, ducks down, and drags his tongue through my slit, I almost yank out all of his hair.

I force his mouth harder against my pussy, his tongue deeper. I lift my hips, and start rocking against his mouth, one hand behind me for balance, the other keeping his head exactly where I want it.

And fuck it feels good.

Diabolically good.

I never want it to end.

Seconds later, I'm already close to coming.

He draws back, licks his lips as he stares up at me. He slides two fingers inside me, beckoning. "Come on, Princess. You know you want to."

Oh God, I'm like fucking putty in his hands. He played the long game and I guess he finally won. I don't have the willpower to resist him anymore.

He licks my pussy again, his fingers still deep inside me, teasing me. Then he starts sliding them in and out. "This could be my cock," he murmurs. "Stretching you. Filling you."

I shake my head. "We can't."

His eyes narrow. "That's not the right answer, Princess."

"Cass, come on—"

He grabs me around the waist and tugs me off the island. His mouth grinds against mine as he drags me back to the edge of the pool.

And I fall for it.

Because I think he's accepted my decision.

We climb out of the pool. He leads me back into the house, not bothering to pick up my robe, not letting me stop for my clothes.

But we don't go upstairs.

He yanks me away from the stairs when I head for them. When I resist, just for a second, he picks me off my feet and carries me to a chaise lounge in the living room.

"Hey, I thought we were—"

"Sorry, my precious little cock tease." He kisses me again, hard, and drops me on the couch. "This is happening."

I push up onto my elbows. "But it's not—"

He grabs my hair, yanks back my head. "Say 'wrong' one more time…"

I stare at him, my jaw bunched.

They treated me like a glass figurine for the last few months. This is the first time one of them is getting even a little rough with me.

Thank *fucking* God.

"It's wrong," I tell him.

He shows me his teeth. "Then I don't want to be right."

Cass straddles me so fast I don't even have time to fight him. He grabs my wrists, slamming them into the chair above my head. Then he claims my mouth again, kissing me like he hates the fact that I turn him on this much.

And I can feel just how much he wants me. Every inch of his cock is rock hard as it slides over my belly.

He shoves a hand between my legs and follows with a knee.

I have no choice but to let him in.

As soon as both his legs are between mine, he goes to his knees and rakes his eyes over my exposed body.

He slaps my pussy hard enough to make me gasp, and then thrusts a finger inside me.

"You're not even wet enough for them, why the fuck do you want to go upstairs?" he says.

I open my mouth, but he doesn't give me a chance to speak.

His lips are on mine, bruising hard, and then his hand is over my slit. He squeezes, massages me, puts pressure on my clit with the base of his palm.

I moan into his mouth, my legs falling open for him.

"That's better," he whispers.

His fingers spread my pussy open. He dips his hips, dragging the crown of his cock over my dripping slit.

"Getting there."

He presses the tip of his dick against my entrance, and then pulls back to smear my arousal over my clit.

The touch is so light, but still electrifying. I lift my hips, trying to increase the pressure, but he just chuckles at me and nips my breast.

I press my nipple into his mouth, and he teases it with his teeth, his hot, erratic breaths puffing against my skin as he slides his cock along my slit.

"Fuck, please," I moan. "Just..."

"Say it, and I'll consider it."

"Just fuck me."

"Hard?"

"Yes!"

"Not slow?"

I groan. "Yes, slow."

"So slow and hard?

"Cass, fuck...please."

I'm about to start sobbing.

He lets go of my wrists. Sits back on his heels. Strokes his dick and studies me. Then he turns his head a little and says, "What do you think, boys? Hard and fast, or soft and slow?"

I jerk under him, my eyes darting to the dark pools of shadow in the living room.

Zach and Apollo step forward. They're still dressed in their pajamas —a pair of boxers for Zach, and a vest and jocks for Apollo.

They're both hard. The lust in their eyes is unmistakable.

Color blazes over my cheeks. Cass slaps my pussy again. "Eyes up here, Trin."

My eyes fly back to him. "Cass—"

"Let them watch," he says, putting his head to the side. "Maybe if you give them a good show, they'll still want you when I'm done."

When he forces the first inch of cock inside me, everything else ceases to exist. My back arches, a soft sigh escaping my lips. He teases me, keeping just an inch of his dick inside me as he strums my clit.

I'm so fucking close to coming I almost unravel the second he finally thrusts into me.

I let out a breathless moan, scraping my nails down his arm.

He folds down, catching my lips with his. His kiss is deep and soulful as he slowly starts fucking me with every inch of his cock.

Slow.

Hard.

His kiss intoxicates me to the point where the room starts spinning. I stab my nails into his back, then his ass, trying to get him to grind harder against me.

He groans, his lips trembling against mine. "Jesus, princess, you're holding onto me so fucking tight."

He's heavy, but deliciously so. And when he starts moving again, it's slow and steady.

"Are you going to come for me?" he whispers.

"Yes."

"Then come, princess. I want to feel you coming all over my cock."

He kisses me again, and slides a hand between us. He massages my clit with his thumb, slowing down until he's barely moving.

Then he rams into me, filling me with every inch of his dick.

Again.

Again.

But he doesn't surrender my mouth. Doesn't stop teasing my clit.

When I come, it's with a shudder and an explosion of bliss deep inside my core.

He pounds into me, and then his cum fills me. He thrusts again, grunting against my lips, like he wants to get even deeper.

Everything down there tingles furiously when he pulls out. He keeps stroking my clit, each caress sending new tendrils of pleasure through my body.

He gives me a last kiss, soft and gentle, as he climbs off me. I lose myself in his mouth, my legs falling open. His cum leaks out of me, and I don't even care if Zach and Apollo see.

He's still kissing me when the couch sinks down between my legs. I try and look, but he grabs my chin and forces me to keep kissing him. And he never stops massaging my clit.

A cock presses against my entrance.

I groan, shift. I want to know who it is, but he won't let me.

But at soon as that first thrust slams into me, I know.

I gasp as Zach fucks me, so hard I can't kiss Cass back anymore. But he doesn't seem to care. He just rains kisses on my lips and chin until I push him away.

It's not fair.

He had me all to himself.

When I face Zach, he stops fucking me. But his cock is still buried in me to the hilt. My eyes flutter, but I force them wide. I grab his shoulder, urge him down.

He moves stiffly, like he's resisting me.

But he's going to have everything, whether he wants it or not.

I slide my fingers in his hair and rock my hips against him, urging him to fuck me again. "Don't stop," I whisper. "You can fuck me as hard as you want."

There's a moment's hesitation, and then he ducks forward and kisses me. His cock draws out, but it slams back a second later.

Pain, pleasure—they mix and swirl around inside me in a dizzying fog.

We can barely keep our lips together, but it doesn't matter. Just the heat of his breath and the caress of his mouth against mine is enough.

That way, he can breathe in every gasp and catch every moan I make as he punishes me.

"Are you going to come for me too?" he asks, breathless, fervent.

"I don't know," I tell him. This is fucking torture of the best kind, but whether I can come when he's fucking me so hard is anyone's guess.

"Make it happen, little girl," he growls. He straightens, grabs my wrist, and slaps my hand between my legs. "And hurry, because I'm not waiting for you."

He grabs my hips, adding even more force to his powerful thrusts.

"Christ, Zach, you're going to break her," Apollo says.

Zach grabs my hand again, and forces me to touch myself. "You never done this before or something?"

Tears leak from my eyes, but I don't know if it's shame or terror or pain or pleasure.

I don't even care.

Cass strokes my hair. "Come on, baby girl."

I touch myself, start massaging my clit.

"Harder," Cass whispers.

Zach's fingers dimple into my hips. I massage a little harder, my mouth falling open as that tiny nub starts sending urgent pleasure signals soaring through my body.

"That's it," Zach says. "Now faster, sweetheart."

I speed up. My head pushes back into the couch. I start moaning and rocking as I lose control over my body.

"Look at me," Zach snaps.

I force my eyes open, but they're blurry as fuck. He starts slowing, but each thrust is now more violent than the last. The impact of our hipbones meeting goes through my body like an aftershock.

"Fuck," he growls. "You'd better come with me." He grinds into me, filling every inch of me with his cock.

I let out a breathless yell, my back arching off the couch as I climax.

"God," he groans. "You're so fucking tight."

One last thrust has my mind coming loose. Zach fills me with his load, and it dribbles down my slit as he pulls out. When he slams back I let out a sob.

He sits back, stroking a last bit of cum from his cock as he watches me shivering under him.

Then he reaches out blindly and grabs hold of Apollo. "You're up."

I lift my legs, squeezing my thighs together. Apollo hesitates, eyes going wide. He opens his mouth as if to ask if I'm okay, and I let my legs fall open again.

He's between them a second later. His cock slides inside me while Zach's cum is still leaking out.

This couch is ruined.

But I don't give a fuck.

I push onto my elbows, let Cass smooth sweat-slicked hair from my face, and then grab Apollo's head for a kiss.

Apollo thrusts deeper into me. Deeper. Deeper. I lift my legs and wrap them around his waist, and force him in the last bit.

"I love you, Trinity," he murmurs.

"I love you too," I whisper back.

We meld together as he gives me a deep, breathless kiss. He pulls back, thrusts into me again.

"But...uh..."

I frown. "What?"

He gives me a grin. "Doggy style?"

I need their help to flip over. My legs are rubber and my knees jelly. But they get me on my hands and knees, and make me share kisses between Zach and Cass as Apollo rubs his cock over my pussy, hunting out my slit.

When he thrusts into me, I let out a strangled gasp of pleasure.

Zach reaches for my clit, but Apollo slaps his hand away. "Mine." It's the closest to a growl I've ever heard coming from his sweet mouth.

I laugh, and that earns me a hard slap to my ass. I moan and rest my head on the couch like the good girl I am.

Apollo thanks me with a groan and a series of hard, deep thrusts that send me spiraling toward another climax.

He comes before I do, giving my ass another hard slap. But he stays inside me as he starts strumming my clit. I push my legs a little further apart, groaning into the cushion as my climax speeds closer.

"What the fuck is going on?"

Apollo yanks his dick out of me. I go onto my knees, grabbing on the back of the couch for support as I try and focus across the living room floor.

"Do you know what fucking time it is?" Reuben growls.

"Half-past three?" Cass says.

"We've got to be at the doctor in five hours."

He's wearing a thick robe, and when he walks closer, it's with a heavy limp. His hair is disheveled, his eyes darkly shadowed.

"Rube, we can expla—" Apollo begins, but cuts off and scrambles off the couch when Rube gets closer.

"This is what you four do when I'm out of it?" he demands, waving a hand in my general direction. "You all fuck each other?"

"Sometimes I read," Cass says.

"Enough!" Rube looks at me, disapproval stark in his eyes. "What do you have to say for yourself?"

I blink up at him, look away, and then start wagging my hips.

Honestly, my brain is mush. If I could have talked my way out of this I would have, but...I've just been fucked seven ways from Sunday.

A big, warm hand caresses my ass.

"Think this is going to fix anything?" Rube asks. "A quick fuck, and all is forgiven?"

"Buddy, you're usually out cold by now," Cass says. "We could have been doing this on top of you and you wouldn't have woken up."

"Doctor said no pills tonight." Rube strokes my ass again. "And no sex, either."

He slaps me.

Fucking hard.

I whimper as my arousal—and possibly three different men's cum—trickles down my inner thigh.

"That's why we didn't—"

"Shut up and hold this."

I look up in time to see Rube handing his robe to Cass. Then he clicks his fingers at Apollo. "Get back in her."

"Man, I would? But..." Apollo cups his hands over his dick and takes a step back. "You scared the bejesus out of me."

"I'll do her," Zach says. "But only if you fucking promise not to rip out those stitches again."

That's the problem with Rube. He thinks he's invincible. *Unbreakable.*

Zach thrusts into me, no teasing, not even a warning. My mouth opens in a gasp, and that's when Rube forces the crown of his cock between my lips.

He was in surgery for nine hours, and walking a week later. That same month, he had to go back in because he'd torn something important—because he'd been fucking me like a goddamn stallion despite the doctor's orders.

The only way we could get him to start healing was to insist the doctor give him a prescription for sleeping pills. And I tried to stay out of his way as much as possible.

Still, it's taken him twice as long to heal as it should have, and if the doctor doesn't like what he sees tomorrow, he could be on bed rest for another week.

So I suck his cock while Zach fucks me from behind, and we put on a good show so that when he comes, Rube doesn't feel left out.

Soon, everything will be back to normal.

No more sneaking around.

No more pills.

Reuben wraps my curls around his fist, guiding his dick deeper into my mouth. "Did they make you come?" he asks.

I look up at him, wide-eyed as I nod.

"Was it good?"

Another nod.

"I don't believe you."

I groan as Cass's fingers trail down my stomach, heading for my clit.

"No, no," Rube murmurs, when I try and move away from his touch. "You said you could handle all four of us." He grabs the base of his cock and forces another inch of himself down my throat. "So handle us, my girl."

When Zach's had his share of my ass, he moves beside Rube. He hasn't come again, and I know why.

My men think I'm even prettier when I'm covered with their cum.

So as Rube's dick starts throbbing in my mouth, and the grip in my hair tightens, Zach starts jerking off beside him, biting his lip as he stares down at me with pure adoration.

Cass shoves his cock into my slit, because I guess they can't help filling every single one of my holes.

And Apollo teases me toward another climax with his fingers.

We don't all come at once...but it's pretty damn close.

And as my climax is tearing through me, Rube demands I look up at him so he can watch me swallow down every drop of his cum.

Side by side, he and Zach are like night and day.

His green eyes so bright, where Zach's are always shadowed.

Light and dark.

All my men have that in them. Both the light *and* the dark.

Thankfully, I've seen more of their light shine through these past few days. I'm hoping, soon, that light will vanquish the dark.

It has to.

The police found enough evidence in Keith Malone's safe house to convict hundreds of child molesters across the country, and lay charges against thousands more. It was the biggest bust in sex-trafficking history.

Keith Malone was dead when they finally excavated the grave. It wasn't that they didn't find a freshly filled-in grave suspicious. The cops were just...distracted.

Kismet.

We brought closure to hundreds of families. Even a decade later, it could still help them heal. The task force assigned to the case is working around the clock to find the rest of the houses still out there.

We brought light to the shadows.

But we also brought hope. And that, I think, is the most important thing.

Because without hope, what is there to look forward to but endless night?

AMEN - BONUS EPILOGUE

CHAPTER ONE
REUBEN

S weat. Blood. Fear. Such a familiar perfume. A triggering scent for me, possibly for all my brothers. But today it's not coming off my skin, or Zach's or any of my brothers. It's the man lashed to the wooden chair in the middle of this cabin that's giving off that unique aroma.

Not even Trinity looks scared, although there's a definite unease in her shifting eyes. Our girl has grown so much these past few years. I suppose just like we did all those years ago in the basement.

What was once terror, transforms into fear. Fear becomes panic. Panic dissolves into anxiety, then unease. The mind cloaks it, knowing it would self-destruct under the constant strain of pure horror.

Did I ever expect our girl to turn into this…this…*machine* though?

I don't think any of us did.

"He's pissed himself," Trinity says.

I can't decide if the shiver in her voice is excitement or alarm. From her deadpan face, it could just be my fucking imagination.

"Don't even think of stopping until you smell shit." Cass is leaning against a wall less than two yards from me, smoking a cigarette, his eyes the color of denim. Smoke puffs from his mouth as he adds, "Fuck that. Make him *bleed.*"

Trinity's eyelids flicker, but that's the only response she shows to Cass's demand. That's how we've trained her, how we've taught her.

Despite the emotion whirlpooling inside your head, when you're with a Ghost, you don't show them anything.

All we saw back in the basement was lust and hedonistic pleasure plastered on grown men's faces as they played out their sickest, most depraved fantasies with our small, unresisting bodies.

It was sickening, terrifying, but in its own disturbing way, it was beneficial too. Those faces told a story. How much the Ghost would hurt us that day. How long they'd take with us.

How much we would bleed.

Before Trinity came into our lives, we'd spend hours planning our revenge on each and every Ghost. How we'd torture them, what we'd yell at them, whisper in their demonic ears.

How we'd exorcise them, Apollo used to say. Which was funny, because he was never a religious type. Not like Zachary, who loves the old testament almost as much as he loves taking the bible out of context.

Definitely not like me.

Trinity holds up the hunting knife she's been clasping for over half an hour already and turns it so that the man bound in the chair in front of her can see it clearly. What little light comes from the single lamp in the corner of the room casts most of the room into shadow, except Trinity's face. Her nose, her chin—a stark relief, an unrelenting silhouette that's never looked this hard...this *clinical* before.

I'm nothing like Zach. I don't get off on other people's pain. But even I'm getting a semi watching her work. This girl, this *woman* is one of us now.

She was broken, just like us.

She scarred over, just like us.

And now she's out for revenge...just like we are.

But tonight it all ends. The final chapter in an epic saga that's taken us five years to complete. Because that man, that disgusting creature of Satan, he's the last.

Not the last pedophile in the world, of course. I doubt we could even put a dent in their population. But the last of the Ghosts.

Our Ghosts.

Trinity leans forward, pressing the hunting knife's blade to the outside of the Ghost's thigh. His legs are already riddled with slashes and oozing cuts, a few of them showing wet bone, but there's not much blood pooling on the floor under his chair.

Because Zachary applied a tourniquet to his legs and his arms. And while that might have slightly desensitized his limbs, we didn't take his sight. More than that—we taped his eyelids up so he can't even blink if he wanted to. He has no choice but to watch as we slice off pieces of his diseased limbs and toss them into the fireplace.

Even when Cass and Apollo are both smoking a cigarette—Apollo spending more time watching out the window than watching the Ghost, of course—the stench of burnt flesh hangs thick in the air.

Once you get over the urge to try and rationalize it, to give it a name, then it's not so bad anymore. It's only when you start confusing the smell with too-sweet pork that stomach's turn.

Well, mine and Cass anyway. I wouldn't be surprised if Zachary was craving a fucking BLT right now.

He's beside Trinity, skin sheened with joy, eyes ablaze with sadistic enthusiasm. He's in his fucking element, and it's never been more apparent. Not from his face, not from the way he watches our girl with obvious pride, chest puffed out and mouth in a smug curl.

"Tendons," Zachary grates, his voice rough and quivering with excitement.

"Now?" Trinity glances up at him, eyes wide and so youthful it makes my heart pang for her loss of innocence.

And God was she innocent. But that was years ago now. When all she'd experienced was violent death and a man sticking it in her without her consent.

That was back then.

She's nothing close to an innocent little lamb anymore. Her white wool is stained with blood and piss and shit.

I'd like to think that there was a different future for the five of us. That, maybe once, a few months after we'd buried Keith alive and moved on with our lives, as the reports began to roll in about the hundreds of pedophiles that were facing trials for their depraved acts, that we could become...normal.

Satan has a sick sense of humor.

That first year, almost fifty percent of the cases were thrown out for processing errors. But we gritted our teeth, and we tried to find gratitude for the meager few that ended up facing prosecution.

It's sickening, how few were actually sentenced. It's disgusting how little prison time they even served.

All those children who were abused, tortured, *murdered*... and the blame all fell on one man.

Keith motherfucking Malone.

Everyone else was just an accomplice. A not-so-innocent bystander.

They were set free, their crimes pinned on a dead man who was already serving an eternity in hell, and probably laughing as he watched each and every trial dissolve into ridiculous "time-served" penalties that wouldn't give any man a second thought to do what he did again, and again, and—

The Ghost yells. Tries to jerk his leg away from Trinity's knife. But there isn't much give in those ropes Apollo tied.

If there's one thing he didn't have an issue with, it was making sure this fucking Ghost wasn't going anywhere. They have history—deep and personal—Apollo and this grunting, panting excuse for a man strapped to the wooden chair in the middle of this cabin.

"Cut all the way through," Zachary says, crouching beside Trinity as she bends to hack deeper into the back of the Ghost's ankles. "Until there's no more tension."

A year or two ago I might have expected Trinity to retch, or go pale. But she merely tightens her mouth into a line and starts sawing blade through flesh.

I'm proud of her too, but not because she hasn't puked in the corner yet.

It should be Apollo in her place, sawing that hunting knife through the Ghost's Achille's heel, but he'd have passed out after she made the first incision. So he asked her to do what he could only imagine, what he could only dream... and she became his angel.

He'd peek back over his shoulder every few seconds—too quick to see much but a blur of blood and shadow, I'm sure—and then face the windows again.

That same pride reflected in his eyes, mirroring Zach's.

Even Cass watches over her with a twisted smirk on his face.

The Ghost's scream is rough and raw. He's been in the chair for over an hour already, and we haven't exactly been good hosts—now or the hours he's been in our captivity before we arrived at Saint Amos. We drove here in a junker Zachary bought for cash at a used-car dealership one state over—something roomy enough for the five of us and our captive.

Cass kept him entertained the entire trip over here with a detailed explanation of what we'd be doing to him once we arrived. When the Ghost passed out, he'd rouse him with the tip of a cigarette pressed into the back of his hand, or his ankle, wherever the skin was thin and the nerve endings shallow.

"Fuck it, I can't stand watching you tease him like that," Cass says, pushing away from the wall and making to flick his cigarette into the corner of the cabin. Zach snaps his fingers, and instead Cass hands him the last two inches of his cigarette.

Cabin might be too fancy a word for this hovel. It was once a hut used for hunting, if the animal bones we found out back were any indication. It's basically one room with a crude fireplace, a rickety table, no windows, and a single door with a bar along the inside.

For when prey becomes predator?

It suits our purposes just fine, which is why we all agreed it would be our torture chamber when Apollo told us what he'd found out in the woods. Usually, Saint Amos students weren't allowed past the cleared areas of the school grounds, but Apollo was always good at bunking off.

But despite what we'd promised each other, this will be our first kill at Saint Amos. It's been years since we've been back here, and seeing the imposing silhouette of the cathedral-like building soaring into the sky as we arrived plucked my heartstrings...in more ways than one.

My memories of Saint Amos are bittersweet. Everything came to a head in this place. We thought we'd lost Trinity forever, Zachary had betrayed us, and we'd lost all hope of ever finding Gabriel again.

But it was also the first place we got a solid lead on our lifelong vendetta against the people who'd tortured and abused us for our entire childhood.

The place where we met Trinity.

Our first love.

Our salvation.

"Move over, my precious little slut."

I snap out of my reverie to watch Cass take hold of Trinity's shoulders and maneuver her out of the way. She gives up the knife grudgingly, but when Cass dips his head and presses his lips to hers, her fingers open.

Everyone's looking, even the Ghost. Who wouldn't? They could be movie stars, Cass and Trinity. Runway models posing for a particularly risqué shoot. Trinity in her form-fitting dress that ends in a stiff skirt just above her knees. Cass with his shapeless clothes that somehow still accentuate his tall frame and toned muscles.

As he turns back to the Ghost, the knife now in his possession, our eyes meet. He pauses, the corner of his mouth quirking up in a half-smile, and then he faces the Ghost.

That crooked smile becomes a leering grin that shows too many teeth to be pleasant.

Adam Fairway is not familiar to me. He didn't speak much when he was down in the basement, and he only ever used Apollo. In the dark, the damp, features weren't always visible. An ordinary man could easily turn into a skull with ink bleeding from its sockets.

Plus, it has been over fifteen years. People change.

Adam didn't recognize any of us. Not even Apollo. Not at first, anyway. But when we refused to answer his pleas, refused to let him out of the panel van, he started staring at each and every one of us, eyes narrowed, brow furrowed.

He worked it out eventually.

We all change...but our eyes can never lie. Apollo had been avoiding eye contact, but the moment he looked over at Adam, the man gasped, clutched his heart, and passed out.

Zachary nearly rolled the car. We all thought he'd had a fucking heart attack. That God had robbed us of this—our last vengeful act.

But he came to when Cass kicked him in the balls, and then it was all just snot and tears.

Fingers wrap around my wrist, and my gaze snaps to Trinity standing beside me. She stares up at me with round, vacant eyes and parted lips. Then she cocks her head to the side, toward the only door leading out of this place.

As I turn to follow, Cass's arm descends in a sharp arc that ends with Adam's breathless yell and the splatter of blood on the floor.

Outside, our breathes plume in the icy air. Trinity shivers, and I immediately slide my arm over her shoulders, dragging her against my body. "You'll freeze out here. Let me get your coat."

"You're my coat," she murmurs, burrowing her face into my chest and wrapping her arms around my waist. "You can keep me warm."

"You okay?" She's shaking in my hands, but I don't know if it's the cold or the fact that she just severely debilitated a man with a hunting knife. I'm not even sure if surgery would ever help him walk again—

The fuck do I care? It's not as if he's leaving the cabin alive. His easy way out came in the van when he almost had a heart attack. It's too late now. He's in it for the long haul, as are we.

"Trinity."

"I'm fine," she says, her voice sharp. "Quit asking." But as if to make up for the snap in her voice, she tips back her head and stands on tip-toes. If there was ever any hope of us kissing, I'd have to bend down, but I watch her for a few seconds first.

Her dark eyes still glow with that honey-gold ring. Her lips are still soft and sweet and pink. But she's changed too. Her face is rounder, her hair longer, her figure fuller. She's turned into the woman us four men needed.

But have we turned into the men *she* needs?

I duck down and slide my hands under her skirt, grabbing her ass and hoisting her up to my waist. Her legs wrap around me in a flash, hugging me tightly as she slings her arms behind my neck.

Her kiss is fierce, urgent with need. She bucks against my body, her spine moving like a serpent, knowing I can't stop myself when she's this insistent.

Even though I know I'll be punished when my brothers find out, I spin around and crush her against the side of the cabin. The wood is rough, unfinished, crude as the grunt she makes when her back slams into the log wall. I rip her underwear to the side with my thumb, wrestling my cock out of my jeans with the other.

All it took was one kiss to make me this hard, her breath whispering against my neck before I'm aching to be inside her.

I thrust, groaning deep when her pussy clenches around me. Compared to the handful of snowflakes sifting down in the icy air, Trinity's cunt scorches. I slam into her, drawing a gasp that makes the hairs on my arms stand to attention.

It riles me that there was a time when I wasn't included. Back when I was still healing from the slugs Keith put in me, when I was on the kind of bed rest that excluded everything except actual fucking sleeping.

There's an unspoken rule in this family. If one of us wants Trinity, we all have her. I think it's because we're all afraid it would feel like being back in that basement. Not knowing where to look when someone you cared for was being fucked. I know it's different, but that doesn't always matter in fractured minds like ours.

Trinity digs nails into my unprotected neck as I fuck her against the side of the cabin. Her gasps and moans aren't loud enough to block out the screams, though, and that just intensifies my thrusts.

I'm not a sadist. I don't experience anything pleasant when I know someone is being hurt—physically or emotionally. Instead, it settles me. It calms the silent storm that's always been raging inside me, the one that gets out when I'm triggered and my brothers aren't around to talk me down.

It's what happened a few months ago while we were hunting down this last runt of a man. I investigated a lead on my own. Anathema, I know, but I'd had a falling out with Zach again, and this time Trinity had taken his side. I had to clear my head, and my route happened to take me past a church where we believed Adam might have been scouting for boys.

It was late on a Tuesday night. The place was deserted. I broke in to take a look at their files, thinking it the perfect time for such misdeeds.

I wasn't the only one.

My misdeeds didn't hold a candle to what I walked into.

Adam's friend, one of the men in the congregation, had a little girl with him. At least...she had been. When I arrived, the Lord had already seen fit to take her to heaven.

Adam's friend didn't survive much longer. I took to him with bare fists, knowing my first blow had cracked his skull and done enough damage that he'd probably be eating through a straw for the rest of his life while nursing staff changes his diapers...but I couldn't stop.

That's what my brothers are for.

They're the only ones who can make me stop.

If Apollo hadn't realized I'd taken off, hadn't tracked the SUV to the church and figured out the rest, I'd be in prison right now. Or possibly a psychiatric ward.

Adam's friend was unrecognizable. Not just as a man, but as a human being. Which is fine, because he never was one. Apollo and Cass got me away from there while Trinity and Zach cleaned up the scene. They buried the little girl under a cherry tree in the church's yard, and scraped what was left of Adam's friend into a tarp and went to go dump him in the desert. Days later, Apollo sent an encrypted message to the family of the little girl telling them what had happened and making it seem as if it came from Adam's friend.

It gave them closure, and hopefully it kept the cops off our trail.

Since then, I haven't gone anywhere alone.

Since then, I've had to take sleeping pills to stop the nightmares from coming back.

There's a sudden manic outburst of laughter from inside the cabin. I'm not sure if it's a coincidence, but that's when I empty myself into Trinity. She sighs, her body going limp, although I know she hasn't come.

The cabin's door creaks open, and Zachary steps outside. His shoes crunch on the slushy ground as he takes one step toward us before stopping. It's dark out here—I'm sure he can't see more than a silhouette.

But he stares at us as if he can.

"It's time," is all he says.

ADAM TRULY LOOKS LIKE A GHOST. His skin is gray, his lips ashen. Sweat-wet hair hangs in ribbons down his forehead, some slicked against his blood-stained skin. That's the only part of him that has any color.

The blood.

He's naked now, putting his podgy, glistening stomach on display. A flaccid dick that barely peeks out between his skinny legs.

It's so much warmer inside than out. Sweat prickles between my shoulder blades as my body struggles to adjust to the heat.

Cass spins the hunting knife on his bloody palm and then closes his fingers tight around the handle. There's a hush in the air, as if everyone's holding their breath—even Adam.

Silently, Cass stretches out his arm, turning the knife and holding it out handle-first to Apollo.

"Cass—" I start.

"It's the price we pay for serenity," Zachary says. He's leaning in Cass's place beside the fireplace where flames sputter and shoot sparks as they chew through the dirty wood we found stacked in one corner of the cabin. "It must be him."

"I'll do it," Trinity murmurs, but before she can take more than a step forward, Cass puts out an arm to stop her. "This is his cross to bear."

I don't know what the fuck comes over me, but before I can stop it, a bark of laughter escapes me. Everyone turns to look at me. I shrug. "Most religious thing I've ever heard coming out of your mouth," I tell Cass.

He quirks an eyebrow. "Then you obviously haven't been paying attention. I say holy shit all the time."

Before he finishes speaking, Apollo snatches the blade from his hand and slashes out with it, a grisly sneer stretching his mouth.

A ragged line of red appears on Adam's throat an instant before his head falls back. Bright blood fountains into the air. Trinity claps her hands over her eyes, but Cass, Zachary, Apollo, and I merely watch as the Ghost's life force pumps out of his severed flesh.

The gurgles begin immediately, but either he doesn't want to hang around any longer in this world, or he just didn't have that much fight in him, because a second later his head sags forward, a permanent slump in his now lifeless body.

A clatter draws my eyes. The knife lays by Apollo's grimy sneakers, his hand dangling limply at his side. His eyes are glazed, his lips parted. He looks like he's high, but he hasn't touched a joint in weeks.

We've had other things on our minds.

"That's it," he says, his voice thick and unusually grim. "It's over."

Zach grunts. "There'll always be more of these sick—"

"It's. *Over.*"

I know I'm not the only one who gets goosebumps at the steel underlying Apollo's declaration.

Cass glances back at me, his mouth working for a second, but he's at a loss for words.

Trinity's eyes are glowing, and when she blinks a crystal tear races down her cheek. She steps forward and lays a hand on Apollo's shoulder. When he doesn't react, when he just keeps staring at the bruised, beaten, bloodied body a foot away from him, she runs her hand down his arm and laces her fingers through his bloody hand.

Some of the man's life juice must have splashed on him when he slashed his throat, but Apollo doesn't even seem to notice.

Usually, he'd be on his back, practically comatose. I've never seen him stare down this much blood and not be in a parallel dimension.

But it's as if he's shed a skin that's been constricting him his entire life. Finally free, his phobias no longer plague him. He's walked away from the scared, pathetic boy he used to be...and grown-up to *this*. To a man who can tell it's over with the kind of authority that makes us believe him.

"It's over," I say, starting to nod.

Apollo looks up at me through his sandy lashes, flicking his head to send a chunk of the same color hair from his eyes. His lips close, and the tiniest crease forms alongside his mouth. It's not a smile, but it's getting there.

"About fucking time it's over," Cass mutters, dusting down his clothes. "I want to travel before it's too late." He cuts his gaze to Trinity, but she only has eyes for Apollo right now. Squeezing his hand, beaming up at him with dare I say almost motherly pride. I can't blame her—my breath is starting to seize up with how my chest constricts.

Zachary pushes away from the wall and rushes out of the cabin, slamming the door open so hard that Trinity yelps in surprise when it crashes against the wall.

"Zach!" she calls out, and for fuck's sake she's about to go after him before Cass grabs hold of her wrist and keeps her back.

I go instead, my jaw already creaking with how my jaw locks.

Of course he's pissed. Zachary could saw off the dick of every molester in the United States and still feel like he hasn't done enough. It's become his obsession, his undying vow, to single-handedly wipe out the surge of pedophiles in this country.

I follow the sound of his boots crunching through the snow. Thank God, he's not heading into the forest—he's heading for the car. Which makes me speed up, because he has the keys to the junker. I'm not sure if he'd leave us stranded, but I wouldn't gamble anything when his mind is in such a wild state.

All of us need a day or two—sometimes longer—to process a killing. And we all do it in our own way. But Zach? There's a brief moment of raging victory, and then he's back to himself. Like a switch flips for a few minutes, and then it's back to business as usual.

It's not healthy. It's not close to normal. But it's Zach…and honestly, I have no idea what *normal* has ever looked like for him.

I grab hold of the driver's side door of the battered mini-van a second before Zach tries to slam it closed. When I wrench it open, he releases the handle with a warning growl, but I just wedge my body in the gap instead.

He opens his mouth, his face a twisted mask of anger, but I don't let him speak. I grab the front of his throat and shove him back into the seat so hard that it creaks in a warning.

His army green eyes go to slits, his nostrils flaring like an animal hunting out a prey's scent.

But I'm not prey.

Not anymore.

"It's over," I tell him.

His lips seal into a thin line, like he'll never allow himself to utter those words. But he doesn't grab my wrists, he doesn't do anything to lessen the pressure around his throat. I'm squeezing hard enough that his face is starting to go red, but he just sits there as if he'd accept his fate if I decided to end him.

"You could go on doing this for the rest of your life, Mason, but then you wouldn't *have* a life. And wasn't that the fucking point? To get our goddamn lives back?"

His lips pop open, and a small cough comes out. He starts to speak, but I know the kind of bullshit he'll spout, so I squeeze even harder.

I'm dimly aware that someone's approaching but I can't break eye contact. This isn't the first time Zachary and I have been on opposite ends of an argument. I know how quickly he can get the upper hand, especially if I'm distracted.

"It's not just you anymore. It hasn't been for years. You'd be a selfish fucking prick if you didn't accept that Adam was the last."

Crunch. Crunch. Crunch....crunch.

Judging from the footsteps, it's Cass. He knows to stay back. Knows to let this duel play out.

"So you're going to say it. Agree that it's over. Close the door to that basement in your mind, and fucking lock it, and swallow the key."

Zach's eyes flare, his lips quirking into a snarl. There's a vein throbbing on his temple, his skin even redder than before. I can hear his breath wheezing through his constricted trachea.

"And if you don't, then I'll just keep squeezing."

He glares at me for a long second, and then croaks out, "Fuck you."

If Cass hadn't jumped onto my back, I'd have killed Zach. I'd have fucking crushed his throat and been done.

But Cass's weight, negligible as it is, breaks my concentration. Zach slams a fist into my solar plexus, winding me and causing a bolt of pain to slice through me.

I stumble back, wrestling Cass off my back and throwing him to the ground so I can get back to Zach. But Zach's out of the van, another fist already flying for my face.

My head snaps to the side when he makes contact, the click ricocheting through my skull like a gunshot. But when he comes at me again, I duck and tackle him to the dirty snow with a roar.

We roll once, twice, slam into the base of a nearby tree. I'm on top, sitting up and straddling Zach's waist as I punch him. He grunts when my knuckles make contact with his cheek, and starts bucking in a futile attempt to get me off him.

He doesn't stand a chance. I have over twenty pounds on him, and a biblical fucking amount of rage boiling through me.

"After everything, you can't even give us this?" I roar, punctuating the sentence with a fist to the other side of his face.

He laughs at me with blood-stained teeth, and then hacks up a mouthful of pink spittle and sprays it on my face. "If you four want to live your perfect fucking lives without me, then do it!" he yells. "I'd never ask you to stop! Never!"

"Because you can't!" Our voices echo around us, wild, but we're miles from civilization.

Miles from anything.

"Exactly!" Zach stops moving, his chest heaving like he ran a marathon. Then he shoves at my chest. "You think I want this? You think I *need* this shit in my life?"

"Guys!" It's Apollo. He sounds out of breath. But I can't spare him any mind right now. My concentration is on Zach.

Lying, full of shit, bastard Zach.

I punch his jaw. The other side—his cheek.

"It's Trinity!" Apollo yells.

A cold shock blasts through me. I spin around, pressing a hand to Zach's chest as I stare over my shoulder at Apollo. If Zach hadn't turned on the van's headlamps, I wouldn't have seen Apollo...or Trinity.

She's bare naked.

My breath hitches. I'm already scrambling up, but Cass is halfway to her already. Apollo is at her side, but she shoves him when he tries to throw a coat over her shoulders.

She's covered in blood.

That's probably why I lose my fucking mind and race at her like a bull with a personal grudge for the matador. Zach leaps in front of me like a goddamn rodeo clown, but I don't fall for it. I snatch the coat out of Apollo's hands and toss it over Trinity's shoulders.

But she pulls some kind of magic trick, and a second later she's naked again, the coat at her feet.

"Stop," she says through a tight jaw, holding up her hands when I duck to pick up the coat. Slamming her foot on the thick fabric, she stares me down like I'm a fool peasant kneeling for my Queen.

One I've just pissed off royally.

She turns, scowls at Zach. "Stop fighting. Stop killing. Stop all of it."

I'm grimacing at her, because all I can think about is how tiny she is, and how fucking cold it is out here, and why the fuck is she covered in all that goddamn blood? I'm searching her pale skin for any sign of damage, a cut or a bruise or anything, but I can't explain it.

"She's lost it," Apollo blurts out. "Just stripped, and then rubbed her hands all over him and then, and she, she's pissed you guys."

"Trinity, put on the fucking coat," Zach growls somewhere beside me.

She pins him with a molten glare. "How dare you?" she whispers furiously. "How fucking *dare* you?"

I swear I can hear him grating his fucking teeth. "Trinity, you can't stand out here in the cold. Let's go inside, there's a fire, we can—"

Her pointing finger cuts me off midsentence. "You can shut the fuck up," she says, showing me her teeth.

They're chattering.

Oh my god, she's freezing.

I rush to my feet, but that finger has a kind of power I still don't understand or even fully accept. Every atom of my being is screaming at me to scoop her up, to run back inside that hovel and snuggle her in every layer of clothing I can find while I cuddle her beside the fire.

But I can't move.

"All of this ends tonight," she says.

Apollo and Cass are nodding furiously, sending me and Zach big-eyed glances meant to impress on us that we should be doing the same.

My jaw clenches, but I manage a nod. Reluctant, grudging as all hell, but I do it.

Zach just glares at her.

"Tonight."

Zach steps forward, his hands fisting at his sides. It takes everything I have not to tackle him to the ground again, just at the thought that he might hurt her for trying to impose her will on him...but she's still pointing at me. Still holding me in place with nothing but deep respect.

I can't explain how it happened, or even when. I suppose it was gradual. As the years wore on, as we grew a tighter-knit family, as the body count climbed...Trinity became the epitome of my hope and my salvation.

We're all still broken. Shards that used to form whole, beautiful children before those wicked men crushed our souls.

But she bound those pieces together. Formed crude structures that somehow resembled who we used to be.

We're happy, now.

Satisfied.

After tonight, fulfilled.

All but one.

The boy who'd been broken so many times, he never could find all the pieces again. But she tried. Over and over again.

"Put the *fucking* coat on!" Zach's voice is shaking with anger, with frustration.

And Trinity's face is cracking. Her blazing anger dissolving, fear replacing it. Dread. I suppose fearing that Zach is, in fact, a lost cause.

We tried to tell her.

She never did listen.

But I can't hold that against her…because we've all said that about ourselves so many times that if she had listened we'd all still be broken and ruined.

There's a crunch as Zach falls to his knees.

My gaze rips away from Trinity's crestfallen face. I watch, comatose, as Zachary puts his hands on the snow and inches them toward the coat Trinity is trampling with her bare, blue-tinged feet.

He makes a sound that could have been a sob or a curse or anything in-between, and then drops his head, letting it hang.

"Please, Trinity. Just…let me go."

Trinity sniffs.

My gaze climbs up her shapely legs, to the shaved V between her legs, to her little belly and plump breasts, to her bobbing throat. "No," she whispers, voice rough and trembling. "You're not leaving us. You're not leaving *me*."

She bends down and puts her finger under Zach's chin, lifting his head and forcing him to look at her.

"You're not leaving *him*."

Zachary's head sags when she takes her finger away and straightens, and then Trinity slides her hands over her stomach, cupping the tiny baby bump rounding out her pale, blood-streaked skin.

"Because if you do, you're dead to us, Mason. Dead to Apollo. Dead to Rueben. Dead to Cass. Dead to me, and dead to your son."

Zach slides as if he lost strength in his arms, but then he's grabbing the coat and trying to tug it out from under Trinity's feet without tipping her over.

"Please," he murmurs. "Please, just put on the fucking coat. Put it on, and I'll leave. I'll never—"

"Feel love again." Trinity's voice is as cold as the air around us. A violent shiver races through her, then she kicks away Zach's hand. "You need us," she says. "And we need you. That's how it's always been. That's how it will be, from now until the end of time."

When we found out Trinity was pregnant, our family rejoiced. Even Zachary lit up like a house on fire. Trinity didn't want to do a paternity test—she told us straight up the child was ours. Each of ours. Boy or girl, she would have four fathers, and even if she had Cass's blue eyes, or Apollo's blond hair, or my build, or Zachary's dimple...she was *ours*.

But we voted. We wanted to know.

Because we were determined to *each* have a child with her. Yes, they'd all be ours, but that's what we wanted.

Even Zachary.

And he has the devil's own luck, because the firstborn son is his.

Little Malachi is this family's first child, and Zachary is putting his life in danger because the fucking prick won't agree to stop killing people.

Typical Mason.

Trinity shivers again, her teeth clattering. Apollo surges forward, but she sticks out a finger at him, and he stops with a grimace that looks as painful as the stab of concern that shoots through me.

Zachary sits back on his heels, his head falling back. Eyes closed, mouth a line, he looks tormented, like Satan himself is inside that twisted mind of his, handling the reins like he has so many of us.

"Okay," Zachary bursts out. He clambers to his feet, making to grab Trinity's shoulders. She steps back deftly, shaking her head. "Okay, you win! It's over." Zach rakes fingers through his hair, his eyes falling to her belly. "You win."

"This isn't a competition," Trinity says.

Zach shares a quick look with Cass and Apollo. Then he cuts his eyes to me, and relief floods my body.

We've learned to speak volumes in utter silence, and tonight is no different.

As soon as Zachary steps forward and cups Trinity's face in his hands, Apollo and Cass duck and drag the coat up to her shoulders. She's still squealing with displeasure when I surge forward and scoop her off the ground, already bundling her against my chest as I make a run for the cabin.

Three sets of feet race after me. Cass sprints ahead, throwing open the cabin door and flattening himself as I shoulder past him and drop to the bare floor in front of the crackling fire.

The door closes quietly behind me. There's the briefest scuffle of feet as if they tried to keep Zachary out, but I guess he forces his way in because the next moment he's beside me, reaching for Trinity's face.

I growl at him, and he stops.

I'm not looking at him—my eyes are locked on the fire. I'm willing it to blaze hotter, to warm the chilled flesh in my hands. But I can see when Zach in my peripheries as he strips off his coat and wraps it around Trinity's legs. Two more coats appear, covering her from head to toe until only her blue nose is sticking out. She grumbles, but when I squeeze her she goes silent.

We sit like that for half an hour, silent but for the crackle and pop of the fire.

Eventually Trinity starts wriggling in my arms, muttering about sweating and that she can't breathe. If the others didn't peel my arms off her, I wouldn't have let go.

She keeps her coat on, sitting in my lap and staring at the fire as we wait.

I guess we all changed tonight.

Even Trinity.

Maybe even Zach.

Because instead of me or Zach speaking up, mapping out the next course of action, Trinity clears her throat and says, "We need to get cleaned up."

We're on our feet in an instant, Cass and Zach heading for the corpse.

"No. Leave him." Trinity gets slowly to her feet and I scramble up a second later. She stares up at each of us in turn, and then pushes Apollo and me aside so she can see the dead man in the chair. "Leave the door open, and let the animals have him."

"That's not safe—" Zachary begins.

"Someone could identify—" Cass says right over him.

Trinity holds up her hand again. "Pull out his teeth. Cut off his fingers. Take his clothes." Her honey-gold eyes study us, and the faintest smile touches her full mouth. "God can decide where his bones will rest."

CHAPTER TWO
TRINITY

I was still groggy when the elevator opened into the penthouse suite of the hotel we'd booked for the night. Couldn't stop myself from falling asleep in the car, especially since Reuben insisted on cradling me in his lap the entire way. They woke me up a few minutes ago and smuggled me through the hotel's foyer—Cassius keeping the receptionist occupied so no one would see my dirty face.

Zach doesn't even wait for Reuben to bring me out of the elevator first. He swarms past all of us and heads straight for the master bedroom down the hall.

I flinch when the door slams, and Apollo lets out a nervous laugh. "Think he's packing his bags?"

"He should," Cass mutters under his breath as he heads for the open-floor kitchen a few yards away. "It's a night for celebrating, not sulking."

I wriggle in Rube's arms until he reluctantly puts me down. "He'll come around."

Cass spins on his heels, eyes narrowed. "I admire your optimism, but sometimes even you have to admit when you're wrong."

I'm tired. I'm dirty. And I feel strangely weightless at the same time. It's surreal thinking we're done. That it's all finally over. But it's as if there hasn't been a second to feel the joy associated with such a momentous achievement...because Zach is hurting.

Zach is *always* hurting.

I don't know what to do anymore. Cass is right—even I'm starting to tire of constantly hoping he'll change. They say you should never get into a relationship with someone expecting to change them, but I can't help that I fell in love with him.

All of them.

"I'm going to sleep," I say, ignoring Cass's imploring stare. He wants to argue, wants to debate, but I don't have the energy. And I'm not the only one.

Apollo slumps onto the closest couch and turns on the flat-screen television, one leg dangling over the side of the sofa, the other propped on the armrest. Reuben sighs and washes his hands over his face.

Usually, we'd all be in bed right now…but no one would be sleeping. We used to celebrate every kill with a night of wild abandon, often staying up until the sun painted the horizon pink and orange.

Before I get halfway down the hall, Zach slips out of the bedroom and pulls the door shut behind him. When he looks up and sees me, he stops.

"I don't want to hear it," I snap, stalking closer and shoving him out of the way when he tries to block me.

He stumbles, and that catches me so off guard that I pause to glance back at him. But he rights himself an instant later, and then pushes away from the wall with a grimace.

As I close the door behind me, I hear Zach say something that sounds like, "Give me ten," but all sound cuts off the instant the bedroom is closed off from the rest of the suite.

I lean my head against the wood for a second before dragging myself into the en-suite bathroom.

Why did Zach leave the shower on?

But I don't bother trying to figure him out—I strip down and climb straight into the gushing water. The temperature is perfect. Most of my men like hot showers, but I can't handle anything hotter than luke-warm. I immediately start washing my face and then move on to shampooing my hair, eager to get rid of every trace of blood covering my skin.

When I hear the shower door sliding open, I splutter out a disgruntled, "Hey!" and try to blink through the suds streaming down my face.

The shampoo immediately starts burning my eyes, of course, and that just pisses me off even more.

Lately, I've barely had a handle on my emotions. Things that normally wouldn't even annoy me, make it feel like the entire universe is conspiring against me. Which makes my men start creeping around me on tiptoes...which pisses me off even more.

"Get out!" I punch out randomly, my eyes squeezed shut because I don't want more soap in them.

I hit solid flesh, but then someone wraps their hand around my wrist and tugs my arm away from them.

"Get—"

Fingers grab my chin and push up. Water hits my head, washing the shampoo from my hair. A hand swipes over my face, wiping away the suds clinging to my forehead and cheeks. Gentle hands. Soothing fingers. Rube or Cass, I'm sure.

When I finally dare to open my eyes, my stomach twists.

Through the steam and the spray of water, I see Zachary standing in front of me. Naked. Grim. Bloodstained.

I quickly scan the rest of the bathroom, but it's just the two of us. And it scares me, because Zach is still broken. He still can—and has—snapped. The meds help, of course, as does the counseling...but a Band-aid is never as good as stitches.

"I'm done," I say, trying to sidestep him. "It's all yours."

"But it's not, is it?" Hands slide around my waist, and I instantly stop moving. Zach's fingers caress the curve of my belly, his dark green eyes moving down my body as he steps closer, drawing me into an embrace.

Is he talking about me, or Malachi? My heart picks up speed—suddenly all I want to do is yell out for the others, to have them close in case Zach acts on the dark promise of those words.

"Malachi is yours, Zach," I say, laying my trembling hands over his as he wraps me in his arms. "And I'm yours too...if you want me."

"You know that's not true," he growls into my ear. "That's *never* been true."

A hard lump lodges in my throat. Pressure builds behind my eyes, and I don't know if I want to cry or scream. "Zach—"

"I'll never be okay with that," he says.

My chest is so tight, I can't breathe. "I never meant—"

"But it's fit in or fuck off, right?" His hands glide up to grip the back of my neck, drawing my head away and forcing me to look into his eyes. "That's how it's always been."

What am I supposed to say? I mutely shake my head, my mouth working as my mind reels.

Something in his face changes. The darkness in his eyes draws back, the tightness around his mouth eases. He blinks, staring down at me as if he's only now seen me for the first time in his life.

Goosebumps break out over my skin, and it has nothing to do with the water, or our proximity, or even the fact that I can feel his dick growing hard between us.

"That's how it's always been, right from the start." He frowns, his gaze latching onto my mouth. "We forced you to fit in. Made you take all of us. Didn't allow you to choose. Would you have, if you could?" He strokes wet ribbons of hair from my face, cupping me in his hands. "Who would you have chosen, if we'd given you a choice down there in Saint Amos's library?"

I shake my head, but he tightens his hands to stop the motion.

"Come on," he murmurs, dropping his head lower, staring deeper into my eyes. "It's just us. No one else will ever know."

My eyes dart between his as I try and read his motives. Because that's something I learned about Zach many years ago—he *always* has an agenda.

"No one," I say.

He blinks, confusion flickering over his face. "None of us?"

"I wasn't looking for anyone—or anything—when I arrived at Saint Amos," I tell him, reaching up and grabbing hold of his wrists. "I'd just lost my parents." My voice hitches, but I soldier on, determined to get done with what I need to say before he interrupts me again. "I was hurting. Alone. Terrified." My eyes narrow. "And then I found you four. You want to know who I wanted? Not a single one of you." My words pick up speed, my voice leveling out and growing stronger. "You scared the living shit out of me. All of you. Psychos, stalkers, deviants."

I dig my fingers so deep into his skin that I'm sure it'll leave a mark. Zach doesn't seem to notice, and if he does, then he doesn't care. He seems fixated on me, on what I'm saying, and that's all I need. Because the others will realize he's not with them, and they'll come looking for me. For us.

Give me ten.

Except if they agreed they wouldn't.

A chill courses through me. It almost snatches me under, but I fight it.

He wants to know? Well, there's no time like the present.

I slap my hand against his bare chest, pushing at him to try and make room between us, but he barely moves.

"We scared you?" he prompts, his eyes devouring me like he's getting some kind of perverted pleasure from my words.

"Of course you did. But that was your plan, wasn't it? Because if I was scared, then I'd do whatever you wanted me to."

"How scared were you?"

"I could barely breathe."

"And when we fucked you that first time? Did that scare you too?" His lips quirk as if he's suppressing a smile.

I was so wrong about him. We haven't made progress. If anything, his visits to the psychiatrist were probably all just some twisted game he was playing. He does that, Zachary. He plays games with everyone in his life. Not the kind where he has opponents, but the kind a little kid plays with a dollhouse. He controls all the people inside that miniature house, staging them just the way he wants, mimicking whatever twisted world view he holds inside his mind.

But I've had enough. He's been pushing for years, but this is going too far.

"I'm not your fucking doll," I hiss, shoving him hard.

He sways, and I take that brief moment to try and slip past him. But he's too fast. Too strong.

Always has been.

Always will be.

An arm slides around my throat. Zach pulls me up against him, my back rubbing against his wet chest. Now it's impossible to ignore the rock-hard cock between us.

Violence excites him. It breathes life into him.

Even the promise of it.

He was so rough with me the day we'd located Adam that Rube gave him a black eye and told him if he ever touched me like that again, he'd kill him.

But they're not here now. It's just me and Zach and the pounding water...

And Malachi.

"Zach, please. Calm down!" I grab onto his arm, tugging at it.

Which is when I realize he's not gripping me tight enough to cut off air—just enough to hold me in place.

His other hand grasps roughly at my breast, tweaking my nipple between finger and thumb hard enough to make me gasp.

"Want to know a little secret?" he whispers in my ear, his hand moving down my belly. "Those times you were so scared...I knew it. I could feel it, taste it, smell it coming off your skin."

"Zach."

"Like now. You're scared now. I can feel you shaking."

I swallow hard. "Please."

His hand moves lower, cupping my belly. Going around and around like I have a tummy ache he's trying to soothe. I want to laugh, want to yell out that it's his kid inside me, not fucking indigestion.

Has he lost touch with reality? Does he even understand what's happening? He must—he's not a fucking idiot—but does he really, truly *understand?* We're bringing a baby into the world, him and I. All of us. How the fuck did he expect the killing to continue? Would we eventually be taking Malachi with us on our hunts? Have him take turns with the binoculars as we scoped out a suspect's house?

Just how the fuck was this all supposed to play out?

But I don't get a chance to ask. Zach's hand moves down, his mouth pressed hard against my ear as he ducks to reach my pussy. He shoves his hand between my leg and drags his fingers over my slit so hard that I can feel the scrape of his fingernails.

A shudder spills through me. My traitorous body responds instantly to his rough touch, coating his fingers with my warm, slick arousal.

"I love it when you're scared, and you want to know why?"

"Because you're fucked in the head."

He laughs, his chest pushing against me, forcing me closer to the wall. We move out of the range of the water, but he doesn't turn it off. It hammers down on the tiles behind us as my cheek slams into the cold wall, as he pushes a hand between my shoulder blades to keep me in place and slides the other between my legs from behind.

"That's true, but it's not right."

He crowds against me, his cock pressing against my entrance. I moan, and I'm not entirely sure if it's with panic or need. Zach must take it as the former, because I feel his cock throb against me as it grows even harder.

His teeth nip at my ear. "When you're scared, Trinity...I'm not."

Zach thrusts into me, driving thought from my mind. I gasp, my mouth staying open as I struggle with the titillating mess of pleasure and pain wreathing through me. He draws out and then slams back in again, immediately falling into a punishing tempo. My core clenches around him, and I let out little gasps of pain that quickly transform into pants of deep-seated need.

Somehow, despite his breathless growls as he slams into me, despite the pouring water, despite my own ringing ears...I hear the bathroom door open.

I would be relieved, but all I feel is that intoxicating rush that fills me when I'm with Zach.

When I'm with any of them. All of them.

As if he knows he's seconds away from losing his only one-on-one time with me in years, Zach thrusts into me and groans deep and hard, filling me with his seed until it drips down my legs. He slides a finger over my clit, toying with the engorged little nub as a stuttering breath washes over my ear.

"When you're scared, baby girl, all I want to do is protect you. Even when I'm the one hurting you, scaring you. And that brief fucking moment is the only peace I ever have inside this twisted freakshow I call a mind." He rubs my clit so hard that my teeth clench. Still deep inside me, he moves his hips, forcing me to feel every inch of him.

"But I don't want you to be scared anymore," he whispers.

Pressure builds inside me, seconds away from tearing me apart. "Zach." His name comes out mangled. His finger picks up speed, his other hand parting my cheeks and stroking a hard line over my backdoor.

"Even if that means I'll never have another moment of peace in my wretched fucking life."

I come with a strangled gasp, slapping my hands against the tiles above my head as I try and hold onto my sanity. A righteous shudder courses through me, and I'm dimly aware that Zachary's suddenly not touching me anymore, that there are raised voices, shouts.

But thankfully another warm body replaces his. Long, graceful fingers slide between my legs, some sliding into me, some cupping my pussy and toying with my clit as I unravel.

Pleasure wraps me up tight and then slowly unwinds, leaving me lightheaded and breathless.

I push away from the wall, letting Cass envelop me from behind. I almost lose myself in the feel of his embrace, but then I hear an unmistakable sound.

A punch.

A groan.

Someone falling.

"No!" I spin around, clutching at Cass's naked body as his embrace suddenly becomes a prison. I fight him, but he pins me effortlessly against the wall. "Cass!"

My eyes flicker to him, but his face is steel. "He said he was going to apologize, not fuck you until you bleed."

"I'm not bleeding."

"You could have been," Cass growls. Anger turns his eyes a sullen navy blue. "That fucking cunt isn't going to keep using you like this. Enough is enough."

"He..." I swallow hard.

Using me.

He was, wasn't he? All this time. He just told me so. I keep his demons at bay. I give him peace...if only briefly.

I stand on tip-toes to look over Cass's shoulder and yell out, "Leave him alone!"

Rube lifts a fisted hand, about to deliver another punch to where Apollo is holding Zach against the bathroom wall, but he pauses. When he looks at me over his shoulder, his brilliant green eyes are narrowed.

"You said it's over," he rumbles, his face twisting. "Well, it's fucking *over.*"

"Rube, no!" I shriek. "Stop!"

Rube shakes his head and lands his fist squarely in the middle of

Zach's face. Blood gushes from his broken nose, and all he does is laugh. "See?" he calls out to me. "Fit in or fuck off, Trinity."

Rube lines up another punch.

I shove at Cass, but he keeps me pinned.

When I let out a frustrated yell, no one even seems to care.

So I glare up at Cass and sink my teeth into his pec.

"Christ!" he yells, pushing away from me. He slaps a hand over his pec and stares at me in shock as blood starts seeping through his fingers. "What the fuck is wrong with you?"

"Rube, stop!" I hold my belly as I move toward him as quickly as I dare. Wet tiles are no joke, especially when I have a baby inside me. One slip is all it will take.

I grab Reuben's wrist, and he jerks me forward with the force of his next punch.

But it never lands, because Rube stops and looks at me with a severe frown creasing his brow. "Let go," he says calmly.

If he'd been shouting, I might have listened. But I've seen this serenity in his eyes before.

People died.

"He told you he wanted to apologize to me," I rattle off, tightening my fingers around Rube's wrist. "Well that's exactly what he did."

His frown deepens. "He was hurting—"

"No." I shake my head, widening my eyes. "No, Rube, he wasn't."

At least, not like they think he was. There was pain, but it wasn't entirely unwelcome. I guess I've changed since they first met me at Saint Amos all those years ago. Terrified, weak little Trinity Malone doesn't exist anymore. Maybe the change has been too subtle for them to register, or maybe they all want to remember me as the timid, innocent girl I was...but it's time they saw me for who I really am.

"I...I think I understand."

"Understand what?" Rube barks.

"Him." I reach past and press a hand to Zach's chest. Then I drag my gaze from Reuben's shocked eyes and stare up at Zach instead. "Why did you wait so long to tell me?"

Zach holds my gaze for a second before he looks away. He clears his throat, and as if that sends a signal to the other men, they're suddenly sharing glances with each other as they move closer. Apollo hands Zach a towel, and he wraps it around his waist before they cluster even closer. Now I'm surrounded by all four of my men, Cass flicking wet hair out of his eyes and tugging at his wet clothes, Apollo gazing at Zachary like he just told us he's going to perform a magic trick, and Rube staring daggers.

But they're quiet, and they listen, and that's all anyone could ever have asked.

"You know how scared you were?" Zachary whispers, trailing his fingers down the side of my face. "Now imagine…" His voice disappears until he clears his throat again. Then he cuts his gaze to his brothers, looking away as soon as they make eye contact. "Imagine feeling like that every second, of every day."

My heart clenches as a sob wrenches through me. "Oh God," I murmur, clapping my hands over my mouth. "Zach."

His throat moves as he swallows, his eyes still downcast. "I used to be scared when I was a kid, before I ever went into that basement." His voice hitches, but he pushes on. As he speaks, Rube starts leaning back as if the weight of Zach's words pushes him away.

"My dad would hit me sometimes, and the worse was I never knew when it would happen. Sober, tipsy, good mood, bad…there was no way to tell what day it would happen. But it always happened at night. Two, three times a week. Sometimes less, sometimes more. It was the not knowing that got to me. That constant panic every time I heard a noise outside my room after dark. But I managed. I had my coping mechanisms." He frowns hard, and then shakes his head as if he's trying to get rid of a horrible thought. But it has to stick, because his mouth trembles a second before the words start spilling out again.

"I'd imagine it was someone else hurting me. A monster that came into my room at night wearing a mask that looked just like my Dad. He was the one who slapped and kicked and beat me. He was the one who'd—" Zach cuts off hurriedly, visibly dragging in a breath that puffs out his chest. He glances up, scans us, and finally ends on me.

His eyes are the color of shadowy moss.

"Over time, that monster took on a life of its own. It would creep out of the pantry on an overcast day, oozing from those dark shadows like a slug. I couldn't sleep anymore—even with my nightlight on, all I could see were shadows. And every shadow was a portal into the monster's realm, a place where it could step through and come visit me with its hands and its fingers and its—"

His throat bobs hard, and he squeezes closed his eyes.

In a rush, he says, "And then they threw me down there in the dark. All day, every day, the dark. There were no portals anymore. No visits." His eyes squeeze shut tighter, and when he forces them open his lashes are glimmering with tears. "Because I was there, in *his* world. And that monster breathed down my fucking neck every second of every day."

There's a long silence filled only with the sound of the pouring water.

"You never said—" Apollo begins.

"Because it promised me if I ever did, it would start hurting you too," Zach cuts in, fast and furious. He lifts his eyes reluctantly. "You already had such heavy fucking crosses to bear...how could I?"

He looks at me, and it's as if a spear pushes through my chest. A hot tear flashes down my cheek. "We can fix this," I whisper. "Your therapist, she can—"

Zach starts nodding. He reaches out an arm and slings it around my shoulder. Then he holds out his other, beckoning his brothers.

But they just stand there, watching. Not moving. My heart spasms painfully, and a sob gets past my defenses. Gently, Zachary draws me into a hug.

"You already have," he murmurs, his lips brushing the top of my head. "I don't get the nightmares anymore." His voice quakes, but he talks louder, strengthening it. "And last night...it was the first time I slept straight through."

I lean back, staring up at him through watery eyes. "Your insomnia...it's gone?"

He shrugs a little. "I don't know. But it was last night." He looks past me at his brothers. "And all I can hope is that it will stay that way."

"So why the fuck all the theatrics back at the cabin?" Cass demands coldly. "When we said it was over, why the fuck didn't you just agree?"

"Because—" Zach stops, takes a deep breath that pushes his chest into mine. "Because I'm scared," he whispers unsteadily. "I'm scared, and I don't know why."

In a rush, his brothers are suddenly clustered around us. Arms wrap us from all around. Four different scents mingle and merge, and I lose myself in that heady aroma.

"Jesus Christ," Cass murmurs. "You just drop kicked my fucking heart, Mason."

I laugh, but it's a muffled sound. As if they realize they're crushing me, my men step back, giving me a little room. I sniff, swiping my hands over my eyes as I twist my head to look at each of them in turn.

"You know what we need, don't you?" I say.

There's a pause. Then Reuben says, "I know what everyone needs," he says gruffly, but his eyes are on Zach. My skin tightens, my heart kicking up a notch at the dangerous glint in his eyes.

"Rube—" I start, twisting so I can try and put myself between him and Zach.

"You, Cass and Apollo need some alone time," he says, his gaze not shifting one iota. "And I need to speak to Zachary."

"But—"

A big hand falls on my shoulder. Rube squeezes me, and then looks down. His mouth curls up into a smile. It's faint, and it's sad, but it's a smile. "There's a lot we need to talk about," he murmurs.

He looks at Zach again. "Wait up. I gotta run some things by you."

There's not a second's hesitation. Zach moves to the side, tightening the towel around his waist, and follows Reuben from the bathroom. When I turn back, Cass and Apollo are watching me like hungry wolves who've just happened upon a lost little sheep.

I won't lie, my insides tangle with desire at that look.

I put a finger in my mouth, looking up at them through my lashes as I twist shyly. "So..."

"Stop acting coy," Cass says, one side of his gorgeous mouth lifting as he steps closer. "We're gonna spread you like a PB and J sandwich."

THEY TAKE me back to the shower, but only to wash me clean. I assume it's so that they can see just how dirty I'll be when they're done—Cass's sweet tooth has moved into the bedroom, and Apollo's never said no to chocolate.

I end up on the king-sized bed, naked and dripping with chocolate and whipped cream. Apollo's between my legs, his tongue driving me to my third climax of the night, while Cass kisses the life out of me.

The fact that I can come at all is shocking. I should be so concerned that Reuben and Zach are alone, that their discussion could come to blows again. That I'm alone with Apollo and Cass, and that's not something we do.

But tonight has been a night of firsts. Apollo's first kill. Reuben and I alone outside the cabin. Zach's emotional breakdown, the first time I've *ever* seen him open up. Now this...

I fist my hand in Apollo's long, sandy hair, grinding my pussy against his mouth as I feel an orgasm approaching. But he pulls away before I can finish, and ignores my sulky moan when he sits up and wipes his mouth.

"I want to make sure they're still fine," he says, cocking his head in the direction of the bedroom door.

"For fuck's sake, they're—" Cass cuts off when Apollo throws him a meaningful look that I recognize but can't interpret. "Although, you really should check."

"That's what I thought," he mutters, half to himself, and then throws on his boxers and pads out of the bedroom.

He shuts the door behind him.

My stomach flutters and I quickly lay a hand on it. Was that a flutter? I've been reading parenting books and stuff, but for the life of me I can't remember during which trimester I'm supposed to be able to feel Malachi moving inside me.

"Twenty, twenty five weeks," Cass whispers in my ear as he snuggles against my side. "Soon, but not yet."

"I'm not in the least surprised you know that," I tell him, turning my head so I can smile at him.

God, he's so fucking gorgeous. There's a small scar beside one eyebrow—he got it during one of our kills when the Ghost somehow managed to escape his binds and used the chair to bash Cass over the head.

That was the last time we used ropes instead of plastic ties. The last time we *ever* left anyone alone with a Ghost.

The last time.

I shiver, and Cass pushes my shoulder so I roll onto my side, spooning me from behind. It means I can't see him, but the warm body pressing up against me is a fair trade.

He slides a hand over my hip and caresses my belly, then starts kissing the back of my neck.

"Cass, we shouldn't—"

"Things have changed, my precious little slut," he murmurs into my hair as his fingers describe sinuous lines over my goosebumped flesh. "And surprisingly, this time, for the better."

He shifts his hips, and I immediately feel the rock-hard length of his cock nest between my ass cheeks. I move back, grinding against him, and the groan he lets out fills me with delicious shivers.

Raining tiny kisses on the side of my neck and my naked shoulder, Cass slides his hand down my leg and gently grasps me under my knee, lifting my top leg and setting it at a right angle to the other.

Cool air touches my wet, exposed pussy, and my core clenches in eager anticipation of his touch. I let out a ragged sigh when he brushes his fingertips between my legs, leaving ghostly tremors in his wake. Dipping a fingertip inside me, he starts stroking my inner wall as his thumb swipes left and right against my clit.

When he's made sure I'm wet enough for him, Cass guides the tip of his cock against my entrance and starts teasing me with it, rubbing it through my slick folds as he nibbles on my earlobe.

"Fuck me," I whisper urgently. "Please."

"Such a greedy little slut." He pushes an inch into me before stopping. "Are you even sure you can take it all?"

"Yes!" I push back, forcing him deeper inside me.

He groans, so I do it again. In seconds, I'm riding his thick, hard cock as he holds my legs apart. His fingers toy with my clit, pinching and rubbing it till I'm seconds away from bursting. He nuzzles my jaw until I turn my head to kiss him, and that's when my climax slams into me.

I gasp, my body locking with my legs sprawled open and Cass's cock buried deep, deep inside me. I can feel his load filling me, oozing out of me as he fucks me through his own orgasm.

Then the bedroom door opens.

If I'd been able to move, I might have tried to get away from Cass, to look less like we were fucking. But before I can gather myself, the bed creaks with someone's weight. Then another. Another.

Oh God. My entire body pulses as I roll onto my back and stare up at my men.

"Get that dick hard again," Reuben grates out, his eyes flicking briefly to Cass. "Then get inside her."

There's a flurry of motion, then I'm lying on my side again, Cass's semi already nudging my back door. He doesn't enter me yet, though. First he drags his fingers through my pussy and makes sure I'm dripping. Zach moves in front of me, cock in his hand and a ravenous light gleaming in his eyes.

A big, warm hand grabs my leg, opening me up as wide as I can go. Cass slips his leg under my hip, lifting me up from the mattress and giving Reuben and Zach just the right angle to fuck me. But first they take turns stroking me, their fingers sending electric tingles through every inch of my body while Cass rubs his cock against my backdoor, reminding me just how full I'm about to be in a moment.

Apollo appears at the top of the bed, a wicked grin on his face as he slides up to me. I smile up at him, and that's all the invitation he needs. He tugs down his boxers and wraps a hand around his cock, urging it against my pouting lips. I suck his crown into my mouth, closing my mouth as a rush of warmth fills me.

A second later, so does Rube.

I barely get a warning before he rams his thick cock into me, taking my breath away as my pussy struggles to adjust to his size. But I don't have much time, because Cass decides he's had enough of waiting and starts forcing his cock into my backdoor.

The stretch is delicious. The friction insane.

My entire body sets alight with unfathomable pleasure.

"Can you handle another cock, or do I have to wait my turn?" Zach grates out. My eyes flutter open, locking with his. He's stroking his cock, alternating between watching me sucking off Apollo and Rube and Cass's cocks thrusting into my dripping holes.

"Her pussy's too tight." Cass groans as he eases more of his cock into my backdoor. "You'll tear her open."

"Fuck that," Rube says. "Our little slut can handle anything we want to fuck her with."

Apollo reaches down and starts stroking my clit as he pumps his dick in and out of my mouth. I moan, my eyes fluttering closed as hedonistic awe washes through me.

A second later, Rube stops fucking me. He leaves his cock buried inside me, though, and moves a little to the side to make space for Zach.

"Fuck, he's doing it," Apollo says, sounding as awed as I feel.

Zach uses his fingers to smear my wetness over his cock, and then pumps it a few times before he dips down and pushes the crown against my clit. Cass starts moving in and out of me an inch at a time, keeping friction building in my backdoor while Rube and Zach negotiate their dicks inside me.

It should be impossible. Fuck, it almost feels impossible when Zach forces the first inch of his rock-hard dick between my pussy lips. But then Apollo starts rubbing my clit again, and arousal slicks my pussy.

"God, you're so fucking wet for us," Zach mutters. "And so tight."

"Go deeper," Rube says, his voice strained. He grazes the top of my knee with his teeth, but his eyes are locked on where Zach is trying to fuck my pussy. "She'll make room."

"Fuck you guys," Cass groans. "I'm so fucking close. Can you hurry up already?"

In a flash, Rube's hand is around Cass's throat, pinning him on his back so his hips are twisted where he's still buried inside me. "You'll wait like the fucking gentleman you are, hear me? And when we're all good and ready, our lady is coming first. Until then, keep your fucking act together."

"Not helping," Cass croaks.

Rube quickly takes his hand away, and instead grabs me around the throat. "Keep your mouth open wide for Apollo," he says, his green eyes blazing. "I want to watch you swallow every drop of his cum."

I moan around Apollo's dick, my body thrumming like it's about to disintegrate. Hot need and lust pour into me, my body growing tighter and tighter the closer I am to coming.

Zach finally fills me another inch, and it's possible they gave each other a signal, because that's when he and Rube begin fucking me in tandem.

Apollo thankfully takes his dick out of my mouth just as I let out a ragged scream of pleasure and pain that seems to fill the entire room.

"I fucking love it when you make that sound," Zach says, his hands on my ass, wrenching me open for Cass.

I self-consciously close my lips, but Cass thrusts hard into me, wrenching another yell.

"I'm going to come," I manage, the words as tangled as my mind.

"Then so will we," Rube says. His fingers tighten around my throat. "I want to hear you scream, little girl."

And I do. I can't help it. When Zach and Rube start fucking me hard, their dicks plunging into me just as Cass is pulling out, my mind explodes.

I'm aware that I catch someone's hand, and that someone's mouth lands on my clit, but I'm in the fucking stratosphere. I hear groans, and feel warm cum filling every inch of me. Apollo's dick presses against my lips, and I swallow him down too, my body bucking in the last hard throe of my orgasm.

Cass pulls out, sounding breathless, but Zach and Rube stay buried inside me, still moving against each other, still stretching me to the limit.

My back slams down onto the mattress, and only then do they slowly pull out of me. Zach and Rube stroke my pussy while Apollo and Cass cover my shoulders and breasts with kisses.

"Oh my fucking God," I whisper.

His lips crooking into an evil smile, Zach cocks his head as he gazes down at me with pure adoration.

"Amen."

CHAPTER THREE
ZACH

The sweet, cloying thickness of cigarette smoke fills my lungs. I'm on the penthouse balcony overlooking the light-studded city sprawled out below, having a cigarette as I try to calm my racing thoughts.

I should be back there, cuddling. But I'd suddenly felt dizzy, overwhelmed, frantic.

Out here, the air is crisp. The stars bright. The city a mass of twinkling lights that blur into big dots when I force my eyes to unfocus.

The balcony door slides open, and Trinity steps outside.

I force a swallow and quickly get to my feet. I was expecting anyone but her—she knows to leave me alone when I'm in a mood. But here is she, fucking glowing, and for the life of me I can't tell her to leave me alone.

Because I don't want her to. I don't want any of them to leave ever again.

"It's cold out here," she says, wrapping her arms around herself. She's wearing the hotel's robe, thick and fluffy, her dark curls pulled into a messy heap on top of her head. "Why don't you come inside?"

"Just having a smoke."

She quirks her mouth. "I thought you were going to quit?" Her hands frame her little belly.

I know what I said, I was there. The instant I knew Malachi was mine, a slew of promises filled my head.

I'd quit smoking.

I'd stop canceling my therapy sessions at the last minute.

I'd actually do the homework my shrink assigned me.

I'd give my brothers less grief.

I'd...be *better*.

I only told them about the smoking part. I guess, in a way, I didn't want to take a chance that I'd fail at all the others. Because I knew I'd fail.

My life was a series of failures, and it showed no sign of changing. Until Malachi arrived, of course. I don't know why my seed was the one that finally took, but I do know that's a question I don't actually want the answer to.

I have a feeling, if Malachi wasn't mine, then I wouldn't have stuck around long enough to know who his father was.

I'm selfish like that.

Trinity knows it. My brothers know it.

This time, the dice rolled in my favor.

I stub out my cigarette and grab the bottle of water I brought out here with me, rinsing my mouth with a few sips. Then I come up to Trinity and scoop her into my arms, hugging her as tightly as I dare.

She says nothing—just clings to me like she'd fall if I let her go.

But I don't plan to.

Not ever.

I cup her face in my hands and lean back so I can look into her bronze eyes. "How could you ever love a wretch like me?"

She frowns. "Now you're quoting song lyrics at me?"

I am? I glance away, but she reaches up and turns my face back toward her. "At first, I didn't. But they did." She cocks her head inside the penthouse.

I stare deep into her eyes, my chest growing tight. Then I shake my head and slowly go down onto my knees in front of her. Mindful of the cold air out here, I tweak open the front of her robe just enough so that I can plant my lips on her belly.

When I tip my head back, tears have gathered in her eyes. She quickly blinks them away, but I'm already on my feet, smoothing the hair away from her face. "Why?"

"Because this is all so..." She sniffs and squeezes her eyes closed. "It's all so perfect."

"What's wrong with that?"

"Nothing!" Her eyes shoot open, angry now. "Perfect isn't a compromise, Zach. It's what everyone strives for."

Everyone but me.

Except...now...staring down at the woman of my dreams, the one who's sheltering my child in her swollen belly, something stirs inside me. It could be many things, but I'm starting to realize that was always the case. I could have gone so many directions with things over the course of my life, but I always chose the negative.

Darkness had been such an integral part of my life that it became familiar to me. When I had to choose, I stuck in my comfort zone.

Choosing the light feels wrong. But I can't be a fucking coward for the rest of my life. I want my son to look up to me. So I'll be brave.

From now on, I'll choose *hope*.

I smile at Trinity, and for a beat it's as if she doesn't know what to do with my expression. Then a flimsy smile graces her own mouth.

"Amen," I whisper.

The End

BOOKS BY LOGAN FOX

FYRE & ASHES SERIES

Healing was Fyre's obsession...until Charlotte Ash walked into his classroom. Now the darkly enigmatic Professor Gideon Fyre has only one objective: to make Charlotte his. Forever.

View all books in this dark stalker romance series.

Playing with Fyre (now available in the **Stalkers Anthology,** see details below)

Under Fyre

Catching Fyre (Coming Soon!)

THE STALKERS ANTHOLOGY

You should never fall for the bad guy...

Over **thirty of your favorite USA Today and bestselling authors** have come together to create an epic collection of forbidden, dark romance stories.

Get lost in this unputdownable mixture of short stories. From heroes to bad guys, there's something for everyone.

Stalkers — All Platforms

A CRIME FAMILY AFFAIR

Nyx Gray, an assassin-for-hire desperate to save her family, attempts a hit on the capo of a powerful Columbian cartel, triggering a war between two crime families and putting herself in the sights of the cartel's brutal lieutenant, Savage Domingo.

View all books in this dark cartel romance series.

Savage Hero

Wild Angel (Coming soon!)

THE SINNERS OF SAINT AMOS

We're ready to die for the sins of our fathers...but is she?

A dark bully reverse harem romance series.

Their Kingdom Come

Their Will be Done

Deliver us from Evil

BAD BULLIES SERIES

View all books in this standalone dark bully romance series.

Brutal Bully — Prince & Indigo

Hateful Bully — Josiah & Candy

THEIR CARTEL PRINCESS SERIES (COMPLETE)

She needs their protection. They need her heart.

View all books in this dark cartel reverse harem series.

Her Merc — Finn, Cora & Bailey

Her Don — Finn, Cora & Lars

Her Capo — Finn, Cora, Lars & Kane

Her Wolf — Finn, Cora, Lars & Kane

Her King — Finn, Cora, Lars & Kane

THE DARK HUNTER SERIES

After a steamy night with the billionaire founder of her rehabilitation clinic, city girl Clover expects to wake up to a gourmet breakfast. Instead, she finds herself naked and disorientated in the middle of the woods, being hunted by the very man she spent the night with.

View all books in this twisted romantic suspense series.

Dark Hunter – Clover & Hunter

Dark Ties – Kane, Hunter & Ziggy

Dark Devil – Clover, Hunter & Kane

Dark Deeds – Kane, Owen & Agony

Dark Reign – (Coming Soon!)

BOUGHT BY THE BILLIONAIRES

She needs money. He wants a new pet.

A dark erotic suspense series. First book is free!

Bought

Bound

Trigger

Printed in Great Britain
by Amazon

83572069R00466